THE WRAITHS OF WILL AND PLEASURE

❧ THE WRAITHS OF WILL AND PLEASURE ❧

The First Book of the Wraeththu Histories

STORM CONSTANTINE

A TOM DOHERTY ASSOCIATES BOOK

NEW YORK

THE WRAITHS OF WILL AND PLEASURE: THE FIRST BOOK OF THE WRAETHTHU HISTORIES

Edited by Beth Meacham

Map by Ellisa Mitchell

This book is printed on acid-free paper.

A Tor Book
Published by Tom Doherty Associates, LLC
175 Fifth Avenue
New York, NY 10010

www.tor.com

Tor® is a registered trademark of Tom Doherty Associates, LLC.

Library of Congress Cataloging-in-Publication Data

Constantine, Storm.
    The wraiths of will and pleasure : the first book of the Wraeththu histories / Storm Constantine.—1st ed.
        p. cm.
    "A Tom Doherty Associates book."
    ISBN 0-765-30346-9
        I. Title.

PR6053.O5134W73 2003
823'.914—dc21

2003040214

First Edition: May 2003

Printed in the United States of America

0 9 8 7 6 5 4 3 2 1

This book is dedicated to all those honorary hara, who have stuck with the world of Wraeththu since the beginning. You all know who you are.

Camphac

HADASSAJ
• Caráway
• Jasminia

ELHMEN

(SAHALE)   Lemarath

• Kar Tatang   WRAKE
• Shappa   TAMYD

                    GIMRAH
                    Strabaloth
                                    • SYKER
            • Ardith
            Kapre •

THAINE

    • Clereness
    • Jael

    FERIKE   Sea

    Saphrax •

FLORINADA

1993
Ellisa Mitchell

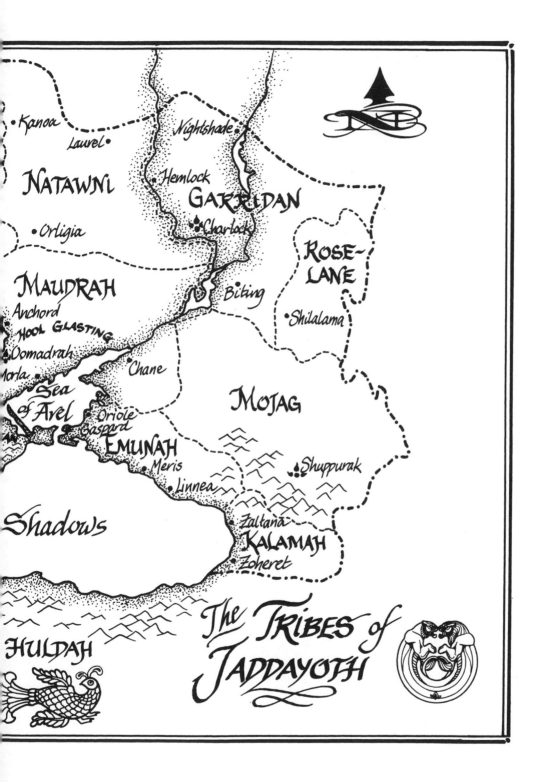

• Kanoa

Laurel •

Nightshade

NATAWNI

Hemlock

GARRIDAN

• Orligia

• Charlock

ROSE-
LANE

MAUDRAH

Anchord

HOOL GLASTING

Biting

• Shilalama

Oomadrah

Morla •

• Chane

Sea
of Avel

MOJAG

• Oriole

Gaspard

EMUNAH

• Shuppurak

• Meris

• Linnea

Shadows

Zaltana

KALAMAH

• Zoheret

HULDAH

The Tribes of
Jaddayoth

AUTHOR'S NOTE

Seventeen years have passed since I first began work on *The Enchantments of Flesh and Spirit,* lead volume of the original Wraeththu trilogy and for quite a few years I had fended off readers' pleas for more stories set in the same world. My argument was that I wrote the original books a long time ago, and I had changed too much as a writer ever to revisit that territory and do it justice. A certain innocence and naïveté had disappeared from my work, and that naïve voice was part of what made the Wraeththu books work. Some fans agreed with me and felt the Wraeththu should be left alone in their world of the past.

However, a year or so ago, I changed my mind. I don't know what the catalyst was exactly, but it was as if I received a communication from a friend with whom I'd lost touch. Suddenly, I knew what happened next, after the end of the trilogy. I wanted to walk once more upon harish territory, but this time with nearly two decades' writing experience behind me. The journey has been wondrous, and perhaps for the first time since the early days of my career, I have basked once more in the heady joy of writing for its own sake.

The original Wraeththu trilogy has remained in print since Tor first published it in the States, and over the years it has attracted a veritable army of loyal fans. Those with whom I have had contact assure me this new Wraeththu story has been long awaited, but I realize that not everyone who picks it up will have already read the original trilogy.

The Wraiths of Will and Pleasure fits chronologically between the second and third books of the original series (*The Bewitchments of Love and Hate* and *The Fulfilments of Fate and Desire*). However, newcomers to this world will find the back story included—I aimed to make this "filling in" as unobtrusive as possible. For those who would like to find out more about Wraeththu history, the first trilogy is still in print, but you can also visit Trish's excellent and informative Web site The Wraeththu Companion, which is an on-line encyclopaedia of events, terms, and characters. The address—at time of printing—is: http://ultrago.com/wraeththu/index.htm

A thought came to me the other day. When I was a child, and a very imaginative child at that, I was always delighted when I met children who were like me and could share my dreams. Together, we'd spend long summers playing in imagined worlds—experiences that obviously contributed greatly to my becoming a writer of fantasy. I just couldn't stop making things up! To me, having readers who get into my made-up worlds as much as I do is like having those like-minded friends from childhood. This is one of the reasons why I encourage fan-fiction (stories set in another writer's world and often using their characters), rather than view it with a disapproving eye. I hope that both new and established readers of my work will enjoy this latest journey into Wraeththu as much as I enjoyed writing it. I invite you to share my dreams.

STORM CONSTANTINE
July 2002

ACKNOWLEDGMENTS

>—+—+>—+—O—+—<+—+—<

Many people supported and encouraged me through the process of writing this book, and I'd like to thank some of them here. Thanks to my husband, Jim Hibbert, for being the patient, tolerant, and gorgeous creature he is; to Eloise Coquio, Wendy Darling, and Paula Wakefield, for their critiques and suggestions—I could never have written a birth scene in such gruesome detail without Paula's frank recollections!; to Deb Howlett for her friendship and convention organization; to Jon Sessions for computer rescue; to my editor, Beth Meacham, for sticking with me; to my agents Robert Kirby and Howard Morhaim for the wheelin' and dealin'; to Ruby for her incredible Wraeththu artwork, which has been a great inspiration; to Mischa and Trish for their fabulous Wraeththu Web sites, and all the visitors to the Stone Inn chat room and the Stormboard discussions on topics pertinent to the book: long live the Internet!; to Gabriel Strange and Lydia for the new Web site; to the rest of my close friends and family not mentioned above, but who have contributed in various ways, either through practical help or else simply by being great mates: Si Beal, John and Norma Bristow, Steve Chilton, Andy and Sue Collins, Claire Cartwright, Bob Forse, Mark Hewkin, Dot and Harold Hibbert, Paul Kesterton, Steve Nash, Ellen Nicholson, Linda Price, Ash Smith, Karen Townsend, Freda Warrington, Caroline Wise, and Steve Wilson.

Finally, I want to thank all the Wraeththu enthusiasts out there, for keeping the world of dreams alive.

Storm Constantine's official Web site: http://www.stormconstantine.com

Information service postal address:

Inception,
6 S. Leonard's Avenue
Stafford ST17 4LT
England

CHAPTER ONE

On the night of the last full moon before the winter solstice, the hara of the desert Wraeththu tribe of Kakkahaar cast off their sand-colored robes and dance naked beneath the stars. It is, for them, the festival of Hubisag, a pitiless hermaphrodite deity of death and dark magic. The Kakkahaar dance around a hungry fire; sparks spiral up into the darkness. Their voices utter mantras to earth and stone. Their fists clench against the sky, then punch the ground. They sway and spin and stamp. Their skins are painted with the blood of sacrifice. They have Medusa hair beneath the moon's stark light. They are proud and fierce, full of secrets and the mysteries of life, and the knowledge that they are superior among their kind.

It is the most important night of the year, when pledges are made to the god and boons petitioned for. It is not unknown for hara to disappear into the desert before the sun rises and never come out again. Hubisag occasionally takes his own sacrifices. He is not partial to prayers.

But the legends of the Kakkahaar speak of a festival night that surpassed all others. It was the night when the world changed. The world of Wraeththu. Perhaps it was when all hara, whether consciously or not, turned purposefully to approach their own potential, rather than career mindlessly along in wild, ungoverned chaos. In Kakkahaar history, two events happened on this night that brought the tribe closer to Wraeththu destiny than they otherwise might have been.

There were no omens in the sky to herald this change, nor in the entrails of vultures into which the shamans of the tribe peered so closely. There was no warning at all. No one knew that somewhere, far away, other hara of other tribes, who also believed themselves to be superior among their kind, made decisions and consequently pulled threads upon the web of wyrd. A decision. An order. A result. Perhaps without thought for how far the reverberations on the plucked web would be sensed. For those who had eyes to see. For those with eyes inside.

Ulaume was not Kakkahaar, although he lived among them. In fact, the tribe leader, Lianvis, had bought him some years back, from a traveling band of Colurastes, who had taken care not to mention exactly why they were prepared to sell one of their own into slavery. Lianvis had seen only the surface beauty—he liked pretty, sparkling things—and had perhaps smelled a sense of danger that reminded him very much of himself. The deal had been concluded with almost indecent haste and very little bartering, which even the Colurastes had known was unusual for Kakkahaar. They hadn't cared about it. They'd simply blessed their gods in silence as the goods changed hands. Then they'd gone away—swiftly.

Ulaume knew his people had been relieved and pleased to see the back of him. He bore little resentment. Slavery existed only in the mind. He felt utterly free. Lianvis approved of most of what he did, and actually seemed pleased when Ulaume did something that he could disapprove of, because there was very little Lianvis wouldn't do himself. From the very first moment he'd looked into Ulaume's eyes, the Kakkahaar leader had known he wasn't looking at a slave. It had been an unspoken message, which Ulaume had been very clear about in his silence. Still, they played the game of master and not-master, even though it was only a game, and a darker, more complex relationship existed between them.

The dwelling of Lianvis was a warren of canopies that looked very permanent, although hara of the tribe could dismantle it within an hour, scour the site to eradicate signs of their presence, and melt into the desert as if they'd never been there. The Kakkahaar were adept at illusion.

Ulaume had his own rooms within the pavilion, where the walls were never still, prey to the insidious breezes that breathed sand into every corner. He had a mirror that was exactly his own height and it was very old. Somehar had stolen it from the silent ruins of a rich human's house and then, sometime later, had sold it to Lianvis, once they'd realized it was actually quite cumbersome to haul around the desert. For this reason, Lianvis had acquired it at a very good price. Its glass was flawless and the frame looked as if it had been designed by an evil witch queen, writhing as it was with smirking demons, which suited both Lianvis's and Ulaume's tastes perfectly. Ulaume liked to admire himself in this mirror and Lianvis liked to watch him doing so.

But tonight, Ulaume was alone. He applied scented oil, mixed with his own blood, slowly and languorously to his supple limbs, his body swaying slightly as if he danced to a distant song. And so he did, because he was of the Colurastes, the serpent tribe, and their hearing is more acute than most hara's. It was the song of the stars Ulaume heard, the song of the moon, calling so softly. All of his senses were especially alert. He could hear the brushwood being dragged across the sand almost a mile from the camp. He could smell the first peppery tang of new flame. This night was important to him because he intended to work a potent curse against somehar who he considered had wronged him. Somehar who had been the cause of the first harsh words Lianvis had ever spoken to him. Somehar who would pay most dearly for their interference, and who would most certainly never forget the name of Ulaume, har of the Colurastes, har of the serpent people.

Ulaume stared at himself in the shadowy glass, his head thrown back, his glance haughty. He smoothed his tawny flanks and tossed his hair, which fell to his knees and possessed properties that hair normally did not have. Sometimes, he had to twist hanks of it fiercely to make it behave. Satisfied with what he saw, Ulaume hissed expressively and made a small pounce toward his reflection. Then he laughed quietly, in utter self-absorbed pleasure. "Pellaz," he said, leaning close to breathe upon the mirror. "Remember me. I wish you the greatest, most exquisite pain."

He leaned his cheek against the glass, then decided he'd had enough self-indulgence and prepared to leave the pavilion for the festival site. Lianvis would already be there, supervising the arrangements. It was supposed to be a wild night of abandonment, but in fact Lianvis planned it very carefully and made sure that nothing was omitted, left at the camp, or overlooked.

Ulaume threw a dun-colored cloak around his shoulders to cover his naked body and padded out into the night. He felt so powerful he was sure his footprints must be smoking, and the sand would turn to glass wherever he trod. Hara would see those footprints in the future and they would say to one another that they were the legacy of the night on which Ulaume of the Colurastes cursed the wretched har, Pellaz. But who was Pellaz? some might ask. A nohar.

It is almost beneath me to do this, Ulaume thought. *Self-righteous fool. Who will ever hear of you, while I, naturally, am destined to be legendary? So, I will make you legendary too, you reeking tower of piety, and you really do not deserve it. Be glad you have offended me.*

Cheered by this idea, Ulaume stalked away from the camp, his cloak blowing about him. What a pretty picture of death I must make, he thought.

Other hara were also making their way to the site, although none of them approached Ulaume or appeared even to notice him. This was not deliberate ignorance, but just an acknowledgment of his status. When he led the dance this night, power would surge to the tribe from the cold distant reaches of the universe. When he sang, stars would shatter in distant galaxies. Ulaume had no friends, other than Lianvis, but possessed a horde of helpless admirers, who all feared him greatly. Such had it always been. It was one of the reasons why the Colurastes had done what they had to him. Ulaume had no time for fear. He despised it in others. Lianvis's lack of it made him worthy of respect. Only one other had not feared him. Only one. Ulaume sneered instinctively, then got control of himself. Anger was weakness. He must remain focused.

Not far from the camp, there were ruins, constructed in ancient times by humans who had possessed more knowledge than their descendents who had lost the world. The Kakkahaar had appropriated this place for themselves and journeyed to its location several times a year for specific rites. The ruins were mostly underground, but for Hubisag's festival, the ceremonies would be held outside, because the god should not be worshipped in hidden, secret places. It would be an affront to his power.

Ulaume noticed Lianvis standing beside the fledgling fire, his arms folded and his expression that of contemplation. He did not know what Ulaume planned to do and Ulaume did not intend to enlighten him, because part of the reason for his incandescent fury was that Lianvis had a soft spot for the loathsome Pellaz, even though he wouldn't admit it. It was this softness that had inspired Lianvis to upbraid Ulaume for his behavior after Pellaz had left the Kakkahaar camp. Ulaume hadn't intended to attack Pellaz physically. He'd had seduction in mind: seduction in the manner he most enjoyed, which invariably involved some kind of struggle for power. Pellaz had not been interested. He'd revealed his contempt, so what other choice had Ulaume had other than to lash out? His hair often had a mind of its own. With hindsight, Ulaume realized it might have been better not to have allowed it to try and strangle Pellaz. Afterward, Pellaz must have whined to Lianvis about the incident, because the Kakkahaar leader had punished Ulaume: first with scorn, then with silence. It had been weeks before Ulaume had won back Lianvis's favor.

Now, the need for secrecy interfered somewhat with Ulaume's desire for everyhar to know what could happen to those who crossed him, but he would work out the details of how to spread the news later. Events were still too raw to be addressed with Lianvis now. Pellaz had been gone for less than a year.

Perhaps Lianvis was now thinking of Pellaz too. He might be remembering the jet-black hair, the jet-black fire of condemnation and virtue that could shoot from Pellaz's eyes. He had despised the Kakkahaar, full of judgment and morality. Stupid, misguided, and outdated human notions. Fear hid inside it all. No true Wraeththu, he. Lianvis must not think of him. No, as a leader, he must be considering other things: his own power, how to increase it. Fair Lianvis. Fair and wicked king. His hair was the color of honey made by bees that feasted on poisonous flowers and was braided into three plaits, each of four sections of hair. Two hung over his breast to his waist, the other trailed like a serpent down his back. His face was like that of an ancient Egyptian pharaoh. His pale robe was embroidered with a grimoire of arcane symbols. By any standards, he looked like a divine sovereign and knew how to behave like one. Ulaume prowled to his side and laid a hand on Lianvis's shoulder. Lianvis started in surprise, then smiled. "You fold out of the darkness," he said.

"Or into it," Ulaume said.

Lianvis took hold of Ulaume's hand and kissed it. "Work well tonight. I've a feeling we have need of it."

"You look thoughtful. What worries you?" Ulaume supposed that Lianvis's sharp, sensitive mind might well be picking up on his own intention. He must allay such suspicions.

"I am unsure," Lianvis said, frowning slightly. "There is a flex to the air tonight. A strange feeling. Can't you sense it?"

Ulaume could sense nothing but his own desire, which was strong enough to eclipse all other sensations, and smelled strongly of smoke and blood. It filled his entire being. "No," he said. "I can't imagine why you should feel like this."

Lianvis gave him a considered glance, because it was rare he could feel something Ulaume could not. "Then perhaps I am wrong," he said, in a somewhat dry tone.

"Perhaps you sense what is to come," Ulaume purred. "Perhaps we shall conjure something tonight beyond our imaginations."

Lianvis laughed. "I am not sure I would like to confront something beyond *my* imagination—or yours, for that matter. But for that reason, it is an idea to cherish."

Hara were gathering thickly around the fire now, which had begun to reach for the stars with more intensity, fed by tinder and intention. The high cabal of tribe shamans was already circling the flames. They dragged carved staffs through the dusty sand, marking an area of sanctity. Ulaume's arrival at the site had signaled the ceremony must begin.

Lianvis judged the moment and stepped away from Ulaume. He raised his arms and immediately everyhar became silent and still. For some moments, he appeared to bask in the hellish light of the fire, his eyes closed. Ulaume stood like a statue behind him, the hood of his cloak shadowing his face.

"Hubisag!" Lianvis called in a hollow, chilling voice. "We call to you, Father of Eternity, Lord of Iniquity, whose stride spans the abyss. We call to you. We conjure and command your presence on this, the night of your holy festival. Hubisag, we are your children, and all acts we commit, we do so in your name. Come to us now! Instill within us the might of your power and wisdom! Hubisag, come!"

The shamans began a low rumbling chant in an unintelligible tongue that was reputedly the language Hubisag obeyed. Out of the darkness, as if they'd manifested from the desert sand itself, a troupe of hara clad only in their own thigh-length hair, insinuated themselves lithely between the motionless lesser hara of the tribe. These were Fire Dancers, of the Pyralis level of the Ulani caste. They prowled around the perimeter of the flames, snarling, their fingers curling on the air. Beyond the circle of the congregation, drummers started up a throbbing tribal rhythm.

Ulaume stirred restlessly within the disguise of his cloak. His body yearned to burst free, now, this moment, but he must judge the right time. It was not yet. The Fire Dancers must weave the web of power before he could dance upon it himself.

The whole tribe had begun to sway in time to the hypnotic rhythm and now the dancers' prowl was punctuated by abrupt leaps and yelping cries. They spun in circles, lunging at members of the tribe, who did not flinch, but who threw back their heads, uttering ecstatic gasps.

Ulaume felt the power building up. He sensed it as smoking blue-white light emanating from the hot skins of the dancers. It too was spinning, swirling counterclockwise around the circle. The drums grew louder and faster, and the hara of the tribe added their voices to that of the shamans. The power was reaching a peak. Ulaume noticed Lianvis throw him a covert glance, as if to indicate that now was the time to join the dance, but Ulaume waited a few more precious seconds. He wanted that power to ache for him, to be taken beyond the point of no return, to demand the release of his body's energy thrust into it. His eyes were half closed and he fancied that he could perceive a gigantic nebulous figure forming from the smoke and sparks of the fire. *Hubisag,* he said in his mind. *Grant me my boon. I will show it to you now.*

With a fierce and guttural cry, Ulaume threw off the cloak and leapt forward, right into the midst of the dancers. The others went for him, growling and lashing out with their clawed hands, but Ulaume spun away from them, around and around the shouting flames. The roar filled his head. *I will show you! I will show you!* He conjured in his mind a picture of Pellaz, offering it up to the god like a severed head on a silver salver. *Now, my Lord of Iniquity, do unto this . . .*

Pain. Total. Instant. Consuming. Ulaume screamed and shot several feet into the air, his body twisting in unnatural contortions. The silent petition was stilled in his mind. It was as if a fist of hard air had reached into his head and squeezed his brain. Agonizing sensations flooded through his body. Every nerve screamed in torment. Something had punched a hole in his head. His life was running out of it. He collapsed onto the ground as if he'd been thrown there.

Movement, voices, flickering light. Ulaume lay panting, facedown, on the sand, his fingers flexing weakly in the sifting grains. He felt like a rare creature that had been shot and awaited the inevitable approach of the hunter for the coup de grâce. He was aware of every labored breath he drew into his body. He could hear his heart slowing down. The drums were fading away. Hara were silent around him. There was only the night and himself. Slower, slower, the heartbeat's drum. His breath was the roar of the ocean, so hard to draw it. So hard.

A flash of lightning pierced his eyes and his body jerked involuntarily. He was both blinded by the light, but also given the most intense clarity of sight he'd ever known. Pictures came thick and fast upon the mind's eye. He saw landscapes of unimaginable strangeness and wonder rush past his perception. He saw mighty cities of black stone rearing against an obsidian sky, devoid of stars. He saw the abyss, impenetrable blackness, and heard the lament of lost souls. He saw hara dancing, beautiful free movement, but their limbs were attached to shining strings, and somewhere, invisibly, a puppeteer tweaked and guided them. Now the puppets began to jerk and wriggle in strangely obscene gestures. There was no beauty to their movement, no harmonious rhythm. The puppet master laughed and it was a sound that filled the universe. Ulaume feared it more than he had ever feared anything. Perhaps it was the first thing he'd feared in his life. Was this death? Was he heading this way? No!

"Hubisag," he said in his mind, *"if I have offended you, I repent me. I am your priest, your child, and I adore you. Show me how I can atone."*

Thinking those words required the most effort he'd ever put into a conscious action. It was as if existence itself fought against his expression and his own life depended upon it.

Take yourself to a sacred place . . .

It was the words of a prayer he heard in his mind, a small echoing voice.

And another voice: *Father, you have murdered me . . .*

What he heard made no sense. He heard a horse scream. He smelled cordite. He saw blood running across sandy soil, dark blood, from somewhere deep inside. The sight of it touched him, moved him, and he felt something he'd never felt before. He didn't know what it was, but it wasn't fear. He saw the face of Pellaz, as he'd appeared when Ulaume had first met him, his eyes full of curiosity and desire. Ulaume's essence was drawn toward those eyes. This time their welcome would not turn to ice. But when Ulaume reached them, they were glazed over and dull. They were dead.

"Ulaume!" Rough hands shook his body, hauled him to his feet. Someone slapped his face hard. "Ulaume! Come out of it! Come back!"

Ulaume blinked, gulped air, sucked it into his body in a powerful rush. Sound and movement hurtled back, his stilled heart raced frantically. The night was confusion and riot around him. He saw Lianvis's face before him, pinched with concern, and slumped against his body.

"What happened?" Lianvis demanded.

Ulaume raised his head, shook it slowly from side to side. The movement filled him with nausea and he had to pull away from Lianvis to vomit copiously onto the ground.

"Tell me," Lianvis said in a low voice. "I must know."

Ulaume wiped his mouth with the back of one hand. "He's dead," he said. "That's all you need to know."

Not all the Kakkahaar were present at the festival that night. Only three did not attend, and they were occupied by what formerly, in the world of humanity, would have been seen as women's work.

For nineteen hours, Herien, a young har who had been incepted to Wraeththu only a year before, had been pacing, pacing around the pavilion he shared with his chesnari, Rarn. He had spent hours weeping. He couldn't sit down. He couldn't lie down. When Rarn had tried to touch him in comfort, he'd pushed him off, his skin too sensitive to bear it. If he just kept moving, it was better, he could just about stand it. The moment he'd stopped, he'd felt as if a captive demon in his gut was trying to push his insides out. Sometimes, he had vomited until his stomach hurt. He couldn't bear the terrible weight of what pressed down inside him. He was exhausted, yet near hysterical. Eventually, he'd fallen to the floor, groaning in agony, but too tired to keep moving.

Now, the time was near and Herien lay supported on Rarn's chest, on a low bed in one of the canopied rooms. Rarn, kneeling on the pillows, held Herien beneath the armpits, while a healer of the tribe, a one-eyed har named Chisbet, peered between Herien's raised knees. The noises that Herien made were like those of a half-slaughtered calf. He was in the process of delivering a pearl, which in human terms had once meant giving birth.

Wraeththu harlings are born in leathery sacs, in which they continue to develop for several weeks. In those days, procreation was a virtually untrodden territory among Wraeththu. They still had too much to learn about their androgynous condition, before embarking upon such an essentially female aspect of their being, and were ill-equipped to deal with it. There were no women to help them, which would certainly have made the transition easier. They were alone with a frightening truth. They were no longer men and this was the most damning proof of it. And they had to cope without much-needed female support, because that was a price they must pay for taking the world from humanity.

Only high-ranking hara were supposed to be capable of inseminating a host, and Rarn was indeed a Nahir Nuri of the tribe, but even he had been aghast at what had happened, one night after too much wine and a desire to take aruna beyond its normal boundaries.

Herien was clearly terrified, perhaps because his memories of being utterly male were too close for comfort. Even in his exhaustion, he writhed and moaned, asking to die, asking for someone to kill him, asking for release. Rarn felt helpless and numb, and willingly surrendered all control of the proceedings to Chisbet, who claimed to have helped deliver a pearl before. Rarn was not convinced of this—the occurrence being so rare among Wraeththukind—but he was prepared to overlook his misgivings. He couldn't have coped with this on his own. It was dreadful. Hideous. The mess. The stink. Was this truly necessary?

Chisbet told Herien to push, and Rarn's gorge rose. He was remembering his childhood and his youth, films and documentaries on TV, whispered conversations of female relatives. He was remembering being human and the life and culture he had chosen to forget. He didn't need this to remind him. At that moment, he would cheerfully have taken a blade to Herien's throat, even though he was immensely fond of him. Anything to stop the noise, to stop this dreadful process.

"Do something," he said to Chisbet. "You do know what to do, don't you?" His tone, by this time, was desperate, and not at all haughty as it usually was.

Chisbet had lost an eye in battle, fighting for the Unneah tribe. The Kakka-haar regarded him as somewhat unsavoury, but he was a good healer, so his eccentric and uncivilized ways were tolerated. "It's more up to him," he said. "This is nature. He's resisting it. Talk to him."

Rarn uttered a sound of despair, anguish, and revulsion. He wanted to say, "This is not nature," but of course it was. He swallowed sour saliva, trying to keep a hold on the writhing har lying against him. "Herien, you must . . . you must do . . . you must *expel* it." He couldn't say "push," he just couldn't.

"Cut it out! Just cut the thing out of me!" Herien screamed. "It's killing me!"

At once, Rarn drew the knife from his belt, but Chisbet's right hand shot out and clasped his wrist. "No. We cannot risk damaging the sac. There are fluids inside it."

Herien's screams had reached a diabolical pitch. His face was unrecogniz-able, screwed up into a tortured monkey mask.

"Do something!" Rarn cried. "He's dying!"

Chisbet appeared calm. "Come on now," he said. "You can do this. Push, Herien."

Herien uttered a final roar and his body lunged backward.

Rarn was almost knocked over, and was sure he felt the muscles in his thighs rip. Something shining and slippery shot out of Herien's body and landed in Chisbet's hands, which were held waiting. It was the size of a har's head. Unspeakable!

Chisbet's shoulders slumped, apparently in relief.

"What now?" Rarn demanded, a tremor in his voice.

Herien had gone worryingly quiet and still. His body was as limp as a corpse as Rarn wriggled out from beneath it.

Chisbet laid the pearl carefully on a cloth and then examined Herien's body. "Looks in order," he said, "but I'll need to stitch and pack him to stop the bleeding. Fetch me the hot water. I'll clean him up."

Rarn stood shaking beside the bed and couldn't bring himself to look at anything but the rugs underfoot.

"Do it, har!" Chisbet snarled. "You made this happen. You help now. You hear me?"

Rarn somehow made his limbs obey Chisbet's command. He couldn't think, couldn't absorb what he'd just witnessed.

Chisbet appeared to read his mind. "Get used to it, Rarn. This is the way of things. How else do you think our race will continue?" He laughed rather cruelly. "Be glad. You have a son—or soon will do, at any rate."

Rarn handed the materials to Chisbet: lengths of linen wadding, suture equipment, and the hot water. He glanced at Herien, whose lower parts looked as if a frenzied maniac had attacked them with a dozen weapons. Herien's eyes were closed and he did not move. Swallowing with difficulty, Rarn looked away. He had touched those precious parts, tasted them. Now they looked like ruined meat.

Humming to himself, Chisbet carefully bathed Herien's soume-lam, his female organs, and stitched up the tearing. His male parts, the ouana-lim, had withdrawn into the body to prevent damage.

Rarn glanced at the pearl. "How long will it take to . . . to come out?"

Chisbet shrugged. "Couple of weeks, that's all. It's not too bad. It's over. Lianvis will be pleased. Stop feeling sorry for yourself. Look at this poor creature here. He's the one who's suffered, not you."

"You must be dead inside," Rarn said. "Can't you imagine how I feel? How can you say those things?"

"Easy. I face reality. This will be common soon—if we're lucky."

"You enjoy it. You're perverse."

"Of course I enjoy it. It's a miracle and I'm proud to be part of it. It's you who's perverse, my friend. Think about it."

Rarn really didn't want to. It was not something he'd have chosen to be part of.

"Go and get a breath of air," Chisbet said. "I'm going to pack the wound now."

Rarn left the pavilion, grateful to escape the abattoir stink. He breathed slow and deep the cool night air and gazed at the glow in the sky, which was the festival fire. A son. Could it possibly be real? He had never felt so exhausted in his life. Even althaia, the changing from human to Wraeththu, hadn't been as bad as this, because then he hadn't been conscious. He'd gone into a coma a boy and woken up a har. This was disgustingly different. It could have been him lying there on that bed with blood and shit running out of him. Hellish injury. Such violation. Too human to contemplate for someone

who believed he'd transcended humanity. It could have happened to him anytime. He'd taken aruna with other high-ranking hara. Nohar knew what they
were risking. Nohar. How could such a rank visceral event result from the
blissful aruna that had caused it? He remembered the night they'd made the
pearl, the feeling of having transcended the flesh, of touching Heaven. The
closeness of it. The bond. Herien, so trusting, so completely surrendered to
love, that a part of himself, deep inside, had opened like a flower: a part that
had never opened before. And a previously unused part of Rarn's ouana-lim
had woken up, drawn by the alluring song of that secret inner organ and had
ventured forth to enter it. In such a way were Wraeththu harlings conceived.

Rarn pressed the fingers of one hand against his eyes. His body shuddered
with dry sobs. So much to learn. So much. He felt full of love and sadness. He
was beginning to understand what it meant to be truly har.

In the pavilion, Chisbet finished off the wound-packing and sat back for a moment to admire his work. Herien had still not come round. Chisbet knew he'd
done a good job on the stitches; the har would be fine in a few days. He
changed the soiled bedding around Herien, made him comfortable, and then
turned his attention to the pearl. Gently, he cleaned it. He had seen this happen only once before, among the Unneah, and that event had occasioned more
upset than this one. He smiled to himself in recollection. Every har in the
tribe had trembled in terror then, as if a plague had come upon them. Chisbet
wasn't distressed by harish birth. He had spoken the truth when he'd called it
a miracle. Until he'd seen this, Wraeththu bodies and all their pleasing accessories seemed only like ornaments. This was real and bloody. To Chisbet, it
was proof that they were meant to be. New life.

Chisbet shed a few sentimental tears from his remaining eye and then laid
the pearl in the curve of Herien's right arm. The pearl was dark in color and
strangely veined. There was a sense of life moving within it. Chisbet wiped
Herien's brow with a damp scented cloth and Herien opened his eyes. His
mouth trembled. He looked so young.

Chisbet stroked his face. "You're fine, my lovely. Fine. All went well. You
are a pioneer, you know. You're blessed."

"Where's Rarn?" Herien asked in a slurred mumble. He hadn't yet noticed
the pearl.

"Taking a breath of air," Chisbet said. "You keep that young one warm
now. Cherish it as a mother hen cherishes her clutch."

Herien glanced down, saw the pearl and went rigid. For a moment, Chisbet
was concerned that he'd throw it away from him.

"That's yours," he said. "Part of you. Don't be afraid."

Herien laid his head back on the pillows and began to weep, but his fingers flexed gently against the pearl. Chisbet held onto his left hand, squeezing it hard. He sighed. It was tough, growing up.

Rarn did not go back into the pavilion for over an hour. He'd needed time alone to recover, then felt guilty about leaving Herien and steeled himself to return. But whatever horror he had expected to confront, he found that even during that short time, Herien had recovered considerably. He was now propped up by pillows, sipping a hot drink that Chisbet had made for him.

Rarn stood at the entrance to the bed chamber, feeling awkward and embarrassed. Chisbet winked at him and left the room. Rarn couldn't think of anything to say. He had a ridiculous fear that Herien would blame him in some way for what had happened, and be angry about it. But Herien looked radiant, if tired.

"It doesn't hurt anymore," Herien said, wonder in his voice. "The pain's just gone, as if it was never there. I can't believe it. I'm just a bit sore now, that's all."

Rarn went to sit beside him. "You were female," he said. "For a time. It looked that way."

"We're all female," Herien said, "*and* male. Isn't that the point?"

Rarn grimaced. "How easy it is to ignore or forget."

"I'll never forget it again," Herien said. "I don't want to now. You should go through this, Rarn. You really should."

Rarn laughed uncomfortably. "I'm not sure. I don't think I can ever forget what you went through. I had a view you didn't, remember."

"But it was worth it. Look." Herien drew the covers back and showed Rarn the pearl, held tight against his body. "Isn't it strange? Isn't it wonderful?"

Rarn stared at the pearl.

"You can touch it," Herien said. "You can feel something moving."

Tentatively, Rarn reached out and laid his hand over the warm sac. The harling protected within it seemed to press against his hand. He glanced into Herien's eyes and felt faint at the sensation of total union that passed between them. Chisbet was right: this was a miracle.

Herien smiled, and Rarn leaned forward to kiss his brow. "You are beautiful," Rarn said, "beautiful and brave and strong."

"I am Wraeththu," Herien said. "Truly so now."

CHAPTER TWO

Not too far away from the Kakkahaar camp, across the desert, lay the town of Saltrock, cradled by gaunt mountains, perfumed by acrid aromas that rose from the soda lakes nearby.

On the night that Ulaume danced before the festival fire and Herien delivered the first Kakkahaar pearl, Seel Griselming, the leader of the Saltrock community, and Flick (who had not elected to take a second name for himself following inception), had invited the shaman of their people, Orien Farnell, around for dinner. Seel was an exotic creature, olive-skinned, with a riot of multicolored braids into which were woven ribbons and feathers. Orien was less flamboyant in appearance, a har who moved with grace and whose long tawny hair fought constantly to escape whatever ties sought to constrain it. Flick always felt too young and awkward in the presence of these hara. His skin was pale, and not even exposure to the sun could conjure forth a honeyed sheen. His hair was intensely black, long down his back but cut short to the sides of his head. One day, he supposed, he might become tall and commanding as every other har in Saltrock seemed to be. A well-meaning har had once referred to him as a "little imp" and Flick had yet to get over the remark. He was not Seel's chesnari, but he was rather more than an employee. Flick himself was never sure exactly what place he occupied in Seel's life, even more so of late.

But tonight, at least to begin with, all was in harmony. Cutlery and glasses chinked and glinted in candlelight and conversation was cheerful. Orien had come to finalize with Seel arrangements for the approaching solstice festival. The hara who lived in Saltrock came from many different tribes and, as yet, nohar had suggested they give themselves a separate tribal name, although they usually referred to themselves as Sarocks, and other tribes had begun to use this term for them as well. Seel was not concerned with such things, considering himself a creature of action and enterprise. His identity derived from his capabilities and his leadership rather than a label, although it was doubtful the rest of his people felt that way. Seel, however, kept them too busy to think about it. He wanted to build a functioning Wraeththu town. He wanted order, for hara to fulfill their potential and not just live from day to day like savages. He'd seen enough of that in the north, following his own inception. In his opinion, Wraeththu needed to grow up quickly, because otherwise they might destroy themselves before they found out what they really were. He was very selective about who he allowed into Saltrock and although this had been criticized quite recently by an old friend, Seel still considered he was doing the right thing. Now, he thought of that old friend and raised his glass to the others. "A toast," he said. "To Cal and Pell, wherever they roam."

"To Cal and Pell," Flick said with enthusiasm.

Orien frowned slightly, then raised his glass silently and clinked it against the others. He took a sip of wine, his expression thoughtful.

Seel cocked his head to one side. "To old friends, Orien? Can't you drink to that?"

Orien smiled rather grimly. "I find it hard to drink to Cal. But I don't like the way that makes me feel."

"You don't like him. Admit it," Seel said, pouring more wine into his glass. "Don't feel bad about it. You're not perfect. You don't have to be."

"Was that a claw showing?" Orien said.

Seel shrugged. "You know how I feel about Cal. He's hag-ridden by his reputation, and your attitude doesn't help, because you are respected and therefore you affect other hara's attitudes too. That's not fair."

"He earned that reputation," Orien said mildly.

"Oh, please don't argue about this again," Flick said. "I'm sick of hearing it."

"Be quiet, we're not arguing," Seel said. "You must admit I'm right, Orien."

Orien put down his glass on the table and moved it around a little. "Don't corner me, Seel. We have to agree to differ over this."

"You can't bear it because he was right about Pell," Seel said. "He found you out, didn't he? You'll never forgive him for that."

"And you'll never forgive him for leaving you," Orien said. "See, I can show claws too."

"Right, that's it!" Flick snapped. "If you don't stop this, I'll pour the rest of the wine down the sink. You've been over this ground too many times. Let it go, will you."

"I can't let it go," Seel said, fixing Orien with a manic stare. "I worry about what's happening to Pell, and that's got nothing to do with Cal. I worry that you won't tell me things. I worry that you're creating a scapegoat in Cal, because that means something might go wrong. Will you ever tell me the truth?"

"No," Orien said. "And as Flick correctly suggested, we should drop this. You know why I can't speak."

"No, I don't actually," Seel insisted, grabbing hold of the wine bottle before Flick could snatch it from him. "It's preyed on my mind for months. I can't talk to you about it because this great wall of silence goes up. We're supposed to be friends, but you won't trust me. If you continue to keep silent, I can only think the worst."

"It doesn't matter what you think," Orien said. "It won't change anything."

"What are you afraid of? Or should I say 'who'?"

At this point, Flick thought, a divine mechanism should intervene: fire from heaven should shoot through a window, or a building should collapse outside. Like Seel, he thought Orien had secrets, but he knew Orien would never reveal them. Nagging him to do so always ended up in argument. Seel should let it drop, but he couldn't, because he and Cal had a history.

As young humans, Cal and Seel had been lovers and they had believed the only path open to them was to cast off their humanity and become Wraeththu, so they could be together for eternity, in complete harmonious bliss, and all the rest of it. But it hadn't worked out that way. Being har had driven them apart rather than bound them together. The first tribe they had stumbled across, who had taken them in and performed, in their particularly brutal way, the necessary procedures to change their being, had been Uigenna. Not the best choice, but then they'd not had a choice, only desperation. Seel hadn't stayed long with them. Essentially, his soul was gentle, whereas Cal's . . . well, nobody really knew what comprised Cal's soul. He'd stayed with the Uigenna though, even when Seel had defected to a less rabid tribe, the Unneah.

Seel had never spoken to Flick in great detail of his early Wraeththu life. Flick knew this was because it embarrassed him as much as it pained him. But Flick did know that things had gone really bad for Cal, so bad that even the Uigenna had cast him out. He'd gone to Seel for sanctuary, but that hadn't lasted long either. By then, Cal had had a disreputable chesnari in tow called Zackala, a har who'd died a short time afterward under circumstances of which the details were disturbingly vague.

The first time Flick had met Cal was a couple of years before, when he'd turned up unannounced at Saltrock. Flick had been jealous of Cal on sight, because his was the lithe, sinuous, lazy sort of beauty that enslaved haras' souls and hearts with no effort whatsoever. It was the kind of beauty that caused trouble, a sort of poison, a narcotic that made you feel good to start with, then sent you spiraling into a gutter, retching your guts out, and wishing you'd never had that first taste. He'd had a lovely human boy with him, who he'd stolen—or bewitched—away from a comfortable home and had brought to Saltrock for inception. Even at the time, Flick had thought this act was perhaps not expedient, but just another way to turn the knife in Seel. But Seel, living up to the image he wanted to portray, had been willing to help, or at least had seemed so. Seel didn't know that Flick had overheard him telling Orien all about this lovely untouched boy, whose name was Pellaz Cevarro. Seel had said there was something different about him. Privately, Flick wondered whether this was perhaps the fact he could hold Cal's interest for more than a minute. Seel had tried to for years without success. Had it been a sense of duty or sour envy that had driven Seel to confide in Orien? Flick still did not know. He did know that Orien had been on the lookout for something, or someone. A high-ranking har somewhere had given him instructions, and in Pell, he'd found what he'd been looking for, or thought he had. Seel had implied so to Orien, which had resulted in Orien making contact with a har who'd arrived at Saltrock with supernatural haste to incept Pell himself. This har was Thiede, a legend among Wraeththu, who hadn't existed long enough to have that many legends.

Thiede was a creature so alien it was impossible to imagine he'd ever been human like the rest of them. He possessed great power and influence, over a race that had little cohesion. It was said that even the Uigenna deferred to him. Thiede had created a destiny for Pell, but nohar knew what it was, only that Pell was innocent and ignorant and very possibly in great danger. Now, Flick thought, Seel tortured himself with guilt about it. It was a complex seethe of emotions that didn't do Seel any good at all. It made him short-tempered during the day and desperate for alcohol and oblivion at night. Flick felt powerless in this situation. He cursed the day Cal had come to Saltrock, even though he'd liked Pell very much and still missed his company. He wished they could all forget about it, because it was over and done, and nohar could change the past. Cal and Pell had left Saltrock earlier that year, because Pell had needed to continue his caste training. Orien had sent him to the Kakkahaar, but they'd heard nothing since. The Kakkahaar were dangerous creatures, supposedly steeped in dark magic, but Orien had wanted Pell to go to them. Why? Was it because he knew Pell would need that dark education in order to survive?

While Flick had been immersed in private reverie, Seel had continued to rant at Orien, who sat bland and composed, infuriatingly tolerant. "I know how you feel," he was saying now, "and I'm sorry." He glanced at Flick. "I think I should leave now."

"Thanks," Flick said bitterly. He didn't want to hear the rest of the rant. He knew it all by heart. At least when Orien was present, Seel directed it all at him. "I don't want these ghosts around us," Flick said. "There's no point to it. It doesn't get us anywhere."

Seel pressed the heels of his hands against his eyes and Flick discreetly removed the wine bottle. Orien stood up, fingers splayed against the tabletop. He stared at Flick as if he didn't know what to say.

Flick made a dismissive gesture. "Get going," he said. "It'll be fine."

Orien nodded, his expression dismal. Flick could tell he hated these confrontations and regretted the worm of suspicion and distrust that had begun to eat away at his close friendship with Seel. Perhaps he should tell the truth, no matter how terrifying or dangerous it might be. At least, it would clear the air and they could face whatever it was together, as a united front.

Orien took his coat from the back of his chair and began to put it on. Silence hung thickly in the room and the candle wax smelled sour. Flick shivered. He felt slightly feverish: it had come upon him suddenly.

Orien appeared to be about to say something, then his eyes glazed over and his body went stiff. Flick glanced around, his skin shrinking against his bones. He was sure Orien could see something in the shadowed corners of the room. "What is it?" he asked quickly.

Orien held his breath, swaying slightly on his feet. Flick realized that he gazed beyond the mundane world. He was looking through a window that neither Seel nor Flick would be able to see. Orien emitted a short strangled sound and clutched blindly for the table to steady himself. His expression was that of naked terror, his eyes still fixed on an impossible distance.

Seel lowered his hands from his eyes, while Flick jumped out of his seat and knocked over his chair.

The air in the room had become chill, in an instant. Something was there with them. Drunkenness dropped from Seel at once—it was plain to see—but before he could do or say anything, Orien fell heavily to the floor.

By the time Flick and Seel reached him, his body was arching in an unnatural way, so that only his head and his heels touched the floor. His hands shook, twisted over his chest.

"What's wrong with him?" Flick cried. "What *is* it?"

Seel knelt down, took Orien's head between his hands. Flick could hear him murmuring: the words of a magical spell or perhaps just of comfort. Orien screamed. It was the most hideous sound Flick had ever heard and he'd heard quite a few nasty screams during other hara's inceptions. "Get me the salad spoon," Seel said.

Flick was nonplussed for a moment.

"Do it! Hurry!" Seel snapped.

The wooden salad spoon had a long handle. The moment Flick handed it to Seel he realized what he meant to do with it. He forced it between Orien's teeth to stop him from ruining his tongue.

The fit seemed to go on for hours. Other hara were attracted by the screams, which had rung out through the peaceful Saltrock night. It was most likely that they were afraid their leader had been attacked. Flick had to answer the hammering on the front door, let them in. When he returned to the dining room, the air stank. Orien had bitten the salad spoon in half and was now lying on his side in a pool of his own vomit, heaving onto the wooden floor. Flick, responsible for all housekeeping, could not help feeling relieved he'd missed the carpet. Seel stroked Orien's wet hair back from his face. The hara who'd come into the house stood around in silence, their surprise at finding their competent shaman in such a state was palpable in the atmosphere. Eventually, Orien stopped retching and groaned.

"Help me lift him," Seel said, and two hara went to assist.

Orien lolled between them, a caricature of his normally elegant graceful self. "It's done," he croaked. "It's done."

Seel and his assistants lowered Orien onto a chair. "What's done?" Seel asked. "What has happened?"

In response, Orien surrendered to a fit of weeping so heartfelt it instilled horror in the breast of everyhar present. Flick had never heard sobs come from so deep within a harish frame before. It was a lament for the world.

Something terrible had happened. Orien held onto Seel tightly, as if Seel could somehow make the terror go away.

"What's happened?" Seel asked again, but it was clear that Orien couldn't answer.

After everyhar had gone, Flick left Seel to help Orien upstairs to a guest room and went out into the night. He knew Seel and Orien needed time alone, bound together in an uncomfortable cocoon where there was no room for him. He walked around the yard behind the house, restlessly pacing. Horses watched him nervously from the corral, unable to sleep so close to his fizzing energy. Flick looked up at the sky, so many stars there. Some of them were already dead, of course. Still beautiful to behold, but already dead. Flick hugged himself. The air was hot, but he felt so cold. He was eighteen years old, but felt ninety. *What are we doing?* he thought. *What are we?*

He glanced back at the house, solid against the sky, a house built by harish hands, but no different from a house that humans might once have lived in. Aeons ago, a flicker in time, Flick had lived in a very similar house, where there was a magnolia tree near the porch and children's toys strewn over the lawn. Now he was here and someone else, but there were too many holes in the story, as if he was dreaming and couldn't wake up.

Have we any right to mimic the past? he thought. *Isn't it a travesty? We should live beneath the stars, howling like coyotes; we should live in tepees or tall towers of stone with no stairs. We should not eat dinner together in candlelight, or drink wine, or talk about inconsequential things. We are not allowed to, and look what happens when we do. The otherness comes creeping in to remind us of what we are. It's done; he said so. But what?*

It was something big, Flick was sure of that. And it wasn't merely going to touch them—it was going to reach down and grab them and squeeze them of breath.

Without realizing he had done so, Flick found he'd gone back into the house and up the stairs to the room he didn't share with Seel, but was regularly invited to. Seel lay on the bed, smoking a cigarette in semidarkness. His multicolored hair was spread over the pillows. He looked fierce.

"We can't hide here," Flick said. "You do know that, don't you?"

Seel exhaled; the smoke looked like his own breath. "Go away," he said.

"Sometimes, I really want to."

Seel said nothing to this, as Flick had expected, although he couldn't have been ignorant of the implications.

Flick went to sit on the bed. "Did Orien say anything else?"

"Nothing that made sense," Seel said. "I've never seen him like that."

"He's afraid."

"Yes. He's a fool. We're our own hara here."

"You—we—invited Thiede in. He's seen us now. He knows us."

"We have no proof that what happened tonight has any connection with that," Seel said. "It would be a mistake to spook ourselves. Orien is a seer. He just had a moment, that's all. It could mean anything."

"Except that it didn't."

"I told you to get out, didn't I? What's keeping you?"

"You were never like this, Seel, not before . . ."

"Get out, Flick. I mean it."

Anger flared up in Flick's heart. "No!" he cried. "I won't. I'm not your servant. I'm not even your whore, although you treat me like one."

"What the fuck are you talking . . ."

Flick sliced the air with one hand. "No! Listen to me. Tonight was all about Cal. You know it was. Something's happened and you're scared he's dead. Isn't that right? You and Orien invited something into Saltrock and you can't undo it. You know it. I know it. Everyhar knows it. What did Orien see? Tell me! I know you know."

"He thinks he's doomed, okay? Does that satisfy you? He thinks he's dead."

"It's not just that."

"Oh, what the fuck do you want it to be, then? Isn't that bad enough for a har to see, to experience?"

"Seel, calm down. This anger is just a defense. What else did Orien see? Why does he feel threatened?"

"His own death. Can't you get it? You want a message for yourself? Is that it?" Seel growled and took a long furious draw off his cigarette. "Are you that important, Flick?"

Flick's heart was beating fast now. He felt dizzy with the hostility that screamed silently around the room. He swallowed slowly and with difficulty, as if past a tumor that had formed in his throat. "You were never hostile. You're becoming like him—you're becoming Cal. Don't do it, Seel. You're better than that."

Seel's lips curled into a snarl. "You have no right to speak to me like that. I won't accept it. Get out, before I do or say something I can't take back."

"You never ran from the truth before. You were in balance, with yourself and with others. Can't you see what's happening? Is this what you want to be?" Flick knew he was heading into very dangerous territory, but he had to speak.

Seel sat up abruptly and it took all of Flick's will not flinch away. He thought he knew Seel, but perhaps all he did know was what Seel wanted to be. Seel had been incepted to the Uigenna. There was wildness in him, even if it was buried deep. Somehow, pushing the fear back down inside him, Flick managed to hold Seel's furious gaze. He had to try and reach him: the real Seel, the person he knew and wanted to love.

Eventually, Seel sighed and leaned over to stub out his cigarette in an ash-tray on the bedside table. "You're right," he said. "I'm sorry. Now will you please go?"

"You should talk about it."

Seel uttered a caustic laugh. "About how I probably changed the course of Pell's life, and through doing that changed all of our lives? We think we know so much. We don't know anything. I lost sight of that. I was too adept at for-getting. Now it's too late, and I know something's happening and I'm partly to blame. I could feel it in that room down there. I could smell it. I smelled Cal, the way he was a long time ago."

"Shutting yourself away won't help," Flick said. "We should all face this together, whatever it is. We mustn't fight amongst ourselves."

"I don't want to go back," Seel said. "That's what it's about. I want to stay here, live the life I've chosen, but I know I can't. That's the worst of it. You're right, Flick, Thiede has seen us all. And we're just puppets to him."

"Is that what Orien saw?"

"I think so, yes."

"What is Pell's destiny? Will you tell me?"

"I don't know and that's the truth. But it's not just him. It's all of us." Seel grimaced. "My guts ache. They ache so much."

CHAPTER THREE

When an abnormal event occurs, it tends to occupy hara's attention, consume them with the emotions it might have inspired. But it is impossible to live in the moment of an abnormal event forever. In the morning, meals still need preparing, a lame horse has to be shod, fires have to be built.

And so it was in the Kakkahaar camp. Ulaume's unexpected fit the previous night had brought a nervous edge to the festival, even though Lianvis had done his best to reassure his hara that it was nothing out of the ordinary. Strange influences might be floating on the ethers and sensitive hara could pick up on them. Visionaries and seers were subject to that kind of episode all the time. It was a risk they took and nothing to worry about.

Ulaume knew this was a lie but appreciated why it had to be said. He wasn't sure himself what last night's events really meant, only that they had affected him greatly. He hadn't been able to curse Pellaz either, and the two things must be connected. Had he incurred Hubisag's displeasure? Surely not. Pellaz represented all that Hubisag did not stand for. Some Wraeththu strove to be pure, enlightened, and compassionate. Some strove to be decadent, enlightened, and dispassionate. The Kakkahaar fell heavily into the latter camp, while Pellaz, who'd been incepted at Saltrock, was influenced by the former.

After his trance, Ulaume had been unable to join in with the festivities, but for the sake of appearances had concluded his dance, a torment for which Lianvis had thanked him warmly afterward. The Kakkahaar leader knew it had been a dreadful trial and that Ulaume had only done it to allay the fears of his tribe. As soon as he was able, Ulaume had slunk off into the desert. He couldn't talk to Lianvis yet, even though he'd felt his leader's eyes upon him as he left the gathering.

Ulaume walked around till dawn, trying to work out the meaning of what had happened. He knew he'd witnessed Pellaz's death, and also that he had not been an instrumental factor in it, but he was overwhelmed by the fact that this knowledge heralded a beginning, rather than an end. In the cold twilight of the predawn Ulaume sat down with his back to a tall rock and faced an unpleasant truth—something to which he was not normally given. He hated Pellaz because Pellaz had spurned him. Pellaz despised him and thought he was evil. Ulaume believed that eventually he'd have been able to turn this pious creature, but unfortunately his companion, Cal, had been a Uigenna, who'd had Ulaume's measure all too accurately and had influenced Pellaz's opinions. Perhaps, then, Ulaume should hate Cal more than Pell and direct the curse at him. But that was pointless, because anyhar could see that Cal was already cursed. He was more kin to Ulaume than he was to Pellaz, and also unreachable. Ulaume now felt annoyed with himself that he'd allowed these hara to affect him. Weakness, weakness, and he'd believed it to be strength. He felt as if he'd had his wrist spiritually slapped and that was a humiliating sensation. The universe had told him emphatically that, in some way, his destiny was linked with Pell's, but how could that be? How could he be linked to a dead har? How could so shining a har, in fact, be dead? He was too vital, too alive, too . . . special. Ulaume ground his teeth. He didn't like having to admit that. He didn't like having to admit that the curse would have involved asking Hubisag to send Pellaz back to the Kakkahaar, so Ulaume could exact his own revenge, the result of which, in Ulaume's dreams, was Pell's submission. It would never happen now.

Ulaume punched the hard cold ground and said aloud, "Show yourself to me, shining spirit. Tell what it is you tried to convey. I am open to your manifestation. Speak to me."

Nothing answered, but in the distance a coyote yipped at the last stars in the sky. Ulaume sighed heavily. There were no answers out here. Perhaps there would never be answers.

He returned to the camp, where the last stragglers from the festival were slouching back to their pavilions, yawning and belching and supporting each other. A few lewd songs could still be heard inside the tents. Ulaume felt depressed by it all. These stupid creatures hadn't realized something of importance had happened. They had abandoned themselves to wild excess and today they'd readjust their masks into those of restrained shamanic adepts, believing they knew all the mysteries of life and death, when in fact they knew nothing.

Lianvis was still awake, drinking coffee in the main salon of his pavilion. Ulaume was annoyed to see he had company, a high ranking har of the tribe named Rarn. Ulaume really needed to talk to Lianvis alone, and thought that Lianvis would have known this.

"Good news," Lianvis said, when he noticed Ulaume skulking among the draperies. "Last night, Rarn's consort delivered a pearl."

Ulaume grunted. To him, that was of no importance. There were more pressing matters to discuss.

"Perhaps this was what your trance indicated," Lianvis said.

"I hardly think so," Ulaume snapped. "I saw death, not birth."

Rarn shifted uncomfortably on the cushions.

"Yes," Lianvis said. "We must speak of this. You told me somehar was dead. Who?"

Ulaume struggled with the anger that rose within him. Lianvis sounded as if he was inquiring about a ridiculous piece of gossip. He was clearly so pleased about the pearl, he had forgotten the enormity of last night's events, the pressure in the air, the feeling of power all around them. He didn't even seem concerned about where Ulaume had been all night. "No har in particular," Ulaume said. "It doesn't matter."

"Today, we must celebrate," Lianvis said. "Our tribe has taken a great step forward."

"Congratulations," Ulaume said spitefully to Rarn.

"We know now that this is something we can all achieve," Lianvis said carefully, appraising Ulaume with a steady eye. "We can create our own pearl."

Ulaume nearly choked. Lianvis thought his waspishness was because he felt jealous of Rarn's consort. "It isn't something I've thought about," he said. "It's not my role in life."

"Surely, it is everyhar's," Lianvis said, and now he sounded stern.

Ulaume slumped wearily inside. So, Lianvis wanted sons. This was the last thing Ulaume could think about. "Whatever you want," he said. "I need to sleep now."

He left the room and once the drapes fell behind him, he could hear Lianvis speaking quietly to Rarn. Ulaume realized he'd received another message from the universe. Whatever had happened, or was happening, to him, he must deal with it alone.

Unfortunately, the universe was not very forthcoming about what Ulaume should actually do. Most nights, he awoke from disturbing dreams, of which he could not remember the details. He woke with a taste of metal in his mouth and a strong desire to leap up and run somewhere. But where? The rest of the tribe, including Lianvis, appeared to forget there had been anything unusual about the night of the festival: Herien's pearl wholly consumed their attention. It was as if they believed that no other Wraeththu had ever succeeded at pro-creation, although Ulaume knew this was not the truth. The tribe would not move on until the pearl had delivered up its treasure and Ulaume felt so rest-less. He took to walking out into the desert at night, willing for whatever en-tity had tried to communicate with him at the festival to manifest once more. If he had a job to do, he must know about it. He should be given a sign. It was strange, but he no longer felt the anger and need for revenge he had before. If Pellaz had died, then he had taken all of Ulaume's rage with him. All that was left was a burning curiosity and a sense of yearning. Lianvis barely noticed Ulaume's protracted absences from the camp, spending most of his time in Rarn's pavilion instructing Herien on how he should bring up his harling, once it hatched.

Herien, privately, often wondered exactly who would be the parents of the child when it finally emerged into the light, given Lianvis's overwhelming in-terest in the proceedings. He began to harbor fantasies of running away, but then he had become very attached to the pearl and the life that writhed within it. He resented the fact that everyhar else was intent on sharing what he wanted to be a private personal experience. His desires were not to be catered for, however, because on the night when the surface of the pearl convulsed and began to fracture, every high-ranking har of the tribe was in Rarn's pavil-ion. The pearl lay on a cushion in their midst and at the moment when a small groping hand emerged from the rubbery coating, every throat uttered a gasp of wonder.

Herien himself could not breathe. He held onto Chisbet's hand, so full of emotion he thought he might explode. Chisbet pulled away from him to help the harling emerge from its external womb. Carefully, he stripped away the withered shell and lifted the child out. He held it up before the others, who were silenced. A creature perfectly formed. A miracle. It stared around itself with knowing eyes, so unlike a human child, it made everyhar feel totally freakish for some moments.

Herien clasped his own throat with both hands, as if to hold onto consciousness. He could not believe what he beheld, but felt in his heart he had given birth to a god. The harling did not look like a baby, but a miniature human child of two years or so. Its fair hair was soft and silky, its expression weirdly benign. It uttered a sound, surely a laugh, and waved its small fists at its audience. And perhaps because they regarded it through a film of tears, none of them noticed the obvious at first.

Rarn fought his way through the goggling throng and put his arms around Herien's shoulders. "Thank you," he murmured.

It was the most complete and wondrous moment of Herien's life, but sadly short-lived.

Chisbet had put the harling down on the cushion in order to inspect it thoroughly and now his expression had become grave and distressed. He knelt up, hands braced on his thighs, and stared down at the harling; his eye held the intense gaze of an oracle.

"What is it?" Lianvis demanded.

Chisbet shook his head and sighed deeply. "Send these hara away, Tiahaar," he said. "I must talk to you and the parents in private."

At once a murmuring started up, but Lianvis got to his feet immediately and asked the company to leave. Reluctantly, they did so.

Herien used this opportunity to seize his harling and hold it close to his breast. He sensed trouble and a lioness instinct took over. If anyhar had bothered to glance at him, they would have seen he was prepared to die to protect his young.

"Is something wrong?" Lianvis asked, once the last har had left the pavilion.

Rarn had wrapped both Herien and the harling in a fierce embrace. "There is nothing wrong," he said in a low voice. "What is this, Chisbet?"

The harling chuckled to itself and gazed in wonder around the pavilion. It made small noises of interest and pointed at various objects. Then it would nuzzle into its hostling's hair.

Herien had closed his eyes.

Chisbet composed himself on the cushions. "What I have to say is not easy," he said. "I have heard of this happening, but have never witnessed it."

"What?" Lianvis barked.

Chisbet scratched his empty eye socket. "Herien," he said, "please put the harling down on the cushion again. It will be easier for me to show you than to explain."

"No!" Herien snarled. "There's nothing wrong with him. Get out!"

Chisbet looked up at Lianvis. "Tiahaar?"

"Do as he says," Lianvis said. "We need to know."

"This is my harling!" Herien snapped. "Mine. Not yours." He held the child tight, and now its small features had become slightly troubled. So the concept of fear came into its life.

"It is not exactly a harling," Chisbet said.

"What do you mean?" Rarn asked. "How can that possibly be so?"

Chisbet held out a hand to Herien. "Please, trust me. Put down the child. Let me show you."

Herien looked into Chisbet's eye, this har he trusted so implicitly and who over the last few months had become one of his closest friends. He saw compassion in Chisbet's gaze and reluctantly laid down his child, keeping one hand upon it.

"Look," Chisbet said, straightening the harling's limbs. "This is not a Wraeththu child, as such. It is not androgynous. It is a half-sex, in this case, female."

For a few moments, everyone stared at the child in silence. Herien felt totally numb. He remembered having a dog as a young boy, and how that dog had been his constant companion, his beloved friend. All his memories of the dog were gilded, but one day the animal had contracted a disease, which had made him no longer a faithful companion. Herien, as a human, had tried to ignore this. He'd been too full of love to care. He would love the dog and that would sustain the pair of them. But one day, the dog had gone, because it was dangerous and Herien's parents had been afraid for him. Old feelings of grief now flooded his body. He picked up the harling and enfolded it in his arms. It didn't matter, surely? It didn't matter. The child had come from his body. They were linked.

"I don't understand this," Lianvis was saying. "What are you trying to tell us, Chisbet?"

"Occasionally, I have heard, harlings of this type appear among Wraeththukind. They are throwbacks, freaks."

"But you have never seen one," Rarn said. "How do you know he won't develop the necessary characteristics later on? You've only seen one birth, you said so. You know only a little more than the rest of us."

"I know about this," Chisbet said, "because the har who trained me told me of it. He told me to be aware of it and how to deal with it, should it occur. It is very rare, among births that in themselves are rare, but my mentor impressed upon me its importance."

"Again, what are you trying to tell us?" Lianvis said in an even tone that normally sent hara into palpitations of terror.

Chisbet appeared most reluctant to speak. Eventually, he swallowed, and said, "We cannot allow creatures of this nature to live."

Herien uttered a moan of dread.

"What?" Rarn cried. "Are you telling me to kill my own son?"

"It is not a son," Chisbet said calmly. "You must face this. We don't know exactly how spiritually elevated aruna creates harlings. We don't know if we always do it right. This is a new and experimental time for us, and as such we must remain objective."

"This is a harsh judgment," Lianvis said.

"I will not do it," Herien said. "I'll leave the tribe, live in exile. I will not do it."

"And I will be with you," Rarn said.

"You cannot," Chisbet insisted. "Believe me, I am as grieved and sorrowful as you are. I feel as much a part of this young one's birth as its own hostling. But the truth cannot be ignored, and as healer of this tribe, given shelter by the Kakkahaar when I most needed it, I must be honest with you. These creatures are dangerous. My mentor told me of it. He told me how one tribe allowed such a child to grow up among them and that it was mad. It was an abomination of a creature, full of bitterness and vengeance. In the end, they had to kill it before it killed somehar else."

"That is only one child," Herien said, surprisingly calm. "You don't know that my harling will be the same. As Rarn said, he might change as he grows. You don't know. None of us do."

"Could it be the host who is responsible?" Lianvis enquired. "Will Herien be able to have normal harlings after this?"

Herien had never heard such a sinister question voiced about himself.

"Yes," Chisbet said. "My mentor told me that the har who created the other half-sex had another harling very quickly, who was completely normal. We don't know what causes this condition, as I said. But for its own sake, the child must be exposed, otherwise we doom it to a life of pain."

"I won't let you do this!" Herien cried.

Chisbet nodded slowly, acknowledging Herien's anguish, and his voice, when he spoke, was soft. "Herien, you must look upon this as a stillbirth, a terrible circumstance that human women had to deal with throughout history. Know that I will do all in my power to make this painless. I will dose the child with a soothing philter, so that the moon may take it in peace, out in the wilderness. Its soul must be given this release. It is the only fair and compassionate thing to do. We are not humans, bound up in superstitious fear of physical death. We are Wraeththu. We are strong. We know the soul is eternal and the flesh but a temporary vehicle. If the vehicle is faulty, the soul deserves to find for itself a more suitable vessel."

"No," Herien said. "No."

Rarn pointed a shaking finger at his harling. "How can you look upon this beautiful being and sentence him to death? Are you insane? We are less than human if we do this thing."

"Tiahaar," Chisbet said to Lianvis. "Emotions run high, which is understandable, but you alone are detached and you are our leader. You cannot present this harling to the tribe as a miracle, because it is not. You should not be swayed sentimentally by its appearance. You must be firm on this matter."

"Betrayer!" Herien cried. "You are doomed too, Chisbet, doomed by my curse. By all the gods, I hex you to eternity!" He appealed to Lianvis. "Do not listen to him, tiahaar. Allow us to leave the tribe. If all proceeds as Chisbet says, then we will deal with it in our own way, but give us a chance."

Lianvis tapped his clasped hands against his mouth. He appeared to be deep in thought. "The bloodline of the Kakkahaar must be kept pure," he said at last. "We cannot afford to slip back."

"This is barbaric!" Rarn cried. "I can't believe you're even giving it consideration!"

But he was appealing to a har who had done terrible things, far worse than exposing a freakish child in the desert. Lianvis did not want the slur of this event to affect his reputation among Wraeththukind. The Kakkahaar were feared and respected, and their livelihood mainly rested upon that. If other tribe leaders had been strong enough to do as their healers had suggested, then so was he. "Bring Ulaume to me," he said. "Let our seer look into this. Then, I will make a decision."

Ulaume, however, was nowhere to be found, as he was out on one of his meditative excursions in the moonlight. How he would have dealt with the situation will never be known, because he never found out that Lianvis had summoned him. Instead, Persiki, one of the shamans of the high cabal came to Rarn's pavilion. Like Lianvis, he was a creature who was intimate with the abyss and all its horrors. His morality was molded wholly by the things that his tribe's high-ranking hara did together in private rituals, away from the prying eyes of the rank and file. He had taken life many times. He had watched Lianvis murder human children to attain power. He was capable of finer feelings, as was Lianvis himself, but he was also merciless.

Herien did not know much about Persiki, but he did not believe he'd have an ally in him. As Persiki cast grains onto a burning charcoal, and breathed in its fumes in order to enter a trance, Herien was planning his escape. He feared

Lianvis enough to know that trying to make a run for it would be fruitless. He was not yet capable of communication by mind touch to formulate a strategy with Rarn, because Herien was only Aralid, the lowest of Wraeththu castes. But there would have to be an opportunity when he could run. Not here, not now, but soon. The harling breathed against him, as still and silent as a small animal who sensed it was in danger. Remaining motionless, and perhaps invisible, was its only defense.

Persiki had begun to rock upon his heels, his hands braced against his knees. He inhaled deeply and exhaled in a gasp. Then he opened his eyes and stared directly at Herien. "You will be blessed, doubly blessed," he said.

Herien could not take comfort in those words; he heard a threat behind them. "How?"

"Two harlings, the seeds of a great dynasty among the Kakkahaar. Their names will be commemorated in stone. Their monuments will touch the sky."

"Is this one of these legendary harlings?" Lianvis enquired delicately, indicating the child in Herien's arms.

Persiki flicked a glance at his leader, like the cold kiss of a serpent's tongue. "No," he said. "This creature will be exposed in the desert."

"Death, then," Lianvis said.

Herien could not speak. There were dancing spots of light before his vision. For the first time in years, he felt utterly powerless, more so than when he'd writhed in althaia, the changing, more so than when he'd striven on a bed of birthing.

"It will be exposed in the desert," Persiki said. "That's all I can say."

"And will you kill me to achieve this?" Herien asked.

"No," Persiki said in a flat tone. "You will do as you know is right. Give this poor creature to the moon and then go to your pavilion. Hubisag will place a balm over your wound. There will be another harling—two. This is the measure of how important it is to renounce this ill birth. The gods will reward you with two harlings should you have the strength to do what is most unspeakable to you. I swear this in the name of all I stand for and believe in. I would stake my very soul upon it. The creature that sprang from your flesh is not yours to raise."

Perhaps it was Persiki's strange choice of words that swayed Herien's heart, or perhaps it was because Herien knew that whatever he thought, said, or did, the harling would be taken from him, in any case. Herien could not tell. But for a moment, a strange feeling, as of being plunged into a cold spring, flooded his body. For a moment, he was bigger than himself and filled with hope and clarity. He had a secret, it had come to him as a divine gift, but he could not voice it. Silently, he handed the harling to Persiki, who held his gaze with steady, knowing eyes. Herien could sense that the breath was stilled in every breast around him. Rarn made a move to retrieve the child, uttering a cry, but Herien stayed his hand.

"Do what you must," he said.

Lianvis exhaled loudly, his hands braced against his knees. "You have my respect," he said, "and will be rewarded."

"That is not necessary," Herien said, still gazing into Persiki's shrouded eyes.

"No!" Rarn cried, a ragged, heartbreaking sound.

Herien felt calm, and not at all surprised that Rarn could not share what he felt. Rarn wept openly now, caught in the same caul of powerlessness that Herien had felt only moments before. It was possible Herien would never be able to share what he knew with his chesnari, but that did not matter. There were other ways to bind an injury. All that Herien knew was that the only chance his child had was if he surrendered it. If the moon had a destiny for it, it was not death. The child was placid again now, as if it too sensed a crucial decision had been reached.

Go with my blessings, Herien thought, and was sure, for the first time, his unspoken words were heard by another mind. *Be strong. Be curious. Live.*

Ulaume had been roaming around the cold desert nearly all night, and now the light had become grey with the promise of dawn. He felt driven, or hagridden, his entire body filled with a compulsion he could not identify. He wanted to scratch himself raw, tear out his hair, scream. The stones beneath his bare feet were sharp and he craved the pain they inflicted. He wanted to leave bloody footprints. A coyote was trailing him curiously, as if it thought he might show it something. Twice, he had paused to throw a rock at it, and the animal had loped away for a distance, only to stand and stare after him, before resuming its pursuit. It looked sick, its belly a little distended. Ulaume was not afraid of the animal. He wanted only to say, "Go away. I cannot give you anything," but a coyote could not understand words.

He could not live like this. It had to be resolved. Was the only answer to confide in Lianvis, and perform some ritual to get information? Ulaume balked from doing that. He hugged his torment to himself jealously. He did not want to tell Lianvis about Pellaz, because the thought of Lianvis's inevitable extreme interest was repugnant. Lianvis would suggest something grotesque, like trying to capture Pell's spirit, which was so far from the point, it was embarrassing. Ulaume was sure Lianvis was incapable of feeling the true meaning of what had happened, even though he was an experienced magician, perhaps the best. He would make something gross and common out of a rare, unique event. Ulaume could not bear it.

I must leave, he thought. *That's it. Leave my tribe. If I live in the desert for a hundred years, alone, perhaps the answers will come to me. If I scour my skin with ashes and eat bitter grasses, if I hardly drink, go mad, howl at the moon, I may be given the truth.*

It was then he realized that the coyote behind him was an aspect of himself.

He could not return to the camp for any of his possessions or supplies. Now the decision was made, he must run with it, into the wilderness. If he could not survive, then it was what was meant to be. Somehow, he didn't think he'd die. Without looking behind, he stopped walking and presently heard the faint sounds that indicated the coyote had almost caught up with him.

"Go ahead," Ulaume said aloud. "Find the way." Still, he did not move.

After some minutes, he noticed the coyote about thirty feet to his left, but trotting ahead of him. He could see now that it was a female and had clearly recently had cubs, as its teats were engorged. Where were those cubs now?

But that creature is me, Ulaume thought, *and I am bursting with something, I am hot and sore. This is just a symbol.*

He followed it.

Dawn comes like a song to the desert, shedding scarlet notes of light over the distant hills. Shadows are stark and alive with creatures once hidden by the dark. Birds wheel high on wide wings in the purple sky. Like a compass they can guide the traveler, not in a particular direction, but to where there is water or food.

Ulaume saw three carrion birds, known to the Kakkahaar as crag rocs, circling quite low some distance ahead of him. The coyote had increased her pace, perhaps making for a water hole. The birds flew lower, landing in a showy flap of wings, ungainly on the ground, uttering squawks. When the coyote ran among them, they protested and lumbered around, raising their wings, but they did not take to the air.

Ulaume approached. The crag rocs had found carrion then, and perhaps he could salvage some of it to cook, share it with his shadow-beast. He picked up a couple of rocks. It was possible he could take out one of the birds themselves. But what made Ulaume throw the stones wasn't the thought of cooked crag roc. It was the fact he heard a soft mewling cry coming from the ground among them. His heart went cold and he ran forward screeching, letting the stones fly from his hands. The coyote, spooked, ran around too, snapping at the air, and the birds rose up in a complaining, clattering flutter.

Ulaume stopped running and looked down. Into a smile. He saw small hands reaching up for him, heard laughter. There wasn't a mark on the child. Not one. Ulaume hunkered down. Who could have left a child out here? Humans? Surely not. And no Wraeththu would do such a thing. Children were too precious to both species; rare and new in Wraeththu, just rare in humans. Perhaps its parents had been killed, but there was no sign of bodies around, no blood or bones. The child was wrapped in a thin cloth, a piece of white linen that looked as if it had been torn from a sheet. "Am I to eat you?" Ulaume asked it. There was something odd about the child. It wasn't a baby, yet it was so small. Was it a midget or a dwarf?

Ulaume unwrapped the sheet and found the child wore a talisman on a leather thong around its neck. The leather was wet as if it had been chewed. The talisman, however, was Kakkahaar, a symbol of protection, stiff herbs bound with horsehair, wrapped in a leather scrap. Ulaume stared at this talisman in disbelief. He knew there was only one Wraeththu child this could possibly be and yet it made no sense. Had he intruded upon some kind of ritual and soon shamans would emerge from the desert to chase him off? He looked around himself, saw only empty desert. The camp was some miles away. That left only one conclusion. The harling had been abandoned here deliberately. So what was wrong with it that the tribe would expose it like this? Everyhar had been so excited about the hatching—too excited, in Ulaume's opinion. Tentatively, he picked the harling up, holding it beneath its arms. It squirmed in his hold, uttering a series of trilling calls, like those of the desert birds, the little hoppers that pecked insects from the scrub. Its legs dangled and kicked. It expressed a robust cry, like a command.

"Shall I eat you?" Ulaume said again and snapped his teeth at the harling.

In response, it laughed, or perhaps it was just another animal sound. Ulaume knew he could not kill and eat the child, but what else could he do with it? Just walk away? He put down the child and stood up. It would be difficult enough to feed himself, never mind a helpless harling and yet it was impossible to ignore the instinct inside him that clamored to protect the infant. It was a gut deep, ferocious feeling, all teeth and snarls. *Must be a female thing,* Ulaume thought, but it didn't help the situation. The coyote was circling the pair of them, her head low, her tongue lolling.

"No meat for you either," Ulaume said, and considered picking up another stone.

The harling, who'd been lying on its back, scrambled onto its belly as Ulaume spoke and before he could blink was crawling at preternatural speed toward the loping coyote. Small stones were thrown up in its wake.

"No," Ulaume said, reaching down to grab the harling. He couldn't believe the child could crawl this fast if it had only hatched hours ago. *What are we?* he thought. *Animals?* He thought of calves and foals, which could walk virtually as soon as they fell from the womb. The harling adeptly avoided Ulaume's hands and he stopped trying to catch it. It seemed to know what it was doing. The coyote was standing absolutely still, her ears pricked. The harling halted a couple of feet away from her and Ulaume could hear it sniffing the air. Then it advanced once more and, reaching the animal's side, groped upward with tiny hands. It pulled itself to its feet, gripping the coyote's fur.

Ulaume shook his head in delight and surprise. "So, the next best thing to being brought up by wolves," he said. In that moment, he thought he had found a kindred soul.

The harling had nuzzled into the coyote's belly and had begun to suck milk from her noisily, while the animal stood passively, allowing it. If Ulaume had instincts, so did the child, an instinct to survive so strong, it colored the air around it pure gold. So strong, it knew about mother's milk, even though, in the normal scheme of things, it would never have tasted it.

CHAPTER FOUR

> ━┥◆〉·✛·〈◆┝━◁

On the day that Cal returned to Saltrock, the air, the very earth, writhed with omens. Pink-edged gray clouds clustered in the sky at midday, lightning stitched through them that never hit the ground. The sun was a gloating eye, peering blindly through the boiling heavens. A group of crows attacked a calf and pecked out one of its eyes. Dogs howled as if a full moon soaked them in lunatic radiance and had to be tied up, while cats fled to the rafters in the attics of every completed house and crouched in the spidery shadows, hissing, their fur erect along their spines. Ghosts walked the rough main street of the town, although only a few hara could see them.

Seel put all this down to the strange weather, although Flick knew better and believed that Seel did too. He wanted to say, "It's coming, whatever it is," but Seel wouldn't hear it. He was clinging with all his strength to a mundane life, as if Wraeththu life could ever be that. Flick pitied him. Hara wanted to go to the Nayati and pray. They wanted ritual, to appease the gods, but Seel wouldn't hear of that either. He marched around the small town, growling orders, inspecting work, his hair livid in the peculiar light. Orien did not emerge from his dwelling at all.

Ever since the episode of Orien's trance, Flick had felt as if life was on hold. He could barely breathe sometimes. After their argument, Seel had made a great and obvious effort to be less grouchy, but the strain of it was clearly wearing him out. Everyone was terrified and didn't know why. Hara approached Flick, because he was the most approachable and close to Seel, but he couldn't tell them anything. They thought he lied to them, and perhaps he did, but there were no words to express what he felt. It was as if the whole of Wraeththu history, such as it was, had only been a preamble to what was going to happen next. How could he tell hara that, when the obvious question to follow it would be "and what *is* going to happen?" Flick didn't know the answer. Orien might, but he had become reclusive. Many times, Flick had knocked upon his door and been ignored. He had shouted, pleaded, but had received no response. Time and again, the thought *He's preparing to die* flashed through Flick's mind, but he pushed it away. Thinking those words made them real; it was the worst magic. Flick realized how special Orien was to him. This was the har, after all, who had led him from the ruins of his human life to a new existence in Saltrock. This was the har who had incepted him, and had always been there for him. Flick wished he could help now, but it was clear that Orien had decided to shut the world out.

So on this day of doom, Flick rode his gray pony, Ghost, out alone beside the soda lake. Leaving the creature to nibble furtively at dry scrub, Flick clambered up one of the spiky crags to gaze out at the eastern horizon, which was invisible in a milky haze. He had come to this place many times with Pell, when Pell had been silent and tense, staring without blinking into the future, which of course had lain to the east.

Flick said aloud, "Is this to do with you, Pell? Are you trying to tell us something?"

And a ghost Pell beside him, who existed only in his mind, said, "You know that I am."

"Then speak plainly."

"You have to imagine it, invent it. You know that."

Flick sighed and rubbed at his eyes, feeling the weight of the eerie sky pressing down upon him. The back of his neck felt hot, as if somehar breathed upon it. He could imagine hands hovering above his shoulders and almost reached up to find them, pull whoever they belonged to through into this reality, but then he thought he heard a gasp behind him and opened his eyes quickly. The sensation of presence vanished and the world seemed stark and raw and without spirit.

A horse was stumbling toward Saltrock along the dusty eastern road. Its head hung low in exhaustion and a shapeless figure was slumped upon its back. The clop of the horse's hooves echoed in the wide cup of the mountains.

Birds rose from the caustic bath of the lake in a shimmering throng. Flick got to his feet and put his hands around his eyes to focus on whoever, or whatever, approached. He heard Ghost whinny softly below—a sound of alarm—and jumped down from the rock. He was aware of a sense of relief. This was it. At last.

He mounted the pony and urged it toward the approaching horse, which lifted its head and found the energy to prick up its ears. Its rider seemed asleep in the saddle.

"Hoi!" Flick called.

At the sound of his voice, the horse came to a halt. Flick could see the rider wore a wide-brimmed hat. His body was wrapped in a dusty, colorless cloak. Flick jumped down from his pony. The rider was motionless; there were flies around him. Could he be dead? Flick remembered instances of disease being brought unwittingly into Saltrock. Perhaps he should be cautious. Scanning the ground, he found a thin black stick and used this to poke the rider in the leg from a short distance. The body twitched and slowly the rider raised his head. Flick saw smoldering violet eyes gazing down at him from a filthy face. He felt paralyzed, even though at first he did not recognize who he was looking at.

"Flick." The voice itself was dusty, like that of a revenant, full of earth. It was dead, without inflection.

Flick didn't say anything. He was thinking of hauntings and curses, and wondered whether he should just leap back onto his pony and gallop hell for leather back to town.

The rider took off his hat, revealing flattened white-gold hair that the dust had not touched. "It's me," he said.

"Great gods!" Flick cried. "Cal." He couldn't think of anything else to say. This was too unbelievable, and surely no coincidence given what had happened a few weeks before.

"I had to come back," Cal said.

"Well . . . well it's good to see you," Flick said insincerely. He frowned. "Where's Pell?" He looked around, which was ridiculous, because the landscape was so empty. "I was just thinking of him."

Cal smiled sweetly and said in a matter-of-fact tone, "Oh. Dead."

"What?" Flick's voice was a squeak. "How? Why?"

"It's what I'm here to find out," Cal said. "This is the end of the path."

It didn't feel real, Pell being dead. It wasn't real. Flick couldn't believe what he'd heard, sure that he'd have felt it in the fiber of his being if it were true. But something had happened. Something. "Come to Seel," Flick said. "I'll take you."

"I know the way," Cal said. "You know I do."

"I'm sorry," Flick said, but they were just words.

"Everyhar *will* be," Cal said.

Flick smiled nervously and clambered back onto his pony. He fought an urge to hurry. It was clear that Cal's horse was at the end of its strength, as was its rider. Cal looked as if he'd fought a battle and lost. He should be dripping blood. Flick had a water bottle with him, containing a small measure of warm stale liquid. This he offered to Cal, who declined it.

"What happened?" Flick asked, fully prepared for Cal not to answer him, because he was used to his questions being ignored. "*Where* did it happen?"

"Near Galhea," Cal said. "Pell was shot there. I had to burn . . ."

"No," Flick said. "This can't be true. It can't."

"Then please tell me it isn't and be right," Cal said, deadpan.

That was when Flick realized it must be true after all. His friend was dead. "No," he said again. "It can't be."

"It is," Cal said. "A mark was put on him, and it was seen, recognized. Just a nobody. A human. But they might as well have been a god."

"But . . . but how?"

Flick wanted to say, "Well, weren't you there to protect him?" Didn't he have Kakkahaar magic behind him?

"I want to know," Cal said. "It is my only purpose now. It's why I'm here."

"You think Orien can help?"

Cal was silent, his face grim. He thought Orien could help all right.

"Things have changed," Flick said. "Orien had a strange turn. He hardly comes out now. He won't speak to me."

Cal still did not speak. If he'd been damaged before, he was clearly ruined now. Flick was anxious to turn this casualty over to Seel. "Perhaps that's when it happened," he said, thinking aloud.

Cal glanced at him.

"When Orien had his turn. Perhaps that was when Pell died. A week or so before the winter solstice?"

Cal closed his eyes briefly. It seemed he'd lost the ability to speak.

"I think Orien saw it," Flick said. "He saw death that night."

Seel was not yet home when they reached the house. Flick told Cal to go on inside while he saw to the horses, making sure Cal's animal was given a full meal and clean water. He spent some time grooming the dusty coat, while the horse munched hay slowly. Flick didn't want to go inside, not yet. He felt numb, yet light-headed. Was this grief or shock or both? Pell's dead. They were just words. They didn't mean anything. It still didn't seem real. Cal's horse sighed and shuddered. It was too thin, its eyes dull. It seemed without hope, eating because instinct made it do so, not because it wanted to live.

Cal was sitting at the kitchen table when Flick eventually steeled himself to go into the house. He had taken off his cloak, revealing an emaciated body from which his clothes hung loosely. His face, though still striking, looked like a grimy skull that somehar had dug up. He had clearly been rooting around the pantry, because he was drinking wine from the bottle. His hands did not shake. They looked strangely strong against the green glass, strong and tanned, the fingers long.

"Are you hungry?" Flick asked.

"No." Cal took a drink. "Where is he?"

"Oh . . . out and about. He'll be home soon, or do you want me to go and look for him?"

"I mean the other one."

"In his house I expect," Flick said. "Do you want me to take you there?"

Cal shook his head, grimaced. "I want a bath."

"Good, yes," Flick said. "I'll see to it." He was relieved to leave the room. After he'd run the bath, he'd go and find Seel. He couldn't cope with this.

Up in the bathroom, Flick sat on the edge of the bath and splashed one hand through the chugging water. His heart was beating too fast. His head was somehar else's. The house was too quiet around him, and the air felt dank. He sensed a presence behind him and jumped in alarm. Cal loomed at the threshold, still clutching the bottle. He was a hideous lich, who had disappeared from the kitchen and manifested here spontaneously without a sound. Flick shuddered. He thought about Cal in the bath and about holding his head under the water. Perhaps that would be a mercy. "Nearly ready," he said. "I'll go find Seel."

"Yes, do," Cal said. He put down the bottle and clawed off his clothes. Beneath them, his body was a skeleton barely covered by skin.

Flick swallowed with difficulty. They would need healers, an army of them.

Seel was in the Nayati, Saltrock's temple. He appeared to be studying a joist, but Flick wondered whether he'd been praying. The cold glance that Seel shot toward him made him speak bluntly. "Cal's here," he said.

"What?"

"Cal's here. He's at the house. He says that Pell is dead."

Seel stared at Flick with a burning gaze for some seconds. Then, without speaking, he ran from the Nayati in the direction of home. Flick was left alone. The air smelled of wood and pitch and dust. Many hara had been incepted here, Pell among them. It was a place of sacrifice and transformation. It was a place of truth. But nothing lived there, even though it was supposed to be the home of the Aghama, Wraeththu's god. Flick sat down on the floor and thought, *I promised Pell I'd find his family, didn't I? I never did. Do I find them now to tell them he's dead?*

There seemed no point. Pell had been dead to them for a long time.

For the rest of the day and the night that followed, Seel kept Cal in his room and didn't come out. Flick could hear Seel's voice, speaking softly, a sound that sifted down like dust through the layers of the otherwise silent house. Flick couldn't hear the words, and eventually everything went quiet. He thought of Seel lying on his bed, holding Cal in his arms, his eyes full of pain. He thought maybe he should go to Orien's house and shout through the door, tell him what had happened, but ultimately did nothing. No hara came to the house, perhaps because none of them had seen Flick taking Cal there. But the town outside was as hushed as the house. Flick realized that there was no need to go to Orien and tell him Cal was here because he would already know. He'd seen Pell's death and hadn't wanted to mention it, because Seel would have held himself responsible. It made sense now. Orien had spoken of his own death because it was easier. He'd made it up, anything to stop Seel's questions. Was Cal's arrival the beginning of making things better? It had to be. The climax had come and only healing could follow.

Cal and Seel appeared at breakfast together, which Flick had already prepared. He hadn't gone to bed, but had slept a couple of hours before dawn on the sofa in the parlor. Cal looked better today, somehow sleeker, more filled out. Seel had no doubt spent the entire night creating this effect, filling Cal with the essence of his love. There was an understanding between them that Flick could feel against his skin. He could reach out and pinch it, if he wanted to. It was clear that Seel thought everything was going to be all right now. He had Cal back, minus Pell, and had the power to heal him. There could be no grand destiny for a dead har, so it was all over. They could begin again. Seel was modestly cheerful, while Cal looked like a romantic, grief-stricken lover who was finding solace and comfort in the arms of friends. They kept touching each other, small touches, an intimate language. Seel did not look at Flick once.

Why does he despise me? Flick wondered. He put ham and eggs down on the table.

"So much is clear now," Seel said. "Orien foretold Pell's death. He saw it."

"It's more than that," Cal said.

Seel frowned. "How can it be?"

"Because Pell had a destiny. It shouldn't have just ended like that. I want to know why it happened, and how. Are you telling me Thiede incepted Pell just to let him die? I don't think so. It doesn't make sense."

It didn't to Flick either, who said nothing.

"Perhaps he was a sacrifice," Seel said carefully.

Cal stared at him with a bone-crunching gaze.

Seel shrugged awkwardly. "It could be an explanation."

"Perhaps that's what Orien knows," Flick said, unable to keep silent any longer. "Perhaps that's what made him keep quiet."

"I want to know what he knows," Cal said. "He can't keep quiet any longer." His even-voiced confidence was somehow unnerving.

Seel went out after breakfast to try and persuade Orien to come to the house. Flick was worried that Cal would hang around, underfoot and causing discomfort, while he attended to his daily chores, but fortunately Cal decided to go and look up old friends in the town. His behavior bordered on normal and it was easy to believe that his healing had begun.

Midafternoon, Seel turned up accompanied by Orien. He must have spent around six hours persuading Orien to meet Cal. Seel was obviously concerned Orien might not wait around too long, so went back out immediately to track Cal down.

Orien sat at the kitchen table. He didn't look ill, dazed or even haunted, just a little uncomfortable. Flick made him some coffee and said, "Why have you been hiding away like this?" It had been always easier to ask Orien questions than to ask Seel. Flick wished now that he'd been more persistent at Orien's door.

"I needed to think," Orien said, a reasonable answer.

"For so long? What about?"

"I was looking for answers," Orien said, "in the ethers."

"Did you find any?"

Orien shook his head.

"Was Pell supposed to die?" Flick asked.

Orien flicked a glance at him and for the briefest moment he appeared furtive. "How can I answer that? Perhaps we were all wrong. Perhaps it was random fate. Perhaps that is the lesson we have to learn. None of us are safe, not even those we believe have a great destiny. In legends, heroes survive against all odds to make a difference, but what if that is the greatest lie, and a chance accident can wipe out the hero who can save the world? Were we looking for that special har, all of us? Had we all, unconsciously, invested something in Pell, just so that we'd eventually have to face that we are ultimately responsible for ourselves?"

"You've been thinking a lot," Flick said.

"My questions created only more questions," Orien said. "Now I have to face Cal and I really don't have the stomach for it."

"You don't feel sorry for him, do you." It was a statement rather than a question.

Orien's mouth was grim. "Another lesson," he said. "Perhaps the hardest of all."

Flick wondered how Cal would react when he came face to face with Orien. Would he go mad and attack him, or would he be insulting? Flick could not imagine it being easy, whatever happened, and he felt so nervous he cleaned the kitchen three times before he heard footsteps in the corridor outside.

Seel and Cal came in, both talking at once, and it appeared they'd opted for an attitude of insincere cheer. Orien stood up and greeted Cal, who nodded to him. They regarded each other politely in the way that hara who mutually despise each other do, when they don't want others present to witness any unpleasantness.

Cal sat down and lit a cigarette. After a while, Orien sat down again too. It was clear he had prepared himself for a difficult interview; he was going to play it Cal's way, whatever that might entail. Flick suspected that a small part of Cal was enjoying this. Seel was obviously nervous too, because he busied himself with making drinks rather than asking Flick to do it. Orien didn't say anything and for some minutes, neither did Cal. He smoked his cigarette, apparently taking great sensual pleasure from each draw. At the sink, Seel broke a cup and Flick jumped in his seat. It sounded like a gunshot. The sharp report appeared to act as a prompt. Cal rubbed his face and said, "You know what I want to hear."

"Tell me," Orien said.

"What was going on? What did Thiede tell you?"

"Very little," Orien said, "and that's the truth. I admit I summoned him."

"Why?"

"Thiede was on the lookout for individuals of an unusual nature, boys arriving for inception who had special qualities. He didn't say why."

"Didn't you question his motives? Didn't it occur to you they might be sinister?"

"No. Why should it? I've known Thiede a long time, and it made sense to me that he would want high caliber hara with the Gelaming. I thought he was merely recruiting such hara, and I have no reason to believe otherwise now."

"So, you're saying that Pell's death was an accident?"

"Yes. I can think of no reason why it wasn't—and believe me, I have been thinking long and hard over these last few weeks."

"You were surprised, though, weren't you, when you realized he was dead. Why?"

"I presumed Thiede would protect him, that's all. As I said to Flick earlier, I think I invested a lot in Pell myself. I thought he was destined to make a mark. It didn't seem right that he should die, but now I wonder whether that was what we were supposed to learn from his death: there can be no miracles or heroes. We have to forge our own way."

"I don't believe you. There's more. I can smell it."

Orien scraped tendrils of hair back from his face. "Cal, you were in love with Pell. You are looking for meaning in the senseless tragedy of his death, but I think you have to face there may be none."

Flick shifted in his seat. He was remembering the words Orien had spoken on the night he'd fallen into trance: "It's done." Much as he'd prefer not to, he had to agree with Cal. There *was* more.

Seel came to the table with steaming mugs of coffee on a tray. He placed it down carefully and said, "You knew he was dead that night, Orien, yet you did not tell us. Why?"

Flick thought that this was a pointless question, because it was so easy to concoct a credible response. It would pain him to hear Orien's predictable reply, so decided to voice it for him. "He was thinking of you," Flick said to Seel. "He didn't want you to feel responsible."

Orien cast Flick a grateful glance, and Flick wondered why he'd decided to conspire in that way. He could easily have let Orien say the obvious and then have challenged it.

"You should have told me," Seel said. "As you should have told me all you've just said. It wasn't some great secret. How could it have mattered if I knew?"

"That Thiede was using your precious Saltrock as a recruiting ground for Gelaming?" Cal said. "Are you comfortable with that, plus the fact that one of your closest friends was involved in it?"

Orien displayed his hands. "Those were my thoughts." He leaned forward. "Seel, I'm not even going to try to justify what I did. In a sense, I did betray our friendship, but Thiede and I have known each other longer, and he asked me to keep what I knew to myself. I made a promise, so I had no choice but to honor it." He clasped his hands beneath his chin. "The fact is, we have all lost a dear friend, and that is a shock. The circumstances surrounding Pell's inception are irrelevant. The two facts are not connected."

Flick watched Cal's face as he lit another cigarette, his eyes never straying from Orien. Did Cal believe what he'd heard? Flick realized he wanted Cal to believe, because even if it wasn't true, they couldn't do anything. It was over. It had to be.

Before Cal could say anything, Seel said, "And is it still going on, this *recruitment?*"

Orien shook his head. "Thiede has not contacted me since Pell's inception."

"Why should he?" Cal said. "He got what he wanted, didn't he?"

"I'm sure that is not the reason," Orien said. "Thiede is involved in many schemes to help consolidate Wraeththu. No doubt I'll hear from him, should he need my help in the future."

"Didn't you think to try and contact him after you had the vision of Pell's death?" Seel snapped. "You must have done!"

Orien inclined his head. "I did. Of course I did. But there was no response."

"You must be annoyed he's cut you out of the web," Cal said conversationally.

"I'm not involved in Thiede's plans," Orien said. "I don't expect to be."

Flick thought it was as if Orien was on trial. He sat there with dignity, answering the prosecution questions in a clear manner. But he didn't have to go through this. He could get up and walk out. In a way, he was right: Cal *was* trying to find meaning in a senseless tragedy. Was that why he was being so accommodating, even though he disliked Cal?

"You should have told me all this," Seel said. "I wonder whether you ever would have done if Cal hadn't come back."

Orien shrugged. "I was coming to my own conclusions, meditating alone. Cal's arrival merely precipitated events, that's all."

"Is there anything else you can tell me?" Cal said, and Flick thought this was perhaps the most important question. It was a nexus point.

"No," Orien said. "I don't think so."

Cal almost looked sad. He sighed and shook his head. "Your choice," he said, "and as you pointed out we have to take responsibility for ourselves, our actions and reactions—and their consequences."

Orien's expression was wary. "I'm not your enemy, Cal. I'm sorry for your loss, but I can't help you find that meaning you so desperately need. The only thing I can suggest is that you seek Thiede out yourself, and put these questions to him. Perhaps that would put your mind at rest."

Cal smiled. "Then, by all means feel free to summon him for me."

Orien laughed uncertainly. "You must know I don't have the power to do that."

"Oh, you do sometimes, Orien. We all know that."

"You could try," Seel said. "It's the least you can do."

Orien exhaled through his nose. "Very well, although I am sure it will be a pointless exercise." He stood up. "I'll go back home now, and put out a call. Perhaps we should meet later."

"Dinner," Seel said. "Flick can prepare one of his feasts."

It was the last thing Flick felt like doing, although he smiled in what he hoped was a convincing manner. "Invite Thiede to dinner," he said. "Perhaps the prospect of one of my feasts will entice him back to Saltrock."

"No slur on your culinary skills, but I doubt that," Orien said.

"So what would entice him back?" Cal asked.

Orien didn't respond. "I'll see you all later," he said.

After Orien had left, Flick suggested that perhaps some of Cal's old friends could also come to dinner and for once Seel agreed Flick had a good idea. "You've got to look to the future now, Cal," he said. "What are you going to do with your life?"

"I have no life," Cal replied. "It died on me."

Seel put his hands upon Cal's shoulders. "You didn't die," he said, shaking Cal a little. "Come on. This is hard, I know, but think of all we've been through together. Think of the hideous things we witnessed and survived. You're strong. You can get through this. I'll help you."

It would not be so easy, Flick thought, looking at Cal's face.

Orien did not reappear for dinner, but sent a young har over an hour or so beforehand to deliver a message. He had put out an etheric call to Thiede, but had so far got no response, not even the faintest ghost of a whisper. He intended to devote himself to amplifying the call for the rest of the day.

Cal went to lie down in Seel's room and Flick started preparing dinner. Seel sat at the kitchen table, watching him cut up vegetables. "Thiede won't come," he said.

"No," Flick agreed. He wondered why the big cook's knife looked so brilliantly silver and sharp in his hand.

"Perhaps Orien should just make something up, to put Cal's mind at rest."

"He'd know."

Seel sighed. "Yeah."

"You're taking on a lot, you know."

Seel scraped his hands through his hair. "I have no choice. I can't let him go on like this."

Flick didn't think it was anything to do with "letting" Cal do anything. He went his own way and always had. All the help in the world would do no good if Cal wasn't receptive to it. Flick thought that Cal was too self-destructive. How he'd survived this long was a phenomenon in itself. Flick wasn't looking forward to having Cal around the house for a lengthy period.

Colt, one of Cal's old friends, arrived early, before the other guests. He, and his chesnari Stringer, had been incepted from a very old race of humans, who had been close to the earth and to magic. Colt was a hawk of a har, whose eyes could see through anything. Now, he sat in the kitchen, getting in the way, as Flick put the finishing touches to the meal.

"Cal doesn't look good," Colt said to Seel, helping himself to some fried chicken. "The one har's help he needs is Orien's, but from what I heard today he won't take it."

"We've got to be patient with him," Seel said.

"In the old world, he'd have been locked up," Colt said. "For his own good and everyone else's."

Flick smiled to himself.

"This is not the old world," Seel said darkly.

"He's sick," Colt said. "You must see that. Sick in the head." He tapped his own brow.

"It's not beyond us to heal him," Seel said. "We're not humans, stuck in the old world. We have the ability now."

Colt shook his head. "We're not gods, Seel. For fuck's sake, do we really know what we are?"

"Yes, we do."

"I don't think so. We're still struggling to accept ourselves, and I think some of us go mad in the process."

The kitchen door opened and Cal sauntered into the room. He must have heard what Colt had said, but gave no sign. Perhaps he had been listening for some time. "Smells good," he said to Flick.

"You could do with feeding up a little," Flick said.

"Orien won't be coming," Seel said.

Cal grimaced. "Now there's a surprise."

"He's still trying to contact Thiede."

Cal nodded. "Yeah, right."

The dinner that night could hardly be termed a riotous success. Everyhar laughed too loudly and made too obvious an effort to cajole and patronize Cal. Flick could tell they were all uncomfortable with him. Most of these hara, having been incepted into northern Wraeththu tribes, had suffered losses time and again. They had watched hara close to them die, but they had also accepted that casualties of war were part of what they were and what they were trying to achieve. They couldn't let themselves fall to pieces, and having somehar around who was literally disintegrating in front of them because a loved one had died filled them with a strange kind of fear. Flick intuited they didn't want to go home that night and find themselves lying in the dark, remembering old faces. It was almost farcical, the way that once the meal had been cleared away, everyhar around the table was clearly formulating frantic excuses to leave. Cal, presumably feeling charitable, expressed a wide yawn, and at once at least three hara were on their feet, muttering about early starts.

Seel saw guests to the door, and Flick could imagine the whispered apologies about Cal's behavior, which had bordered on autistic for the entire evening. Colt, along with his chesnari, Stringer, were the last to leave. Colt put his hand on Cal's shoulder and said, "We can't help you, old buddy. It's up to you."

Cal flicked him a cold glance. "There are no 'buddies,' Colt. Not anymore. We left all that behind."

"Yeah, well there's a lot more you could leave behind," Colt said.

Stringer put on his jacket. "Let's go," he said. "See you around, Cal."

Cal said nothing.

Flick could tell Seel was bursting to say something like, "You could have made an effort, Cal," but instead he brought out his treasured bottle of old brandy, perhaps the last he would ever drink.

Seel poured out three measures and the fragrant aroma of the drink filled the room. Cal lifted his glass and said, "I want to sleep in our old room tonight, the one Pell and I stayed in."

"It's not made up," Seel said, which was a lie. Cal probably knew it was. He'd have visited that room already.

"That doesn't matter," Cal said. "I want to sleep there."

The room that Cal and Pell had used when they were last in Saltrock. The room where Pell had gone through althaia, the changing. The room where Cal and Pell had first taken aruna together. Seething with ghosts.

Let him, Flick thought. *Let him wallow in this grief.*

He wondered why he felt impatient with it, and why so many of Cal's old friends did too. Grief, under the circumstances, was normal. It should be respected, accommodated for. But in Cal, it seemed weirdly like self-indulgence.

"Flick, can you sort out the room?" Seel asked.

Flick nodded and stood up. He'd change the bedding, root out the striped coverlet that was on it the last time. If Cal wanted ghosts, he could have them.

"No," Cal said. "It's fine as it is. Don't go in there."

Flick sat down again.

"Perhaps you need to erase some of the memories associated with that room," Seel said. "It's probably right that we sleep in there."

Cal didn't look up from the table. He was turning the brandy glass around and around. "I'm sleeping alone," he said.

"Fine." Seel raked a hand through his hair. "Can you finish up, Flick?"

"As always," Flick replied, thinking, *Don't leave me with him.*

But Seel was already out of the door.

Flick started to rise from his chair, then Cal's right hand shot out and grabbed his wrist. "I want to talk to *you*."

"Let go," Flick said coldly.

Cal did so. "You know, I think you must see and hear a lot of what goes on around here," he said. "Quiet little Flick. You must know quite a lot."

"Not really," Flick said, gathering a few glasses from the table. "I can't tell you anything."

"Tell me about Orien."

Flick dumped the glasses in the sink, turned on the faucet. "What about Orien?"

"Where did he come from? How did Seel meet him?"

"Seel met him while he was still with the Unneah. They came here together originally, I think."

"Orien's an adept. Who trained him? Was he incepted to the Unneah?"

"I don't know," Flick said. "Why don't you ask him?"

Cal uttered a bark of caustic laughter. "You think I'd get the truth?"

"What I think is that Orien isn't the sinister dark character you believe he is. Why don't you speak to Seel about this? I don't know anything."

Cal stood up and came to stand behind Flick at the sink, very close. Flick could smell him: a warm spicy aroma of fresh hay. "I'm not sure I believe everything Seel says either," Cal said.

Flick could barely move. He realized, with a strange kind of detachment, that he was terrified, but there was something else . . . "You're joking. Seel adores you."

Cal touched the back of Flick's head. "I bet you hate me for that, don't you?"

"Not for that particularly, no. Get your hand off me."

"What *do* you hate me for, then?"

The fact you can intimidate me so easily. The things I don't know about you. The horror inside you. Your power.

Flick managed to turn around and wriggle away from the sink. "It's not hate, Cal. I don't know you, and I don't think anyhar can. You're freaky, that's all, and I think you get off on unnerving others."

Heart, slow down.

Cal laughed and folded his arms. "You're not afraid of me, are you?"

Utterly. "No. Should I be?"

"I don't know. I'm so full of hate I'm fairly unpredictable."

Flick shrugged. "You're nothing to do with me."

"You and Pell were pretty close. I'm surprised you're not more upset."

"I am upset," Flick said. "I'm dealing with it in my own way. Look, just go to bed, Cal. Leave me alone."

"What did Pell say to you before we left Saltrock? I know he said something. I watched you together. You looked weird."

"Nothing," Flick said. "I don't remember."

"Lies, lies," Cal sang. "What are you afraid of?"

"Okay. He asked me to find his family, that's all. We're not supposed to do that, are we? Wraeththu don't have human families. We have to forget them. So I never spoke of it. Satisfied?"

"And did you find them?"

"No, of course not."

"Some friend."

"There would have been no point. The chances are they'd have been attacked by one of the rogue tribes by that time, anyway."

"Possibly. It's not that far, you know. I remember every step of the journey, every rock, every stone."

"Then you go," Flick said. "I'm sure they'd be delighted to see *you* again."

"God!" Cal put the heels of his hands against his eyes. "The smell of that place. I can remember it so well. The sight of him. So beautiful. God!"

The wrong one was shot, Flick thought. *If this were Pell here now, and Cal had been killed, he wouldn't be like this.* "I can't help you," Flick said. "I think you should let it go."

Cal lowered his hands. "Yeah," he said quietly, resignedly.

Flick watched as Cal went back to his seat and poured himself some more brandy. He looked frail, as if some kind of wildfire had died inside him.

"You want a coffee with that?" Flick said.

"No. Some company would be nice though."

Flick sat down. He might as well have another drink too. An image of Seel flashed across his mind. He'd be lying awake, dealing with being hurt. Flick sighed. "I wish you'd go," he said. "You're trouble."

Cal took a drink. "I *can* be nice. Pell loved me back, you know. It's not just me."

"I thought you wanted to be alone tonight."

Cal grimaced. "Just not with Seel. I can't cope with all that *concern.* It drives me nuts. Now you—you're refreshing."

Flick thought it best to ignore that remark. "You do some talking," he said. "Tell me about Seel. How did you meet?"

"When we were kids," Cal said. "He was a lot like you then. Makes sense, I suppose. Finding a younger version of himself to have around."

"He was never like me," Flick said. "Why say that?"

"Why not? Do you want hear this or not?"

"Tell me."

It was fascinating to listen to the picture Cal created. Seel was so intrinsically Wraeththu, it was hard to imagine him as human, let alone as a child. He and Cal had lived in the same area, attended the same schools, until Cal had corrupted him enough to stop bothering. Cal would have been the wild kid, always in trouble. Flick already knew Cal came from a rich family, but it was hard to imagine. He seemed to have "deprived childhood" written all over him. "As soon as we found out about Wraeththu, I wanted to find out more," Cal said. "I wasn't scared like most of the others. We heard they were just gangs, some weird kind of cult. I always knew it was more. Sensed it. Seel wasn't into it at all. It was only once his mother found us together in his bed that I managed to persuade him it was our destiny. He couldn't face the flak at home and didn't have a choice but to come with me. I was going and he didn't want to be left alone."

"You were cruel even then," Flick said. "You took advantage."

Cal shrugged. "Maybe. He doesn't regret it now though, does he?"

"No." Flick put down his glass. He had drunk too much. Cal didn't seem affected by the alcohol at all. If anything, he seemed the brightest he'd been since he'd arrived in Saltrock. He looked radiant, the har who had seduced Pellaz Cevarro away from home. Flick could remember the names of some of Pell's family now. They came back to him, sister Mima, closest brother Terez. Already dead, no doubt. Flick rubbed at his face and Cal reached out to touch his arm. "Are you okay?"

Flick nodded. "Just tired."

"So what's your story?"

"Not now."

His arms lay on the table and now Cal had taken one of his hands. His skin felt smooth and dry and cool. *Oh God,* Flick thought. *What have I done?*

"Nothing yet," said Cal.

Flick snatched away his hand. "Stop it. Don't pry. Don't play with me."

"Oh come on. At the very least, it would really *really* piss Seel off. At the very most, you would enjoy me immensely. Think about it. Seel treats you like a dog and there you are, the obedient little puppy, coming back with your tail wagging after every kick. He doesn't see you for what you are, does he? He doesn't even know you. You're stunning, Flick. Seel's stupid not to realize what he's got."

"Shut up."

"It's true, isn't it? Even Pell noticed the way Seel treated you so dismissively. We talked about it." He reached out and took Flick's hand again, and even though Flick wanted to so badly, he couldn't pull away this time. "Everyhar is so full of advice for me," Cal said, "but here's some for you. Stop being a shadow. Stand up and shine."

Flick looked into Cal's eyes and couldn't think of a reply, witty or otherwise. He knew it was the truth.

"You won't stay here forever," Cal said. "If you think you will, you're wrong. Oh, it's painful to think about. You don't want to think about it. So don't. Forget it. It's what everyhar wants me to do, isn't it?"

Flick felt as if he'd been punched in the head. He didn't know what he felt.

Cal took some minutes to finish his brandy and they sat together in silence. A thousand thoughts tumbled through Flick's head, too fast and chaotically for him to understand them. Then Cal stood up and pulled Flick to his feet. "You coming?"

Flick raised the hand that Cal was holding. They stood there, palm to palm, for some moments, until Flick laced his fingers through Cal's. "Let's go."

Seel must have heard them go up the stairs, but he did not come out into the corridor. As soon as they were inside Cal and Pell's old room, Cal shut the door and pushed Flick up against it. He took Flick's face in his hands and then they were sharing breath, savagely, strongly, tasting thoughts so deep they came from another life. Flick searched vainly for a part of himself that was aghast, disapproving, or even mildly surprised, but could not find it. It seemed the natural conclusion to the evening to be here in Cal's arms, bruising against his mouth.

When they broke apart, Flick said, "Your madness is infectious. This was not part of the plan—ever."

Cal laughed. "How do you know?"

"Do you want to playact seducing a young Seel again? Is that it?"

"If you want."

"Sick," Flick said, but all he could see was that finely drawn mouth, the lazy eyes, the heavy yellow hair. All he could smell was the burning, spicy aroma that was essentially Cal. Pell had never stood a chance, it was obvious. And neither had Seel.

"You want to know," Cal said. "Admit it."

They stumbled over to the bed, crashed onto it. The sound reverberated through the silent house. "There go the springs," Cal said. He pushed Flick onto his back, lay over him, holding his arms above his head. "Grrr!" he said.

Flick laughed. "Fight you for it!" Cal had lost his fitness. It was easy to roll him off and pin him down.

"Oh, fiery!" Cal said. "How Uigenna of you."

"You should know."

"See how good I am for you. Already you have rediscovered your forgotten male half."

"Shut up," Flick said. "Stop wittering. God, you're so skinny. Don't break apart on me."

"You can leave a pile of mashed bone and blood in this bed if you want," Cal said. "It's all one to me."

Flick grabbed hold of Cal's jaw with one hand. Cal stared back at him, passive. Flick knew he shouldn't be doing this. It would hurt Seel and that was what Cal wanted. He wanted to hurt hara who cared about him.

But he can't hurt me, Flick thought. *And he respects it. That's the strangest thing.*

"I once wanted to find Immanion, the Gelaming city," Cal said. "I wanted to find it with Pell, to find Paradise. Take me there. Now."

Flick laughed softly. "Cal, from what I know of you, I suspect you're quite capable of being king of Immanion one day. You could flirt your way there." He lowered his head and breathed over Cal's closed eyes. He slid a hand over Cal's starved flank. "We have small paradises," he said. "This is one of them."

CHAPTER FIVE

It was not just Cal's physical appearance that made him so attractive. Flick realized Cal's true charm was the way he could make a har feel. Walking out of Cal's room the following morning, Flick felt about ten years older and six feet taller. He had been manipulated, played with, and—in one sense— abused, but he'd never felt so good about himself. Cal could turn his attractiveness on and off at will—Flick had witnessed that the previous night. He could make you feel special, better than anyhar else, and when you were with him, you could tell he meant it. That was powerful magic. Or it was like the camouflage that desert creatures were born with. It was Cal's method of survival.

Seel was already up when Flick went into the kitchen. Flick steeled himself for hostility, but Seel only grinned rather sadly at him, and said, "Was it good?"

"Okay," Flick replied, sidling to the cooking range.

"*That* good." Seel shook his head. "We have to be careful. What was I thinking of?"

"Seel—"

"No, listen. There's something not right. I remember what it was like before—this division, this playing hara off against one another. Just watch out. It could be a trap."

Flick said nothing. Half of him suspected Seel might be right. At least the Seel sitting at the kitchen table today was more like the har he used to be. Cal had reached inside him, searching for Seel's heart, but he'd grabbed his anger by mistake. He'd crumpled it into a ball and thrown it away.

Cal slept for most of the day, and while he was sleeping Flick resolved not to play Cal's game. He didn't want to be part of it. When Cal eventually emerged, heavy eyed and languorous, he behaved as if nothing had happened the night before, which had to be for the best. Perhaps, in Cal's own mind, something had fallen into place. They'd simply helped each other.

Orien put in an appearance that evening to tell Cal he couldn't contact Thiede, but that he'd keep trying.

"I didn't expect anything else," Cal said. "You don't have to try again, not on my account."

Seel and Flick exchanged a glance at that point. *Something* was better, wasn't it? This couldn't just be a deceptive calm.

While Orien was still talking to Seel, Flick went out to see to the horses. He stood in the gloom of the musty stable, taking in all the warm scents and the comfortable sounds of contented animals snorting and munching hay. It was like a warm giant hand around him. Then came a breath of cold air and there were living hands on his shoulders, in his hair. He turned round. "No, Cal. No."

He could have pulled away at any time. He could have been cold and harsh, but it was beyond him. Cal was using his strongest magic.

An unspoken vow passed between them that night. Their liaisons would henceforth be kept secret. If Seel suspected, he did not say so. Cal wanted to revisit all the sites of significance for him. It was as if he was trying to imprint Flick over images of Pell. They took aruna together in the Forale House, where Pell had suffered alone the day before his inception. They writhed together on the inception slab of the Nayati, surrounded by feathery shadows. In this place Thiede had put his mark on Pell forever, and by default on Cal as well. They lay side by side next to the shore of a soda lake with crystals forming in their hair, watching the stars wheel across the sky. And Cal spoke of Pell, he spoke of the journey they had shared, the hara they had met. With eyes closed, Flick lay at Cal's side, walking in his mind through the shadowy canopies of the Kakkahaar, the cracked ruins of the Irraka town, the dark splendour of the Varr enclave. He heard the names, like those of mythical he-

roes: Lianvis, Spinel, Terzian, and he imagined the smoky mystery of the alluring seducers that had crossed Cal's path: Ulaume of the Kakkahaar, Cobweb of the Varrs. Flick loved to hear these stories, but part of him wondered
how much of what he was told was true. To Cal, it was perhaps an exorcism,
as the touch of Flick's body was an exorcism of Pell—or so Flick told himself.

One time, Flick said, "What do you want from this?"

And Cal replied, "Everything I'm getting."

Flick wasn't quite sure what that was, but despite his earlier resolution, he
was playing Cal's game, so much so he found himself saying, "Where else,
Cal? Where else do you want to go around here?"

They were lying in the fodder loft above the stables, where once Cal had
surprised Pell while he'd been working. He and Flick had rolled in the linger-
ing atoms of earlier love. "I don't know," Cal replied. "Where else is there?"

Flick pondered. Between them, they'd drunk a lot of wine and it was almost dawn. "There's only one other place I can think of," he said. "Orien's
house."

"We were never together there."

"I know, but it was where Orien trained Pell in the arts of aruna magic."

Cal laughed. "You know what that means?"

Flick didn't like the tone of the laugh. "No. What?"

"I have to have Orien there, not you." He narrowed his eyes. "Maybe I was
waiting for a sign. Maybe you're an oracle. Maybe it won't be there."

It was too late to take the words back. It was as if the whole time, from
when Cal had first arrived, Flick had been maneuvered into this moment, to
say those words. They could never be taken back.

Five days later, Orien came to Seel's house for dinner. The air was electric
that night, and metal all over the house seemed to shine with a weird light.
Flick felt jumpy and hot. Cal slunk around him in the kitchen as he prepared
the meal, and Flick's body ached for him. He could imagine a red mist descending before his eyes, so that he'd sweep all the vegetables and pans off
the kitchen table and throw Cal onto it, ravish him there. And no doubt Orien
and Seel would come in and—No, the image was just comical after that.

Cal picked up the cook's knife and ran its point down Flick's spine. "Like
that?" he said.

"Too much," Flick replied. "Make yourself useful. Cut something up."

"Okay. What?"

"The meat."

Cal threw himself down into a chair and began chopping up the steak, his hair hanging over his eyes. *You are a monster,* Flick thought, *devastating and terrible. You are also a drug and extremely addictive.*

Flick could tell from the beginning of the meal that Cal was planning something. He had come to recognize a certain calculating air about Cal and that it signaled trouble. Orien was like a trusting doe, tied to a stake as bait for the predator. Cal stalked him, circled him, then attacked. Flick had never witnessed such precise and surgical verbal assault before. It was the same as before: the accusations, the suspicions, but with a new and bitter malice. Cal sounded drunk, but Flick knew he wasn't. Cal raved about Pell, about Thiede, about how it wasn't over. It really wasn't and he wouldn't rest until those who were responsible had paid the price. Was this the preamble to a seduction? If so, it didn't sound like it.

"Cal, stop it!" Seel yelled. "You've been over this a thousand times. It does no good."

Cal appeared to have worked himself into a frenzy. Flick just wished he would stop. It was an act, a play, but what final scene was in store?

Orien had had enough. "You're insane," he said coldly. "Look at you. You're an insult to our kind. You're selfish, vain, arrogant, and sick."

Cal laughed hysterically. "Then I'm a mirror," he said.

"I'm sure you'd like to be. The fact is, you're so busy looking at yourself in it, you can't see anything else."

Cal leapt from his seat and before Seel or Flick could act, hauled Orien up and threw him against the wall. "You killed him!" he screamed. "You!"

Orien looked frightened. In the moments before Seel and Flick managed to pull Cal off, Flick saw that terrible fear and realized then he'd been playing with fire. He thought he could control it, but he couldn't. He'd just made it burn hotter. Cal had deceived him. He was so much more than he appeared to be, and so much worse.

Orien made a hasty exit and Cal slumped back in the chair that Seel had pushed him into. "You've gone too far," Seel said. "Too far, Cal. I won't have this. If you can't get a grip, then you have to leave. I won't let you abuse my friends in my house."

Flick had never thought he'd hear those words. He wondered just how jealous Seel was and how much he had guessed.

Cal put his head in his hands. "I'm sorry," he said. "I'm sorry. I'm sorry."

Seel folded his arms. "Go to bed," he said. "Sleep on it, and tomorrow we talk about your future." He glanced at Flick. "I want *you* to come with me tonight."

For once, Flick was glad responsibility for the rest of the night had been taken from him. He knew that if Seel hadn't said that, he and Cal would have ended up together, and everything felt too sour and stagnant for him to face that. He felt physically sick.

In Seel's room, Flick said, "That wasn't meant to happen tonight. I'm sure it wasn't. Something went wrong."

Seel pulled off his clothes. "What went wrong happened a long time ago," he said. "Don't make the mistake of thinking you understand him, Flick. You don't. You're just under his spell."

Seel had clearly come around to sharing the thoughts of hara like Colt. When Cal had decided to glamorize Flick, so it seemed the scales had fallen from Seel's eyes. Perhaps Cal was too weak to glamorize more than one har at a time.

Seel made no move of affection toward Flick, who was both grateful and disappointed. He had changed. Surely Seel could see that? They lay side by side, not touching, listening to the creaking timbers of the house. Cal would leave soon, Flick was sure of it. It was something he both craved and dreaded.

In the weird hours of the night before dawn, Flick woke up. Seel was snoring gently beside him, looking vulnerable and achingly beautiful in sleep, all the lines of anxiety smoothed away from his brow. Something had roused Flick. He had been dreaming, and the dream had made his head throb, it was so chaotic and intense. He couldn't remember it now. He got out of bed and pulled on his trousers. Outside the bedroom door, the house was bathed in a strange blue twilight. He could hear it breathing. Cal's door was open and Flick knew, deep in his gut, that Cal wasn't in the room. Had he gone to Orien's house? Surely not.

Flick padded down the stairs. The eerie light blurred his vision. He couldn't see properly and sometimes the steps beneath his feet felt wet. The house seemed odd, as if the atmosphere had been stirred by an invisible yet burning presence. Flick went into the kitchen and walked around it, touching the worn implements he used every day. There was a finality to everything. It was like saying good-bye. The wooden block that held his knives lay on its side on the counter next to the range. Flick righted it and noticed the biggest knife was missing. His flesh froze, slowly, from his heart to the surface of his skin. He ran out into the night.

The streets of Saltrock seemed to have become wider, the buildings along them taller. Everything appeared skewed and out of proportion. Flick didn't know this place. It scared him. He ran around in tight circles, afraid of whatever might lurk behind him. He needed to put his back against something solid and crouch there until dawn.

The Nayati loomed black and sinister against the stars, a haunted place. A ghost was coming out of it, a ghost haloed in light. Flick stumbled to a halt on the dusty road. He felt dizzy and the buildings swayed around him. "Cal!" he said. He wanted to shout, but it came out as a whisper. He couldn't shout, mustn't. Had Cal been to the Nayati to pray? Like Flick, he was naked from the waist up. But for his bright hair, he looked like he'd been tarred.

Flick walked toward him slowly. Cal had come to a halt and was staring ahead of him, his gaze unfocused. His face was a warrior's face, smeared with fierce gouts of darkness. Light was starting to fill the sky, an unhealthy light. Perhaps it wasn't the dawn at all, but the end of the world.

Flick reached out and touched Cal's chest. The skin was icy cold, and stickily wet.

"What have you done?" Flick said.

Cal did not look at him. "Go home," he said. "You're dreaming. Go home."

"Cal . . ."

"I'm not here. I never was."

Cal brushed past him and began to walk toward Seel's house. Flick went after him, grabbed his shoulder. "You're drenched in blood," he said. "What happened?"

Cal glanced at him then. "He came back, that's all. You want to see? Go look. I've left an offering in the temple."

He took Flick's hand and pressed something into it. "Here. This is yours." It was the kitchen knife. Flick dropped it at once. It lay shining in the dirt, brilliantly silver and brilliantly red. Impossible in this light, yet there it was. When Flick managed to tear his gaze away from it, he was alone.

His mind was in turmoil. Part of him was already running back to Seel, waking him, dragging him from his bed to discover whatever terrible thing awaited them in the Nayati. But his body wouldn't comply with this image. It just stood there, paralyzed. Even when Flick heard the galloping hooves leave the town, he could not move.

When the roosters began to crow, he picked up the knife and went back to the house. He washed the blade in the gushing water at the sink, retching, swallowing bile. He dried the knife carefully and replaced it in the block. With a wet cloth, he wiped away a bloody handprint from the back door. He ignored the rest. Then he went up the stairs, not looking down at what he might be treading in. He crawled into Seel's bed. And slept.

Seel woke him late. Presumably, he'd slept deep and long too. "Flick, get up, there's a problem," he said.

"What?" For a moment Flick couldn't remember what had happened during the night. He thought he'd had a bad dream of some kind.

"Cal's room. It looks like an abattoir and he's not in it."

Flick could feel the color drain from his face, which Seel would think was only natural under the circumstances.

"We'd better organize a search," Seel said. "It's possible . . . it's possible he might have cut his wrists or something, although that's not what I'd have ever expected of him." Seel's expression was remarkably calm, but he kept swallowing hard. His olive skin looked sallow and damp.

Flick got out of bed.

"There's blood in the corridor, on the stairs, everywhere," Seel said. "You run over to Colt's and Orien's." He shook his head. "Fuck, what the hell has he done?"

Flick couldn't speak. When Seel left the room, he went to the bathroom and washed his feet, without looking at the color of the water that spiraled down the plug hole. Then, he returned to the bedroom and stripped down the bed. He didn't look at the sheets, at the marks that might stain them where his feet had lain. He dressed himself with care and brushed out his hair, then plaited it slowly. Seel's head reappeared round the bedroom door. "Get a move on! Flick! Snap out of it! We have to deal with this."

Flick nodded and followed Seel to the stairs. He faltered at the top, seeing the glutinous trail of red that led to the bottom.

"Don't look at it," Seel said. "Just go and fetch Colt, Stringer, and Orien. I'll see to this later. Just go! I'll start searching."

Like an automaton, Flick walked to Colt and Stringer's house. They were already up, and Stringer was working on some arcane-looking piece of machinery in the yard. "Can you come . . . ?" Flick said.

Stringer looked up. His face was smeared with grease. "Sure. What's up?"

Flick saw the sun go red. Everything was red.

"Flick?"

He felt hands upon him and he was sprawled on the ground, looking up at the sky. The sun burned into his eyes. He felt so cold.

"What the hell's happened?" Stringer demanded.

Flick clawed himself into a sitting position, hanging onto Stringer's shirt. "Something terrible," Flick said. "Sorry. Sorry . . . Just come, that's all."

"Come where?"

"Seel's . . ."

Colt had come out of the house.

"We have to go to Seel's," Stringer said. "Something's happened. Something bad."

"So much blood," Flick said. "Seel needs you."

Colt and Stringer looked at him for a moment, then Colt growled, "That shit!" and ran off.

Stringer lingered. "Go," Flick said. "I have to . . . I have to tell . . ." He waved a hand in Stringer's direction.

Alone, Flick sat in the yard, picking at weeds between his raised knees. He couldn't face going to Orien's, he just couldn't, and yet he'd seen nothing with his own eyes. Cal could have slaughtered a horse and put it in the Nayati. "Slaughtered a horse in his bedroom," Flick said aloud to himself. "Yeah, that's *so* possible. Idiot!"

He got to his feet. If he could only throw up, he might feel better, but the insides of his body felt like dust. Slowly, he walked toward the Nayati. Surely, somehar must have looked in there by now. And so they had. It must have been simple for Seel to follow the trail of blood.

Flick saw a crowd had gathered at the Nayati door. Colt stood at the threshold with his arms outspread, preventing hara from going inside. Numbly, Flick pushed his way through the crowd, and they parted to let him pass, because they thought he was close to Seel. At the door, a gray-faced Colt said, "You don't want to go in there, Flick. Take my advice. Don't."

"What have you found?" Flick asked.

"It's not Cal," Colt said.

"Then who?"

Colt glanced above Flick's head at the crowd. It was clear that not everyhar yet knew what grisly secret lay within. "Just not Cal," he said, "but somehar who ran into Cal."

"Let me through," Flick said.

"If the sight of what you saw at home made you pass out, you won't take this," Colt said, but he lowered an arm.

Flick walked past him. The darkness of the interior was intense after the sunlight outside. He saw Seel, Stringer, and a couple of other high-ranking hara doing something at the far end, near the altar. They were limned in light coming through a high window, framed in the act of cutting something down. There was a smell: terrible, meaty, sweet, and foul. Flick turned his head away. He had seen a white, blood-streaked, dangling arm. He closed his eyes for a few moments, taking deep breaths, then went back outside.

"Can I do anything?" he said to Colt. "Does Seel need me to do anything?"

"Are you up to cleaning the mess at home?"

Flick nodded slowly, his lips drawn into a thin line. "I could do that."

The house was quiet, but for the lazy buzzing of flies in the kitchen, circling endlessly in the center of the room. There air was sickly sweet. Flick went into the pantry and pulled out a mop and bucket. He filled the bucket at the sink. The water was bright and sparkling like diamonds, the sound it made so loud. Slopping water onto the floor, he lifted the bucket from the sink. He'd overfilled it: water went everywhere, over his clothes, his feet.

He began by the door, and by the time he'd reached the table, he had to change the water. He felt light-headed, disorientated, as if he was watching a movie of himself. This blood would never be cleaned away. Too much of it. He was just spreading it around, a thin film of Orien throughout the house. He kept seeing Orien's face before his inner eye. Orien, smiling, laughing, his tawny hair hanging in tendrils around his face. Orien, who had brought him to Saltrock for inception. Orien being kind when Flick was sad. Orien's words of wisdom. Silenced forever. It seemed to Flick as if the whole floor were red. He threw down the mop and surrendered to a fit of weeping, sinking down until he was crouched against the wall, surrounded by bloody handprints that looked like ancient cave paintings.

Seel found him there a couple of hours later. Seel had tied up his hair, but his shirt and hands were red. Without saying anything, he hunkered down and took Flick in his arms, kissed his hair. Flick fell against him, choking.

After a while, Seel hauled Flick to his feet and gestured at the mop. "Don't bother with this," he said. "I'll get somehar to come and do it. Go to the other room. I'll get us a drink."

Flick fumbled his way, half blind, into Seel's parlor and lay down on the couch. There was no blood in here.

Seel came in and gave Flick a glass of brandy. "What's left of it," he said dryly.

The taste, even the smell, made Flick feel nauseous. He remembered those hands on his body, the laughter, the smell of Cal. But he took the glass and drained it quickly.

Seel sat by Flick's head and stroked his hair. "We have to suppose," he said carefully, "that Orien came back here last night. It's clear that . . . it happened upstairs. The body was dragged from here to the Nayati." He paused. "I know this is tough, Flick, but I have to ask. Did you see anything at Orien's house when you went there? Any evidence or clues?"

Flick shook his head. "I . . . I didn't go."

"Why?"

Flick shrugged. "I felt sick. I was looking for you. Saw the crowd at the Nayati."

Seel shifted a little beside him. Flick knew what he was thinking. Why wouldn't Flick go directly to Orien's house, which was nearer than Colt and Stringer's? Why wouldn't he run to fetch the one har on who they depended? Flick realized he should have lied.

Flick could hardly breathe in the silence. He could feel Seel becoming tenser beside him. Eventually, Seel said, "Flick, you didn't *know,* did you?"

"No, no, of course not! I just didn't know what I was doing. I thought Cal was dead."

"Well, don't be relieved because he's not."

"Seel!"

Seel touched his shoulder. "Sorry, that was foul. This is . . . This is just the worst thing."

The worst thing, Flick thought, *is that I didn't come directly to wake and tell you last night. Now I have to hide in a nest of lies. Cal has made me like him.*

Flick felt responsible for Orien's death, as if his silence had prevented help getting to Orien in time. But in his heart he knew Orien had already been dead by the time Cal had dragged him to the Nayati. "How did you find him?" Flick asked. He didn't want to hear the answer, but to punish himself he had to know.

"Hanging," Seel said and paused before saying, "by his guts. Hanging by his guts. He was butchered."

The pain of those words was like a penitent's whip across Flick's mind. "Why did he come back here? *Why?*"

"God knows," Seel said. "To talk to him, I suppose. To try and help him. We'll never know."

"We should have heard," Flick said. "Seel, why didn't we hear and wake up?"

Seel had the fingers of one hand pressed against his eyes. "I don't know. Perhaps the bastard made it happen like that."

"I didn't realize how much he hated Orien, how much he blamed him."

"I think we had a glimpse last night," Seel said, "but I'd have never believed he'd go so far. It's his Uigenna blood."

"But you have it too."

"Uigenna indoctrination, then. I wasn't that affected."

"How do we go on from here, Seel? What will we do?"

"I don't know. In the old world, we took so much for granted, criminals being hunted down and brought to justice. What do we do now? Hunt him down ourselves? He's long gone, and an experienced traveler. We'd never find him. So, we tell the Gelaming? That's the nearest we have to a peacekeeping force isn't it? Do you think they'll find him for us?"

"I don't know."

"They won't," Seel said, standing up. "They're dealing with whole rogue tribes, intertribal wars, and such like. One bad har won't mean much to them."

"So, he just gets away with it?"

Seel sighed, shook his head slowly. "There's nothing we can do," he said. "We're powerless. He came here to do this. It was his purpose. He played with us all, like a cat with its prey, then he made his kill. I'm just gratified he'll never be happy, never get true satisfaction from this. I tell myself to think of his hell, which he lives in continually. It's the only comfort."

Before they went to bed that night, Flick told Seel he wanted to change the bedding. He said he wanted to put the previous night well behind them. Seel accepted this and let Flick get on with it. Flick wanted to burn the sheets, even though the marks on them were scant. Perhaps it hadn't really been necessary to change them, but that was Orien's blood that would be pressed against his skin as he slept. Even if there were only a faint stain, it would burn him like acid.

The blood could be cleared away, the body burned, but the wounds Orien's murder left on the Saltrock community would take a long time to heal. Hara found it inconceivable that anyone could infiltrate their safe haven and commit such an atrocity. Seel organized a lengthy ceremonial funeral for Orien, and his body was burned on a great pyre in the middle of the town. Hara stood around numbly, confused. This was never meant to happen. How would they carry on without Orien, their shaman, their rock? Who was there to replace him? No har.

The day after the murder, Seel went to Orien's forlorn empty home and collected all his cats, but they kept running away from Seel's house, back to their old home. After a couple of days, two hara moved into Orien's place, just to look after the animals.

Flick rode out to the soda lake, taking with him the cook's knife from the kitchen. He threw it into the corrosive bath of minerals and steam, and said a prayer. He did this alone, although in the shimmer above the waters, he thought he saw shadowy cloaked figures walking toward him, carrying staffs and dressed in long black cloaks. But they never reached him.

Over the following weeks, Seel and Flick moved awkwardly around each other, as if they'd lost their senses. Cal had duped them both, but this shared mistake didn't bring them closer together. Flick didn't have the energy to look after the house, and Seel spent nearly every day in his office, where the plans for a greater Saltrock lay spread out on his desk. He sat with his back to the window and his head in his hands, staring at the marks on the papers as if he'd never seen them before.

One morning, Flick went into the room without knocking. Seel looked up blearily.

"I have to go," Flick said.

Seel just stared at him.

"I'm sorry. It's the only way. I can't stay here. There's a promise I made. I mean to keep it."

"Flick, don't leave me," Seel said.

"I have to," Flick said.

"Where will you go? This is your home. You're an important part of Saltrock."

"It doesn't matter. None of it matters. I can't live with myself here. Don't you understand?"

"No," Seel said. "I don't. It wasn't your fault, what happened."

"I could have prevented it," Flick said.

"You couldn't. Don't kid yourself. He used you."

"I'm going," Flick said. "You can't say anything that will change my mind."

"Then he's won completely," Seel said. "This is what he wants—Saltrock to fall apart. Let me guess. He told you that you should leave?"

"This is my decision," Flick said.

"You mentioned something about a promise," Seel recalled, his eyes narrow. "What did you mean?"

"It doesn't matter."

"Don't let him use you still," Seel said. "Please, Flick, be careful of what you're doing."

Flick nodded. There was nothing else to say. He couldn't thank Seel for all he'd been given. He couldn't promise to come back one day.

Outside, the afternoon was just beginning, the sun high in the sky. Flick saddled his pony, fixed his supplies and a tent to it. Seel didn't come out of the house.

Flick mounted the pony and urged it out of Saltrock. There was no har to say good-bye to. He headed toward the northwest. The sun was leading him down the sky. He was heading toward the past.

CHAPTER SIX

>━┤━◄┣━・⊖━・◄┣━┤━◄

During the day, when the sun was at its most deadly, Ulaume would find somewhere for him and the harling to crouch: beneath an overhang of rock, or among the spiky fingers of a spindly bush. He used the piece of fabric the child had been wrapped in as a canopy for them both, and while they waited for the sun's fierce eye to close, Ulaume would talk constantly to his companion. In the mornings and the evenings, they would travel, but in the cold tomb of the middle of the night, they would sleep, huddled together for warmth. The coyote had stayed with them, albeit at a distance, but she led them to water at sundown. Sometimes she led them to caves, where blind bats huddled in a creaking leathery mass, only to pour forth after dark like a curse. Ulaume found it easy to acquire food. It was as if what he was doing now was meant to be. He killed the small desert hares, and quick emerald serpents. He knew which roots to dig up and chew. And while they ate, he would observe the child of wonder sitting before him: straight-backed, legs poking out, gnawing on a bone.

From the very first day, the harling rode upon Ulaume's shoulders, fists plunged deep into his hair. It was only when he'd felt the liquid running down his back that Ulaume was faced with the task of keeping the harling clean. Whoever had exposed it in the desert had wrapped its loins in absorbent cloth.

Now it was soiled. Ulaume lifted the child down and untied the cloth. "Don't piss on me," he said, knowing with a sinking heart the harling could not yet understand. He hoped it would learn such things as swiftly as it had learned to crawl. The harling laughed and kicked at him. "You're pretty, so you'll get away with a lot, but not this," Ulaume said. He was surprised to discover the harling did not have fully developed sexual organs, but perhaps that was because of its age. He did not know how Wraeththu were supposed to develop, but it crossed his mind this might be why the harling had been exposed. If so, it seemed stupid. Were the Kakkahaar so frightened and ignorant they would shun this precious gift, just because it didn't yet look like them? It didn't make sense, yet the harling seemed perfect in all other ways. The more he thought about, the more Ulaume believed that Lianvis wouldn't have rejected the harling unless absolutely necessary. Then the thought occurred to him that the child might be dangerous in some way, but if so, he couldn't imagine how. It was a delightful creature, full of joy and curiosity.

Ulaume realized the only way to train this wise little animal was through example, so he made the harling watch him urinate and defecate, and explained how it was important to bury the result. He indicated they should do this duty together, at certain times of day, and very quickly the harling realized what was required. It was so gratifying, Ulaume realized it would not be a great trial to teach his new charge anything.

The harling nibbled constantly on the talisman around its neck, until after only a few days it disintegrated. Ulaume gathered up the bits, feeling they shouldn't be lost. He felt strongly that the harling's hostling had tied the talisman there. There was a resonance within it of grief and love. Inside, among twigs, feathers, and leaves, he found a scrap of parchment, and upon this was written the word, "Lileem." He did not know this word, but decided it must be the harling's name. "You are Lileem," he told it. "And I am Ulaume. Yoo-Law-Me. Can you copy that?" He touched the harling's throat gently. "The noise comes from here. Ulaume. Say it."

The harling grinned at him, but didn't attempt to make a sound.

Ulaume had no idea of where to go. He was heading roughly northwest, driven by the conviction that eventually he'd arrive somewhere important. It was as if the landscape itself aided his journey. The desert wilderness was treacherous and harsh, and many hara had died in it who were experienced desert-dwellers, yet every day Ulaume found food without too much trouble, and the coyote sniffed out water. Every time he and Lileem needed shelter, he found it almost at once. And the harling developed with alarming speed. It was as if he had been designed to be on the run shortly after birth, and perhaps because Wraeththu were in some ways usurpers in this world, that was the idea. Ulaume thought of the child in terms of "he" rather than "it" now, because the young personality was blossoming. Lileem embraced life with a loving madness. He raced about, naked and free, mimicking the sounds of the desert creatures, of the wind whispering through the scrub. He had an impressive array of yowls, clicks, and whistles, but so far had not tried to talk. He was a demonstrative, affectionate creature, who would throw himself against Ulaume's legs and grip them fiercely. Without ever having been shown how, he planted wet kisses all over Ulaume's face before they went to sleep. He sang to himself in a sweet wordless way. He sang to Ulaume's witchy hair and made it dance like snakes.

Often, Ulaume thought about the hostling who had abandoned this child. He did not even know the har's name, and the idea of Rarn's consort was shadowy in his head. They must have met countless times, but no face remained in Ulaume's memory. Once, when Lileem's wileless behavior had been exceptionally enchanting, Ulaume lay awake in the night, his arms about the harling, and sent out a strong, clear call to say that Lileem lived and was well. He didn't know what level Rarn's consort was at magically, or whether he'd be able to pick up the message, but felt he had to try. He was sure the har wouldn't have surrendered Lileem willingly. It was as if a mist of his love still lingered about the harling, like a wistful ghost.

Eventually, they reached the mountains that the Kakkahaar called Hubisag's Crown. Here, in the foothills, Ulaume lit a sacred fire into which he cast a lock of his own hair. It writhed within the flames and made a sound, as it burned, like a high-pitched scream. Ulaume prayed to Hubisag and thanked the deity for helping them through the desert. As he prayed, Lileem danced around the fire, singing, and nearby, upon an overhanging ledge of rock, the coyote also sang to the stars.

His rite concluded, Ulaume crouched beside the fire and wondered where his instincts would lead them next. He imagined Pellaz sitting opposite him, on the other side of the fire, almost invisible through the dancing flames. "Do you have a task for me?" Ulaume asked. But, as ever, there was no response, either in reality or imagination.

The following morning, Ulaume sniffed the air to decide which way to go. He really needed to find somewhere he could acquire clothes for Lileem. The harling was clearly a hardy creature, and rarely seemed affected by cold or heat, but beyond the desert there would be greater temperature variation in the seasons, and Ulaume knew it could get very cold, even though he had never been to such places before. His own clothes were hardly suitable for traveling, and he had a strong sense that now they had left the wilderness realm, they had fallen into reality where physical needs would become more pressing. The flight from his tribe had so far seemed like an agreeable dream, but here the air smelled sharper and more immediate, rocks were spikier beneath the feet, and there was a danger of running into rogue hara of inhospitable tribes.

A mountain path led to the west and Ulaume chose to follow it. Lileem wanted to run ahead as he usually did, but Ulaume called him back. He felt wary now. Lileem was not pleased to be restrained, but Ulaume took hold of the harling's hand firmly. "You have to learn about danger," he said. "It's not always safe to run about. You've seen me kill hares and snakes? Well, you should know that some hara might want to do the same to us."

"Eat us!" Lileem said, which were the first words he had spoken.

"Yes," Ulaume said, "well done. You've found your voice, then."

Lileem didn't say anything else, but began to sing.

"Hush," Ulaume said. "If we make noises, we could bring danger to us."

Lileem sighed and his shoulders slumped.

Late in the afternoon, Ulaume smelled smoke. He bid Lileem to be quiet and to wait for him behind a rock. Uttering a low bird call, he beckoned the coyote to him. For once, she seemed totally in accord with his wishes. Ulaume crept ahead along the path and presently came to a burning cart, which was surrounded by charred corpses. If there had been horses or mules, the attackers had taken them. Ulaume's first thought was that whoever had done this had made it impossible to steal clothes from the dead, which was most inconvenient. The charred twisted remains were barely smoking, which suggested the carnage had taken place some time before. He didn't sense anyone else about. The coyote nosed at the carrion and Ulaume did not bother to stop her. He thought the corpses were human, therefore little more than animals. Still, it must mean that he was approaching areas of habitation. He examined the wreckage and some distance from it found a striped blanket draped over some scrub. This he took and rolled into a bundle. But that was the only loot to be salvaged.

He ran back to Lileem and found the harling still crouching wide-eyed behind the rock where he'd left him. "You've been very good to stay here so still and quiet," Ulaume said. "We're going to have to be even more careful from now on." He held out his hand. "Come on."

Lileem looked the most troubled Ulaume had ever seen him. "Smell," Lileem whispered, wrinkling up his nose.

"I know. It's horrible. Some humans are dead up there."

"Bad meat," said Lileem. *"Bad."*

"Yes," Ulaume agreed. He thought that Lileem was sensitive to vibrations in the air left by the slaughter. "Come on now. We'll run past it."

Lileem scrambled out of his hiding place and took hold of Ulaume's hand at once.

As they passed the wreck, Lileem blew out his cheeks and shut his eyes, clearly holding his breath. The coyote was still occupied with gnawing bones, and Ulaume let her get on with it, knowing she'd find them once she'd sated her appetite. He began to run, the harling beside him, and the more he ran, the less he felt like stopping, ever, but eventually, he sensed Lileem tiring and slowed down. A kind of panic had affected him. He knew in his blood that Wraeththu had been responsible for what they'd seen at the side of the road and they were not the kind of Wraeththu he wanted to run into. Ulaume had no fear for himself, particularly, as he was afraid of very little, and felt more than capable of dealing with any foe. All he had to do was be himself, even if they were faced by hara of the Uigenna tribe, who were reputedly the worst of all. But he was concerned for Lileem. It would not be good for the harling to fall into the wrong hands and no matter how adept Ulaume might be at protecting himself through the powers of seduction and witchery, he might not be able to prevent Lileem being taken from him, and then indoctrinated into twisted, ignorant ways. He could not bear to think of Lileem's boundless joy for life being corrupted by hara like the Uigenna, who he considered to be little more than human, but more dangerous than human because they had Wraeththu powers. He did not believe anyhar would kill a Wraeththu child, as they were worth more than gold, but then he glanced down at Lileem. What if some ignorant har made the mistake the Kakkahaar had made? The more he thought about it, the more Lileem actually looked like a girl child, but surely that must be the way of things, and male characteristics would develop later on. He didn't want to risk arguing the case though.

They came to the settlement an hour before sundown. The first thing they saw was a windmill, its sails turning slowly against the red sky. Creaking wood was the only sound. Ulaume smelled smoke again, and his instincts advised him that this place had also suffered an attack. There was no sign of life, but perhaps survivors were hiding among the ruins, ready to strike out in terror at whoever came near. Ulaume gestured for Lileem to crawl into a dry prickly bush beside the road. "Wait here, don't move," he whispered. "I'll scout ahead."

Lileem obeyed, and hugged his knees among the spiky branches. He said nothing but then held out a hand in desperation, his face forlorn.

"Don't worry for me," Ulaume said. "Listen for my heart. It will remain with you."

Lileem frowned earnestly. He pulled the branches around him.

Ulaume crept forward, towards the sinking sun, every muscle taut and quivering. He could hear insects scuttling among the grasses. His steps were light and silent like a coyote's. His body bent low to the ground, but moved swiftly. Ruined buildings were silhouetted against the long sunset. They might have been empty for a thousand years, and yet Ulaume thought he heard the cries of recent ghosts. He sniffed the air constantly, analyzing the different scents. The smoke was old, perhaps older than that of the wreckage they had seen earlier. There was a rank air of death and fear, a stink of attic dust and mold. Ulaume's hair shifted restlessly. He felt he might have to defend himself at any moment, yet the scene ahead of him appeared devoid of life. He thought of Lileem crouched motionless amid the scrub, as still as a wild creature under threat. He could not risk his own life, because then the harling would be alone, with only the coyote for company. He must be as cautious as if Lileem were still at his side.

Flat fields surrounded the settlement on all sides, but the crops had been burned like the buildings. Scorched land, cursed land. There would be bones poking through the soil. No birds called; a sure sign of terrible history. Ulaume's flesh squeezed tight against his bones as he prowled along the ramshackle main street, keeping close to the buildings, to the shadows. Sunset dyed the world red; even the shadows were crimson. He supposed this to have been a human settlement, because a smell of humanity remained: a psychic rather than physical scent. There was no one here, he could sense it strongly, yet still he felt unnerved and edgy. Whatever had happened here had been unspeakable. The land was soaked in its memory; so much so, Ulaume had to fight the urge to sink to the dirt and weep. He had no sympathy for humans, but something about this place affected him. There was a message here, almost as if it was written in the dirty windows, the dust on the road, the splay of naked tree branches. Could it have been a Wraeththu town after all? The only one he knew of near this area was Saltrock, and that was miles away. But things changed quickly in the outside world, things that not even Lianvis knew about. What Ulaume had to decide now was whether it was safe to bring Lileem here. There was a chance they could find supplies and clothing, because not all of the buildings were razed. It was strange there was no sign of conflict, other than the burned areas. There were no corpses, no blood. As far as Ulaume knew, Uigenna did not generally tidy up after their massacres. Perhaps something worse than them had happened to this place.

On the other side of town was a graveyard, and it was clear the ground had been recently dug. There were no headstones on the fresh graves, not even wooden markers, only the oblong patches of raw earth that spoke of endings. Someone had stayed behind to bury the dead. That suggested survivors to Ulaume rather than attackers. Perhaps the bodies he'd seen on the road earlier were the remains of this community, who had been hunted down and killed like their neighbors. But it didn't make sense. This town had been attacked weeks, perhaps months, ago, and the carnage on the road had been recent. Why would aggressive Wraeththu leave survivors to their own devices, and then slaughter them once they decided to leave the town? Ulaume wandered among the graves. Some seemed very recent indeed. Survivors who had died of their injuries? There had to be people around. There was no other explanation.

He saw a flash of light in the corner of his vision and leapt down instinctively behind an old gravestone, tense and motionless. But then he realized it had merely been the dying sun, glinting off the windows of a big house that stood on a hill outside of town. Perhaps that was where the survivors lurked, but no lights burned there. The house seemed to contemplate the end of the day, immense and inviolable. It was too late to investigate now, because it was almost dark. He must go back for Lileem. They would camp near the road tonight, and return here in the morning.

Ulaume walked back through the town, and now he kept to the center of the dusty road. It wasn't really a town at all, just a cluster of dwellings and workshops. Whoever had lived here hadn't been a threat to anyone. It appeared they had been farmers, clinging to a dying way of life. Ulaume chastised himself. He mustn't think that way. If these humans had still lived, they'd have killed him and Lileem, whether they'd been simple farmers or not. It did no good to pity the enemy. Yet still came the urge to weep, to feel compassion, to be outraged. Ulaume had been incepted at a very young age, and could remember hardly anything of being human. Tribes like the Gelaming would frown on such a practice, as they only incepted boys at puberty, but perhaps for no good reason. Ulaume had grown up Wraeththu. His inception had been different from most hara's, because the Colurastes were different from most hara. His initiation had not been consummated with aruna: that had come much later. He had been given to a foster hostling, and had been allowed to finish his childhood. Manual procedures had been carried out upon his body to activate his Wraeththu organs, but it had been a clinical passionless operation. Aruna, when it happened, had been a time of celebration, a rite of passage. When Ulaume was old enough to appreciate this difference, he'd been grateful, although the Colurastes troupe he'd been part of had eventually come to regret taking him in. It hadn't been his fault. He had his nature, they had theirs. He had been born wild, and reborn even wilder. Why should he think of this now?

He paused in the purple twilight, and it seemed to him as if the air smelled of rain. He shivered. He could hear a strange grating sound, like stone being drawn against metal. There was a sense of immanence around him. This place was holy.

Ulaume closed his eyes for a moment. Emotions poured through him, as if a thousand ghosts flew through his flesh. He was here for a reason.

Ulaume hardly slept that night, and Lileem shuddered against his body, whimpering softly. The coyote had returned, and stood sentinel high above them, occasionally offering her song to the gods of night.

At dawn, Ulaume roused Lileem and before they even took breakfast, led the harling by the hand into the ruined settlement. Lileem was fretful, more fractious than Ulaume had ever seen him. He tried to pull away from Ulaume's hand. He wept.

"What's wrong with you?" Ulaume said. "There's no one here."

"He's still crying," Lileem murmured. "It's in me."

Ulaume swallowed the sour taste that rose in this throat. It was clear that Lileem could feel whatever had happened here. "We have to investigate," Ulaume said. "There's *something* here. That's what you feel. But it's not alive. It can't hurt us."

Lileem's expression showed he wasn't sure about that, but he fell silent and allowed Ulaume to lead him.

By day, the settlement was less spooky but revealed as more desolate. It was full of sound now: the bang of windows and doors in the wind, the creaking of the windmill sails, the hiss of brushwood scratching along the road. Ulaume investigated some of the buildings, and was pleased to find items of clothing, cooking utensils, and even some tins of dried fruit. He made caches of the things he wanted.

At one house, he opened the door and a scream flew out.

Beside him, Lileem squeaked and ducked down, as if to avoid heavy wings.

But there was nothing beyond. "Trapped ghost, that's all," Ulaume said. "We set it free."

Always, Ulaume was edging toward the hill on the outskirts of town. He watched it through the corner of his eye, drawn, yet also repelled. Something may be waiting there. Hope or revelation. Sometimes, Ulaume forgot he was on a quest or pilgrimage associated with the impressions he'd picked up of Pellaz's death. Lileem had consumed his attention for the quick months that had passed since he'd left the Kakkahaar. But, in the back of his mind, deep in his heart, it was always there: an insistent murmur, a sense of anticipation and excitement. He was perplexed as to why this dismal, violated settlement should seem part of that.

Ulaume saw the graveyard just up ahead, and tightened his hold on Lileem's hand, in case the harling was upset by whatever emanations might seep from the recently opened ground. Lileem, however, broke free of Ulaume's hold. He seemed delighted by the place and scampered among the humps of earth, bending down to place a small starfish hand on each one. Ulaume decided he would never fathom the minds of harlings. This, surely, should be the creepiest place, but now Lileem seemed far more relaxed. Perhaps it was because the town was behind them. The graveyard, in its own way, was clean. Everyone who had come here had already been dead.

Ulaume allowed the harling to play and shaded his eyes to gaze up at the house on the hill. It was made of pale stone, and didn't seem to fit comfortably into its landscape. "Leelee," Ulaume called. "Come here."

The harling came to him directly.

"Look," Ulaume said, pointing. "Look at that big house. What do you think about it?"

Lileem took hold of one of Ulaume's knees. "It's sad," he said. "Not bad."

"Do you learn all your words from me?" Ulaume asked.

Lileem grimaced. "Shapes that say things," he said.

"You're a freak, you know," Ulaume said. "You're too old in the head."

Lileem grinned widely, apparently pleased with this pronouncement.

Ulaume was unsettled to think the harling had understood exactly what he'd meant. "Is anything in there?" he asked.

Lileem studied the house for a moment. "It isn't dead," he said. "We can go there."

"What else?" Ulaume said, wondering how quickly a Wraeththu child could learn to be economical with information.

Lileem shrugged. "Won't hurt us."

Ulaume was convinced Lileem sensed something about the true nature of this place. As to why the harling wouldn't or couldn't voice his thoughts was intriguing.

A narrow road wound around the hill that led to the house. Although at first it had appeared to be standing in splendid isolation, as they grew nearer, Ulaume could see that behind the house were stables, outhouses, and a barn. Ulaume said, "I've never seen such a big house."

"What's it for?" Lileem asked.

"Living in," Ulaume replied. "You live there all the time, if you have a house like that."

"Have you ever had one?"

Ulaume laughed. "No. Where we come from, hara don't have houses."

The big front door was stuck, as if rain or tears had warped the wood. But it was partly ajar, and Ulaume could peer into the dim hallway beyond. He saw a checkered marble floor and drifts of crinkly leaves. The windows were all locked, none broken. Ulaume could hear something creaking in the wind, and thought of gibbets, but when he and Lileem rounded the corner of the house into a yard full of stables and outhouses, it was only a stable door harried by the breeze. Strands of yellow straw were caught between the cobbles, and Ulaume could imagine the clop of shod hooves against the stone. He felt strongly that he must go into the house and leaned against the back door. This was unlocked and unwarped. It swung open onto a corridor lined by kitchens and pantries. But try as he might, Ulaume could not conjure up the ghosts of quick steps, of industry and the smell of domesticity. This house had been forlorn long before what had happened recently. No screams would fly out of doorways here, because the ghosts who had always been present were silent and glum.

Lileem came into the house also and looked into the rooms. "It's dark," he said.

"Yes," Ulaume agreed. And it was not because this side of the house faced away from the sun. It felt strange to be standing in a house that humans had lived in. It was like going back into ancient history or uncovering a forgotten tomb. If he blinked, none of his Wraeththu life might ever have happened. He could have been born in a place like this. Not like Lileem, with no history and no memory of all that had once been. He stared at the harling as he scampered in and out of the rooms and thought to himself. *It is real.*

Lileem appeared to sense something was troubling Ulaume. He ran to Ulaume's side and gripped his legs fiercely.

"I've just woken up," Ulaume said.

They investigated the house from top to bottom. Lileem was clearly fascinated by the moth-eaten furniture that smelled of old cologne and dust. These were arcane and puzzling objects to him, but somehow attractive.

Ulaume did not want to sleep in rooms where old beds soaked in memories moldered in the shadows. He found a room with bare floorboards right at the top of the house, where a skylight opened to the stars. Here, he made a nest of blankets he had found folded up in a chest, scented with sprigs of withered sage.

Lileem watched the proceedings with a dubious expression on his face. "Stay here?" he said.

"Just for a short while," Ulaume answered. "I need to make plans. We are without a tribe and I am without all that I seek. I want to stay here."

Lileem pursed his lips and glanced around the room. Already he had opinions, and had learned enough to keep some of them to himself.

"We are not in danger here," Ulaume said.

Lileem had never slept beneath a roof before, and it had been a long time since Ulaume had been enclosed by solid walls. Neither of them felt particularly comfortable as they prepared to sleep that night, and Ulaume wondered whether they'd be better off finding a secluded corner of the garden to sleep in. The coyote would not come into the house but padded around the yard, making odd yelping sounds. A wind had started up, blowing in off the burned fields, carrying with it a faint acrid smell.

Ulaume lay awake, yet he knew he was dreaming. It was the kind of dream you can't wake from, because you can't convince yourself it isn't real. A face hung before him in the dark. Despite the lack of light, he could see its eyes, and they were the eyes of an animal, empty of all but a mindless cunning. Then he was outside, walking down the road toward the settlement. Rain fell softly, barely more than a mist and every building was robed in steam. He heard the sound of grating metal again. Figures moved around him as blurred shadows. The buildings seemed more real than life. He came to a house with a wide wooden veranda, where a human boy sat sheltering from the rain. He ran the blade of a knife down a stone. The boy was Pellaz. Ulaume ran forward. He meant to seize this dream by its shoulders, shake it, make it speak. Pellaz looked up. He appeared so young, his features less set than when Ulaume had met him. "Hello Ulaume," he said. "You must go away. I don't know you yet."

"Pell," Ulaume said, but he could no longer move. An invisible wall had sprung up before him, and what lay beyond it was now dimming out of existence. "What do you want of me?" Ulaume yelled. "I am here. Tell me."

There was no reply, yet he could hear the sound of hooves upon the road behind him. Was an older version of Pell approaching, one who would speak to him? Ulaume turned. He caught a brief glimpse of a horse, a rider, a feral grin, and then the apparition passed right through him. A black wave of terrifying emotion pulled at his flesh, his mind. He was in hell.

Then he was awake and panting in the dark attic room of the big house, his breath steaming on the air. Lileem slept soundly, curled against his side.

And there was a face above him: its long black hair hung down right onto Ulaume's chest. Eyes wide, whites showing all around. Mad and vacant. Ulaume held his breath, afraid that the slightest movement would dispel the dream image. "Hubisag," he whispered beneath this breath, "let the ghost speak that is the essence of knowledge, knowledge brings wisdom, wisdom brings courage. Hubisag, let all be known that I should know."

The face above him turned to the side quizzically. He saw a flash of white teeth and then it was gone. There was a sound like a rat scampering down the stairs, swift and light. Ulaume leapt from the nest of blankets, casting aside Lileem, who whimpered and rubbed at his face. Ulaume made a quick signal for silence and sped toward the door. Someone had been here. A real person of flesh and blood. His flesh tingled as he ran down the stairs, his feet barely touching the steps. It was as if he followed a column of smoke. There was only a faint sense of presence left behind.

CHAPTER SEVEN

$\rightthreetimes\!\cdot\!\leftrightarrow\!\cdot\!\cdot\!\ominus\!\cdot\!\cdot\!\leftrightarrow\!\cdot\!\leftthreetimes$

If somehar had told Seel that Flick might walk out on him and that if he did Seel would feel as if a part of his life had been cut away, he wouldn't have believed it, which just goes to show how a har who believes himself to be self-aware can be so wrong.

After Flick left the office on that last morning, Seel sat staring into space, unable to take in the fact that Flick had somehow found the courage and independence to leave Saltrock. Like many strong partners in relationships, he'd taken Flick for granted, and it's only when the other partner walks out that the dominant half suddenly finds themselves bereft, hopeless, and grief-stricken. It struck home most of all when Seel felt hungry. He'd sat in the office all day, doing nothing but chain-smoking. At sundown, his stomach complained and he went to the kitchen. He'd have to cook for himself and he didn't know where half the things were kept. For dinner, he had bread and some dry strips of meat Flick had been keeping in the larder to give to Orien's orphan cats. As he ate, he read the letter that Flick had left for him, propped up against the saltcellar. It was full of rambling explanations that made little sense, but for the part that Flick had decided to seek out Pell's family. What idiocy? Why was he doing this? It would achieve nothing, and might well be fatally dangerous. "You little fool," Seel said to the empty room. "This is what he wanted. Cal has won."

Seel couldn't face going out or telling anyone that Flick had left him. He felt ashamed, as if he'd done something really bad. And he knew exactly what that was. His own harsh and indifferent words to Flick echoed round his head in an endless cruel mantra. Why had he taken out all his fear and bitterness on the one person who'd been there for him for the past few years? Why had he been so stupid? He had been careless. Cal had used this opportunity to worm his way into the hole in Flick and Seel's relationship and sever the final ties. Seel also found it impossible to dispel the nagging doubt that Flick had known rather more about Orien's death than he'd said. He didn't think Flick had done anything wrong, but just that he'd covered up for Cal rather more than he'd needed to. He believed, deep in his heart, that Cal had told Flick something that terrible night. And Cal had pressed Flick to silence, perhaps for no other reason than to widen the yawning chasm between Flick and Seel.

Will we ever be free of him? Seel thought. *How long will the spiteful reverberations of his hate linger?*

For two days, Seel kept to the house, other than when he crept out to the stables to feed the animals. Sometimes, he considered saddling up his horse and riding off to find Flick, but he knew Flick would not want that. The letter was too final. He had turned his back on all that he knew. He and Seel had never been chesna: ultimately, there had been little for him to walk away from and only an emptiness to bring him back to.

Seel ignored the heavy pounding on the door when Colt came to the house. Colt shouted through the door. "Are you all right, Seel?"

No, I most certainly am not, Seel thought, but hid in the kitchen anyway. He knew that very soon Colt would come back with others and break into the house, perhaps afraid that Seel was ill, dead, or had gone mad. When Colt stomped away, Seel went out to the stables. This was his town; he couldn't abandon or neglect it. He would have to face his friends and tell them the truth.

After allowing himself the luxury of cursing aloud the day that Pell and Cal had first come to Saltrock, Seel went back into the house, where he washed and changed his clothes. As he'd anticipated, Colt came back a couple of hours later, no doubt after protracted discussion. He had four other hara with him, who Seel could see from the bedroom window. Stringer was not with them, and Seel knew this was because Stringer was aware he needed time alone, for the blood to congeal, for the initial healing to take place. By this time, Flick's absence would have been noticed and few hara would draw the wrong conclusions.

Seel uttered a single long sigh, then went down to open the door before Colt could damage it. He reflected that Colt had changed very little since he'd been incepted. He was still very much the macho type, in his own spiritual warrior way, and Seel had to admit that sometimes there was comfort in that. When Colt was around, hara felt safe.

"I'm not dead, in case you were worrying," Seel said, as Colt came up the wooden steps to the porch.

Colt said nothing, waiting.

Seel folded his arms and leaned against one of the porch posts. "Flick's gone," he said. "Walked out on me two days ago."

Colt dropped his gaze from Seel's, rubbed his chin, then said, "We thought so. I'll find somehar to help you—you know, help with the house."

"Okay," Seel said. "I'm helpless. I need feeding." The words were light, but his heart felt like damp clay. Stringer would be easier to talk to about this.

"The dust will settle," Colt said in a determined tone. "This is the last of it, Seel. We can carry on."

"I know," Seel said, "but *you* still have Stringer."

Colt looked embarrassed. "Come over to our place," he said. "Eat with us."

As Seel walked away, surrounded by those whose best interests lay in him remaining sane and functional, he looked back. *Perhaps I need a new house,* he thought. *That one will be haunted now, by more than one ghost.*

The sky was dark above the roof and glistening with stars. It seemed to shimmer as if it were just a veil hiding another reality. As Seel stared up, a strange feeling stole through him. Something was wrong. Something felt out of place. Slowly, the velvet night became milky and shot with arrows of white light. Seel blinked and realized it wasn't an effect of the tears in his eyes and caught hold of Colt's arm. "What the hell is that?"

The sky was fracturing.

Before Colt could offer a reply, there was a deafening crack like thunder and the night shattered. Something burst out of it like a gigantic comet. At first, all Seel could see was a boiling cloud, his body gripped by a paralyzing sense of wrongness. He knew he was seeing something that didn't naturally belong to this world.

They came in slow motion at first, pouring down from the hole in the night: white horses, nostrils flaring, manes flying with shards of frost. As they hit the ground in front of Seel's yard, they threw up a spray of dust and sparks, and then somehow galloped into real time, fast and shrieking. They careered up the street, bringing with them a vapor of frozen air and a smell of ozone. Blue lightning crackled between them and ice crystals flew from their steaming flanks. Their riders were wrapped in silver-gray hooded cloaks that swirled like foggy air.

"What the hell . . . ?" Seel realized he had grabbed hold of Colt in terror and now pulled away from him. This wasn't a vision: it was real. The ground was shaking.

There were five horses and the leader of the troupe brought his mount to a prancing halt a few feet in front of Seel. He threw back his hood and gazed down imperiously. A mane of red hair fell forward over his shoulders and he shook it, making it writhe like fabric under water. A terrifying and beautiful vision, nightmare made flesh.

"Thiede," Seel said. He should have known. Who else would make such a grand entrance? Seel knew he had to catch his breath, gather his senses, no matter what outlandish illusion he'd just witnessed. He would need his wits about him if Thiede were here. "You are too late," he said, surprised and pleased at the steady tone of his voice.

"Good evening, Seel," Thiede said and dismounted. "Fortunate to catch you here so quickly."

The other riders remained motionless in their saddles, their faces still covered. Seel wondered who, or what, they were, and whether Thiede would elect to tell him. Now, Thiede towered over him, alien and discomforting. Had he ever been human? No, of course not. Thiede was a creature of magic that could fly through the air on an enchanted horse. He couldn't possibly be real, but he was.

"Orien is dead," Seel said, "but I suppose you know that."

Thiede nodded once. "Yes."

"He called for you, many times."

"I could not prevent what happened," Thiede said. "Nor could I accept Orien's messages. I was engaged in business that prevented communication."

"I'm sure," Seel said. "What do you want?"

"I had to come," Thiede said. "Orien was my oldest friend."

"You've come to see the grave then? There isn't one. We burned him."

"I have come to see you," Thiede said. "There is much to discuss."

"Like the truth about Pellaz Cevarro?"

"Yes, among other things."

Seel turned to Colt. "May this meeting take place at your house?" He glanced back at Thiede. "My home is no longer fit for guests."

"I hope that will not matter in the long run," Thiede said.

Seel frowned at him in perplexity.

"Sure," Colt said. "What about them?" He gestured at the silent riders. "We don't have a big place."

"They are my personal guard," Thiede said. "Gelaming warriors. They will wait for me here."

"Are they alive?" Seel asked.

"Of course," Thiede answered. "The spectacle of our arrival will have dismayed you, but that was my intention. I wanted you to glimpse some of Wraeththu's potential."

"How did you do that? Illusion?"

"Not at all." He patted the neck of his horse, which though more beautiful than any animal Seel had seen before, seemed earthly enough. "These creatures are *sedim,* vehicles that traverse vast distances in minutes. They can step out of reality and journey the otherlanes, the route between different dimensions."

"Oh," said Seel. The whiskers around the horse's nose were still crusted with ice crystals. It nudged Thiede affectionately with its head.

"You sound skeptical, and I understand that," Thiede said. He laughed. "I like these creatures. In appearance, they are an ancient and primitive form of transport, and yet in reality the most sophisticated and advanced. It is like a joke, yes? Years back, we dreamed of silver ships to sail the universe, but this . . ." He patted the horse again. "It is a fine joke."

"My sides are splitting," Seel said coldly. "Shall we go?"

Colt and Stringer's house really was too small to contain such a massive presence as Thiede. Seel had to smile at Stringer's horrified expression as Thiede ducked beneath the doorway and strode into the kitchen. It was as if an angel had come to earth.

"Guests for dinner," Colt said darkly.

"Please be at ease," Thiede said, squeezing himself into chair at the head of the table: Colt's place. He would be totally aware that ordinary hara could never be at ease in his presence. "Something smells good. Traveling always makes me hungry."

You are enjoying this so much, Seel thought. He sat down and said to Stringer, "Any chance you could break open a few bottles of wine?" He looked at Thiede. "Stringer makes the best wine. He can make it out of anything."

Stringer nodded distractedly and left the room.

"So?" Seel said.

Colt remained standing, arms folded. His expression was that of utter disapproval, but certainly not fear.

You have your guards, but I have mine, Seel thought, a bolt of pure affection for Colt shooting through his heart.

"So," Thiede said, spreading his fingers against the tabletop. He wore two huge rings, set with glittering stones. "Do you believe in destiny?"

"Maybe," Seel answered.

Thiede cast him a wry look. "Perhaps not the best start," he said. "Very well. I am sorry you have had to go through some rather unpleasant experiences, and more than sorry that Orien lost his life. I did not intend for that to happen."

"What did you intend?" Seel snapped.

"The first part," Thiede answered. "You found Pellaz for me. You helped incept him."

"Orien did that," Seel said. "I wouldn't have become involved if I'd suspected any of what might follow."

Thiede paused and smiled. "Don't delude yourself, Seel. You *did* suspect. You were quite prepared to go through with it then and you'd no doubt do the same again. What irks you is that you do not know its purpose. You are a proud har and you resent being kept in the dark. I am here to enlighten you."

Seel shifted uncomfortably on his seat. Stringer had returned with open bottles of wine and now dispensed the drinks around the table. Thiede took a sip and nodded in approval. "Tasty."

"Enlighten me," Seel said. "What was Pell's purpose and how did it go wrong?"

"It didn't," Thiede said.

"What?"

"Cal went entirely wrong, but that was out of my control."

"Pell is dead. What was the point?"

"He is dead yet he lives," Thiede said and took another sip of wine.

Seel just stared at him, trying to absorb the words. After a while he said, "Go on."

"It will take some time, but eventually Pellaz will rise again, reborn and perfect. It is my intention to make him a divine king of Wraeththu."

Seel laughed nervously. "Okay, fine."

Thiede made a tutting sound. "Again, the skepticism. Look inside your own trousers, my dear, and tell me the impossible can't happen."

"You can do this? Raise a person from the dead?"

"Not exactly. And no, I'm not here to reanimate Orien's corpse, although even if I could you've left little for me to work with."

"It's a disgusting thought. Absolutely wrong."

"I agree. What I'm doing with Pellaz is recreating him, his essence, his being, his energy, but with the personality intact."

"How? How is that possible?"

"I'm not about to reveal my working secrets to you," Thiede said, grinning.

"But if you can't bring Orien back, how can you bring Pell back? His body was burned too."

"Well, let's see," Thiede said carefully. "I was, shall we say *prepared* for Pellaz's death. Orien's, on the other hand, took me by surprise."

"I find it difficult to accept or believe," Seel said. "You must appreciate that. How do you do it?"

"I am able to, that is all," Thiede said. "I am not like you, Seel, nor any other har."

"Why? What are you? I wonder whether you are Wraeththu at all."

"Let's just say I am different, more Wraeththu than most. I am what your children will become. And before we get sidetracked into a discussion about procreation, yes, you will have heirs, Seel. But now is not the time to talk about it."

"I don't believe you've just come here to tell me you've reanimated Pell," Seel said, still unable to believe a word of what he'd heard.

"Indeed not," Thiede said. "I wish with all my heart that Cal had not come back here and committed such a dreadful atrocity. It makes my job more difficult, because your mind and feelings are clouded by the horror of it. You blame yourself, of course, as do many others. But I want you to try and put it aside for now, to listen to me."

"I will listen."

"Pell will need hara around him whom he trusts. I want one of those hara to be you."

Seel drew in his breath slowly. "I see."

"It *will* happen, Seel. You must accept it."

"What are you asking of me really?"

"I want you to come to Immanion, to see for yourself."

"Cal's dream," Seel said bitterly. "He always wanted to find Immanion. I thought it was a fantasy."

"Far from it. Come with me to Almagabra, Seel, for that is where Immanion lies. It is a dream come true, and you must walk its streets to see for yourself."

"You're asking me to leave Saltrock?"

"I'm asking you to visit, that is all. You do not yet have to leave here permanently. You will have a few years to make the necessary arrangements."

"No," said Seel. "This is my home. I built it, and I intend to carry on building it. I don't want any part of your schemes, your glamours. It's over, Thiede. Forget Saltrock. Do what you have to, but leave us out of it. We played our part for you and look how it ended up. No more, I swear it. No more."

Thiede laughed quietly, a terrifying sound. "I will not accept 'no' for an answer, Seel. What harm will it do for you to visit the city? Have you no curiosity? I think you have plenty. You are merely being difficult for the sake of it." He paused. "And because you have no liking for me."

"True."

Thiede leaned back in his chair. "Then I see we need more valuable currency to persuade you. Name it. Name your price."

Seel gazed at Thiede's face and realized, with incredulity, Thiede meant it. He would pay anything. *Am I that valuable?* Seel thought. *Why? What does he really want of me?* "Well, there is one thing," he said.

"Name it."

"This is the cost for me to come and visit, nothing more. I will not be your plaything, Thiede. You have far too many of those already."

Thiede inclined his head. "What is the price?"

"Find Cal, punish him."

"That might not be easy."

"If you are so powerful, you can do it."

"Very well." Thiede held out his hand. "Do we have a deal?"

Seel stared at the hand, so much bigger than his own, yet elegant and attenuated. "Yes," he said.

Thiede withdrew his hand. "Then let's eat whatever smells so tempting and afterwards return to Immanion. Are you prepared to see your vision of reality come crashing down about your ears? Believe me, after traveling the other-lanes and seeing Immanion, you will never be the same again."

"I am prepared to endure whatever you show me."

Thiede laughed again. "I like you, Seel. I have great admiration for you. Perhaps in time you will come to view me as less of a monster."

Seel glanced up at Stringer, who said, "I'll serve dinner then, shall I?"

Seel reached for Stringer's hand, squeezed it. "Please."

Colt, who had said nothing the entire time, sat down opposite Seel. Without looking at Thiede, he said, "Tell him I will come with you. It's not right you should go alone."

Stringer set down a tureen on the table with force. "Colt, no!"

"It's not right," Colt said stubbornly. "Seel's Saltrock's heart. He shouldn't be placed in danger."

"It's all right," Seel said, but Thiede interjected.

"Your friend is right. It would be a symbol of trust if more than one representative of Saltrock came to Immanion." He smiled up at Stringer. "Please don't worry. He will be quite safe."

"I want to see it," Colt said. "If it's real."

"You would be aghast at what is real nowadays," Thiede said and tasted his meal. "Mmm, I miss simple cooking."

During the meal, Thiede informed Seel that two of his Gelaming guard would have to stay behind in Saltrock so that Seel and Colt could ride their *sedim*. The country of Almagabra lay on the other side of a great ocean, and it was necessary for Seel to use Gelaming transport to get there quickly. Seel was not entirely happy about Gelaming strangers remaining in Saltrock while he was gone. He wondered if, as Thiede's agents, they would set about making changes and indoctrinating hara the minute his back was turned. Grudgingly, he offered them accommodation in his home, sure they would be poking into everything.

Seel returned to his house to gather a few things for the journey, and found the Gelaming sprawled on the porch, laughing together and sharing a drink. They seemed more like ordinary hara now. But what specimens they were. These were the kind of hara Thiede had instructed Orien to find for him: the best. The cream of Wraeththu.

Seel took his unexpected guests around the house, pointing out where things were kept. He wasn't completely sure he was awake, for these were creatures from a dream. They were so much taller than him, and somehow so much bigger in more than a physical way. One of them went unbidden into the room Seel had shunned since the night of Orien's death, Cal's old room. The Gelaming looked around it without speaking, then came out again, closing the door behind him. "We could clean that for you," he said.

"Yes," Seel said. "Yes. Whatever." The room was clean of blood already, but he knew what the har meant.

The other Gelaming said he'd be happy to care for Seel's animals, so a tour of the stables and yard was also necessary. As Seel indicated where the feed was kept, the Gelaming said, "You mustn't fear. Immanion exists at the end of your journey. It will be worth it."

"Mmm," Seel murmured in a noncommittal tone.

"You won't wake up and find this is a dream," said the smiling Gelaming. "Believe it."

Outside the house, Colt was already mounted on a Gelaming *sedu,* which was prancing around, tossing its head. Colt, however, looked perfectly at home. "It's like sitting on a time bomb," he said to Seel, grinning. Colt was an excellent rider.

Thiede handed the reins of another *sedu* to Seel. "Mount," he said.

Seel paused. "How do we do this?"

"Just mount."

The minute he was on the horse's back and had gathered up the reins, Seel was aware this was no ordinary beast. It felt, if anything, like a machine that was designed to obey his commands. There was a sense of quivering power, and of alien intelligence that he could almost feel pushing against the boundaries of his perception.

"The *sedu* will follow the others," Thiede said. "He's well trained, so you don't have to worry. Our intention will be strong enough to carry all five of us."

" 'Intention . . . ' " Seel said.

"Intention and will are the aids these horses obey," Thiede said, swinging up into his own saddle.

The other two Gelaming positioned their mounts behind and to the left side of Seel and Colt, Thiede in the lead. Seel cast a glance at Colt. "We're not doing this, are we? I mean . . ."

Colt shrugged. "Let's see, shall we?"

Thiede raised his hand and the *sedim* began to walk down the main road. Once Thiede's horse started to trot, the others followed, their pace increasing all the time.

This is like taking off in a plane, Seel thought. *They will take off any minute.*

He couldn't help laughing out loud, because the sense of power beneath him was so strong and so awesome. The horse felt as if it was revving up, the muscles roaring with energy.

But the *sedim* didn't gallop up into the night sky. Suddenly, there came a crack of thunder once more and the air splintered around them. Seel's breath was knocked from his lungs. He lurched forward and had to grip the horse's mane. Its neck reared up and hit him sharply in the face. There was no reality. It was beyond dreaming, unimaginable. No harish mind could conceive of this even in dreams. He was aware of other presences around him, but knew he had no body, no substance. In this no place, he was pure essence, clinging like a leech to a presence more at home in this environment. It would be so easy though to lose his grip, to float off into the void, be lost forever. Cosmic winds he could not feel buffeted his being, trying to rip him from the *sedu*-essence. There were entities in this wind, but he could not perceive them properly, just sense they were near. These presences were malevolent, eager to claw him away from his companions.

Just when he thought he was lost, hard air splintered around him and the *sedu* was plunging, as if having taken a high jump, down onto a road in daylight. Seel was freezing cold. His hair was full of ice. The horse's reins dangled free. His hands were knotted in its mane, frozen into place. He feared his fingers would break like glass if he tried to move them. His vision was obscured, so he could barely take in the landscape around him, but was aware of the smell of the sea and the vague shapes of tall poplars that lined the road.

Thiede pulled his horse to a halt and both Seel's and Colt's mounts slid to a stop behind it. Tears of ice streaked Colt's face. He gathered up the horse's reins, shaking frost from his long braids. "No words," he said. "None."

Thiede had turned his horse and now came to Seel's side. "Are you all right?"

Seel managed to nod. "So cold."

"It can be," Thiede said. "Now you must admit that has to be the finest of my illusions, eh?"

"It was . . . awakening," Seel said.

"Forgive me if I sound smug, then," Thiede said, and gestured down the road, which sloped towards the white towers of a city that hugged the coast beyond. "Behold Immanion."

It was both an old city and a new one. A crystal blue sea sparkled beneath it, and in the quay, long prowed boats pranced upon the incoming tide. The boats looked both ancient and alien, as if they'd been plucked from the oceans of far worlds. The city itself was like a mixture of Classical and Far Eastern design: pagodas and pillars, domed roofs of gold and flat, tiled roofs of red. It was surrounded by high white walls and constructed upon a series of hills. Nowhere did there seem to be any scruffy corners. Long banners flew from towering minarets, emblazoned with the recently designed arms of the high-ranking families. Upon one hill, Thiede pointed out, were the villas of the city's governors, while along the coast a short way, lay the sprawling barracks complex and training grounds of the Gelaming army. In the center of the city was the High Nayati, the greatest of temples, and one day, in this place, Thiede intended to crown Pellaz Cevarro as Wraeththu's king.

Seel could see all this as they rode down to the gates. He had never beheld or imagined a city so beautiful. It was all that Cal could have dreamed it could be. But even from this distance Seel could tell there was no place for hara like Cal in Immanion.

Thiede said he would take them to his villa on the outskirts of the city. Once upon its streets, it was clear a lot of building work was still in progress. Old buildings were being torn down and others put up in their place. Humans were working alongside hara, perhaps slaves. Almagabra was a beautiful country, but once humans had densely inhabited it. Clearly, the Gelaming had applied themselves to removing evidence of recent human construction, which must not have been as aesthetically pleasing to the eye, or the soul, as Immanion was. From the city, the coastline appeared mainly empty of buildings and towns: a sweeping vista of open land, where sheep grazed in the sunlight. Questions began piling up in Seel's mind. He must remember them all.

The villa was situated on the crown of the hill where all the prominent Gelaming families lived, and boasted a fine view of the city below. As they rode up the curling drive, Seel caught sight of a huge edifice, half built and surrounded by scaffolding, on another hill in the city center, near the Nayati. Thiede caught him staring. "That will be Pell's palace," he said. "Phaonica: a diamond that will shine so bright all the cities of the world will by lit by its radiance."

Saltrock, in comparison to this, seemed a pathetic experiment. Thiede obviously had far more resources than Seel had had, but then he had elected to build his city right in the middle of what had been human land, rather than hiding away in the wilderness as Seel had done.

"You are a builder," Thiede said, probably having been prying in Seel's mind. "You belong here. You will be able to indulge your dreams to the full."

Seel could say nothing, because there wasn't anything to say. If Thiede had been covertly recruiting hara from Saltrock to bring them here, how could it be seen as wrong? Where would they rather be, given the choice? Seel had never felt more humbled in his life. He had never had the breadth of imagination to believe this was possible and had scorned those who had.

"Don't be hard on yourself," Thiede said. "There is much to be said for skepticism. Blind faith never does anyhar any good. I wanted you to see. Now you are here."

"But how have you achieved so much so quickly?" Seel asked. "This city looks as if it has stood for a thousand years. How did you organize hara so well?" He shook his head. "I'm stunned by it. It's amazing."

"There have been some hara," Thiede said carefully, "who have criticized my decision to seek out the best of Wraeththukind. I have plucked enterprising, bright, and visionary souls from the wastelands. I have followed the dim beacons of shining spirits to the farthest corners of the world. This is why. I am not interested in posturing, preening fools, or those who wallow in the basest aspects of our being. I am looking for those who are fit to inherit the world and who will be its wise custodians." He made a sweeping gesture with one arm. "This is but an intimation of all we can achieve. When I look upon it, I see a beginning, an experiment. Immanion may be the first, but it will not be the best."

"Is there dark in Immanion?" Seel asked.

Thiede smiled. "Only at night."

The villa itself was not too large and ostentatious, as Seel expected, but of simple and elegant design. Its tiled floors were cool beneath the feet and every room smelled strongly of lilies. Seel and Colt were shown to a guest room by a deferential house-har, where scented baths awaited them and a change of clothes.

"We may be dead," Colt observed as he pulled off his boots. "He could have killed us and brought us to his heaven."

Seel ran his fingers over a white marble statue of a naked har that stood in a corner of the room. "That is possible." He walked out onto a balcony and leaned against the rail, breathing deeply a scent of pine and roses. Bees hummed lazily in the heavy blooms that climbed the walls of the villa. In the garden below, a har with honey-colored hair hanging to his knees gathered flowers in a basket. Water ran in landscaped streams throughout the gardens and birds were streaks of metallic light among the lush trees. In a place like this, the dead could come back to life.

Colt, wearing a belted robe, joined Seel on the balcony. "I should be tired, but I'm not. I feel as if I've just woken from a good night's sleep."

"There is something about this place," Seel said inadequately, then paused. "What do I do? Do I come here for good? Is Pell really going to come back?"

Colt sighed through his nose. "Don't know about that. I think maybe that was the bait Thiede used to get you here. He does want you for something though. Can't you just accept it might be because you're good at what you do and would be of immense use to him in creating his ideal society?"

"Its design . . ." Seel said, narrowing his eyes at the horizon. "It's made to seduce you, to glamorize the senses. It's like drinking the waters of forgetful-ness. Is that good or not? I'm not sure. I think if a har stayed here too long he'd forget everything else."

Colt leaned on the balcony rail beside him. "Thiede is more powerful than any of us thought."

"Will he find Cal, do you think?"

"No," Colt replied. "Did you ever believe he would? I think you just wanted an excuse to come and look without appearing to give in too easily."

Seel laughed and punched Colt in the arm. "That's so wrong!" He sobered. "I meant it. I won't let him forget it either."

They spent the rest of the day exploring the villa and its grounds, Seel taking time to chat with the household staff. Everyhar appeared contented and en-thusiastic about the future. Everyhar knew who Seel was. They told him they hoped he would come to join them for good. Clearly, Thiede had primed them thoroughly.

In the evening, Thiede reappeared and announced he had invited guests for dinner, who were important for Seel to meet. "The governing body of Wraeththu, whose seat shall be here in Immanion, is to be termed 'the Hege-mony,'" he said. "Most of them I have already chosen: charismatic hara from around the world who have done much to further the advancement of our race. You will meet some of them tonight. These are not savage barbarians or mindless hedonists. They have brains. There is a place for you too, Seel, high in the administration."

Seel smiled thinly. He felt as if he were on a roller coaster, unable to con-trol its speed or destination.

Thiede's staff laid out a magnificent feast, mainly of cold food, in a spa-cious dining room that overlooked the gardens. Beyond its huge window doors, a wide balcony hung over a large pool covered in lilies. Seel and Colt were conducted into this room to meet Thiede's four guests. Their names were Dree Uvayah, Tharmifex Calvel, Cedony Mithra, and Ashmael Aldebaran. It was obvious to Seel that these were hara of high caliber, who had perhaps at-tempted projects similar to his own at Saltrock. They were first generation Wraeththu, hara who had witnessed the very inception of their race. Memo-ries lay deep behind their eyes. They appeared young, yet were old. Seel was especially intrigued by Ashmael, for he felt this har's attention on him very keenly throughout dinner. General Aldebaran was supreme commander of the Gelaming armies. Seel knew it was only a matter of time before Ashmael spoke to him about the subject that fairly blasted from his aura: Pellaz.

The time came as the party rose from the table to go out on to the terrace for drinks and to bask in the balmy Almagabran evening. Ashmael signaled to Seel to hold back, which Seel did.

"May we talk?" Ashmael asked.

"Yes."

Ashmael closed the window door and the sound of cheerful voices from outside was silenced. "We must be quick. Thiede will notice our absence, and this is a conversation he'd seek to quell. You are friend of this har Thiede wants to bring to Immanion?"

Seel nodded. "I knew him. He is dead."

Ashmael grimaced. "We have heard that, *and* the mumbo jumbo Thiede spouts to explain why this is not actually so. It mustn't happen. It is an abomination. If there is any truth in this matter, it is that Thiede seeks to create a freakish homunculus to govern for him. He speaks of hegemonies, of cooperation, but it is clear to the most stupid har there are dark forces at work. If the fact of this Pellaz is true, it is unnatural and wrong."

"I don't disagree with you," Seel said. "But neither can I wholly believe it."

"Thiede wouldn't say it if it weren't true," Ashmael said. "He never loses face, nor can bear to appear fallible. If he says he can do it, he can. We must accept that, however difficult it is. It is up to you to stop it."

Seel laughed uncertainly. "Me? How?"

"Do you want to see a friend of yours, some reanimated corpse, come lurching back into your life? What do you suppose he will be like? Have you thought of that?"

"I cannot stop it," Seel said. "I know nothing about these things. I am a stranger here."

"Not for long," Ashmael said bitterly. "Build your nest well, tiahaar. You will live in it here for a long time. Think about what I said." He opened the door. "We had better rejoin the company."

Seel did think about what Ashmael Aldebaran had said, but couldn't see how he would have the power to halt Thiede's plans. The more he saw of Immanion, the less he was inclined to think Thiede was the monster he'd once thought him to be. Seel had planned to remain in Almagabra for only a few days, but the days stretched into weeks, and neither he nor Colt felt a strong desire to return to Saltrock immediately. There was so much to explore and so many interesting hara to meet. It was hard to believe that students of science, engineering, and medicine had survived the transition from human to Wraeththu, but some had, and Thiede had devoted himself to finding them. These were the jewels of harakind who would help to build a civilization upon the earth that was superior to all that had gone before. Seel was shown the new hospital where hara were trained in healing of both traditional and original skills. Here, students learned how to focus and amplify that natural healing energy that hara could channel through their bodies. They experimented with the use of sound as a therapeutic medium. The building itself was more like a temple than a hospital. Nohar would ever fear having to go there.

Throughout the city, universities and training facilities encouraged Gelaming hara to learn new skills, to create and invent. Beyond Immanion's walls, spreading farms grew an abundance of crops. Cattle, sheep, and goats roamed free upon the hillsides, feasting upon sweet grass and flowers.

In the evenings, after long days exploring Immanion's wonders, Seel and Colt would sit upon Thiede's terrace drinking wine or else visit other hara they had met in the city. Seel knew this was only a holiday, and that if he ever agreed to move there permanently, he would no doubt be working eighteen hours a day, but for now he was happy to bask in Thiede's dream. Pellaz had hardly been mentioned and as Thiede was rarely around to be questioned, Seel put the matter to the back of his mind. He could not imagine a day when he would stand looking over the city with Pell at his side.

CHAPTER EIGHT

> ⊱—⊱•⊙•⊰—⊰ ⊰

The moment Flick could no longer see Saltrock behind him was the moment of his rebirth. He thought to himself, *I do not know this world. I am new in it and it is new to me.* Despite this revelation, he also felt numb. No strident harpies of emotion clawed at his heart or haunted the shadows of his dreams. He did not feel regret or loss or grief. He could not even feel ennui, traveling the bleak landscape toward the west. It was difficult to recall familiar faces, and past events seemed like stories someone else had told him, a long time ago.

What he would actually do should he find Pell's family, Flick did not know. The quest seemed like an excuse. He was not driven to fulfill a promise, but merely to escape. Other hara, who had worked hard on training themselves, might be able to use their psychic talents to quest the path. Flick had neglected that side of himself. He was blind inside. All he had to follow was the map of Cal's romantic recollections, which he had listened to so many times.

The cruel cliffs around him did not fill him with dread. They were silent, tranquil, enclosing him in their eternal dreams. Flick could believe easily there was no world beyond this landscape, and that, should he wish, it could extend for infinity. It was a hinterland, but one that he embraced wholeheartedly. He knew that it had taken Pell and Cal only about a week to reach Saltrock from Pell's old home. A week was not enough time to be alone. So Flick tarried often among the crags. He sat on ledges, gazing out at the horizon. He watched the slow then sudden progressions of dawns and sunsets. He ate sparingly of the provisions he'd brought with him. And he thought about how he knew so little, and was less a creature of magic, than a creature of clay. But perhaps the time would come for change.

The universe hears all focused thoughts. It listens hard. And when the student is ready, if they are lucky, the universe sends them a teacher.

Flick delayed reaching his destination by two days, but it loomed before him all too quickly. And he was clearly too late.

Pell's old home was a dead place. Flick's own prophecy to Cal had come true. As he reined in his horse at the edge of the settlement, he looked upon a scene he might have devised in his imagination. Perhaps the moment he'd spoken the idea to Cal, he had made it happen. For some moments, he considered he might not be at the right place, but then the landmarks that Pell had given him all stood before him in evidence. The three windmills, the white house upon the hill to the north of the town. And the fields. Spread out, as far as they eye could see, they were supposed to be full of the cable crop. Now, they were only burned earth. Flick's pony, Ghost, flexed his neck, pulling against the bit, yawning. He was not disturbed by the stink of death, because any evidence of it had blown away. All that remained was a sense of desolation, as if the settlement had lain untenanted for many years.

There was no point investigating the empty staring buildings, because their forlorn silence told Flick all he needed to know. Everything had died, past, present, and future. A scythe had fallen across the world. Flick knew that no one was left alive. There was no one to whom he could tell his news. He was absolved. What had happened to his warm heart? If he felt anything now, it was simply relief.

Flick turned Ghost toward the south and urged him trot away from the settlement. They could not go back to Saltrock. But where else could they go? Flick's provisions would not last forever and he was ill used to traveling alone. The thought of introducing himself to a new Wraeththu tribe was daunting. He would have to abide by their rules, their way of looking at the world. He was, he realized, a tribe of one.

By sundown of the third day, he had ridden aimlessly for many miles, and had reached the foothills of an ancient cordillera. He had to make a decision and it seemed increasingly that he had no alternative but to return, abashed, to Seel. But he had made such a grand exit, the thought of that was humiliating. It would prove to Seel that Flick could not live without the comforts Saltrock provided. It would prove that what Cal had said to him about living in Seel's shadow was right. Cal had offered a challenge: live life for yourself. Now, in taking up the challenge, was Flick living in Cal's shadow as much as he had in Seel's?

Flick rode among dark leaved shrubs that clustered in groups like malevolent hags. Shadows gathered among them; dark familiars rustling through their skirts. But there was a pool of water nearby, fed by a hurrying stream, and the pony went directly to it and drank deeply. Flick dismounted and unpacked what remained of his provisions. The cured meat he'd brought was beginning to go green, and the cheese had sweated itself into an unappetizing sticky lump. The bread was dry and spotted with mold. Even though he was hungry, the sight of this food did not stimulate the appetite. Instead, he drank water from the pool, which was brackish. A cloud of mosquitoes hung grimly over the water. If he stayed here, by morning he would be bitten raw. This landscape was probably full of things he could eat, but apart from hunting small animals, Flick was at a loss. He knew that the fruit of the prickly pear could be eaten, but was it in fruit just now? Perhaps he should return to the ruined settlement, and try to find food there. It seemed unlikely he had enough to sustain him for a return journey to Saltrock. He'd have to exist on water alone.

Nibbling on a piece of the cheese, Flick investigated his immediate surroundings. Large rocks littered the landscape, and the stream ran over shingle between them. A group of old stones close by reminded him of an ancient monument, as if human hands had placed them there in the distant past. The stones were huge and smooth, with spindly trees growing from the cracks between them. Flick ran one hand over the stone. He sensed energy flowing from it, like a faint vibration coursing up from deep within the earth. There was power here.

For the first time since Orien's death, Flick felt a jolt of interest reawaken within him. The evening was suddenly more alive around him, its scents and sounds more intense. His hand could feel the grain within the stone. It was as if a drugged torpor had fallen from his mind.

Leaving Ghost to graze, Flick ventured farther into the shadow of the stones. They loomed over him, full of presence and sentience. Stars had begun to prick through the darkening sky above and the stones were solid black against them. The sandy ground underfoot was damp. Flick left deep footprints. The stones leaned closer together to form the entrance to a cave and Flick ventured within. Moonlight fell in a silver beam from a chimney above the center of a high natural chamber. Around the edge of the cave, the ground was strewn with dried grasses, as if people went to sit there regularly. Evidence of a fire lay in a blackened ring of fist-sized stones, directly beneath the opening in the ceiling. When Flick went to investigate, it was clear that the last fire had been lit here a very long time ago. But he felt strongly that this was a sacred place. It was so tempting to lie down upon the prickly grasses that still smelled faintly of hay. The moonlight, through his half closed eyes, was a white goddess standing before him, who held in her hands the balm of sleep.

In Saltrock, Wraeththu met in the Nayati to acknowledge the divinity of the Aghama, their god. Seel did not like religion, and in fact thought it stunted personal growth, so he discouraged anyhar from trying to establish personal relationships with gods. He believed in magic, not prayer, in will and intention over supplication. But to Flick lying alone on the cusp of he knew not what, that seemed an arid and comfortless belief. He wanted a goddess in silver, with moon-white skin and moonstone eyes, to stand over him and douse him in grains of sparkling dust that could erase all care. He wanted divine intervention, a higher power to rescue him from his life. Did he want to go back, further even than Saltrock, so that his life would rewind until he was a child again, and Wraeththu would not happen? How easy that life might have been, and yet how incomplete. He did not want to give up the part of himself that was akin to the goddesses of the world.

Come to me, Flick thought. *Come down from the moon and scatter your silver incense over all that is female within me.* He closed his eyes.

Sleep did not come easily. Even though he felt tired to his bones, Flick could not let go of consciousness. Thoughts gushed through his head in an unending stream: images of Cal, the smell of blood, Seel's face at his desk on the morning Flick had left Saltrock. He tried to dispel these images, to think of mundane things. But his mind would not rest. He sat up and put his head in hands. He remembered Seel as he'd first known him: the touch of his hands and eyes. His laughter, and the long carefree days. A changeling had taken Seel's place, soured the friendship. Where had it all gone? How could such a thing happen? Flick felt tired to the innermost core of his being, and his head ached.

Perhaps if he stood up and walked around for a while, peace might come to him. But the cave was so large, and there was a danger of falling into the abyss. The ledge he sat upon was very narrow, and he was sure there were creatures flying around him in the darkness. He could sense their claws. There was no moon in this place. It had crashed into the lightless sea millennia before. He did not realize he was in a different place. He felt he had been there for years.

I cannot invoke the moon, he thought, *but I must try to invoke the other light. What is its name?*

He couldn't remember.

A human woman walked up to him along the ledge, carrying a basket of keys, which were rusty. He could see the woman clearly, even though he was surrounded by darkness. "Where are the locks?" she asked him. "I need to find them before the keys are dust."

"I don't know," Flick replied. "Where is the light?"

"It is coming," the woman said. "I heard its scream."

"Must I wait here?"

The woman shrugged. "It is as good as any other place."

"Can I have one of your keys?"

"You already have one," she said. "It is very small."

"What does it open?"

"The gates." She looked behind her. "I must go. There isn't much time."

She vanished into the darkness.

Flick held his breath. He could sense something approaching him. There was no sound, no change in the temperature of the air, but he could still feel it.

Aghama, he said in his mind, *be with me. Help me.*

But the words meant nothing. Aghama was not his god. He did not have one. He was alone in a void.

Flick felt his way to the edge of ledge and leaned out over it. He could see nothing but knew a bottomless abyss fell away from him below. He was too high to call out to whatever might fly and tumble in it, but he could see specks of golden light, far away, winking like distant stars. As he stared upon them, one of them grew steadily larger. Flick dared not blink, sure that if he did the star would vanish. His eyes burned. The light grew brighter and brighter, fizzing up toward him. It was a sphere, then a spiral, now a spinning column with golden wings. It was an angel, a furious spirit, a heart of fire. Pellaz.

"Tell me now that you are dead," Flick said, still not daring to blink.

The vision hung before him, the face compassionate. Pellaz was made of gold light. He had no wings. He was simply a blade of radiance hanging in the void. He held one finger to his lips and the other hand was raised beside his head, two of the fingers curled over the palm. "Seek me within," he said, although his lips did not move.

"Are you a god now?" Flick asked. "Is that it? Is that the answer Orien was seeking?"

"I will not be your god," Pellaz replied. "You are your own. Open your eyes and take what is given to you in full sight. Seek me. I will not remember this meeting, but you will do so. I am to be reborn, and for these scant moments before it happens, I know all. I can see it all, Flick, so clearly."

"Orien is dead," Flick said. "He died, in a way, for you."

"He sought death," Pellaz said, "but not for any reason you yet know. We are so much more than we know. So much. Nothing is as it seems."

"How? In what way? What is our purpose?"

"You are the guide. Your teaching will take the student to the place of all knowledge."

"What? Who? Pellaz, explain it to me!"

There was a mighty crash, as of mountains tumbling into the abyss, and a great flash of light. Flick jerked backward, his hands across his eyes. When he lowered them, he found himself in the small cave, with a single beam of moonlight falling down in the center. He was lying on his back on a bed of straw. He couldn't stop the tears. He wasn't psychic. He didn't have visions. And he couldn't trust his dreams.

Flick woke again some hours later before the dawn, feeling very cold. The moon had slipped away and the cave was in darkness, but for a strange impression of light that seemed to emanate from the walls themselves. Flick's body ached with stiffness and his mouth was as dry as if he'd drunk himself into a stupor the night before. He remember he had left Ghost to wander about outside. The pony might have disappeared into the wilderness, leaving him stranded in this place. Flick jumped to his feet. How far would he get without a horse? How long would he survive? A bewitchment had taken him, stolen his mind.

He'd almost reached mouth of the cave when his senses became alert to another presence. Freezing, he saw a motionless figure standing in the shadows, staring at him intensely.

For some moments, Flick did not move. Perhaps here was the time when he had to face hara of a different tribe, explain himself, appease.

Then a voice hissed out of the darkness. "Get out of here, girl!"

Flick still thought that he was looking at another har, a har, who for some reason or another had made a gross mistake concerning his own identity. He had seen hara similar in appearance to the one before him, in that blurry time between the decision—or calling—to leave his humanity behind, and when

Orien had plucked him from inception into a tribe whose name he'd never known. He'd seen copper-skinned hara before, with feathers in their hair and stark-black patterns tattooed onto their faces and arms. Flick's second impression was that now he might be in danger. If there was one har, then others might be around. But both impressions were brief. He realized he was looking only at solid rock, grayed by the predawn light that came down through the chimney of stone. There was no one there at all.

Spooked, Flick ran outside. The first thing he saw was Ghost standing by the pool. The pony's head was turned toward him, ears pricked. The air seemed to shimmer with unseen power, and reverberate with an eerie humming just beyond Flick's perceptions. The landscape looked odd, as if drenched in ultraviolet, yet the light was dim. His first instinct was to mount the pony and gallop away from this place at speed. Ghost whinnied in apparent pleasure to see him and ambled toward him. He butted Flick with his head, as if to offer reassurance. Flick cupped Ghost's ears in his hands, leaning his cheek against the broad forehead. The warm smell of horse was like a memory of a lost gilded time, and he remembered the stables in Saltrock, the lazy hours he'd spent there, working at his own pace as he replaced the straw and fed the animals, without a care in the world. "Damn you, Cal!" he said aloud. He had no choice but to go back to Saltrock. It was all that he knew and he belonged there.

But as he swung up into the saddle, gathering up the trailing reins, he heard a voice call out. "Not yet, not yet!" It was so clear, ringing through the air that was brightening with every moment.

Flick looked around, but could see no one. Was this another ghost or illusion conjured by his imagination? *Ride away,* he told himself, *do it now.* He turned the pony in a circle, reluctant to leave, yet desperate to do so. "Who are you?" he cried. "Show yourself."

Wind sighed soft as a purr over the rattling grasses, and in the arms of the mesquite trees, but there was nothing else.

Sighing, Flick dismounted. He led Ghost to the entrance to the cave, and the pony was not averse to going inside. This must surely be a good sign. If there were anything bad about this place, Ghost would surely balk, flare his nostrils, throw back his head, and refuse to move. Instead, he went to investigate the dried grass around the edge of the cave and began to eat. Flick prowled around the edge also, running his hands over the stone. As the light became brighter, he could see that there were carvings in the stone, worn with age. He did not recognize their style as belonging to any culture that he knew, and they were clearly ancient carvings. Near the back of the cave, pleats of stone concealed an entrance leading farther back. Shadows were cast in a way that made the wall appear solid, but it was not. Flick ducked down and peered into the tunnel beyond. Dim light illuminated the scene before him, revealing a sandy floor unmarked by the passage of harish or human feet. Flick did not feel as if anyone else was around. He ventured into the tunnel.

What was here for him? Would he find bones up ahead, or evidence of a vanished race? Anything seemed possible. The passage eventually opened out into another chamber, where natural holes in the stone ceiling provided illumination. Ledges had been cut into the rock and looked like seats or hard beds. The floor was strewn with dried grasses and reeds from beside the pool. Flick was sure someone had—or did—live in this place. There was a strong smell of fungus. Beneath one of the upper windows a kind of garden had been created. Plump white mushrooms grew from a bed of dark soil. It was the sight of these mushrooms more than anything else that made Flick decide that he would stay here for a while. In his mind, he saw himself going to fetch his belongings from the back of Ghost's saddle, placing them on one of the stone ledges and unpacking them. He saw himself harvesting some of the mushrooms—their soft pale flesh like effulgence of the moon itself—and cooking them on a fire of sweet grass and sticks in the blackened rings of stones in the outer chamber. He could already smell the delicious aroma. And before too long, he was doing exactly that. Another bewitchment had taken him.

After his meal, which had felt more satisfying than it surely should have done, given the fact Flick had with him none of the condiments, herbs, and accessories that had earned his cooking its reputation, he went to explore the landscape around him more closely. Near to the cave, he found a patch of earth with a few stringy root vegetables growing in it, but it was clear no one had looked after it properly for years. He was thinking in terms of how he could survive here, and how he could spend some time alone to order his thoughts and make decisions for the future. It might be, he conceded, he'd stay here till he died, but as nohar yet knew the full extent of Wraeththu lifespan, he might have a long time to go slowly mad in his isolation. Every other har he'd met had been recently incepted, during the last five years or so. Even Seel, it seemed, because Seel professed to be young. Was this the truth? Was it all an illusion? A stultifying moment of disorientation came over him. None of it might be true. He should perhaps check his body again just to make sure all of it had really happened. How had the last few years passed so quickly? None of it felt real now. He wasn't completely sure how long he'd spent in Saltrock. He wasn't sure how he'd got there. He knew the story, and could tell it to others, but couldn't remember the feelings, the experience. The world seemed suddenly too big, confusing, and dangerous. Flick fought an urge to flee back to the cave and crouch in the shadows. He was alive and breathing. He must make the best of it.

For the rest of the day, he tended the patch of earth, pulling up weeds and carrying water from the pool to scatter over the wilting stems. He'd unsaddled his pony and let him wander free, sure he would not stray far. The way Ghost looked at Flick, the way they found comfort in each other's presence, made Flick feel more horse than har. Perhaps Ghost felt the same. He rolled pleasurably in the dirt then shook himself. He sniffed things like an oversized dog. *Ghost appears,* Flick thought, *to be strangely happy in this new place.* At home, they'd never felt so close.

Near sundown, realizing he was hungry, Flick went hunting and caught a rabbit. It would not offer much meat, but its strong taste would go well with the mushrooms and the fat from its flesh would serve as cooking oil. It was dark when he sat down to eat in front of his fire and the moon had already begun her stately journey across the sky. Ghost shared his accommodation, and Flick was just mulling over the fact that pony dung would be useful as both fertilizer for his small garden and fuel for his fires, when he realized that he was not alone. He was alerted to a presence by a shrinking sensation in his flesh. At once, he turned and found himself looking up into a stern countenance.

The tall figure Flick had glimpsed the night before had emerged from the inner chamber and had crept up beside him. Flick saw at once that this was a man, human not har. He had dark skin and a hawklike countenance. Flick did not say anything, but immediately offered up his tin plate of food, in what he instinctively hoped was a friendly gesture.

"I told you to leave," the man said. "I told you clearly. Did you not hear me?"

"I thought you were a ghost," Flick said. "I didn't think you were real." He hesitated. "Do you live here?"

The man took the plate and sniffed the contents. Then he handed it back to Flick. "This is my space," he said. "It is where I am."

"I needed shelter," Flick said. "I don't mean to intrude. I have nowhere to go."

The man nodded his head once. "That is sufficient," he said, and sat down on the opposite side of the fire, staring at Flick intently.

Flick found it impossible to eat under such close scrutiny. The day before, this elusive being had thought him a human female. He might not be so accommodating once he realized the truth. And where had he been hiding all day? "Will you share my meal?" Flick said.

A smile flickered briefly across the man's face. "Share my produce," he said.

"I took only a few." Flick only had one plate, but he scooped another portion from the skillet onto it, and offered it across the fire.

The man took it and began to eat. "You are far from home, you are lost," he said between mouthfuls.

"Mostly," Flick agreed. "Someone died. I had to leave home." He realized this sounded somewhat sinister. "I didn't kill anyone," he added hastily.

"I can see that," said the man, "but you cannot wash the blood away."

"No," Flick said. He looked at his hands, remembered the knife, the floor, the mop, the useless task of cleaning up the blood. "I made a promise to someone. I had to come here, but it was too late. It has all gone."

"Not all," the man said. "You should look with clear eyes."

"A settlement near here," Flick said. "That has gone. It's abandoned. I was looking for people there."

"I did not think you people could go back," said the man.

Flick's flesh tensed. "What do you mean?"

"The past is cut away from you, so much that it feels like a dream. You should not attempt to go back. It serves no purpose. In that, your people are right."

Flick waited a moment, then blurted, "You know what I am?"

"Yes." The man put down the plate, licked his fingers.

"You said I was a girl, you called me that."

"And you're not?"

"Not in the way I thought you meant."

"You are lost," said the man, "but it is no doubt meant to be. I have been alone a long time and this is pleasant, talking across a fire."

Flick was silent. All humans should hate him. He was a symbol of their decline. Was it possible a sinister motive hid behind the apparently congenial words? Perhaps this man still didn't know what Flick was. He might have lived here alone for so long he didn't know about Wraeththu, but that seemed unlikely. This place wasn't that far from habitation. Also, he did not look that old. He could almost be har.

"Don't be afraid," the man said. "You do not intend me harm, nor I you. You were brought to me, and perhaps that is my purpose."

"Your purpose?"

"To help you walk your dreams."

"I would like to stay here for a while," Flick said. "If that's okay. My name is Flick."

"Thank you," said the man, inclining his head. "You may call me Itzama."

Itzama said that the cave was a place of initiation that had been used by his people for countless generations. Who were his people? On this, the man was vague. He had the look of someone native to the land, and yet Flick was also aware he could equally be of Latino stock and had elected to become someone else. Itzama also evaded giving details of why he was living there, alone and so young. He seemed to have no history, but then Flick could empathize with that. He felt the same way. They could conspire their fictions together, if that was what the man wanted, because Flick had no intention of revealing anything about himself that was remotely true. Itzama claimed he was a shaman and had clearly decided it was his task to teach Flick the shamanic way. Flick vacillated between thinking this might give him some answers, or at least some questions that made sense, and that it was a complete waste of time. He had no faith, that was the trouble. When he saw a brilliant star in the clear night sky, where the potential of the universe seemed written in light, he thought of gases and not of gods or angels. His goddess of the moon had been an ephemeral creature. He was har. He couldn't have goddesses. They had died out with the human women, pulling their hair and lamenting. Har itself meant nothing. Wraeththu had come to replace humans, but nothing had been learned and nothing gained. Hara killed each other as humans had killed each other. There were more differences between individuals than similarities, and everyhar was selfish. Pellaz might come to Flick in a visionary dream, uttering words that dripped with meaning, but in the cold clear light of day, it was just a dream and Pellaz was dead. Flick no longer wanted to go back. He wanted to find pleasure in the veins of a leaf or in the rill of water over stones, but it was empirical pleasure.

Itzama, though still implying he was the guardian of great knowledge, appeared to respect this. He disappeared throughout the day, clearly a device designed to make him seem more mysterious, and would reappear at sundown, when he and Flick would eat together. Then he would talk. Flick realized the man had been silent for too long, and now could not stop himself speaking at every opportunity. He spoke of the legends of his people, whoever they were, stories of magical creatures that had come out of the heavens to create the world: spiders, pumas, mythical birds, and the trickster coyote. "I have prowled with the puma in the night air of the mountains," said Itzama. "I have trailed Coyote through the poison plains. He gave to me a talisman, which he spat onto the path. These spirits you too will know."

Flick liked the stories. Listening to them made him feel relaxed and sleepy. Itzama would talk throughout the night, and Flick fell asleep to the soft deep tones of his voice. When he awoke, he was always alone, and there was no trace of Itzama's presence within the cave chambers. *One day, I will stay awake,* Flick thought. *I will watch you through half-closed eyes, and I will follow you.* But he never did.

During the daylight hours, he roamed his surroundings, climbing the rocks, following the trail of the stream. He gave names to trees, plants, and animals that were his alone. He redefined his landscape. Yet somewhere, always, in the back of his mind, Saltrock went on, and Cal went on, and the ruined settlement to the north went on. An empty promise hung on a spiky mesquite tree, flapping in the wind like an old torn scarf, and though it might become more ragged every day, it still clung to the twigs and wound itself around the trunk. It was bloodstained and burned, and it belonged to a dream, and Flick could see it sometimes, on the edge of his vision.

CHAPTER NINE

Flick's caste training within the Wraeththu belief system had never progressed very far. It wasn't that he hadn't been interested in pursuing his studies, or that Seel had openly discouraged it, just that life hadn't really called for it in Saltrock. Flick had lived very much in the real world. If he had used magic it had been nothing more than pouring intention into a meal or into the work he did with the animals. He had liked order and simple rituals of existence.

But magic is in us, Flick thought. *We are awake to the world, and that is part of it.*

One night, Flick resolved it was time to do something about it. Itzama reappeared as usual, as Flick was cooking the evening meal. Flick smiled to himself, thinking that the preparation of food seemed to have become his role in life. Itzama came to him at sundown as Seel had always done, hungry after a day's work. Flick did not mind about it. He enjoyed cooking. When he handled the ingredients and worked his personal magic on them, conjuring up the mouth-watering aromas, he felt at peace. He had not realized that before either.

Flick handed Itzama a plate of vegetables fried in rabbit fat, along with the ever-present mushrooms, which had become part of every meal. "This is magic," Flick said. "I take the raw ingredients and create something different from them. I use the energy of fire to transform them."

Itzama sat down cross-legged beside the fire. "Yes," he said, and began to eat.

"So teach me," Flick said.

Itzama glanced up.

"Isn't that what you said you'd do?" Flick asked. "Among my people, I am Neomalid, that is the second level of the first tier in our caste system. Caste is not to do with social position, as in the old world, but with magical training. I have been taught the basics of manipulating energy, but have hardly put it into practice. If anything, I've forgotten all I know. Now, I need to remember it, and learn more. I need to know myself, and how to transcend fear."

Itzama smiled. "I was presumptuous, perhaps, to assume I could teach you anything."

"You are a shaman, you say. What does that mean? How is it different to what I do?"

"People like me have a specific function. We leave our bodies to work for our community in the other world. I was taught to alter my state of consciousness in such a way I could walk with the spirits. The spirits give to us the knowledge. We learn from them and pass on what we know to our people."

"Spirits like Coyote."

"Yes."

"Then I must do this also. Take me with you. Coyote is a trickster, but I have him by the tail and I won't let go."

"You are a very beautiful woman," said Itzama.

"Coyote tricks," Flick said. "It won't work. I know what I am."

"You people have a wonderful gift that you think is a toy," Itzama said. "You have passed beyond human, yet you can't let it go."

"I don't disagree," Flick said. "You're not telling me anything I hadn't worked out for myself. But there are those among us who do have great knowledge and who use the gift properly, if not wisely."

Itzama paused for a moment, then said. "I would like to hear the story of how you came to be here. I wanted to ask before, but the time was not right. Are you ready now to tell me?"

Flick laughed. "I would have thought you'd have read my mind and found that out for yourself."

Itzama rested his elbows on his knees, and cupped his chin in his hands. "It is your turn for the story."

"It began," Flick said, "when a har named Cal came to Saltrock, the town where I lived, some years ago."

Itzama shook his head. "No, that is not your story. How did you come to be here as you are? What is your beginning?"

Flick put his hands over his face. In the darkness, he looked into the past. "I'm not sure," he said, his voice muffled through his hands, "It is like a dream."

"Try."

"Something . . . something had happened," Flick said. "I was at home, and we were preparing to leave. Packing. My mother was crying and my father wasn't there. A truck was coming for us and we were going to go someplace else. There was a war going on, but inside the war, yet outside of it, was Wraeththu. It was like a ghost haunting us, a scavenger at the edge of the battle zones, seeking the weakest. There were drugs I had to take, because when the call came no one could ignore it. You just got up, like you were sleepwalking, and went out of the house. You'd find yourself with your nose pressed against a fence, so desperate to get through it, you'd want to push your flesh through the wire and fall into a thousand pieces. You believed that if you did that, on the other side, your body would remake itself and you could walk away, find the source of the call."

Itzama said nothing. The only sound was the pop of twigs in the fire and the soft call of a nightbird beyond the cave.

Flick looked up, directly into Itzama's eyes. "I didn't stop taking the drugs, not once. I remember going outside, carrying a box that was so heavy. I remember thinking about all I'd had to leave behind, and I was afraid for the future. They told us there were safe havens, but I couldn't believe it. Everything was falling apart. It felt like the end of the world.

"I saw the big truck and our neighbors were getting into it. People were running around and there was so much noise. There was fire in the sky to the east and the sound of explosions. I remember standing in this little pool of quiet, looking around. Sound just faded away, and it was like watching a silent movie. Then I saw him. Among the trees in the yard opposite. Tall and dark. I saw his long coat, his big boots. He just looked at me. I wasn't afraid. I wasn't even curious. I just thought, that is another way, another road, and it is looking at me. I put down the box and went to him.

"He was har, of course, slinking like the ghost I believed them all to be among the panicking human population. On the lookout, seeking souls. I couldn't hear the call, because of the drugs, but I could see the road. Does that make sense? I had to get away. There was nothing left. It was like a portal opening onto the land of the dead, and it was so easy to walk down it, to walk away. It didn't matter that I might be giving up my life. I was so tired. I wanted to get away from the noise and the fear and the uncertainty. What I felt when I looked at him, was sureness. This was an illusion, but it didn't matter. Something inside me knew that this was perhaps my only chance.

"He took me to a place that was some miles away. We walked there, and hardly spoke. He offered me a drink and it felt good to be walking beside him, swigging liquor like an adult, in this . . . this unbelievable calm. All around us, the city was burning, but it was like we were spirits, and it couldn't touch us. Military vehicles were screaming past us, and we walked through a place where there was gunfire, but I'm sure that any bullets would have passed straight through me without damaging my body. I didn't even know his name.

"We went underground beneath this half-fallen tower, and there were about a dozen hara down there, as well as a lot of human boys who'd obviously been taken from the mayhem above. It was then I met Orien. He came to each of us in turn, and asked us questions. Can't remember what. His voice was soft, and he looked to me like an angel, not man, not woman, but something of both. When he put his hand on your head, you could not be afraid. Light came out of him. Before the morning came, he said to me, 'I will take you somewhere.' Just me. None of the others. We went up into the morning, and the city was obscured by smoke. It wasn't real any more. Everything was so quiet. I thought we would walk into eternity, but Orien had a military jeep and we drove in that instead. We drove for days. Orien took me to Saltrock, and there he incepted me. I became Wraeththu, and it seems as if that was when my life really began. Orien chose Seel to be the one to initiate me into the mysteries of aruna, and we stayed together afterwards. It was perfect, until Cal came . . ."

Itzama's expression had become troubled. He was staring at the fire.

"How did you escape it?" Flick asked. "How are you still human?"

"I'm not of this time," Itzama said.

Flick made a sound of exasperation. "I've told you about myself. At least repay the compliment."

"Let's just say it passed me by," Itzama said.

"You were strong enough to resist the call, weren't you," Flick said. "But was that the right thing to do?"

"I was not chosen as you were," Itzama said.

"I was not special. Everyone was chosen. Wraeththu were trying to save those who were left."

"It must be an amazing thing," Itzama said, "to find a person and to change them in that way, to make them like you."

"I can't incept you!" Flick said.

"That was not what I meant. I was simply imagining the great power of it. Hara must enjoy that very much."

"It's not selfish."

Itzama uttered a caustic laugh. "No, it makes the world a better place, does it not? You pass on the change, the awakening, and then everyone is enlightened and aware."

Flick bridled at the sarcasm. "You asked me, I told you. I'm not prepared to justify my kind."

"The gift is abused. You still fight amongst yourselves, each thinking they know the one true way. None of you do. Not yet. And you will have to work hard to find it, otherwise you will suffer the same fate as humanity." He made an abrupt gesture with one hand. "I see now that inception is only the beginning. It does not bestow mastership. It is merely the initiation, like a key to the door of the mysteries."

"The key . . ." Flick nodded. "I dreamed of keys the first night I was here." He waited a moment, then said, "Am I the first har you've met?"

"In waking life, yes," Itzama replied. "It has been interesting to observe you."

"I'm sure," Flick said coldly.

"Tell me the rest now," Itzama said. "The story you want to cut free."

Even as he was telling it, Flick was thinking, *This is not a good story. It taints whoever hears it. I feel as if I'm betraying my tribe for revealing us to be barbaric and stupid, like humans. Yet what loyalty should I have to Wraeththu? I have been betrayed and abused by my own kind, and the only unconditional kindness shown to me has been by a human, a member of the race we have come to replace, to expunge.*

Itzama did not look at him as he related the tale. He stared into the fire, as if seeking insight in the flames. And Flick found the more he talked, so the easier it became, and he remembered details he had forgotten. Suddenly, the gleam of morning light upon the handles of his knives in the kitchen seemed as important to the whole as the sight of Cal walking away from the Nayati. Suddenly, the story of his flight from humanity seemed more real than the one he was relating now. This couldn't have happened. It was too terrible, too unbelievable. And yet it had happened.

At the end of it, Flick was weeping. Itzama made no sound, nor reached out to touch him. After some minutes, Flick raised his head, and cried, "I hate them! I hate them all! How could I have been so stupid, so taken in?"

"It is yourself you hate," Itzama murmured.

"Yes!" Flick punched his own thighs with both hands. "I am a fool. How could I let Seel treat me like that? How could I have played Cal's game so willingly?"

"You did it out of generosity," Itzama said, his voice still quiet and calm. "You only gave, and if in your innocence, that was abused, you should not judge yourself for it."

Flick shook his head vigorously, and the cave spun around him. "I can't help it. I was weak, and yet it was Cal who did it. He ruined our lives. He turned Seel into somehar else. He bewitched me. He bewitched Orien too. All of us."

"It cannot be undone," Itzama said. "There is no point in placing blame. You are far from it now, but you cannot move forward until you let it go from inside."

"I am so full of hate," Flick said. "And it's terrible, the way it makes me feel. It makes me a bad person." He glanced up at Itzama. "That is what Orien said, on the night when he fell into trance. He said that his feelings for Cal made him a bad person, and Orien was never that."

Itzama made a languid gesture with both hands. "Then that should tell you. Your friend Cal is very damaged, and his pain has become his whole reason for being. Do not follow his path. Do not let this tragedy become your life."

"I don't want to," Flick said, "but what is left for me? Where do I go? What do I do? I think maybe I should go back, but then I know I shouldn't."

Itzama smiled. "The whole world is yours, Flick. This is the sanctuary, and you should use your time here to heal yourself. Then you will move on, and find your true path."

"I miss Seel," Flick said. "I miss the har he used to be."

"Let it go," Itzama said. He rose to his feet and stretched, then padded into the other chamber of the cave.

Flick sat motionless before the fire. His heart was beating fast and he felt he was in shock, as if Orien's death had just happened. His whole being was weighed down with pain. He could see how easy it would be to become this thing forever, to assume it was the only part of himself that was real. This was what had happened to Cal and possibly was happening to Seel. He could see now that he'd done the right thing in leaving Saltrock. If he'd stayed, he'd have helped create the world of pain and cement it into place.

Itzama came back to the fire carrying a small clay cup. "Are you ready to walk the spirit road?" he asked.

Flick looked up at him, nodded. "Whatever it takes. I'm not a great visionary, whatever you might think."

Itzama handed him the cup. "Drink this," he said. "We will enter the otherworld, and there seek guidance."

Flick sniffed the contents of the cup, smelled fungus, earth, and a bittersweet perfume. "What is this?"

"The key," Itzama said. "Drink half of it."

Flick held his gaze and half drained the cup. He felt at once as if he wanted to vomit, but swallowed it back. Wiping his mouth, he held out the cup to Itzama.

Itzama took it and sat down beside him. He finished the drink and carefully placed the cup by the fire.

"How long?" Flick asked, still swallowing hard. He suddenly felt very cold.

"Some minutes," Itzama said. "Don't be afraid." He took one of Flick's hands in his own and a sense of warmth crept up Flick's arm. "You are not alone," Itzama said.

The physical contact kindled a small flame in Flick's belly. He thought of aruna, of the last time he had been with Cal. Wraeththu needed aruna: what would he do when the desire for comfort and closeness became a sizzling need? If Itzama had been har, they could be together and Flick could experience healing on other levels too. But Nature, or whatever had created Wraeththu, had created safeguards to prevent humans and hara coming together in that way. Thinking aloud, Flick murmured, "You know what I am? I am poison to you. Do you know that?" He was sure Itzama wouldn't know what he meant, but he had to say it.

Itzama smiled and squeezed his fingers. "You are the princess in the tower, above an ocean of thorns. I know that. Relax." He pulled Flick against his body, and Flick rested his head on Itzama's chest. He could hear the man's heart beating, steadily, like a ritual drum.

Flick had almost drifted off to sleep when Itzama shifted and said softly, "Open your eyes. It is time for us to leave."

"What?" Flick raised his head drowsily. The flames of the fire had taken on a bluish hue and cast stark shadows upon the uneven walls of the cave.

Itzama's flesh was shining a little in the weird light. He got to his feet and held out a hand. "Come." He led the way outside and once beneath the eye of the moon, Flick uttered a cry. The landscape had transformed into a strange world of nebulous lights and patterns. He could still see the yucca trees, the ancient mountains and the pool, but they had changed. All the plants were surrounded by glowing halos, the water sparkling in the stream sang with the voices of a thousand spirits and sparks of light flew off it. The pool looked like a cauldron of rainbow mist. Overhead, the stars fizzed through the sky, as if a thousand daily revolutions took place within a single minute. Yet strangely, the full moon hung motionless overhead, bigger than Flick had ever seen it. He was sure that if he looked hard enough, he would see the moon spirits dancing upon its radiant surface. And there was one star standing still also, a bright point of light to the north.

"It's so beautiful," Flick murmured.

"This is the realm of dreams, of the moon," Itzama said. "One of many other worlds."

"It is healing just to look upon," Flick said. "I feel better already."

Itzama smiled. "Already? We must walk the North Star Road. Come."

Flick could see it now, a shining ribbon stretching before them. It disappeared into a sparkling mist but overhead the North Star shone fiercely. As they trod upon the road, so the stones and earth seemed to give slightly beneath Flick's feet. It was as if he walked upon a living creature.

They came at length to a great tree, whose trunk reared toward the sky. Flick could not even see its canopy of foliage, although he knew instinctively it was somewhere high above. At the base of the tree sat a veiled figure, dressed in silvery gray. The figure was dwarfed by the size of the tree and was perched upon a seat fashioned from the enormous gnarled roots that grew out of the earth. The roots appeared polished, as if innumerable creatures had sat there and worn them to a sheen. At the feet of the veiled figure, were two round holes in the ground, surrounded by patterned mosaic.

"They are the Wells of Forgetfulness and Memory," Itzama said. "The Wife of Bones will draw water for you, if you ask her."

The Wife of Bones unnerved Flick. She was so still; she might have been a statue. He was sure something hideous lurked beneath the veil and a sense of unbelievable antiquity poured out of her in waves.

"Do not be afraid," Itzama murmured, close to Flick's ear. He pushed him forward a little. "Approach. It is why you are here."

Slowly, Flick did so. It took all the strength he possessed to take each step. He felt as if he were walking upon knives. He paused a few feet away from the tree and bowed his head.

"Child," said the Wife of Bones. "Come to me."

Flick looked up and as he watched, the Wife threw back her veil. At first, he thought he was looking at Thiede, because the face beneath the veil was not female and the hair was the dark red of fresh blood. The skin was whiter than the moon and the eyes were reflective pools of silver. But Flick quickly realized this was not Thiede. As he gazed upon her, so the Wife seemed one moment female, the next moment har.

"You will see me as a reflection," said the Wife. "I am the Lord of the Underworld and yet the Queen of Faery. I am the Mistress of Bones and King of the Wild Hunt. I am the one who stands at the threshold of being, who welcomes in the souls of the dead and who guides them to rebirth."

"Are you our god or goddess?" Flick asked. "Is this what I'm being shown?"

"You do not yet have the terms to describe me," said the Wife, "nor any of my aspects. This is because you do not yet have the terms to describe yourselves. But I am here, as I have always been here, the triple form of harling, har, and harun."

"What is 'harun'?" Flick asked. "Is it when a har's aspect is more female than male?"

The Wife slowly shook her head. "No, it is the aspect of old age, and none of you yet have reached it or reaped its benefits. You must discover for yourself the godforms of Wraeththu, of hardom. There are many and this will be your gift to your people. The gods are but magnified mirror images of those who inhabit the earth. When you look into the mirror and see divinity looking back at you, you will know. The gods are not to be found outside yourself."

"We have a god. He is the Aghama," Flick said. "Is this one of the aspects?"

"Aghama is the Child of the Cosmos," answered the Wife. "He is one aspect, that of learning. The mistake you have made is to believe you are not human. Once you can accept this, then you may move on to fulfill your potential. As long as you resist all that you fear, you exist within it, you *are* it. A man and a maid war within you, child. It is a war that shakes the world. Now, will you drink?"

Flick did not hesitate. "I must drink from the Well of Memory, mustn't I? I need to remember, not to forget."

"It is the more difficult path," said the Wife, "but not necessarily the better. In forgetting you start with a blank page, whereas the page of remembrance is covered in marks, which are difficult to decipher. Many hara have written there and some of them are mad. Think carefully before you choose."

"I don't want to forget," Flick said. "I am sure of it."

The Wife leaned forward and lifted a metal cup on a thin silver chain from the well to her left. "Then drink."

Flick took the cup, and as he did so, his fingers touched the Wife's hands. Her flesh was cold and hard like bones without flesh, yet there was comfort in their strength and durability. These bones would never fade to dust. Flick drank, drained the cup, and the metal was icy against his lips. He had to tear it away and felt his skin rip. The water was the clearest and purest he had ever drunk. Utterly without taste, it burned his throat as it slid into his stomach. Before his eyes, a thousand images flickered and danced. He saw many different trees, in different parts of the world. All had water at their roots, wells, cauldrons, or pools. Some were situated at crossroads, others in barren landscapes of twisted trees. All had figures beside them: crones, veiled women, men whose faces were shadowed by wide-brimmed hats or cowls, frightening trinities of hags or vicious maidens, three-headed animals, or humanoid figures with the heads of three animals. These were things that Itzama had told him about in stories, over the long nights they had sat together. He knew then that this was the gateway, the crossroads between the worlds. Every culture held within its memory an image of this place. He was creating the tree and its guardian in the image of his kind, visualizing the latter as a veiled hermaphrodite. Perhaps he was the first har to do it. If he climbed the tree he would pass to the Land of Youth where the blessed spirits dwelled. If he went through the roots and tunneled down their labyrinth, he would come to the underworld, where a dark river roiled and lost souls mourned their plight in the lightless reaches of the Asphodel Fields.

"Where do I find my friend?" he asked aloud. "He is named Pellaz, and his death caused terrible things."

The Wife held his gaze with silver eyes. "The one you seek has passed beyond these realms. You are not here to climb the tree, nor to burrow its roots. You came here merely to drink of the waters. Return now to your world. You will undertake a period of learning, which shall last exactly a year and one day. On the eve of the last day, slaughter a creature of the wilderness, and prepare it as for a feast. Pour out its blood upon the earth. This act will raise a spirit of the dead to speak with you. You may give to the dead the animal you prepared, as the dead are very hungry in your world. Ask of the dead the questions you wish."

Flick bowed his head. "Thank you, Wife of Bones."

The Wife of Bones smiled, and suddenly she became nothing more frightening than a beautiful young har sitting among the roots of an ancient tree. The har held a finger to his lips for a moment, then beckoned Flick to lean forward and whispered, "Remember the North Star Road, and the destination you will find at its end. You will walk this path many times, as you seek the bed of history. Dream new dreams, love new loves. Know that my blessings go with you."

Flick was impelled kiss the Wife's cheek, but found his lips pressed instead against the smooth bark of the tree. The Wife had vanished.

"Come," said Itzama, "now we return."

The next thing Flick knew he was opening his eyes in the cave, gazing upon the last smoldering embers of the fire. It was not yet dawn. He raised his head from Itzama's chest and realized he had drooled over the man's shirt. His mouth was filled with a rancid taste and he craved water. Itzama was still unconscious, so Flick eased away from him slowly and crept out of the cave. Never, in his life, had he experienced anything so magical as a vivid visionary journey. It was the result of drinking Itzama's narcotic brew, of course, but even so, it had felt so real. Other hara did things like that all the time.

Flick looked toward the North Star, hanging brilliantly in the sky. He could hear small creatures scuttling through the bushes around him. He could hear the creak of trees and soft shushing of the night wind. The pool was a dark mirror and Flick lay down beside it. He plunged his head beneath its icy surface and sucked water into his mouth. He exhaled bubbles and thought he could remain there for hours, without needing to take a breath, but then there was a soft touch upon his shoulder and he raised his head, gasping.

Itzama stood over him, his hair hanging down over his chest. "You all right?" he asked.

Flick sat up, scraped back his sodden hair. "Yeah. Needed a drink. That was wild tonight. Thanks. You must have given me some pretty strong stuff."

Itzama made a noise in his chest that was part laughter, part disgruntlement.

Flick realized he had said the wrong thing and probably should have prolonged the moments of otherworldliness by saying something profound, deep or mystical. "Where did all that come from?" he said.

"All what?" Itzama hunkered down beside him. "I did not share your visions."

"I saw a goddess sitting at the base of a big tree. Then she was har, and she said things. I drank from the Waters of Memory. Those things I saw, they're the same for everyone though, aren't they? The symbols. I got a strong sense of that, even though no one's ever told me about it. Is it the drink you gave me that makes it happen?"

"It opens doors," Itzama said. "It allows us to step from our limitations for a while."

"It was amazing. It told me so much. But is there really a goddess who spoke to me, or did it come from myself?"

"Both," Itzama said. "You must learn to walk the fine line between belief and skepticism."

"She told me I could create gods for Wraeththu," Flick said. He laughed. "I already have! I can't even call the Wife 'she' because he wasn't."

"Language is a great barrier," Itzama said. "The beauty of walking the spirit path is that you converse free of its restrictions and boundaries."

Flick frowned. "Hara like Orien must know this. There are great adepts among Wraeththu. Why should special revelations come to me, who does nothing to look inside what we are?"

"You did look inside. It's irrelevant whether others have trodden the same path, at least for now. This is your time."

Flick exhaled through his nose. "I feel it's so important, but already it's fading away, like a dream. I've imagined a term for old Wraeththu. It's 'harun.' What will we be like when we're old?"

Itzama shrugged. "Do you have a word for mother?"

Flick glanced at him. "Hypothetically. We hear rumors that some hara have had children, but I've never seen it myself. The children are called 'pearls' and the har who carries them is a 'hostling.' As far as I'm concerned, it could all be made up, or wishful thinking."

"Then, if you will forgive the suggestion, you could see tonight's events as the first meeting, for your entire race, with the Hostling of Bones, wishful thinking aside."

"Has a good ring to it," Flick said.

"Hermaphrodite gods will be an interesting idea to work with." Itzama grinned. "For me as much as for you. I'm grateful to you for giving me this opportunity."

"You can be so formal," Flick said. "We've done something incredible to-night."

"Have we?"

Flick noticed at once a certain edge to Itzama's tone. "What's wrong?" he asked.

Itzama shook his head. "Nothing. Dreams, that's all." He took one of Flick's hands in his own. "One thing you should know, Flick. You look upon me and you see a man. But consider I might be as different from humanity as you are. My people have always known that one day your kind would come. It is our belief that you have returned rather than come anew."

"Who are your people?"

"They have long gone," Itzama said. "I cannot speak to you about it, because I don't really know why I'm here. I was called, and perhaps it was you, or the spirit of your kind, that called to me."

"I don't understand what you're trying to say."

"I was waiting," he said, "and you came. You are the Star Maiden, beautiful and beyond my reach. You are remote and cold and brilliant."

"I'm not cold," Flick said. "Neither am I far away. I am not a maiden and that is perhaps the worst thing. Stop looking at me as if I'm female, Itzama. I'm not. Don't kid yourself for a dream. Look into my face, really look, and you'll see the truth of it. Nothing you say is right. Nothing."

He held Itzama's steady gaze, not sure himself what he was doing or why. "Do you see?" he murmured.

Itzama closed his eyes for a moment, turned his head away, making a small sound of distress, then lunged at Flick, took him in his arms and kissed him with an ardor that could only stem from long abstinence. A rational detached part of Flick's mind, which always had something to say in moments such as these, told him this was selfish and cruel. This wasn't sharing breath, where the minds and souls of hara mingled like smoke. This was purely physical, the demands of human sexuality with its need for instant gratification. But Flick could not even offer Itzama that. He pulled away, stared into a face that appeared both terrified and inflamed. "We cannot do this," he said, raising his palms as if to fend Itzama off. "You must understand that we can't."

"I accept what and who you are," Itzama said in a surprisingly even tone.

"It's not that. It could hurt you, perhaps kill you. It is said our secretions are like acid to humans. Can you imagine a worse death?"

"Frankly, no. But is it true? Have you see it with your own eyes? All I know is that when I look at you I want you. I want to revere you in the act of love."

Flick had to try hard not to smile at that last remark. It was made with such earnest conviction, but at the heart of it, surely, lurked only the male desire for conquest. "There are some things we can do," he said. "You are not poison to me: at least, I don't think so."

Itzama looked uncertain.

"How can I ignore that heartfelt cry you uttered?" Flick said. "Don't think of revering me. Let me do the revering. Come here."

CHAPTER TEN

All houses have personalities, and the older they are, so the character becomes more entrenched. A house soaks up all that happens within it, and stores events as memories, saying nothing, like a silent paralyzed observer, doomed to be buffeted by the emotions of quicker, more ephemeral beings. The spirit of the white house was ponderous, gloomy, and given to sighs. To Ulaume, it was like an old despairing man, a spirit that moved slowly from room to room, carrying with it a black cloud of regret that affected the surroundings and turned the wallpaper dank. Patches of mold on the walls looked like sorrowful faces and every floorboard creaked in a complaining voice. A long time ago, Ulaume had lived in a house himself, when he'd been human, right back at the beginning when Wraeththu was hardly more than a germ of an idea in the consciousness of the world. But he didn't remember much about it. The Colurastes, those who had taken him in, were nomadic, as the Kakkahaar were. Unlike the Kakkahaar, who lived solely under canvas, the Colurastes sought out caves as temporary homes, for they liked dark places from where they could emerge at night. They called themselves the serpent tribe, but really the Kakkahaar were far more serpentine, for they lived in the sun and were burned by it, and their blood ran cold inside.

Like houses, caves had personalities, but tents and canopies did not. They were raised and lowered too many times to find any kind of permanence in the world and their flapping, flimsy fabric was not so disposed to recording events as stone was. So for Ulaume, his new home was unfamiliar in many different ways. He could not say he liked the feelings that crawled just beneath his skin, but they fascinated him. It was as if an unseen story went on all around him, continually. If he remained in one spot for long enough, he would become part of it. There was never a moment he did not feel he was being watched and whenever he entered a room, it felt as if someone had just left it. He sometimes wondered if it was Pellaz he sensed around him, for he was in no doubt that this place was somehow connected with him, and yet Ulaume's instincts also told him that Pellaz had never lived in the house. The visions and dreams he'd had implied that Pellaz's family had occupied one of the smaller houses beyond the hill. For some weeks, Ulaume did not venture there, savoring the moment when he would. He knew he had a lot of time, as much of it as he wanted and for this reason he decided to expand outward into his environment slowly, to soak up as much as he could in minute detail.

Lileem liked the white house a lot, and wherever Ulaume was, he could always hear the thunder of Lileem's feet as he charged about the rooms, slamming doors in his wake. At least, Ulaume presumed it was always Lileem. The sounds were too alive and energetic to belong to the resident ghosts, who were more the dragging, groaning kind.

For the first few weeks, Ulaume concentrated on claiming a portion of the house for himself and Lileem. He allowed the harling to run wild, do whatever he pleased, and did not expect him to become involved in the home-building project. To Ulaume himself it was absurd, an aberration. All his life he had expected his environment to mold itself around him and had never considered putting his own mark upon it. He had enjoyed pinching and hissing at the young Aralid hara who were Lianvis's staff, employed to create a homey ambience around the tribe leader. Ulaume had never had the slightest interest in what was perceived as comfortable and what was not. But now, in some small way, he did care. He realized he was not so much concerned with making a home, but with trying to reconstruct a picture that might tell him something. He wanted to bring the house back to life, so that its energies would flow down the hill like a breath of spring perfume and resuscitate what lay below. This was the heart of the place.

Lileem spent a lot of time outside, racing around the tattered gardens, where canes rattled in the wind and tall yellow grasses looked like the nesting ground of bitter female spirits, who might sit in the puddles of their long black dresses, watching the empty windows. Black hens roamed the gardens, and Lileem would bring in their warm brown eggs for Ulaume to put in a bowl in the larder. Ulaume had found clothes for the harling to wear, which had been a little too big, but had clearly once belonged to a human child. While Ulaume adjusted the garments with scissors and teeth, Lileem fidgeted and stamped. He was as eager as a young hound to be out in the air or pioneering through the attics. Ulaume found other clothes packed in trunks, which he appropriated for himself. These were from an area where he believed the servants of the house had lived. On some days, he'd dress in shirt and trousers, on others in long peasant skirts. He liked the feeling of fabric sweeping around his calves as he walked. He felt the woman they had once belonged to had walked with purpose and determination, and part of her personality clung to the cloth. Ulaume swept floors and clawed cobwebs from the corners. He chose one of the kitchens to be his own, even though his knowledge of preparing food was no greater than that needed for survival. Among the Kakkahaar, when Lianvis had called for food, Ulaume had generally slapped the nearest servant and demanded them to fetch it. Fortunately, the cellars of the house were well stocked with vegetables, cured meat, and even dusty bottles of wine. This house had not been abandoned long. There was a walled kitchen garden near the stables where vegetables were slowly breaking ranks, but still growing. In the larder, there were barrels of flour that didn't look mildewy or infested, so Ulaume attempted to make bread. His first efforts were surprisingly edible, if somewhat misshapen. On a shelf above the flour, Ulaume found a listing row of old books on cookery, gardening, and the husbandry of bees and chickens. He congratulated himself, and thanked the spirit of the house for his fortunate discoveries. They would contribute greatly to his and Lileem's survival.

Every evening, by candlelight (and there was stock in the cupboards to illuminate the longest apocalyptic dark), Ulaume read, and learned the skills that once he would have scorned. He would light a fire in the kitchen and try to exorcise the damp. How could a house be clammy in such a dry climate? Damp with tears perhaps. He had yet to learn Wraeththu created its own ghosts, in unimaginable ways.

Ulaume experienced very vivid dreams in the house, and he took the vision he'd had on the first night there to be one of them. He thought he'd seen Pellaz, a younger version of him, and it did occur to him that maybe, years ago, Pell had once happened upon a stranger asleep in the attic. Ulaume knew that sometimes the paths of time could cross, and the vision had seemed very real. But the one thing wrong with this idea was that he was still sure Pell had not lived here, nor could he imagine him creeping into the house surreptitiously.

Rich humans had once lived here, and Ulaume knew Pell had not come from affluent stock. The vision had belonged very much to the here and now, so there was a mystery. Soon, he must walk down to the cluster of farm dwellings and confront what might lie waiting for him on the porch of the largest one, but not yet. He must put the pieces of the puzzle together in the right order. The house had called him. It had something to say.

The ghosts were watching them, night and day. Everything in the landscape quivered with a nervous sentience. Ulaume felt that Lileem's and his living energy was affecting the environment, waking it up. He realized this was not a pleasant feeling, but Lileem seemed oblivious. He grew swiftly, like a quick-growing vine snaking up a wall in the sunlight. At times, snuggled up to the harling beneath their shared blanket at night, Ulaume felt very close to him. At other times, watching him absorbed in his own inner life, playing alone with no need for company, Ulaume thought they were creatures of two entirely different species. Wraeththu's young were perhaps as different from their parents as the incepted were from humans. He felt a fierce love for Lileem, but occasionally a kind of frightened disgust. All around, creatures of male and female perpetuated their species, be they insects, birds, or mammals. The world was a dualistic place and Wraeththu was apart from it. Thinking of this made Ulaume feel disorientated. It made him wonder whether he was, in fact, an abomination and not at all part of something that was destined to save the world from human predation.

This is why we live in tribes, he thought. *In isolation, we think and then we go mad. Together, we intoxicate ourselves with each other, with aruna, and in that ecstasy, we have no need to reflect or consider. We can simply be, in the moment, with no future and no past.*

He had been taught that aruna was the lifeblood of Wraeththu, essential to well-being, and thought perhaps he understood now the true meaning behind those words. Aruna was a euphoric drug, and without it, the world revealed itself as it truly was. Alone, a har began to drift free of the common will, that which kept him sane and accepting of the unbelievable thing that had happened to him. Ulaume thought that if he could survive estrangement from his tribe, then he might become truly har. He would understand what he was and why he existed. He would be purged and strengthened by the fire of solitude, his body aching for the touch of another, and in that pain learn something marvelous. Lileem's mere existence proved something, but Ulaume wasn't sure yet what it was. One thing he felt completely sure about was that there were Wraeththu somewhere who did know, shadowy hara who had created the tribes and the customs they followed. Ulaume was convinced, in his heart, that not everyhar slept in ignorance.

Ulaume dreamed often of Lianvis and the Kakkahaar. He dreamed of waking up in Lianvis's canopy and that he had never left the tribe at all. The night of Hubisag's festival was yet to come, and when it did, nothing would happen. In the dream, Ulaume resolved not to try and curse Pellaz, which would mean everything would turn out all right. Waking from this dream, he would find tears upon his face and desolation in his heart so intense it could only be marveled at. It was the most pure feeling Ulaume had ever experienced. He did not mourn for Lianvis, but for his own ignorance. What bliss it had been, living out a fantasy. He had created himself in a wondrous image, a Wraeththu femme fatale of deadly strength, but there were no hara to appreciate this image now, so it had withered and died. It could not survive without an admiring audience. To Lileem, Ulaume was simply the equivalent of a mother and Ulaume realized he had become this thing. He tied back his hair in tight plaits, so it could barely move, and in truth it had nothing to move for. If it could not help to build a fire or cut logs or mop a floor, it might as well be dead hair, like anyhar else's. More than once, Ulaume imagined cutting it all off, and he felt it would not scream as he did so. It would fall to the floor in lifeless hanks.

Never once, in Ulaume's dreams, did Pellaz appear to him. Then, one night he did, as if he'd been waiting for the right moment. It was not comforting.

In the dream, Ulaume was tending the garden outside the white house. He was trying to plant bulbs, but the soil kept rejecting them, pushing them back out. He tried to hold them down with his hands, but they felt like fingers wriggling beneath the surface. Their sharp nails scratched his palms. Someone called his name and he looked up. There was no one there, but a gate had appeared in the garden wall. A voice called to him from beyond it.

The moment Ulaume stepped through the gate he realized he was dreaming. He fell at once into a black void and the rush of flight pushed the air from his lungs. Fortunately, he did not need to breathe. A light appeared below, a deep hellish red. Ulaume now saw he was falling through an immense abyss. On the walls around him, he saw many scenes, souls in torment, holy temples filled with adoring worshippers, demons torturing the damned. Angels flew around him, screaming and tearing at their own wings, while devils knelt in prayer upon the air. In the center of the abyss reared an enormous wooden pillar, the trunk of a tree with branches splaying out from it the size of highways. Pale figures were climbing the tree or descending it. Ulaume flew toward it and saw Pellaz hung upon it, like a sacrificed king. As he drew nearer,

Ulaume saw that the tree was drawing Pellaz into itself: he was sinking into the bark and it appeared to be growing around his body.

This is the underworld, Ulaume thought. The realm of the lost dead.

"Pell," he called, "you do not belong here. Break free! Rise up!"

Pellaz's head lolled forward upon his breast. His hair hung in lank strands. Ulaume took hold of Pell's face between his hands, tried to raise it.

"My brothers," Pellaz murmured. "I cannot find them. They are not here."

"If they are not in this terrible place, they have moved on," Ulaume said, "as must you."

"I am being reborn. It takes me into itself, scours away my flesh. It is the only way." Even as he spoke, the ancient wood creaked around him and he began to sink farther within the trunk.

"Pellaz," Ulaume said, holding tight onto Pell's face, "I am in your old home I think. I am there for a reason. Have you led me there? If you have a message for me, tell me now."

"Those who walk the path alone will make the maps of it," Pellaz said. "You are not wrong. A thousand worms gnaw at the roots of the tree, and they are the blight of the world. You are the witch of the dark, who can see where others cannot. You are the cruel one, she who gives a thousand wounds, he who spears the soul. Help those whom I love."

With these words, the trunk shuddered and emitted a terrible groan and then snapped shut around Pell's body. All Ulaume had left in his hands was a perfect mask of Pell's face, made of carved bone.

Ulaume woke with a start, but was gripped by the paralysis that sometimes snares the abruptly woken body. For some moments, he could not even open his eyes, could not breathe. The conversation with Pellaz had seemed so real, despite the utter surreality of the abyss.

Then his eyes snapped open and there was a face inches from his own. He could smell breath scented by herbs, feel the damp heat of it. It was the face from his dream: Pellaz.

"You live!" Ulaume hissed and lunged to catch hold of what he thought was a revenant. His hair, perhaps awoken by the scent of the one who had once defeated it, lashed out like snakes.

But it wasn't Pell. Ulaume realized it very quickly. The creature who struggled in his hold, feral and snarling, skinny as a stray dog and perhaps as rabid, was human and female. He glimpsed small breasts through the holes in her ragged shirt, felt the difference of her beneath his fingers. But her face: it was so similar to Pell's. "Who are you?" Ulaume demanded.

Lileem had awoken and had begun to cry, pressing himself against Ulaume's side. The girl made no sound as she writhed in Ulaume's hold. Only the pant of her breath could be heard. She managed to free one of her hands and punched Ulaume full in the face. As he reeled from that, she went for his eyes with her clawed fingers and he had to lunge away. In an instant, the girl had fled the room.

Ulaume pushed Lileem from him and sprang after her. He heard her racing down the stairs, the rasp of her breath. How many times had she observed them as they slept? She must be the unseen presence he had sensed. He followed her out into the garden. She was running so fast she seemed to skim the ground. Her hair flew out behind her.

"Pellaz!" Ulaume called.

For a moment, the girl faltered, skidding to a halt. She glanced behind her, but only for a moment. With the agility of a cat, she was off again, and over the wall. By the time Ulaume reached it and clambered after her, she had vanished into the night. Ulaume gripped the top of the wall, straining to see into the dark, but there was no moon. He was filled with a sense of conviction. He had uncovered a secret of the house. "I know you," he murmured into the cool, quivering air. "You are his sister."

Ulaume walked slowly back to the brooding house, his heart full of a strange and excited wonder. She was as androgynous as her brother had been, beautiful. Wilder perhaps, but what had happened to her? How had she survived? What of the rest of her family, the brothers Pell had spoken of? Tomorrow, Ulaume knew, he must go down the hill. It was time.

In the attic bedroom, Ulaume found that Lileem had lit some candles and now sat hunched among the blankets, looking scared and—most strangely— slightly guilty.

"What is it?" Ulaume snapped.

The harling looked away from him.

Ulaume sat down on the bed and took Lileem's face in one hand. "You have seen that person before, Leelee? You must tell me."

Mouth pursed, brow furrowed, Lileem nodded gravely.

"It is not a har, Lee," Ulaume said, his heart softened by the harling's expression. "Why didn't you tell me? It's a human, not one of us. Dangerous."

Lileem pulled away from Ulaume's grip and shook his head fiercely. "No! Not bad! He is a friend."

"It's not a 'he' " Ulaume said, "but a she. A human female."

Lileem's expression was now defiant and also scathing. "He. My friend."

Ulaume expressed a sigh. "You must never keep secrets from me. It's too dangerous. Did you think I'd be angry?"

Lileem shrugged. "He said not to. No, didn't say, but I knew. Inside. Promised to hide the words. Promised."

"Tell me about it now. Whatever promise you made means nothing anymore. The truth is out, so tell me."

Lileem just stared at Ulaume, mouth still firmly pinched shut.

"Then I will tell you something," Ulaume said. "That girl, I think she is the sister of a har I once knew called Pellaz. I think he lived here with his family when he was still human." Ulaume paused. "This means nothing to you, does it. You don't even know what you are."

Lileem's face seemed to be carved of stone. Defensiveness oozed from every pore of his small body.

"Do you want to know?" Ulaume asked.

Slowly, Lileem nodded, and the hardness dropped from his features. "I'm scared," he murmured.

"I'm not surprised," Ulaume said dryly. "It is a terrifying, but also wondrous story. If you don't understand anything I say, you must stop me and ask me to explain. It's important you understand it clearly. I don't want you to get things wrong in your head." Ulaume reached out and stroked Lileem's hair. "You are such a baby. I forget that sometimes, because you are also like an animal that grows up so quickly. I want to explain what we are to you now, and perhaps I need it more than you do. Perhaps you can tell me things in return that will help me understand you. I am not your hostling, Lee."

"I know," Lileem said. "He weeps for me. I hear him sometimes. I feel him inside me."

Ulaume had never told Lileem what a hostling was. Now, in the shuddering candlelight, he shivered. "You are what I am supposed to be, I think," he said. "What we are all supposed to be."

It was well past dawn by the time Ulaume had finished his lesson. He told Lileem the history of Wraeththu, all that he knew, aware even as he talked that some of it must be lies. He explained about how the world was before, what humans had been like and what it had been like to be human. He described the wars, the disease, the famine, the pollution, the scream of the world. He told of the death and the phoenix that was Wraeththu rising, ash strewn, from the burned ruins. Lileem hardly interrupted his narrative, his eyes depthless pools that seemed to absorb the words. Perhaps he could read Ulaume's feelings and intuit the truth from them. By the end of it, Ulaume's throat was sore. He had talked for hours. Stretching, he picked up the jug of water he kept by the bed and drank it all. Lileem sat motionless, but even with his back to the harling, Ulaume could feel intense energy pouring out of him.

Ulaume put down the jug and curled up beside Lileem. The harling nestled against his side. "Are you still scared?" Ulaume said.

Lileem's eyes were so dark, they seemed to have no whites to them. They glittered with unshed tears. "There is only me," he said huskily.

"I don't think so," Ulaume said. "There will be other harlings. There must be. You must not feel alone."

Lileem shook his head, looking so much older than he was. "No, just me. I'd hear their inside voices if they were out there. There is nohar like me."

"Indeed not. Everyhar is unique. And we are far from other hara here. You might not hear or feel others because of that. We don't know. But you have me, and I will be with you for as long as you need."

"I know," Lileem said. "But the girl, he—she—is like me. When I saw her, I felt it. I knew her."

Ulaume did not respond immediately. He thought about the differences from normal hara he had noticed in the harling's body. Could it be possible it was not something that would change as Lileem developed? Perhaps this was the reason Lileem had been exposed in the desert. Could a har give birth to a female child? But Lileem was clearly not human, because he grew so quickly and was weirdly wise. A Wraeththu female? Impossible, surely.

"Tell me the quiet things aloud," Lileem whispered. "Please, Lormy. Tell me. What is the scared feeling when you look at me sometimes? Why does my hostling weep and why aren't I with him?"

Ulaume uttered a groan and kissed Lileem's head. "I want you to be happy," he said. "Happy and free. I don't want you to worry or be afraid."

"I am happy *and* afraid," Lileem said. "I want to know."

"Your head is a thousand years old," Ulaume said. "All right. But I can stop at any time. Just put a finger to my lips."

Lileem only reached out and touched Ulaume's mouth when the story was finished. He gently traced the shape of Ulaume's lips with his fingers. Ulaume could feel him trembling. "You see," he said. "There is only me."

"What have we discovered?" Ulaume murmured and drew the harling close to him held him tight. "Oh Leelee, I don't know. I don't know."

They slept for a couple of hours, then Ulaume went downstairs to prepare some breakfast. He couldn't help glancing around him continually, sure he would catch a glimpse of the strange girl, but she was nowhere around. In daylight, it was hard to believe he'd actually seen her.

Lileem came trailing into the kitchen, rubbing his eyes. He yawned and started poking around at the eggs Ulaume was preparing, rolling the empty shells beneath his fingers. "I came from something like that," he said.

"In a way," Ulaume said. "Sit down."

Lileem perched on a chair. "When Pellaz died, he cried out to all the world," he said.

Ulaume froze. "The girl told you that?"

"No. I heard it. In my warm place where I was curled up."

"He died the moment your pearl was born, I think."

Lileem nodded. "Yes, but I'm not him. You just thought that, didn't you?"

Ulaume smiled, surprised to find he was not as unnerved by that remark as he perhaps should be. "I know you're not him, Leelee. But you're quite the little oracle, aren't you. I never realized how much. Also, I should tell you it's rude to pry into people's thoughts. Don't do it unless you really have to."

"You heard his cry too," Lileem said. "It was a big wind that swept around. It was inside me when we went through the desert, and I didn't know what it was. Now I do."

"Is the girl his sister?"

"You think she is."

"What do you think?"

"Don't know. I'll ask her."

Ulaume continued to beat eggs. He was aware he must proceed carefully. "When, Lee?"

"Don't know."

"When do you see her?"

"In the gray times, at morning and at night mostly. Then you call me in for breakfast or supper and she has to go."

"Where does she live?"

"Don't know."

"Perhaps you could ask her that as well."

"She won't talk to you," Lileem said. "She thinks you're like the others, who did the bad things. She wants to kill you, but I've told her not to."

"Thanks!" Ulaume said, in a harsher tone than he meant to use.

"I like the 'she' word, it's soft," Lileem said wistfully. "Can I be she?"

"Be what you like," Ulaume said. "It doesn't matter. You are what you are, whatever that is."

"Two things, one thing!" Lileem said and giggled loudly. "Two things, one thing. She he she he she he. I'm a she she she."

"That's enough," Ulaume said. "It might change, Lee. We don't know yet. Just *be,* and don't get attached to one idea. There's enough of that goes on among Wraeththukind, and it causes half the problems, I'm sure."

After breakfast, Ulaume let Lileem go out alone into the gardens, hoping that the girl would show herself to the harling. He had no doubt she would not appear if he was around, so it seemed he had no choice but to leave the hill. He realized he had been putting this moment off for weeks. He dressed himself in shirt and trousers and walked barefoot down the rough road.

As he walked, clouds drew in from both the east and west, turning the sky a strange greenish purple. Though he could not see it, Ulaume knew that lightning stitched itself within the boiling vapor. He could not hear it, but he felt thunder in his bones. Past the creaking windmills, the stable doors banging, the empty yards, the staring windows. Gradually, the sounds around him folded themselves away into the air, and he walked in a silence that vibrated like a plucked wire. Some terrible ghost awaited him, and it had been waiting long.

Nothing looked real in the strange light. The house before him now looked like an image from a grainy photograph. Ulaume closed his eyes. He must open up, summon back the parts of himself he'd sought to bury beneath domesticity and mundane routine. In his mind, he saw a boy on the porch, sitting with his knees up, intent on sharpening a knife. His eyes held the same dull metallic glint as the metal in his hands. The air was full of a misty rain and the boy, who had been Pellaz, was part of it, a creature of mist who might vanish in an instant should Ulaume reach out and touch him. Then, as before, he sensed a presence bearing down from behind, the sounds of hooves slow-clopping on the damp earthy road. Ulaume paused. He could hear thunder, or was it the rhythmic boom of someone pounding metal, or the sound of a giant marching ponderously across the cordillera to the east, taking in forests with each stride? It was his own heart, amplified and intense.

Ulaume felt the entity enter his body and it passed right through him. He was drawn onto tiptoe as it did so, unable to breathe, his chest constricted with terrible pain. Then, released, he saw it, as he had not done before: Cal on a red pony riding away from him, having passed through Ulaume's heart. He rode toward Pellaz, and Ulaume knew this must have been the first, fateful meeting between them.

Pell looked up, his eyes dull silver. In his hands, the knife shivered with blue fire. Cal's first words were, "Behold, I have come to take your life," but these words were unspoken. Ulaume heard him speak aloud and he said, "I am Cal." He might as well have said, "I am the demon of the darkest corner of your soul." Anyone could see he was already cursed.

Ulaume opened his eyes, and for a brief instant could still see the two of them on the porch. Then, the image wavered and shattered like glass, pieces of Pell and Cal flying out in all directions. Thunder broke in the west and a charge of lightning struck down in the fields beyond the settlement. Ulaume would not let himself think or evaluate. He walked on, his feet now treading the steps to the porch. He reached out to unfasten the door but it was already open.

In the kitchen beyond, the Cevarro family sat eating a meal around a table. Ulaume heard laughter, the scrape of cutlery against plates. He saw Cal sitting among them, and from his fingers silver threads emanated, each hooked into the heart of someone at the table. Their eyes were milky and blind—but for two. Ulaume recognized her then, a younger, innocent image of the wild girl who had run from him the previous evening. She could see clearly, and so could Pell. Pell stared only at Cal and the girl stared only at her brother. Cal was so busy he hadn't noticed she could see. If he'd known, he wouldn't have cared anyway. Or maybe the Uigenna in him would have killed her for it. Ulaume stood at the threshold and saw something he'd never had, but which he'd sometimes, in the most secret moments of childhood, longed for. The Cevarro family was wrapped in a golden caul of light. There was an intimacy between them that while it included others also excluded them. Pellaz was loved. He'd always been loved. Perhaps it was part of what had impelled Cal to steal him away. Without even being aware of it, he'd been jealous of what Pell had and had sought to destroy it.

Perhaps I would have done the same, Ulaume thought. *I would have been full of derision and contempt for this. I would have stolen him too, broken their cozy intimacy. Something has happened to me. I have lost myself.*

At that moment, Pellaz turned his head and stared directly into Ulaume's eyes. "I did not choose what I was meant to be," he said. Around him, the image of Cal and his family continued to converse. Pell had stepped outside of the vision.

"What were you?" Ulaume asked. "Have you changed me? Have you brought me here?"

"Help them," Pellaz said. "You are strong, Ulaume, and you can do it. I will not remember this. I have much to learn. I will despise and condemn you, but now, in this moment, I know you are the one."

"Are you really dead?"

"None of us are ever really dead."

"Please answer me."

Pellaz rose from his seat and came to take Ulaume's hand. He seemed small and childlike, and his skin was warm. "I am dead," he said, "but I live. Come."

He began to lead Ulaume away from the room, into the house, and when Ulaume glanced back, he saw another Pellaz still sitting at the table, gazing at the destiny that was Cal.

The house was in darkness, but breathed softly around them. Pell's fingers felt very real in Ulaume's own. "I have seen your sister," Ulaume whispered. He dared not raise his voice.

"She is strong, like you," Pellaz said. "She survived, as I survived."

"You want me to help her?"

"She does not need your help in the way you think, but you might help each other."

They had come to a closed door. Pellaz put his free hand flat upon it. "In this room, we first shared breath," he said. "Cal showed me everything and nothing. I did not know him, and I will not know him for a very long time, but our souls are one. He is me and I him. Look."

He pushed open the door and Ulaume saw Pell lying on the bed, next to another, who lay snoring, presumably one of his brothers. On the floor, wrapped in a blanket, lay Cal, his violet eyes open, staring wildly. He was planning, feverishly. And Pellaz, taut as a frightened hare, did so also. It was inevitable they should be drawn to one another. Pellaz no longer stood beside Ulaume at the threshold. Now, he was on the floor, beneath Cal's blanket and Cal's hand was upon his face.

Ulaume heard a noise from the bed, and began to back from the room. He did not want to see them take aruna together, and yet how could they have done, when Pell had still been human? Pell's brother on the bed was writhing beneath the blanket. Ulaume could see his breath steaming in the air, which had become suddenly icy. Ulaume was shaken back to reality. This was no vision.

The room looked abandoned, wrecked, and it was daylight now. Someone, or something, writhed upon the bed among a debris of withered leaves and shattered glass. It squealed like a frightened pig. Ulaume cautiously approached. He drew back the blanket, saw brown skin, and a back with the spine sticking out of it so far it looked as if it grew on the outside. So thin, and it stank of shit and blood. Human or har? Impossible to tell, but whatever it was, it was sick or dying. Ulaume reached out tentatively, put one finger upon it and at once the creature sprang up. Ulaume fell back, uttering a shocked cry. The face was terrible, huge eyes protruding from a skin-covered skull, the teeth too large and long. This apparition threw itself from the bed. Upright, it jerked like an animated puppet, careening from wall to wall, legs stiff, arms held out. Its hair was a filthy mane of tangles and twigs. It uttered hideous strangled squeals.

Ulaume had never beheld anything so vile. The mere sight of it seemed anathema to life and reality. It went beyond surface appearances, which in themselves were terrible. It was a great wrongness.

Before Ulaume could flee the room, the thing had lurched past him and its dreadful noises diminished as it moved away. Ulaume felt dazed. He could barely move, although his flesh crawled with revulsion. What had Pell shown him? Was this what Pell had, or would, become?

Back at the white house, Ulaume could not find Lileem. He searched all the rooms and the gardens, calling the harling's name. He must be with the girl and would no doubt reappear at sundown. Ulaume's heart beat fast all day. Wherever he was, he kept glancing out of windows, sure he would see some terrible vision shambling up the hill. The image he'd seen in the Cevarro house would not leave his mind. He felt nauseous, light headed.

As Ulaume predicted, Lileem reappeared when the evening meal was ready. "You should come in earlier," Ulaume said sharply. "It's time you began to help me more. Look at you. You're half grown up already."

Lileem didn't say anything, but went to wash his filthy hands in the sink. It looked as if he'd been rolling in mud all day.

Ulaume dished out the food and said carelessly. "Did you see the girl today, Leelee?"

"No," the harling said, tucking into his food with relish.

"What have you been doing, then?"

"I waited for her, but she didn't come," Lileem said. "I went to the water mill and saw some silver fish."

"That's in the town," Ulaume said. "Don't go down there, it's not safe."

"It is," Lileem said.

"I saw something today," Ulaume said. "I think there are other things here apart from the girl."

Lileem said nothing.

CHAPTER ELEVEN

For over two weeks, Lileem claimed he no longer saw the girl. Ulaume, unsure of the harling's truthfulness, stooped to spying on him, to no avail. Perhaps the girl had moved on, spooked by Ulaume catching sight of her. Neither did he see again the creature he'd come across in the Cevarro house. He rarely left the hill and told himself what he'd seen had been part of a vision, nothing more. He tried to create some kind of routine. He would bring Lileem up in this place. The past was done, but always he could feel the unseen tugging at the locks on his senses, trying to find a way in.

One evening, he said to Lileem, "Do you think the girl has left this place?"

Lileem paused before answering, enough to alert Ulaume to a forthcoming untruth. "She's not here," Lileem said.

Ulaume said nothing more, but he felt angry inside. Lileem was cunning, as only a child could be. Cunning in innocence. The girl was still around and she was positioning herself between Ulaume and Lileem. She was luring the harling away.

Ulaume said nothing more on the subject and did not let his anger show. He remembered how he used to be, how nohar ever got something over on him, how he always got revenge.

The following morning at breakfast, he said to Lileem. "I have to go back

down to the Cevarro house today. I must meditate there. I need to know answers. Do not follow me, and do not stray into the town. I will be gone all day.
Will you be all right alone?"

Lileem nodded, without even glancing up.

"Good," said Ulaume.

After they'd eaten, he left Lileem to see to the dishes and left the house. He
had no doubt the girl must be watching him, so he went slowly down the hill,
heading toward the Cevarro house, although he had no intention of going
there. Nothing would entice him back into that afflicted place. Instead, he
went into another house and there set about shrouding his thoughts. It was
clear to him that whenever Lileem had been with the girl, he'd utilized his
psychic abilities to warn himself of Ulaume's approach. Ulaume intended to
put a stop to that. He waited a couple of hours and then let down his hair, so
that it fell around him in a cloudy veil. He went out into the sunlight and
squeezed himself into the spaces between the air, so that nohar could see him
and nohar could feel his presence. *Now let us see,* he thought.

He heard their laughter before he saw them. There was an outcrop of rock
on the side the hill that was part of the garden. Here a landscaped waterfall
slipped down a series of carved chutes and bowls shadowed by hardy ferns.
Ulaume already knew this was one of Lileem's favorite places, even though
he'd warned the harling that the rocks were dangerous. He crept through the
trees and saw them playing together, the girl splashing water over the harling,
while Lileem waded noisily through the ponds, shrieking and giggling,
soaked to the skin. There was an intimacy between them that made Ulaume
furious at once. Lileem had lied to him, after all that Ulaume had done. He
could have left the harling to die in the desert, but he had not. He had given up
his life for this child and this was how he was repaid.

So have it, he thought bitterly. *You are a freak, Lileem, and now I will leave
you here in the care of a creature who will grow old and die, who can teach
you nothing about yourself, and who will not be able to protect you from
strangers. I will return to my tribe, as I should have done before. Pellaz is
dead. I owe him nothing.*

But first, he could not resist revealing himself.

He folded himself out of the air and for some moments hid among the
trees, projecting intention toward the harling. Lileem soon picked up on this
and froze. The girl did not notice and continued to play. Ulaume stepped forth
from the trees. He felt his hair rise around him. He felt the fire in his own eyes.
"Lileem!" he said.

An expression of pure horror convulsed the harling's features and even though Ulaume was so angry, he could not help but be affected by that. It hurt him, but also fueled his fury. "Come here!" he cried.

Lileem panicked. Instead of obeying Ulaume's command, he sought to escape the other way. It happened so quickly. One moment, he was clambering up the sheer rocks, the next he was falling, arms flailing. Ulaume's heart stopped. It seemed the harling fell in slow motion down to the next pool, where cruel rocks protruded from the water. He landed with a mighty splash and spray flew everywhere. Ulaume leapt forward and so did the girl. She reached Lileem first, expelling animal cries of alarm. She lifted the small limp body in her arms, gazed at it. Blood poured from a wound on Lileem's forehead. His eyes were half open.

Ulaume felt as if he were trying to force his body through glutinous syrup. He could not move fast enough. He could not reach Lileem's side. As he watched, the wild girl bent her head to the wound and began to slurp at the swiftly rilling blood.

"Get away from him!" Ulaume roared and lunged across the last few feet between them. He struck at the girl's head, which snapped back. She recovered quickly, clasping Lileem to her breast, snarling up at Ulaume, her bared teeth red. She was like a cornered rat: in the position of disadvantage but unafraid and prepared to fight. In the few brief moments while Ulaume considered how best to deal with her, she looked away from him and began to lick the harling's head once more. There was too much blood for her to consume. It ran over her fingers. She uttered soft crooning sounds. It was at this moment that Ulaume realized she wasn't feeding but trying to heal. His anger flowed out of him and ran with Lileem's blood downstream. He hunkered down in the water a few feet away from the girl and said, "Let me have him. I can make it better. Let me have him."

The girl stared at him through wild tangles of hair. The whole bottom half of her face was red and scarlet streams were swirling out into the pool around her.

Ulaume held out his hands, projected from them the healing power he had learned during his caste training. Perhaps the girl could feel it. Slowly, he edged forward. The girl tensed and scrabbled back a short way. Lileem's limbs dangled bonelessly in the water. He did not move. Ulaume continued to murmur soft reassurances and then his hands were upon Lileem's face. He exhaled and realized he'd been holding his breath. He was aware of the warmth of the girl's body, her heavy breathing. He could smell her: a mixture of sweat and sage. Ulaume traced the wound on Lileem's head and projected the intention to close it, to cauterize the capillaries, to clot the blood. It made his head ache; he'd rarely bothered with healing before. He wasn't doing it right, because he could tell he was using too much of his own energy rather than channeling that in the environment, but there was no other way. It had to be done now. He did it for too long perhaps, because when Lileem stirred beneath his fingers, Ulaume fell to the side, his face in the water, unable to move. He was partly breathing in water, but was powerless to help himself. Through one eye, he saw the girl place Lileem tenderly on a flat rock, then come wading toward him. She caught hold of his hair and dragged him to the bank, so that his head lay on the smooth rock, his body still submerged. She kicked him savagely in the side, then went back to Lileem.

Ulaume lay panting and coughing, desperately seeking strength from the living trees around him, from the water itself. The girl could make off with Lileem now. Then what would happen? Ulaume knew he hadn't yet done enough to effect a complete healing. Lileem needed gentle handling and proper care.

He watched the girl squatting over the harling, touching his hair, his limbs, making soft sounds of concern. She kept shaking her head like a cat, as if she had something in her ears. She stood up, waving her hands around her face as if warding off a plague of flies. She staggered on the rock, uttering strange sounds.

Ulaume hauled himself from the water and lay on the bank. He absorbed the green balm of the trees, the light of the land. He was struck by the absurdity of their situation. Lileem lay semiconscious on a rock, while he himself was paralyzed by exhaustion. The girl, their strange companion in drama, was reeling drunkenly through the pool, screeching and fighting off invisible enemies. Ulaume knew why, and he could not help smiling about it. Lileem's blood had poisoned her.

Ulaume carried Lileem back to the house and put him to bed. As far as he could discern, the harling had suffered a mild concussion, but there was no fracture of the skull. Because his healing skills were not that advanced, Ulaume resolved to give Lileem hands-on treatments every few hours. But from now on, he must be careful not to deplete himself.

After a couple of hours, Lileem woke and clung to Ulaume fiercely. "You betrayed me," Ulaume said, stroking his hair. "Look what happened."

Lileem wept softly. He was, after all, only a child.

Once he was satisfied Lileem was comfortable and sleeping normally, Ulaume went back to the pools. Lavender dusk was stealing in and the trees were full of cicadas. He expected the girl to be dead, but she wasn't. She was curled up beneath an acacia, shivering and muttering to herself. A twinge in Ulaume's side reminded him of her vicious kick. He observed her for some minutes, but she didn't seem to realize he was there. She was so like Pell, it was uncanny: the lush black hair, the perfect face, and the graceful slim body. In the vision, Pell had said, "Help those I love." He'd also mentioned that this female creature could help Ulaume. Presumably, her supping Lileem's blood had not been part of Pell's plan.

Sighing, Ulaume squatted down and let his right hand hover over the girl's head. She was giving off a lot of heat and energy, but he couldn't sense death approaching. She might rear up and attack him at any moment, but vulnerable and defenseless as she was now, it was difficult not to feel pity. She had lost everything, even her humanity to a degree, and Wraeththu had caused that. It was a miracle she had survived.

Ulaume lifted her in his arms and took her back to the house. She was limp and did not stir in his hold. He made up a bed for her on the floor in the kitchen, next to the stove, where it was warm. She shivered beneath the blankets, her lips surrounded by a white crust of dried foam. It looked to Ulaume as if she was going through althaia, the changing. But no females had successfully mutated into Wraeththu. Lileem, of course, could be different from normal hara, not just in physical appearance, but also because he was pure born, and had never been incepted. Perhaps pure born hara could incept females. Perhaps Ulaume would now find out. He composed himself in a chair and watched her through the night, accompanied only by a couple of bottles of wine he took from the cellar. Occasionally, he'd go to check on and give healing to Lileem, whose breathing was deep and regular and who now sported a large discolored lump on his forehead.

Before dawn, Ulaume dozed off, and was woken up some hours later by Lileem pulling on his arm. He opened his eyes and looked down into Lileem's familiar grave expression. A quick glimpse across the room assured him the girl was still comatose beneath the blankets.

"Sorry," said Lileem.

Ulaume reached out and touched the harling's face gently. "I won't punish you," he said. "I think you've learned a lesson."

Lileem glanced at the bundle on the floor. "You brought her here . . . Is she ill? What happened?"

"There is something wrong with her, certainly." Ulaume stretched languorously; his limbs were stiff. "Perhaps you are not as different from me as we thought."

Lileem frowned. "What?"

"We will have to wait and see," Ulaume said, "but I have an idea of what's wrong with her."

For three days, as in a normal althaia, the girl writhed and screeched beneath her blankets. She ran a high fever and her skin was flaking and sore. Ulaume did what he could for her. She was like a wild creature, a bundle of defensive instincts. When she'd been vicious with him before, he'd hated her, but now could feel only pity. Also, she was beautiful in the way a wolf is beautiful: unapproachable, best admired from afar. He smoothed her tangled hair and bathed her face with cold water. She didn't know he was there. Sometimes, among her animal noises, he thought he heard her whispering Pell's name, but he couldn't be sure.

Twice, Ulaume woke in the morning to find damage had been done to the garden outside and yet he never heard anything during the night. He remembered what he'd seen in the Cevarro house and told Lileem not to stray. The girl might have been his only protection from whatever roamed out there.

On the evening of the third day, the girl's fever abated and she slept easily. Whatever had happened to her was over, but Ulaume had no idea what he should do next, if anything. A Wraeththu har's inception was consummated by aruna, but there was no one to do that for the girl. He certainly wouldn't, or couldn't, himself. She was not har. She was something else and it was as if his sexual senses couldn't recognize her.

Lileem had found some old board games, only partly chewed by mice, and sat at the kitchen table making up new rules as to how to play them. Ulaume sat reading a book on chickens. He heard the girl moan and put down his book. She had rolled onto her back and cast off the blankets, one forearm pressed against her eyes. Ulaume stood up. This was the moment he'd both dreaded and looked forward to with curiosity.

"Can you understand me, girl?" he said.

For some moments, she did not lower her arm, but when she did her eyes were black and furious and terrified. She glanced around, clearly still too weak to move, but even so seeking an avenue of escape.

"We mean you no harm," Ulaume said, which even to him sounded unconvincing. "I am a friend of Pellaz Cevarro. You know him?"

"He's dead," she croaked, her voice sounding rusty with disuse.

"Not anymore—apparently," Ulaume answered, "but then, I'm not sure. He has spoken to me here. You are his sister, yes?"

"There's nothing left for you here," the girl rasped. "Go."

"I am not here to take anything," Ulaume said. "I came here only looking for sanctuary for myself and Lileem, the harling—the child. We are alone. I am not a warrior. I don't even have a tribe, but I knew your brother."

"I have no brothers," she said, "only monsters. They are gone."

Ulaume drew a deep breath. "A har called Cal brought Pellaz to my tribe. Pell had been incepted to Wraeththu at another settlement. He came to us for training."

The girl turned onto her side and put her hands over her ears.

Ulaume sighed deeply. "You are right. He is no longer your brother. He cast off all that he was the moment he became Wraeththu. There is no point in talking about it."

He turned to Lileem who was sitting absolutely still, no doubt taking in every word. "Ask your friend if she wishes to eat. You can prepare something for her."

"Child stealer!" hissed the girl, still with her back to him.

"I did not steal Lileem," Ulaume said coldly. "He is not human, whatever you think. He was born of Wraeththu and is as much your enemy as I am. His blood poisoned you." He did not wait for a reply but left the room.

Outside, in the murmuring garden, he took deep breaths to calm himself. He must not let this human affect him, if indeed she was still human. Creatures stalked this place and none of them was normal. He'd seen something vile in the Cevarro house and he must find out what it was. The girl had spoken of monsters. He had seen one. But where did he progress from here? He did not expect the girl to take to him, it would be unrealistic to imagine so. But she held the answers. She had the history in her.

Ulaume narrowed his eyes and scanned the night. He sensed a dark cloud hanging over the hill, although the night was clear.

"Her name," Lileem said, "is Mima."

Ulaume and Lileem were sitting in the garden. The girl would not move from her place by the stove, other than to visit the small bathroom off the kitchen. She had lived there, a silent, brooding presence, for another three days. She would not acknowledge Ulaume existed, and he pretended she wasn't there.

"You must ask her something," Ulaume said. "I want you to ask her to examine her own body. Ask her if there are any changes."

"Why?"

"I think you incepted her accidentally."

Lileem grinned. "Made her like me? Is that possible?"

"How should I know? It's as much of a mystery to me as to you. But perhaps, if we find out, we'll learn a little about how you might be one day."

Ulaume's heart clenched at the sudden flowering of delight and hope in Lileem's face. "You can also ask her how she feels, if she's noted any differences about her perceptions, that is, how she sees the world and hears it, and what she does not hear or see but somehow *knows*."

Lileem nodded vigorously. "I will! I will!" He hugged Ulaume fiercely. "Thank you, Lormy. Thank you for giving this to me."

Ulaume laughed uncomfortably, remembering his own bitter thoughts at the poolside before Lileem's accident. "I did nothing: you did."

"You could have left her to die. You helped her live."

"That is true. Perhaps I am a nicer har than I think I am."

Ulaume waited for Lileem to come back to him with answers, and was therefore surprised when Mima herself addressed him in the kitchen the following morning. It was preceded by a punch in the face, which took him even more by surprise. As he was picking himself up from the floor, fully prepared to defend himself in the most vigorous manner, Mima pushed back her hair and said, "The child says something has been done to me, the same thing you do to boys. Is that true?"

Ulaume merely flared his nostrils. "When you can behave with dignity and courtesy I may be moved to answer your queries." He stalked out into the garden and began picking berries from a rather straggling bush.

Mima followed him and hovered behind him. Ulaume hid a smile. He could sense Pell strongly. After a while, Mima said, "There are changes. I am different."

Ulaume waited a moment, then glanced around at her. "That is perhaps unfortunate. I can do nothing to help you now and Lileem is only a child."

"What do you mean?"

He shrugged carelessly. "Well, in Wraeththu, you have to take aruna after inception. But no females become Wraeththu, so you're probably not har. I don't know what you are."

"I don't know what you're talking about. Explain."

"Aruna is sex. You need it to finish the inception. But there's nohar for you do it with. You are not har. I can sense it. Maybe you don't even need it. Who knows?" He turned back to the berry-picking.

"I am not the same as I was. Is this what you are, what Lileem is?"

Ulaume shrugged. "I don't know. I'm not even sure what Lileem is. He was exposed by his parents in the desert to die, so you can be sure he's not normal."

Mima screwed up her eyes, rubbed her face in confusion. "The child is a girl, anyone can see that."

"Well, perhaps that is the reason then. But if so, he—or she—is not a human girl. He's a freak, and so are you."

"I do not feel like a freak," Mima said and her tone caused Ulaume to stop what he was doing and pay her more attention.

She squatted down in front of him. "May we talk?"

"If you can keep your hands to yourself, yes."

"I have lived a nightmare, can you understand that?"

He nodded.

"I have lived in a dark world, watching myself. Whatever has just happened to me brought me back. I awoke a few days ago and I was back in the real world, no longer just a spectral observer. It has taken me some days to accept this, for it had been my decision to leave my own mind."

"What happened?" Ulaume asked.

Mima stood up, and gazed down upon her old home, hands on hip. "We were attacked, as many people warned us we would be. Nearly everyone was killed. They took my brothers, as Pell had been taken, but one I managed to help escape."

There was a silence, which Ulaume intuited Mima wanted him to fill. He had a history and answers that she desperately wanted too. "Did you take him after he'd been incepted?"

She made a sound of exasperation and kicked the dirt. "They had done something to Terez, yes, if that is inception. He was very ill. We'd heard months before there might be some physical change involved in becoming Wraeththu, but I'd not believed it. Not until I was forced to."

"I think I've seen him," Ulaume said. "You shouldn't have done that. Do you know what you have done?"

"Know? I tried to save someone I loved, after everyone else was dead. Is that so wrong?"

Ulaume stood up also. "Yes, in this case. If you have lived in a dark world, then he exists in a grotesque half world. I shudder to imagine."

"Do you! What happened to Terez, what happened to me, to my parents, to my sisters and brothers, it is beyond understanding, beyond hell. I had to leave it all behind."

"Yet you survived," Ulaume said. "In that, you are very similar to Pell."

Mima grimaced. "He chose that life. I hated him for it. I hated him for leaving us."

"You shouldn't. The alternative might have been another Terez. At the very least, you would have lost him anyway, and probably to a barbaric tribe. You should know that he received the very best and most gentle inception. He was trained well, so well in fact, it appears he may have survived physical death. He still cares about you, when so many hara have cast off their human past completely. He has spoken to me of you."

"Did he send you here?"

"No, it was coincidence, if such a thing exists. But perhaps not. Pellaz certainly inspired me to leave my tribe, and if I had not done so, Lileem might well be dead now."

Mima's eyes were round. "Tell me. Everything."

"We have much to speak of," Ulaume said. "In essence, it is difficult to know where to start."

"The beginning," Mima said. "The truth about Wraeththu, what you are. All I know is what travelers told us. I look at you, and at Lileem, and I can see you are different to those who murdered my people. It is of this I want to know."

"Let's go inside," Ulaume said. "Lileem should be with us while we talk."

Later, Ulaume reflected that Pellaz, had he been Mima, would very probably have reacted in the same way his sister did to this enormous and stultifying catalogue of revelations and unbelievable fact. After hours of discussion, she went quiet, then announced she needed time alone. Not once during the proceedings, had she revealed anything about herself or her new condition. Ulaume realized she was not self-obsessed. In some ways, her body was incidental to her. She knew she had learned things that the majority of humanity never had nor ever would. She sensed the responsibility of this knowledge and also the fact that Fate had plucked her from madness and/or death. She was too bright and aware not to realize this was a second chance, for which, whatever the circumstances of it, she should be grateful. But unlike those hara who had initially resisted inception, only to wake from althaia and realize they would be stupid not to make the best of it, Mima did not have the support and guidance of others like herself. She was, to Ulaume's knowledge, unique. She had learned what Wraeththu was. She had yet to learn how she fitted into the picture, and for the answer, she would look within herself. As she left the house, Ulaume could only admire her courage.

Mima became part of their household, and a very useful part, as she had domestic and farming skills Ulaume did not, and was familiar with the terrain and its flora and fauna. Despite her earlier hostility, she was clearly grateful to have companions once more, and because they lived apart from the world, it did not matter what kind of creatures they were: how different or how similar. Ulaume learned they lived in the house Mima's people had called the Richards House, or simply the white house, and that it had once belonged to a hermitic landowner named Sefton Richards. The Cevarros had worked for him and the farming settlement they lived in was known either as just the Richards Place, or else as Casa Ricardo, in the native tongue. Mima explained to Ulaume that when the rogue Wraeththu had come to destroy the farm, she'd been lucky. She'd been away from home, buying tools from a neighboring farm some miles away, and had seen the smoke from a distance when she'd returned. For some days, she'd haunted the shadows, seeking evidence of whether her family had survived or not. The Wraeththu had remained there until the althaias were over, because they'd incepted every suitable young male. Mima had found Terez before he'd regained consciousness. With the stealth of a mountain lioness, she'd crept into the house the Wraeththu had been using for their inceptees and had stolen him away from beneath the noses of his captors. But when he'd regained consciousness, he'd been wild and mindless. She'd had to tie him up and take him out into the desert to wait for the Wraeththu to move on. "I had another brother, Dorado," she said, "but I couldn't find him. I was just relieved I was able to rescue Terez."

Ulaume winced as he listened to this story, imagining Terez's terror, his instincts that would have craved to be with the ones who had made him like them. It must have felt as if his limbs were being torn off.

"Eventually, I untied him," Mima said. "He went for me like a wild animal and I had to run for my life. He didn't know me then, and he hasn't since. Well, you've seen what he is now."

She had returned to Casa Ricardo and had buried the bodies she'd found there: these were the graves Ulaume had seen at the base of the hill.

"After that, which was the most terrible thing anyone should ever have to do, I lost my mind," she said. "It went all in one go, just like a light going out. I laid the earth over the final grave and I died too, and yet I didn't. All I can remember is running around screaming, and then everything gets muzzy. There was no day or night, no thought. Terez and I must have been occupying the same territory, but we never met up. We were both animals. He still is, of course. It began to change for me when I met the little girl—Lileem. I felt like a big dog, wagging my tail for her. I just wanted to please her and be with her. The rest . . . you know what happened."

"I found dead upon the road near here," Ulaume said. "More recent than what happened to your people. Did the rogue Wraeththu return?"

She shook her head. "No. Most likely, Terez did that. He eats anything."

Ulaume swallowed with difficulty.

"The bad Wraeththu must have attacked every farm around here," she said. "So there must have been some survivors seeking an escape."

Pell's prophecy, or wish, had come true. Ulaume and Mima had found each other, and together they could keep Lileem, and each other, safe. Ulaume only hoped the outside world, and all that was evil in it, would pass them by.

CHAPTER TWELVE

Saltrock felt different now. Seel walked the familiar streets and it was as if revisiting a childhood haunt. He'd been away only a short time, although longer than he'd planned, and even in the few weeks of his absence, new buildings had sprung up. As he'd expected, the Gelaming had been determined to make their superior presence felt and had lost no time in ingratiating themselves with Stringer, who being an affable soul had seen no sinister motive in their behavior. For Stringer, it had no doubt been astounding to realize that he was effectively in charge of Saltock. With Orien gone, and Seel away with Colt, the inhabitants had invested him with authority. They had gone to him with queries and to seek advice, because there'd been nohar else to turn to.

Seel had to admit that Stringer had done a good job. He'd even been around to tidy up Seel's office and Seel felt strongly that his plans for the town had been inspected thoroughly. Was it time to hand over the reins of Saltrock to Colt and Stringer, who were more than suitable for the role? Evidence seemed to point that way, but Seel felt uneasy, because this was what Thiede wanted, and therefore he had to suspect that Thiede had somehow engineered the situation.

Seel discussed it openly with Colt, who said, "We don't want power,

Stringer and I, but after what I've seen, I think maybe Immanion is the place for you, and we'd gladly care for Saltrock while you're away."

It seemed so neat and easy, perhaps too much so, and for this reason Seel put off making a decision. Thiede didn't hassle him about it, which in itself was suspicious.

Some six months after his return to Saltrock, Seel received a visitor. Early one morning, there was a knock at the front door while he was eating breakfast, and when he went to answer it, he found Ashmael Aldebaran on the porch. Seel stared at him in stunned silence for some moments and Ashmael said, "No, Thiede hasn't sent me, in case you were wondering."

"Come in," said Seel, aware at once that Fate was handing him an information update on a plate. He was also aware that his initial reaction on seeing Ashmael had been pleasure.

"It must be difficult to construct an idyll in a place like this," Ashmael said as Seel led him to the kitchen, which was where he spent most of his time nowadays. "You have to admit Thiede chose a better spot."

Seel did not deign to comment on this, but made Ashmael some coffee and sat him at the table. Like Thiede, he seemed too big for Saltrock, an anachronism. His thick fair hair was cut fairly short by Wraeththu standards, but fell across his face seductively. He brushed it out of his eyes continuously, a boyish gesture that seemed at odds with his appearance and position. Perhaps he knew that and it was a conscious conceit.

"Your hara are intrigued by Gelaming," Ashmael said, sipping the coffee. "I attracted quite a crowd before I found your house. Luckily, everyhar wanted to show me the way. They are keen for you to take up Thiede's offer, aren't they?"

Seel realized he hadn't considered that. Nohar had said so, but perhaps it was the case. A close alliance with Immanion could only benefit the town and most hara there probably did harbor secret desires to be Gelaming. "I haven't made up my mind," he said. "You know why. What is more pressing in my mind is the reason for your visit."

"First, I'd like to say I think it would be a good idea for you to come to Immanion, but I'm not here to persuade you about that. It is the other matter."

"Pellaz," said Seel.

Ashmael nodded abruptly. "Have you thought about what I said?"

Seel folded his arms on the table. "Yes. I'm still not convinced it's possible for Thiede to bring somehar back from the dead."

"I'm aware of that. However, the Hegemony have a proposal for you."

"Which is?"

"How would you feel about asking Thiede to show Pellaz to you? We understand he is incarnate, at least in some form."

"I would like evidence," Seel said carefully. "So your request is not unfeasible. I presume you want me to report on what I find. Why can't one of your hara do it?"

"Thiede won't let anyhar near Pellaz, but we are sure you would be an exception. He wants you in Immanion, Seel. You don't know how desperately. You gave him a condition once—do it again."

"He hasn't captured Cal though, has he?"

"Not that we know of, but this request would be easier to fulfill."

Seel frowned. "You clearly believe Thiede is capable of reincarnating a dead har, so I can't understand why you want my evidence. I didn't know Pell that well and I imagine that if what you say is true the har who lives now must be very different from the young boy who was incepted here. What's the point of this?"

"It's not just your evidence we want," Ashmael said.

"What else?"

"We want you to kill him."

Seel laughed at the absurdity of these words. "Really! You think I'd do that?"

"Why not? In one sense, he is already dead and I know you are disgusted by the idea of what's been done to him as I am. The Hegemony does not want Pellaz brought to Immanion, Seel, but our hands are tied. Thiede has great power, not only in a personal sense, but also throughout Wraeththukind. We are aware our own limited powers could be taken from us very easily. We do not want some zombie puppet of Thiede's ruling in Immanion. The idea is unthinkable. Don't get me wrong. I admire Thiede and know that we need him in order to construct our society, but in this he is misguided. It's some bizarre personal dream he has, and more than a few of us think it has the mark of insanity upon it."

"It's obvious Thiede is a little insane," Seel said. "And perhaps Orien died for what he knew." He hesitated.

"This abomination must be disposed of," Ashmael said quickly, "and you can do it."

"You're asking me to throw away my life, I think. Thiede wouldn't take kindly to losing his dream, would he?"

"There are rumors," Ashmael said, "that this is not the first time Thiede has tried this procedure. It has failed before. Whatever he's doing, it must be a risky process and the revenant is fragile. We believe that is why he keeps hara away. Dree managed to grill him for information and Thiede told him the entire process takes several years. We don't know how he does it, or what state the revenant is in during this time. I know what I'm asking you to do. I know the risks, and there's nothing I can offer you in return, other than the Hegemony's support. But we feel strongly this process must be aborted before it reaches fruition. Surely you agree with this. It is a crime against nature. If you won't do it for us, do it for the friend you once had in Pellaz."

Seel considered and a frightening image of an undead Pellaz flashed through his mind. Would Pell want Seel to end his life again? Would it be release rather than murder? Those were the salient questions. In Pell's position, Seel would not want to live, not in the manner Ashmael implied, but until he'd seen Pell for himself Seel couldn't know what was the best thing to do. "How would I do it?" he asked.

"I don't know. I can't give you any prior intelligence. You would have to use your initiative. It may be that you will find the task impossible. We know that. We just want you to try. If we leave it for much longer, it might be too late."

"Thiede would kill me if he found out. I don't want to die just yet."

"We have faith in your creativity," Ashmael said, leaning back in his chair. "If there is a way to do it without arousing suspicion, we are sure you will find it. You need only to convince Thiede the reason you want to see Pellaz is because you are concerned for his welfare. Thiede will believe this, because he'll want to believe it. You are the only har he knows who was close to Pellaz. Orien would have been better, of course, because he was always at Thiede's beck and call, but that avenue is closed. He needs you, Seel, and none of us really knows why. You are part of the process, clearly. And we know you have a good heart, that you will do what's right."

"That is a big assumption. You hardly know me."

"We know enough."

"How flattering."

"Thiede has left you alone, but he's jittery. I don't think a day goes by your name is not mentioned in the Hegalion. He's building you up, making sure the Hegemony think well of you. And we do, but not for the reasons Thiede might want. He will contact you soon, be sure of it. That is the time for you to make your request."

"Very well, I will ask him, but can make no promises other than that."

"It is all we ask. You know our thoughts and I think I know yours. Of course, should it ever arise, this meeting never took place."

"Naturally."

"I too am taking risks, Seel."

"I appreciate that, although perhaps you should have made a more covert approach to my house. I expect there isn't a har in Saltrock who's not aware of your presence here today."

"So? We are friends, aren't we? I won't hide the fact of my visit, only some of the content. The official story is that I have come to see you because I couldn't get you out of my mind after spending time with you in Immanion. Is that unreasonable?"

"No. How far am I expected to go to maintain this cover story?"

"As far as you like. Thiede would be delighted if our friendship were to deepen. He would see it as a means to further his cause."

"Mmm." Seel considered the har before him, who was arrogant and confident, supremely attractive and determined to get his own way. It was amusing to be in such demand.

"More than one har in Immanion has dreams," he said. "I'm not what you think I am."

"It is not my intention to be coarse," Ashmael said. "This aspect of my visit has revealed itself in rather a cumbersome way."

"Clinical, I'd say. The implication is that you are prepared to endure my company in order to achieve your aims."

Ashmael pulled a rueful face. "That's not the case. I'm sorry. When I said I couldn't get you out of my mind, I wasn't lying."

Seel stood up. "Would you like to see the town?"

Ashmael stared at him through narrowed eyes. "That is courteous of you, tiahaar."

"Courtesy costs nothing," Seel said.

A group of younger hara had appointed themselves as grooms to Ashmael's *sedu* horse, which stood near the center of town, idly stamping its hooves and devouring the food offerings made to it. Ashmael went over to the group, and chatting affably told them they could ride the horse if they wanted to. This offer was met with unrestrained cries of delight. The hara were not simply pleased by being able to ride a Gelaming horse, but because Ashmael had spoken to them.

As they walked away, Seel said, "Is that wise, Ash? I don't want my hara disappearing into thin air."

"They won't open a portal, don't worry. Zephyr is a wise beast. He'll trot round like an old nag for them."

"You like a well-trained creature, disciplined to an inch of its life."

"On the contrary. I prefer spirit. Is that your Nayati? How quaint."

Seel took him inside the temple. It felt unused and forlorn since Orien's death, even though hara still used it regularly. It had become a shrine to Orien's memory. Some of them prayed to his spirit there.

Ashmael admired the carved wooden columns that supported the roof and praised the artistic skills of their creators.

Seel only shuddered. "This place should be knocked down and rebuilt," he said, rubbing his arms. He knew the Gelaming had performed banishing and cleansing rituals before the altar, but for him the air would always smell of blood. It was no longer a spiritual place.

He only realized he had closed his eyes when he felt Ashmael's hands on his shoulders. "It's bad for you, Seel," Ashmael said softly. "Let it go. This is part of why you should leave here."

I don't want to fall into your arms so easily, Seel thought, doing so. He didn't want to share breath either, but was powerless to resist, because his heart and body desired it.

"This place is a tomb," Ashmael said. "You don't belong here."

"It is not," Seel snapped. "It's recovering. It will recover."

"It's not your life's work to heal Saltrock's heart," Ashmael said. "You proved something in building this place. It's time to move on."

"Are you sure Thiede didn't send you?"

Ashmael laughed. "You know that he didn't. You want to be what I am. I know you do. You covet what you see in me. And you can have it."

"That's offensive," Seel said. "I'm not like that." But he didn't pull away.

"Aren't you?" Ashmael murmured, running his fingers through Seel's hair. "It's the truth, isn't it? You know you are bigger than what's been given to you, and you deserve more. I respect you, Seel. You will not find betrayal in me." He took Seel's face in his hands to share breath once more, and Seel knew that Ashmael had been referring, if only partly, to Flick. The Gelaming knew all about his private life, because they saw it as their business to know. And who was Flick in comparison to these shining stars of Immanion? Who was he to apportion blame and walk out of Seel's life? A flicker of resentment and grief burned briefly but hot in Seel's heart. In that moment, his decision was made.

Colt and Stringer saw Seel's new relationship with Ashmael as a positive healing thing. They were not aware of the darker undercurrents and Seel didn't enlighten them. Ashmael took to visiting Saltrock fairly regularly. Seel always looked forward to these visits, but somehow they didn't feel real. In bed, Ashmael taught him things he'd never dreamed possible, all the while respecting Seel's pride and pretending Seel already knew of them. Seel felt as if he were being groomed for something. Taking aruna with Ashmael was like being trained to explode the world. He could feel immense power simmering around him and yet he could not dispel the suspicion, however slight, that Thiede's hand was behind it. He was under no illusion that this relationship was permanent.

One day, a few months after Ashmael's first visit, he turned up with Thiede. Seel was not surprised, although would have appreciated some kind of prior warning. It annoyed him that Thiede clearly thought he had won, but he swallowed his pride. It would be stupid to reject what was being offered to him. The glamour of Ashmael's visits had served the purpose of highlighting Saltrock's limitations. His talk of life in Immanion hadn't failed to make an impression. Seel found himself dreaming of living an idyllic life in the sun, which was filled with potential and promise. Thiede had the grace to appear that he thought he still had a lot of convincing to do, so Seel played the game also.

At lunch, Thiede said, "Will you ever come to Immanion, Seel? Must Ashmael forever be absent from the Hegalion coming here to you?"

"It's a big move," Seel said. "There are many things to consider."

"I know the harder I push you, the more you'll dig in your heels, but even so . . ." Thiede shrugged. "It all seems a little pointless and tiresome now."

"I'll need a month or so to sort out my affairs," Seel said, gazing at his plate. He could feel Thiede's immediate tense stillness across the table.

"Whatever time you need. You know that. Any help I can offer . . ."

"And I want to see Pellaz before I make up my mind for definite."

Seel could sense Thiede swapping a sharp glance with Ashmael. He could imagine Ashmael's insouciant shrug, but he didn't look up. Not until he said, "You said you wanted me in Immanion for Pell. Prove to me that's the real reason."

Thiede's silver-gray eyes were like glittering stones. He was not pleased, but also knew he was cornered. "I don't expect you to take my word for it. Of course, you may see him, but he won't be as you remember him. The process is far from complete."

"If I can recognize him, that's enough," Seel said. "I want to do this before I move from Saltrock."

"Am I right in assuming Lord Ashmael's curiosity is at work here as well as your own?"

"This is personal," Seel said, wiping his mouth on a napkin. "Ash can't influence my decisions in this matter."

Ashmael raised his hands. "I wouldn't intrude on such a delicate situation."

"Very well," Thiede said, "although I would have preferred you to wait a little longer until you saw Pellaz."

"Now or never," Seel said. "You didn't produce Cal in chains, but at least you can grant me this."

"The first matter is not forgotten, I assure you," Thiede said. "And I promise you I will fulfill my promise. We had a deal. But as a mark of trust, I will grant this request also."

"Thank you," said Seel. His heart was beating too fast, his ears zinging with white noise. Soon, there would be no going back.

The journey to the place where Pellaz was kept would take no time at all, not in the otherlanes. Thiede assured Seel he could be back at Saltrock in time for supper. Seel was unnerved. This was all too quick. He would need time with Pell, and it was clear Thiede wasn't prepared to give it. When Thiede went to the bathroom, Seel couldn't even discuss it too openly with Ashmael, because both of them were aware that Thiede was too close for comfort and might eavesdrop on them psychically. "You'll be fine," Ashmael said. "Don't worry."

"I'm not looking forward to what I might see," Seel said. He felt cold, although the room was warm. His jaw ached. "If this is for real, every instinct inside me is screaming for me to keep away."

"You don't have to put yourself through this," Thiede said. He stood at the doorway.

"I do. For Pell," Seel said. "Will he know me?"

"No," Thiede said. "That's impossible."

"What am I going to see?" Seel asked.

Thiede smiled cruelly. "Squeamish? I wouldn't expect that from a har who once ran with the Unneah."

Ashmael reached out and gripped Seel's cold hands, which were knotted together on the table. "I will be waiting," he said. "Zephyr will take care of you."

The *sedim* broke through into the world in a place that was as icy as the otherlanes. It was clearly a far northern country, hardly touched by human or harish hand. Snow covered the ancient pine forests and sound was muted. A short distance away, on a sheer hillside, a castle of white stone nestled at the edge of a forest. Lights glowed in the windows. It was nearly dusk.

"This is where I conduct my most secret experiments," Thiede said in an arch tone.

"Where are we?" Seek asked.

"Oh, a very cold place. Private. Come, let's make haste. I dislike the cold."

The *sedim* galloped over the hard-packed snow, their glistening coats appearing drab against the aching whiteness, where blue shadows were forming. Seel's coat was not thick enough to keep him warm. Thiede hadn't warned him about the cold. By the time they reached the castle courtyard, Seel's hands and nose were numb, even though they'd ridden for only a half-mile or so.

Hara were waiting in the yard, as if they were expecting Thiede. He must have sent advance notice of his visit. "Warm drinks, if you please," he ordered, striding past the grooms who took the reins of the horses.

Seel followed him into the castle. Inside, it was very warm and comfortably furnished. The rooms were much smaller than Seel expected and had a strangely unlived in ambience. Thiede marched into a sitting room and went to stand before the hearth, where a ferocious fire devoured a mountain of pine logs. "I'm glad you've decided to join us in Immanion," he said, holding out his hands to the flames.

Seel went to stand beside him, conscious of Thiede's immense height. In his presence, Seel felt like a child. "There was only so much resistance I could put up," he said. "After a point, it becomes futile, if not self-indulgent. I know what you are offering and I'm flattered by your opinion of me. I only hope I deserve it."

"You do. Don't think you'll just be Pell's companion. I have work for you, great work."

A deferential har appeared at the doorway carrying a tray of steaming mugs. The delicious smell of hot chocolate spiced with liquor eclipsed the scent of burning pine. Thiede took both mugs from the tray and handed one to Seel. "Don't worry about seeing Pell. It's not that dreadful."

"I have accepted many impossible things in my life," Seel said, "but I never thought I'd have to accept this. I feel very . . . strange."

"That's quite natural. I will have a hard job convincing the Hegemony about Pell, you know. And he will have an even harder job living up to my expectations. We will both need you, Seel."

"What about his mind?" Seel asked. "How will this . . . process . . . affect it?"

Thiede shrugged and took a sip of his drink. "Impossible to predict. I'll do what I can for him, believe me."

The drinks were finished too soon for Seel's liking. He felt he needed more time to compose and prepare himself, but Thiede was already ushering him out of the door.

Seel followed Thiede up several flights of stairs and through a maze of corridors. There didn't seem to be many hara around, although Seel could sometimes hear the sound of doors closing in the distance and the pad of feet on the carpeted floors. He felt completely disorientated. He didn't want to see this. And yet he did. The thought of murder was far from his mind. He hoped only to live through the next few minutes with his sanity intact.

It can't be any worse than what happened to Orien, he thought, *and you coped with that. Remember who you are, and what you've seen. You can do this.*

Thiede stopped at a white door and turned the key that stuck out of it. They kept something inside that room, locked up. Seel swallowed sour saliva.

Thiede pushed open the door. "Here we are. Would you like me to come in with you, or would you prefer to do this alone?"

"Alone," Seel said. He realized he might never leave this place, because his conscience could force him to do something inside that room for which Thiede would punish him severely. Now, it did not seem to matter. Only an hour before, he would never have put himself at risk in this way, but the feelings of horror, which it took all his strength to control, made him acknowledge that some things might be more important than his own life. He closed his eyes as he stepped past Thiede. He found himself uttering a prayer to Orien's spirit. "Be with me, old friend."

The door closed behind him and he opened his eyes. It was a white room, too white, and almost empty but for the structure at its center. Seel's first impression was that it was a kind of vat, a processing machine. Thick coiled pipes that were like intestines rose from its sides and disappeared through padded holes in the ceiling. It was surrounded by long, diaphanous curtains that moved slightly. There was no draught in the room, but Seel smelled a strange lemony, musky scent and perceived an almost inaudible humming sound. He stared ahead of himself for agonizing seconds, then walked quickly across the room and threw back the curtains.

The structure was made of some transparent material that was not glass: it appeared organic, like an immense pod from an alien plant, and was roughly oval in shape. It was full of milky green liquid and rested on a plinth of pipes and struts. Something hung inside it, a drowned thing. A body with long black hair that floated around it. Snaking narrow pipes like tendrils of black vine grew into its flesh. The arms were bent up against the chest, the hands twisted claws. The head was turned to the side, its face clouded by hair.

Seel steadied himself and placed the palm of one hand against the pod's surface. It was warm and a faint vibration passed through his fingers. He felt light-headed and nauseous. He must not think that what he saw before him might be a dead body brought back to life. No, Cal had burned the body. This was something else. For some moments, he took deep breaths and calmed himself, willed his disorientation to abate.

"Pell," he said aloud. He couldn't tell if the body in the pod was Pellaz or not. It was not as hideous to behold as he'd feared, but there was no way he could be sure of identifying the har within. The body hung motionless, lifeless.

Seel lowered his hand, exhaled slowly. He glanced up at the coiling pipes, which must surely provide life support of some kind. Should he attempt to sabotage the pod now? He couldn't be sure. He didn't know what he was looking at. Impulsively, he knocked against the surface with his knuckles, not really expecting a response, but at once the body within the pod jerked violently.

Seel jumped back in alarm. Inside the pod, bubbles streamed from the har's mouth, and his hair threshed around him. The head snapped back, eyes closed.

"Pell," Seel breathed. There was no mistake. He knew that face, still beautiful. Dreamer Pell was living the ultimate dream, hanging there in an unnatural womb. "You didn't die," Seel said. "You couldn't have. Thiede fooled Cal, didn't he? That's what happened. It must be." But how could a har live in liquid?

Slowly Pell's head turned this way and that and then the eyes opened. Only he had no eyes. Then Seel realized there were orbs in the sockets that were completely black. Pell's lips peeled back in a snarl, and his teeth were yellow jagged stumps. The inside of his mouth was livid green and raw red. Not perfect, far from it. There was no sense of intelligence, personality, or soul in what hung there.

"Kill it," Seel murmured to himself. "Do something." He felt remarkably calm.

Pell's clawed hands unfurled and he reached out. He placed his long fingers against the inside of the pod's surface. Seel was impelled to raise his own hand again, press it against the outside. They were almost touching. He closed his eyes for a moment and the briefest, lightest mind touch brushed against his thoughts. "I am here."

Seel opened his eyes. "Tell me quickly," he said, in mind touch. "Do you want release from this?"

The black eyes regarded him without expression. "I . . . Am . . . Pellaz . . ."

There was strength behind the thought, the instinct to survive. With his lips closed, he looked beautiful again. His black eyes were full of stars like the depths of the universe.

"You will come back to us," Seel said, more to himself than to Pell. "You really will."

"I . . . Am . . . Loved . . ."

"Yes," Seel said. "You are. A har has died because of that love. Do you know me?"

"I . . . Am . . ." Pell's eyelids flickered and closed, and the light mind touch faded away. The effort of communication had clearly exhausted what little strength he had. Had he sensed Seel's intention and dragged himself from whatever deep place his being inhabited to stop Seel killing him? Seel believed so. He stepped through the curtains and rearranged them carefully. Thiede came into the room. Seel could not look at him.

"You couldn't do it, could you," Thiede said.

"I did. I'm not that squeamish."

"You know what I mean."

Seel glanced at him and began to walk toward the door.

Thiede caught hold of his arm. "You came here to kill him. Don't think I didn't know."

Seel pulled his arm away, walked out of the room.

After locking the door once more, Thiede followed him. "I knew you wouldn't, just as I knew that Ashmael would ask you to."

Seel stopped and faced Thiede. "Would you have stopped me if you'd been wrong?"

"Of course, only I knew there was no danger. It was necessary, this visit. It will prove to the Hegemony I'm right. I bear no malice about the incident. In Ashmael's place, I'd have done the same, as I would in yours. I never underestimate my most valued hara. It is what makes them special."

"I couldn't kill Pell, but that doesn't make it right, what you're doing."

"Save your opinions until you have witnessed his return," Thiede said, "then you may talk to me of whether I'm right or wrong."

"But why let him die only to do this? Why didn't you just take him from Saltrock with you and train him yourself?"

Thiede laughed softly. "Oh, Seel, do you seek to pry my secrets from me? I'll tell you this. I incepted Pell, and he became part of me because of it, but not a big enough part. I was prepared for his death . . ."

"Because you arranged it?" Seel snapped. "That's barbaric."

Thiede didn't respond to the question. "I was able to net the essence of his being in . . . let's call it 'transit.' You must appreciate that I have access to advanced technology, the like of which has not seen on this world before. The *sedim,* for example. The incubation pod you saw in Pell's room is from the same origin. It will take time, but eventually, Pellaz will be in the condition to accept more of my life essence, not through blood, or through aruna, but something more. He will become more than any other har."

"More than you?"

"I wouldn't go *that* far. Wraeththu need something, or somehar, to bind them. They need a figurehead, a divine ruler. I am making one for them."

"Did Pell have a choice about it?"

"Unfortunately, no. He will resent that for a time, I expect."

"I'm weak. I should have killed him when I had the chance."

"Don't delude yourself," Thiede said in a sharper tone. "Pellaz wants to live, as all living creatures do. He just can't help it. It's a biological imperative. Thankfully, he'll retain no memory of your murderous impulses. He will never know you saw him in that state."

"Take me back to Saltrock," Seel said. "You've got what you wanted."

"Indeed I have. You will visit Immanion soon to see the house I've had built for you. I expect you to move in within a month. You will be pleased to know I've allocated a *sedu* to you. Your training in controlling it begins in two days' time. I'll send a teacher to Saltrock with the animal."

"We're all your puppets," Seel said angrily. "We are all hanging in pods, hooked up to pipes, breathing fluid. I can't fight you, Thiede, but I have your measure."

"Good. I wouldn't expect anything less of you." Thiede put an arm around Seel's shoulder and began to lead him up the corridor.

Seel glanced back once at the door. He felt numb.

CHAPTER THIRTEEN

The gods came to Flick at any time of day or night. He would be walking in the hills, and a name would come to him. One time, as he watched a flight of birds erupt from the canopy of trees and spiral, screeching, into the sky, he heard in his mind the name Miyacala, and an image came to him of a tall, white-haired har, whose eyes were milky blind, but whose forehead burned with a silver star. Flick knew then that Miyacala needed no physical eyes to see, for his sight was of the psychic kind. He was a god of initiation and magic, and those hara who studied and honed their skills walked in the prints of his sacred feet.

One night, as Itzama lay beside Flick, breathing softly in sleep, and Flick's body ached for a release that Itzama could never give it, he saw a black deity, with serpentine hair, whose eyes were burning red. He was a fearsome god, and he reigned over life, aruna and death. His name was Aruhani and he could smite as quickly as he could bless.

The third god that came to Flick was Lunil, a creature of the moon, whose skin was blue and whose hair was a smoke of stars. These were the dehara, harish gods.

Sometimes, Flick dreamed of returning to the world of Wraeththu, coming like a prophet with a sacred text to inspire and enlighten. Then he asked himself:

why should anyone listen to what he had to say? It was his own imaginings, and his pantheon was personal. If he went to Seel with his creations, Seel would only scoff, and the imagined humiliation of this made Flick's face burn. But mythologies continued to pour from his mind and occasionally he would catch brief glimpses of spirit faces among the trees, or hiding amid the rocks. He heard their voices in the rill of the stream, in the cry of birds and in the wind in the mesquites. There were no more dreams of Pellaz, but perhaps he too had become a god. Pellaz, god of martyrs.

There was no need to write any of this down, because once Flick had a thought, it stayed with him. It was as if he'd known these imagined entities all his life and had always respected and honored them. Itzama told him that certain god forms recurred throughout every human culture, therefore it was no surprise that Wraeththu should have their own. "They are not Wraeththu's, they are mine," Flick said, and realized he was uncertain he wanted anyone else to believe in them.

Sometimes, Flick remembered that the Hostling of Bones had told him he would train for a year and a day, and when this recollection came to him, he always pushed it away. He did not want his life to change again—not yet. He did not love Itzama, even though the man was handsome, kind, and devoted. It was pointless to fall in love, because Flick knew that they would not be together for long. With experimentation, they had devised ways to enjoy physical intimacy, but it was not aruna. Itzama derived more pleasure from it than Flick did. Despite this, they had a companionable relationship and there was an easiness between them that Flick had not experienced before.

Itzama never revealed his background, and Flick often wondered whether he was an outcast and had committed a crime. He could not imagine why else such a sociable creature would choose to live alone. On the night of visions, he'd spoken briefly and vaguely about having been called to this place, but he would not expand upon it. He'd implied he wasn't quite human, but Flick saw no evidence to the contrary. There was definitely a secret, but on the few occasions Flick tried to press the matter—the best time, he discovered, was after sex—Itzama was not merely vague; it seemed as if he himself didn't know the answers. Maybe, he'd suffered an injury in the past that had affected his memory. One time he said, "When you leave, then I will go too," and Flick thought, not without discomfort, that Itzama meant to accompany him. He knew that one day he would have to return to the world of Wraeththu in one way or another and he couldn't take Itzama there, not as a human.

"You would have to be incepted," he said, rather abruptly, and Itzama stared at him with a confused expression on his face.

"No," he said at last. "I didn't mean that. When you leave this place, I will leave it too, because I think you are the only thing that anchors me here."

"Where will you go?"

"Where I came from," Itzama replied. "The place I have forgotten."

"There is no future for you if you remain human," Flick said. "Perhaps you should consider inception. It seems such a waste if you just grow old and die. You are too beautiful for that."

Itzama only smiled and Flick sensed the man did not believe he would grow old and die. He was never around during the day, and it did cross Flick's mind that Itzama might be a ghost after all, but how could a ghost have a living body? Whatever the truth of the matter was, Flick and Itzama had an understanding, and eventually Flick did not even ask questions. They were living outside the real world, where the strange and perplexing were the natural order.

When nearly a year had passed, Itzama reminded Flick of what he had learned in his vision quest. "You must speak with the dead," he said. "Remember what you were told."

Flick didn't want to be reminded of this, because it meant he would have to make decisions about the future. Also, he had no desire to talk to someone dead. It would all be in his head, or a product of one of Itzama's hallucinogenic concoctions, and Flick was hardly eager to find out what his mind would conjure up. At the very least, it would be Pellaz, uttering further impenetrable riddles. "This is my life now," Flick said. "Here with you. Learning. Magic. It's all I want. I'm not yet ready for changes."

"It cannot be," Itzama said. "You cannot receive all this knowledge and then keep it yourself. It belongs to your people. The shaman goes into the otherworld to help his tribe. This is your duty. You have your gods, now you must communicate with them."

"No one can call up the dead," Flick said. "I don't believe in it."

Itzama smiled his slow lazy smile. "The shaman can do anything if he has a suitable source of power. You have one, so use it."

On the appointed night, to keep Itzama quiet rather than to please himself, Flick killed a large rabbit. He carried it to a small ritual site he used among the stones and tumbling waters of the stream near the cave. There was an area where the water flattened out and ran more smoothly in a wide shallow pool beneath an overhang. Here, Flick drained the body of the rabbit of blood and collected it in a bowl. The moon burned fat above him and the North Star was a god's jewel in the sky. Shadows were like velvet, and the undergrowth rattled as if shaken by spirit hands. There was a presence to the air, but perhaps this was because of what he was doing. It felt primitive and powerful, a primal rite from the dawn of time.

Flick lit a fire and stood before it. He wore only, wrapped around his loins, the skin of a coyote that had been given to him by Itzama. He loosed his hair and held his arms to the sky. Now, he must do it. Now, he must believe. He would call upon one of the deities he had named. In his mind, he saw Aruhani, his braided hair like snakes. This was not a comfortable image, for Aruhani was capricious and sometimes sly. But he was the god of life, sex, and death, so the most appropriate in this instance. Flick concentrated on the image in his head. He tried to feel the deity as well as see him. He took a deep breath and called, "Aruhani, I call you! Come to me now, in the name of the Aghama, the principle of creation! I command you! I bring blood as an offering. Hear me and approach!"

Flick's heart was beating fast. When he opened his eyes, the whole night seemed tinged a reddish-purple and a high-pitched hum vibrated on the edge of his perception. He poured a little of the blood into the folding ripples of the stream and in the bright moonlight saw its black streak spread out and slip away. Flick dropped to his knees beside the water, his hair hanging forward to wave upon the current, black as blood. He gazed at the glittering depths and then was compelled to jump to his feet. He ran out into the stream, beneath the dark shadows of the overhanging rocks and he danced in the water. He chanted the name of Aruhani, spinning around faster and faster, sending up a spray of sparkling motes. Itzama had told him that magic without a source of power was not magic at all, but simply a game, a play, a deceit. He had to feel the power, really feel it, before continuing, because otherwise it would be pointless, an empty rite. He spun round until he felt he was about to collapse into the water, then flung himself onto the bank of the stream.

Lying on his stomach, he said, "Aruhani, open my eyes that I might see. Open my ears that I might hear. Open my heart that I may sense the dead approach, open my mouth that my voice will be heard beyond the realm of this earth."

The night had become still, listening to him. Even the plash of the water was quieter. Flick hauled himself to his feet and went to sit beside his fire. He threw some sage wood into it. Sparks sizzled up toward the moon and the astringent smell of the herb filled the air. Flick held out his hands to the flames. He should feel cold, but he didn't. When he spoke again, his voice sounded lower in tone; it vibrated in his chest. "Aruhani, come forth to me. Give strength to my hands that I shall be strong, that I may keep the dead within my power."

He then took up the bowl of blood and spilled it over the earth. Black blood. Slick and shining, like the blood down the stairs, as ancient as the handprint over the doorframe, as sweet as the smell in the Nayati that morning, when the sun came through the windows in precise perfect rays and a white arm dangled down. Flick swallowed thickly. He must not think this, he mustn't. The images would be too terrible. Aruhani was with him, but the dehar was not a creature of sweetness. He had fangs and claws and his shadow was long. Flick closed his eyes again. He had to speak. His hands dangled between his knees.

"I conjure you, creature of darkness. I summon you, creature of spirit. I summon and call you forth from the abode of darkness. I evoke you from your resting place in the caves of the earth. I summon your eyes to behold the brightness of my fire, which is the fire of life. I evoke you from your resting place. I summon your ears to hear my words. Come forth, dead spirit, who might speak with me. Come forth in the name of Aruhani, dehar of life and death, whose word binds you. I command you to come forth."

He could hear the crackle of the fire, smell the sage mixed with the scent of burning charcoal. He could taste blood in the back of his throat, so he must open his eyes now. He must.

Orien sat on the other side of the fire, smiling mildly. His tawny hair escaped his braid in soft tendrils, as it always had. He did not appear remotely dead. Flick was so surprised he scrabbled backward, and yet wasn't this what he'd worked for and believed in? Did he trust himself so little?

Orien put his head to one side, but said nothing. There was a sadness in his eyes, which Flick thought might be pity.

"Speak!" Flick managed to say. From this moment, his entire life had changed. He should be driven insane by what he saw before him, but it wasn't frightening at all. That was the strangest thing. Perhaps Itzama had fed him some drug and he hadn't realized it.

"You have come a long way," Orien said.

"Not as far as you," Flick said. "Can you remember, Orien? Can you remember what happened?"

"You were nearly there, but the diversion was perfect. The last of the human tribes called the shaman here, but they went away and you found him."

"What do you mean? Itzama?"

"The people of this land were a very ancient race. When Wraeththu came, the wisest among them called upon an ancestor of strong magic to aid them. They called him forth from the past, they danced the spirit dance to call him. But they were driven away before he came, so he had no purpose, until you."

"Itzama isn't a ghost, but he isn't exactly *real* either," Flick said, to himself rather than Orien. "He is never around during the day. Where does he go?"

"You cannot see an ancestor spirit in sunlight," Orien said. "There is a purpose to everything. You must go back. You carve the words from stone, but they already exist in stone. Aruhani is a stone book in the library that no one ever wrote before. You have written him and read him. He has taken your mentor, Itzama, back into himself, to release him from his bondage to this world. He has served the dehara in giving you his knowledge."

"Has he been taken already?"

"It is time now for what will happen next."

"Orien, do you know me?"

"You missed the message, in the air, in the clouds. You walked passed it. But it is time now. There is something to be brought forth, but it is in need of nurturing. It is a secret, hidden. One of many, but this one is yours, even if it is not yours alone."

He looked beautiful, serene as he'd ever been, but Flick knew that Orien could not really see him. Orien was only a perfect shadow. He could never *be* again. He wasn't answering questions; he was a spirit with a message, no more than an image programmed by the energy of a god. But perhaps there were some questions he would answer, namely the ones Flick was supposed to ask. "Should I go back to Saltrock, or to the settlement I passed?" he asked. "I command you to tell me."

"The birthplace of Pellaz Cevarro, that is the place. It is the fountainhead."

"Thank you," Flick said. "I release you. Go in peace."

Flick didn't even blink, but in a splinter of a second, Orien was no longer there. He might never have been there, and from the moment he vanished, Flick began to doubt what he'd seen and heard. But at the same time he knew it was the most real experience he'd ever gone through. He had seen the image of his dead friend. He could have reached out and touched him, but, if he had, Orien would have broken apart like a reflection in a pool.

For some minutes, Flick surrendered himself to grief. He wept for the tragedy and the senseless waste. He wept for Cal, who was so damaged and for Seel, who had tried hard to escape his beginnings. But tears would not wash away the past. They lanced the infected wound, but could not eradicate its scar.

Flick rubbed his face and scattered damp sand over his fire until it sizzled out. He got to his feet and thanked Aruhani for his aid, bidding him to depart. It was clear, from the feeling in the air, that the dehar had already gone.

Flick went back into the cave, hoping to discuss with Itzama what had happened, but not sure what he would find. From the moment he set foot inside, Flick could tell that Itzama had indeed gone. Their home was no longer a living space, but an empty cavern of stone. It was hard to believe he had ever lived there. Itzama and Flick had been almost like lovers, but now Flick could not mourn Itzama's disappearance. He had been called to this world and abandoned. It was only right he should be released.

The fabric of the otherworld, in which this site had been caught for over a year, was breaking apart like rotten silk, and Flick knew he should, at the very least, be disturbed, but he felt strangely calm and centered. Outside, the night bristled with sentience and power, and a road led to the northwest. At the end of it, ancient mills creaked in the breeze and secrets slithered through the shadows. The past came back in a surge like a tidal wave. A year ago was only yesterday, the rest a dream. He had missed something. He must return.

CHAPTER FOURTEEN

The settlement had changed within a year. The burned fields were a riot of new growth and in the late autumn were full of unharvested crops. Weeds had spread throughout the little streets and grew upon the roofs of the houses. The landscape looked softer, greened over as it was, as if it was melting back into the earth. There was sense of wistful melancholy, for all that had gone before and vanished, and as Flick rode Ghost among the buildings, a fine misty rain began to fill the air. On a day like this, Cal had come here. Flick knew the story by heart because Cal had told it to him countless times. If Pell had not responded to Cal, or had been somewhere else at the crucial moment, none of what followed would have happened.

Ghost's hoofbeats echoed between the walls of empty dwellings, which seemed to have moved closer together since the last time Flick had seen them. His spine crawled as he passed into the shadows.

The last thing flick expected was for someone to jump down onto him from an overhanging eave. He didn't expect to be pushed from his horse, nor to land heavily on his back in the damp dirt with strong thin hands already around his neck and bony knees forced into his chest. All he could see was misty air and the writhing vines of thrashing black hair, hair that was so heavy it could only move in slow motion. It was at this moment that he realized a ghost had come to kill him. His head banged painfully against the ground and when he grabbed hold of the skinny wrists above him, he felt the bones grind beneath the brown skin. "Pell, stop!" he managed to croak. "Didn't I do what you asked? Didn't I?"

The apparition on top of him let go of his neck and straightened up, tucked its hair behind its ears. "Who the fuck are you?" it snapped, and it wasn't Pell at all, but could only be *of* Pell, so therefore a surviving relative.

"Get off me and I'll tell you," Flick said.

Reluctantly, his assailant got up and stood with folded arms before him or rather over him, because at first Flick was too winded and dizzy to move. "Well?"

"My name is Flick," he said. "Pell asked me to come here, to find you, to tell you."

"Tell me what? My brother is dead. He became one of you and he died. What else is there to say?"

Flick got to his feet. Ghost had run off and now stood staring fearfully some yards away. "Pell wanted me to come. He told me he had brothers. I never hoped to find one of you alive."

"You didn't. I'm his sister. Or I was . . ."

"You still are," Flick said, privately wondering how a female could possibly be as androgynous as her phenomenal brother had been, without the benefit of the changes Pell had undergone. "He never forgot you. You are Mima, yes?"

"Yes." She sighed heavily, scraped her hands through her hair. "You're too late. I'm the only one left, and not much use to you. You might as well leave."

"Can't we talk? Don't you want to know what I have to say?"

She was silent for a moment. "His friends are always turning up here. Wonder who will be next? I hope it's Cal, I really do. I hope he finds his way."

Flick could tell she wanted to settle the score with Cal, but there were few people who didn't. "Who else? How many?"

"Just one, actually. He's a Kakkahaar."

"A friend of Pell's." Flick wracked his brains for the memory. "Lianvis?"

"No, Ulaume."

"Really!" Flick exclaimed. "From what I heard he was hardly a friend."

"I know the story," Mima said. "Ulaume is obsessed with Pell." She shrugged. "Maybe there will be others like him. This place has become a shrine. Ulaume doesn't think Pell's really dead. What do you think?"

Flick answered carefully. "He was important. There is more to the story than we know. Our story. I'm from Saltrock, where Pell was incepted."

"Ulaume's told me about that place."

"Cal returned to Saltrock," Flick said. "He killed one of my dearest friends, because he blamed him for Pell's death. The story isn't over. Everything is still rippling or vibrating or something. I had to come here."

"Ulaume is up at the white house," Mima said. "Perhaps you two should talk."

Mima kept guard over the settlement because, despite Ulaume's assurances to the contrary, she feared that one day the Wraeththu who had devastated her home and family would return to finish her off. She wasn't concerned for herself so much as for Lileem, who she loved passionately. She could tell when someone was Wraeththu or human immediately now. She had perceived a spectral light around Flick and knew it for what it was. She had also realized he'd posed no threat but had attacked him regardless, because even though she'd known they'd end up talking, it helped scratch the nerve of pain inside her to beat him up a little before this happened. She had new strengths and most of them she enjoyed having. She took Ulaume and Lileem for granted because they had become like family, but this new har intrigued her. He looked like a boy, pale-skinned and elfin, with his long hair in braids. Perhaps Ulaume would take aruna with him, because it seemed so important, and the thought of this intrigued Mima even more. Despite her rages and resentments, she had become a precarious part of Wraeththu, forever excluded from its mysteries in some ways, but nevertheless attached and curious. She found she did not want Flick to think of her as a human female, but also felt shy of telling him anything to the contrary. It would sound embarrassing and coarse. Ulaume would have to tell him.

Flick had calmed his pony and now walked with Mima up the hill to the house.

"This was where the owner of the farm lived," she said. "Sefton Richards. He's dead now, but who isn't?"

"Did Ulaume save you from the raiders?" Flick asked.

"No, I saved myself. Ulaume came later, but not much later. Just as well. They would have done something awful to him, and the harling."

"Harling? Ulaume has a child?"

"Not his own. Lileem is . . . well, different. You'll see."

"I've never seen one, hardly believed it was possible."

"Perhaps it isn't. Maybe you're not meant to breed."

"What do you mean? Is something wrong with the harling?"

"No, she's perfect."

"Ah . . ." Flick smiled to himself. "I *see*."

The harling in question came bounding out of the house as Mima and Flick were putting the pony into one of the empty stables. "Mima, Mima, *who's this?*" it demanded. To Flick, the child looked very much like he'd imagined a Wraeththu harling would look: neither male nor female, but something of both. As it should be. It appeared to be around four or five years old, with the somewhat exotic look of the Kakkahaar in the catlike eyes and golden skin.

"Leelee, this is Flick," Mima said, "a friend of my brother's." She pulled the harling back against her, who leaned against her legs, staring up at Flick in unconcealed curiosity.

Ulaume had come out of the house and his expression was hostile. "A visitor," he said, "how nice."

"Behave," Mima said, "be friendly. Flick is from Saltrock."

"The home of fine upstanding hara," Ulaume said. "The ones that transformed your brother into a little pillar of piety."

"Flick wants to talk to you," Mima said, wondering how long it would take for Ulaume's fur to stop standing on end. He was so much like a cat sometimes. How much ritual spitting and hissing, and occasional swipes would there be, before he settled down to purring and curling up to exchange licks, or whatever it was they did?

"We don't get many visitors," Mima said to Flick, "and look what that has done for some of our manners."

"It's okay," Flick said. "I don't care about manners. Could use a drink though."

"Come in," Ulaume said spitefully and marched back into the house, slamming the door behind him.

"Lormy is so rude!" said the harling.

"It's territory, kitten," Mima said, "that's all it is."

Destiny had brought Flick to Casa Ricardo and there had been a dysfunctional family waiting there for him. From the minute he stepped into the house, Flick knew there was work to be done and that his fingers were itching to do it. This was not a home. It was makeshift, unkempt, and unloved, although it was clear that cursory attempts at comforts had been made. But it was a far cry from the amenities of Saltrock. He had come here to give Mima the information about Pell, and this he did at once, but there was more than that. Mima told him about Lileem, while Ulaume remained stubbornly silent on the matter. There were questions that needed answers. Orien had directed Flick to come here. Was it simply to help these people? Flick did not tell any of them about his visions, not at first. He must wait and see. Lileem was perhaps part of the future he had been brought here to witness.

That first night, after dinner, which Flick had cooked for them, Mima said, "What are you going to do now, Flick? Where will you go?"

"I don't know," Flick replied. "I need to think about it. I wonder if I might stay here with you for a time."

Ulaume made a noise of annoyance and left the table. He slammed the kitchen door as he left the house.

"Don't mind him," Mima said. "He'll come around."

"Perhaps I shouldn't stay," Flick said.

"No, *do* stay!" Lileem cried. "Please, please, please!"

Mima wiped bread around the gravy on her plate, then consumed it with relish. "I, for one, look forward to more of this! How about a deal? You cook for us, we let you stay."

"Yes!" Lileem yelled.

"I'll more than cook," Flick said. "Believe me, I'm adept at housekeeping *and* at fixing the plumbing."

Mima laughed. "Wonderful. I think I like you, Flick from Saltrock."

He inclined his head. "Likewise, Mima Cevarro."

"Sorry I beat you up earlier."

"Forgiven."

For some months, the house consumed Flick's attention. He worked on the water-heating system, which was similar to the one Seel had constructed for the house in Saltrock. He repaired the roof and replaced broken windows with glass from the dwellings down the hill. With Lileem's and Mima's help, he cleared rooms and reorganized furniture, so that they could have proper bedrooms and a living room, as well as the kitchen. He said that when four individuals lived together, they needed more than one comfortable room, so that they could get away from one another sometimes. This was an offering to Ulaume, although if he realized it he did not show it and certainly wasn't grateful. They also had a proper dining room, that they had yet to use, but envisaged would be suitable for birthday celebrations and such like.

Flick took Mima and Lileem out into the fields and beyond to round up what remained of the old farm stock: a few goats, sheep, and cattle and—most useful of all—a family of burros. Now, they could ride together to neighboring farms, which were often more than a day's journey away, to collect samples of surviving crops to plant in their own land, as well as any further stray animals, which they could add to their breeding stock.

Ulaume watched all these activities with the same sour expression he wore while eating Flick's meals. He would not become involved in them and rarely spoke to Flick directly. Flick knew that Ulaume wished he would leave and that it would be a good idea to try and include Ulaume more in what they were doing. Lileem and Mima constantly praised Flick's efforts, and this made Ulaume feel superfluous and useless. Flick thought this was a shame, because whatever Ulaume was like, he had brought Lileem to safety and had done what he could to create a home. But Flick's pride balked at the continued sullen behavior and he couldn't bring himself to extend a hand of friendship until Ulaume realized it would be better to thaw than continue to freeze. There was no indication this would happen in the near future.

If it hadn't been for Mima and Lileem, who Flick grew to love very quickly, he would have moved on from Casa Ricardo. Fortunately, the warmth of the others more than made up for Ulaume's frigid silences and the stultifying atmosphere he seemed to carry around with him like a bad smell. Flick felt slightly guilty about it, because he knew that Ulaume thought his life had been spoiled. Flick didn't want to be Ulaume's enemy, or to cause him hurt in any way, but he couldn't see how the matter could be put right. He couldn't be so selfless as to leave the settlement just to please the Kakkahaar.

Each night Flick would go out beneath the stars and perform small rituals to Aruhani, with whom he felt a particular affinity, and occasionally to Lunil. He did this to keep in touch with the dehara. He sought further information, although none was forthcoming. Perhaps he needed Itzama's potions for that. He had brought some of the fungus with him from the cave, but shrank from using it alone.

One night, Lileem followed him in secret, waited until he'd finished his devotions, then emerged from cover to ask him what he was doing. Flick sensed immediately the burning curiosity within the harling, the hunger for experience and secrets. He told her all he knew and Lileem sat listening, her eyes wide, brimming with new ideas. Occasionally, she would interrupt him to add to his story. "Lunil keeps a bird with silver feathers who has three heads. One speaks only the truth, another only lies, while the third speaks in riddles."

Flick wasn't sure whether Lileem genuinely added details to his pantheon or was just making it up like a fairy story, but perhaps it didn't matter. She was imaginative and he liked the things she invented. Lileem clearly loved the idea of the dehara and would pester Flick for stories all the time. She insisted that one night she had seen Lunil with her own eyes. He had flown out of the moon as a flock of ghostly owls, only to transform into a silver-skinned har with blue hair, who had danced in the tree outside her bedroom window and sung to her. Lunil was an especial favorite of hers. Together, she and Flick created myths. He began to teach her how to read and write, and was astounded at her brightness and eagerness to learn. Lileem practiced her new skills by making up illustrated stories about the dehara, using pencils she and Flick had found in an old desk in the house. Sometimes, they used one of her drawings as a focus during ritual, in the way that a statue might be used. Flick told Lileem about cult statues and the harling immediately thought about how they could make their own. She used mud from the streams, but was not pleased with the results. Her fingers couldn't reproduce the fabulous entities she saw in her head.

Lileem was a constant source of wonder to Flick. She was impossible, yet perfect, an ideal companion, who shared his new love of the mysterious and unseen. They worked well together, like a magician and his apprentice. She learned quickly. He was curious about what she actually was and for some weeks debated about whether to ask her intimate questions. Eventually, he introduced the subject and found she didn't mind talking about it. She told him that once she had thought about it all the time, how different and how similar she might be to Ulaume, but now she didn't consider it much at all. It no longer seemed important. "Not since you came," she said. "You're showing me better things."

She looked as if she were a human child of five or so, yet her manner and her intelligence were far more mature. "Will you show me something, Lee?" Flick asked. "I want to understand about you. Can I see what your body is like?"

She hesitated for a moment, then shook her head. "No, I don't want to do that. It wouldn't feel right."

"That's okay. Don't worry about it."

"Perhaps when I'm older," she said gravely.

"There may be others like you," Flick said, and Lileem cast him a strange, furtive glance.

"Maybe," she said. "Maybe we'll never know."

Sefton Richards had owned quite an impressive library, and Flick began teaching Lileem from its books. They would sit together at the wide desk in the old dark room, with the morning light falling in upon them, making a pool of radiance near the window.

One day, Lileem pored over an old biology book, studying the diagrams of human bodies. "How strange to be so . . . ," she wrinkled up her nose, "*incomplete.*"

"Perhaps you could try drawing what a har looks like, what you look like," Flick said carefully.

"Okay." She pushed her hair back behind her ears and began to draw slowly. "Men and women must have been really jealous of one another."

"That's an interesting way of looking at things."

Lileem grinned, because she liked compliments. Presently, she handed her drawing to Flick and he had to suppress a smile. "Lileem, there are all sorts of extras on this! Don't tell me it looks like you."

She shrugged. "It's what I want to be like. We should have wings everywhere, shouldn't we?"

"In a perfect world, maybe! Here, let me draw something for you. I'm no artist, but it'll give you an idea."

Flick gave Lileem a very badly drawn diagram of Wraeththu physiology and told her to keep it. She glanced at it, folded the paper twice and put in the pocket of her trousers. Flick sensed she still felt her body was very private, perhaps because of careless things Ulaume might have said in the past. To Lileem, there was no need to dwell on what she was. She was only a child, and the vast reaches of time stretching before her obviously meant little. But Flick knew that she couldn't hide away here forever; none of them could. They could live for a long time and eventually Wraeththu society would reach out and touch them in some way. It was not inconceivable that other hara had already been compelled to find the birthplace of Pellaz Cevarro. He had no doubt met many people on his travels with Cal and had affected them like he'd affected Ulaume. One day, Flick was sure, others would find them here. And by then Lileem might be adult. She was an enigma, and there was neither prurient nor morbidly curious intent on Flick's part when he'd asked to see her body. He felt it was essential he should know and privately scorned Ulaume for not investigating the matter when Lileem had been younger. It showed, in his opinion, a lack of responsibility. Now, Lileem was shy about such things and not even Mima knew what secrets she hid beneath her clothes. Ulaume had only seen her naked when she was very little and said that although the ouana organs had appeared atrophied the soume-lam had seemed fairly normal, but how could they tell? None of them had seen a Wraeththu harling before. Lileem insisted she was more female than male, and Mima, perhaps for reasons of her own, tended to agree. Lileem wanted to be termed "she," but this might only be because she knew she was different and not because it was a correct label for her difference.

As for Mima, Flick thought that being around hara had changed her. She was so like Pell, it was uncanny, and not just in physical appearance. There was a strangely familiar aura around her and when it touched Flick as they worked together, he felt there was another har beside him, not a human female. He was not drawn to her sexually. Instead, it inspired a kind of comfort within him. He felt he could trust her utterly and sometimes he was sure she could hear his unguarded thoughts. Occasionally, he would experiment by sending out a clear mind call, but to these Mima would never respond. Flick, however, could not dispel the impression this was deliberate and that she was concealing her abilities.

But these enigmas were put aside in the spring, when a new mystery presented itself to Flick. He had long accepted that the white house was a haunted place, and thought it no surprise, considering the many violent deaths that had taken place in the locale. He had often felt strange tinglings in his spine as he worked in the garden or walked though the settlement seeking tools and other supplies in the empty houses. Then, it came to Flick's attention that Mima was taking food from their stores and disappearing into the settlement with it. He followed her on a couple of occasions, and found that she laid the food out behind the old Cevarro house. Eventually, he cornered her in the kitchen one morning and asked her outright what she was doing.

"They are offerings," she said.

Flick was interested at once. "Offerings for spirits? Your family?"

Mima frowned. "Not exactly . . ." She sighed deeply. "I feel awkward about this, but there's no point keeping it secret, really. I have two dead brothers, Flick, but one still walks."

And so the story of Terez came out. Flick's initial reaction was of complete shock, not because a har had failed to complete an inception, but because Ulaume had done nothing about it. To Flick, this was typical Ulaume behavior.

Mima came to Ulaume's defense. "There's nothing anyone can do. Terez is a walking corpse, but he can't die. He won't let me near him. He is terrified of those who live. Perhaps the kindest thing to do would be to kill him properly, but I can't do it. I can't. So I bring him food. Because of all that you've done, we live well now. I want Terez to share that in whatever small way he can."

"You must take me to him," Flick said. "There must be something we can do."

"There isn't," Mima said. "I'm responsible for what happened, Flick. I have to live with it."

Flick thought about it for a while. "You acted out of ignorance, but not with malice. It's not your fault. I think we could try to repeat the inception."

Mima's expression brightened. "We could do that? Is that possible?"

"Ulaume should have thought of it before." Flick frowned. "But how? We lack the proper equipment. Blood has to be transfused."

Mima stared at him steadily. He looked into her eyes and saw a small, fearful hope within them. She wet her lips with her tongue, swallowed. "Could we not . . . could we not *feed* him blood?"

Flick shook his head emphatically. "No, it doesn't work that way."

"Are you sure?"

"Yes, of course. I've seen hundreds of inceptions. We are not vampires, Mima."

"I think we should try it, all the same."

Flick was alerted by a certain tone in her voice, and the fact that her aura seemed to condense around her like a protective blanket. "What makes you say this?"

"Nothing, a hunch . . . What harm could it do?"

"It's more than that. I can sense it. Why won't you tell me?"

Mima stood up and walked away from him. She went to the window by the sink, rubbed at a new pane of glass where some of Flick's finger marks were still visible, close to the frame. "You might not approve of what you hear."

"Don't be ridiculous. Tell me."

She sighed. "I suggested it because it . . . because it was what happened to me."

Flick stared at her for some seconds. "What?"

Mima turned to face him again. "Can't you tell? I know you can. You've sensed it. I was waiting for you to ask."

"You have drunk Wraeththu blood?" A dozen hideous images splashed across Flick's mind.

"Yes," she answered, "but not in the way you're thinking. Before you came, but not long before, Lileem fell badly and was injured. I was . . . ill then, mentally ill. It was because of all that had happened, but . . . Anyway, when Lileem was hurt, I wanted to help her, but I didn't know how, so I licked her wound, like an animal would. I don't know why I did it. I can't remember what it was like to be me then. The blood affected me. I became . . . different. Not completely har, but different."

"Do you realize what you are saying?"

"Not as much as you do, obviously."

"This is astounding. The implications are immense. Have you changed physically?"

"Yes, and before you ask, I'll not show you. Forget me. What I'm trying to say is—"

"Forget you?" Flick interrupted. "You can't just skim over this, Mima. You don't know how important this is. So many women have died during inception. As far as I know, no female has survived it. Hara should know about this. It should be investigated, studied . . ."

"Be quiet!" Mima snapped. "We are stuck out here in the middle of nowhere, and I have no intention of letting curious hara *investigate* me. If it's happened to me, it'll inevitably happen to someone else—if it's meant to— and they can be investigated. Ulaume said my experience was probably an anomaly, a one-off, and maybe it is, but the same process—of ingesting blood—might work for Terez. I should have thought of this before. It seems obvious now."

Flick considered this, simultaneously attempting to accept the enormity of what she had told him. He shook his head. "I don't know. I've never heard of anyone trying that. And the results might be unpredictable. You are not completely har, as you said yourself."

Mima came back to the table, thumped it with a closed fist. "We must try. Look at me. I have my wits, my health, and quite a bit more besides."

Flick raised an eyebrow.

"Strength, increased psychic ability and—yes—some puzzling physical adjustments. I don't think we could use my blood though, or Lee's, but yours or Ulaume's might be suitable."

Flick sighed, rubbed his face. "Mine then," he said wearily. "I predict Ulaume will not approve of your plan."

Ulaume was indeed scathing of the idea. Later that day, while Mima took some blood from Flick's arm in the kitchen, Ulaume stood with folded arms behind them, saying, "You are both mad. This won't work. What happened to you, Mima, was a fluke."

"You don't know that," Mima said.

"At best it produces an incomplete inception," Ulaume insisted. "You are evidence of that. You are not har."

"But I'm not dead either," Mima snapped. "Aren't women supposed to die?"

"We don't know anything," Flick said, wincing as Mima sliced into his arm with a sharp knife. "We have always accepted that women can't be incepted. But now we are faced with new evidence, in you and Lileem. More things are possible than we know. I remembered something today. Don't our own legends tell us the Aghama created the second Wraeththu by letting him feed upon his blood?"

"Legends," Ulaume snapped. "Only that. Otherwise inception wouldn't be what it is."

"Perhaps transfusion is a more effective and direct method," Flick said. "And Terez has already received one. What he lacked was the proper care during althaia and presumably the aruna that completes the process. If we could somehow awaken the harish parts of himself, the inception might progress as normal."

"Aruna with *that*?" Ulaume laughed cruelly. "Good luck, Flick. You haven't seen what Terez has become."

Mima took up the small bowl of Flick's blood and soaked bread into it, adding herbs and chilies to make it more appetizing. This, she carried to the shadowed corner behind her old home, where she habitually left food out for Terez. This time, Flick accompanied her. Usually, Mima would not hang around, because Terez would not appear if he sensed her near, but this night, she and Flick concealed themselves on a nearby roof to keep watch. Mima was still unsure Terez would make an appearance with them so close, even though they took care to shield their thoughts. Terez was damaged, but his senses were acute. They stayed out all night, huddled in blankets, and never heard a thing, but in the morning, they saw that the offering had been taken, and hopefully by Terez rather than a passing animal.

"Now what?" Mima asked.

"We'll need to sedate him," Flick said. "Capture him. I'm hoping the meal will affect him in some way, perhaps revive him, but I believe there is only one thing that will truly make a difference. The energy centers within the soume-lam have to be reactivated. It initiates a chemical process, I think, which is why aruna after althaia is so important."

"I don't think aruna is an option," Mima said. "Ulaume is right about that. Terez is monstrous, Flick. Could you really do it? Think about it?"

"The centers could be activated manually," Flick said fastidiously. "Even you could do it."

"This is bizarre," Mima said. "You are all freaks."

"And so are you. Get used to it. At least I'm in a majority of freaks, you are unique."

"As far as you know."

"As far as I know. Have you any ideas what we could use as a sedative?"

"Spider agave," she said. "It's a man-made strain like the cable crop that we used to grow here. Its sap could be made into a painkiller or an anesthetic. The Santos place, a few hours away, used to grow it though I guess the Wraeththu marauders burned most of it. We could go and look for some."

"You go," Flick said. "Take my pony. It'd be quicker than if one of us rode a burro."

"Okay." Mima began to clamber down from the roof.

Flick leaned over the eaves. "If you find any, bring as much as you can. Bring roots, seeds, whatever. We need to add this plant to our own collection."

"You sure? It's a devil plant. The leaves are like blades and can pierce the thickest leather. I have seen men lose a leg to it. Unprocessed, its sap is a poison. I should have the proper equipment or at least protective gloves to try and harvest it. It resists being useful, believe me."

"Sounds like a Wraeththu plant," Flick said.

Mima grinned. "I'll do what I can. There must be something I can wrap around my hands."

"Cut up my saddle bags," Flick said.

Mima nodded and dropped to the ground. Flick watched her running steadily and gracefully along the narrow alley between the dwellings. She was as tall and slim as a har, her hair swinging out behind her. He wished, for a moment, that Seel could meet her or, more interestingly perhaps, Cal. Now that might be amusing.

Mima did not return until long after sundown, by which time Lileem was frantic with worry. Ulaume too was moved to show some concern and suggested he should take one of the burros and go and look for her, even though none of them even knew in which direction the Santos farm lay. However, in the midst of rescue debate, Mima walked into the kitchen and dumped a collection of wicked looking foliate knives and lances onto the table. "Only one wound," she said, displaying a bloodied rag wrapped around her left forearm. "It'll need stitching. Lee, go find needle and thread."

Lileem ran from the room, while Mima washed herself at the sink. Ulaume went to examine her wound, while Flick carefully inspected the leaves on the table.

"Extract the sap and boil it," Mima said. "If there's anything more to the process, I don't know it. We'll have to hope for the best."

"What about dosage?" Flick asked.

She shrugged, pressing a towel to her arm. "I've no idea. We'll have to guess."

"That wound is bad," Ulaume said. "You must let me give you healing after you've stitched it."

"A scratch," Mima said, grinning, although Flick noticed the skin around her mouth was sallow and damp and there were shadows beneath her eyes. He hoped her semi-Wraeththu condition might prevent any serious effects from the agave wound.

The following evening, it was clear that Mima was running a fever, albeit a minor one, but she was insistent she must help with capturing her brother. Whether through concern for Mima, or a genuine interest, Ulaume offered his assistance also. Flick had made darts of the tips of agave leaves, which had been no easy job as it seemed the spirit of the plant was intent on causing damage to tender living flesh whenever possible. Even lying dismembered and inert on a table, the strong hard leaves presented dangers. Accidentally brushing against the blade of a leaf caused a painful cut. Flick told Lileem there was strong magic in the plant and she said that perhaps there was a dehar of agave, who was a god of weapons, pain, and war. "That is his name, of course," she said. "Agave. Perhaps we should make him an offering and say a prayer, so that he'll help you get Terez."

"We could," Flick said.

"The offering should be blood, not yours or Mima's, as you've already given, but mine or Lormy's."

Flick's flesh went cold for a moment as Lileem innocently put her request to Ulaume, presumably because she was a little frightened of the cruel agave. Flick expected Ulaume to glance at him contemptuously and say something like, "Now who's been filling your head with this rubbish?"

Instead, because he was gradually proving himself to be a creature of surprises, he said, "Tell me about it." His strong brown hands worked dextrously with the agave. Of all of them, he had received no wounds.

Lileem described Agave and his preferences in terms of offerings, then said gravely, "Flick has seen the dehara, the gods. We see them together now. They are pouring out of the stars."

"The Kakkahaar have a dehar," Ulaume said. "His name is Hubisag, and he sounds similar to your Agave."

"I remember you calling on him," Lileem said, "though you don't do that now."

"I am far from home," Ulaume said, "and in a landscape of agave. I will acknowledge its god, if that is what it takes." Now he looked at Flick directly. "I danced in Hubisag's honor for my tribe. Perhaps I miss it. I like these ideas you have. They make sense."

Astounded, Flick could only nod and turn away feeling embarrassed. Ulaume's approval was somehow worse than his scorn.

Much to her annoyance, Lileem was told to remain at the white house while the rest of them went hunting. "You might be a prodigy," Ulaume said, "but you're still a child and you've never done anything like this. Show your maturity now and accept you might mess things up."

Grudgingly, she agreed, and watched the rest of them forlornly from the lighted window as they crept down the hill. It was clear in her face she was aggrieved to miss the nearest thing to an adventure since Flick had arrived at the settlement.

Mima had brought a more sumptuous meal than usual: a whole freshly cooked chicken in herbs, which filled the night air with mouth-watering fragrance. This she laid down in the usual place and the three of them took up their positions, each armed with an improvised blow gun, created from some hollow metal tubing Flick had found in the stable block behind the house. The guns were armed with agave darts. They waited for most of the night and Flick was beginning to think that Terez was wise to them and wouldn't show, when his senses detected a furtive movement in a stand of sumac bushes. The movements came closer to his position, shaking the leaves of a feathery esperanza. He became utterly still and strained all of his senses out into the darkness. He could sense also the alert tension of his companions. Suddenly there was a soft rushing sound and the esperanza shook violently. Someone, possibly Mima, had fired a dart.

Flick saw a dark scrabbling shape emerge from the bushes and scuttle on all fours across a narrow open space, heading for the other side of the settlement. He was too far away to fire, but then the shape jerked almost upright, its feet leaving the ground. It uttered an enraged shriek and tried to run. At that moment, Ulaume dropped down from his hiding place on one of the roofs, clearly having fired a dart. Terez was so quick, like a monstrous spider. Flick saw a brief struggle, heard a cry. There seemed to be a dark, noxious smoke hanging over the whole scene, and Flick feared that Ulaume would be consumed by it. A sickly putrid smell like rotting vegetation filled the air. Flick called out, and his voice sounded low and slurred. Ulaume snarled and cursed, then Terez had managed to wriggle away from him. Like a black wraith, he shot off into the shadows between the buildings.

"Damn!" Flick said aloud.

Mima jumped across from a neighboring roof, wiped her upper lip, which was sweating. "I think he took Ulaume's dart. We can follow."

She leapt down to the ground, landing on all fours, her hair swinging wildly as she glanced around her. Quickly, she glanced up at Flick. "Come *on*!"

It was her brother they were trying to capture. Her only surviving brother, in whatever form he took.

Flick jumped down beside her. Close by, Ulaume was trying to examine the top of his right arm by starlight. "Bit me," he said, "felt like to the bone."

"Which way did he go?" Mima asked.

"He'll have got away by now," Flick said.

"No, he took the dart in the neck," Ulaume said. "I saw it."

"Which way?" Mima almost screamed.

Ulaume indicated with a jerk of his head. "That way."

She was gone in an instant.

Ulaume crumpled to his knees in the dirt, holding on his arm. "That thing smacked me in the head too. It has a lot of strength."

Flick squatted down beside him. "You should go back to the house. Clean the wound. Get Lileem to give you some healing. I'll go and find Mima."

"Be careful," Ulaume said. "That thing's unnatural."

Flick stood up, but hesitated before following Mima.

"I know what you're thinking and you're right," Ulaume said. "This was a stupid idea. You don't know what you're messing with."

"It is our responsibility," Flick said. "You know that."

"It's a big one, Flick. If you catch the thing, it's only the beginning. By Hubisag, even just being near it makes me sick."

Flick found them on the porch of one of the buildings. Dawn had begun to gray the sky and the light was magical and strange. Mima was hunched over an awkward tangle of splayed limbs. She was rocking back and forth, weeping, her hands over her nose in a position like prayer. From yards away, Flick gagged on the stench. He steeled himself and approached, reaching out a hand to Mima's shoulder. It felt hard and bony beneath his fingers. For a moment, he was back in time, comforting Pell when he was so afraid of inception. Flick closed his eyes, willed himself back to the present. He had to keep swallowing to keep himself from vomiting. Terez was semiconscious, viscous fluid leaking from his upturned eyes. His skin was a mass of sores, which can sometimes happen during althaia, but they had never healed. He had never risen reborn from inception, as perfect har, but had lingered in some abominable hinterland. What remained was like the dark soul of Wraeththu, the terrible things that hid deep inside. *And what now?* Flick asked himself.

"He needs a transfusion, we have to find a way," he said.

Mima looked round at him then. "It's too late, isn't it? I've never been this close. Oh God!"

"We began this," Flick said. "We finish it. Help me carry him."

"Back to the house?"

"Where else? You want him back, Mima. We start by bringing him into our fold."

"But Lileem . . ."

"Lileem is far more robust than any of us. She can take this, probably better than we can. She'll be of help. We don't have to worry about her."

He hoped he was right.

CHAPTER FIFTEEN

$\rightarrowtail \cdot \dotplus \cdot \multimap \ominus \multimapdot \dotplus \cdot \leftarrowtail$

Over the following weeks, Flick wished many times that he had Orien or Seel to turn to for advice. As Ulaume had told him, he was out of his depth, but felt he had to carry on. They had to keep Terez sedated all the time, because on the only occasion they let him surface to full consciousness, he tore up the room he was being kept in and smeared excrement around the walls. To Flick, Terez was like a mad monkey, uncontrollable, spiteful, and sly. He was also very strong. It was hard to feel pity for this creature, who screamed the entire time he was awake and emitted foul fluids from every orifice when asleep. Flick did not know how to give a transfusion, the best he could manage was to cut his own arm and press it against a similar wound he made on Terez. Every day he looked for improvements, and it seemed that Terez's skin was slightly clearer and Mima was sure he was putting on weight, but his mind would not come back.

Once, Ulaume said to Flick in private, "You know what we should do. A pillow. It'd be quick. Better than this living death."

But Flick could not give up. Perhaps Saltrock sensibilities could not concur with those of the Kakkahaar, but he felt there must be hope. He resorted to something that he felt was bound to work by letting Lileem put her hands on Terez. She sat cross-legged behind his head, her fingers resting lightly on his twisted face. Surely the innocent purity of a child would reach and heal him? It seemed not.

"What do you think?" Flick asked Lileem, as she sat, lips pursed, brow furrowed, concentrating on the sick creature before her.

"He is similar to how Mima was," she answered. "His mind is far away." She glanced up. "He will never be like you."

Flick had been telling himself that he was looking for some signs of improvement before he considered the arunic aspects of Terez's condition. He realized now it was something he was trying to avoid. Everyone knew—or at least had been told—that aruna after althaia somehow made permanent the changes of inception. If only he knew more about the mechanics of it—what exactly aruna did. Was it to do with receiving the energy or essence of another har, or chemical changes within the inceptee's body stimulated by the act itself?

To Ulaume, it was becoming increasingly obvious that he must intervene in the Terez situation. He harbored resentments for Flick, the har who had swept into his life and taken over his household. He couldn't deny the benefits of Flick's presence, but he had a prejudice against Sarocks that was difficult to dispel. Ulaume had come to care for Mima, and Flick was wrong in assuming that Ulaume hadn't thought long and deeply about what should be done for Terez. Ulaume had simply come to the conclusion that he could do nothing alone and that Flick couldn't, either. Neither could Mima or Lileem assist. Ulaume knew there was only one thing they could try. He wasn't sure it would work in the way that everyone would want or that a perfect har would arise from the husk of Terez afterward. He wasn't sure if his idea wasn't dangerous. But at night, he had to listen to Mima weeping softly in the room next to his own, or hear her pacing the creaking floorboards, and he knew that eventually he would have to do something. It would mean thawing with Flick and that was the second thing that prevented him acting, because Ulaume took a long time to forgive or to drop a grudge. Flick reminded him of what he considered to be the worst aspects of Pell. They didn't look that similar, but there was a certain manner and attitude, presumably deriving from Saltrock inception itself, that they shared. Capable, industrious, considerate, and disciplined. Perhaps the opposite of everything Ulaume thought himself to be. But in this instance, the combination of personalities, however at odds, might work in Terez's favor. No doubt, if Terez could be healed, he would be another fawning devotee of the accomplished Flick, which would be extremely annoying, but if it brought harmony back to the house, then it would be worth it.

Once the decision was made, Ulaume brooded over it for several days, chewing each detail in his mind to try and divine possible outcomes. Lileem knew he was considering something important, because she kept casting him knowing glances, but he'd reveal nothing to her. He and Flick must do this alone. It was their territory.

One evening, while Mima and Lileem addressed the unpleasant task of feeding and cleaning Terez, Ulaume went into the kitchen and found Flick there, cleaning Ghost's saddle and bridle by lamplight. The mere sight of this industry initiated a spasm of annoyance in Ulaume's heart, but he gritted his teeth and went to sit opposite Flick at the table. Flick glanced up, smiled tightly. Ulaume could feel discomfort pouring off his skin. Flick hated to be alone with him.

"This Terez business has gone on for over a month now," Ulaume said. "The meal of blood did not work, and neither have your other experiments."

Flick shrugged awkwardly. "There is a gradual improvement. His skin is clearing and he's put on a bit of weight."

"Don't kid yourself," Ulaume said. He paused, then added, "There *is* something else we could do."

Flick's hands fell idle. "Has it anything to do with pillows, poison, or blades?"

Ulaume smiled. "No, not at all. It might work, it might not. I don't think we could guarantee what would come out of it, but we could try."

"What do you mean?"

"Grissecon," Ulaume said. "Ritual aruna to create a healing elixir."

Flick began cleaning the bridle again, perhaps with too much concentration for such a mundane task. "I have seen that done, but it takes hara of high caste to do it. I've never done anything like that."

"I have. Not for healing exactly, but I'm familiar with the process."

Flick's brow was furrowed and his face was flushed. Ulaume had never seen a har so riddled with discomfort. "We are not friends, I know," he said, "and this won't come easy. But you were the one so keen to do something about Terez, and this is a possible solution. Are you no longer prepared to try anything?"

"I don't think you mean it," Flick said suddenly, throwing down the bridle in a clatter of harness buckles. "I think this is just another way to make life difficult for me here. Maybe a Kakkahaar can take aruna with somehar they despise, and maybe you know I can't. I'm not stupid."

"I didn't realize you despised me. Thanks for being so honest." Ulaume couldn't help laughing.

"I don't . . ." Flick shook his head. "I didn't expect this. Not from you. I can't help but suspect your motives."

"The motive is to help Mima. Not sure about Terez, because I'm still not convinced he isn't beyond help. But if there is a chance, we should perhaps take it." He paused. "Wouldn't Pell want us to do this?"

"That's low," Flick said.

"Not at all. It's the truth. I can't believe I'm trying to persuade you to do this. I don't have to. I don't have to listen to insults." He stood up.

"Give me time," Flick said. "I have to think about this."

"We are Wraeththu," Ulaume said. "Perhaps we have forgotten that, living here. We have run away from our lives, and we have tried to detach ourselves from all that we were. But you were the one who said Terez was our responsibility. You were the one who wanted to help him. The rest of us are just living with the consequences, and they are not pleasant. That is what you should think about."

Ulaume left the room before Flick could say any more.

The following day, Ulaume avoided Flick to give him space to think. He had to admit to himself that the idea of becoming close to another har again was not without its delights, even if that har was Flick. He was physically very attractive, despite his annoying traits. Ulaume had trained himself not to miss aruna, but the desire was always there, deep within. *If we do this,* Ulaume thought, *it will initiate many things. It will create changes.*

Perhaps these were needed changes. Ulaume believed Flick wanted their home to become the new Saltrock. Many times, the possibilities of other hara finding them there had been discussed, albeit lightly. Ulaume knew that Lileem desperately wanted it to happen.

Before dinner, Ulaume went outside to watch the sunset. A beautiful purple-red light tinged the land. Cicadas purred in the acacia trees and the coyote made her song to the night. In the early days, Ulaume had thought the animal might become a sort of doglike pet, but once they'd moved into the house, she'd gone back to her wild ways. Sometimes they heard and saw her, but the time they'd been almost like friends had long gone. She'd had a small but important part to play in their little drama, but now it was over.

Flick came out of the house, wiping his hands, which were damp from peeling vegetables, on a ragged towel. Already, appetizing smells were drifting out of the kitchen window. Flick sat down beside Ulaume on a shallow flight of ornamental steps that led to a pond with a dry fountain. He cupped his chin with his hands, his elbows resting on his raised knees. "When?" he said.

Ulaume pointed up at the sky where a waxing moon pulled herself out of the distant cordillera. "Anytime between now and the full moon," he said. "You know that."

"Hmm." Flick shifted uneasily. "Tell me what you propose, apart from the obvious."

"Outside, at the falls. It is a good place. We call upon one of your dehara—you should decide which one and how to address them—and we tell them what we want to do and ask for their help. Then, we perform the Grissecon. It's not that different from any other ritual really, apart from the aruna aspect. I will be ouana, you soume. That seems the best approach."

Flick nodded slowly. "I can see that. Should we tell the others?"

"We tell Mima we are doing something, but mustn't get her hopes up too high. We will ask her to keep Lileem inside, who will be bursting with curiosity to observe. I would prefer to do this without an audience."

"Me too!" Flick exclaimed. He rubbed his nose with both hands. "Tomorrow night. That will give me time to write something down. I need to think about it."

"You spend too much time thinking, but okay. Put some ideas together and show them to me."

"The only rituals I've done here with the dehara have been with Lileem and they were just light, nothing much. This will require something more powerful and focused."

"Good practice, then. You'd better see to dinner. I can smell burning."

As Ulaume thought, the mere mention of a new idea to help Terez caused Mima to become a fountain of hope. He trusted he and Flick wouldn't disappoint her. Somehow, he didn't think they could fail. This Grissecon would involve a sacrifice, that of their own feelings toward one another, and he was sure this would empower the ritual. "Sit with Terez," Ulaume said to Mima. "You and Lileem can concentrate on his well-being. I think it will aid what Flick and I intend to do."

Mima, who never touched anyone impulsively apart from Lileem, wrapped Ulaume in a quick, fierce embrace. "Thank you," she said. "I know what this must be costing you."

"Actually, you have no idea," he said lightly. "It's a cost I'm willing to pay."

Over a frugal dinner of salad and water, Flick produced his ideas for the ritual. Mima had already taken Lileem to Terez's room.

"I thought that Aruhani should be the focus to start with," Flick said, "but then decided it should be Miyacala, who is the dehar most associated with inception. We must ask him to guide Terez back into himself, to complete the process that was arrested." He glanced at Ulaume. "You must use your knowledge to create the elixir."

"We should alter our state of consciousness," Ulaume said. "Usually, Grissecon is an elaborate event, with drummers, shamanic trance, the lot. We shall have to improvise."

"I have something we could use," Flick said. "A fungus that grows in the desert caves. I've used it before."

Ulaume pushed his plate away from him. "I'm still hungry, so that should aid the process."

Flick exhaled a shuddering breath. "I'll prepare it now," he said. "We should get going."

He stood abruptly, knocking the table with his hip so that a glass fell over.

"Calm down," Ulaume said. "You are a jangle of nerves. You're making me nervous."

Flick mixed up a fairly noxious brew and he and Ulaume sat at the table to drink it. Flick was tense and silent and Ulaume was almost amused at how much of a trial this seemed to be for him. On the other hand, it wasn't very flattering either.

When the drinks were finished, Flick clasped his hands on the tabletop. "Is this the reason we're here?" he asked. "For Terez?"

"For him, for Lileem, for Mima—who knows? Maybe all three. Maybe there is no reason and everything is coincidence."

"You and I meeting here? Coincidence?"

Ulaume sighed through his nose. "Let's go."

The night was almost too beautiful. Flowering vines that grew up the side of the house released a subtle fragrance and the breeze was warm. Overhead, the sky was encrusted with stars, so thickly that it seemed a thousand new galaxies had been born overnight, or a thousand dehara were trying on new jewels. Ulaume felt powerful and serene. In one sense, he was coming home.

When they reached the falls, Ulaume said, "This is where Mima became . . . well, whatever it is she's become."

"I know," Flick said. "She has brought me here before."

"What *are* Mima and Lileem?" Ulaume said. "In my tribe, the shamans would strap them down and take a good look."

"In your tribe, they expose them in the desert," Flick said dryly, then softened. "I don't know what they are. Part of me thinks we should take them somewhere—like to the Gelaming or something—and find out, perhaps find help, while another part thinks they're safer here in isolation."

"Those are my thoughts also," Ulaume said.

Flick began to unpack some lanterns he had brought with him in a bag. Each held a candle, which would be protected by glass from the gentle breeze. Flick arranged them in a circle. He placed some on the rocks around the water and hung others in the acacias. In the soft yellow light, he looked young, pure, and troubled, and Ulaume felt a thousand years old with a dark history that dragged behind him like a lame hag. "You must consecrate me," he said abruptly, voicing a thought that had come unbidden to his mind.

Flick glanced at him and frowned. "What?"

"You heard. Surely you know how. Sarocks must consecrate everything."

"No, we don't, but why do you want to do that?"

"Because it is necessary."

Flick stared at him for a few moments. "In the water," he said. "Go into the water."

Ulaume took off his clothes and waded out into the largest pool. The moon was captured there, the water full of its cold white essence. Flick undressed with care and placed his folded clothes in a neat pile next to the untidy heap of garments that Ulaume had left on the bank. His skin was so pale he looked like a moon creature himself. It occurred to Ulaume then that Flick was afraid that this rite might contaminate him in some way. Flick knew the Kakkahaar reputation for dark magic and Ulaume could not reassure him, because he wondered the same thing.

Flick stood before Ulaume in the water, some inches shorter than his companion. He raised his arms to the moon and said, "Lunil, dehar of the moon and of magic, I call upon you now and ask that with your white cleansing power, you consecrate this har, Ulaume, who is of the Colurastes and the Kakkahaar. Descend now from the mansions of the moon into this water and lend us your cold pure light. Enter into this har and cleanse him of all that is dark and unclean. Lunil, I ask this in your name, dehar of the moon and of magic."

Flick leaned down and scooped up some water, which he poured down over Ulaume's head, stretching up to do so.

Ulaume closed his eyes as the icy streams ran down over his face. Then he plunged himself wholly into the pool, opening his eyes upon glittering darkness. "If only for this night," he prayed in silence, "make me worthy of this." Flick's narcotic brew must already be having an effect, for Ulaume could see small pointed faces in the ripples and bubbles around him. He could smell the moon.

He came up gasping and shuddering, hardly able to breathe, because the water was so cold. Flick's flesh was pimpled with goose bumps.

"It is done," Ulaume said and, taking Flick's arm, waded back to the bank. Here, he rubbed himself down with his shirt and Flick did likewise. The atmosphere was electric, but also sacred. Magic crackled in the branches of the acacias and sizzled in the blades of needle grass.

In the circle of soft lamplight, Flick called upon Miyacala. Ulaume had read the invocations Flick had written, but it appeared Flick had decided to discard them. Now, he spoke from the heart, saying whatever came into his mind. It was a hypnotic mantra, repeated phrases tumbling over and around each other. At some points, Ulaume was moved to add his voice to the chant, and sometimes he was silent. With eyes closed, he could feel power circling around them, like a great beast attracted to a campfire in the desert. He fixed his entire being upon this force, because he must call it into himself. This was the power they must capture and weave into their union. This was the fire that would make liquid stars of their essence, with the power of the universe within it, the power to create and destroy. Miyacala, dehar of inception and initiation. Ulaume could feel this being's presence. He could see him in his mind's eye: immensely tall with long white hair, his eyes milky blind orbs, but whose brow blazed with a white star, which represented his true sight.

Flick had fallen silent. He squatted before Ulaume, who knelt upon the ground, and took Ulaume's hands in his own. "He is here," he murmured. "Give him the image of Terez. We must do so together."

Ulaume pulled Flick's head toward his own and in the sharing of breath, so they conjured the image of the injured and incomplete Terez. Ulaume forced the image to change, to grow, to become whole. He could only offer an image of Pellaz, because that was the single template he had to go on, and he presumed Terez must look similar, under normal circumstances. Flick's skin felt hot and feverish against his own. Ulaume was filled with a strange, immense stretched feeling as if he were part of the sky and it was yawning.

Flick drew away and lay back on the ground, offering himself. In the moonlight, his soume-lam gleamed like pearl. He was not as reluctant about this as he'd seemed.

Ulaume knelt before him and summoned the power into himself, directing it down to the root of his being. His ouna-lim had become the dark flower of creation, a spiral coral to slide into a spiral shell. The ocean, the sky, the moon. Elemental powers, circling stars. Ulaume uttered a cry of command. He was har, awake and alive, and he had just come back to his kind.

Flick collected their combined essence in a small glass bottle. They held it up to the light of the moon. It was luminous, spiraling slowly, glistening with tiny stars of light. "It's alive," Flick murmured. "Something different." His fingers were glowing with it.

"Let's use it now then," Ulaume said. "Perhaps don't tell Mima exactly what it is."

Back at the house, they found Lileem and Mima in an excited mood. "A little moon came in through the window," Lileem cried as they entered Terez's room. "A ball of white light hovered over the bed and then sank down into his chest."

"It was incredible," Mima said. "Did you do that? He's been quiet ever since."

"It sounds hopeful," Ulaume said.

"You are shining," Lileem said, "like the moon. What did you do?"

"We made a medicine," Flick said.

Ulaume watched as Flick took the glass bottle out of his pocket. He could still taste Flick's skin on his tongue.

"That's sooo pretty," Lileem breathed. "Liquid moon. How did you make it?"

"Moonshine and starlight and Lunil's tears," Flick said and leaned over the bed. He took the stopper out of the bottle and poured the contents between Terez's cracked lips. Flick had told Ulaume that in Saltrock, they would simmer a Grissecon elixir with milk, liquor, tea, or herbs, but as Terez wasn't conscious, they might as well just pour it into him neat. He'd never know.

Flick attended to this task, then they all sat back to wait. Bats threw themselves against the window: they could hear the soft little slaps. Moths came to worship at the oil lamp next to the bed. Terez's lips shone like nacre in the gentle glow. Ulaume knew he should care about what might happen next, but all he wanted to do was get Flick upstairs alone, so they could carry on making up for lost time. His whole body felt like a plucked wire.

After what seemed like an hour, but was probably only a few minutes, Terez opened his eyes. Ulaume saw at once that they were no longer milky and dull. They were black, like Mima's eyes.

Mima uttered a soft cry and sat down on the bed. She stroked her brother's face, pushed the lank, lifeless hair back from his face. He didn't blink and made no sound, but Ulaume knew he was *there*. Flick caught his eye and nodded once. There had never been any doubt. They'd both known that what they'd done would succeed, and that the long abstinence they'd suffered was what had heightened their power. They might never be chesna, like lovers, but never again would they be enemies, and they would share their bodies as Wraeththu did.

"Give Terez more of the sedative," Flick said. "Let him sleep."

"I'll stay with him," Mima said. "I'll be with him when he wakes tomorrow."

"Mima . . ." Flick paused. It was clear he wasn't sure how to say what was on his mind.

"What?" Mima asked sharply.

Ulaume put a hand on her head, stroked her hair briefly. "Don't expect too much. I think that Terez will be har, and in that way healed, but he might never be the same in his mind."

"Tomorrow, one of us will do what has to be done," Flick said.

Ulaume intuited Flick hoped it wouldn't be himself. "We have to be careful with this, Flick. We can't force aruna on him, because that would be pelki, and hardly part of an althaia."

Flick frowned. "What do you mean?"

"Pelki is forced aruna, rape. It is supposed to be anathema to our kind. We'll just have to hope Terez is compliant, but if his mind is still . . . *odd,* it might be difficult."

"Then I will do it," Mima said.

Ulaume and Flick stared at her for some moments, a certain pressing question eager to escape their lips, which both were too embarrassed to voice.

"I *could,*" she said fiercely.

"You are not har," Ulaume said gently. "Even though he might trust you more, you could damage him rather than help."

"Then let me be with you when you do it," she said.

Ulaume glanced at Flick, who inclined his head discreetly. "Very well," he said. "We should do this together." He turned to Lileem. "Apart from you, Leelee. And no arguments!"

"I understand," Lileem said. "I'm not old enough."

Ulaume was alert for sarcasm in her tone, but found none. "There's nothing to worry about, Lee. We'll be all right."

Lileem smiled weakly. For once, it seemed, she accepted this was adult business and wanted no part of it.

CHAPTER SIXTEEN

><<>>•⊖•<>>—<

Before Ulaume or Flick awoke, and while Lileem slept in a nest of blankets on the floor, Mima gently shook her brother from sleep. Outside, the air was full of the cry of birds and the light changed from gray to pink. Terez opened his eyes and fixed his gaze upon his sister. She could tell that he knew her, and that he would not let go of her image. He dared not even blink. She leaned down and kissed him. "You are safe," she said. His breath came quick and shallow, poisoned by fear. "Come," Mima said. "Get up."

She held his hand and helped him to rise. Today, his body was not stooped and twisted, but his shoulders were hunched, his head held low. "We are in the Richards house," she said. "We live here now. Don't be afraid."

He let her lead him from the room.

In the garden, Mima saw the dawn breaking over the cordillera to the east and the hill was bathed in early sunlight, while the settlement below still lay in shadow. Terez stood beside her, taller than she was, silent but for his shuddering breath. She took him to the waterfalls, and there bathed his body. As she washed him, flakes of skin came off and his body was smooth beneath. She brushed his hair and the knots came out in her hands, but what was left was clean and glossy. She made him lie beside the water and cleaned his fingernails, biting away the ragged ends. Because she could, she examined what made him har and saw for herself how different and how similar she was to Wraeththu. He never spoke, but simply kept his eyes upon her as if afraid the moment he looked away she would be gone and some unimaginable terror would return.

"We are different now," she told him softly. "The troubles came upon us, and most of us are dead, but we two have survived. Life is beautiful, Terez. Whatever has gone before, we must forget it. You are Wraeththu, as Pell became Wraeththu. I know now it is not the terrible thing we thought, but only a different thing. I am no longer human either, because Wraeththu has touched me too. We are new, do you understand?"

Terez only stared at her, but she sensed he did not want to run away. He could hear her, even if he could not yet fully understand her words.

"Today, some friends and I will make you better still. You must trust me, and them. We will not hurt you. You want to be well, don't you?"

Barely perceptibly, Terez nodded.

Tears welled in Mima's eyes. "You *will* be better," she said.

Terez reached out and traced her tears with his fingers. She closed her eyes to his touch, pressed against his hand. He was all she had left of her family.

"Mima," he said huskily and she opened her eyes.

"Yes, it's me."

"We are not all dead. Dorado . . ." His voice was scratchy and low, as if it came across a vast distance.

"No," Mima said firmly. "Don't think about him. He's beyond us."

"Wraeththu," Terez said and his eyes were troubled. "We are the same." Slowly, he sat up beside her, and Mima could see that with each passing moment he was growing stronger. It was like watching a dragon fly emerge from its chrysalis. Soon, the great wings would open out. They'd shimmer.

"Dorado's gone," Mima said, "as Pell is gone. There is only us. We must think of the future."

"Dorado called to me in the darkness. His voice . . ." Terez put his head into his hands, pressed the fingers against his temples. "I heard him, but it was so dark I couldn't find him. His voice got fainter and then I couldn't hear it at all. He wanted me to follow him, but it was too dark and I was all messed up."

Mima's mouth had gone dry.

Terez lowered his hands and looked at her. "I was meant to be with them, to follow. But something happened and it left me in the darkness with the . . . *things*. I was lost. I have been in that place forever, until I saw your eyes."

"Your inception went wrong," Mima said. "My harish friends have helped you, made it right."

"But I was in the light and then something pulled me into darkness. The Wraeththu were not the darkness."

"They killed our family!" Mima said. "Remember that. They were bad Wraeththu. My friends are not."

"There was a call," Terez murmured. "Like a song. I could smell it and taste it."

"It's over now," Mima said. "Please, Terez, be with me. Live this life."

He did not answer but stared out over the landscape, his eyes so dark no light could escape them.

Ulaume came looking for them, sure that Mima had taken matters into her own hands. He found them as they were making their way back to the house.

"What were you doing?" Ulaume demanded.

"I wanted to talk to him, bathe him," Mima answered.

She was surrounded by a dark cloud. As Ulaume had feared, the results of their actions were not entirely to her liking. Terez himself appeared greatly improved, if distant. He was not that much like Pell, because he was so grim and a little taller, but perhaps the grimness was to be expected.

Flick had prepared breakfast and Lileem had put some flowers on the table, but whatever plans they might have had for a cheerful celebratory breakfast was dampened by the dour presence of Terez. Ulaume could not decide what was worse: a mindless creature with whom they could not communicate at all or this looming presence who was now destined to be part of their lives.

That morning, Ulaume wanted to celebrate because he and Flick had spent the entire night in ecstasy. Ulaume wasn't even tired, and he knew Flick felt the same. He wondered how he could have lived without aruna for so long. It was bizarre, but he no longer felt even slightly annoyed by Flick's habits and quirks. He wanted to touch Flick all the time, swim in the tide of his breath, fill and be filled by him. But any affectionate behavior felt entirely inappropriate in front of Terez. He was like a stern disapproving adult dampening the spontaneous play of children.

After the meal had been consumed, Ulaume carried the dishes to the sink, where Flick was washing up. "We can't do this aruna thing together," Flick whispered, leaning back slightly to press against Ulaume's body. "Face it, we can't do it at all. He's like a black mountain."

"We have to," Ulaume said quietly. He kissed the back of Flick's neck.

Flick sighed in pleasure, then said, "*You* can. You know the dark better than I do. I can't go near him. I know it."

Ulaume groaned softly. "So is this my penance for what you consider to be my questionable experiences? Thank you."

"In this instance, I think your experiences are useful," Flick murmured. "It won't frighten you. I'm sure you've done worse."

"Taking aruna with that will be a travesty after being with you." Ulaume put his arms around Flick's waist, pulled him close.

"Lie back and think of Wraeththu," Flick said. "Believe me, I'm not happy about this. I'd far rather spend the day locked in the bedroom with you than sit down here picturing what's going on with you and Terez."

Ulaume sighed deeply and returned to the table. He found Terez's eyes upon him and realized he'd heard every word of the conversation with Flick. "We need to talk," he said.

"Yes," Terez said.

"Somewhere else," Ulaume continued.

Terez stood up.

"I will come with you," Mima said.

Her brother put a hand upon her shoulder. "No, Mima." His voice was firm.

Ulaume led the way to his room high in the house rather than the sick room where Terez had spent the past days and that no doubt still stank of diseased flesh and rank despair. Terez sat down on the bed and Ulaume realized there was a certain acceptance within him. He knew what would happen and there was no question of resistance or reluctance. Perhaps, in the prison of his madness, he had thought only about this one thing all the time. He had been incepted after all.

The silence in the room was tangible and it poured from Terez like a black mist.

I will need wine for this, Ulaume thought.

"Excuse me a moment," he said. "I just have to fetch something."

"Wait," Terez said.

Ulaume paused with his hand on the door handle.

"Why?" Terez asked.

"Just to make us more relaxed."

"No. Why did that bad thing happen to me? Why was I left behind here? I can remember almost everything but for the darkness when I went away from myself."

Ulaume carefully shielded his thoughts, folding them in on themselves like petals. "The Wraeththu who incepted you were marauders, rogues. They weren't organized. Something went wrong and they left without you. We're trying to make it right now."

"It's too late," Terez said.

Ulaume went back to the bed, sat beside him. "No, it isn't. You are back. It'll take time, but you'll be fine. Mima is here."

Terez shook his head. "You are trying to make it right, but the light I should have had, with the one who was waiting for me, it is gone forever."

Ulaume put an arm around Terez's shoulder and pulled his head down to his shoulder, which took some effort, because Terez didn't want to be comforted. Neither was Ulaume particularly adept at being a consoler. Eventually, however, Terez relented and relaxed against Ulaume's side. He exhaled long and slow: it was more than a sigh. "There are many lights," Ulaume said. "You must believe it. I think your brother Pellaz is alive, even though everyone thinks he's dead. Flick thinks we're all here for a reason and perhaps we are. If I can ease the pain, I will. It's all I can offer."

"I should not be here," Terez said. "I should be with the one who was waiting for me."

Ulaume had expected many responses: anger, confusion, resentment, fear, and hatred. But not this. He realized now that Terez had been a willing convert to Wraeththu, perhaps having thought about it for a long time after Pell had left with Cal. Had Mima known this? Was this why she had dragged him away from those who'd incepted him? The situation was far more complicated than Ulaume had thought, and it was not the kind of thing he enjoyed dealing with. If anything, it was Flick's territory.

"It has to be you," Terez said abruptly. "Not the other one. You. It is my choice."

"Don't do that," Ulaume said. "Don't listen in. That's one of the first rules."

"I've been listening for a long time," Terez said. "I have heard many things and soon I will know what they mean." He glanced at Ulaume. "You wish you had not done this thing, and you wish you could walk away now. If you were meant to do this, you don't want to, but you care about what the others think. You care what Pellaz thinks, because he thinks badly of you."

Ulaume stood up. "That's enough."

"I know what you all wanted," Terez said in a chilling monotone. "I would be mad and you would play with me, like you play with a sick animal. You would lead me from room to room and feed me and comfort me. You did not want me to be what I am. I was never mad, Ulaume, just lost. I forgot how to live in this vehicle of flesh, but I will remember. It survived without me for a time, and now it needs my attention because it has not cared for itself."

"Where were you?" Ulaume asked.

"In this world, there are no words to describe it, although of all of them here, you would be the most likely to understand it. It is why you are here now, but don't be afraid. I won't take you back there."

"I could walk from this room," Ulaume said. "I have no obligation to you. If I did, would you go back to that dark place?"

"I will not go back," Terez said. "You will give me what I need." His eyes grew wider and they were completely black. "Look at me. There are things in me you desire. I slept beside Pellaz every night of my life, from the moment I left my mother's breast until he went away. You want to see through my eyes, hear my stories of the past. Give me your essence, Ulaume, and this flesh will look more how you want it to look. I am happy to indulge your fantasies."

Ulaume had unconsciously moved back until he was pressed against the door. The creature before him now was more horrific than the thing he'd stumbled across in the Cevarro house. It was intelligent and powerful and determined. It was like a dark Pellaz, not evil certainly, but possessed of knowledge that Pell had never had.

"You are rarely afraid," Terez said, unwinding his long body from the bed like a black cobra. He could move quickly, and in that too he was like a snake. In an instant, his hands were on Ulaume's face, powerful head-splintering energy pouring from his fingers. His skin smelled like bitter chocolate. "Listen," Terez said.

He put his mouth against Ulaume's own, and Ulaume tensed himself for some kind of terrible fight, but Terez poured into him a series of images from the past. He could smell the cable as the seedpods burst in the fields. He could hear Pell's laughter as he ran toward the sunset. Thunderclouds swept over the cordillera and white-tailed deer fled before a storm. Pellaz crouched before him, surrounded by blue stem grass and the spikes of agave. His loose shirt was very white in the strange storm light and his hair very black. His eyes were full of humor. There was no guard there, no caution or judgement. This was the Pellaz of whom Ulaume had once dreamed. Pellaz said, "I think, if we try hard enough, we could change the weather."

Terez broke away and Ulaume put his hands against his eyes. He wanted to pull Terez back to him, because the vision had been so real.

"You would do anything to see him again," Terez said, "and you know I can help you. First, you must help me."

Ulaume had met few hara he considered stronger than himself. In Terez, he feared he might have met his match. The Cevarros were clearly a singular breed and their inception to Wraeththu could mean more to harakind than any could have envisaged—for good or ill. Somewhere, another one could still be running around with a rogue band of hara. It was anyhar's guess how Dorado might have developed, but Ulaume doubted he was a faceless rank and file har of low caste.

For two days, Terez kept Ulaume in the high attic room, and it was not as if Ulaume wanted to leave particularly. Something inside him was faintly repulsed by the dark force that surrounded him and took possession of him, but it was also intriguing and in some ways addictive. It reminded Ulaume of his best days with Lianvis, when they had explored higher realms together, lost in the delirious waves of focused aruna. Terez was careful not to deplete Ulaume, because he clearly did not want to damage the thing that could replenish him. He seemed to be knowledgeable and skilled in the arts of aruna, which should be impossible, because he couldn't have been trained prior to inception. It occurred to Ulaume that Terez might have received otherworldly instruction or else he acted upon instinct. What was certain was that Terez was hungry for energy and power. And he was cunning, because he knew that in pleasing Ulaume, he got what he wanted. Part of the contract between them was information.

Ulaume heard about how Terez and Pellaz grew up together, Terez being a year younger than his brother, while Dorado was a couple of years older than Pell. Pellaz had not known it, but Terez had been awake for most of the night while Cal had conducted his big seduction. He had heard some of what had been said, even though Pell and Cal had talked, for the most part, in whispers.

"I fell asleep, and dreamed I left home with them," he said, "but when I awoke, it was too late, because they were gone. For a long time, I hated Pell for that, even as I mourned his loss. But I knew I only had to wait, and I was right, because eventually the . . . others came."

"Who killed your family," Ulaume said. "Didn't you feel anything about that?"

"They were no longer my family," Terez answered. "I could not allow myself to feel pain. I had to endure whatever it took and be strong enough to do so. I had to follow Pell."

As perhaps, Ulaume thought, he had always done.

"Do you ever think of your human family?" Terez asked.

"No," Ulaume said, and it was true.

"Then don't expect me to," Terez said.

"But Mima is here. She is . . . well, we're not really sure what she is, but she's not quite human anymore."

"She and Pell were very close," Terez said. "She was never like the other girls. If she has found a way to survive in this new world, then I respect her for it."

"There are some tribes," Ulaume said, "that . . . even within Wraeththu have a bad reputation. There is a darkness to you, Terez. I'm sure you know that. Could it have come from your inception? Who were the hara that incepted you? Can you remember anything about them?"

Terez glanced at Ulaume keenly. "I was with them for such a short time, but one of them, he taught me many things. He told me about Kakkahaar, your tribe, and some of the others. He told me who were his enemies and who were not."

"Are Kakkahaar enemies of his?"

"They are not to be trusted."

Terez had spent a week with the hara who'd ransacked his home, and at the end of this time, one of them had incepted him. Althaia had caused him to lose track of what happened next. Mercifully, he could not remember that it had been Mima who'd dragged him away from his newfound family.

Flick or Mima brought trays of food to the room and left them outside the door, which Ulaume regularly collected. On the evening of the second day, he took all the scraps and plates downstairs and found his companions in the kitchen, who went silent when he walked in.

Then Flick said, "We were just debating whether to break down the door to your room. We wondered what had happened to you."

"Still alive," Ulaume said. He glanced behind him, closed the door by leaning on it, then went to the table and put down the trays. "Listen, I must speak quickly. Mima, all of you, guard your thoughts. Guard them well, at every moment. Terez is something more than we all imagined."

"What do you mean?" Mima hissed.

"Don't let him know what you did, Mima. Never!" Ulaume said. "He would hate you for it. He wanted to be Wraeththu and he is angry at what was taken from him."

Mima turned away. Lileem only stared up at Ulaume, her face white, her eyes wide.

"What are you trying to tell us?" Flick asked.

"I don't know," Ulaume said. "Just that we've got more on our hands than we bargained for. Terez is no addled, wandering soul. He's back with a vengeance."

"He will never be like you," Lileem said, in a small voice. "I told you that."

"You didn't listen to me, did you," Ulaume said to Flick. "I cautioned against this. Now, we must cope with the consequences."

And the consequences made themselves known swiftly. Terez appeared shortly after Ulaume had come downstairs. He had taken a bath and dressed himself in some clothes that Ulaume had found for him. Flick uttered some awkward remarks about making dinner, but Terez ignored him. He spoke directly to Mima. "We will leave tomorrow," he said.

Mima looked flustered, which was not a usual state for her. "What do you mean?"

"I am going to seek my brothers. I acknowledge that, because you have been changed, you should fall under my protection. You will come with me."

"No," Mima said. "I don't want to do that."

"That is your choice," Terez said, "but I think it is what Pell would have wanted."

"He's dead," Mima said. "We have no real proof otherwise."

"You have no idea what death is," Terez said. "We will find him."

"How?" Mima said. "It's a big world out there. Dorado could be dead too, for all we know. Stay here a while, heal yourself. Then think about the future."

While Mima was speaking, Ulaume silently begged her to let Terez go. Nothing but trouble would come of him remaining among them. They had done their job in bringing back his mind, now they should let him do what he wanted. But Mima blocked out his call. She was obsessed, full of guilt.

"This place is not fit to live in," Terez said. "It should be allowed to return to dust. It is wrong what you are doing here. If you want to survive, you must learn to become har, and you won't do that here."

"What if I can't become har?" Mima snapped. "What if I'm safer here, where hara don't want to kill me?"

"Nowhere is safe," Terez said, "not without a tribe. I learned this before I was taken into darkness."

"Then go!" Mima cried, then shook her head, raking her hands through her hair. "But not yet. Please. You are the only one left. Stay here a while with me. Help me become har, if that's what I should do."

Ulaume exchanged a glance with Flick, who stood mortified by the sink. Neither of them knew how to defuse this situation. They had brought something into the house and it was not what they'd thought it was.

Flick went out into the garden and Ulaume followed him. Now, there was a reticence between them, as if their night of bliss had never been.

"I'm sorry about this," Ulaume said. He wanted to take Flick in his arms, but sensed Flick didn't want it. No doubt he was repulsed by the aura of Terez's essence, which must be hanging around Ulaume in a foul cloud.

"It's all right," Flick said, bending down to pluck out some weeds from the flower beds. "I know what you have to do."

"He just needs strength," Ulaume said.

"I know. It was me who suggested it. I'm okay, really."

"Flick."

Flick sighed and stood up. He turned to face Ulaume and his expression was resigned. "We had a job to do. We did it. We had fun doing it. Now, you have another job to do."

The coldness in his tone made Ulaume's heart freeze. "Fine," he said and went back into the house.

He did not see Flick crouch down again and put his hands against his face.

One of the first things Terez did was to go down among the dwellings below the hill and set fire to them. Flick was furious about this pointless waste, and realized that he was watching his dreams of a new Saltrock go up in smoke. He watched Terez from the hill, a tall dark figure against the flames. The flames were his anger, his bitterness. He would purge the landscape where he had lived as an animal for so long.

Terez slept with Ulaume every night, because he needed aruna to make him strong. It was clear that Ulaume had ambivalent feelings about this, although he did not speak to Flick about it. Flick realized he had succeeded in freezing Ulaume off, which was not what he had intended. Mima told Flick that Ulaume had confessed to her he was drawn to Terez's dark force, and also that he wanted to hear as much as he could about Pellaz's childhood. Wraeththu were supposed to cast off the past, but perhaps in Pell's history lay the secret of why he was so different from other hara. So far, no useful information had been forthcoming. Pell had not been born in a thunderstorm or a hurricane. He had not appeared psychic as a boy. He had not had prophetic dreams. It was obvious he had been enchanting and the most favored son in the family, but Ulaume hoped to find something deeper than this. If Terez knew more than Mima did about their brother, he was keeping the information private.

Flick felt resentful of the way Terez commanded Ulaume's attention. He had opened himself up to aruna again only for it to be denied him. There were no illusions that he had fallen in love with Ulaume: Flick knew the feelings he had were entirely physical. He knew that Ulaume was aware of how he felt and probably would have been happy to share his time with Flick, but Flick couldn't bear the thought of being intimate with a har who was intimate with

Terez. He also thought that Ulaume was scared of Terez, and that was mainly why he took aruna with him so often, but Ulaume would never admit that, even to himself. Terez *was* frightening. He was an implacable force that was entirely self-serving. He was not really har, because half of him was missing: the feeling half. But, as each day passed, Terez grew more physically attractive. One day, he would be devastating, and Flick imagined that the only har who might be able to contain him then was Cal. Terez had a disturbing gaze, not because it was empty, but because it was so full of things Flick could not understand or interpret. Sometimes, it felt as if Terez might leap up, kill, and devour him. Terez despised them all, including Mima. The closeness they'd experienced at the falls had been ephemeral. Flick wondered whether Terez suspected the truth about his sister. If so, she might be in danger.

After a month or so had passed, it was clear to Flick that Mima's tolerance of Terez's strange behavior was wearing thin. She wanted to love him and be loved by him, but he barely acknowledged her existence. He didn't remain at the white house because of her, but for some other reason, about which Flick could only conjecture. Flick was sure Terez didn't regard either Mima or Lileem as abominations to be expunged; he simply wasn't interested in them at all. Mima's eyes became haunted and sad. Therefore, when the household woke up one morning to find Terez gone, along with Flick's pony, none of them were really sorry. Flick was angry and saddened to lose Ghost, but perhaps the sacrifice was worth it, if it meant Terez was no longer around. They had performed their incautious charitable act, borne the unforeseen consequences, and now it was time to move on.

That night, Ulaume came to Flick's room and Flick said nothing. He merely opened up the covers and allowed Ulaume to climb in beside him. There was no point in condemning Ulaume for his absence. He was his own creature, perhaps more like Terez than he was like Flick. They shared breath, and Flick pulled away, because he could taste something dark and sour.

"Make it go away," Ulaume said. "Please. You are stronger."

So Flick poured his heart and soul into Ulaume's being, a fierce radiance to cast out the shadows. As ouana, he had the power to command the darkness to depart.

Lying in Flick's arms, Ulaume asked, "What have we learned from all this, Flick?"

"That we shouldn't expect gratitude," Flick replied. "I was an idiot, and you were right. We should have put a pillow over his head months ago."

The Cevarro house had burned to the ground, and all the ghosts in the settlement had fled. Tonight, the breeze that came in through the window smelled of charred wood. "Perhaps we should move on now," Ulaume said. "Find somewhere else to live."

"He won't come back," Flick said. "Don't worry about it."

"It's not just that. I don't feel safe here now and it's nothing to do with Terez," Ulaume turned his head to the side and the fact that he was anxious kindled a similar feeling in Flick's heart.

Long after Ulaume had gone to sleep, Flick sat by the window, staring out over the dark landscape. Just before dawn, he saw the serpent of lights.

CHAPTER SEVENTEEN

$\succ\!\!-\!\!+\!\!\succ\!\!-\!\!\bigcirc\!\!-\!\!\prec\!\!+\!\!-\!\!\prec$

Flick shook Ulaume awake, pointed wordlessly at the window, then hurried to Mima and Lileem's room to wake them too.

"Get up!" he hissed at Mima, shaking her roughly.

She sat up quickly, instantly alert. "What is it?"

"Company," Flick said. "And I don't feel good about it. Go to the wine cellar. Take Lileem. Hide."

"But who . . . ?"

"Don't ask questions. I don't know. Just hurry."

As he left, he heard Lileem's sleepy voice murmuring querulously, and Mima's soft response.

He met Ulaume in the corridor outside his room. "There are twenty-two hara below the hill," Ulaume said.

"I warned the others," Flick said. "Told them to hide. There are twenty-two you can see, there may be more."

"They are probing us. I felt it."

"Who are they?"

"I don't know. They are more organized than a rogue troupe. Perhaps we've been wrong all along about what kind of hara initially ransacked this place, and perhaps the ones responsible have returned."

"Have they come back for Terez? Did he call them? Is he with them?" Flick did not expect answers to these questions and Ulaume did not provide them.

"This could be bad," Ulaume said. "We should think about escape."

"How? They obviously know we're here and no doubt have us surrounded. It couldn't be your tribe, could it?"

"No," Ulaume said. "They're not Kakkahaar." He narrowed his eyes, thinking. "We have no choice but to try and be friendly, compliant. You might not like what you'll have to do, but it could mean your survival."

"Will they have picked up on Lileem and Mima?"

"I hope not. They were scanning for harish life force. It does mean they have a powerful shaman with them. They must be from an established tribe."

"So what do we do?"

Ulaume took Flick's arm. "Come on. Let me do the talking. Shield your thoughts. Act dumb."

By the time they reached the kitchen, the intruders had entered the garden. They were moving through it purposefully and slowly, destroying plants underfoot. They had weapons, man-made guns from an earlier time. Flick could barely breathe. Their expressionless faces were painted with savage stripes and their hair was molded into fierce spikes. These were warrior hara, the kind who'd prowled the perimeter of his childhood home and who had eventually breached its defenses. They were not at all like the Wraeththu with whom he was familiar.

"We are har," Ulaume said. "Remember that. We mustn't show fear, only respect and dignity."

"You handle it," Flick said. "I'll quite happily forget how to talk."

Ulaume went to the kitchen door and opened it. At once, guns were raised and pointed right at him. Flick lurked in the shadows. He saw Ulaume limned against the light, raising his hands in a nonthreatening gesture.

"Greetings," Ulaume said and bowed a little.

One of the hara stepped forward. When he spoke, Flick could see his teeth had been filed into points. He carried facial scars and could not be termed beautiful. Clearly, he had opted for a fearsome appearance instead. "You are not the one," he said. "Where is he?"

Ulaume lowered his hands. "You are looking for somehar?"

"He was known as Terez."

"He still is, but I'm afraid he's no longer here. If he has called you, then he must have gone looking for you."

Flick could see that this suggestion was accepted by the savage har, and it also seemed as if the threatening troupe were on the point of leaving, because the spokeshar turned to them, muttered abruptly, and they lowered their weapons. But then another har arrived on the scene, riding a beautiful black horse. His hair was like the halo of the sun and his gray gaze looked as if it could melt steel. He was clearly the troupe leader and his horse trampled the flower beds that Flick had nurtured with his own hands.

"What is this?" the troupe leader demanded.

"The lost one is no longer here," said the fanged har.

"You!" The leader pointed at Ulaume. "Come out where I can see you."

Ulaume slunk from the shadows of the house. Flick could not see his face, but could imagine its expression: sultry and sensuous. Ulaume had gone into survival mode.

"A har was stolen from us," said the leader. "We thought him dead. Then we receive a call from him and we come back. Where is he?"

Ulaume put his hands together and bowed slowly. Pure grace. He straightened up and shook his hair, which in the still air moved as if in a breeze. "Terez was sick because of the incomplete inception. I re-incepted him and he decided to leave, to seek you out. He must have been calling to you since he regained his wits." A pause. "And I can see why."

The troupe leader's expression did not even flicker. "What are you doing here? Why are you in this human house? Who else is with you?"

"There are two of us," Ulaume said. "We are staying here temporarily."

"You have no tribe. Why?"

"We are shamans, taking leave of our kind in order to study."

"And who are your kind?"

Flick perceived Ulaume's brief pause and hoped the others did not. He must be debating whether to say Kakkahaar or Saltrock.

"Kakkahaar," Ulaume said.

"Kakkahaar do not roam alone. They are scavengers who travel in packs."

"I am Kakkahaar," Ulaume said. "Why should I lie when you could so easily find out for yourself?"

The troupe leader curled his upper lip contemptuously, then gestured at the fanged har. "Taste it!" he said.

What the fanged har did could not be described as sharing breath, because he simply grabbed hold of Ulaume and sucked the air from his lungs. Flick cringed, shrinking back against the table in the darkness of the kitchen. He imagined those monster teeth grinding against his own mouth. His heart was beating so fast, he thought he might lose consciousness. He realized he had never truly been afraid in his life before.

Outside, Ulaume was thrown to the ground, where he crouched gasping.

"Kakkahaar," confirmed the fanged har, wiping his mouth.

"Intriguing," said the troupe leader. "Was it cast out?"

"No. He has secrets, but it was his choice to leave his tribe. He is concerned for the other one inside, who is not Kakkahaar. He couldn't hide that."

"Bring it out," said the troupe leader. "I wish to view it."

Aruhani, be my strength, Flick murmured. *Aruhani, creature of magic, be with me now.*

He knew he had to summon courage and perhaps there was the suggestion of a dark shadowy form hovering in the shadows of the kitchen. He must not let these savages into the house so they could drag him out. He must remember dignity.

Flick took a deep breath, clenched his fists at his sides and went to the doorway. At once, two hara took hold of him roughly and dragged him before the black horse, which was dancing nervily among the trampled flowers.

"And where are you from, little white ghost?" asked the troupe leader.

"Saltrock," Flick said, chin high.

The troupe leader laughed. "This is an amusing alliance! Kakkahaar and Sarock. What is your reason for being here?"

"I came to fulfill a promise," Flick said, "for a friend who is dead. I met Ulaume here. You don't need to steal my breath to know that this is true. Sarocks do not lie."

Again the troupe leader laughed, and Flick was surprised and relieved that his surly demeanor seemed to have found more favor than Ulaume's attempts at seductiveness. This was important. "What promise was it, little one?"

"A promise to Terez's brother, who was incepted at Saltrock. I came back for Terez and I found him. Ulaume and I healed him and now he has left. There is nothing else to tell."

"I think there is probably a great deal more to tell," said the leader. "And I think that you will reveal it to me. I shall enjoy the experience."

"Who are you to infringe my freedom?" Flick snapped.

"I am Wraxilan," said the har on the horse. "I am the Lion of Oomar, Lord of the Uigenna, and this is my territory now. All those within it are mine."

The Uigenna took Flick and Ulaume to their camp, which they had established in the cable fields. They scorned human dwellings and clearly had no desire to set foot in the white house. They separated their captives and confined them in tepees with guards at the entrances. Flick sat in brown gloom, surrounded by the stink of untanned leather. He sat with his forehead pressed against his knees, his arms curled around his head. *Think, think, and call upon the dehara.* How much time would he have?

The one called Wraxilan will come to me, he thought, *and I must take aruna with him. I must win my freedom through winning his trust. I can do this. I must do this. We are both har. His first instinct cannot be to slaughter other hara. He just craves power over them and I will let him think he has it over me. But not easily. Remember Ulaume. Remember the Uigenna seemed to respect you more.*

But Wraxilan did not come to the tepee. Some hours later, another har brought Flick food and water. He did not appear to be hostile and Flick said, "What will he do to me?"

The har set down the food and shrugged. "What do you think? Comply, if you have any sense. You have no tribe. You could have one. Think yourself lucky. He likes you."

"What of my friend, Ulaume?"

"He's Kakkahaar. He'll survive. They always do, through deceit and cunning. He might exhaust himself in the process, but that's not your worry. Think about yourself and just do what the Lion wants. It will please him to have a Sarock in his troupe. You will be a novelty."

From this har, whose name was Morail, Flick learned that the Uigenna group who had found them was Wraxilan's select guard. The tribe as a whole had established themselves throughout the land, and farther north the bulk of them remained to build their own town on ground that had never been settled by humankind. Wraxilan had left trusted commanders in charge, while his personal troupe engaged in the process of flushing out remaining pockets of humanity, looting for provisions and tools, and subjugating weaker Wraeththu tribes. It seemed they had no intention of attacking Saltrock, or even the Kakkahaar. Saltrock offered little to them, situated as it was in such isolated hostile country, while the Kakkahaar were secretly feared. Morail did not say this in so many words, but Flick could tell that was the truth of the matter. For this reason, he thought, Ulaume would receive rough treatment from them.

"You think we are just barbarians," Morail said, apparently without resentment. "But we're not. Wraxilan has made strategic alliances with the Varrs and the Unneah. All other tribes will be absorbed. We will create unity. You are lucky we found you, because now you have an easy way in. We are respected among Uigenna, so you've come right to the top."

Flick had heard about the Varrs from Cal—and therefore knew them to be another belligerent tribe like the Uigenna—and he knew of the Unneah, because of Seel. The Unneah appeared to ally with the strongest tribes around them. Flick imagined that this suspect and certainly unstable coalition would be strongly opposed to the Gelaming. There would inevitably be conflict and suffering. History repeating itself.

Before Morail left him, Flick asked if he had heard of a har named Dorado. "He was the brother of Terez, who you came looking for."

Morail shrugged. "We incept many hara. I do not know of him. He is not with this troupe, but if you intend to seek him out when we return north, remember that many hara change their names after inception."

"And the one who incepted Terez, is he still with you? Who is he?"

"His name is Agroth. He was close to the Lion, but he was taken, some months back."

"Taken? Who by?"

"The Gelaming have spies in this land. They were probably responsible. Agroth will die before he tells them anything, but because of him, the Lion took heed of the call when it came. It was why he went back for Terez."

Once Morail had gone, Flick considered the irony of having to become Uigenna and what Seel would think about it. Cal would no doubt find it extremely amusing. He hoped that Mima had the sense to keep herself and Lileem in hiding. They might have to fend for themselves now, but would be safe in the white house until the Uigenna moved on. *Damn Terez, and damn the moment when the stupid idea of trying to help him sprang to mind.*

All day, Flick pondered how he would behave with Wraxilan and what he should say. Before sundown he must have played a hundred scenarios over in his head. It would happen tonight. It must do.

As darkness descended, Flick heard the hollow rhythm of drums start up outside, soft at first, like distant thunder, but becoming louder and more intense. He heard a strange chant begin to rise and fall, like the song of coyotes. The Uigenna were preparing for a ceremony.

The tepee entrance lifted and a Uigenna guard stood at the threshold. He gestured to Flick. "Come."

He would be taken to Wraxilan then. That made sense. Wraxilan, who believed himself to be a king, would not stoop to go to anyhar.

The har took hold of Flick's arm, which was totally unnecessary, and led him roughly through the camp. In the center, a large fire had been built and here the drummers were playing. A group of hara enacted a tribal dance around the flames, and some of them were chanting. Eyes shone in the darkness, like the eyes of cougars. Feet stamped and hair and feathers flew.

Flick's guard held him before the fire, but no har paid them any attention. Flick looked around for Ulaume but could not see him.

Then Wraxilan stepped from the largest tepee and all fell silent but for the hungry crackle of the flames. The Uigenna leader stared across the fire directly into Flick's eyes and for a moment. Flick understood the point of it all. This was so different to anything he'd experienced since inception. He'd never met hara like this. Their raw, savage power skittered like electricity over his skin. They were reputed to be cruel and were clearly barbaric, yet he could not deny that in their pride they possessed a certain primitive nobility. These were the kind of hara who had changed the world. They did not hide in the wilderness, they overran it.

Wraxilan made a gesture and Flick's guard inclined his head. "Lie down for him," he said to Flick.

"What?"

The guard did not repeat the instruction but knocked Flick from his feet by kicking him in the back of the knees. Instinct took over and Flick immediately tried to rise, to run, but other hara, uttering fearsome cries, ran over and knelt on his limbs.

It is only pelki if you see it that way, Flick thought. He closed his eyes. There was no point in fighting. It would be over sooner if he did not resist.

He could feel Wraxilan's approach and knew when the Uigenna leader stood over him, because his hot power burned into Flick's skin.

"You will be initiated into our ways," said Wraxilan. "Know this is a privilege and be grateful."

Flick would not open his eyes. He tried to distance himself, concentrate on his breathing, think of other things. He would not be a victim. He would be remote. He would not acknowledge the pain in his arms and legs where bony knees dug into him.

"Prepare him," said Wraxilan.

The hara who held Flick down got up and virtually tore off his clothes. Flick kept his eyes closed tight. He wouldn't utter a sound. Hands pulled his legs apart. He thought of the North Star, its brilliance and Wraeththu spirits dancing in its light.

He heard Wraxilan's voice, closer now. "Look at me, white ghost."

He wouldn't. Wraxilan could do as he wished with his body, but his mind and his eyes were his own.

"Look at me!"

Flick swallowed with difficulty. He anticipated the blow before it came. He felt his lip split, tasted blood. *I have a choice,* he thought. *I can open my eyes or get beaten up, and the outcome will be the same.* He opened his eyes.

Wraxilan knelt between his legs. "That is better, white ghost. Be here, not somewhere else."

I want to spit on him, Flick thought, but knew it would only make matters worse. He would look into Wraxilan's eyes, and he wouldn't show contempt. He'd show nothing, which would be more insulting.

The Uigenna's song had changed to a soft haunting mantra. Wraxilan reached out and lightly touched Flick's broken lip. "You were wrong to make me do that. It is not my wish to hurt you." He leaned down and kissed the cut, licked the blood away. Flick could feel the rhythm of the drums in the ground beneath him. "The Aghama has made me your lord," Wraxilan murmured, close to Flick's ear. "With me, you are sacred and what we do is sacred."

This was not what Flick had expected. Wraxilan's breath curled into him like smoke. Flick was powerless to prevent it and could not ignore its influence. In the sharing of breath, hara become one, and it is an act of surrender to each other, when innermost thoughts mingle and collide. Performed in this spirit, it can never be an act of violation. Flick saw a high mountaintop and eagles soaring. Then he was an eagle himself, riding the currents of air, and another eagle swooped beside him and the tips of their wings were touching.

Don't let him take me to this place, Flick prayed. *Aruhani, don't let this happen. I call upon you now. Don't.*

But Aruhani was the dehar of aruna and Flick had dreamed him into being. He was dancing now to the throb of the drums, his dark braids flying, his skin as black as oil from a hidden kingdom. He had been invoked. Wraxilan would not be violent. He was gentle and that was the greatest cruelty. Betrayed by his body, his own being, Flick lost himself to aruna, and was only partially aware that it was no longer Wraxilan upon him, but another har, then another, and another. Each of them were different flavors, different colors, that he could weave together. A shining plait of souls. Flick became like Aruhani, chaotic desire with a necklace of bones, with soume-lam that bled fire.

Ultimately, in a moment of clarity, he found himself looking into Wraxilan's eyes once more and he thought, *It is in all of us. I am no different from him.*

For a few brief seconds, Flick felt he had become Cal. He was wrapped in the familiar sensations of being with Cal, his smell, the subtle emanations of his being. He was Cal, young and naive, and Wraxilan was inside him.

The world fractured and reality exploded into splinters of light. Flick's consciousness shot up into the air and he looked down upon himself, heard himself scream. Then he smashed back into his own body and he was gasping for breath, hair across his face.

Wraxilan stood up, staggered backward. He looked disorientated, as if he'd been beaten. His voice was a raw, ragged gasp. "*He* trained you," he said.

From the moment that Pellaz Cevarro had set foot in Saltrock, the magic of coincidence had begun to pile up. Flick realized it should come as no surprise that Wraxilan was the har who'd incepted Cal. It would have perhaps been more unusual, given the mounting synchronicities of the past few years, if he hadn't.

He was taken to Wraxilan's tepee, because of course they now had to talk. Flick realized he had reached a major fork in the path of his life. He could easily become Uigenna now. He could almost predict every forthcoming moment if he made that choice and it would not be a difficult life. Because of Cal, he could have influence with Wraxilan, and probably status too. But then, there was Lileem and Mima, waiting tense and frightened in the cellar of the white house. Flick could sense their thoughts and feelings. He could taste the sour fear in their breath. He knew Mima had felt something happen to him and that she didn't know what it was and was afraid it might be death. And apart from his concern for his friends, he was sure that his fate did not lie with the Uigenna. He was destined to be more than a concubine of the Lion of Oomar. All of his senses were heightened. He dared not stare in any one place for too long, because otherwise the fabric of reality would break down and he would see what lay beyond the illusion.

Wraxilan reclined on cushions, wrapped in a loose robe of black cloth. Hara waited upon him. One poured wine into goblets from a metal flagon, while another combed out the Lion's mane. Wraxilan indicated that Flick should sit down before him. Flick realized he too was dressed in a robe and couldn't remember putting it on. Everything had gone strange.

"You must tell me," Wraxilan said.

"About Cal," Flick said. "You knew him, didn't you."

"You could say that. Did he speak of me to you?"

"No, I just saw it. I saw you incepted him."

Wraxilan nodded distractedly. "From the moment I first laid eyes on you, I must have sensed his presence around you. I didn't realize it and it was stupid of me. You could have killed me."

"I couldn't."

"Sarocks do not lie, but neither do they realize the truth, it seems. You could. You had my heart in your hand, believe me. You could have torn it out."

"That was not me exactly. It was . . ." Flick paused. He thought this would be a legendary moment, when he revealed the existence of his gods to some-har new. "It was Aruhani. He is a god of aruna, a dehar. I channeled him, accidentally."

Wraxilan sat up a little straighter. "Explain. Is this something Cal taught you?"

"No. It is what I have learned away from my tribe. And I could give this knowledge to your hara too. If I do, you must let Ulaume and I go free."

"What is the knowledge?"

"That we can create gods, which I call dehara. You could create your own and I can show you how."

Wraxilan was silent for some time. "There is no reason why you cannot stay with us. You have nothing else."

"I do not want to be part of a tribe."

Wraxilan narrowed his eyes. "No, there is something else. You have another reason. Tell me."

Flick lowered his eyes, building barriers around his thoughts. He must not betray Lileem and Mima to this har, let no light of their being seep through the cracks in his defenses.

"You know where he is, don't you," Wraxilan said in a low voice. "You are waiting to go to him."

"No!" Flick said. "It isn't that!"

"You will take me to him."

"I can't," Flick said. "I don't know where Cal is now. Part of the reason I left my kind is because of him. I need to be alone, to finish my work. That is all."

"I am not interested in your work," Wraxilan said. "You will tell me all you know of Cal. I want to hear your history with him."

Flick found there was power in revealing just as much or as little as he wanted to. He didn't tell the whole story, for he owed Wraxilan nothing. He sensed Wraxilan would not let him go free, whatever he said or did. The Lion was a collector, who liked to own unusual hara. Flick realized his only hope was to lull his captor into believing he wanted to be Uigenna and then plan an escape. For a moment, it had seemed he could bargain his way to freedom, and that he might have been able to introduce the Uigenna to the dehara, but it had quickly become clear the only god Wraxilan believed in was Cal. Once, some years ago, Cal had had his habitual devastating effect on this har and changed his life forever. Wraxilan had never forgotten and never would. He believed that Aruhani was Cal, created by Flick in Cal's image. If the dehar's skin was black where Cal's was white, it was because it represented Cal's great power, that of the hidden places where no light penetrated and the color white could not exist. Flick knew this was not so. Aruhani had nothing to do with Cal, who was a damaged and ultimately pathetic creature, no matter how much charisma and beauty he might have. If Flick was ever to share his dehara with others, it was not to be among the Uigenna.

Sometime, in the hours before dawn, Wraxilan said, "I made a mistake in teaching you how powerful you are. Now, I will risk my life when I take aruna with you. You are of Saltrock, but you are also of Cal. You can never be light again, no matter what you think."

This was not a pleasing thought and Flick hoped it was wrong, but then, only hours before, he had become something else. He had writhed in the dirt and had turned a violation into a sensual feast. Maybe he did have it in him to kill, as Cal did. Maybe he wasn't who he thought himself to be at all. Ulaume would be proud. So Flick said nothing and merely smiled.

Wraxilan indicated the cushions beside him. "A life without risks is a dull life indeed. Come, show me what else you can do."

CHAPTER EIGHTEEN

Mima's worst fear had been realized. The Wraeththu who had slaughtered her family and stolen her brothers had returned. She could sense their presence and it was familiar. This cellar, where she crouched with Lileem pressed firmly against her side, could be a sanctuary or a prison. She might be safe here or she might be trapped. Her thoughts were too confused and frightened for her to make sense of them. She couldn't make plans, couldn't even clear her head. The savages had done something terrible to Flick. She had felt his soul cry out. Ulaume was invisible. She could not sense him at all.

We are alone now, she thought. *And I don't know what to do.*

Lileem trembled against her. "Will they come looking for us?" she murmured.

"I don't know," Mima said.

"Do you think we should try to run away? What's happened to Flick and Lormy? Can we save them?"

"Hush!" Mima snapped, harsh because she had no answers.

"Flick has called upon a dehar," Lileem said. "I felt it."

"Then let us hope his gods can save him," Mima said. She pushed Lileem away from her gently and cautiously approached the cellar steps. At any moment, she expected the door above to burst open and for death to come pouring down. Slowly, she crept to the top of the steps and put her ear against the door. All was silent beyond. She extended her senses and could not discern the tingle of living energy. Still, her instincts told her not to step outside. Not yet. But they couldn't stay down here forever.

They had lanterns, but Mima was nervous of lighting one. Earlier, a few feeble shafts of light had come in through a grille at ground level, but now the sun had sunk and it was completely dark. Her semi-Wraeththu senses enabled her to perceive objects, but this was not a comfortable hiding place. Lileem was frightened and hungry and Mima's own stomach had begun to growl demandingly. All they kept down here was Sefton Richards's old stock of wine, and alcohol was the last thing she should drink now. Her head must be clear.

That night, Mima and Lileem slept in a nest of musty rotten sacks that were stiff with mildew. At one point, Mima woke up to hear Lileem weeping softly. The harling was attempting to muffle the sound in her hands. "Sssh," Mima said. "We must be strong. I will look after you."

She woke early, as thin beams of light falling in through the ventilation grille stole across her face. Today, she must steel herself to going outside. They would starve to death down here. Lileem was still asleep, so Mima eased herself away from the harling's side without waking her. She suspected Lileem had been awake most of the night. Slowly, Mima climbed the cellar steps. Her whole body itched, probably because the sacks she'd slept in were full of fleas or lice. Her skin felt sticky and her hair was stiff. Her mind was full of the image of the inviting pool by the waterfalls. At the top of the steps, just as she reached out to turn the handle on the door, it opened wide. Mima was so astonished she fell backward a few steps. Light blinded her. She didn't even have time to feel afraid.

"Mima!"

For a moment, she thought it was Ulaume and relief flooded her body, but then her eyes adjusted and she saw that it was Terez. Her throat closed up. She could not utter a sound.

He came and took hold of her arms. "It is safe. You can come out now."

Mima pulled herself away from him. Her fury was a high-pitched whine inside her head.

Lileem had woken up and had followed Mima up the steps. "You called them here, didn't you!" she cried. "They've taken Ulaume and Flick. It's your fault."

"Come out. They've gone," Terez said.

Mima took Lileem to the kitchen, where they wolfed down some of Flick's homemade bread and hunks of goat cheese. Mima could not bring herself to speak to Terez. Her rage and disappointment were a boulder in her neck, past which no sound could squeeze.

Lileem, however, could not keep silent, even while she was stuffing bread into her mouth. "You're evil!" she screamed, bits of chewed food flying from her lips across the table. "Flick and Lormy brought you back and you betrayed them. You should die!"

Terez stood with folded arms, leaning against the wall, apparently regarding Lileem's tirade with indifference. When the harling had exhausted her stock of complaints, he pushed himself away from the wall and went to fetch water from the sink. He placed a cup of it next to Mima's plate. She sniffed in contempt, but drained the cup. He filled it again and handed it to Lileem.

"There is something you should know," Terez said.

Mima uttered a choked laugh. "And what is that? That we were fools to help you?"

"The Wraeththu who incepted me, and who came back for me, they are Uigenna."

"Ulaume told me Cal was Uigenna," Mima said, the first thought that came into her head, followed by the second, which derived from what Flick and Ulaume had told her about the Wraeththu tribes. "They are monsters! You should have told us this! You lied to us. You said you didn't know what tribe they were."

"I learned many things in the darkness, Mima, and one of them was how certain other tribes regarded the Uigenna. I could not tell Ulaume about this. He might have realized I could call to them, because they are strong, and that they would hear my call and return. I let him think some rogue hara attacked this place."

Mima bared her teeth. "And you let Flick and Ulaume fall into their hands? What will they do to them?"

"I don't know. How can I? I only know the one I was seeking was not with them. Neither was Dorado. I came back here because I sensed my call had been answered."

"You're too late," Mima said. "You shouldn't have bothered coming back. They've left without you again."

"They will be easy to follow this time," Terez said. "You will wait here for me."

"What?" Mima picked up her plate and threw it at him. It bounced off his head then shattered on the floor. "How dare you!"

Terez raised a hand to his brow, rubbed it. "You are angry," he said. "I understand that, but I'll bring them back. I have to."

"Bring them back?" Mima leapt to her feet. "What do you mean? Will you hand Lee and me over to them? Is this how you'll wheedle your way back in with them?"

"Ulaume and Flick," Terez said. "I will bring them back, and then you must move on."

"Why should you care?" Mima said. "You have made your feelings about us very clear."

"Pell has told me to do this."

"Oh, has he!" Mima said. "I don't believe you."

"He came to me," Terez said, "and I realize Flick is precious to him. I will bring them back."

"Why would he come to you and not to me?" Mima said. "He would never have done that. You know it. I was the one he was close to, not you, and you are jealous of it, always have been."

"You tried to keep him to yourself, I know," Terez said. "But you're wrong if you think I was jealous. Pell had his own way with Dorado and me, a different kind of closeness shared only between brothers. You were never part of it, and that is why he came to me now and not you."

"You're insane!" Mima cried. "We should have let you die. We should have killed you, like Ulaume wanted to."

"You don't mean that," he said. "I know you don't."

Mima slumped back into her chair. "This is a mess," she said. "A hideous mess."

Terez sat down beside her. "I dreamed of Pell and perhaps the voice that spoke to me was my own, but I knew I had to return. I knew what would happen and that it wasn't right. Ulaume and Flick did what they could for me. I can feel their fear and their pain. I will bring them back and the score will be settled."

"You are not my brother anymore," Mima said.

"No, I'm not." Terez stood up again. "Keep watch, but I think it will be safe for you to stay here until I return."

"If you return."

Terez said nothing, but walked out of the kitchen door, closing it gently behind him.

Mima raised her eyes and looked into Lileem's wide accusing stare. She shrugged. "What can we do but trust him, Lee?"

Lianvis had fallen in love with Ulaume's wiles at first sight and Ulaume had known how to manipulate the situation to his advantage. He'd thought he'd known the rules, what strategy to use. But now, none of it would work. For a start, Wraxilan had no interest in him, so Ulaume had no opportunity to ingratiate himself with the Uigenna leader. Second, it was clear the Uigenna harbored the greatest suspicion and contempt for the Kakkahaar. It gave no advantage to understand this was because they feared the desert tribe, because now they had a Kakkahaar alone. He was outnumbered and they could do what they liked to assuage the resentment they felt. The Uigenna were amoral. They had the highest respect for aruna, but could also turn to its darker side without shame. Pelki stripped the sanctity from Wraeththu's most sacred creed. It was denial of the individual; it could unmake a har.

Like Flick, Ulaume realized that cooperation was the best strategy. If he complied, then what they did to him could not be pelki. But this could not stop their taunts, their laughter. Ulaume could not be himself. He could only be an object of ridicule. That first night, a few of Wraxilan's closest hara came to the tepee where Ulaume was confined and amused themselves at his expense. He endured this and gave up trying to please them, because it did no good. Neither did they care if he was remote or not. He was just an object. Sometime, half through the night, Ulaume had had enough. He retaliated.

It happened involuntarily. One moment a har was pawing at his body, the next Ulaume's hair had wrapped him in a strangling embrace. Ulaume squeezed hard, felt the life start to trickle out. His ears were filled with a buzzing shriek. He could hear panicked voices around him only faintly. His fingernails dug into tender flesh. He felt them sink in, like a blade through softened butter. If he dug hard enough he'd reach through muscle and flesh and find something more vital to tear at.

Then came the terrible pain. His head exploded with it, as if lightning had struck him. He was on fire. Ulaume uttered a roar, lashed out with clawed hands, but someone was sawing at his hair with a serrated knife. They held his limbs, punched his face, his stomach. It lasted for an eternity.

He was on his knees, trying to breathe. On his knees in a swamp of slippery tawny locks. And around his face, each severed hair was bleeding. His head was a cauldron of pain.

The Uigenna stood around him in a circle, perhaps revolted by what they saw. He could hear their heavy breathing. The dying serpents of Ulaume's hair writhed and flopped around him and what was left bled in thin threadlike streams onto his shoulders and down his chest. Since the day of his inception to the Colurastes, Ulaume had never cut his hair. Although he had imagined it when he'd first arrived at the white house, he knew he would never have done it. His instincts wouldn't have let him, and this was why. It had never been dead.

"Freak!" One of the hara kicked him in the side.

"Let's get out of here," another said, and even in the delirium of pain, Ulaume heard the fear in his voice.

Left alone, he knelt on the ground, hands braced against it. His breathing was labored. Eventually, the bleeding stopped and his head went numb. He dared not move. There was no way out of this. He was lost and his power was lost.

The following morning, the Uigenna struck camp. Ulaume was dragged naked from his tepee and taken to a covered wagon. Inside, was a cage in which a mountain lion crouched: Wraxilan's pet. Beside it, was another cage: empty. The Uigenna threw Ulaume into the empty cage and locked it. He hunched there, almost mindless, his hair hanging over his face, stiff with dried blood. His face was a bloody mask. He stared at the lion and the lion stared back. They had nothing to say to one another.

When the lion was fed, Ulaume was fed. He was let out of the cage to re-lieve himself. He didn't know in which direction they were heading or what would happen to him. His life was this: confinement. Perhaps when they reached the Uigenna town, Wraxilan would give him as a gift to one of his fa-vored aides.

It seemed that months passed, but it was only a few days. On the evening of the third day, the cages were unloaded from the wagon. Through the bars, Ulaume could see that the Uigenna were making camp, and it appeared to be more permanent than the last few nights. There must be something in this area that demanded their lengthy attention. A har, who Ulaume now regarded as his keeper, came to open the cages. He put a leash on both Ulaume and the lion and let them out. The lion must have been kept in this way since it was young, because it had no spirit. It did not lash out with its great paws and knock the har senseless, as it surely could have done.

"You're to clean yourself up," said the keeper to Ulaume. "Somehar wants you tonight."

This was not welcome news, but perhaps Ulaume might be lucky and find himself with har who could be influenced by his charms—what was left of them.

The keeper led his charges to a deep watering hole, surrounded by high rocks. Here the lion crouched to drink. Ulaume went into the water and sub-merged himself, joined to the land by the leash. He wondered if he had the courage to drown himself. The har who held him did not yank the leash or pull him back. Ulaume relaxed, let his limbs float free. He felt the blood melt from him and drift away. His hair would grow again. He rubbed at his face with his hands, then smoothed his body. He must remember hope and strength. As long as he was alive, he had the power to make changes.

As he thought this, the leash jerked. Ulaume gulped water and floundered a little. Stupid har! His first instinct was to grab the leash and pull back, haul his hated keeper into the water, but he realized this would not be a good move. If he failed to overpower the har, he could end up dead. Now, he was being pulled back to the bank of the water hole. Breaking through the water's surface, Ulaume coughed and blinked. He pushed wet hair from his eyes. Above him, standing on the bank, he saw a tall dark figure that looked like a manifestation of Aruhani himself. It seemed to emanate dark light. This figure crouched down and held out a hand. Ulaume took it and a familiar sensation of rushing dark energy coursed up his arm. Terez had returned to the Uigenna, then. Ulaume saw the lion cowering some feet away and a bundle of cloth and limbs that looked very much like a dead har. It appeared Terez had not returned to be a part of the tribe.

"Terez," Ulaume said. "That *is* you, isn't it?"

Terez hauled him from the water. "Yes. They've made a mess of you." This observation was delivered without feeling.

"Thanks to you. Have you killed that har? Why? This isn't a rescue, is it?"

"Yes it is," Terez said. "Stop gabbing and take that leash off."

Ulaume did so. "Well, well. Did guilt actually get to you?"

Terez exhaled impatiently through his nose. "I have been observing the troupe for a couple of days. Needed to be sure of where you were being held. Now, we will release Flick. Strip the Uigenna of his clothes and dress yourself. Be quick."

Ulaume wondered whether this might be a dream: dressing himself in the clothes of a dead har, rescued by a living dead har. His keeper had worn a tasseled scarf around his head. Ulaume took this and beneath it hid his butchered hair. He unleashed the lion and hoped it might go free, but it probably wouldn't. It would sit there shivering until somehar came for it and discovered its keeper was dead.

"Do you know where they're keeping Flick?" Ulaume asked.

"More or less, but it'll be easy to find out precisely."

"I hope you can do it, then," Ulaume said. "My senses aren't what they should be at the moment."

"Yes." Terez threw back his head, closed his eyes and inhaled deeply. After a moment, he opened his eyes again and without glancing at Ulaume said, "This way. Keep to the shadows."

There was little security in the Uigenna camp, because they clearly didn't think they had anything in this area to secure themselves against. Some hara were busy erecting tepees, building fires and cooking food. Others were attending to animals, horses, and the small flock of sheep that accompanied the troupe. There were no idle hands. Ulaume and Terez picked up a bale of fodder each that they found in a pile next to a newly erected tepee and made their way round the edge of the camp, keeping a distance from every har else. Flick was being kept apart from the main camp, which was most convenient. Even as they approached, Ulaume could feel the familiar warmth of Flick's spirit, and it was like coming home, even though he could tell Flick was far from happy.

Two Uigenna guards were stationed at the entrance to the tepee. Terez called to them and they both looked his way. Ulaume had taken a knife from the lion keeper. His strength had returned with his hope. In an instant, he leapt forward and cut a har's throat. Terez dealt with the other one by twisting his neck. Ulaume heard the damp snap of bone. Terez then finished off the har whose throat Ulaume had cut. It was over so quickly. Together, Ulaume and Terez dragged the bodies behind the tepee, before anyhar noticed something was amiss.

"Get Flick," Terez said. "Meet me back at the water hole. I'll fetch horses." He backed away into the shadows.

Ulaume went into the tepee and saw Flick crouched on a large silk cushion. He was pale, with dark circles beneath his eyes, dressed up like a Kakkahaar whore. Ulaume could not imagine what he might have lived through over the past few days.

"Come!" Ulaume said. "Now Flick. We're leaving."

Flick looked confused for a moment. "Ulaume?" He stared at the fresh blood on Ulaume's shirt.

"Quick, no time for talk. Come on." Ulaume grabbed hold of Flick's left hand and dragged him out of the tepee, desperate to get him beyond the light of the camp torches. He was afraid that somehar would pass the back of the tepee and spot the dead bodies. Then the alarm would be raised.

Without words, Ulaume and Flick ran to the water hole. Terez wasn't there. "By Aru, I hope he makes it!" Ulaume hissed. "You won't believe it, Flick, but it was Terez who rescued us."

Flick was staring at the dead har. The lion had wandered off after all. "Terez," Flick said weakly. "I wish we'd killed him." There was a bitterness in Flick's voice that Ulaume hadn't heard before.

"Well, if we had, then the Uigenna might still have returned, and we'd have had no knight in shining armor to save us," Ulaume said, "so maybe you were right about Terez after all."

Flick merely grunted.

Ulaume heard the sound of hooves on the packed earth and then Terez appeared out of the darkness with the reins of three horses in his hand. One of them was Ghost. The animals stomped and snorted behind him. Terez put a finger to his lips for silence, then indicated they should mount up. He began to climb onto Ghost, but Flick pushed him aside and swung into the saddle himself. Terez shrugged and mounted another horse.

They walked the animals for about a hundred yards from the camp, then urged them into a gallop. *The trouble with desert travel,* Ulaume thought, *was that you left a very obvious trail.* A mile or so from the Uigenna, Terez directed them east, toward the cordillera.

"They'll follow us," Flick said.

"We have the lead," Terez said. "We must keep it up."

At dawn, they had passed beyond the foothills and were in a deeply forested region. Here, Terez decided it was safe for them to rest the horses for a couple of hours. Ulaume and Flick were so shocked and exhausted, they were happy to let Terez take control. They would have to take it in turns to keep watch. Terez offered to do so first.

Flick and Ulaume did not contest this. They climbed into a wide hollow tree and here Ulaume took off his scarf.

"Oh no," Flick said. "Your hair. Your face." He reached to touch Ulaume's head, but Ulaume pulled away. He couldn't bear for it to be touched now.

"It'll grow back," he said. "And bruises fade. How are you?"

"All right. Better than you." Flick reached out and gripped Ulaume's right arm. "I'm so sorry."

"Terez is the one who should be apologizing, not you," Ulaume said.

"Why did he come for us?"

"I don't know and I don't care. I'm just glad he did."

"We can't let them take us again."

"We won't. I'll die first."

Ulaume knew they should sleep, because they'd need their strength, but it was difficult to surrender to it. His senses strained to pick up sounds of pursuit. The best he could hope for was a short time out of saddle. He wouldn't sleep until he felt safe.

Flick clearly felt the same. He explained how Wraxilan was obsessed with Cal and believed that Flick was in touch with him. "He wouldn't listen to me. It was what he wanted to believe. I felt that at any moment, one night, he'd go mad and try to beat it out of me, the information I don't have." He paused. "Ulaume, those hara are . . . The things I did . . ." He shook his head. "I can't speak of it."

Ulaume stroked his face. "We escaped. We survived. That is all that matters."

Flick sighed. "Yes, I suppose so." He paused. "We won't be able to return to Casa Ricardo and live there as before, will we."

"No," Ulaume said. "It would be safer if we moved on."

"Where will we go?"

"Just away," Ulaume replied. "Ask your dehara. Quest for the advice we need."

Flick uttered a strange sound of angry despair. "I'm not sure I trust the dehara anymore."

"Why not?"

"I don't want to talk about it."

"Okay," Ulaume said carefully.

Flick snuggled up against Ulaume for warmth, and Ulaume put his arms around him. Ulaume was just drifting off to sleep when he heard Flick say, "There is something terrible in us. We are no better than humanity, just stronger and more dangerous."

Ulaume did not answer. He'd known that for a long time.

CHAPTER NINETEEN

><->-O-<->-<

Five years after Cal had witnessed the death of Pellaz Cevarro in Megalithica, Thiede brought his reborn Wraeththu king to Immanion. The Tigron was renamed Pellaz-har-Aralis, and through his sons would begin to create the great Aralis dynasty.

Seel was not in the city when Pell arrived there. He was in Thaine, a country to the northwest of Almagabra, supervising the building of a Wraeththu settlement. A message came to him via an otherlanes courier to return to Immanion at once. Thiede wanted him to be there for Pell's coronation.

That night, Seel sat up alone, shunning the company of his friends, and drank himself into a stupor. Now that it was about to happen, he dreaded having to face Pell. The following morning, he sent a message back to Immanion, informing Thiede he would not be able to get away from his project for two weeks, and he hoped this would be acceptable. A message returned quickly to say that it was. Thiede must know Seel needed time to compose himself for the forthcoming meeting.

However, the thought of two weeks of anxiety eventually got to Seel. Perhaps it would be better to get this over with. After only two days, he saddled up his *sedu* and traveled to Immanion.

The city had grown even more since Seel had last been there, and that had only been a couple of months before. The last of the scaffolding had come down from the walls of the Hegalion, where the Hegemony sat in council several days a week. Its great roof had been covered in gold leaf and Seel saw a new forked banner flying high from the tallest staff. He knew from designs that Thiede had shown to him that it sported the colors of the Tigron: purple and gold. A rampant flying horse dominated the center. This must signify, Seel presumed, that Pellaz was present in the city.

Seel went directly to Thiede's villa and hoped he would be home. Thiede had an apartment in the palace Phaonica as well, but usually returned to his villa to sleep. Fortunately he was in residence, and his steward conducted Seel into his presence. He was still taking breakfast, wearing his dressing gown and appeared quite surprised that Seel had arrived so early.

"How is he?" Seel asked, not wishing to waste time or mince words.

"Perfect," Thiede answered, gesturing for his steward to pour Seel a glass of coffee. "I am delighted with my success."

Seel sat down at Thiede's table. "What have you told him about me?"

"That you were reluctant to leave Saltrock, but are prepared to come here to be part of his staff."

"Why not tell the truth? I am a fawning lapdog of yours like everyhar else."

Thiede laughed. "Never that, tiahaar. We'll go to Phaonica as soon as I have dressed. Let's surprise Pell, shall we?"

Seel had not set foot in the palace Phaonica before. Thiede had often invited him to look around it, but a kind of squeamishness had always prevented Seel from accepting. He hadn't wanted to think about how one day a living dead har would call it home. It was a magnificent building, as the abode of the Tigron would have to be. Situated at the top of a hill, it was surrounded on all sides by tiered gardens that had been landscaped by the most creative of Wraeththu gardeners. Phaonica was like a small town within the city proper. Every need of the Tigron would be catered for. Produce would be grown for him in the kitchen gardens, fresh eggs laid by a flock of sleek black hens, milk and cream given by gentle dairy cows. The palace was so huge, it was bewildering and Seel wondered how a humble farmer's son from southern Megalithica felt to be living in such a grand place.

They found Pellaz in the library of the palace with another har, whom Thiede informed Seel was now Pell's personal aide. The doors were open and Thiede indicated they should approach quietly. In this way, Seel had the advantage of being able to stare at Pell for several seconds before he looked up from what he was reading. Thiede was right. Pell was perfect. He was taller than Seel remembered, and so beautifully formed (there was no other way Seel could describe it to himself) that he appeared unearthly. Seel felt dizzy. The dead had come to life. A more beautiful version of Pell had been snatched from some heavenly realm and the reality of him was disorientating. Seel still wasn't sure whether a knife to his throat would not be the best option.

"Pell," Thiede said. "You have a visitor."

Pellaz raised his head and those luminous dark eyes stared right into Seel's gaze. Pell froze.

Seel inclined his head. "Hello Pellaz. You look well."

"Seel," Pell said in a bewildered voice. "I knew you were coming but . . ."

"I managed to get away early."

Pell nodded. "Yes . . ." He smiled, head enchantingly tilted to one side. "Oh, Seel. It's wonderful you're here." He ran across the short distance between them and wrapped Seel in a tight embrace.

Seel staggered a little, felt winded. He could smell clean hair and exotic perfume. He could feel the warmth of a living body. After a moment, he thought he'd better return the embrace and did so. "Well," he said awkwardly, "whoever would have thought it would come to this."

"Thank you for coming," Pell said, drawing away from him. "I'm so glad to see you."

"I'm rather amazed to see *you*, but—"

"I know," Pell said. "I understand." He led Seel to a chair and pressed him into it, then sat on the wide arm of it. "You must tell me all about Saltrock. How is everyhar there? Thiede told me Orien is dead. It's terrible. What happened?" He gestured at the rather haughty red-haired har who was his aide. "Vaysh, bring us some refreshments."

Seel couldn't speak.

"Later," Thiede said smoothly. "I think Seel is rather more interested in hearing about you."

"Yes," Seel said. "I am. You look incredible, Pell. I can't take this in."

"I'm going to be king—Tigron," Pell said. He sounded like an excited child.

"I know," Seel said. He wondered how long it would take for the responsibility of that to knock all vestiges of innocence from this radiant har. Pellaz was reborn in every sense. He was like an unmarked page. Seel couldn't dispel discomforting images of the way Pell had appeared in the pod at Thiede's ice palace. He found himself wondering whether this was just a beautiful shell, and the real Pellaz was all rotten and black inside.

"I need friends," Pell said. "Hara here are suspicious of me."

"Hmm," Seel murmured. "Well, here I am."

"I don't have an inception scar anymore."

"No, I don't suppose you do." Seel glanced at Thiede darkly. This was hideous. Pell had no idea how uncomfortable Seel felt.

"There's this har called Ashmael," Pell said. "You must meet him. He hated me, but I don't think he does as much now. He's quite scary."

Seel had spent two exhausting nights with Ashmael before leaving for Thaine. He wished Thiede had told Pell the truth, that Seel had been part of the Gelaming administration for some time. He foresaw future difficulties.

Thiede rolled his eyes in their sockets behind Pell's back. He was grinning. Seel grimaced at him. Pellaz was such an innocent. Seel felt sorry for him. He was completely ignorant of everything, a condition in which Thiede most likely preferred to keep him.

"We'll all dine together later at my apartment here in the palace," Thiede said. "I think you should let Seel leave now, Pell. I just wanted him to drop in and see you. He no doubt wishes to refresh himself after his journey here."

"Of course," Pell said, rising from his seat.

Seel stood up and Pell held out his hand to him. His expression was kind, but there was a hint of arrogance about it. Not self-aggrandizing, but merely that of a har who knew in his blood he was born to be served. Seel took the hand, pressed it to his lips and his brow. It was an involuntary gesture of respect. He bowed his head. Without doubt, Thiede had created a king.

For some time, Seel managed to hold off Pell's incessant questions about Saltrock and Orien, which was difficult because Pell wanted Seel to be near him most of the time. Seel did not want to be the one to tell Pell about Cal, because he knew the information would hurt Pell very much. The potential Tigron talked about Cal as if they would be together again one day. "He goes to Saltrock sometimes, doesn't he?" he asked Seel. "Thiede doesn't want me to see him again, I'm sure, but you could get a message to him for me. Perhaps we could even meet at Saltrock."

Comments of this kind were excruciating to Seel. But it was when Pell finally mentioned Flick that the dam broke and Seel revealed all.

The coronation was only a few days away and Seel was in Pell's dressing room, keeping him company while a gang of costumiers fussed over his coronation regalia. At some point in the conversation, Pell asked Seel why he hadn't brought Flick to Immanion with him.

Seel knew then that the time for prevarication had past. *Just tell him,* he thought. *Once it's out, it's out. Tell him everything.*

So he did. He told it as succinctly as possible, all the time watching Pell sink into a terrible despair. He couldn't tell it quickly enough. By the end of the story Pell was slumped in a chair, his head in his hands. "*I* did that," he said, over and over. "*I* did that."

Seel knew that Pell perceived no distance or awkwardness between them, because up until this moment he'd been so enmeshed in the heady experience of being alive in a wonderful new body, about to become Tigron of all Wraeththu. A fairy-tale ending to a marvelous story. Now, Seel knew he had shattered it. The first bits of Pell's childlike wonder and innocence had been chipped away. Perhaps it would have been better to keep him in ignorance, but how could he be a true Tigron if he remained that way? Seel thought that if he was to conspire in Thiede's plans at all, it must include teaching Pell some autonomy, guiding him to wisdom. He could not embrace Pell spontaneously, because of all that had happened, but now he forced himself to cross the room and take the shuddering slender body in his arms. He murmured words of consolation. Pell couldn't blame himself for this. If anyhar was responsible, it was Thiede and Cal's insane stupidity or stupid insanity.

"You hate him, don't you," Pell mumbled, against Seel's chest. "You hate Cal now."

Seel only tightened his arms around him. *It's more than hate,* he thought. *So much more.*

Two days later, the whole of Immanion turned out to line the streets for the Tigron's coronation. The holiday would last two days, with continual feasting and parties in all corners of the city. It should have been the best day of Pell's life. He rode through the streets to the High Nayati in a carriage decked with garlands, surrounded by cheering hara. Ashmael's select guard, mounted on glossy *sedim,* led the procession. Hara threw olive sprigs and flowers into the carriage. They touched their brows in gestures of respect. Some, as they gazed upon Pell, wept openly. Pell kept a smile upon his face, but even so Seel knew the whole experience was now blighted for him by the bitter knowledge he held in his heart. When he swore allegiance to Wraeththukind in the High Nayati, his voice rang clear and true and perhaps only Seel heard the note of sadness that lay deep within it. At least Pellaz had a cause to which he could devote himself. As Tigron, there would be little time for him to dwell upon the past.

A private feast for the Tigron was held after the coronation in Phaonica. The salons of the palace were crammed with Gelaming dignitaries as well as representatives from many foreign tribes. In the main room, where Pellaz held court, tirelessly being nice to an endless procession of faces, Ashmael took Seel aside. They hadn't met since Seel had returned to Immanion. "Well?" Ashmael said. "What do you think?"

Seel shrugged. "He'll do the job. Anyhar can see that."

"He's as green as a lettuce," Ashmael said and took a long drink of wine. He had already consumed quite a lot.

Ashmael had never condemned Seel for not being able to kill Pell when he'd had the chance, because he respected Seel's judgment, but he was still not at all happy about Thiede's protégé becoming Tigron. Mainly, Seel thought, this was because Ashmael had fancied the role for himself. Thiede was right not have chosen him though. Ashmael had a tendency to be hot-headed and he could easily have become a dictator rather than a Tigron, who deferred to the Hegemony in all matters.

"Give him a chance," Seel said. "He didn't ask for this."

"Oh, I will," Ashmael said darkly. "But the minute he starts trying to throw his weight around, he's carrion."

Seel snorted. "Oh, for the Aghama's sake, Ash, that's not going to happen. Look at him."

Ashmael glanced over to where Pell sat, a picture of regal splendor. They could hear the Tigron's laughter: spontaneous, warm, and genuine. "Power does things to hara," Ashmael said in a grumpy tone. Seel noticed his gaze lingered for few moments on the Tigron's aide, Vaysh.

"Doesn't it just!"

Part of the reason Ashmael was, to put it mildly, cautious about Pell was because of Vaysh. Pell had told Seel that Pell's aide was another protégé of Thiede's, one who had been kept completely secret. Vaysh had been an earlier candidate for Tigronship, and had undergone the same traumatic death and re-birth experience that Pell had. But Vaysh was one of the less successful attempts that the Hegemony had heard rumors about. Something had gone wrong, and although Vaysh appeared physically perfect on the surface, the resurrection rite had affected his fertility, so he could never produce heirs, either as soume or ouana. This was not desirable to Thiede; his Tigron had to be perfect. Unfortunately, Vaysh had once been Ashmael's chesnari, and perhaps initially Thiede had beguiled Ash into becoming Gelaming for the same reason he had beguiled Seel. As Cal had with Pell, Ash had believed Vaysh to be dead, but their story had not ended with a happy reunion. Ashmael had only realized Vaysh was alive when he'd turned up in Immanion with Pell. Seel could only imagine what Ashmael must have gone through over the past weeks. He was not a har prone to displays of emotion and as far as Seel knew the only har with whom he'd discussed the matter had been Pellaz himself, which was odd given his feelings for the Tigron. Now, it was clear that in some peculiar way he held Pell partly responsible for what had happened to Vaysh.

"Pell is a good har," Seel said. "Don't let your personal feelings cloud the issue."

Ashmael cast him a sharp glance. "Meaning?"

Seel stared at him meaningfully. "*You* know." He paused. "Why don't you just go and talk to him? Pell told me everything, Ash."

"Charming. That was supposed to have been a private conversation."

"He didn't tell it like gossip. He feels for you. Have you even spoken to Vaysh since he came here?"

"That's none of your business, Seel. Back off."

"You're repulsed by him, aren't you, which must be pretty grim because you still love him too."

"Shut the fuck up."

"You have the honeyed tongue of a diplomat."

Ashmael finished his drink. "Sorry, that's a sore spot."

"I know how you feel," Seel said. "Pell spooks me too sometimes. He is possibly the most beautiful har in the whole world, but the thought of touching him makes me shudder."

Ashmael regarded Seel thoughtfully. "That's the gist of it." He helped himself to another glass of wine from a tray carried by a passing house-har. "You know, I think it must be because we knew them before. For example, even though I can't help feeling our beloved Tigron is a bit of a dizzy idiot, I could quite easily carry him off for a night of abandoned passion, whereas my flesh crawls at the thought of Vaysh. Just out of interest, what do you feel about him?"

Seel grimaced. "Mmm, difficult. He can freeze blood at twenty paces. If he wasn't so stony, I could probably endure it."

"He wasn't always like that," Ashmael said wistfully. "He was a creature full of joy and love. I hate this thing that has stolen his face. It's not right."

"It's not his fault, Ash."

Ashmael sighed deeply. "I know. Still . . ." He drained his glass. "I'm bored. Fancy coming back to my place for a frolic?"

Seel found he had to glance over at Pell to make sure the Tigron didn't need him. He was annoyed at himself for it, but couldn't help checking. Pellaz, however, was still in the thick of an adoring throng and clearly had no need for support. "Sounds good," Seel said. "Let's go."

Although Pellaz was now Tigron and began to learn quickly how to fulfill his potential, he was also very fragile, because his love for Cal had left a gaping wound in his heart. Seel felt protective toward him, in spite of himself, and never told him the full story of when Cal had returned to Saltrock. There was no need for Pell to know. The bare facts were enough to wound him deeply. Still, he was made of sterner stuff than Cal, because he hadn't gone mad or maudlin. Mostly, he kept his thoughts to himself and maintained a cheery face.

Seel watched Pellaz all the time. He saw how certain members of the Hegemony sought to humiliate their new Tigron, yet Pell was always gracious with them. Seel had to admit that Thiede had chosen well. Pell had dignity and respect for others. He would never lose his temper and end up yelling regrettable things in meetings like Ashmael often did. He had to meet new hara endlessly, as representatives from various tribes showed up in Immanion, wanting to be part of Thiede's new world, and determined to be treated with the esteem they thought they deserved. Pell was always courteous to them and gave the appearance of being interested in everything they had to say. His generosity of spirit seemed limitless. In his place, Seel would have lost patience many times. As time went on, Pell inevitably became somewhat imperious, but his positive aspects more than outweighed his autocratic manner. The Tigron could not be a groveling fool. He had to stand tall and proud. And he did.

Occasionally, Pell would mention Flick, in a cautious way, and say that perhaps he should look for him. "Don't you wonder where and how he is?" he asked Seel. "We are here, living a privileged life, and Flick should be also. He was a good friend to me at the beginning. He helped me through inception, and we don't even know if he's still alive."

"Let it go," seel advised. "You knew a lot of hara before, Pell. You can't look up every old friend. You are Tigron." Another thing Seel had kept from Pell was that Flick had left Saltrock to look for the Cevarro family.

"Don't you care about him anymore?"

"Of course I do, but sometimes, you know, you just have to walk away. It was over between him and me a long time ago. We weren't that close, not really. Flick just grew up, I guess. He moved on." Seel didn't mention that he believed Flick would have no desire to see him again. He still harbored guilt about the way he'd treated Flick in the past.

Eventually, Pell let the matter drop, but Seel knew he was rather puzzled by Seel's apparent lack of concern.

A difficult time arose some months after Pell's coronation when a har named Caeru Meveny turned up in Immanion, claiming to be the hostling of the Tigron's son. Thiede, who had been looking out for a consort for Pell, leapt on this glad coincidence with the zeal of a famished tiger. While Pell was still reeling from the shock of Rue's arrival, he found himself bonded in blood to this virtual stranger, who should—in Pell's words—have remained as nothing more than a one-night stand, doomed to be forgotten. Pellaz was furious, because Thiede tricked him into taking Rue as consort. Seel could not quite understand what had possessed Pell to create a pearl with a har he'd barely known, but Pell's excuse was that he hadn't realized how easy it would be for him to do it. It had happened very shortly after Pell had left Thiede's ice palace, in a town en route to Immanion.

Now, in an almost indecently short space of time, Rue had been installed as Tigrina of Immanion. Although Seel wasn't that impressed by him, and Pellaz would quite happily have wrung his neck, the populace swiftly took him to their hearts. As Thiede pointed out, Rue was perfect for the job. He had once been a singer in a band. He looked good, was an excellent performer in public and knew how to win over crowds. Pell, however, simply regarded him as an adventurer who had effectively stolen a place that was reserved—at least in Pell's heart—for Cal. Seel had never seen Pell be hostile to a har before, nor could have imagined he was capable of it. He had always appeared to like every har he met, so the strength of his feelings, and the uncharacteristic behavior they inspired, were shocking. His biased but eloquent opinions had a strong effect on Seel, who privately wondered whether his own antipathy toward the new Tigrina was also encouraged by the fact he had white-gold hair like Cal's.

Seel comforted and supported Pell through the first grueling months of his bloodbond with Rue, and it was as exhausting for Seel as it was the Tigron himself. Public appearances were horrific. Rue was a strange mixture of heartbroken grief and calculating manipulativeness. He was either a besotted wretch or very clever, because Seel never saw him do anything but try to please Pell and win him over. Hara noticed this. They witnessed Pell's steely distant demeanor and they did not approve. Seel could tell Rue loved Pell passionately, but for how long? What love could stand up to such repeated battering? Seel considered that Pell was doing himself no favors in forcing that strength of feeling to become hate. Rue would make a tough adversary, and Seel could envisage a day when the veiled hostilities might descend into a humiliating and public popularity contest. One thing was certain: no matter what hara in the street perceived or were shown, Pell and Rue would never be chesna. A blood-bond was supposed to be sacred and hallowed; not to be undertaken lightly. What the Tigron and Tigrina had was the nuptial equivalent of pelki. Not even their son brought them together. Abrimel was closer to his hostling than to his father. Seel noticed the contemptuous way the harling looked at Pell, and guessed he'd been subject to some fierce indoctrination from Rue. Pell did little to improve his relationship with his son. Abrimel witnessed some ugly scenes between his parents.

Observing most of the unpleasantness firsthand, Seel made a mental note to himself: *Don't ever do anything like this. There are no hara in the world who are worth bonding in blood to. There are no relationships of that kind that truly endure. Humans were obsessed with marriage, and that was a sham. As Wraeththu, we have aruna, we are grown up. This is pathetic.*

One time, Pellaz said to Seel, "I don't know what I'd do without you. Don't ever leave me."

And Seel promised that he wouldn't.

Thiede, however, had other ideas. He waited until Pellaz had settled firmly into his new life and had won around the most intransigent members of the Hegemony. He waited until he knew for sure that Ashmael supported the Tigron. He waited until Seel was complacent and then, with the brutal precision that was his mark, he summoned Seel to a private meeting.

Ever since Seel had moved to Almagabra, the Gelaming had been involved in conflict in Megalithica. They were strongly opposed to warmongering tribes like the Uigenna and the Varrs, and their objective was to oust these hara from power, so that they would not oppress weaker tribes. That was the propaganda, in any case. A cynical mind might suggest that the Gelaming were just as power-hungry as the Uigenna and the Varrs, and that this was simply a war over territory. Ashmael was often away for months at a time, supervising the movements of the Gelaming army. When he was home, he often wanted to discuss the minutae of his campaigns with Seel, but Seel wasn't really that interested. Even the mention of Megalithica's name made him feel uncomfortable, as if there was something important he should have done and he couldn't remember what it was. To Seel, there was no point in talking about it. He took it for granted that Thiede would achieve his aims, whatever they were, and he had no desire to hear about combat. He did not think, for one moment, that eventually Thiede's inevitable success would affect his own life in a colossal way.

Thiede received Seel in the office of his Phaonica apartment, and when Seel entered the room, Thiede was impatiently rifling through a pile of papers on his desk. "I can never find anything in this place," he said to Seel. "My assistants try to tidy everything away and then things are lost forever."

Seel waited, but without any foreboding. He presumed he was there to discuss some trifling matter.

"So," Thiede said at last, having found the particular piece of paper he was looking for, "I have a job for you."

"Fine," Seel said. "What is it?"

"You will have heard our troops took the Varr leader, Terzian, into custody last week."

"Yes, I did hear talk."

"This is a very positive development. Soon, Megalithica's barbarians will be utterly disempowered."

"Well, that is good news." He paused. "What has this to do with the job you have for me?" It did not occur to Seel that there was any threat in Thiede's words. He believed his duty was to be at Pell's side for his entire life.

"Can you put your affairs in order? I want you to go to Imbrilim, our enclave in Megalithica, next week."

Seel felt his mouth drop open in shock. "What? Why?"

"Oh, because eventually I want you to become the consort of Terzian's heir."

"Am I dreaming this?"

Thiede considered. "No. Even before you came here, I did tell you I had important work lined up for you."

"Which I have been doing, to the best of my abilities," Seel said. "Does Pell know about this?"

"Not yet. Don't worry. It's hardly as if he'll lose your friendship."

"I don't want to be anyhar's consort. Really, Thiede, this is too much. Do you expect me simply to comply with this outlandish suggestion?"

"No, I expect you to argue and rant, as Pell did about Rue. Don't waste your energy. I've picked well for you. The child will be perfect."

Seel sat down, before his legs gave way. "I'm dreaming," he said. "A nightmare."

"You are among the most privileged of hara," Thiede said. "Privileges have a price tag. I want you to host a pearl for this har, and I want you to be Immanion's presence in the Varrish noble house in Galhea. It's a strategic alliance."

"Why me?" Seel said. "Pell needs me here."

"No he doesn't. I need you in Megalithica more. Don't argue with me, Seel. The decision has been made."

"You are as barbaric as any Varr," Seel said. "It's like something out of medieval history, the way you force hara to take consorts, bond in blood, and produce heirs. Aren't we supposed to be more enlightened than that?"

For the first time, Thiede appeared stern. "Seel, you have eaten your dinner off my plate for years, and have lapped up every crumb. You are not a common har, who can fondly dream about living up to ideals. You are part of an administration that has a monumental task on its hands. Humans made alliances like these because they were useful. It has nothing to do with being civilized or enlightened, believe me. The har you will be with is named Swift. He is quite presentable, I understand."

"And you believe a Varr will be as delighted with this idea as I am?"

"He's barely more than a harling, but he is good stock. I want him to take his father's place, but as a Gelaming governor. There's no point in installing a complete stranger in Galhea. The Varrs can be a belligerent lot, but they adore Terzian and therefore will adore Swift. He doesn't know my plans yet. He is still under the impression he can carry out a mission to save his father. Terzian, of course, is being held here in Immanion. Swift will never find him, but he *will* find you. By the time he does, he will have dreamed of you for months and will be like Rue is with Pell, a drooling yearning hound."

"This is disgusting. This is torture."

"I don't intend to pull out his fingernails. Aruna with you can't be that terrible."

"I really hate you," Seel said.

Thiede smiled. "I know, but it won't be forever. One day you'll thank me."

Seel uttered a low, gibbering growl, which was the most he had to say to that remark.

"One other thing before you go," Thiede said. "Before you conceive the harling, I want you to perform Grissecon with Swift. The elixir will be useful in toppling Ponclast's forces. Quite ironic really, using the essence of a son of Varrs against them."

The last time Seel had performed Grissecon had been with Cal, years ago. He had started to sweat.

"Don't look so beaten," Thiede said. "This is an honor and you know it. Once you get your teeth into Galhea, you'll be in your element. Terzian has done little to change the town since he appropriated it from humanity. It's very old-fashioned by our standards. You know that building communities is your forte. Well, what do you think?"

Seel knew there was no point in saying any more. As had been pointed out to him, he'd willingly accepted all of Thiede's gifts. In the back of his mind, Seel had always been aware that if a price for them were ever named he'd have to pay it. Now, he simply rose from his seat and walked out of the room, leaving the door open. On the way down the corridor outside, he allowed himself the indulgence of kicking over and smashing a priceless vase full of peacock feathers that stood on the tiled floor.

"Seel!" Thiede called him imperiously from the threshold of his office.

Seel froze. He was too afraid of Thiede to keep on walking.

"There is another aspect to this task you will appreciate."

Seel turned, said nothing.

"I never forget a promise," Thiede said.

Seel felt a chill pass through him. "Go on."

Thiede folded his arms, leaned against the doorframe. "You should know that during your friend Cal's travels with Pell, he ran into Terzian in Galhea. Terzian was just like most other hara and fell for him like a wounded bird out of the sky. So, after Cal's indiscretion in Saltrock, he had a suitable bolt-hole primed and waiting. He returned to Galhea. He is still there, Seel, with Terzian's family."

Seel walked back down the short corridor. Suddenly, all the things Thiede had told him in the office seemed unimportant. "The Gelaming will arrest him now?"

"No need," Thiede said. "Cal will be brought to you in Imbrilim. The Varrish heir will take Cal with him on his fruitless quest and will unwittingly deliver him into Gelaming custody."

"Does Pellaz know this?"

"No, and you won't tell him."

"How, in the name of all that's sacred, have you arranged this?"

Thiede laughed. "Strategic friendships, my dear, how else?" He sobered and narrowed his eyes a little. "I am very fond of you, Seel. If you want your sport with Cal before he's brought to Immanion in the chains you've dreamed of so fondly, then everyhar will turn a blind eye. You have my sanction to do whatever you please with him. Just don't damage him too much. He must be brought to me alive and intact." With these words, Thiede stepped back into his office and closed the door.

Imbrilim was not just an army camp, but also a center for refugees, both human and harish. Because of his prior experience, Seel found his time was consumed mainly with accommodating and organizing this horde of helpless creatures, who all looked upon the Gelaming as holy saviors. Sometimes, Seel fell into bed late at night, fully clothed, and was up again in only a couple of hours, dealing with the next influx. It was important to keep disease in the human population under control and sanitation was the biggest project. Various members of the Hegemony were in residence continually to assist with organization, and Ashmael's right-hand har, Arahal, was the camp commander. Seel depended totally on this capable and tireless har. Without him, Imbrilim might well have fallen into chaos.

Chrysm Luel was the youngest member of the Hegemony and many hara said that he and Seel could have been brothers. They did look alike, although Seel considered that Chrysm was far too frivolous and disorganized to be worthy of the name Griselming. It was a puzzle to Seel how Chrysm had actually secured a place in the Hegemony, but no doubt it was the result of one of Thiede's strategic friendships. However, out of all of them, Chrysm was the one who noticed when Seel was on the verge of collapse. One afternoon, late in the summer, he virtually hauled Seel out of a ditch in a field, took a spade from his hand and said, "What the hell are you doing, digging like this? You look terrible. Go and rest."

A large gang of humans and hara were helping to dig, but Seel could only think about how he needed this task out of the way, because there were so many others to attend to, and the best way to get something done was to do it yourself. "This has to be finished by tonight," he said, reaching for the spade.

Chrysm laughed and jumped backward. "Oh no you don't. Tell you what— *I'll* dig. I'll take your place, when I could be wandering around the meadows composing poetry. See? You've no excuse. Go and sleep."

Seel sighed and relented. He knew very well that the moment he'd left the area, Chrysm would throw down the spade and wander off, whistling cheerfully, but he was so tired he could perhaps grab a few extra hours sleep. A bath would be nice too.

Back at his pavilion, Seel's staff prepared him a bath and then spent an hour or so pampering his body. Seel relaxed in warm steam and thought about how he actually enjoyed his work in Imbrilim more than running around after Pell back home. His life had purpose again now. He liked getting his hands dirty, being involved in actual construction work. As yet, there'd been no sign of Swift the Varr and Seel sincerely hoped he'd fallen into a marsh and drowned, or perhaps Cal had gone mad on the journey and slaughtered his companions. Wishful thinking, even if it wasn't totally unlikely.

Seel wandered into his sleeping quarters and threw himself face-down on the bed. He groaned in pleasure. Ah, sweet sleep . . .

Half an hour later, Arahal was at the threshold. Seel sensed an emergency and was fully awake in seconds. He saw that Arahal appeared troubled. "What is it?" Seel asked, reaching for his clothes.

"You'd better come," Arahal said. "Our scouts have reported the approach of a party from Galhea."

Seel threw down his clothes again. "Oh no! Fuck!" He sighed and picked up his trousers. "Can't you arrange a tragic accident?"

Arahal grimaced, then laughed rather uncertainly. "I'll wait outside, okay?"

"I meant it," Seel said as Arahal left the pavilion.

They found one har at the Varrish campsite, which was in a small clearing near a river. The Varr was quickly overpowered. Two hara held him on his knees, while Seel began an interrogation. "Where are they?" he asked.

The Varr spat at him. Seel sighed. He turned away and hunkered down by the meager fire that the Varr had just built. "Arahal, search the area." He did not look at the Varr, but addressed him. "You should tell us where they are. We'll find them anyway."

Then he heard a panicked cry from beyond the camp, "Swift, go back! Go back!"

"Too late," Seel said softly to himself. He looked up and there he was: Cal. He stood at the edge of the clearing, his hair reddened by the evening sun. He looked exactly how he used to look in the early days. He never changed. He never would. He was more like a physical expression of dark desire and danger than a living har. Seel wondered whether he did, in fact, want to kill Cal or not. He didn't feel anything, strangely. A younger har stood in front of Cal. He looked terrified and angry, but also brave. *Here goes your life, little one,* Seel thought. He stood up and turned his back on them. "Arahal, take charge."

Seel walked from the clearing and mounted his *sedu.* He thought about riding back to Imbrilim, but changed his mind. He wanted to ride just ahead of

Cal all the way back. He would be silent and in that silence would be the threat that he held the key to Cal's life in his hand. It looked like iron, but it wasn't. He could snap it in two very easily.

There wasn't much time. Thiede had informed Pellaz of his plans for Swift, and because the House of Galhea was such an important one, both he and Thiede knew that Swift should be greeted by hara of the highest rank. The Gelaming wanted to impress the young Varr and also to make him feel valuable. Pell had said that once Swift was at Imbrilim, he wanted to come to Megalithica himself to meet him. Thiede, carefully, managed to get the Tigron to change his mind and suggested he should send Rue instead. Seel knew this was because Thiede didn't want to risk Pell running into Cal. Thiede had already told Seel he wanted Cal well out of the way by the time the Tigrina came to Imbrilim. News would be sent to Immanion immediately, but it would not reach the ears of the Tigron or Tigrina for some days. In that time, Seel realized, he had to decide what, if anything, he wanted to do to Cal.

The Varr was an innocent, as Pell had been an innocent, but even to a casual observer, it was obvious he was, or would be, a har of substance. Seel could not believe that eventually he'd have to do the things with Swift that Thiede wanted. It seemed unthinkable. Swift didn't know about it yet, but already his mind and feelings were being manipulated. Hardly a marriage made in heaven.

Over the next few days, as Arahal began the preliminary indoctrination of the hapless Swift, Seel noticed the young Varr came looking for him whenever possible. He didn't dare approach Seel directly, but Seel could feel Swift's eyes on him all the time. It felt like burning and was far from unpleasant, surprisingly. Swift was a very handsome creature, slender yet strong, with thick brown hair and the most enormous dark eyes Seel had ever seen. Under normal circumstances, he wouldn't have objected at all to initiating aruna with a har like Swift, but it made him feel nauseous to imagine what was going on in the young Varr's mind, what Thiede had done to him. Often he wanted to tell him, "Look, you don't feel these things for me, not really. It's all an illusion," but of course that would oppose Thiede's plan and was therefore impossible. Seel felt real sympathy for the Varr, but slightly despised him because of his tribe and his loyalty to Cal. He also resented him, because if he didn't exist, Seel wouldn't have to go and live in Galhea and start breeding. Thiede sought to make a prince out of a barbarian. It was the sort of task Thiede enjoyed immensely and he would succeed, as he always did. *Then the prince will be mine,* Seel thought. *Is this real?*

After a few days, Arahal said to Seel, "You have to decide what to do with the Uigenna." He meant Cal. "He asks for you constantly."

"He wants my mercy," Seel said.

Arahal smiled grimly. "He won't get it. Thiede says we're not allowed to kill him."

Like many others who were aware of Cal's history, Arahal thought death would be the most merciful option for him.

"Take him away from his companions," Seel said.

"Where shall we take him?"

"The old human fortress to the south. Take him there."

"You'll see him, then?"

"Give him the putiri drug. Leave six hara with him, and never let anyhar remain alone with him. Do you understand?"

Arahal bowed his head. "It will be so."

"Where is Swift at the moment?"

"With Ashmael."

"Don't let him see anything."

"As you wish."

In the early evening, Seel rode out to the fortress. He could have reached it in minutes via the otherlanes, but spent an hour making the journey on solid ground. He needed time to think. The fortress was a ruin, and had never been used by Wraeththu, but some of its rooms were still secure.

One of Cal's guards came out into the overgrown courtyard when he heard Seel's horse trot under the gate arch. "Do you wish to see the prisoner?" the guard asked.

"It's why I'm here," Seel said. "Take me to him."

Seel's mouth was dry as he climbed the dark stairway that led to the room where Cal was confined. He had no idea what he was going to say or how he would behave. It was impossible to make plans in this situation.

The guard opened a door at the top of the stairs and Seel walked past him into the room. It was empty of furniture. They'd given Cal no comforts. He sat on the floor beneath the window and it was clear they had taken no chances with him either. He was sprawled in a drugged stupor. Five other hara sat on the far side of the room, playing dice. They jumped to their feet when Seel walked in. "Is there water here?" Seel asked.

They all nodded.

"Bring some," Seel said. "Find buckets or something. Wake this thing up."

While he waited for the water, Seel stood in front of Cal and stared at him. Cal's head was sunk onto his chest. His hair was filthy. His hands trembled where they lay in his lap. He was beautiful. Seel remembered their childhood, their first kiss, the smell of Cal's body. He remembered how he would have died for Cal and how he nearly did—of a broken heart. A fog of grief had spoiled the first few years of his Wraeththu life, because he'd had to face the fact that Cal did not love him in return. *You stole my youth,* Seel thought. *You made me love you and you made me Uigenna. I gave up everything for you. Now look at you.*

Two guards returned with water, which Seel directed them to throw over the prisoner. Cal came to his senses a little, cried out, and flailed his arms.

"Look at me!" Seei said.

It appeared that Cal did not recognize him, but why should he immediately? The old Seel had gone for good. What stood in front of him now was a Gelaming aristocrat, with smooth tawny hair and elegant clothing. Cal blinked a few times, grimaced then said in a small voice, "Seel?"

"That's right," Seel said. "You understand you are in Gelaming custody?"

"What are you doing here? Where am I?" Cal looked around himself, his movements sluggish.

"I represent the Hegemony of Immanion—"

Cal laughed, butted in: "You? No way!"

"And I am here to tell you are you will be punished for the murder of Orien Farnell at Saltrock."

"Seel, this isn't real, is it . . . I mean this is a dream or something. You are back at Saltrock, sitting in your little office making plans and I am asleep somewhere."

"No, if you remember, you were traveling with Swift the Varr and we took you captive. You have been in our camp, Imbrilim, for some days."

Cal appeared confused, but Seel noticed a certain expression of recollection steal across his face.

"Listen to me," Seel said. "I work for Thiede now, and it is his wish—our wish—that you should pay for your crimes."

Cal just stared at him, stupefied. Seel could tell Cal didn't believe this was really happening. Perhaps it had been a mistake to drug him.

"You're not dreaming," Seel said. "I'll show you."

He knelt down and grabbed Cal by his hair. He poured his breath into him and showed him every detail stored in his being of the day when he had discovered Orien's body. Cal tried to pull away. He made pitiful sounds, but Seel didn't let go for a long time.

When he finally stood up, Cal was virtually unconscious again. He moved feebly, like a newborn animal.

"So, now you appreciate this is for real," Seel said, "you can pay attention to what I'm saying."

"I believed you," Cal said weakly. "When you said you had nothing to do with Pell's death, I believed you. You said you didn't work for Thiede, and you did, all along."

"I had nothing to do with what happened to Pell. That was not a lie, not that I have to justify myself to you. Pell is not dead, in any case."

Cal's eyes opened wider. "What?"

"Pell isn't dead, Cal. I have worked for him for some years. He is Tigron of Immanion, Lord of all Wraeththu. This was the plan that Thiede had for him, from the moment of his inception. He was never meant for you."

"You're lying."

"No, I'm not. You saw Pell die, and he did, but Thiede brought him back. He is more beautiful now than he ever was. You should be pleased for him. He has a consort and a son. He has a wonderful life. I wonder if he even remembers your name."

Seel wasn't sure what reaction he expected to these disclosures, but Cal simply appeared to shut down, just like a machine switched off. He went inside himself, perhaps. His eyes stared blankly ahead.

"You committed murder for no reason," Seel said coldly. "A magnificent har died because of you, and you are nothing. You are scum. The worst tragedy in the world is that you live while Orien does not. And the only comfort I get is from knowing that your whole being is consumed by your love for Pellaz Cevarro, and that now you know he is still alive and he does not want you. If you are wise, you will find a way to kill yourself, because Thiede will not kill you and neither will I. We will find a way to make your life as agonizing as we can. Or maybe Thiede will kill you and then bring you back, again and again. He might give you release only to bring you back to bondage. Who knows? Whatever happens it won't be enough to atone for Orien's death." Seel fell silent and became aware of the guards standing behind him. He'd spoken too openly in front of them and regretted it. He should have sent them from the room.

Cal did not speak. His face ran with tears, but his features were immobile, showing no expression. How was it possible to love and hate somehar so much at the same time? Seel wanted to take Cal in his arms and he wanted to beat him until the blood ran.

"I have waited years for this moment," Seel said softly. "Now, I shall leave you and we'll not meet again. Think of me sometimes, Cal. You will have a very long time in which to do it. Think of me being with Pell, of me taking what you love, as you have done to so many others. Think of him glad that you no longer have your freedom. Think of his contempt for you. Then, think of me living in the house that was recently your home, my being erasing every atom of your presence there. Think of me with Swift, for no doubt he is one of your blind slaves too. Think of him being Gelaming, of embracing your enemies. I am going to Galhea, and you will never see it, or your friends there, again. It, and everything in it, will be mine.'

With these words, Seel left the room and closed the door behind him. His heart was beating fast, as if he'd been running. He went slowly down the stairs and when he reached the bottom he heard one terrible, lamenting cry come from the room at the top. It was the pain of all the world.

Seel stepped outside. The sun had set and bright stars filled the sky. He would go to another life now. The past was over. He thought of Swift and his beautiful eyes and he thought, *I can do this now. I will do this now. May the gods forgive me for my heart.*

CHAPTER TWENTY

>━┥◆〉━◯━〈◆┝━<

Lileem did not miss the desert lands. She liked the cold of winter in the north and the different moods of the seasons. She liked the brightness of fall, the strange sensuality of high summer, with its hidden thread of dark magic that walked the hills at midday. She loved the spring when hope found its way through the dark earth and the landscape sang in a voice so loud it deafened the inner ear, even though it sounded only like pretty birdsong to the every-day senses. If anyhar had asked her, she would have said that her life was complete and perfect.

They lived on a large riverboat, called *Esmeraldarine,* for which Flick and Ulaume had battered some years back. It seemed the best way to live, because constant traveling meant they made no close friends, and nohar ever became suspicious of them. The territory they roamed belonged mainly to the Un-neah, who had no real love for Uigenna or Varrs, and were happy to offer sanctuary to fugitives from the warlike tribes. It was a common circumstance to them. They had paid lip service to Wraxilan in order to maintain a peaceful existence, but if a stronger tribe came along and killed every Uigenna down to the last har, the Unneah would dance on their graves, then pay lip service to whoever took control after.

After Terez had rescued them, Flick and Ulaume had returned to Casa Ricardo for Lileem and Mima, and even before the day was over they'd packed up what they could carry, and, taking a couple of burros as well as Ghost and the two Uigenna horses, had ridden hard to the north. Once they'd reached Unneah territory, Terez left them again. There had been no fond farewells.

Ulaume and Flick had worked for a Unneah tribe leader for nearly two years to pay for the boat, and during that time, they had all lived in a small wooden house on a hillside, some miles away from the nearest habitation. The Unneah had not bothered them particularly, which was fortunate, because Flick and Ulaume were wary of making friends. Lileem knew this was because of herself and Mima. Flick and Ulaume had isolated themselves to protect them. They had perhaps sacrificed other lives they could have lived, but they didn't resent it. When the time had come for their lives to change again, and they took to the water, Flick had sold Ghost. He said the pony deserved a better life than constant flight.

A year or so ago, they'd heard that the Gelaming had invaded Uigenna and Varrish lands and that both tribes had been subjugated. But whether that was true or not, Uigenna still roamed the more heavily populated areas, so it was safer to keep to the wild places, where few hara lived. The Unneah who inhabited these hills wanted no part of the outside world, and respected reticence in others. Lileem and the others felt the same. They had made a life for themselves and nothing else mattered.

But it wasn't as if all the things they had gone through hadn't affected them in various ways and degrees. To Lileem, Flick appeared harder and was certainly less idealistic. Ulaume had taken a long time to get over his injuries. The hair that had been severed never grew again—it was truly dead and eventually, each hair dropped out. Like any other har, he had to wait for new growth to replace the old and that was a gradual process. Lileem offered him healing whenever she could, and when she placed her hands upon his head, her mind filled with thousands of tiny hissing voices, the lament of serpents who'd been cut in two. Nohar was sure whether Ulaume would regain the unique ability he'd had before, and that upset him greatly, although he wouldn't show it. Mima still tortured herself over Terez and wouldn't share her feelings with anyhar. Lileem intuited she blamed herself for what had happened to Flick and Ulaume. But perhaps the Uigenna would have come back to the white house one day, regardless, and if Terez hadn't been there, Ulaume and Flick might have been lost forever. Who could tell?

Terez had made it clear that he did not want to be Mima's kin. Despite this, he came to find them sometimes, perhaps twice a year. None of them knew why he did, because Mima found it too painful to be near him and his presence was always accompanied by a sour unpleasant atmosphere. He didn't care for any of them, not really, but still he kept in touch. He could sniff them out wherever they were. He had not found Dorado, and Pell's ghost had remained silent. Lileem quietly respected Terez for not making up stories about Pell speaking to him. He could easily have done so, and she suspected that if he had Ulaume would have believed him, too. Terez was a loner. He had not joined the Uigenna, perhaps because the har he had longed for among them had disappeared. He might be dour, aloof, and without finer feelings, but he was honest. That counted for something. Of all of them, Lileem had the most time for Terez. She had forgiven him for calling the Uigenna to Casa Ricardo. There was something about him she couldn't help but like. Over the years, his personality had gradually revealed itself. He had a sharp sense of humor and didn't hold grudges. He accepted that he wasn't truly liked by Mima and the others, and didn't appear resentful of it. He told fascinating stories about his travels, and all the different tribes he'd met, and when he visited *Esmeraldarine,* liked to sit up all night drinking and talking. The others said they only tolerated his visits because they got to hear the stories, but Lileem noticed that not even Mima went to bed early when Terez was there, even if she did sit away from the rest of them, showing them all how good she was at being moody. Terez had many fine qualities, Lileem thought, and often she wished he were still with them all the time. He'd had a bad start, that was all. These opinions she kept wisely to herself.

They had run from the sierras and cordilleras of the south, into much greener territory. Now, they traveled up and down the great river hara called the Cloudy Serpent, trading what goods they could produce of wood and clay and leather. Majestic mountains soared around them, wreathed in mist. Life was movement and the undulating coils of the serpent ever beneath them. Lileem was not afraid of hara finding out she was different, because she no longer felt she was. When they had to meet others, she kept her secret to herself and became "he" again. On the outside, she looked no different to a Wraeththu har. She had grown into a lithe and sinewy creature, a harish adolescent, who was only eight years old but appeared like a human would have done in their midteens. Mima too had camouflaged herself more than adequately. She wore her hair in braids and smoked a long pipe, and when she sat on top of the boat at sunset to smoke, she sprawled with her limbs splayed out in a manner that Flick said was utterly unfeminine, but Lileem didn't really know what that was. Although both Lileem and Mima possessed the vestiges of feminine breasts, these were not prominent enough to warrant extra disguise. A loose shirt was enough to conceal them. Ulaume also said he'd met true hara who had possessed similar attributes but who had otherwise been Wraeththu in every way. Flick said that in the past, a human's voice had been the biggest giveaway concerning gender, but that harish voices were, like their bodies, not exactly male or female. Mima had this voice, as did Lileem herself. Animal camouflage, a cry through the trees.

One late afternoon in summer, they docked at a small Unneah settlement, where they had made acquaintances. It took several years to reach that stage of friendship with the privacy-loving hara of this area. Lileem went with Flick to pay respects to the community leader and he offered them a meal. Soon the sun would begin to set. Usually, Flick made excuses to avoid social situations, but for once he accepted the invitation. Lileem knew then that Flick had finally lost the fear of hara guessing she was unusual. They could risk being sociable.

The Unneah was named Rofalor and he lived with his chesnari Ecropine in a house with a wide veranda that overlooked the river. They had a harling, who was only a few months old and very shy. Lileem was naturally intrigued by this young har, not least because it was obvious to her, if not to Flick, that he did not possess the abnormalities that she did. Lileem could just tell; she didn't know how.

After they had eaten, they sat around a table on the porch, smoking pipes and listening to the song of the great river. Flick asked questions, carefully seeking information. They never told anyhar that Lileem was a second-generation har. They always let other hara think she'd been incepted.

"I've heard," Flick said, "that sometimes Wraeththu births can be dangerous, that they can go wrong and produce—well—freaks. Have you heard that?"

"I've heard of it," Rofalor said, "but I think that as time goes on, we are more at home in our skins, and such risks become less. I think that those incidents were caused by a lack of focus during the aruna that creates the pearl. We know more about it now. We take precautions."

"Have you ever seen a harling that was damaged at birth?" Flick asked.

Rofalor grimaced. "No, thank the Aghama!" He smiled at his son, who was lurking beneath the table. "The worst thing for us will be when we have to hand over our son to another har for feybraiha."

"What's that?" Lileem asked.

"Coming of age. I suppose it's rather like althaia. It's when aruna becomes a pressing need." He sighed. "For us, childhood is even shorter than it was for humans. In some ways, that is sad."

Lileem had not considered things like this and a chill passed through her.

She thought fearfully of Terez and wondered whether the future held some terrible madness and decay for her. "When does it happen?" she asked. "How old is a harling when it does?"

"Oh, around six or seven, I think," Rofalor said. "It won't be a worry for us until a few years have passed and you can be sure I'll keep my eyes peeled for the right har for the job from now until then." He smiled. "You're presentable and gentle, Lileem. Perhaps I'll choose you if you still ride the river at that time."

Lileem must have looked stricken, because Flick announced it was time for them to get back. He virtually whisked Lileem off Rofalor's porch. She stumbled along beside him up the winding path back to the boat, her arm limp in his grip, her legs barely able to work. "Aru, Aru, Aru," she murmured beneath her breath.

Flick did not take her directly back to the *Esmeraldarine*. They climbed some rocks that hung over the river and lay on their stomachs looking down at the dark waters below. The moon was beginning to rise above the hills opposite. Trees heavy with leaves, in full summer regalia, dipped their branches toward the water. All was beautiful, yet now in some way spoiled.

"We don't know about this," Flick said. "You are already eight. It might not happen to you."

"But if it does . . . ?" Lileem dug the heels of her hands against her eyes. "What if it does? I might just have a slower body clock than normal hara."

"You must tell me," Flick said, "if you feel anything strange, or if your body starts to change in some way. You must tell me at once."

"I don't want to end up like Terez," she moaned.

Flick reached out and squeezed her shoulder. "You won't. No har on this earth could be like Terez! If it happens, then perhaps we'll know you're just har, who's a bit different, and that's that." He paused. "To be honest, Lee, none of us know how different you are, do we."

"I looked in the books back at the white house library," she said. "*I* know."

"But perhaps with this feybraiha thing, everything will become normal. Damn, I should have asked Rofalor for more details. We just skirted the issue and didn't find out anything really."

"Maybe you could go back tomorrow and ask him," Lileem said.

Flick grimaced. "I don't know. I'm still cautious of inviting too much attention to ourselves."

"Why are you so afraid for me? Hara treat me like normal. What difference would it really make?"

"I don't know," Flick said. "But my instincts advise me to be careful, that's all. You and Mima are special, but I'm not convinced all hara would think that way."

Lileem already knew that when one significant event occurs, then others are waiting to manifest, impatiently in a line. Therefore, when they returned to the *Esmeraldarine* and found Terez there, sitting with Ulaume on the roof, she was not surprised. He hadn't sought them out in so long, she had begun to wonder if he ever would again, but now, here he was, the creature of dark, sharing a drink with Ulaume in the last of the sunset. Lileem was pleased to see him.

"Terez wants to talk to us," Ulaume said as Flick and Lileem jumped aboard. His tone was tense. "Flick, you must persuade Mima to hear this. It's important."

Flick sighed. Mima would be hiding below deck, seething with all the complicated bitter emotions Terez's proximity inspired in her. While Flick went to reason with her, Lileem sat down. Her head was aching in three different places. She felt dizzy.

"You have grown a lot since the last time I saw you," Terez said to her. "It's uncanny."

Lileem had nothing to say to this. "Have you brought us anything?"

Terez produced a leather bag. "Not much. Some trinkets." He pulled an object out of the bag and passed it to her. "Here, it's yours." It was a small white carving of a har, very beautiful. He wore an ornate headdress and the detail was astounding.

"It's lovely," Lileem said, turning it in her hands. "So delicate. I wish I could carve like this. Does it represent anything?"

"Yes," Terez said. "It is the Tigron."

"Somehar's god?"

"In a way. I'll explain when the others are here."

Lileem held out the little carving to Ulaume, but he would not take it. He was frowning, and his composure was ruffled. This meant Terez had told him something he didn't like, something that endangered his control of life. Ulaume always hated things like that, especially so since the episode with the Uigenna. He was superstitious about the carving. Lileem was so full of curiosity, she forgot about how frightened and threatened she'd felt only minutes before. She enjoyed mysteries.

Flick emerged from below deck, with Mima following, her face set into a surly expression. She had her arms folded and everything about her was closed in and hostile. She would never forgive Terez for what he'd said and done in the past and she couldn't forgive herself for what she'd done, either. Lileem wished Mima would let it all go. Terez had been denied a life with the Uigenna, but surely that was for the best. What did Mima have to feel bad about now? Terez did not appear unhappy. He didn't appear anything. Well, perhaps, there were reasons for regret, after all.

"What's so important?" Flick said, sitting down beside Terez.

Terez held out his hand to Lileem. "The carving," he said.

Lileem handed it to him and he passed it to Flick.

"Somehar else is inventing gods," Lileem said.

Flick examined the carving. "It's well crafted, but what's so important about it? If other hara are creating dehara, it's not that surprising." He held out the carving to Terez.

"Look again," Terez said. "That is the Tigron of Immanion, the king of the Gelaming, if you like. The ruler of all Wraeththu."

"Well, they were bound to do that sooner or later," Flick said. "They think highly of themselves. Personally, I don't have a king and never will. I won't buy into Gelaming power fantasies."

"His name is Pellaz-har-Aralis," Terez said. "The carving is stylized, of course, so don't look for resemblances."

Flick glanced again at the carving, then fixed Terez with a stare. "What are you suggesting?"

"I travel widely in this land," Terez said. "I get to hear many things. I make sure I do. I've never stopped searching for my brothers, and my feet led me to what was once Varrish territory. It was there I met a har who came from Al-magabra. He was Gelaming, attached in some small capacity to the noble house of Parasiel in Galhea, the home of Swift the Varr, now presumably Swift of the Parasiel, who has earned himself fame as a Gelaming lapdog. The har I met told me that Thiede had created himself a king and that his name is Pellaz."

"No," Flick said. "Don't think it. It's impossible."

"No it isn't," Ulaume said, in a low voice. "You know that. This is what everything has been leading to. It makes sense of your story, Flick, about Pell's inception and Thiede. This was the plan no har knew about. He never died. Cal was deceived."

"He couldn't have been," Flick said. "It was too raw and real for him. I don't believe it."

"But you have seen Pell in visions," Mima said. Her arms were unfolded now, though her skin looked sallow. "He spoke to you, and Ulaume never believed Pell was dead. By Aruhani, this is it! He sent you to us, Flick. He sent you to care for us, because he is a Wraeththu king, all powerful. Because he *can* do it."

"Then he could have come for you himself," Flick said. "Don't jump on this, Mima. There could be any number of explanations. Not least that Thiede just decided to call this king he made Pellaz. It could be anyhar."

"I agree," Terez said, "so I investigated further. It transpires that a har named Cal went to Galhea a few years back and that it's rumored he once had a connection with the Tigron. That is more than coincidence."

"When I felt Pell die," Ulaume said, "and when your friend Orien had that psychic episode, it must have been the exact moment when Thiede took Pell away from Cal. We misinterpreted what we felt. It was a transformation, not death."

"Cal burned the remains," Flick said. "I'm sure he didn't make it up. You didn't see him, talk to him. He knew what he saw and experienced, and it *was* Pell's death. He had half his head blown off. There can be little mistake under those circumstances. I know Cal visited the Varrs. He did so with Pell. The stories are getting mixed up, that's all."

"No, this was more recent," Terez said, "certainly since he murdered your friend at Saltrock."

"Why are you trying to explain this away?" Mima said. "Flick, it is the answer. It's why you and Ulaume were drawn to us."

"But if it were true, then surely Pell would have tried to make contact with you himself," Flick said. "Mima, please think about this. Don't give in to wishful thinking. If he lives, he's obviously not thinking about you, or Terez, or Ulaume, or me. Not even Cal. Maybe he wanted this. Maybe he was in on it from the start. But, if he is this Tigron, he doesn't care about you. You must be dead to him, as I am, as we all are."

Lileem was watching Mima's face. She noticed the way Mima recoiled from Flick's words. They were harsh, but true, and despite everything, Mima was no fool.

"Flick's right," Terez said. "It would once have been my instinct to believe this fully, without question, but now I am wiser. I'll go to Immanion and find out for myself, and if there is any truth in this story I will find you and tell you."

"Hara don't just 'go' to Immanion," Flick said. "You must know that. Many don't even believe it exists. The Gelaming create legends about themselves, and one of those legends is that no har finds the city unless the Gelaming invite them there."

"I will discover what is truth and what is myth," Terez said. "I don't need invitations. You cannot do it, because you need to remain here in hiding. But think of this, if Pell *does* live and he *is* Tigron, then he could provide the protection you need for Mima and Lileem. This must be important to you all."

"If he lives and is Tigron, it's my thought that he's abandoned all aspects of his past," Flick said. "I wouldn't count on an offer of protection. He could have done that anytime. He might not even acknowledge you as kin."

"We *are* protected," Lileem said abruptly. "We don't need anyhar else to do it. We have ourselves." She was filled with a fear of her life disintegrating around her. She didn't want change. There was nothing that needed changing. Whatever happened that she couldn't handle herself, Flick, Ulaume, and Mima would deal with it.

"I have to agree with Flick," Mima said, "even though it hurts to do it. I want Pell to be alive so much, yet if he is, I have to face that he has no interest in us. If he wanted to find us, he could have done, but as yet, he clearly hasn't bothered trying."

Lileem was surprised that Mima had changed her mind so quickly, but then again she could see in Mima's face all those difficult feelings she couldn't straighten out. Mima felt abandoned, all over again.

"I hope to all the dehara it isn't true," Flick said in an uncharacteristically cruel tone. "Because if it is, then it means Orien died for nothing and I lost Seel for nothing. Cal went insane for nothing and has blood on his hands for eternity. If Pell lives, he's as much responsible for what happened in Saltrock as Cal was."

Lileem opened her mouth to offer some comfort, because she could see how upset Flick was but, before she could speak, he threw down the carving, leapt off the boat onto the bank and marched off into the trees. For a moment, all was silent.

"I knew this news would be difficult," Terez said. "I had thought of the implications in it too."

"You must find out if it is true though," Mima said. "I have to know."

"I will do what I can," Terez said.

Lileem picked up the little carving Flick had discarded and held it out to Terez.

"Keep it," he said. "I have no need for it."

Lileem put the carving of the Tigron in a drawer in her cabin, although she liked to get it out at night, when she was alone, and study it. Not for one moment did she ever doubt that what Terez had told them was true. Neither did she think that Pellaz had coldly and consciously abandoned his surviving kin and friends. She was sure he just didn't know about them, that other things occupied his attention. If he had truly died and been resurrected, perhaps he couldn't even remember his human family. Everyhar was reacting in a very personal way, but Lileem had never had business with Pell. She had no expectations of him, and no disappointments in him. If anything, the idea of him intrigued her greatly. All her life, she'd heard about him, and the way he affected others made him all the more fascinating. Lileem liked both Mima and Terez very much, and considered them to be beautiful, dashing, and daring creatures. It made sense to her that a Cevarro should end up as king of all Wraeththu. It was terrible to her than any of the family had been killed, because she was sure they had all been special people. Flick, Ulaume, and Mima lashed out against Pellaz in hurt and resentment. Terez merely set himself the task of discovering the truth. Lileem herself simply decided to wait. This was a story that had yet to reach its conclusion.

Flick would not return to Rofalor's house for more information about harlings, so the morning following Terez's arrival *Esmeraldarine* left the Unneah settlement and headed north. Terez departed before they left, riding one of the Uigenna horses he'd stolen years before. Lileem stood on top of the boat and watched him gallop off into the morning, where an early mist hugged the ground. *I wouldn't mind being like him,* she thought, *not if I could look like that, riding a horse. Not if I could be a walker of shadows, like he is, and never be flustered, unsure, or frightened.*

"Hey!" Flick called to her. "Are you dreaming? There's work to do!"

"Sorry."

Flick looked at her strangely and she found her neck was burning.

It began two weeks after Terez had come to them, two weeks after the conversation at Rofalor's. Lileem was ashore one afternoon, walking in overgrown fields next to an abandoned farm. Feral horses galloped in the sunshine and the air was full of insects, murmuring lazily in the summer warmth. Lileem walked to a gigantic oak and sat down against the trunk. She leaned back and closed her eyes, breathing deeply, absorbing all the scents of the land. Why had she ever been afraid? She was a part of the world, at one with it. She could feel every ray of sunlight as it fell on her skin, coming down through the softly rustling leaves overhead.

"Lileem!"

She opened her eyes at once. There was no har there, and yet the voice had sounded so close. She jumped up and glanced around herself, but the field was empty of all but horses, which had stopped cavorting around and now cropped the grass nearby, their tails swishing to ward off the flies. It must have been one of the others, putting out a mind call to her, but it hadn't felt like that at all. She had heard her name spoken, not in her head, but with her physical ears. Neither had she recognized the voice.

This could be a haunted place. Humans had once owned the ruined farm. They may have been slaughtered in this field. Unnerved, Lileem ran through the sunlight to the shelter of trees and the woodland path that led back to the river. Just when the world feels right and good, something peculiar happens to remind you that nothing is certain.

Lileem didn't mention anything to her companions about what had happened, but for the rest of the day she felt slightly disorientated. Her ears had started to ring, and it was a strange ringing that sounded like the distant lilt of a choir. If she put her hands over her ears in order to concentrate on it and hear it properly, it went away. But when she was speaking or others were making noise around her, she could hear it again, faint and insistent within her.

That night, she was plagued by troubling dreams. All of them involved voices shouting her name. They were calling to her desperately: *Come to us!* But she didn't know who or what they were. In the single word of her name, repeated endlessly, she perceived the message: *You belong with us. Come quickly! It is time.*

She wondered if it could be her hostling, and in the morning felt she had to confide in Flick about the dreams. She asked him to go for a walk with her in the woods, because for some unknown reason, she didn't want Ulaume or Mima to hear what she had to say. Flick listened to her account of the call in the field the previous day and the events of the night. He did not interrupt, which was unusual, and unsettling.

"Is it the Kakkahaar who was my hostling calling to me?" Lileem asked, making a conscious effort not to wring her hands together. She couldn't stop shivering.

"I don't know," Flick said. "I doubt it. Maybe it was just a bad dream."

Lileem could tell he didn't believe this, because his expression was deeply worried. "Is it . . ." she began. "Is it the . . . *other* thing? Is this what happens? A call from somehar I don't know, the har who's supposed to . . ."

"No!" Flick said quickly. "I'm sure it's not. It could be something to do with the landscape here. We'll move on. Let me know if anything else happens." He paused. "There haven't been any other changes, have there?"

Lileem's face burned. "No. I'd tell you."

Flick nodded. "Okay. Don't worry. It's probably nothing."

The walked back to the boat in silence and Lileem considered how much

Flick had changed since she first met him. It was as if she were seeing him for the first time. He no longer appeared so fey and vulnerable. He was strong and his hands were calloused. They rarely talked of the dehara nowadays, although Lileem had kept up her devotions to them privately. Flick had lost faith in all that was wondrous, as had Ulaume. Flick had always believed the world would be fair to him, and it hadn't been. What had started in Saltrock had only been compounded by the events with Terez and the Uigenna. Flick never spoke of those things either, but sometimes Lileem could feel self-loathing coming off him like a black flame.

All day, Lileem felt nauseous. Her face was hot, her ears were singing, and her head felt as if it was stuffed full of cotton. It was inevitable that both Ulaume and Mima noticed she was out of sorts. "You're flushed," Mima said. "Do you feel all right?"

Lileem wanted to escape them all. She was terrified that the dreaded time of feybraiha was upon her. What would happen? What must she do? As the hours passed, the voices in her head became louder, calling her name insistently. She must be going mad. She would become like Terez had been, a half-creature lost in darkness.

Just before sundown, it became unbearable. One moment, Lileem was sitting down on deck to begin the evening meal with her companions, the next she was on her feet, screaming aloud. She jumped off the boat and landed in the icy cold water with a great splash.

Deaf to the cries of her companions behind her, she swam strongly toward the eastern bank and climbed from the water. She wanted and needed to run, to keep running. Clawing her way through thick, thorny bushes, she headed east. It was the only way to go, and the faster she went and the longer she ran, the more the pressure let up within her. This was the way the voices wanted her to go. They lay in this direction, waiting. She found she was both laughing and crying as she ran.

Breaking free of the bushes, she hurtled down an old road that was cracked and half hidden by weeds. Here, her limbs took flight. She had never run so fast and it had never felt so good.

She ran for half the night and only stopped running when she fell exhausted in her tracks. Flick found her before dawn. She was still panting.

He wanted to take her back to *Esmeraldarine*, but she could only screech and lash out at him with her fists when he tried to make her do that. She couldn't go back. It was far too painful. "This way!" she yelled, pointing to the east. "I'm going this way and you won't stop me. I have to."

Flick crouched before her, his hands hanging between his knees. "Why?" he asked.

Lileem gripped her head, squeezed it. "It's a call," she said, trying to think clearly. "So strong. I have to obey it. There is no choice."

Flick stared at her and she stared back, breathing heavily. She couldn't slow down her breath. After a long minute or so, Flick said, "All right."

"All right what?" she cried. The singing in her ears was so loud now she had to shout to hear her own voice, never mind Flick's.

"We'll go east," he said. "I'll come with you, if you have to go."

Lileem threw herself against him. "Thank you." She realized she had never wanted to go alone.

He held onto her tightly, for just a moment, then held her shoulders at arm's length, gazing into her eyes steadily. "I'll go back to *Ezzie,* tell the others, see what they want to do. Okay? Will you wait for me here for a just a while?"

She nodded vigorously. "Yes."

He stood up. "If you really have to go, leave signs. I'll be as quick as I can."

Lileem watched him lope away from her and when he had vanished from her sight, began to weep. He hadn't questioned her desire. He accepted it, and he would be with her. Her breast ached as if something inside it was about to burst. She had never felt so happy, yet at the same time, so sad.

It was difficult not to give in to the desire to leap up and keep running, but Lileem managed to control herself. She knew she should feel hungry, because she hadn't eaten anything since lunch the day before, but she had no hunger within her. She was simply itching to move and had to keep pacing around. While she did so, she prayed to Lunil, her gentle dehar. *What is happening to me? Help me.* But it was daytime and Lunil's influence was weak. She shrank from calling upon Aruhani, because of his arunic associations and Miyacala did not feel appropriate. Her own particular invention, Agave, could give her strength perhaps. For some minutes, she spoke to him, and maybe it was her imagination at work, but her body did begin to feel less agitated. It was fortunate she'd not strayed as far from the river as she thought she'd done, because Flick returned to her just past noon.

"Ulaume had an idea," he said. "It might take strength for you to go through with it. There is an eastern tributary to the Serpent a few miles north. You should come back to *Ezzie* and we'll head that way. It'll be quicker than traveling on foot."

Lileem considered this. "It's a good idea, but I don't think I can."

"You could try."

"But it hurts so much. You don't understand."

"We don't know who or what is calling to you," Flick said. "It would be better if we could all stick together. Try speaking to these voices in your head. Tell them your intention is to go east, but that you need to go back west first for quicker transport."

"Okay, I'll try." She took a few tentative steps toward Flick and it was as if a giant fist closed about her mind. She uttered a cry, clasped her head, stepped back. "I can't!"

"Lileem, you are strong," Flick said. "Fight back!"

Lileem screwed up her eyes and cried, "Agave, be with me! Give me your strength, your fire."

"That's it!" Flick urged. "Take my hand. Come to me."

Lileem reached out and his fingers curled around her own.

"I will feed you strength," he said. He pulled her toward him.

It was like being hauled through a thicket of blades, perhaps the blades of Agave's sacred plant itself. But then, a warm wave of energy coursed through Lileem's body: Flick's strength and love. For a moment, her head was completely clear. "Run!" she cried.

As they ran toward the west, Lileem imagined the immensely tall figure of Agave on the path behind them, blocking the way of any pursuers. He held a lance and a sword, and his being protected her.

CHAPTER TWENTY-ONE

The tributary to the Cloudy Serpent, called Little Drake, pours down from the eastern mountains. At first, it is fierce and white, as it tumbles over precipices and between narrow rocky channels, but gradually, it curbs its temper and flows smoothly, if purposefully, through fields and forests toward the southwest.

In the early days, when the Varrs first fell to the Gelaming, you could travel up the river and see the signs of old battles all around you: blackened ruins, some with smoke still issuing from the timber, months after the initial fires; burial mounds that blocked out the sun, with ragged standards drooping at their summits; a general reek of unease and pain. Any Varrs you might meet, who were not even allowed to refer to themselves as such anymore, were generally suspicious, dispirited, or stultified. Gelaming commanders supervised rebuilding, and scouting parties still roamed the hills, rooting out the last of the Varr leader, Ponclast's loyal followers. The Gelaming regarded themselves as a force for good, and in many ways they were, but they were also inexorable and their compassion could often feel like oppression.

Flick and Ulaume could not help but feel skittish passing through this territory. They were not, nor ever had been, Varrs, but strangers could very easily be mistaken for Varrish warriors in disguise and neither Flick nor Ulaume relished the idea of having to submit to interrogation.

It wasn't until they began their journey east that they realized how vast the Varrish empire had spread and that the Uigenna had really only been minor players in the war with the Gelaming. One thing was upon everyhar's lips, however: the Uigenna Wraxilan's days were numbered. The Gelaming had a price on his head and he would not escape it. This gave the travelers some small comfort, because none of them had ever lost the fear that the Uigenna might pursue them, even if none of them spoke of it. But perhaps the Gelaming might be worse than the Uigenna, especially so if Mima and Lileem should be discovered. They advocated a kind of Wraeththu purity, which even in the least educated breast kindled feelings of discomfort and unease, echoing as it did similar obsessions by earlier human conquerors.

To Flick, it was like emerging from a dream. Orien had whisked him away from the scenes of conflict to hide him in Saltrock, and his life since leaving his first Wraeththu home had been one of isolation. He hadn't heard much news, only rumors, and the stories that Terez had told them, but now they were traveling through the real world and it drew them into itself. Wraeththu fought for power, and stronger hara could affect the lives of those weaker than themselves.

Lileem appeared to be fairly comfortable, although Flick suspected she still kept a lot to herself. The voices in her head and the presences in her dreams did not leave her, but they were less strident as she continued to head east. As to where they came from and what might be waiting for her at the end of the journey, she did not know, but Flick was reassured by the fact that she did not appear to fear it. She had turned to the dehara for comfort, and Flick knew she was disappointed that Flick appeared to have lost interest in the gods he had dreamed up. Ulaume, however, had taken up where Flick had left off, and was quite happy to meditate with Lileem, so that they could gather visualized imagery about the dehara.

Once, Lileem confronted Flick and told him that Aruhani was displeased he had turned away from him.

"No he isn't," Flick snapped angrily. "Don't make things up."

"Wasn't that what we were always doing?" Lileem countered. "Didn't you say we couldn't really make anything up, that everything we can think of exists in the universe somewhere already. What happened, Flick? The dehara were yours. Why don't you like them anymore?"

Flick could not tell her how he had come to believe that Aruhani was a terrible and perverted force. It was Aruhani who had made him enjoy being with Wraxilan, who had encouraged him to perform disgusting sadomasochistic acts with the Uigenna leader for several unforgettable nights. Flick could never forgive himself for that, and he thought that in conjuring dehara, he'd been playing with a force that was far too strong and unpredictable. He knew that if he spoke of it, Lileem would disagree and try to persuade him otherwise. It was unthinkable he'd ever tell her what he'd done, in any case. Not even Ulaume knew. Once, not long after they'd left Casa Ricardo for good, Flick had thought longingly of Itzama and his serene wisdom. If he could speak of his problems to anyone, it would be him. But so many years had passed, and his time with the strange shaman was like a dream. None of what happened then seemed to have any bearing on the reality of life. Flick's excitement in discovering the dehara had been crushed. The gods were capricious. They could smite as well as bless. But only Flick thought this.

"The voices that call to me," Lileem said. "The dehara know what they are. They give me strength and courage. I am not afraid."

Many times, Flick wondered whether it was actually Pellaz calling out to her, drawing them all to him through her, but he could not decide if this was wishful thinking or paranoia. Part of him still could not believe that the Pellaz who sat upon a throne in Immanion was the same har who'd been his friend at Saltrock and yet, looking back, there had always been a faint autocratic air about Pell. Given the right conditions, his willfulness and stubbornness could very easily have slipped into arrogance and pride. Sometimes, Flick's heart ached for Cal, and he thought that the Gelaming perpetrated atrocities upon the world. He wanted no part of them, so therefore became troubled when he discovered they were traveling closer to them than might be safe.

In these lands, Mima and Lileem kept below deck whenever the boat passed other hara or settlements along the river bank. But they still needed to stop for supplies, and for some months the constant traveling had meant they'd had less time to devote to their crafts, which was how they generally earned their living. Also, the defeated Varrs weren't that interested in charming little talismans of bark, feathers, and leaves, or Lileem's carefully worked clay statues of the dehara. The boat needed fuel, so quite often Ulaume and Flick had been forced to seek work along the way. Flick did all that he could to make himself appear unattractive and he noticed Ulaume did the same thing. They bound up their hair beneath turbans of dirty scarves and didn't wash themselves for days. They went barefoot and their toenails were black. It was safer that way. They didn't want to invite attention.

When they took aruna together, Flick felt sad, because these times of freedom, when they could be themselves again, were too brief. The years they'd spent at the white house seemed like a lost idyll; the future was uncertain.

The landscape was draped in fall robes when the boat docked at a tiny sagging jetty by a village that was fringed on the river side with ancient yellow willows. It looked beautiful in the late afternoon, with red sunlight kindling jewels and flashes of bronze in the bright leaves. The little settlement was carpeted in crimson and gold and the hara there did not appear so dour as others the travelers had come across. There were no walls or palisades to protect the dwellings. They soon found out why.

Flick and Ulaume went ashore and made for the center of the village, where there was bound to be an inn of some kind, which was always the best place to look for work. Sure enough, they found a hostelry next to a green that was strewn with leaves from the copper beeches that surrounded it. Tables were set outside the inn, and it was still warm enough to enjoy a mug of ale in the open air. It was too early in the day for many hara to be drinking, for this was the time when the land had to be prepared for the long winter ahead and there was much work to be done. Flick and Ulaume were grateful that they could settle themselves and take in the surroundings before applying themselves to the task of seeking a temporary employer.

The pot-har was a curious, talkative creature, which again indicated this area had not seen much conflict. He said it was good to meet new faces, and the first drinks were complimentary. Flick was wary of this, used as he was to Unneah caution and he could tell that Ulaume felt almost threatened, even more so when the pot-har sat down next to them.

"You're from the west, aren't you," he said.

"No," said Ulaume.

"Yes," said Flick.

The pot-har laughed. "You don't look like Uigenna!"

"We're not," Flick said and Ulaume shook his head.

"We are just traveling hara who like to keep our heads down in these troubled times," Ulaume said.

Again, the pot-har laughed. " 'Troubled times'? You've been traveling too far and too long, tiahaara. There is nothing to fear around here. This is Parsic land."

"Parsic?" Flick frowned. "What's that?"

"Swift the Varr, who is the son of Terzian, a great Varrish warrior, toppled Ponclast with the help of the Gelaming. After that, the Varrs became the tribe of Parasiel. We are no longer Varrish but Parsic."

"I see," said Flick. "We have been out in the wilderness for a long time. This is all news to us."

"You can let down your defenses now. Come, wipe those suspicious frowns from your faces. Rejoice, as we all do. The Golden Age has begun."

There was a fanatical edge to these suggestions that Flick balked at. Ulaume caught his eye and grimaced. *We belong to nohar,* Flick thought, *and that's the way it's going to stay.* "It's good you feel that way," Flick said. "We've seen a lot of devastation on our journey east."

"It will soon be cleared away," said the pot-har. "Lord Swift will see to it." He stood up. "Well, I'd best be back to the kitchen, because this place will be heaving with hara within the hour. Enjoy your ale, tiahaara."

"Well!" Flick said, after the pot-har had disappeared back into the inn. "This is all a bit surreal."

"Swift the Varr," Ulaume said, his eyes narrow with thought. "Didn't Terez mention him in connection with Cal?"

Flick sighed deeply. "Yes. The name is familiar. I think Cal mentioned him to me too, but I can't remember what he said."

"We are in his lands," Ulaume said. "Flick . . ."

"I know," Flick said. "We could use this opportunity to glean information about Pell."

"You don't sound happy or enthusiastic about it."

"We are here because of Lileem. We shouldn't take risks of being delayed or worse."

"You don't want to know, do you?" Ulaume said. "Not really. You want Pell to stay dead."

Flick merely shrugged.

"Have you ever thought he might be responsible for what's happening to Lee?"

"Yes, I have," Flick answered abruptly.

"Then . . ."

"You don't understand, Lor," Flick interrupted. "It's complicated for me. My feelings for it all are so mixed up, I don't know what they are."

"We don't talk about him," Ulaume said. "We don't talk about anything seriously, and perhaps we should." Unconsciously, he'd reached up to touch his head. His hair had grown past his shoulders, but he was too careful about it, kept it wrapped up when he didn't need to. "If the Parasiel and the Gelaming rid the world of Uigenna, can they be all that bad?"

"I thought the Kakkahaar scorned Gelaming," Flick said.

"I am no longer Kakkahaar. We are unthrist, Flick, without a tribe."

"By Aru, you're not pining for it, are you?" Flick asked, louder than he intended. "I thought you liked it this way, just the four of us."

"I was simply stating a fact," Ulaume said. "To be honest, I don't know what I want."

The hara who came to drink at the inn all appeared sleek, well fed, and fit and were more than happy to talk to strangers. Everyhar suggested that the best place to seek work was in Galhea, which was only a few miles northeast. The biggest farms could be found there, which always needed extra labor to make ready for winter.

Flick could tell Ulaume took this as an omen, and wondered whether they'd be arguing about it later. There might be little to argue about though. Galhea was a big place and Swift a prominent figure. Flick and Ulaume were inconsequential, small hara in a vast world. There was no reason why they shouldn't seek work there for a while and do some investigating at the same time. Any newcomer to the area would be interested in recent history. Flick and Ulaume's questions wouldn't be seen as suspicious and they had learned how to be unnoticeable.

On the way back to *Esmeraldarine,* Ulaume was silent, and Flick intuited he was formulating the right spell of words to invoke the response he wanted. For a while, Flick let him struggle, then said, "We could go tomorrow. We probably have enough fuel."

"Are you sure?" Ulaume asked.

"No, but you are."

"I am," Ulaume said. "Thanks. I was expecting a fight over it."

"I know. So was I."

Ulaume laughed and wrapped an arm around Flick's shoulder. "We know each other too well now."

Domestic crisis awaited them at the boat. When they went below deck, they found Mima comforting a distraught Lileem in the main salon.

"What's happened?" Flick demanded.

Mima indicated he and Ulaume should go above deck with her. Lileem had not even acknowledged their arrival. She appeared inconsolable.

Out in the crisp night air, Mima hugged herself. Her expression was pinched.

"Well?" Ulaume said.

"Something's happening to her," Mima said. "She told me what she learned from the Unneah Rofalor. She thinks this feybraiha thing is happening to her."

"I'm sure it isn't," Flick said. "She's just afraid it will. I think she's likely to manifest symptoms because she's scared of them."

"What's feybraiha?" Ulaume asked.

"You explain," Flick said to Mima. "I'll go talk to her."

"You?" Ulaume said. "I think we both should. What's going on?"

"Let Mima explain," Flick said. "I'm sorry, Lor, but this something Lee and I have talked about before. I'm sure she'll talk to you too, but for now, just let me handle it."

Lileem was a pathetic sight, appearing more like the child she really was than the young har whose origins it was easy to forget. Flick sat down next to her on the couch, where she was sprawled face down, her head in the cushions. He put a hand on her shoulder. "Hey, it's me."

For a moment, Lileem didn't move, although her sobs subsided to snuffles.

"We're going to Galhea in the morning," Flick said. "That's where Terez said Cal went to after Saltrock, remember?"

Lileem turned over. Her eyes were swollen, her face red and blotchy. She'd clearly been crying for hours. "Why?" She rubbed her eyes and nose with her hands.

"For work, but Ulaume wants to do some detecting too."

"Will it be safe for us?"

"I think so. It's a big community and therefore it'll be easier for us to stay invisible."

Lileem wriggled up the cushions into a sitting position. She clasped her knees with her arms. For some moments, she was silent, her expression intense as she stared at her hands, then she looked up and said, "Flick, I think it's happening."

"Okay. Why?"

Lileem's face and neck had gone scarlet. "I had a weird feeling today. My body went all hot, and . . . I don't want to say, it's so vile. I hate it."

"Have you told Mima?"

"Not really. I don't know if I can. Is she like me or is she something else? I don't know what to do."

"Have there been physical changes?"

"A bit. Sort of."

Flick lowered his head and pressed the fingers of one hand against his brow. He sighed. "Lee, we can't mess around like this. We have to know. You're going to have to show one of us, and tell one of us everything, then we might know how to proceed."

"I can't," she said. "It's just so embarrassing."

"Lee, it could make you ill if you don't start helping yourself. None of us know how to deal with this, and we need more information. Yes, it'll be embarrassing, but it'll be over in a moment. We are your family. You don't have to feel ashamed or scared. Okay?"

Lileem writhed uncomfortably on the cushions. Fresh tears spilled from her eyes. "Why is this happening? Why? I don't want it!"

"We don't know if it is yet," Flick said gently. "Now, tell me what happened."

"It was so sudden," she said. "I was just sitting on deck in the sun and I was making a new model of Lunil. It was going really well too. Then this pain just shot up my body, like I'd been stabbed or something. Some liquid came out of me. I knew at once it was something to do with . . . well, growing up, I guess. I'd read in books about puberty in humans and how girls menstruate. Do you know about that?"

Flick nodded. "I think I can just remember."

"Well, at first I thought it was that, and it would prove I was female, har but female. And that would be good, wouldn't it? Because I might not need aruna, but . . . Anyway, I went below deck and looked, thinking I'd find blood, but it wasn't blood."

Flick was silent.

Lileem put her hands against her eyes. "By Aru, Flick, it was awful. Just strange stuff, almost like the elixir you made for Terez. Does that make sense?"

"Mmm, a little."

"I was all swollen and sore, it was so weird. And this is the worst . . ." She uttered a nervous giggle. "I touched myself to see if I was okay and I nearly bit my own hand off!" She put her fingers over her mouth and shook with laughter, although tears still coursed down her face. "I'm sure there were teeth."

Flick struggled not to laugh as well, although he was bursting to. "Oh, well, if you ask me, that sounds fairly har. But there are no teeth, Lee, just strong muscles and an instinct. Did you notice anything else?"

"Yes. My ouana-lim has changed as well. It's more there than it used to be." She groaned. "It *is* happening, isn't it."

Flick drew in his breath. "Something is, obviously. Will you show me or would you like Mima or Ulaume here instead?"

Lileem covered her face with her hands again. "Oh, I don't know! I know I have to but I don't want to. Give me a moment."

They sat in silence, while Lileem rocked on the cushions, uttering a low humming sound. It was the sort of noise she used to make as a child. Eventually, she lowered her hands. "We could all do it, all see. That would be best, wouldn't it? Then we'd all know about each other."

"Lee, I don't think so. That would be . . . well, I don't think it would be right."

"Why not? If I was truly har you wouldn't think twice about it, would you? That means you think I'm different, you look down on me."

"No, it doesn't."

"I won't show myself unless you all do. It's only fair. What are you afraid of?"

"Instinct," Flick said. "I'm afraid for you. If hara shared a moment like that, I know how it would end up. You're so young."

"And that wouldn't happen if it was just you and me?"

Flick stood up, agitated. This conversation was heading into territory he had not anticipated. "I'll talk to the others," he said. "Wait here."

Outside on deck, he took deep breaths. How stupid not to consider that if Lileem ever did come of age, like a normal harling, one of them would have to be her first aruna partner. But that might not even be possible. She could be poisoned by it, or worse.

Mima noticed him standing in the darkness and came over, Ulaume following. "Well?" she said.

"She will show herself to us, but only if we show ourselves to her at the same time in return."

Mima turned away abruptly.

"That's reasonable," Ulaume said. "We shouldn't prod and poke her like a freak. She should be as aware of the similarities and differences as we are."

"Mima?" Flick said. "Could you do this?"

She would not look at him.

"This is a hurdle that needs to be overcome," Ulaume said. "For too long there have been big secrets between us. Once it's out in the open, we're all a lot wiser and there's nothing to fear. We live together as family, but we don't even know if we're the same species."

"No," Mima said. "You do it, if you want to, but I won't. I'm not a sideshow."

"What good does this attitude do you?" Ulaume said. "For Hubisag's sake, Mima, stop being stupid and coy and start being har. It's what you want, isn't it?"

In response, Mima jumped off the boat onto the bank and ran up the path beside the river.

"Sensitive of you," Flick said.

"It's senseless," Ulaume said. "We've indulged them too much, Flick. We should have known these things years ago, now it's so much more difficult." He clasped Flick's shoulder. "Mima can stew for a while. Maybe she'll come to her senses. Let's go to Lileem."

Ulaume was the best har for the job. Flick was amazed it was ultimately so easy, and wondered why he'd put himself through those awkward moments with Lileem. Ulaume made it fine, because he was so matter of fact about the whole procedure.

They returned to the cabin and Ulaume said, "We've talked about what you asked, Lee, and we agree to what you suggested. Mima hasn't, and she's charged off in a huff, but if you want to know about me, you're welcome." He began to unbutton his shirt. "One thing about being har is not to be ashamed or frightened of your own body." Off came the shirt. "Perhaps it's my fault, and I should have been more open with you from the start." He pulled off the rest of his clothes and stood before her. "So, let's compare."

"Okay."

Flick could tell she was so fascinated by the sight of a naked har, she had lost some of her own fear of revealing herself. Lileem's rampant curiosity was often a blessing. She began to undress and Ulaume said, "Come on, Flick, take part. I can give Lileem a biology lesson with you as the subject for dissection."

"Thanks," Flick said.

Never could Flick have imagined that one day he'd be lying on his back, legs spread, while someone described his parts and their functions to someone who'd never seen anything like them before. Lileem explained to Ulaume what had happened to her and Ulaume said, "When the soume-lam is stimulated, it can bite, believe me! It has five energy centers within it, almost like five clitorises. Humans would have loved to possess such a thing. It often has a mind of its own, more so than the ouana-lim, which is a bit of a reversal to the way things used to be with humans. The ouana-lim itself is refined as a male organ, and much improved. I can vouch for it."

"It's quite pretty," Lileem said, pointing at Flick. "I saw the pictures of humans and they were scraggy."

"As you can see, we do have organs similar to testicles, but they are smaller and can be withdrawn into the body during aruna and I expect during birth. You can push them up yourself, like this."

"Have you quite finished!" Flick said, flinching. "This is a bit much."

"Okay, let's have a look at you," Ulaume said to Lileem.

"I'm not the same, not quite," she said shyly, sitting down.

Ulaume gently pushed her back and parted her knees. "Hmm. That's interesting. Flick, what do you think?"

The soume-lam looked normal, but the ouana-lim was less developed than in a normal har and she had vestigial seed sacs. Her body was slightly wider around the hips than a normal har's and there was still the suggestion of breasts upon the chest. "She's not completely female," Flick said, "but the male side of things does appear to be underdeveloped."

"I think," Ulaume said, moving away, "that you are har, Lee, but you have physical abnormalities, like a birth defect."

"Oh," Lileem said, sitting up again and clasping her knees. "So, what does that mean for me?"

"I think it means we need to know more. Try stimulating the soume-lame yourself and see what happens. I don't think we should rush into anything, because you're still so young."

"But Rofalor says feybraiha happens when harlings are six or seven," Lileem said, "so doesn't that mean I'm more than old enough?"

"Your feminine aspects are dominant," Ulaume said. "Hara don't have breasts, but you do, even though they're small."

"You said once that some hara do. I remember."

"I know, but it's not the same. In humans, some men had quite fleshy chests and in hara it's no more than that. Your body is also more female shaped than ours. I don't think we should take risks. If feybraiha is upon you, and you need aruna, you must try to do it yourself."

"Oh." For a moment, she appeared almost crestfallen, then she grinned. "I'm glad we did this. I feel so much better. There are no secrets now."

"But for Mima's," Flick said. "I wonder if she is the same."

Mima was back on the boat by morning, but reluctant to speak to anyhar. Flick could tell she was suffering and eventually could bear her silence no longer. She was sitting alone on the prow and he went to sit beside her. "It's no big thing, Mima. Forget it."

"Did you find out what you needed to know?"

"Yes, I think so. There's no doubt in my mind that Lee is harish rather than human, but just that she has certain abnormalities. Ulaume called them birth defects. I think he's right."

"I'm not like you," Mima said. "I can't be blasé about this. I'm not even like Lee, who has no feelings of shame or guilt. I don't have Wraeththu innocence."

"We are not innocent," Flick said, "don't ever look on it like that."

"Does she still want to be called 'she'?"

"She hasn't mentioned it. The female aspect is very strong in her though."

"I don't," Mima said. "I don't want to be what I am. If I have to be alive, I want to be like you, but I'm not."

"How do you know?"

"It won't work with me," Mima said. "Forget it. I don't have things happen to me like Lee did. I'm dead in that way."

"Well, if you ever want to talk about it . . ."

"Don't patronize me, Flick. I'm sorry I went off like that last night, but it's just so hard for me."

"Be at rest," Flick said. "We are heading into new territory and this should concern us more than anything. We could find out about Pell in Galhea."

Mima nodded, staring ahead up the river. "Yeah."

Just after midday, a Parsic patrol ordered them to halt. They were a magnificent sight: black-clad hara, wearing black plumed helmets on horses with black glossy coats. There were five of them and at their signal, Ulaume steered the boat over to the bank. They carried guns.

"What is your business, tiahaara?" inquired their leader.

"We are seeking work in Galhea," Ulaume said.

"How many travel on this boat?"

"Four," Ulaume replied. "Do we need permits or something?"

"We will escort you to the council house in town," said the Parsic, "but first we must search your vessel."

"Of course," Ulaume said.

Flick, lurking behind him, went cold. Mima and Lileem were below deck. As the Parsic troupe leader and his deputy dismounted and came aboard, he shot into the main cabin and hissed, "Look busy. Look as if you're working, not hiding. We have guests."

Fortunately, Lileem and Mima were already sorting through some of the materials Lileem had collected on their journey. While Ulaume and Flick worked in the fields, they planned to create more artifacts to sell.

The two Parsics came into the room and Mima stood up and bowed. "Greetings, tiahaara. May we offer you refreshment?"

The leader took off his helmet and a long brown plait fell down over his shoulder. "What have you got?"

"Wine and coffee from the Unneah."

The Parsic leader inclined his head. "A measure of wine would be most welcome."

Lileem got up rather furtively. "I'll see to it."

The Parsic sat down at the table, while his assistant made a cursory search of the room. He rifled through Lileem's collection of stones, feathers, leaves, and bird bones. "What are these?"

"We make charms," Mima said. "We sell them for fuel and food, and so on."

"Travelers," said the troupe leader. "What was your tribe originally? Are you Zigane?"

"We come from all over," Mima said smoothly. "You know how it is. We just met up and became friends and decided to live on the water. We like it."

Flick was impressed by her cool.

"Were any of you connected to the Uigenna?" asked the Parsic.

Mima laughed. "You think we'd admit it if we were?"

He laughed back. "I doubt it."

"But we weren't in any case. We had to head east because they took our little settlement from us. They wanted slaves. They are disgusting."

"You won't have to worry about them anymore," said the Parsic. "If you send a petition to Lord Swift, Parasiel might even be able to help you reclaim your land."

"Really? That's amazing," said Mima as Lileem put down cups of wine on the table. "But, you know, we've kind of got used to traveling. It's great to see the land, and experience the seasons. We really love this life now, even though we were forced into it really."

The troupe leader narrowed his eyes at her. "You know, you look slightly familiar."

"How so?" Mima asked brazenly.

The Parsic shook his head, laughed beneath his breath. "No. It's nothing. I pay no heed to the stories that say the Tigron sometimes travels in disguise among his hara."

Mima shot Flick a hot glance. "You say I look like him? Have you met him?"

Flick stared at her hard, willing her not to block his thoughts: *Shut up!*

"Not met exactly," said the Parsic. "I went to Immanion once, with Lord Swift. Caught a glimpse, that's all."

"You've been to Immanion?" said Mima, eyes round. "I'd love to hear about it. It's like a dream."

"Perhaps we could meet while you are in Galhea," said the Parsic. "I am Chelone. You can look me up at the barracks."

"Thanks," said Mima. "I'll take you up on that."

After the Parsics had left, and Ulaume had gone with them to acquire official permission for them to dock their boat in Galhea and work there, Flick gave vent to his feelings. "Are you insane? Don't you dare go the barracks, Mima! It's far too dangerous. You know what he wants from you? Would you risk being found out?"

"He thinks I'm a charming har who looks like the Tigron," Mima said. "What harm would there be in having a drink with him one night? This is what we came for, isn't it?"

"Ulaume and I won't let you," Flick said. "At least . . ." He sighed. "Not alone."

CHAPTER TWENTY-TWO

Mima knew exactly what she had to do and that she must do it alone. Flick and Ulaume cared for her, but there were certain things in life you could only do by yourself. If she endangered herself through doing them, so be it. It was a gamble she was prepared to take.

The night when Lileem had revealed herself to the others, Mima had done a lot of thinking, not least: *Who am I?* Ulaume was wrong to call her coy. It wasn't that. She was quite sure she was Wraeththu, if not completely har in the way her incepted companions were, but where boys had the big dilemma of having to deal with female parts of themselves after inception, in some ways her own dilemma was more disorientating than physical changes. She could not call or think of herself as "he." It didn't feel right and it didn't sound right and to do so would somehow murder Mima, the person she had grown up to be. So much power in so small a word. She wished it away, but it wouldn't go. It gnawed at her, so much so, it was like having a disease that she couldn't tell anyone about, all the while knowing it was killing her. They had learned that it was possible for females to be incepted and maybe it wouldn't work every time, and maybe it required abnormal hara like Lileem to accomplish it, but there it was, an incontrovertible and vexing fact. On the outside, with her clothes on, Mima looked almost the same as she'd always done, because like her brothers, she'd always been fairly androgynous in appearance, but inside, she was changed. Her identity had been wrenched inside out.

She had promised Flick and Ulaume she wouldn't go wandering around by herself in Galhea, and for a week or so she didn't, because it took time to summon the courage. But one morning, after they'd gone to work early, she left Lileem asleep and crept off the boat. It was another beautiful, crisp fall day, like all the days in gilded Galhea seemed to be. She had no doubt the other seasons were as perfect, because this was essentially Gelaming land and they would not tolerate anything less.

Everyhar she passed nodded good morning to her and she was not nervous about asking directions. Other hara saw nothing unusual in her; she was just a stranger needing help. The barracks were in the south of the town, approached by a busy main street lined by market stalls and surrounded by a high wall, where sentries in black uniforms ambled back and forth, dark silhouettes against the deep blue sky. The air was full of swirling leaves, but the breeze wasn't cold. The scent of frying sausages from the food vendors' stalls made her mouth water. From a blacksmith's workshop came the ring of iron on iron. Mima absorbed each sensation, thinking she must remember this day. It was important.

The guards on duty at the gate looked her up and down when she asked for Chelone. She could tell what they were thinking and tossed back her hair to show them she wasn't just any common har. Perhaps he was already out on duty, patrolling the river, or perhaps it was his day off and he wasn't here at all. If he wasn't, then it would be a sign and she'd go back to the boat. But even though she had to wait for a good fifteen minutes, which under those circumstances felt like an eternity, he eventually came strolling across the yard toward her. She could see him approach through the bars of the gate: a prime harish specimen with dark brown hair drawn back into a long plait. His face was well sculpted, his mouth finely drawn. He would do.

Chelone stood on the other side of the gate, not smiling particularly, but not hostile either and she said, "Do you remember me? From the boat you searched a week or so ago?"

And he thought for a moment, then said, "Yes, of course."

She realized he'd recognized her straight away, but didn't want to appear too eager. He had been waiting for her to come.

"Well, here I am. When do you get time off? Can we arrange to meet?"

She didn't know if this was the way hara were supposed to speak to each other, if it was too forward or not forward enough.

Chelone did not appear to find her approach unusual. "I could change duties today, seeing as you're here, because I'm busy for most of the week."

He didn't have much to do clearly. What, in Galhea, was there to guard against? He must be bored.

She had to wait some minutes longer while he made arrangements for cover and then he was at the gate again. He had let down his hair and brushed it. Mima felt weak. What was she doing? This could be disastrous.

He took her to a quiet inn near the river and here they ate breakfast together. She asked him about Immanion and he told her, what he knew of it. It was a real place, but now it didn't seem that important. "Tell me about the Tigron," she said.

Chelone made an airy gesture, wiped his mouth with a napkin. "What is there to say? I didn't speak to him, because lowly hara don't. He glows. They say Thiede made him and it's probably true. He's unearthly, like Thiede is, but then a Wraeththu king could not be anything else, could they? We are all perfect, so our divine ruler has to be more perfect than us." He laughed and took a drink of coffee.

"Do I really look like him?" Mima asked, resting her chin in her hands. "Or was that just a line?"

Chelone glanced at her. "There is a resemblance. You are of the same race, certainly."

"Is it true a har called Cal came here a while back? A friend of a friend of mine thinks they once knew him."

"Oh yes." Chelone's dark tone indicated at once it must be the same Cal.

"Did you meet him?"

"Occasionally. We were not close friends. He was only interested in Terzian, who was our leader then. Cal collects high-ranking hara, that is my opinion."

"Is he with the Tigron now?"

"Nohar knows where he is, other than that the Gelaming have him. He won't be dead, technically, but who knows? They destroyed Terzian by ruining his mind."

"Do I detect some dissatisfaction with your saviors?"

"I didn't say that," Chelone said. "Nohar criticizes the Gelaming, if they know what's good for them."

"I hope you don't mind me asking all these questions, but we've been out in the middle of nowhere for years. I've lost track of things."

"That's okay. It's the excuse for us meeting, isn't it?"

"Yes. It is."

It was so easy to be arch and flirtatious. Perhaps too easy.

"I don't even know your name," Chelone said.

She didn't pause. She just said, "Mima."

And he replied, "Nice name."

"You mentioned that Lord Swift might be able to help us get our land back. Could you arrange for me to meet him?"

Chelone laughed. "If I remember correctly, you told me you liked your water gypsy life now. It's not the land you want—you just want to meet a star of Wraeththu, I think."

"It's not that," Mima said. "I do want to meet him, and—yes, okay—I'm not that bothered about the land. There's something I need to talk to him about."

"Is this to do with Cal?"

"Partly."

"So what's the story?"

"I can't tell you yet. I hardly know you."

"I'll tell you this. Cal is anathema to the Gelaming: everyhar knows it. They hate him because he is a somehar and they want him to be a nohar. He is the flaw in their plan, not least because the House of Parasiel is very fond of him. If you want to go to Swift with more bad news or complaints about Cal, forget it. He's Cal's only champion."

"I don't want to complain about Cal. But we can discuss this another time. What can we do today?"

Chelone was giving her a considered stare. "I could show you round the town, some of the sites outside of it. I can show you Swift's house from the road, if you like."

"Sounds good."

"How come you're not working like your friends?"

"I'm supposed to be. I'm being bad. They don't know I'm here."

He grinned. "Okay. Let's go then."

She watched him as he went to the bar to pay for the meal and watched his hands as he pulled money from a purse. She thought to herself, *I can't believe this. He's real and alive and this isn't a dream or a fantasy and I'm probably heading into territory where I really don't want to go, but what the hell!*

Later, Mima would reflect upon that day and consider it to be one of the best of her life. She was truly herself. She didn't have to act or pretend. Chelone accepted her totally as har, more so than her friends had ever done. She had enjoyed brief dalliances with boys when she'd been human, and what astounded her most was Chelone's attitude to her that was so different to any human male's. There was equality between them and, because of that, easiness. No difference, no obstacles, no misunderstanding. Was she deceiving him or not? Mima could not make up her mind about that.

They visited the sights and finally came to stand at the iron fence that surrounded Swift's house on a high hill outside the town. "It is named," said Chelone, "We Dwell in Forever."

"That's beautiful," Mima said, her hands gripping the bars. "It reeks of romantic stories."

"And there have been many in that house," Chelone said, "not all of them with happy endings. My best friend Leef was rather a casualty! And . . ." He shook his head and spoke softly. "Some things are best forgotten."

Mima reached out instinctively to touch his arm. She spoke the words that sprang into her mind and knew they were true. "Somehar died, didn't they? Somehar close to you?"

He took her hand. "That was extremely sensitive of you. But then, I'm not surprised. I wasn't that close to him, not really, but he made an impact on me."

"Perhaps we can share our stories one day."

"I would like to. One day."

It will never be, Mima thought sadly, but she wished it could be true. He drew her to him, and she let him do it. She let him put his mouth against her own and then her head was full of sparkling mist, of wonderful visions. For a moment, she surrendered to the sensation totally, but then realized she must guard her thoughts. He must have felt the barriers go up, because he drew away, still holding onto her face, stroking her cheeks with his thumbs.

"You almost showed me something," he said. "Darkness."

Her lips were tingling. "Sorry." She pulled away from him and shook her head. "I didn't mean to."

"I'm flattered. You felt relaxed enough to forget for a moment." His smile was ironic.

Her heart was racing. She felt faint. "I'm hungry. Can we go and eat?"

His expression was slightly puzzled now. "Of course. But what about your friends? Shouldn't you tell them where you are?"

"Probably," she said. "But it doesn't matter. I want to be here, now, with you."

"Are you chesna with one of them? Is that it?"

"No. They are just very protective, because of things that happened to me once. I feel safe with you. It's okay."

"They'll be worried."

"Chelone, don't!" She raised her hands as if to ward off his words. "I want to eat. If you want me to go afterwards, I will, but I have to eat."

She felt as if she was losing control of the situation. It was spiraling somewhere. She was pushing him away. The others were standing there between them and she wished he didn't know about them. She should have lied earlier, said they knew what she was doing.

There was a tense atmosphere between them as they walked back to the town. Chelone tried to disguise it, but Mima knew he harbored suspicions about her now. He sensed there was a heavy history attached to her and perhaps he thought it might be too much to take on. Soon, she must leave him, but just for an hour or so, she wanted to remain in his company. She had shared breath, done a harish thing. He had tasted her soul.

Chelone took her to an inn much busier than where they'd taken breakfast, which was probably a sign how things had shifted between them. Other hara he knew were eating there and already wine and ale was flowing copiously. This was a warrior's watering hole and their energy was fierce and overwhelming. Mima sat at a table in a corner, feeling miserable. She'd ruined everything now. Damn.

Chelone came to join her, having ordered a meal at the bar. "What's wrong?" he asked.

"I want to go back in time," she said, "to the moment before we shared breath. I'm sorry. I'm no good at this. I want to be, but I'm not."

"Because of the things that happened to you?"

She nodded. "Yes."

He reached out and hauled one of her hands from her lap, where her fingers were clenched together. "I'm not offended. If you have secrets, that's your business. I enjoyed being with you today. I like you a lot, Mima."

"You might need more than a lot of like, if you knew everything about me."

He laughed. "I'm willing to take that risk. You don't turn psychotic during aruna and kill, do you?"

"Not that I'm aware of."

"Well, I should be okay then."

Mima drank in one long gulp the glass of wine he'd put before her. He was watching her again and she wanted to tell him to stop it.

"It's been a while, hasn't it," he said at last. "You know what I think—you were looking for somehar, and you chose me. Just how long has it been, Mima?"

She stared at him directly, took a deep breath. "Since forever. My inception went wrong, because the hara who incepted me left me behind, before it was completed. My friends found me and healed me, but I've never taken aruna, Chelone. That is the problem."

He'd gone white. "I see. Then . . . how . . . ?"

"There are ways," she said. "Use your imagination."

"Why me? Why now?"

"Because I don't know you," she said. "Because you're not so damned concerned about me. Because, with you, I have no past. And also, because I like you a lot too. Will that do?"

He looked uncertain.

"Was I supposed to ask first, or something?" she said. "If so, I'm sorry. This isn't the big responsibility you think it is. Really."

"You don't have to ask. You just took me by surprise, that's all. I wasn't expecting it." He squeezed her hand. "I will be honored."

Mima took a deep breath, wondered why she was having difficulty focusing on his face. "I have only one requirement."

"Which is?"

"We both get drunk first."

When he took her to his apartment in the barracks complex, Mima was aware her life might be in danger. She had shared breath successfully, but there was no proof that his essence couldn't kill her. *Why am I willing to take this risk?* she thought. Because it had to be done. She couldn't go on unless she knew. If she was a freak and an accident, then maybe she'd be better off dead, but if she was something else, and proved it, then she could live fully and happily.

She made him turn out the lights, because she didn't want him inspecting her too closely. He held her naked on his bed and his strongly beating heart made her body vibrate. His breath smelled of alcohol and his hands were hot. She wilted beneath the heat of him. He put his fingers inside her and ignited five fires, one by one. "The soume aspect is strong in you," he said.

She didn't answer, trying so hard not to break her teeth, because her jaw was clenched tight. Reality was breaking down all around her. She was the earth and a great mountain was thrusting up from the soil. It made a sound like the heavens cracking. There was no pain, only a sense of something immense occurring, like the birth of a world or a universe. She was not in her own body anymore. The mountain would erupt and hot lava would cascade down its sides, perhaps bringing death. The earth might be scorched, or might

bear it. The earth might be stronger than the mountain. The fires inside her became volcanoes. She was erupting too and the whole world was flame. For a
moment, she opened her eyes, expecting reality, but it had gone. This was no
vision. It was real. She was looking upon an alien place so bizarre she could
not identify the objects around her. The air was like glass and it had begun to
splinter. She felt a rush of heat within her and thought that if these were to be
her final moments, she must live them in the steam of his breath. She pulled
his mouth toward her, sucked in his scream of repletion and the universe shattered around them with a mighty crash. A wind that smelled of nothing Mima
had ever smelled before seared over them. She felt it move her hair.

Chelone collapsed onto her heavily, his breathing labored. She was alive.
Was she starting to burn up? No. If anything, she felt cool now. The room had
reappeared, all the normal things like chairs and lamps, and clothes strewn on
the floor.

Chelone raised his head. "I don't know what happened to you in the past,"
he said, "but you just took me to a very weird place. I thought we were dying.
I thought we'd just shatter and disappear."

"We nearly did," Mima said. "Isn't that normal?"

"No. No." He rolled off her. "It felt to me like we left this world. What are
you, Mima?"

"I don't know," she replied. "Nohar does."

Mima knew she should return to the boat now, because Flick and the others
would be beside themselves with terror for her, but before she did, there was
one other task to accomplish. She could tell Chelone was nervous of having
her touch him, because he didn't want to go back to that strange place. She
had proved to herself she could take aruna as soume and not be killed, but the
biggest test was to see whether she was capable of being ouana. That would be
the strangest thing, but the absolute proof she was har. Her ouana-lim was not
as developed as Chelone's was, but she already knew it was functional, having
experimented herself with it many times. He hadn't noticed its deficiency, because the ouana-lim always shrank and retracted when a har was soume.

They had lain in silence for some minutes, but now she leaned over him
and breathed over his face. He stared at her rather wildly and when she
reached down to touch him, he stayed her hand. "Please," she said. "Let me."

He closed his eyes, let go of her. He felt beautiful, slippery and silky, and it
stirred her. She could smell him and it reminded her of lilacs. He made a
small sound when she entered him and his soume-lam contracted to seize her.
Reality did not splinter this time, not so drastically. She kept her eyes open

and watched the room, while waves of sensation coursed through her body like a pulse. She saw the air begin to fold around itself and light from somewhere else seep through. She could tell that their union created this and that it so easily could engulf them. It was dangerous, uncontrollable. Light had become hard, made up of geometric shapes. She should stop. She knew she should, but she couldn't. Fortunately, release was quick. She realized she could make it happen that way, although hara probably wouldn't normally do that, opting instead for a slow languorous climax. Chelone didn't complain. When he opened his eyes, he looked terrified.

"Thank you," Mima said. "I had to know. You do understand that, don't you?"

She saw his throat convulse. He couldn't speak.

She got up and went to the window. It was very late. No doubt Flick and Ulaume would be searching for her. She felt wonderful, as if her body was made of white light. Slowly, she pulled on her clothes. When she was ready, she stood at the foot of the bed.

"Will you help me?" she asked.

Chelone raised his head. "I think you have to be careful," he said. "Something's not right. I can't help you with that. I wish I could, but I can't. You need an adept, a Nahir Nuri, or something."

"No, I mean with meeting Lord Swift."

His head flopped back. "Oh, that. Yes . . . maybe. I'll ask Leef."

"We are still friends, aren't we?" she said.

He propped himself up on his elbows. "Okay, I have to ask. I've been lying here thinking . . . *Are* you the Tigron in disguise?"

Mima laughed. "No! Really I'm not. But thanks. I'm flattered."

"We're still friends," he said, lying back down again, his hands over his eyes. "Go! I don't want your companions beating down my door."

Mima ran down the stairs outside his door and through the apartment complex. She thought she could very easily fly now, if she put her mind to it. She ran through the town, waving a greeting to any har she came across, and there were not many, because it was so late. When she arrived back at *Esmeraldarine,* she was greeted by a tearful Lileem, who told her the others were still out searching for her.

"Where have you been?" Lileem cried. "Were you with that har? Flick and Lormy think so. They went to the barracks after work, and somehar told them you'd gone off with him. How could you? What happened?"

"Hush!" Mima said. "I can't tell you when you're gabbling."

Lileem sat down on the couch, pulling Mima with her. She stared at Mima's face for a moment, then her jaw dropped open. "By Aru, you didn't! Tell me you didn't!"

"I did," Mima said. "I took aruna with another har. In fact, I'm absolutely rooned out."

Lileem squeaked and pressed her hands against her mouth for a moment. "But couldn't he tell about you?"

"No, not a hint of a suspicion. This is it, Lee. We don't have to hide anymore. We have our secrets, and our differences, but we *are* har. I'm sure of it."

CHAPTER TWENTY-THREE

In Galhea, the old seasonal festivals were strictly observed, which is a tradition that began long before Terzian had taken over leadership of the local Varr factions. And despite their reputation as warriors and conquerors, the average Varr had always been a farmer; well-tended farms surrounded Galhea. It might be that the Varrs in that area had been drawn mainly from the sons of the humans who'd once owned the land, but in any case, the Galheans knew how to get the best from the soil.

Four of the major festivals celebrated the harvest, beginning with Cuttingmas, the summer solstice, when the first sheaves were cut, to the great festival of Shadetide, the Rite of Death at the end of Fall, when the last of the fruit was gathered, already bitten by the first frost.

The hara with whom Ulaume and Flick worked were already talking about Shadetide, which would take place in two weeks time. There would be huge fires throughout the countryside, on every hill and in the gardens of the bigger houses. Ulaume became almost sick of the invitations to join a party that were offered every day. There was only one house he wanted to be invited to, and he wasn't yet sure how to wangle it. From where he worked in a har named Gortana's fields, he could see the hill where We Dwell in Forever crouched amid a court of ancient cedars. Sometimes, he could see figures moving in the

gardens, carts and horses going up the wide drive. Cal had been there and perhaps even Pell too. Flick and Ulaume habitually remained taciturn with
strangers, in order not to attract interest, and this was a habit that was now
hard to shake off. Ulaume, however, once asked a har he worked with how he
could get to meet Lord Swift. The har merely laughed at him. Swift was too
busy and too important to bother with every traveler that came to Galhea.
Ulaume was tempted to mention that he knew the Tigron, but guessed this
would be met with equal amusement, if not utter disbelief. So, in the dawn of
the day when he and Flick returned to *Esmeraldarine,* having been searching
for Mima all night, he was not as angry with her as Flick was. She had made a
contact, and all she wanted to tell them was that her new friend would try to
organize a meeting with Swift.

"What have you been doing all night?" Flick demanded.

"Talking," she replied.

She wasn't telling the truth, of course, and both of them knew it, but Mima
had already proved herself to be quite a private person. Clearly, whatever had
happened to her had not been upsetting or dangerous. She was glowing. When
she felt ready, she might reveal what she'd done, but no amount of interrogation would prise the information from her. Flick knew this too, so he didn't
push it.

He and Ulaume went to their cabin to sleep for a couple of hours before go-
ing to work. Flick sat on the narrow bed and whispered, "What do you think?"
The walls were thin on the boat and they could still hear Mima murmuring to
Lileem in the main salon.

"We both know," Ulaume answered. "It's pouring out of her like smoke."

"She must be different to Lileem, then."

Ulaume shrugged and pulled off his shirt. "Perhaps. I think that if you
weren't looking for abnormalities, you might not notice them."

Flick got into bed. "I wonder. Maybe she told him the truth."

"Mima?" Ulaume grinned. "I doubt that very much."

"She's very like Pell," Flick said. "Headstrong and willful."

"It's her life," Ulaume said. "I understand why she did what she did. It
must be eating her up. She wants to be har, Flick, that's all. I just hope this
Chelone can organize a meeting for us."

"He might only be able to get Mima in."

"And you, of course, don't *want* to go. Why?"

Flick frowned. "I don't know. I feel strange about it. Part of me wants to
know everything, to have the answers we've sought, but another part doesn't
want to set a toe over the threshold of that house."

Chelone did not make contact for over a week, and Ulaume could see Mima getting restless about it. He knew she was considering going back to the barracks, but pride prevented her doing so. Whatever had happened between her and the Parsic, he clearly wasn't eaten up with desire to see her again. He finally turned up early one evening, a week before the festival. Mima was up on deck with the others for a tidying session when Chelone rode his magnificent horse to the river bank and dismounted. Ulaume noticed that Mima flushed vigorously when she saw the Parsic. He was without doubt a fine specimen.

Chelone came aboard and uttered a formal greeting to all present, then said to Mima, "Do you still want to go to Forever?"

She nodded. "Yes."

"So do I," Ulaume said quickly.

Chelone cast him a glance. "I can get two of you in, on the festival night. I have an invitation, and so does my friend, Leef. Two of you can come as our escorts."

"You go, Lor," Flick said. "I'll take Lileem to the party in the town."

"Fine," said Chelone. "Come to the barracks just before seven. Dress up— if you can."

"We'll be there," Ulaume said.

Chelone nodded shortly and made to leave the boat. Mima took hold of his arm and said, "Thank you. I appreciate it."

He looked at her hand. "I said I would."

She let go of him quickly.

Everyhar finished work early on the festival day, so Ulaume and Mima had plenty of time to get ready. Ulaume realized he had quite a task ahead of him, because he hadn't taken much care of himself recently. Flick applied himself to the same restoration work, because Lileem wanted him to do so, and now he resembled more the idealistic and somewhat wide-eyed har whom Ulaume had first met. His heart turned over as he looked at Flick. He felt sad for him, which was odd.

Mima was silent and moody, and Ulaume could feel tension building up, which he could tell was about to explode. At half past six, the explosion happened.

Mima was brushing out her hair, when she uttered a cry and threw the hair brush across the cabin. "I'm not going!" she announced.

"What?" Ulaume turned her to face him. "Why not? You have to."

"I can't," she hissed. "The way he looked at me. I just can't."

"Thanks," Ulaume said. "That means I can't go either, and it's what I've been waiting for, as you full know."

"Oh, you can still go," Mima said caustically. "He won't mind if I don't turn up. You saw the way he was. Take Flick instead."

"I don't want to go," Flick said hurriedly.

Lileem suddenly looked hopeful, but Flick said to her, "And you certainly won't be going!"

"I can't go alone, it'll look odd," Ulaume said. "Mima, stop being stupid. This is what we're here for: answers about Pell. Who cares what the Parsic thinks of you?"

"I care," Mima said. "I don't want to see him again. It was a mistake."

She must have noticed that neither Flick nor Ulaume asked the obvious question of "what was?", but she didn't comment upon it.

"Flick, you have to come with me," Ulaume said. "Please."

"Yes, *please* do go with him," said Mima. "I just can't face it."

Flick hesitated a moment, then said, "Oh, all right. If I must. But I don't feel good about this. I've a feeling there will be unexpected consequences, and they won't be to our liking."

"Well, I don't feel that at all," Ulaume said, "and it was once my job to feel things like that. It's you. You're paranoid. Are you scared you'll run into Cal there or something?"

"No," Flick said, visibly bristling. "It's not that."

He looked so drawn, Ulaume could tell Flick had a real fear, but his own desire to get information, to possibly find an avenue to Pellaz, shouldered aside any empathy for Flick.

On Shadetide night, it is traditionally the time when the veil between the worlds is thin, and things can slip through from the other places. Ghosts ride the winds on ragged clouds and fly from the face of the moon. The trees talk loudly and if a har is lost in the thick woods around Galhea, sometimes he might find himself understanding their words. On this night, the past can come back.

Ulaume and Flick walked to the barracks, and Ulaume's heart was beating fast in anticipation, even though Flick was dragging his feet. Ulaume put a hand through Flick's right elbow, in an apparent gesture of affection, but really to speed him up a little. "Mima is a temperamental creature," Ulaume said. "I can't understand why she backed off like this."

"She liked him," Flick said.

"So? That's all the more reason to see him again. She must've freaked him in some way. She could make amends somehow, I'm sure."

"No, Lormy, you don't get it. She *really* liked him. And she feels rejected. Mima is a dab hand at feeling that, as you know. She *does* want to see him, but can't bear the thought of it, because he won't look at her in the way she wants him to."

"Oh. I wonder what happened."

"Why don't you ask him? When he came to the boat, he looked worried, if you ask me, not hostile. He was scared of something."

"Well, it is the night for it."

Flick grimaced. The wall of the barracks loomed before them. "Here we are. You do the talking."

The guards on duty had clearly been told to expect them. They had to wait only a couple of minutes before Chelone and another har, both resplendent in black Parsic uniform of leather and steel, came to the gate. Ulaume understood why Mima might be upset. These were hara of dignity and presence. Nohar would want to be cast aside by such creatures.

"Where is Mima?" Chelone asked at once.

"Sh . . . Shy," Ulaume spluttered.

"He changed his mind," Flick said quickly. "Is that okay? Can I come with you instead?"

Chelone shrugged. "Well . . . I suppose so." He indicated his companion. "This is Captain Leef Sariel, a close friend of Lord Swift."

"He's Flick," said Ulaume. "Just that. I am Ulaume har Colurastes."

Chelone and Leef exchanged a glance.

"Interesting," said Leef.

Stable-hara brought out a gleaming open carriage drawn by two horses, into which Chelone indicated they should climb. Another har in uniform leapt up into the driving seat. "A little cold tonight for this kind of transport," Chelone said, "but we thought you'd appreciate the view."

They drove through scenes of celebration, past vast bonfires. The scent of cooking meat filled the air and the sweet-sour tang of apple beer. In one place, apple trees lined the road and Chelone stood up in the jolting carriage to pluck a soft fruit right off the branch. He handed the apple to Ulaume. "Tonight, the spirit of the fruit can be eaten with the flesh," he said.

Ulaume bit into it, and found it so cold it made his teeth ache, but the taste was like perfume. Opposite him, Flick sat hunched up beside Leef, not saying anything, and Leef looked bored.

Chelone was happy to talk about Galhea, and everything the incomparable Lord Swift had achieved since his father's death. By the time they reached the gates to Forever, Ulaume was already thinking that Swift would be unbearable, full of himself and righteous. Still, he could put up with that if this meeting produced any results.

The house was a blaze of light and a large fire was already burning on the grass outside the front door. A big crowd of hara was gathered in the dark, drinking apple beer and sheh, the local liqueur distilled from apples and spice. Two whole lambs were roasting on spits over fire pits, where the fat dribbled down onto baking potatoes.

Their driver took the carriage round into the stable yard where many others were parked. Stable-hara ran around attending to the stamping horses.

Chelone got out of the carriage first and told the driver they'd meet him later. He offered his arm to Ulaume, "Shall we join the party?"

Leef and Swift followed behind, awkward companions.

Before they reached the crowd, Chelone said in a low voice, "I've upset Mima, haven't I?"

"Yes," Ulaume said. "Did he upset you first?"

Ulaume could barely see Chelone's face in the darkness, but the silence was eloquent. "I just don't think I can help him," he said at last. "I wanted to come and see him, but . . ." He was quiet for a moment. "I hoped he'd be here tonight. I needed to explain."

"Mima is a proud creature," Ulaume said.

"It says a lot that you and your friends haven't helped him either," Chelone said. "I guess you know the problem."

"He is not a great one for sharing," Ulaume said.

"But to have that happen, the inception thing . . ." Chelone shook his head. "It must have been vile."

"Mmm," Ulaume murmured. "What exactly did Mima tell you?"

That Mima had used Terez's story as her own delighted Ulaume: what a good idea. Chelone didn't go into grisly details about the aruna, but it was clear something had happened that had unsettled him greatly. Perhaps later Ulaume could pry for more information.

As they wandered through the crowd, Chelone pointed out hara of high rank. "That is General Ithiel Penhariel, who commands the entire Galhean militia. Oh, I see we have a couple of Gelaming with us . . ."

Ulaume froze. "Who?"

"Don't know them. They appear to be of pretty low rank, probably officials attached to the Hegemony in Immanion."

"Where is Lord Swift?"

"Can't see him yet. We'll go inside. He may be there. You should see the house, anyway."

Ulaume glanced around, but Leef and Flick had headed off in the direction of the food tables, no doubt for Flick to fortify himself with liquor.

At one time, a very rich human family had owned Forever, and it seemed that none of its finery had been lost during the wars. It was a mansion, far larger than the white house, where it had been clear that many of the rooms had never been used. Here, a large staff ran around carrying trays of drinks and food. Hounds barked at newcomers and cats looked down disdainfully upon the revellers from high vantage points on the furniture. This was a home. It had a warm atmosphere and there were domestic animals. Hara had grown up in this place; Swift was a second-generation har like Lileem.

As they walked through the vast entrance hall, Ulaume looked up the sweeping stairs and saw a vision of Wraeththu beauty descending them. His hair hung, like Ulaume's once had, to his thighs, and he was dressed in loose white shirt and trousers that were of the finest softest matte silk. He wore a wreath of autumn leaves and small crab apples as a crown. Even from a distance, it was possible to see his eyes were deepest green, because his skin was so pale. He was not tall, but he radiated power and confidence.

A calculated entrance, Ulaume thought. "Who's that?" he asked.

Chelone glanced up and smiled. "That is Cobweb, Swift's hostling. A legend." He disengaged himself from Ulaume's arm and went to the foot of the stairs, where he bowed deeply.

Cobweb continued a slow descent then extended slim arms to embrace Chelone rather coolly. "You look well," he said. "Who is your companion?"

Chelone brought Cobweb over to where Ulaume stood, somewhat dumbfounded, feeling inadequate. He wished he'd had hours to get ready and expensive clothes to slide into, like this har evidently had. "This is Ulaume har Colurastes," he said. "A visitor to Galhea."

"Colurastes?" said Cobweb in a low husky voice. The voice, of course, just had to be as beautiful as the flesh. "I've never met one of your kind before, but the idea fascinates me. I hope we have time to talk."

Ulaume inclined his head. "I would very much like to."

"You do not have a drink," Cobweb said. "We must do something about that." He led the way into the main room through vast double doors. The room was lit by candles and a huge fire snarled in the immense hearth. Here, the stars of Galhea were gathered.

"Mima reminds me of Cobweb," Chelone said softly, close to Ulaume's ear. "A strong soume aspect, almost like a human woman."

"Almost," Ulaume said coldly. "But not human."

"Well, quite. I didn't mean to give offense."

Ulaume squeezed Chelone's arm briefly. "None taken, but would you voice such a remark to Cobweb himself?"

Chelone wrinkled up his nose. "No. He *does* take offense at things quite easily."

"I can imagine."

Cobweb raised an arm and imperiously gestured for a servant to bring them drinks. "You must meet my son," he said to Ulaume. "I know he'd be really interested to make the acquaintance of a Colurastes too."

"I would very much like to meet him," Ulaume said. "I've heard so many good things about him." He was privately quite astounded at how the fortuitous meeting of Chelone and Mima had occasioned this priceless invitation into Galhean high society.

Another har came to join their small group and again Ulaume sighed inside. Was every har as lustrous as Cobweb in this place? He wished he hadn't let himself go so much during his travels. The newcomer was olive skinned and had smooth tawny hair. He moved like a panther.

"We have an interesting guest," Cobweb said, taking the newcomer by the arm. "This is Ulaume of the Colurastes."

Ulaume inclined his head.

"And this," said Cobweb, "is Seel Griselming, my son's consort, and hostling to my divine highharling, Azriel."

Ulaume felt his jaw drop open as if someone had punched it. It didn't seem to belong to him.

His expression of surprise conjured an immediate response in Seel. "Do I know you?" he asked abruptly.

"No," Ulaume shook his head. "Forgive me. I have heard of you, but I did not expect to find you here. You *are* Seel Griselming of Saltrock?"

"Was," said Seel, his eyes dark and cold. "Might I ask who told you about me?"

Immediately, Ulaume knew, there was a ghost in the room between them, but he didn't think that ghost was Flick. "Somehar who once lived in Saltrock," he said. "Somehar who knew you."

"Who?" Seel insisted.

They held each other's stares for a while, and Ulaume could feel Chelone and Cobweb's consternation thickening around him. He thought of Flick and Flick's pain and then realized there was no reason to lie. Flick had never done anything wrong. "Flick," he said at last. "The har who used to live with you, the one who once thought he was *your* consort."

He shouldn't have said it. He knew he shouldn't, but he couldn't resist it, because Seel was living here in all this luxury, complete with consort and harling, while Flick had gone through such troubles.

"Flick," said Seel. He appeared dazed, and Ulaume knew the invisible punch had been returned. "How is he?"

"Surviving," Ulaume said. And he wanted to say, "You can see for yourself," but realized this was what Flick had been dreading. His instincts had forewarned him of this, and now Ulaume knew he must get Flick away. It would be excruciating. He turned to Chelone. "Our companions," he said in a meaningful tone. "I think we should find them."

Chelone looked puzzled, but he wasn't stupid and was in the process of putting two and two together. He wouldn't want a scene either. "Yes," he said. "We should."

"This is all very dark and mysterious," said Cobweb in a playful tone. "What's going on?"

"Nothing," Chelone said. "Leef's outside. We'll go and find him."

He and Ulaume fairly ran from the house. "Why didn't you tell me?" Ulaume demanded. "You must have mentioned every damned har in Galhea but for that one! Why has nohar here ever mentioned him? It doesn't make sense."

"If you're talking of Seel, few do mention him," Chelone said in a caustic tone. "He took somehar else's place and there are still those among us who are not pleased about it."

"Typical!" Ulaume said. "Just typical." He scanned the crowd. "Where the hell is Flick? I have to get him away. Now!"

"You're right," Chelone said. "If there's a scene with the Incomparable Seel, Cobweb will either be furious or highly delighted, and both moods, in his case, lead to trouble."

"It's Flick I'm worried about," Ulaume said. "You have no idea what he's been through."

They searched the crowd, but there were so many hara milling around the fire now, it was difficult to see clearly. Ulaume knew, with a sinking heart, he'd probably just scuppered any chance of meeting Swift, and it really wasn't like him to put somehar else's feelings before his own, which must prove how fond he'd become of Flick. He remembered the day when Terez had told them that Pellaz was Tigron and Flick's hurt words: "I lost Seel for nothing." Seel clearly wasn't missing him.

Eventually, they found Flick and Leef in the gardens around the side of the house. Small lamps had been hung in all the trees next to an ornamental lake and tables had been laid out there. Flick was sitting beside Leef at one of the tables, and appeared to be deep in conversation with a human female, sitting opposite. She was dressed in an artfully tattered robe of some dark color, her shoulders covered by a shawl with a long silk fringe. She wore a lot of ornate jewelry and her pale hair was confined with jeweled combs in a tousled heap on top of her head. Escaping locks fell over her shoulders and breast.

"Who's that?" Ulaume asked, sure Chelone must be sick of that particular question tonight.

"It's Tel-an-Kaa," he replied. "She must be here for the festival. She's of the Zigane, which is a gypsy tribe of hara and humans. We thought you were of their kind, do you remember?"

"Humans and hara together?" said Ulaume. "That's odd. Even more so that a human is an honored guest at this house."

"Tel-an-Kaa is no ordinary woman," Chelone said, "as your friend has obviously found out. She is a good friend of the family here. Swift has made many changes in Galhea, not least a tolerant attitude towards humanity."

Ulaume ignored this comment on the illustrious Swift's philanthropy and hurried up to the table. "Flick," he said. "Flick, we have to go."

Flick glanced up and Ulaume felt the woman's attention fix onto him immediately, but he took no notice of it.

"Why?" Flick asked. His face looked pinched and vulnerable in the soft lamp light.

"I've said something," Ulaume said. "Put my foot in it. We have to go."

Flick rolled his eyes. "Oh no! I was just beginning to enjoy myself too. Can't we just sit here? Not many hara are around. Whatever you've done can't be that—"

"Flick!" Ulaume said sharply. "We have to go. I'll explain later." He wasn't looking forward to the explaining part.

Leef had stood up. He appeared faintly aggressive. "You go," he said. "I can bring Flick back later."

"No," Ulaume insisted. "He has to come now."

"But why?" Flick said, his expression confused.

Then his face went blank. He was no longer staring at Ulaume but past him. Ulaume turned at once, but he already knew Seel would be standing there.

Cruel, he thought. *Too cruel.*

"You don't have to go," Seel said. "Not on my account."

Flick clearly could not speak. Seel was the last person he expected to run into, even if he had, as Ulaume suspected, harbored private and conflicting hopes of finding Cal here.

"It's good to see you," Seel said, approaching the table. "We were all very worried about you, Flick. It's been so long. It's good to know you're all right."

What an assumption, Ulaume thought.

"Seel," Flick said. "I never . . . What are you doing here?"

Ulaume thought Flick would be angry, because in his place Ulaume certainly would have been. But in Flick's voice, he heard that terrible sweetness, which was just too much.

"He is Swift's consort," Ulaume said. "He lives here now." He went to stand behind Flick and put his hands on Flick's shoulders. "There's nothing to say, believe me. This is why we should leave."

"What did you say to him?" Flick said bitterly. "What?"

"Nothing bad," Ulaume said. "Come on." Flick's body was rigid beneath his hands.

"You can't just leave," Seel said. "We should talk."

"What about?" Ulaume snarled. "How you treated him, froze him out, ordered him around like a slave, let him walk out of your life without a single word, and then forgot about him so easily?"

"Lor, shut up," Flick said. "Don't."

"It was years ago," Seel said, "and none of your business, har." He dismissed Ulaume from his attention. "Things happened back then, Flick; many I'm not proud of. Why are you here? If Fate didn't want us to meet, you wouldn't be, surely."

"We're here to see Swift, not you," Ulaume said. "Not that there'll be much chance of that now."

Seel sat down opposite Flick, who was staring at his folded hands on the table. "What do you want to see Swift about? Maybe I can help."

Flick glanced up. "It's—"

"Don't tell him anything," Ulaume said, digging his fingers into Flick's shoulders. "Don't." At that moment, he caught the eye of the silent woman sitting beside Seel, and for some reason he got the impression she was strongly with him on that point. Had Flick told her about Mima and Lileem?

"We heard Pell was alive, that he was Tigron," Flick said. "Is it true?"

Seel nodded slowly. "Yes. It is true."

Flick lowered his head to the table, and rested his forehead on his hands for some moments. All was silent; Chelone and Leef no doubt desperately wishing they were elsewhere.

Flick raised his head again. "You have seen him?"

"Yes," said Seel. "I went to Immanion. I went to work for Thiede. Things were not how they seemed."

Ulaume could not see Flick's expression, but he could feel the shudder of his breath. "So Orien died for . . ." Flick swallowed thickly. "Cal didn't need to kill him."

"There was never any reason why Cal should do that, whether Pell was alive or dead," Seel said. "If you hadn't left Saltrock, you would have been part of this, Flick. It's just that none of us knew. Pell will be relieved to hear that I've seen you."

"Oh, come on!" Ulaume spat. "You're not being hard enough! Surely you can think of something more cruel to say than that!"

Seel glanced up at him, his expression cool. "Will you keep out of this? I don't want to have to ask Leef and Chelone to remove you. I know who and what you are, Ulaume. I remembered while I was following you here, because I've heard all about you. It does not cheer me to find Flick in your company. You call yourself Colurastes, but that's not the whole truth, is it?" He smiled coldly. "You are, after all, Ulaume of the Kakkahaar, aren't you?"

"Was," said Ulaume. "Might I ask who told you about me?"

"Pellaz," said Seel, clearly also recalling the earlier conversation in the house and how Ulaume was mimicking it, "but you were never a consort of *his,* were you?"

"Stop it!" Flick said. "This does no good. We came here to find out about Pell and this is part of it." He reached up and touched one of Ulaume's hands. "I know," he murmured. "I know why you're doing this and I'm grateful, but there's no need."

Ulaume was pleased to note the gesture was not lost on Seel, because he appeared momentarily sour.

"Why don't we all go back to the house," Seel said. "You can meet Swift and we'll tell you all we know. Come on now. This should be an occasion for celebration, not harsh words. Old friends are finding each other again."

It was obvious that Seel didn't want Ulaume to be included in the party, but Flick insisted. Ulaume knew he needed the support. It was not good for Ulaume to discover that Pell had spoken badly about him, but hadn't Pell once told him in a vision, albeit obliquely, that might be the case? Ulaume felt old feelings well up within him, the old resentments. He could smell the festival fire of the night when he'd been determined to curse Pell. *Things never work out how you expect.*

As they returned to the house, Tel-an-Kaa came up beside Ulaume and put a hand upon his arm, indicating with a pointed glance that he should hang back from the main group with her. "What?" he asked coldly.

They continued to walk slowly behind the others.

"We are all here for reasons," she said, apparently not offended by his un-friendly tone. "I know about the individual in your care. I know how much you have cared for her. I do not share the Parsic view of Ulaume of the Kakkahaar. I believe no har but you could have looked after the child as you did. You are her guardian, as is Flick, but she is also a concern of mine."

"Flick told you," Ulaume said. "Risky of him. I know of your tribe, how you mix humans and hara, but you should know that Lileem is not a human. She is har, just different, that's all."

"I know she's not human," Tel-an-Kaa said, "as I know she is not har. Flick said nothing to me. She has been called, hasn't she? Isn't that partly why you're here, heading east?"

"Yes," Ulaume said, coming to a standstill. "Did you call her?"

Tel-an-Kaa took his arm and led him onward. "Say nothing to Swift and the others about the girl," she said. "Say nothing. This is most important. Her safety depends on it, and you have to trust me on that for now. You must inti-mate this to Flick too. I couldn't speak earlier because the har Leef was pres-ent."

"Did you know we'd be here tonight?"

"No," said Tel-an-Kaa. "That was a fortunate coincidence. I felt Lileem's presence near and have been drawn here for the purpose of finding her. I ar-rived only this morning and have had to spend the day observing the niceties of social behavior with the family. Now, it seems, I won't have to work to find the one I seek. Etheric influences move in our favor."

Ulaume, rather than feeling hostile as he usually would, was sure he could trust this strange human. It was most bizarre. "There is more than one," Ulaume said. "It appears, although we don't know how, that Lileem managed to incept a human woman too. She is with us. She is . . ." He took a deep breath. "She is, or was, the Tigron's sister."

"Aah," breathed Tel-an-Kaa. "Even better."

CHAPTER TWENTY-FOUR

$\succ\!\cdot\!\vdash\!\blacktriangleleft\!\succ\!\cdot\!\ominus\!\cdot\!\langle\!\blacktriangleright\!\dashv\!\cdot\!\prec$

Too much is happening at once, Flick thought. His head ached and he found it hard to concentrate on what hara were saying to him. They treated him like a celebrity, but he wasn't. He was conscious of Seel standing so close to him, a familiar face who was a stranger. This wasn't the Seel he knew. All the edges had been planed off. His hair was straight and sleek and all one color. His clothes were less flamboyant. He was Gelaming now, no matter how much his new family might want him to be Parsic. He was Thiede's eyes and ears in this house. Flick couldn't be bothered to be hurt or angry. He thought wistfully of *Esmeraldarine* chugging up the river, the moonlight on the water, and the laughter of his companions. He dreaded now that the life he had grown to enjoy was gone forever, and that he must do all that he could to resist the onslaught to his senses and will that was sure to come.

Seel wanted him to go to Immanion almost immediately: he wanted to show off his find to Pell, like a good hunting dog returning with a plump kill. Flick didn't think he could face it. None of this felt like real life to him, not like living on the river did. And what about Lileem and Mima? How could he explain them? Also, Ulaume would not be involved in any journey to Immanion. As far as the Gelaming were concerned, his kind were scum.

It was hard to meet Swift and witness the obvious affection between him and Seel, an affection that came so easily and so genuinely. Swift had a handsome, open countenance, and rarely did not smile. His smile was very attractive. Flick wondered if he could muster the energy to be jealous of, or hateful toward, this splendid har, but it seemed like too much effort. Then there were the harlings. To add insult to injury, it transpired that Seel had borne a pearl for Swift, and nohar had to remind Flick how rare and special that was. He could not picture ever having felt that close to Seel and could not help imagining what it must have been like for him and Swift. And then, the greatest revelation of all: a sulky young har with pale yellow hair, who stood on the edge of the party, moodily watching the proceedings. Flick felt his eyes drawn to this individual time and again, until Seel said, "Ah, you've noticed the resemblance. Your eyes do not deceive you. That's Tyson. He looks like Cal, which is hardly surprising, because he is Cal's son."

"Is that legal?" Flick couldn't help blurting, wondering how anyhar could want to continue Cal's tainted bloodline.

Seel laughed. "It's all that Terzian ever wanted."

"He told me," Flick said. "Cal told me that Terzian tried to persuade him to stay here when he visited with Pell."

"He told you a lot," Seel said. "Don't think I wasn't aware of it."

There is so much hurt in the world, Flick thought, *so many intrigues and complex politics in the realm of relationships. As hara, we're supposed to rise above all that, but it's not true. We are just as bad at it as humans ever were. Now Seel is remembering how jealous he used to feel about Cal and me.*

And in Seel's tone and the eyes of the harling in the corner of the room, Flick guessed that Tyson had to pay for his heritage, in small ways, every day.

"You know Cal came back here after Saltrock?" Seel said.

Flick nodded. "Yes, a friend of ours told us."

"Who?"

"You don't know him. He visited Galhea and heard the gossip."

"Well, Cal's had it now. Thiede finally got him. He promised to me that he would and he did."

"You think highly of Thiede now, then?"

"He is unique," Seel said. "And he kept his promise."

He bought you, Flick thought, but because he wasn't Ulaume, he didn't say it aloud.

"So how come you're with the Kakkahaar?" Seel asked.

"We met up. Coincidence," Flick said. "Everything is coincidence."

"I presume Cal told you about him too."

"Yes. I form my own opinions of hara. Ulaume is my closest friend and we are unthrist. We only have each other and we like it that way."

Seel gave him a considered stare.

There is no way I'm going to tell you about Mima and Lileem, Flick thought. *We are going to get out of here and we're going to have our proper life back, wherever it leads us.* "What will the Gelaming do to Cal?"

"They will attempt to rehabilitate him, which will be a complete waste of time. It's not my concern. He's suffering now. That's all I care about."

"And Pell? Is that all he cares about too?"

Seel took a breath through his nose. "Pell has a consort called Caeru. It's all history."

You both forgot about all of us, Flick thought. He felt sick.

"Don't think about that," Seel said. "It's dark history and it's best forgotten. You'll love Immanion. It's all we ever dreamed it could be."

"Mmm," Flick murmured.

These hara are no longer my life, he thought. *In coming here, I have been given release.* A feeling of gratitude flooded his body. He felt weak with it. Ulaume caught his eye from across the room and winked. Flick smiled at him. *My friend,* he thought. Ulaume appeared to have taken a shine to Tel-an-Kaa, which was surprising, but then the woman seemed to be one of the few present who wanted to speak to him. Even Chelone kept his distance now, no doubt fearful of incurring Seel's displeasure.

"Where are you staying?" Seel asked.

"On a riverboat," Flick answered. "It's ours."

"Come and stay here," Seel said. "Swift would be more than pleased. Any friend of Pell's is a friend of his."

Flick put the glass he was holding down on a table. "Seel, get this straight, we can't just . . ." He scraped a hand through his hair. "I can't forget what happened to me and I can't call myself Pell's friend. Friends keep in touch, don't they? Respect what I am and let me be."

Seel frowned. "You're here now."

"Did I have a choice?" Flick sighed. "I'm sorry. This is all a bit overwhelming."

"No, it's me who should say sorry," Seel said softly.

Flick looked into Seel's eyes, and his heart turned over, but then Seel said, "I just take it for granted, all this. I understand how you must feel, being swept along in this great current of change. You need time. That's okay." He reached out and touched Flick's face and it took all of Flick's will not to flinch away.

"You're not going anywhere," Seel said. "Not tonight."

Just for a brief moment, Flick was back in the tepee of Wraxilan the Uigenna. He must get away as soon as he could.

Seel, however, clearly did not intend to let Flick drift from his side and Swift kept away, no doubt believing Seel and Flick wanted to catch up on old times in private. Flick wondered how much Seel had told Swift, and how it would go when he finally had to insist he was leaving.

Hara began to leave the party around two in the morning. By this time, Flick had drunk quite a lot but he didn't feel intoxicated by it. Seel had told him the story of how he'd met Swift, when Swift had taken Cal to the Gelaming. "Swift thought he was looking for his father, but in reality he was delivering a criminal into custody," he said. "It was the way it was meant to happen."

"How did Swift feel about that?" Flick asked. "I heard he thinks fondly of Cal."

"Swift rarely has bad thoughts about anyhar," Seel said. "He feels sorry for Cal, that's all. He has a big heart."

"How is Saltrock?" Flick asked. "Do you ever go back there?"

"I don't have the time, really," Seel said, without a flicker. "Colt and Stringer run it more than adequately, I'm sure."

You gave up your dreams, Flick thought. *I'm not sure I even like you anymore.*

"We had good times once," Flick said. "I miss them. But life moves on." He paused. "Seel, I don't want to go to Immanion. It was . . . interesting . . . meeting up with you like this, but I'm already pining for the river. I have to go."

Seel blinked at him. "Don't be ridiculous."

"I'm serious. Please don't argue about it." He took a deep breath. "No matter who and what you've become, you can't order me around anymore."

"It's not our decision," Seel said. "Don't you understand? Pell would want to see you and he *is* Tigron. He's never stopped mentioning you, Flick. He was devastated to hear we'd . . . to hear you'd left Saltrock. It is my duty to take you to him, and yours to comply. If you don't want to remain in Immanion after that, it's between you and Pell, but he'd never forgive me if I just let you slip away again."

"Then don't tell him!" Flick snapped. He glanced around desperately for Ulaume, sure that if he tried to make a run for it, Seel would order hara to restrain him.

"Sleep on it," Seel said. "Sleep here. We can talk more tomorrow."

"And Ulaume?" Flick asked. "Can he sleep on it too?"

"Ulaume is not part of this," Seel said. "He never was. You know what happened between him and Pell once."

"So . . . let me get this right. You are taking me away from my chesnari? I have no choice?"

Seel laughed. "You are not chesna with him. I appreciate you might have seen qualities that have passed others by, but . . . Flick, you can't reject what's on offer. I tried to once, but I don't regret going for it eventually. Look what I have now."

"You used to say that," Flick said bitterly. "You used to say that, when kids were scared of inception. I remember."

"So, it's another kind of inception. Your point being?"

"Call your guards," Flick said.

"What?"

"Call them. It's the only way you'll force me to stay here."

Seel stared at him. "Don't make me do that."

"What? Don't make you put the knife in me, don't give me the blood? Oh, but you can't because I know too much now, don't I? I know the truth and truth is dangerous. I know hara died and went mad so that Pellaz could become Tigron. I know that Thiede turned a har of integrity and vision into a tame dog. Not everyhar in the world waves the Gelaming flag, Seel, and you know it. So, you can't have loose cannons running about, can you?"

"You never doubted being incepted."

"Pell did."

"And where is he now?"

Flick closed his eyes for a second. He saw the inevitable conclusion, but why waste any more time? "I mean it," he said and turned for the door. Ulaume could follow him, if pursuit was a possibility.

From the corner of his vision, Flick saw Seel press his hands against his face briefly, then make a gesture. At once, two hara came to his side. "Escort tiahaar Flick to one of the guest rooms," he said. "A secure room, and have the Kakkahaar escorted to the boundary of the estate."

"Seel," Flick said dismally, still disappointed, despite his fears. "No . . ."

But before he could make a scene, he was firmly and swiftly led from the room. The last thing he saw was Tyson watching him knowingly from among the drapes by the tall windows, where the last light of the fire came in to conjure animal fierceness in the harling's eyes.

When they'd returned to Forever after the war with the Varrs, Swift and Seel had made Terzian's master bedroom their own. It had been redesigned since the days when the Varr leader had slept there. It was now a much lighter, airier place, and warm memories had been imprinted over less wholesome ones. But that night, the atmosphere in the room was sour and tense and the light seemed too bright.

Seel sat on the window seat, staring moodily out over the dark gardens, while Swift stood over him, glaring. It was not a common expression for Swift.

"What the hell are you doing?" he demanded. "Have you gone mad? You can't just lock that har up like that."

"So release him," Seel said. "You explain to Pell why you did it."

Swift sighed heavily and it sounded like a snort. "Pell doesn't have to know. You're well aware of that. This is about something else and we all know what."

"Enlighten me. I can't wait."

Swift was silent for a moment. "I don't know you," he said. "This isn't you, Seel."

"Yes it is, or has your memory been wiped? Remember when we met."

"I don't care about that. I want to know why you imprisoned one of my guests. What has this to do with your insane obsession with Cal?"

Seel pressed one hand against the cold glass of the window, thought about pressing until it broke. "I don't want to feel this way," he said. "Flick was . . . he was an essential component in all that happened. Pell wants to speak to him and so do I. I never asked him much about what he knew of Orien's death. I treated him badly, took out my anger and hurt on him."

"And this is the way to make amends?"

Seel closed his eyes. "No. I just want to take him to Immanion."

"You can't force him. It's wrong."

Seel leapt up from his seat and Swift backed away a little. "I know it's wrong, but I have to do it. Flick's just being stupid and awkward. If I don't make him do this, he'll regret it later, when it's too late. Pell is very fond of Flick. He's been concerned about him from the moment he found out that Flick left Saltrock alone."

"Is that so?" Swift said. "Strange. I was sure this was really something to do with Cal."

Seel was silent for a moment and when he spoke again his voice was low. "All right, Swift, all right. The truth is that Pell hides what he feels, but every day a part of him is dying. Can you understand that? For a long time, I've kept a lot of the truth from Pell, to protect him, but now I think differently. He has to speak to Flick and Flick has to tell him what he knows. Nohar knows what

Pell is going through, his pain. Nohar but me, because he can't show it. He is Tigron and Cal is a dirty stain in his past. Flick was there the night Orien died. I believe Cal spoke to him."

"You want to believe that. You have no proof."

Seel thumped his chest. "I do. In here."

"You and Pell encourage each other in unhealthy love and unhealthy hate," Swift said. "You shouldn't draw Flick into that nest of snakes."

"Oh, will you just stop being the voice of reason," Seel said angrily. "I'll take Flick to the city, then bring him right back. Give him gifts, adorn the Kakkahaar with jewels, or whatever it is they like. Make amends in whatever way you see fit, but I won't be swayed on this."

"He will hate you for it, as if he doesn't already have enough reasons. Don't go back to that bad place you used to live in. Don't revive the worst aspects of the past."

"Do you know," Seel said, his eyes narrow, "I get sick to death of having to be nice, gentle, compliant Seel. Sometimes, I just want to be the absolute bitch I really am. I'm sick of pretending."

"You are not a bitch," Swift said. "You're the same as anyhar else: some things bring out the worst in you."

"Yeah, like the har you love so much, the archangel Cal. I sometimes wonder what is the point of having any relationships, because at the end of the day, we are all obsessed with that bastard. All of us. We are all his chesnari, helpless, pathetic, and sick. You are probably the worst of us, because you're always so damn nice!"

Swift's eyes looked completely black, in the way that Cobweb's did when he was so angry he could unmake the universe with a glance. "Fine. Go then. Go to Immanion. I hope it makes you feel better." With these words, he marched out of the room and slammed the door so hard all the pictures shook on the walls.

Seel threw himself on the bed. He wanted to go to Flick and unlock the door that constrained him. He wanted to unsay the words he'd said to Flick, undo the past. He wanted to go back in time, take Flick by the arms and say, "You're not going to leave Saltrock. I won't let you go, because I love you." That would have changed everything and he might never have met Swift, and that wasn't what he wanted either. They shouldn't have argued tonight. Seel didn't mean the harsh words, not really. What obsessed him, more than Cal himself, was exactly why he had killed Orien. Seel wanted to know what Cal might have said to Flick on that terrible night, and whether there was any justification in it. However hard Seel might be on himself for his lapses, the real reason he was looking for some kind of light in Cal was because he wondered if, somehow and in some way, Cal could be redeemed. Seel knew he should have questioned Cal, in a reasonable and controlled manner, when he'd had the chance in Imbrilim, but instead he'd just fired dart after poisoned dart into Cal, while he was weak and helpless. Lies, terrible lies. *What kind of friend am I to Pell, really?* Seel thought. He knew that if Pell ever found out about Seel's meeting with Cal, it would ruin their friendship.

Seel had private motives in wanting to question Flick, but he also wanted to take Flick to the Tigron. Whenever Pellaz was good to him, Seel felt guilty about the things he'd said to Cal. He couldn't change that, but he wanted Pell to be pleased to see a familiar face from the past. Since Cal had been taken from Imbrilim, Thiede had hidden him away. He was unreachable. What Thiede's plans were for him, nohar knew, but Seel was sure they didn't include a reunion with Pellaz.

Seel's heart was full of love: for Pell, for Swift, for Flick. So many mistakes.

Because Swift and Seel had gone upstairs to argue almost immediately after Flick had been escorted from the room, they did not know how events had turned out downstairs.

Ulaume was standing near the fire, still talking with Tel-an-Kaa, when a Parsic guard came up to him and said, "You're to come with me, tiahaar."

"Why?" Ulaume asked.

"You must leave the premises."

"What? Where's Flick?"

The Parsic took hold of Ulaume's arm. "Please don't make a fuss. Come this way."

There might have been an almighty and unseemly struggle, but at that point Cobweb suddenly appeared, as if from nowhere, and said, "Take your hands off that har at once, Oriel. What is going on?"

The guard bowed. "Seel has ordered that the Kakkahaar is to be escorted from the estate."

"Kakkahaar?" said Cobweb lightly.

"Yes," Ulaume said. "And no. I lived with them for a while."

"I see," Cobweb said and then addressed the guard. "Well, Ulaume is also a guest of mine and I will countenance no such thing as him being removed in this manner." He waved a hand at the guard. "Off you go. The matter is in my hands now, and if you are questioned, this is what you will say."

The guard backed off, still bowing. "Of course, tiahaar."

"Thanks," Ulaume said. "I think I should find Flick and leave anyway."

"You can't," Cobweb said. "Seel has locked him in a room upstairs."

"What?" Ulaume cried.

"Hush," Cobweb said. "Don't attract attention." He inclined his head to Tel-an-Kaa. "My lady, would you care to join us for a walk in the gardens?"

"A delight," said Tel-an-Kaa.

Outside, it was now bitterly cold and a moaning wind had started up, which shook the cedars and screamed around the peaked roofs of the house. Cobweb was muffled in a big fur coat and had lent one to Ulaume also. Tel-an-Kaa was wrapped only in her shawl, but didn't appear affected by the temperature. They walked quickly to the lake, where there was an old summerhouse. Inside, it was derelict, but at least it offered shelter from the wind. Cobweb had brought a lamp with him and now he lit it, setting it on the edge of a dry pool that was choked with weeds.

"It is my thought," said Cobweb, "that you must leave here at once."

"I can't leave without Flick," Ulaume said. "Why has Seel locked him up?"

"He wishes to take him to Pellaz," Cobweb said, "and Flick is resisting. Anyway, you don't have to leave without him. I have already made arrangements for his release, once things have quietened down in the house."

"You work quickly."

"The best way."

"I never noticed a thing."

Cobweb smiled. "Nothing that happens in Forever escapes my notice. I am as much a part of the house as its bricks and beams. It speaks to me. However, that aside, it's likely Seel will send hara after you. You cannot escape by boat. I will provide horses."

"I don't understand," Ulaume said. "Why are you doing this?"

"The Kakkahaar once had close associations with the Varrs," said Cobweb. "Did you know that?"

"Not really. I'm not Kakkahaar, I'm Colurastes. I merely lived with the Kakkahaar."

"Whatever. They helped us once, so now I help you. Also, Thiede has collected enough captives for now. He has Cal and there's no sign he'll ever release him." He paused. "You must understand that Pell is a dear friend of mine. He has been through enough, in my opinion, and I can't see that Seel's plan will do anything to make things better."

"Have you seen him recently?" Ulaume asked. "Since . . . since he came back?"

Cobweb nodded thoughtfully. "Yes, as often as I can. He has learned to become a great actor, but inside he is still the Pell I knew. He saved my life once, and I will never forget it."

"Seel told me Pell has . . ." Ulaume made an anguished sound. "He has no liking for me, and yet, I feel I am connected to him in some way. It's hard to explain."

Cobweb smiled. "Hara like you and I, Ulaume, we are often misunderstood, often feared. I wish we had more time to talk, because I think we'd find we have much in common. You must know that Pell is a great figure among Wraeththukind now, and hara jostle for his attention. There are many knives concealed behind smiles, many plans to trample over rivals and competitors. The Pell you knew may well have thought ill of you, because he was naïve and often misguided. He is older now and in many ways, much changed. He has done cruel things, as you have done cruel things. I wouldn't listen too much to what other hara say. One day, you might be able to find out for yourself exactly what Pell thinks."

Ulaume grimaced. "I doubt that. It seems to be becoming a less and less likely prospect."

"You never know," Cobweb said. "One day, I will tell him I've seen you. Not yet. First, we have to get you away safely, with Flick, and let the dust settle. If Seel succeeds in getting Flick to Immanion, Thiede would most likely intercept his plans and carry Flick off to some hidden corner of the city before Pell ever gets to see him. These things happen. The time of Pell's inception was a nexus point and it's still an etheric vortex. Anyhar associated with it has to be in Thiede's clutches, as Seel is. It amuses me to thwart his plans now and again."

"Are you putting yourself in danger?"

"No. I'm not afraid of anyhar, not even Thiede, and he knows enough about me to respect me."

"What about Swift? Will he back Seel's attempt to pursue us?"

"Swift, my beloved son and a great leader, is in many ways still an innocent," said Cobweb. "He fits comfortably around Seel's little finger on many occasions."

"I have a suggestion," said Tel-an-Kaa, speaking for the first time.

"Yes?" Cobweb said.

"Ulaume and Flick can travel with me. I can take them to a safe place, if you can provide an escort through Parsic territory."

"That sounds like a good idea," said Cobweb. He turned back to Ulaume. "You have other companions, yes?"

"We do," said Ulaume. "They went to a party in town, but I expect they're back at the boat by now."

"Find them and go to the old oak on the east side of town." He turned to Tel-an-Kaa. "You know this place?"

"Yes. I can take them there."

"Good. Wait in the shadow of the tree and Flick will be brought to you, with horses. How many, my lady?"

"Five. I'll take none of my people with us."

"That's settled then. Go at once." Cobweb shivered. "There are wolves in the wind. A fell time." He stood up and left the summerhouse, lost almost immediately in the screaming elements.

"Come," said Tel-an-Kaa, taking up the lamp. "There are many currents mixing and roiling this night, and Lileem has been hidden among them. This is good. Let us go to her."

"One thing," Ulaume said. "Thiede is all powerful, right?"

"Very powerful," said Tel-an-Kaa.

"If he wants all these hara under his control, why hasn't he come for Flick before?"

Tel-an-Kaa pulled a face, rocked her head from side to side a few times. "Mmm, well, let us say that there are other powerful influences in the world that pay just as much attention to events as Thiede does. Those powers can hide things from him sometimes. If he knew of Lileem, for example, he'd want her very much, but he doesn't, so that's good. Come on. Let's not waste time."

As Ulaume had anticipated, Mima and Lileem were already back at *Esmeraldarine*. Lileem was quite drunk and was dancing around on deck, being buffeted by the winds. Ulaume jumped aboard and Lileem threw herself upon him, hiccupping. Tel-an-Kaa stood on the bank, watching.

"Settle down," Ulaume said to Lileem, unwrapping her arms from around his neck. "Where is Mima?"

"Below deck," Lileem said. "She's moody and has sat with a black face all night. I had a good time, a very good time."

"Gather up some clothes," Ulaume said. "We have to abandon *Ezzie*."

"What?" Lileem stood swaying before him. "Why?"

"I'll explain later. Sober up, Lee. We're in trouble." He hurried below deck and could hear Lileem stumbling after him. Mima was lying on the bunk in her cabin and he shook her, thinking she was asleep. But she raised her head at once and wiped her face. She'd been crying. "We're leaving," Ulaume said.

"There's trouble. I've met a human who will help us. Get some stuff together. I don't think we'll be coming back."

Mima just stared at him. "Pell?"

"No. I can't explain now. Help me get Flick's stuff too."

She sat up. "Okay."

Lileem found it difficult to gather her belongings. She couldn't decide what to keep and what to take. In her drunken state, she couldn't think too much about what might have happened. She trusted Ulaume and if he said they must go, then they would. But where was Flick? If something bad had happened to him, she was sure she'd feel it, but maybe she was too drunk to notice.

With a bulging bag, from which the arms of garments dangled, Lileem went back on deck. She saw the tall silent figure standing on the bank. "Hello," she said.

"Lileem."

It was a woman, or appeared to be. But maybe . . . ? "Are you like me?" Lileem said. She staggered over to the side of the boat, wondered if she could get ashore without falling in the water.

"I am here for you," said the woman. "I am Tel-an-Kaa."

"Are you my voices?"

"One of them."

"Great." Lileem jumped awkwardly onto the bank and Tel-an-Kaa steadied her. "They won't make my head ache anymore, then?" Lileem asked in a slurred tone. "The voices, I mean? Not if you're here."

"No, your head won't ache. We will go east, for I have wonders to show you."

"All of us?"

"Yes, all of you. You and your guardians."

CHAPTER TWENTY-FIVE

>⊶⊷⊙⊶⊷⊰

As if being locked up against his will wasn't bad enough, Flick found the room he was staying in very oppressive. It was furnished tastefully, and was very comfortable in a physical sense, but there were undercurrents. Flick had to pace around, sure that if he stood still or lay down, something would fold out of the air before him that would send him mad.

The Uigenna had once confined him, and they were supposedly the worst of Wraeththukind, but now the supposed best had done the same thing. Flick did not want to be important to others like this. He just wanted a small comfortable life. The thought of not seeing his companions again was too painful to contemplate. He could only hope, if he was forced to go to Immanion, that he could appeal to the new Pellaz for help. Unfortunately, the only image of Pell he could conjure in his mind was of a stem autocratic bully. The har who'd raced with him beside the soda lakes, laughing and horsing around, just wouldn't come back. That particular har could never have become a king.

Gradually, the sounds in the house faded away as the last of the guests left the premises. Lights were extinguished in the trees outside and Flick could hear the savage wind tearing at the eaves outside his window. He couldn't sleep, although he felt exhausted. He wondered whether Seel would come to him, but as the night wore on, it was clear that wouldn't happen. But in the dead hours between night and dawn, he heard the sound of the lock being turned and the door to the room opened.

Flick froze. Was he to be taken away now? A young har came into the room, and he saw that it was Tyson, Cal's son. Tyson put a finger to his lips and gestured for Flick to follow him. Quickly, sensing this was nothing to do with Seel, Flick complied. He went out into the corridor, his flesh tense against his bones, but there was nohar else there. Following Tyson, he crept toward the stairs. The hall below looked enormous, and a few of the staff were still passing back and forth through it, clearing up after the party. Tyson paused, peering over the banisters. "Another way," he murmured. "Come."

Flick followed him deep into the heart of the house, a heart so dynamic and present, he was sure he could hear it beating. He sensed that many important things had taken place within these walls. Cal had lived here. How he wished he could hear the story of that time.

Tyson led them to narrow, dimly lit corridors, probably the territory of servants, for there was no carpet underfoot. "Where are you taking me?" Flick asked, presuming it was now safe to talk.

"To your friends," Tyson said. "Cobweb has arranged it."

Flick didn't ask why. He was grateful enough not to question Cobweb's motives.

Eventually, they descended some perilous twisting stairs, and emerged into a small yard at the side of the house. This was not the main stableyard, but an area where, in good weather, laundry was hung out to dry. A mandala of lines, which vibrated in the wind, crossed it overhead. There were seats and tables near the wall of the house and Flick imagined that in summertime the house-hara would sit out here to eat their lunch.

The yard was empty, but for the spirits that rode the wind.

Flick shivered. He hadn't got his coat. "Thanks," he said to Tyson.

Tyson just nodded gravely. He clearly didn't think thanks were necessary. After a moment, he said, "You knew my hostling."

"Yes," Flick said. "A long time ago."

"I can't remember him," said Tyson. "The Gelaming took him from us."

"I know," Flick said. "I'm sorry." The circumstance of offering sympathy to a harling of Cal's under these conditions was absolutely surreal. He couldn't imagine Cal as a parent.

"My father is dead," said Tyson. "The Gelaming killed him."

"I know."

"I wish I could come with you," Tyson said. "I hate this place. I want to travel, like my hostling did. I want to be free."

"Well," said Flick awkwardly, "when you're older you can do what you like."

Tyson sneered. "Don't be stupid. You need powerful friends. If you didn't have them, you'd still be locked up in that room."

Flick considered for a moment. "Your hostling, Cal, he leads a troubled life, Tyson. There are many different ways to live. His is not the best."

"You hate him, like everyhar else does," Tyson said with contempt. "Hara hate him because he doesn't come to heel. Swift told me that."

"I don't hate him," Flick said. "Not anymore. Hara tried to use him, but they picked the wrong har. It ended up very badly."

Tyson nodded glumly and Flick wished that circumstances were different, that he was here for other reasons, that there was no Seel, and that he could spend some time with this troubled soul to try and spread a little balm on his hurts. It was clear that, like Cal, he was full of heat and resentments. Flick's instinct was to nurture and help. He couldn't bear to think of Tyson living here every day being punished because of who had given him life. But maybe Tyson, like Cal, only punished himself, and others were helpless outside that nest of pain. The main difference between hostling and son could be that it was not too late to help Tyson, not too late to guide him onto a firm path.

These bleak considerations were curtailed by the arrival of two shadowy figures in the yard. Tyson peered into the dark. "They're here. You have to go."

The hara crossed the yard by keeping to the walls, away from the meagre light of a lamp that burned above the door to the house. Flick was surprised to see that they were Leef and Chelone. They appeared tense and wary, muffled in long coats with the collars turned up.

"Come," Leef said. "We must hurry."

Impulsively, Flick embraced Tyson and said, "I will think of you," knowing it would probably mean nothing. The harling was stiff and unyielding in his embrace and did not speak. When Flick let him go, he went directly back into the house.

Chelone led the way through a maze of outhouses, stables, and barns to a small road that wound down the hill, on the opposite side of the main driveway. It was lined by tall maples, which were currently being tortured by the gale and stripped of their last bright leaves. Here, another har waited among the trees, holding the bridles of several huge black horses, which were jostling uncomfortably against each other. The wind spooked them, filled as it was with memories and moans.

In silence, the company mounted, the unnamed har leading another four animals. They were about to descend the road, when a voice cried, "Halt!"

Leef signalled for quiet and presently a dozen or so cloaked figures emerged from the woods. They held weapons and now these were pointed directly at the group. Flick's heart fell.

"Identify yourselves!"

Flick heard Leef sigh. "Ithiel, it's me."

"Late to be out riding, Leef."

Leef dismounted, but Flick and the others didn't. Perhaps if Leef could divert these hara, they could make a dash for it.

"Go back to the house," Leef said. "You haven't seen this."

"The Gelaming have left Galhea," said the har Leef had called Ithiel. "They had an interesting spectacle to observe tonight, and no doubt are reporting their findings as we speak. Don't be a fool, Leef. Don't do this, whoever has given you orders. Ultimately, we all answer to Immanion."

Flick could tell that Leef was not prepared to concur with this undoubtedly wise suggestion, but before he could say a word, another horse galloped down the road toward them. Its rider brought it to a rearing halt and Flick realized it was Lord Swift himself. His heart, which had sunk low, now felt squashed beneath his feet. There could be no escape now, because Leef would surely not disobey Swift.

"Predictable," Swift said, scanning the group behind Leef with a cold glance. "You are following my hostling's orders, I presume."

"Yes," said Leef stiffly.

Swift rode nearer to Flick and the others. "Come out here," he called to Flick. "Let me see you."

Flick urged his horse forward.

Swift fixed him with a stare. "You won't get far. You do know that, don't you? Our Gelaming guests witnessed what happened, and have returned to Immanion already. Also, it is Tiahaar Griselming's wish for you to go to the city. He might already have contacted the Tigron's office."

Flick didn't know what to say. He was sure there was nothing he could say that would influence events. Whatever was on Swift's mind, it was already made up.

"You cannot hide forever," Swift said. "You are still part of it all, Flick. None of us can escape it."

"Maybe I'm not ready yet," Flick said. "I don't want to go to Immanion."

"No," Swift said dryly, and it occurred to Flick that Swift was going to let him go, perhaps because he didn't want Seel to be alone with the har who had once shared his home.

"Here," Swift said and threw a dark object to Flick, who just managed to catch it. It was a heavy purse, full of coins. "Parsic currency, but it might be of use wherever you go. I wish you luck, tiahaar. I fear you'll need it."

Flick said nothing.

"We will have much to answer for," Swift said to Leef. "Go about your business and return. There may be repercussions."

"Does Seel know you are here?" Leef asked. *A rather impertinent question,* Flick thought, which indicated just how good a friend Leef must be of the Parsic leader.

"No," Swift replied. "I suspected Cobweb would plan something like this after I heard he'd slipped off with the Kakkahaar." He looked at Flick. "We are not Varrs. We have worked hard to shed that reputation. We are not oppressors. There are things I will not tolerate, as long as I remain lord of this domain." He gathered up the reins of his horse, urged it forward and it galloped off, back along the road toward the house.

"Fur will fly," Leef muttered as he remounted his horse.

Ithiel took hold of Leef's horse's bridle. "We should keep out of these things," he said. "This will be remembered, Leef. You know that."

"We all have loyalties," Leef replied. He made a clucking sound to his horse and jerked its head. Ithiel let go of the reins. The horse began to trot away down the road and the others followed.

Flick could feel eyes upon them until the darkness, and a curve in the road, hid them from view.

Chelone and Leef had arranged for a friend of theirs to take *Esmeraldarine* downstream, in the hope that any pursuers from Forever would assume they'd headed back west. They would ride through the night to the northeast, because Leef said there was somewhere they could hole up in that direction, somewhere of which Seel would be unaware. Despite surface appearances, it appeared the House of Parasiel was not as idyllic as the hara who paid fealty to it supposed. There were dark undercurrents beneath its smooth domestic facade, and their cause emanated from Immanion in Almagabra.

Strange influences were abroad that night, perhaps a symptom of the season. The wild wind was unnatural. Flick was sure that if he listened carefully, he would hear words he understood in its furious scream. Leef and Chelone took him directly to the meeting place that Cobweb and Tel-an-Kaa had prearranged. Here, the others were waiting, Lileem still very drunk, slumped beneath the oak tree. The chaotic elements made it difficult to take note of Mima's reaction when she saw Chelone, but Flick imagined she would, at the very least, be surprised he was there. However, much fuss could be made of getting everyone mounted on the horses, especially Lileem, who had to be hoisted aloft by Ulaume, and personal issues could be ignored. The har who had accompanied Leef and Chelone and whose name Flick never learned, gave Flick his heavy coat to wear. Without it, Flick was sure he would have died of exposure.

They rode to a covered bridge west of the town, and once across the river, galloped through the fields toward forested hills in the north east. It was impossible to talk, because even a shouting voice was snatched away by the wind. The Parsic horses seemed to become part of the furious elements. The wind was behind them and they almost flew through the autumn meadows. Flick had never ridden such a magnificent horse in his life. It obeyed his slightest command and galloped so smoothly he could almost have fallen asleep.

Once they reached the trees, Chelone, who was leading, slowed the pace a little, to allow the horses to cool down and recover their strength. Here the thickly clustered ancient pines muted the voice of the wind and the sound of the horses' hooves on the compressed needles underfoot was muffled. Flick could tell that both Leef and Chelone weren't happy about the slower pace. The horses wound single file along a narrow deer path, and Leef kept to the rear of the line. Often, Flick noticed, he trotted his horse back along the path a short way and waited for a few moments, as if listening for pursuit.

Eventually Flick had to ask, "Will Seel really follow us? Surely, Swift and Cobweb will make sure he doesn't." He couldn't imagine Seel riding out by himself in pursuit, and surely all other hara in Forever were loyal to Swift and his hostling. Could Seel give orders over Swift's head?

"It isn't pursuit from Forever I'm worried about," Leef said. "Seel has a strong link with Immanion. He might do something rash. And our Gelaming guests clearly made haste to leave tonight."

"I don't understand what's going on," Flick said. "Why is the house divided over this? Why is it important?"

"It's like this," Leef said. "Fairy stories have happy endings, right?"

He waited for a response, so Flick said, "I suppose."

"Well, after the happy ending, life carries on. It has carried on. End of story, or rather next installment of story."

"That tells me nothing. Anyway, nohar from Immanion could reach us in time. Or are there Gelaming warriors nearby?"

"Flick, hara from Immanion could be here in seconds," Leef said. "They don't use conventional methods of travel. They have unusual horses that perhaps aren't animals at all. They can travel through space and time."

"What?"

"Don't even think of questioning it. It's true. We need to immerse our-selves in the landscape, let the Zigane use her witch powers to hide us."

"A woman can do that? Hide us from the Gelaming?"

"I believe she can," Leef said. Once again, he turned his horse and rode back along the path.

Mima was riding just ahead of Flick and now she urged her mount to the side of the path and gestured for Flick to squeeze his own horse in beside her own. "I want to ask you something," she said, in a low voice.

Flick could guess what it was. "You want to know why I wouldn't go to Im-manion, don't you?"

"Well, as the plan has always been to find out the truth about Pell, I am a lit-tle confused as to why we're not *all* going to Immanion now. Ulaume told me what happened with Seel. Please don't tell me I'm not going to be reunited with my brother because of your problems with an old flame."

"It's more complicated than that."

"Why are we running from the Gelaming? How are they a threat to us? They are Pell's hara. Are you afraid of him?"

Tel-an-Kaa must have been eavesdropping. Now, she turned in her saddle and said, "Mima, it is out of the question for you and Lileem to go to the Gelaming."

"Why?"

"It just is, and soon I'll explain why. You should be afraid of them."

"But what about *you*, Flick?" Mima said. "There's no reason for you to fear them, is there? Don't you want to meet the Tigron?"

"I'm staying with you, Ulaume, and Lee," Flick replied. "And I don't like anyhar trying to push me around. I've had my fill of that."

In the gray moments before dawn, they emerged into a clearing surrounded by cliffs on three sides. To the left a treacherous narrow path led up through the rocks. The thick trees and the darkness had hidden the bones of the land from view. The path had grown steeper for some time, but now, Flick could see clearly that the landscape was more mountainous, the air more rarefied. Clouds were caught in the high branches of tall sentinel pines and carrion birds called hoarsely. As the light grew stronger, so their charnel song became a cacophony. The trees were robed in moss, and it felt as if no one, human or har, had visited this area before. Flick felt unnerved. He didn't like being out in the open.

Chelone passed around water and food, the latter being hunks of meat and some greasy bread he must have grabbed from the remains of the ritual feast. Lileem looked exhausted, no doubt held in the grip of a savage hangover and Mima was sullen and silent, remaining on the edge of the group. Chelone made no attempt to speak to her.

Tel-an-Kaa stood in the center of the clearing, hands on hip, scanning the sky. "The wind has dropped," she said to Leef.

"Some of it remains, circling high," said Chelone. "We should not stay here."

Ulaume went to sit next to Flick. "Some party that turned out to be," he said. He was still wrapped in the fur coat Cobweb had given to him.

"Everything has changed," Flick said. "Again. Will we ever find peace?"

Tel-an-Kaa again did not attempt to hide the fact she'd been listening to them. "I will take you to a safe place," she said. "There, you will find the peace you crave."

"Where?" Flick asked.

"It's a long journey," she replied. "We must cross the ocean. Our journey's end lies on the other side of the world."

"How long will that take?" Ulaume asked.

"Some time," she said.

Leef came to join them. "Chelone and I will ride with you to the coast," he said. "From there, you are in Tel-an-Kaa's hands."

"You won't get into serious trouble for this, will you?" Flick asked.

Leef smiled rather grimly. "Swift was taken from us," he said and then walked away to confer with Chelone at the edge of the clearing.

"Well, that makes a lot of sense," Ulaume said scornfully.

"They are still Varrs," Flick said softly. "*That's* what it is. They resent the Gelaming."

After only half an hour or so, Chelone told them they must continue their journey. "We must proceed to the safe house. It is not far now, only an hour or so's ride away."

Lileem was so tired and sick, she was on the verge of tears. Flick could tell it took every ounce of strength she still possessed to haul herself back into the saddle. "There are no voices in my head now," she said mournfully to Flick, "but I just can't enjoy it, because I feel so bad."

"You're probably still too drunk to hear the voices," Flick said.

Lileem frowned. "No. Don't you know? Tel-an-Kaa made the call to me. She came to find me."

"Why?" Flick asked.

"I don't know," Lileem replied. "There's been no time to discuss it. But I don't feel worried about it inside, so it must be okay."

"Hmm," Flick murmured. "What interest does a Zigane have in you, how did she know about you and how did she manage to call you? There are a lot of questions here, Lee."

"I know, but all I can care about at the moment is lying down and going to sleep."

The safe house was little more than a sprawling shack high in the mountains, surrounded by ancient trees. At one time, it might have been a logger's cabin. Leef said that Varrish patrols used to scour these mountain forests for refugee humans. He didn't relate the fate of those unfortunate captives.

The cabin had fallen into disrepair somewhat, but there were still bunks and blankets within, running water, and chopped logs stacked outside for firewood. Leef and Chelone didn't appear at all tired and set about lighting a fire. Lileem went straight to the nearest bunk, threw herself onto it face down and was snoring in minutes. Four beds were in one room, a further six in another, more than enough for a competent Varrish patrol. Ulaume and Flick went into the other room and pushed two of the narrow bunks together so they could sleep wrapped in each other's warmth. There was no way either of them wanted to undress: the beds looked gritty and moldy.

"Is it safe to sleep?" Flick wondered aloud.

Ulaume sniffed in distaste at the damp mildewy blankets. "If the Parsics think so, then yes," he said. "You can tell they're antsy about pursuit, but they obviously feel safe here."

The Parsics allowed them to sleep for only five hours. Flick and Ulaume must have dropped off straight away, because they hadn't heard Leef and Chelone come into the room and lie down on two of the other bunks.

Lileem had recovered considerably and went outside with Mima to hunt for breakfast. Leef went to prepare the horses and Chelone left the cabin to bring in more wood for the fire. Flick and Ulaume used this time to corner Tel-an-Kaa. They wanted to know about her connection with Lileem.

"I cannot tell you yet," she replied to their low-voiced questions. "The Parsics are too close. Know only I have Lileem's best interests at heart, and yours also. Mima falls under my protection as well."

"Mima did not hear a call like Lileem did," Ulaume said.

"No," said Tel-an-Kaa, "and that is unusual, but she is still what she is."

"That being?" Ulaume asked.

Tel-an-Kaa smiled. "Once we are free of the Parsics, I will explain everything to you all. Once we are at sea."

And unable to get away from you, Flick couldn't help thinking. He liked Tel-an-Kaa, and did not feel particularly uncomfortable around her, but there was something nebulous he felt unsure about and he sensed Ulaume felt the same. It was almost as if she wasn't quite real, that at any moment the illusion might shatter and reveal something entirely different. Also, Flick didn't like the way the Zigane seemed to think Lileem, and Mima too, were now her responsibility. He wondered how much of the truth they would eventually get and couldn't help wondering whether the influence of Immanion was somehow, deep down, at work here too.

"Are you human?" Ulaume demanded unexpectedly.

Flick noticed Tel-an-Kaa wince a little. "What do you see?" she asked.

"Someone who won't answer my question," Ulaume said. "Well?"

She hesitated, then said, "Not exactly. I will explain. You have my word."

Leef came back into the cabin, which curtailed any further exchanges. It was apparent to Flick that the Zigane was relieved about that.

"If we can reach the eastern boundary of the forest by nightfall, there is another cabin we can use," Leef said. "It isn't that far. From there, we could take the eastern road to the coast. It's about a week's ride."

"Shouldn't we keep off well-used roads?" Flick asked.

"My guess is that if the Gelaming are looking for you, they'll begin their search to the west," Leef said. "They won't imagine you'll head east, especially across the ocean, because that is where Almagabra lies. They'll think you'll want to melt back into the Unneah wilderness."

"I hope you're right," Flick said. "I can't help thinking that if Thiede's involved, we can't hide anywhere."

Leef smiled mordantly. "Look on the bright side," he said in a sarcastic tone. "I would."

For the rest of the day they rode up steep hills and down into plunging valleys. The Parsic horses seemed tireless, even though they must have covered three times as much ground than if they'd been traveling across a level landscape. By sundown, the cabin Leef had spoken of had not yet materialized, and Flick was beginning to worry they'd have to spend the night outdoors, but the Parsics insisted they keep traveling and about three hours after the sun set, they rode into the tiny clearing where the cabin lay. This place appeared to have been used more regularly than the last one, and Chelone explained that hunters from tribes on the lower plains no doubt used it all the time. Thankfully, it was not occupied at the moment.

The most fortunate discovery inside the cabin was a stock of homemade sheh, which must belong to the hara who used the place regularly. Leef and Chelone obviously now felt they were not in danger of capture by Gelaming, because they joked about how tonight the harish hunters would be stripped of some of the moonshine liquor. Flick felt compelled to leave some of the currency Swift had given him in its place.

There was indeed a faint but definite celebratory air to the late evening meal. They cooked three rabbits that Mima and Lileem had caught earlier in the day and Ulaume found a barrel full of old potatoes, sprouting but still edible, in a shed behind the cabin. Flick saw to the meal, which conjured back a comforting sense of familiarity. In the cabin's main room, there was a blackened old potbellied stove. Leef helped Flick build a fire within it. "This reminds me of old times," Leef said, "when I travelled with Swift and Cal."

"Oh? You traveled together?"

"Yes," Leef said bitterly. "We were looking for Terzian, who had vanished, but instead we delivered Cal into the hands of his enemies."

"You were a friend of Cal's then," Flick said. "A rare creature."

"Cal had friends among the Varrs," Leef said. "I hated him for a time, because he took something special from me, but you get to know somehar really well when you're on the road with them. We all became very close."

"Who did he take from you?" Flick asked, knowing full well it wouldn't be a "what," not if Cal had been involved.

Leef glanced at him, then fed more twigs into the fledgling fire. "Swift," he said.

"That's a big 'who'!"

Leef shrugged. "I was chosen for Swift's feybraiha, it was all organized, but then . . . well, you know Cal, so I don't think I have to explain."

"No," Flick said. "I can imagine."

"I wasn't Swift's first, as I'd longed to be," Leef said, "but it wasn't really Cal's fault. He just has this effect on hara. Anyway, ultimately, it didn't matter, not until we went to the Gelaming camp of Imbrilim and the Incomparable Seel came into the picture. He played with Swift like a cat with its prey. He was vicious, in my opinion."

"Go on," Flick said, eager for details.

"Thiede made Seel take a special kind of aruna with Swift. He wanted them to conceive a harling, and they did. Swift was smitten from the start, and eventually it seemed Seel reciprocated his feelings. Who can tell? He is

prominent in both the House of Parasiel and Immanion now. He hasn't come
out of it badly at all."

"You know I lived with him once?"

"I kind of gathered, yes. You were the cause of some pretty meaty gossip at
Shadetide."

"Well, there's one thing you should know, which may be useful when you
return to Forever," Flick said, "and that is that Seel has been in love with Cal
since they were human. He was jealous of Pellaz even before Pell became har.
And you say that Swift was close to Cal too? Draw your own conclusions.
Seel professes to hate Cal, but he's just furious because Cal isn't interested in
him. Whatever Seel says to the contrary, don't believe a word of it."

Leef laughed. "I'll remember that."

Flick took a deep breath. "I can't believe I've just been so catty, but it felt
really good."

Leef reached out and briefly clasped his arm. "I didn't hear anything bad, I
just heard the truth."

The cabin was larger than the last one they'd stayed in, and had two bedrooms as well as a main living area. Chelone built fires in all three rooms and
by the time they sat down to eat the place was quite homey and cheerful. Flick
was strongly aware that he must remember this time, because it was another
important moment. It was, perhaps, the lull before the storm. They did not
know where Tel-an-Kaa was taking them. They had no idea whether the
Gelaming would come after them or not. Tel-an-Kaa had assured them they'd
find peace in the east, but Flick could not be sure of that.

To some extent, the alcohol and the warmth banished Flick's anxiety and
fear. For some hours, it was possible simply to be, with no future and no past.
Leef sat beside him, on the floor before the stove, and when he took Flick in
his arms to share breath, Flick didn't pull away. He could feel Lileem's curious scrutiny, Mima's hot discomfort and Tel-an-Kaa's somewhat weary resig-
nation. Across the room, Chelone was running his fingers through Ulaume's
hair, and when Flick glanced at them for a moment, he was sure he saw that
hair slowly lifting and falling of its own accord. Perhaps it needed the ca-
resses to remember itself once more. Ulaume sat cross-legged, with his head
thrown back, basking in the attention. It would only be a matter of time before
Chelone leaned forward to kiss the column of his throat. For a moment, Flick
felt sad for Mima, but wasn't this the way hara were supposed to be, giving of
each other unconditionally? Whatever she was, Mima was not har. She could
never be part of something like this.

Leef took Flick's hand and said, "Shall we go to the other room?"

"It might be best," Flick said, and Leef laughed softly.

As they passed Chelone and Ulaume, Chelone looked up and caught Leef's eye. Leef made a discreet gesture. Flick saw Chelone glance at Mima and back to Leef. Some unspoken dialogue was going on here.

In the bedroom, Leef said, "Chelone wants to help Mima, but he's afraid. He thinks maybe we could help him together."

"I don't think . . ." Flick began, but Leef didn't want to hear it. He was drunk with desire and it was infectious.

Flick thought that maybe it would all work out fine, maybe this was what was meant to be, but in the event, he need not have concerned himself about it. When Chelone and Ulaume joined them in the bedroom, they were alone.

CHAPTER TWENTY-SIX

M ima realized that the worst pain in the world was having to watch someone you wanted desire someone else. From the moment Chelone had turned
up with the others at the oak tree, a maelstrom of conflicting feelings had consumed her. From that point on, her entire being had been absorbed in fanta-
sizing conversations and possible outcomes, none of which had come to pass.
She couldn't bring herself to look Chelone in the eye, but had spent a lot of
time gazing longingly at his lean back.

Jealousy and misery filled her up when she realized that Chelone planned
to spend the night with Ulaume. It was so unfair. He'd cast her off as if she
was something repellent, and maybe she was to him now, but at one time, he'd
liked her. Then, the moment had come, after Leef and Flick had left the room,
when Chelone just turned to her and spoke her name. She was so surprised;
she must have stared at him like an idiot.

"Would you like to join us tonight?" he asked. Just that. No explanations,
apology, or any attempt to disguise the offer. So harish. But she could see,
from the expression in his eyes, that he truly wanted her with them. Perhaps
he'd needed to get drunk to face this. The situation was so enormous, Mima
could barely breathe. It was as if she was out of her body, floating somewhere

near the ceiling, watching a person who looked like her saying, "Yes." She even watched this person begin to stand up.

But then Tel-an-Kaa's right arm whipped out like a striking serpent. The Zigane grabbed hold of one of Mima's wrists and suddenly she was back in her body, surrounded by the falling dust of a shattered dream.

"No!" said the Zigane.

Chelone stared at her coldly. "What business is this of yours?"

"I have to speak to Mima. It is personal and private. You go and have your fun, har. Leave Mima out of it."

Chelone looked as if he was prepared to fight, and attempted to stare Tel-an-Kaa out, but it was he who dropped his gaze first.

Mima was frozen. She couldn't speak for herself, even though she wanted to. She had to watch Chelone and Ulaume go into the bedroom and close the door.

Once they'd left, she recovered her wits and pulled herself out of the Zigane's hold. "Excuse me," she said coldly. "I don't need anyone to make my decisions for me."

"Stupid creature," murmured the Zigane. "You clearly do. You are no longer a girl, so stop lusting after beings you perceive as boys."

Mima was so shocked Tel-an-Kaa had realized she was not an ordinary har that she sat down again. "What did you say?"

"You heard. You are not Wraeththu, Mima, no matter how much you might think you want to be. Have you taken aruna with a har?"

"That's none of your concern," Mima said.

"Answer me. It is important."

"Yes," Mima said, "because I am har too."

Tel-an-Kaa shook her head. "You are a fool, and lucky to be alive. You have no idea what a risk you took. You and Lileem are something other than har, and now I wish to speak of it to you. This is between the three of us. You must respect that, but I think that once you know the truth, you will."

Lileem sidled closer. "What are we?"

"I know what we are," Mima said. She was still wondering whether she dared to stand up and go through to the other room.

Tel-an-Kaa ignored her remark. "I am not human," she said, her voice so low that both Mima and Lileem had to lean close to hear her. "I am not quite how I appear. I can make myself look like a human woman, because it is my chosen disguise. It enables me to help surviving human women who need it. It allows them to trust me."

"What are you?" Mima demanded.

"I am Kamagrian," she replied softly, "as are you."

"What's that?" Lileem asked in a rather staged whisper.

"Wraeththu believe that only males can be incepted, but this is not so. Females can be changed also, if not exactly in the same way. This is what has happened to you, Mima. The circumstance has arisen since Wraeththu learned how to procreate. Certain individuals born to hara are different—as Lileem is—and these individuals can incept human females. We are a species hidden within Wraeththukind. They do not know how many of us there are, and when we do appear, we are feared, because hara do not understand what we are. They are afraid that the birth of a Kamagrian among them signals that somehow inception is being reversed, that Wraeththu might come to an end. This is not the case."

"How are we different?" Lileem asked. "Ulaume thinks we're just freaks of nature."

"The main difference is that the first Wraeththu devoted himself to incepting others, to creating a new species. The first Kamagrian, on the other hand, isolated herself from the world, which is perhaps one of the reasons why Wraeththu are more prevalent than Kamagrian. My personal view as to why she made this decision is that is it easier for human males to accept being Wraeththu, because they do not change that much physically. What makes them different is hidden, and the one thing that marks them indelibly as inhuman, namely procreation between hermaphrodites, can be ignored for some time. For a Kamagrian, from the very first moment they open their eyes after althaia, the world shatters, and I think this is why our progenitor at first chose not to pass her difference on. After inception, for a woman, gone are the things that made up her identity. She has male organs, developed to a greater or lesser degree, but far more shocking than the discreet soume-lam. She loses her cycles of menstruation, and for many this feels as if they have been unwomanned. They lose their female shape somewhat: the breasts wither, the hips become narrower, fatty tissue is redistributed around the body. In the old world, a boyish shape might have been desirable for a woman, but the reality of actually having a boy's body is something else entirely. It feels as if something terrible has been imposed upon them, that they have mutated into monsters."

"I have felt some of this," Mima interrupted, "but I have striven to be har. It *is* what I am, I'm sure. The problem I have is with thinking of myself as 'he,' which of course I'm not, but it did not feel right to me simply to shift gender in terms of how I thought of myself. I have to, in day-to-day life, because of course to do otherwise would be stupid, if not dangerous. But the problem lies in the words, just the words. Surely, we should just think up a new term between us, that is neither 'he' nor 'she,' then we can all live together comfortably."

"There is some truth in your observations," Tel-an-Kaa said, "but the other reason why you can't think of yourself as truly har lies beyond mere terminology. It is because aruna between Kamagrian and Wraeththu is not possible."

"It is," Mima said.

"Really," said Tel-an-Kaa flatly. "Then tell me your experience of it. Did it progress as normal aruna should?"

Mima felt a defensive wall spring up within her. "How should I know? There were . . . well, the har concerned knew there was something different about me, but everything worked. I could be ouana with him."

"Of course you could, but physical aspects aside, what was your experience?"

Mima was silent for a moment. "The world went a bit peculiar. I felt I could have been sucked out of it."

"Exactly. The essence of Kamagrian and Wraeththu do not mix. It causes anomalies in reality. In effect, it can break reality down, to the point where you are taken from it. Forever."

"Where do you go?" Lileem asked.

"Nowhere you can return from," Tel-an-Kaa said. "We don't know exactly, because no one has come back to tell us about it. Therefore, we can only look upon it as death."

"So," Mima said, "you're saying that a har gave birth to the first Kamagrian, and that even though she came from Wraeththu, she is somehow set apart from it? That doesn't make sense. It doesn't sound like nature."

"The first Kamagrian did not come from a har," said Tel-an-Kaa. "It had nothing to do with nature."

"Then *where* did she come from?"

"The same place the first Wraeththu did. We have no proof, and neither do Wraeththu, but the most enlightened among us all believe that humans created both Wraeththu and Kamagrian. They were genetic experiments. Wraeththu is a refined form of Kamagrian, which we think came first. It would make sense for someone wishing to create a hermaphrodite to use the female as a template, as all human embryos begin life as female. Who knows what genetic cocktails were concocted?"

"But if the first Kamagrian was created in the same way as the first Wraeththu, why was one known as 'she' and the other 'he'?" Mima asked. "It doesn't make sense."

"We can only conjecture," Tel-an-Kaa replied. "For all we know it could have simply been an executive decision. As females, among humanity, gave birth, perhaps it was decided that a hermaphrodite would be better referred to as 'she.' Also, as you probably already know, the ouana-lim is not as developed as it is in hara. Kamagrian children appear virtually female; it is only after althaia or feybraiha that the male aspect tends to become active. In some Kamagrian, this hardly takes place at all. There is no normal physical condition for us, merely a place on a scale. Certain other feminine aspects remain, in rudimentary form, which hara never have." Tel-an-Kaa shrugged. "As I said, we know so little. Whoever created us all is either dead or has purposely abandoned their creations. Perhaps the first Wraeththu was also created from female material. We really don't know that either. All we can do is observe the results. Kamagrian are part of Wraeththu, yes, and sometimes they are born to Wraeththu, like throwbacks maybe, but until someone discovers the truth about how both species were created, we are in the dark."

"But why were we created?" Lileem asked. "Why would humans do that?"

"The threat of extinction through infertility is my guess," said Tel-an-Kaa. "Or perhaps a scientist genius somewhere did it simply because he or she could. Perhaps they had an insatiable curiosity to tamper with the clay of life, to create new and wondrous beings. One day, we might find out, but for now we have to deal with the simple problem of Wraeththu fear and conceal ourselves among them. There are too few humans left for us to incept and unfortunately we have not yet been able to procreate. This is perhaps evidence that in some ways we were the failed experiment and Wraeththu was the more successful one. Too many questions, and no answers."

"This is astounding," Mima said.

Lileem appeared troubled and Mima sensed it was because Ulaume and Flick were their family and now Tel-an-Kaa had somehow taken them away.

"You cannot live openly among Wraeththu," Tel-an-Kaa said, and her words were the death sentence. "You must come with me to Jaddayoth, where our tribe, the Roselane, live. Our progenitor, Opalexian, has established a Kamagrian city there, called Shilalama. There, you can be trained and live in safety. There are some hara there too. It is a spiritual place."

Mima went cold. She and Lileem stared at one another for some moments, and Lileem's eyes were full of tears. Mima knew they were both thinking, *We could run. We could kill this Kamagrian and run. We've done it before, we could do it again.*

"Kamagrian are called to Roselane," Tel-an-Kaa said. "It was the call you felt within you, Lileem. It is where you belong."

"I wasn't called," Mima said.

Tel-an-Kaa appeared slightly uncomfortable. "That is unusual, and perhaps somehow connected with who your brother was."

Mima glanced at her sharply. "You know about him?"

"I know you were the Tigron's sister when he was human, yes. Ulaume told me."

Mima wasn't pleased about that. She wished Ulaume had kept his mouth shut. "I should be with him," she said.

"No," Tel-an-Kaa said. "You can't. Not yet. Things may well change, but this is a delicate time for Wraeththu. It is essential they do not yet become aware of Kamagrian. Elements within Wraeththukind would seek to exterminate us."

"I don't believe that," Mima said.

"I don't care whether you believe it or not," Tel-an-Kaa said. "It is the unpleasant truth."

"Can Ulaume and Flick come with us to Roselane?" Lileem asked.

"If they so wish it," Tel-an-Kaa replied. "Given their own situation, I think it would be the best option for them. One thing you should be aware of is this: Kamagrian have far greater powers than Wraeththu. Psychically we are more developed and are able to channel the life force of the universe more effectively. In some ways, we lack what Wraeththu have, but in others we are greatly superior."

"Can we tell Ulaume and Flick about all this?" Mima asked.

Tel-an-Kaa nodded. "Yes, but not yet. We need to shed the Parsics first. I need also to be absolutely sure your guardians are trustworthy."

"They are!" Lileem cried.

"I am not criticizing them," Tel-an-Kaa said. "I just need to reveal this information to them gently and observe their reactions. If they are not what I'd expect, then certain details must be kept from them. You must respect this, Lileem, because should the information land in the wrong ears, many lives would be at stake. In telling you all this, I am burdening you with a great responsibility. I hope you appreciate that I admire you enough to trust you. Initially, I wasn't going to speak to either of you until we'd left Megalithica, but in the short time I've known you, you've impressed me."

"We love them," Lileem said simply and the tears finally spilled over onto her cheeks.

Mima reached out to take one of Lileem's hands and Tel-an-Kaa placed cool fingers over both of them, where their hands were joined before her.

"There should be no grief," she said. "You were always separate from them, and you cannot shelter in ignorance. Now, you can love them freely, without fear or confusion or doubt. You just have to love them as brothers."

Lileem dissolved into tears, because she was young and a little drunk and Mima held her closely. They had wanted to be har, yet be themselves also. Hadn't they now been given this gift?

"My hostling," Lileem murmured in a choked voice. "He never knew. He was made to give me up. I'll never know him."

Mima kissed her hair, rocking her gently. "Sssh, I know. I know."

Tel-an-Kaa went quietly to fetch them some more drinks. When she returned, Lileem pulled away from Mima, scrubbed at her wet face with her hands, then accepted the drink and drank it in one long gulp.

Tel-an-Kaa sat down again. For a few moments, she closed her eyes and breathed deeply. "Can you feel them?" she murmured. "Can you feel their passion?"

Mima couldn't feel anything. She was too shell-shocked by what she'd heard.

Lileem closed her eyes and said, "I can see silky feathers, angel wings. It smells like springtime." She opened her eyes. "Ulaume and Flick are always taking aruna together. Sometimes, on the boat, pictures would come through the walls to me. All kinds of strange things: alien landscapes, mythical animals, and clouds. It was like a waking dream." She looked at Mima. "After I had that talk with Ulaume and Flick, I used to touch myself when I knew they were together. It seemed to help. I could make my own visions then."

"Come," said Tel-an-Kaa, standing up. "It is time for you to share that experience."

Lileem looked uncertain. "Now?"

"It has been time for months, probably," said the Zigane. "Don't be afraid. We are parage, as hara are har. Parazha. This is the term you can use."

They went into the other bedroom, where the only light was the fire. Mima put more logs onto it. She felt nervous, which was ridiculous, given that she'd earlier been quite happy at the prospect of taking aruna with four other hara present. She could hear the sounds of aruna coming through the wall and it ignited a fire within her.

Tel-an-Kaa came to kneel beside her and spoke softly while, behind them, Lileem arranged the beds. "You look upon Lileem as your child," the Zigane murmured, "but she is not. Parazha and hara are not children for long. She is adult, Mima, and it is only right, as her closest friend, that you are here for her

now. It is the most important time is any parage's life. Let go of those awkward feelings you have, because they are vestiges of your humanity. Look at
her with new eyes, the eyes of Kamagrian. Watch me."

The Zigane stood up and began to remove her clothes. As each layer
came away, so her true self was revealed. She cast off a glamour and appeared to grow taller with each breath she took. Beneath the disguise,
which went beyond mere physical apparel, lay a creature that appeared essentially har. The firelight softened the planes of her body, which was angular and lean. Her shoulders were strong and she had a black, curling
tattoo down one side of her breast, like a stylized dragon. "You see," she
said. "This is what we are. Some hara lean more to the female side than to
the male and vice versa. We are no different."

Mima went to her and took Tel-an-Kaa's face in her hands, as Chelone had
once done with Mima herself. She shared breath a little fiercely, as if to challenge this creature who had deceived them into thinking it was female.

The Zigane pulled away with a gasp. "Your blood," she said, "is very
strong. You are very strong."

"You taste har," Mima said. "I think you are making differences where
there are none."

Tel-an-Kaa said nothing to this, but turned to Lileem who was crouched
defensively on the bed, knees up to her chest. "I will leave you for some time.
I wish to communicate with our tribe."

She went to sit before the fire and composed herself for trance, dressed
only in the shawl of her hair.

Mima climbed up beside Lileem. "Do you want to do this?" she asked.
"You don't have to."

"I do," Lileem said rather archly, "because you'll be so disappointed now if
I don't. The Zigane made you feel roony."

Mima laughed. "Yes, but I won't be cross, Lee, really I won't."

Lileem regarded her gravely for a moment. "I'm not afraid of you," she
said, "just afraid of what I don't know. I can't imagine what it's like. That's
strange, because I know in a short while from now I will know and everything
will be different and I can never go back to how I was before."

"That's pretty much, it," Mima said.

"Share breath with me, then. Show me what it's like."

Mima wondered, even as the desert song of Lileem's soul washed through
her, whether the hara in the next room would hear them. She thought initially
she should be ouana, the guide and tutor, but then she found she had coaxed
Lileem's ouana-lim into blossoming life, and maybe Lileem should experi-

ence that aspect first, even though she had never been female. Mima realized that perhaps unconsciously over the years she'd trained Lileem to think of herself as predominantly female, because she'd tried to mold a kindred spirit. *I must unlearn myself,* she thought, *and find what I really am. Chelone was the beginning, but this is where it led, and I already have so much to teach her.*

Thinking of Chelone, and the mistrust and suspicion in his eyes after their time together, made altogether more satisfying the fact that Lileem was very noisy during aruna. Her cries of delight could not fail to penetrate the thin wooden walls of the cabin.

In the morning, Mima met Flick outside as he gathered some wood for the stove. They would have a last meal together in the comfort of the cabin before continuing their journey.

"What were you up to last night?" Flick asked. "I know what it sounded like, but . . ."

"I took aruna with Lileem," said Mima. "Is that what you mean?"

Flick pantomimed a double take. "You what? Wasn't that a bit . . . Were you drunk?"

"Not really. Were you?"

"Yes, actually, and I did things I never would have imagined before, but that's not the point. Where was the Zigane while all this was going on?"

"In the room with us."

Flick laughed nervously. "Mima . . ."

"Oh, it's okay, she was in trance at the time. I don't think she noticed anything."

"You're kidding, aren't you?"

"No."

"Did it help you get over your 'problem,' as Chelone refers to it?"

"Yes, it did. There is no problem now. Want a hand with that firewood?"

"Wait a minute. How's Lee? Is she okay?"

"She's fine, Flick, stop nagging. You should be happy about it."

"I am, I suppose," he said with a sigh. "To be honest, I thought that one day Ulaume or I would have to take aruna with her, and the idea of that never felt right to me."

"Well, you are both like hostlings to her," Mima said. "It's best this way. I wanted to be like you, Flick, but I have to accept now that I'm not. With Lileem, I have a chance of the happiness hara have, and so does she."

Flick narrowed his eyes. "The Zigane told you to do it, didn't she? She knows something. Are you going to tell me about it?"

"I will," Mima said, "but not until we get away from the Parsics. You'll love what I have to say, you really will. You won't believe it."

On the day following Shadetide, Seel woke up fully clothed on his bed, with the nagging feeling that something was wrong. A few moments later he remembered the events of the previous night and his entire body went cold. Swift had not come back to the room. Seel groaned aloud. What had possessed him to behave in that way last night? It was almost as if some outside agency had taken control, made him fanatically determined to take Flick to Immanion, whatever the consequences. This morning, it seemed ridiculous. A suspicion stole across Seel's mind. What interest could Thiede have in Flick?

That's just a convenient excuse, Seel thought. *You were bad, and you know it.*

He bathed and changed his clothes, then went to the room where Flick had been confined. His heart was heavy. He had no idea how to make amends. But he found the door unlocked and the room beyond it empty. Swift must have let Flick go. Seel rarely argued with his consort, and he felt shaken by the harsh words they'd exchanged the previous night. It took a lot to make Swift angry. Seel reflected, rather bitterly, that Thiede had been right. Whatever manipulations had occurred during the initial stages of his relationship with Swift, genuine feeling had quickly superseded them. Seel liked living in Galhea, even though he knew that some hara harbored grudges and resentments about him. His occasional bad temper, which he fought to control nowadays, had contributed greatly to his life in Saltrock with Flick being ruined. He must not make the same mistake again.

Glumly, having no idea what to expect, Seel went downstairs. The family were gathered in the dining room, sitting around the large table, eating breakfast. Cobweb was the only one to say, "Good morning."

Swift wouldn't even look at him, and both Tyson and Azriel quickly left the room, embarrassed. Cobweb stared ruefully at his half-finished meal, then sighed and said, "I suppose I should go as well. Don't take too long making up, will you? We have guests later."

After Cobweb had left the room, Seel said, "Did you let Flick go?"

Swift inhaled long and slow through his nose. "Cobweb and I did, yes. What are you going to do about it?"

"Nothing," Seel said, and sat down next to Swift, who was at the head of the table. "Do the words 'I'm sorry' carry any weight?"

Swift glanced up at him. "I'll consider them."

"I mean it. I was foul. You were right to let Flick go."

Swift paused for a moment, then said, "Do you still want him?"

"What? No! It wasn't about that."

"It was about several things, I think. Will you tell Pell you've seen Flick?"

Seel nodded. "I think I should. Our Gelaming guests will no doubt have taken care of that, in any case. I'd like to ask Pell to come here for a day or so, if that's okay. This might sound like an excuse, but I'm not sure I was totally myself last night. I think Thiede might have had a hand in how I felt. Pell and I should discuss the implications of that."

"You can go to Immanion if you want to. You don't have to ask Pell here just to please me."

"I don't want to go to Immanion," Seel said. "It would be preferable for Pell and I to talk here."

"Do what you think is right." Swift pushed his plate away from him and stood up. "I have things to do."

"Swift," Seel said, "please forgive me. I didn't mean half of what I said."

"I love you with all my heart," Swift said, "but at the moment I'm angry with you. It'll pass. You're forgiven, but I need time to forget." As he walked behind Seel's chair, he let his hand rest lightly on Seel's head for a few moments.

After he'd gone, Seel closed his eyes and basked in the atmosphere of the room. He spoke aloud: "Thiede, you are a sly and manipulative beast, and I don't know what you're up to, but I'd just like to say this: you were right about one thing. And I will fulfill the prophecy you made: Thank you."

Pellaz came to Galhea the same day. While Cobweb and Swift entertained some Parsic dignitaries from a neighboring town, Pellaz and Seel sat upstairs to talk in private. Pellaz didn't want anyhar knowing the Tigron was in Galhea and it hadn't gone beyond Seel's notice that Pellaz also preferred to avoid running into Tyson, perhaps for obvious reasons. Seel talked about Flick and his suspicions concerning Thiede, but once the story was out, Pellaz only said, "Why didn't he want to see me, Seel?"

Seel sighed. "Pell, I've never told you everything about Flick and me, because some of it does not show me in a good light particularly. He didn't just grow up and move on from Saltrock. I drove him away."

"I'm not stupid, Seel. I can remember the way you were with him. I read between the lines."

"Also, I think that . . . I *know* that Cal had a hand in encouraging Flick to leave me." There was an awkward silence. Cal's name was rarely mentioned nowadays and when it was, it sounded like the most obscene of curses.

"You haven't answered my question," Pellaz said stiffly. "Why didn't Flick want to see me?"

"Okay, this might come as a shock, but Flick has a . . . well, he calls it this . . . a chesnari. Ulaume of the Kakkahaar."

Pellaz laughed. "No! That is the most unlikely combination I can think of."

"I know. But it's true. Ulaume came here with Flick to the festival. We had a verbal scuffle."

"I've had scuffles with the Kakkahaar too," Pellaz said. "How, by all that's hallowed, did he end up with Flick?"

"I don't know," Seel said. "Flick wasn't exactly that forthcoming with information, but I gathered he and Ulaume have been through a lot together. Maybe they aren't that impressed with how we've ended up. It might be jealousy, resentment, or just that they think we have pretensions to grandeur. Flick really didn't want to go to Immanion, but I'm not sure whether that means he doesn't want to see you. It's too complicated. What do you think about Thiede? Is he interested in Flick?"

Pellaz glanced away. "Probably."

Seel wondered what the Tigron was hiding. "How did he know Flick was here?"

"Who knows? The whole world is a web and Thiede crouches in the middle of it like a great bloated spider, interpreting the vibrations of the strands. I'll keep my ears open. It might also be of value to keep tabs on Flick and Ulaume. I won't infringe on their privacy, but I'll keep an eye on them. Thiede is too fond of plucking hara from their lives and making them dance to his tune. If that is his plan for Flick, we should prevent it. Did you send anyhar after Flick?"

"No," Seel said. "In the cold light of day, I felt stupid for what I did last night."

"No matter. I'll send out a troop of my most trusted hara, who will be able to track them down. I'll provide an escort to wherever it is they wish to go. If Flick wants to see me, that can be arranged, but if not I have to respect his decision. I'm just pleased to know he's alive."

"Will you speak to Thiede about this?"

"Only if he mentions it to me. We have no proof he's involved, and if he isn't, we don't want him to know about Flick. It would no doubt give him ideas."

Seel hesitated, then said, "Pell, do you ever get the feeling something big is going on behind our backs?"

"All the time," Pellaz said. "It takes all of my energy to try and keep up with Thiede. I follow him down the wide avenues, but I think there are many dark alleys I've never found."

"Mmm," Seel said. "Pell, do you know who or what Thiede really is? He's not like the rest of us, is he? He's told me as much himself."

Pellaz stared at Seel for a few moments. "Yes, I know," he said softly.

Seel raised his hands. "Well?"

"It's not common knowledge. Thiede doesn't want hara to know, for understandable reasons. He is . . . Seel, he is our progenitor, our father. He is the first of all Wraeththu. He is the Aghama."

This did not come as a shock to Seel. It made complete sense. "I should have realized," he said.

"There is something else you should perhaps know," Pellaz said, his tone grave.

"I'm listening."

"The second Wraeththu was Orien."

"What?" Seel almost choked. "Really?"

"Yes. It's bizarre, isn't it? I remember being incepted and Orien telling me the story of how Wraeththu started. He was talking of Thiede and himself."

"When did you discover this? Why the hell didn't you tell me?"

"I discovered about Thiede very soon after I reached Immanion, because Vaysh told me. You must understand that Thiede hides his feelings utterly. He acts as if everything and everyhar in the world is beneath him. This is not a true picture. I noticed that on one particular day of the year, Thiede goes to the High Nayati and spends some time in prayer there alone. He stays there all night. He never does that normally, and it became obvious to me he was marking some kind of anniversary. I asked him about it eventually and that's when he told me. It is the day of Orien's death."

Seel couldn't speak. He felt numb.

Pellaz reached for a lock of Seel's hair, ran it through his fingers. "You might not want to hear this, but I'll tell you anyway. When Orien died, Thiede felt it. He felt every knife thrust, Seel, every wound. He felt Orien's terror and pain. You think he found Cal just because you asked him to? Don't ever believe it. It is part of why I can never expect him to let me near Cal again. All he wants is to be the devil in Cal's hell for the rest of his life. I don't condone it. I hate it. But, in some ways, I also understand." Pellaz dropped his head. "Thiede would be furious if he knew I'd told you these things. You must promise never to repeat them to anyhar, not even Swift."

Seel nodded. "I give you my word. But why doesn't Thiede want hara to know? Surely, it could only help his numerous causes?"

"There are some hara in the world who might not believe it," Pellaz said. "That would do more harm than good. Thiede doesn't want to be bothered with unexpected repercussions. He's happy with the way things are. Aghama might not be a god if he was revealed to be a har of flesh and blood, and Thiede believes Wraeththu need gods."

"Everything makes sense now," Seel said. "About Saltrock, about you . . . I wish Orien had trusted me enough to tell me."

Pellaz shrugged. "Now you have to forget that you know."

"Thanks for telling me," Seel said. "I realize you didn't have to."

"There have always been too many secrets," Pellaz said.

Seel's smile was tight. Some could never be told.

CHAPTER TWENTY-SEVEN

From the mountain forests, the road winds down to wide plains, where a number of harish tribes took over human towns in the early days of Wraeththu. Eventually, the Varrs absorbed them, but some differences remain in customs and beliefs. It is a strange landscape, because the rigid human dwellings are still crumbling away and more organic Wraeththu structures are forming within them, as if rising up through the rubble, pushing it aside. Hara conjure the green of the land and it creeps over stone and cement. It consumes the ugliness of the past, crushes it beneath its inexorable advance, and the new dwellings appear little different from the trees that sprout from the ruins. There is no place in this landscape for houses like We Dwell in Forever, such buildings are only empty shells, sinking back into the earth. But the wide road remains, in places repaired with slabs of stone, and it is a ribbon to the sea.

Leef and Chelone led their company fast down this straight highway. At night, they would camp in ruins, and sometimes presences could be felt outside. The local hara were not hostile, and neither were they reputed to be particularly discouraging of strangers, but they clearly did not want to have direct contact.

Flick had told Ulaume what Mima had said to him, and it seemed that now Lileem had discovered the delights of aruna she wanted to indulge in it all the time. She and Mima were always creeping off somewhere to be alone. Flick thought back wistfully to his early days with Seel and a similar passion. He remembered the newness of being har, the terror and the delight, and the feeling that anything in the world was possible, that he was charmed.

It appeared that Seel had done nothing to initiate pursuit, which Flick thought was both a relief and something of a disappointment. Clearly, Seel had forgotten about Flick again already. Flick didn't want to have Gelaming warriors bearing down on them, nor to be carted off to Immanion, but it would have been good to have some proof that he was in some way still important to Seel. So, on the last day of their journey, when they could already smell the sea in the air, Flick was silent, lost in his thoughts. He felt melancholy, but it was not a terrible feeling. Soon, he would leave this country behind and it was for the best. There was nothing left here for him.

The day was overcast, the air still. Tel-an-Kaa said she thought it felt as if it might snow, there was a heaviness in the sky, but then it didn't look like a snow sky and it was too early in the year for it anyway.

"No," Ulaume said, "it feels more like thunder. Perhaps a storm is coming."

The sky was thick and white. It didn't feel like a storm to Flick at all. But it did feel wrong.

Leef brought his horse up alongside Flick's. He looked pale in the unearthly light, almost green. "I don't like this," he said. "It's not natural."

Tel-an-Kaa, riding just ahead, turned in the saddle. "I am alert. Don't worry."

Leef and Chelone kept their eyes on the sky with such intensity, it made everyone else do the same. Flick kept looking back. The high forest was black on the distant horizon. They were far from Forever now. Surely they were safe.

Then Lileem said, "What's that?" She had turned her horse around and now pointed at the sky.

Flick looked back. There was a dense core to the clouds above the mountains. It looked like the pulsing pyroclastic flow of a volcano. Could it be smoke?

Tel-an-Kaa trotted her horse back to the others, squinting at the horizon.

"Well?" Leef said.

The Zigane was silent for a moment, then glanced toward the coast town, clearly calculating how quickly they could reach it at a full gallop. "I think maybe it is time to put heel to flank," she said in a surprisingly calm tone.

"What is it?" Lileem demanded.

Flick could see threads of lightning in the boiling clouds now, which were getting closer. It could be just a storm, couldn't it? But a storm wouldn't travel that fast.

"A gate is opening," Tel-an-Kaa said. "Gelaming. It's a big gate, because it's taking a time to manifest. That is not good news. It indicates a large number of hara approach."

There was a grove of oaks to the side of the road and Tel-an-Kaa said, "Ride to the trees. There is no time for flight."

"What good will that do?" Ulaume said. "We can hardly hide there."

"Do as I say," said the Zigane. "Trust me."

In the shelter of the trees, Tel-an-Kaa dismounted and walked around the grove, touching each trunk. Flick could hear her muttering.

An immense crack of thunder shook the sky. Lileem uttered a yelp and crouched down on the ground, pressing herself against an oak. Mima hunkered down beside her to reassure her. Ulaume and Flick went to the edge of the trees. Flick was terrified, but he had to see this. A wind had started up and it smelled of ozone, rushing from the west.

The strange clouds seemed to implode, but then with another mighty crash they split asunder. About three dozen creatures poured from the hole in the sky, like warriors of an angelic army. They were white, pure white, against the dirty clouds.

"We're fucked," Chelone remarked laconically.

"No!" Tel-an-Kaa snapped. "Go into the center of the grove."

The Zigane arranged them all in a tight huddle and then began to walk around them, touching each one with her icy hands and chanting softly, in a language they had never heard. She murmured certain phrases, over and over, and soon the sound of the words echoed in the heads of everyone in the grove.

Ulaume began to take up the chant also, whispering beneath his breath, and presently the others followed his example. The chant conjured a web of power around them.

Through the trees, Flick could see a company of white horses galloping down the road toward them. Their riders were dressed in silver and their flying hair was the same color as the horses' manes. Gelaming. He had never seen anything so beautiful. *If these are the angels,* he thought, *then we must be the devils.*

They were so close now and the chant was rising in pitch. Surely the Gelaming could see them standing in the trees and hear their voices? Soon they would veer off the road and surround them.

The voices sounded feverish now, chanting so fast the words melted into one another. Flick could feel the spiraling power they had conjured, but how could it be enough? Couldn't angels see through everything?

Tel-an-Kaa suddenly screeched, "Release!" and Flick, like the others, was compelled to throw up his arms. He felt something tear out of him, like part of his spirit. He imagined a shining cloud bursting out of them all, a cloud which then drifted down over them like a caul.

The ground shook, and the Gelaming horses thundered by, so close. Flick could see crystals flying off their manes and tails. He could see their distended nostrils, the sweat upon their necks. They could not really be horses. He could see the hands of the riders upon the reins, and their stern countenances. And then he saw only the dust of their passage and the sound of hooves grew fainter.

He released his breath, realizing he had been holding it for a long time. The group broke up, each wandering towards the edge of the trees.

"Will they come back?" Lileem asked. "Will they search for us in the town?"

"We do not leave the boundary of this grove for some time," Tel-an-Kaa said. "Step back, Lileem. Do not break the web."

"They were magnificent," Mima said in rather a dazed tone. "And they are my brother's tribe?"

"Beautiful to behold," said Tel-an-Kaa, "like a snake with its jeweled coat. Do not be deceived. They are ruthless."

Tel-an-Kaa made them wait until sunset before they left the grove. They kept off the road and galloped through the fields toward the town, the horses jumping over sagging fences that had fallen into disrepair. They careered through farmyards and woods, until they could hear the song of the ocean as it threshed against rocky cliffs. The clouds had dispersed and now moonlight illumined the narrow road they took down to the little port of Atagatisel, renamed for an ancient goddess of the sea.

Tel-an-Kaa had sent a mind-touch message to parazha of her tribe who patrolled the northeastern coast, looking for Kamagrian wanderers. The Zigane had made sure that a boat would be waiting for her party. The town was dark and quiet, almost too much so, and Flick could barely draw breath. It was built on a sheer hillside and all the narrow streets sloped alarmingly. Every time they passed a side alley, Flick expected to see a ghostly Gelaming horse materialise before their eyes. Seel had sent hara to find them, after all. What did this really mean?

Tel-an-Kaa did not take them to the main harbor, but to a private jetty just outside the town. Trees that grew right to the shoreline hid it from prying eyes. Here, a har was waiting for them in a small rowing boat.

"He will take us to the ship," Tel-an-Kaa said. "He is one of Opalexian's most trusted agents, and as foxy as any Gelaming. His name is Zackala."

"No," said Flick. "That is just too much of a coincidence."

"What do you mean?" Ulaume asked.

Flick shook his head. "Nothing. Cal was once chesna with a har named Zackala, but he is dead."

"Like Pell is," said Ulaume. "There are no coincidences."

"No, there aren't," Tel-an-Kaa said, "but there are many lies."

The Zigane rode up to the jetty and dismounted, and Zackala jumped out of the boat to hold her horse. "Hurry," she called to the others. "Leef, Chelone, you had better get going, very quickly. Ride south and then go across country back to the mountains. The Gelaming are near, but my colleagues in this area have emitted an ether fog to beguile them. It will not fool them for long."

Flick dismounted and patted the horse affectionately. He'd miss it. Leef and Chelone didn't even dismount. They gathered up the reins of the horses between them.

"Good luck," Leef said to Flick. "I hope we meet again one day."

"I doubt very much I will return to Forever," Flick said, "but it was good to know you for this short time. Thanks for all you've done."

"Our pleasure," Chelone said. "May the Aghama smile upon your journey."

With these words, they set off, without a backward glance.

"Poignant," said Ulaume in a cynical tone.

"Hurry," Tel-an-Kaa said. "Get into the boat. I'm picking up impressions of two distinct Gelaming groups. They are passing in and out of this reality continually. They will find us very soon if we don't leave here."

Zackala helped them aboard. It was difficult to see what he looked like, because a black scarf hid his head and most of his face. His garments too were black and he did not speak. As soon as they were safely seated, he untied the boat and began rowing powerfully out to sea. Flick kept his eyes fixed on the shore. It was happening so quickly, it was surreal. Only minutes ago, they'd been part of a larger company and now everything had changed. He felt dizzy with it.

Lileem was sitting beside him. Now, she leaned close and murmured, "Look at the cliff top, to the right of the town."

A shudder went through him, but he did what she said. He saw a lone white horse up there, standing so still it could have been carved from marble. A figure was mounted upon it, swathed in a pale hooded cloak that flapped in the wind. Flick felt as if the eyes concealed by the hood could see every detail of the passengers in the boat. The horse might take off at any moment and gallop a road of light across the sea to them. He was filled with an emotion he could not name, but which made him want to both laugh and cry hysterically.

"The others can't see it," Lileem whispered. "I think the image is for you."

"Why?" Flick hissed.

"Don't tell Mima," Lileem said. "She must never know. That is her brother Pellaz."

In those days, but for hara like the Gelaming, most Wraeththu had recourse only to primitive methods of transport. Natural reserves of fuel might remain deep within the earth, but few tribes were yet organised enough to mine them. Powerful hara closely guarded remaining stocks. Much of the sophistication of earlier human culture had disappeared. In the beginning, Wraeththu were little more than children, fierce and primitive barbarians, who were so fueled with blood lust to destroy the old order they didn't for one minute think about how they would live once the fighting was over, when there was no one left to fight but other hara. Many skills had been lost or had to be relearned. What did education matter when your only thought was to run wild through the night, celebrating, or perhaps trying to forget, the impossible excesses of your new being?

Therefore, among many other difficulties, crossing the great ocean that Wraeththu called the Girdle of Tiamat was a lengthy, if not hazardous, undertaking. Once, humans had flown over it in silver birds in a matter of hours, or great engine-powered ships had cleaved its fretful waters in days, but now the best vessels were modeled on ancient sailing ships from the past and the journey could take weeks. It was fortunate that once hara began to grow up, the best among them discovered they were resourceful, creative and worked well with their hands. Eventually, they would go on to create machines and vessels far superior to anything humanity had invented, because they could pluck the very stuff of the universe from the source and shape it to their dreams, such as Thiede had done with his *sedim*. But most hara were still working their way up, experimenting with designs and mastering their crafts, and a reliable and efficient alternative power source lay some distance into the future.

The ship, *Night's Arrow,* was of Roselane design, and its crew were harish. Shamans among them were adept in affecting the weather, singing to the sea to quiet its tempers and calling up the winds to speed the journey. This was the harish equivalent of powerful engines and navigation systems. It seemed strange that the Roselane had developed the skill of shipwrighting, seeing as their territory was landlocked, but they had a strong presence in the domain of the Emunah, which extended widely around the Sea of Shadows and the smaller Sea of Arel that was connected to it.

Tel-an-Kaa explained to her companions that they must cross the Girdle, heading northeast, skirting round the eastern continent. There was a quicker way to Jaddayoth, which would mean going southeast past the vast temperate country of Almagabra, passing right through Gelaming waters, which the Zigane didn't think was advisable. So, once they had made landfall on the eastern continent, a long and arduous journey lay ahead of them. They would have to cross the lands north of Almagabra and head toward Jaddayoth, which lay around the cold Sea of Shadows in an ancient landscape. Once at Jaddayoth's border, they must sail down the Eragante River, passing through Elhmen, Gimrah and Maudrah territory, make their way to the Maudrah port of Morla on the Sea of Arel, and from there, journey upriver to Roselane. It seemed such an impossibly long way away, with so many dangers in between. Flick and Ulaume discussed the fact they must accept that traveling was to be their way of life for a considerable time to come.

Flick did not tell Ulaume what he'd seen on the cliff top as they'd left Megalithica. Had it really been Pellaz?

Lileem had been sure it was. "I carry the carving of him in my pocket all the time," she said. "When we were in the boat, the stone went very hot. I could feel it right through my trousers and I was compelled to look at the cliff top. Don't you think that means it was him?"

Flick wasn't sure, but if it had been Pellaz, he had watched them leave. He knew they were on the ocean, and while Flick could not help but feel strangely warmed by the Tigron's lone vigil of their departure, he knew it could spell danger also. What kind of creatures had Pell and Seel become, thinking they could interfere in other haras' lives like this? They were no better than Uigenna.

Mima had no intention of keeping to Tel-an-Kaa's plan of leaving Flick and Ulaume in the dark about the Kamagrian. While the Zigane might have to wait to assure herself they were to be trusted, Mima had no such reservations and neither did Lileem. Tel-an-Kaa was always around, so it was difficult to talk in private, but two days after their sea journey had begun, the Zigane went to her cabin to commune with her tribe and Mima and Lileem used this opportunity to speak with their companions. They gathered in the cabin Flick shared with Ulaume, while outside the Roselane shamans sang to the wind like birds.

Ulaume had not taken well to ocean travel and felt wretched. He said he'd been sick so many times, he'd soon be vomiting up internal organs, which none of his companions were particularly delighted to hear. While Lileem offered him hands-on healing, Mima repeated what Tel-an-Kaa had told her. Occasionally, Lileem would add a comment or an opinion, but for the most part let Mima narrate the tale. They had to impart all the information very quickly, before Tel-an-Kaa reappeared.

At the end of Mima's story, Flick simply asked a typical Flick question: "How do you feel about this?"

"Pleased in some ways," she replied, "but also wary of us being dragged into something against our will. The Zigane has very clear views about Lileem's and my future."

"Do you want to go to Roselane?"

"I'm curious," Mima replied. "I have to be, but I'm not sure I'll want to stay there once my curiosity has been satisfied."

"By which time it might be difficult to leave," Flick said. "I hate all this, other hara—or in your case, parazha—making decisions about our lives. We were perfectly happy living on the Serpent until the Kamagrian started shouting in Lee's head."

"We have a right to know about ourselves," Lileem said. "Don't we?"

"Of course." Flick shook his head. "I don't know. Are the Kamagrian hostile to Wraeththu? What are we getting into?"

"I don't think they are," Mima said. "Although I get the distinct impression there is some friction between Roselane and Immanion."

"I'd expect nothing else," Ulaume said in a muffled voice from beneath Lileem's hands.

She lifted them from his face. "Better?"

Ulaume sat up, grimacing. "Yes, much, thank you." He rubbed the back of his neck, stretched. "I think we should go along with the Zigane for now. As you said, you have a right to know everything about yourselves. We're resourceful, and we're not sheep. We've already dealt with many tricky situations. This can be no worse, surely."

"Except we don't have Terez to help us," Lileem said, a remark that conjured an awkward and tense silence. "He won't know where we are anymore. Will he?"

"We need to find out about ourselves, our strengths, our abilities," Mima said. "One day, I will go to Immanion, I swear it, and my life does not lie in the hands of others."

"Don't you want to see him again?" Lileem said to Mima. "Of course, he might already be in Immanion. He said he'd go there. In that case, he'll be on the same continent as us. So he might be able to . . ."

Mima had fixed her with a cold stare. "Be quiet. That's quite enough! As far as I'm concerned, I have only one brother, and I even have issues with him. I don't want to hear another word about anyhar else." She was painfully aware how not one of them believed her, and she didn't truly believe it herself either. Unfortunately, there was a lump of pain in the way of rational thought, and Lileem was probably right: Terez could not track them down once an ocean lay between them, unless he'd already crossed it himself.

The worst aspect of such a long journey was the boredom. There were only so many times you could sit playing cards for hours on end, without feeling you'd like to rip every one into little pieces. The tortured writhing of the ship in the late fall seas did nothing to make the experience more pleasant.

At first, Flick and Lileem had harbored hopes that the Roselane navigators might share some of their occult secrets with them—Lileem especially savored the thought of being able to conjure up sea spirits—but they were a closed society, and while not rude, made it clear their most useful knowledge was not for the uninitiated. They were, however, more than happy to share their folklore with strangers. Among the Roselane, the King of the Winds is the mighty Chairom, Lord of the North. Beneath his rule are Ishliya, in the East, Tarsis in the West and Kerkutha in the South. Their sons are Nayutha in the southwest, Abathur in the northwest, Muzania in the northeast and Gauriel in the southeast. Chairom is feared most among harish sailors, because his temperament is unpredictable. Shamans control him through song and also through whistling. When they wish to call upon the winds, they whistle a certain refrain, supposedly pleasurable to the wind concerned. Lileem was keen to learn how to do exactly that, but the shamans only laughed and told her she would have to train in the Roselane city of Shilalama for many years to earn that privilege.

During the journey Zackala remained an enigmatic presence, who spent most of his time with the crew. Both Flick and Ulaume privately wanted to question him and discover whether he was the same har who had once known Cal, but he obviously didn't want to get to know them.

One night, Tel-an-Kaa gathered everyone together to reveal the devastating information about what Lileem and Mima actually were. Ulaume and Flick had to act surprised, ask the right questions. Mima had already discussed with

them how they should react to the Zigane's news, and it seemed she had prepared them well. Tel-an-Kaa did not appear displeased with their responses.

This kind of behavior galled Ulaume, who liked to speak bluntly when it
suited him. He wasn't disposed to accommodating others if he didn't feel like
it. His initial opinion of Tel-an-Kaa had changed somewhat. She was a de-
ceiver, and Ulaume knew enough about deception to remain on high alert
around the Kamagrian. If she could lie so convincingly, and with more than
words, about the simple state of her being, what other political lies could she
weave? Ulaume found it difficult to believe the Kamagrian were the retiring,
solitude-loving ascetics that Tel-an-Kaa described. She, for example, was far
too worldly to fit into that picture. As with Wraeththu, it might be that the majority of parazha were fed a strict diet of things to believe in, while their self-
styled leaders did and thought as they pleased. Ulaume was quite interested to
find out if his assumption was correct.

Although he didn't speak of it in detail to Flick, Ulaume found it hard to
accept everything Tel-an-Kaa had said to them. Mima was perhaps as cynical,
but Lileem appeared to embrace the concept of Kamagrian wholeheartedly.
Ulaume couldn't help wondering if the insistence that Wraeththu and Kamagrian could never come together in aruna was not a simple tactic of division.
Mima now felt relaxed enough to describe some of what she'd experienced
with Chelone, and even she was not totally convinced by Tel-an-Kaa's dire
warnings. Something unusual had happened, and she felt she hadn't the experience to deal with it, and aruna with Lileem was far more comfortable, but
one day the issue should be examined properly.

Throughout the journey, the shamans on *Night's Arrow* had called to Tarsis,
the west wind, and he blew the ship all the way to the shores of the far land
known now as Attaris, the domain of winter. Before land was in sight, but
when birds could already be seen wheeling high above, the sea became calm.
This was unnatural in those waters and the shamans set about at once their
whistling and singing, but Tarsis had turned his back on them and had taken
his sons with him.

The air was very cold and everyone huddled on deck, scanning the horizon.
Zackala joined Ulaume and Flick at the prow, and for the first time deigned to
speak to them. Although his head remained covered in a black scarf, his face
was now visible: a dark countenance with a certain rakish gypsy appeal to it.
"This is unnatural," he said. "Prepare yourselves for Gelaming activity." The
prospect appeared to delight him.

"Have they calmed the wind?" Flick asked.

Zackala glanced at the sky. "More than that. They will wait for night to fall. We must hope our wind-singers are capable of combating it." He directed a wolfish grin at them and departed.

A strange twilight crept in from the west. Ulaume could feel all the small hairs on his body twitching, and he had to keep scratching his head. "Now might be a good time to reacquaint yourself with the dehara," he said to Flick.

Flick shook his head. "No. The ones I know of are inappropriate in this situation."

"Aruhani is your patron . . ."

"He is not!"

Ulaume raised his hands. "It was just a suggestion."

Flick frowned. "I know. Sorry. I just feel odd." He gripped Ulaume's arm. "Look! Did you see that?"

Ulaume looked to where Flick was pointing along the deck. "No. What?"

"A black, scurrying thing." He grimaced. "Nothing. It's my imagination. The wind-singers told us that the black djinn come aboard ships before a tempest strikes."

"That is good news," Ulaume said laconically. "There's nothing there, Flick." He peered up at the thick clouds overhead. "I don't sense a storm. Something else. It will be a portal opening again."

The eerie song of the shamans filled the cold motionless air. Ulaume could not see them from where he stood, and they might as well have been mer creatures, their voices rising up the darkest depths of the ocean. He shuddered.

A call came from the high rigging. "Land, ho!"

"Thank Aru," Flick murmured.

Ulaume thought it best not to comment upon Flick's choice of oath. "We're not that close," he said. "I won't be happy until there's ground beneath our feet. At least, then, we can run." He could not see land ahead, but his eyes were not trained to see it from this distance and the light was bad.

"Somehar has lit a lamp above the sails," Flick said. "It's weird. Must be a spirit lamp or something."

A flickering blue-white flame could be seen at the top of the mast. "Nohar has lit that," Ulaume said.

Flick was silent for a moment. "No, they haven't," he said softly. "It is the cloud fire."

"Don't tell me: it's a bad omen," Ulaume said.

Flick smiled. "Not exactly, but it means strange influences are about."

"We should go to the others."

Flick nodded. "Yes."

Lileem was with Tel-an-Kaa and Mima on the main deck. The Zigane was the most anxious Lileem had ever seen her, which did not bode well. The Gelaming were coming and soon they'd cut open the sky and pour down like icy rain. Lileem shuddered as she looked at the thick cloud. It was too congested, as if the sky itself was infected with disease.

Ulaume and Flick came to join them and Tel-an-Kaa said, "The Tigron searches for you most earnestly, my friends." The comment sounded like a criticism.

"I don't know why," Flick said, "he hasn't bothered before."

"I just hope Immanion hasn't caught scent of Lileem or Mima," said the Zigane.

Flick grimaced. "I don't think it's that."

Neither did Lileem, but she kept silent. All too often now, she was keeping silent. She felt like a watcher, observing life from the outside. It pleased her to think that none of her friends really knew her. It pleased her to think that one day she would know herself.

A breeze started up and it smelled sour. It came from the north and it felt unnaturally warm and clammy against the skin. *Soon,* Lileem thought, *it would happen.* Her fingers reached inside her coat pocket for the carving of the Tigron. It was cold as ice. *It isn't him,* she thought. *It isn't Pellaz coming for us.*

Lightning threaded its spiky way through the clouds, illuminating a dense pulsing core to the bubbling clouds. They resembled the fruit of dry rot, which Lileem had discovered in certain parts of the white house: a sticky spherical gauze of livid yellow and sickly white that looked as if it would explode in a smoke of a million poisonous spores if you poked it. When the Gelaming came, would she and her friends have to fight them? They had come so far. They couldn't just surrender themselves now surely. "Will you hide us again?" she said to Tel-an-Kaa.

"I will do what I can," she replied, "although the sea is not my natural element. If I can hide just one, it will be you."

This did not sound encouraging.

It was almost as if the Gelaming were teasing them, because for over an hour, the impending portal merely hung above them in the sky, emitting weird pulses of light and occasionally grumbling with thunder. The Roselane shamans uttered mournful cries to the winds and to the creatures of the sea, but it did not appear they were heard.

They are trying to break our spirits, Lileem thought. *It is so strange. Why are we that important to them?*

Then, the clouds opened. The sky filled with a heavenly white light, a radiance so brilliant that everything—the sea, the ship, its passengers, and crew—were bleached of color. Everything appeared spectral, as if made of light itself.

Tel-an-Kaa began to mutter beneath her breath, but she didn't suggest that any of them join her in her magic. She put a hand upon Lileem's shoulder and the center of her palm radiated an energy that was neither hot nor cold, but something of both. Lileem squirmed away and the Zigane looked at her sharply. In the strange light, her eyes were pinky red, like an albino's. *I won't let you just protect me,* Lileem thought clearly, trusting the Zigane would pick it up. *We are all in this together.*

"Where are the horses?" Mima asked, squinting up at the sky. "Is anything coming out of there?"

"Not yet," Tel-an-Kaa said. Her gaze was still on Lileem.

The shamans of the ship had gathered on the main deck in a circle, and now uttered bizarre cries that shattered around them. Shards of sound caught in Lileem's hair. She could taste the words. It wouldn't work. Nothing they could produce would combat this power.

Ghostly shapes began to spiral out of the sky, circling the ship. They could have been horses, but it was difficult to tell. They brought with them a strong wind that smelled of flowers, of trampled greenery with a strange metallic undertaste. The ship began to roll upon the newly agitated waters. Its timbers groaned as if in pain.

Lileem was thrown against the side of the ship and Flick pulled her back. "What can we do?" she said to him. "What?"

"Nothing. We can do nothing."

The ship was surrounded by what looked like a white twister. It had no form, and was sensed rather than seen with the physical eyes, but Lileem caught the impression of flying manes, of sharp hooves slicing the air. There were no riders though.

The Roselane shamans were now shrieking out their invocations, to no avail. The ship began to turn, slowly at first, but with increasing speed. The waters around it were becoming a whirlpool.

"They mean to take us!" Tel-an-Kaa cried. "They will carry the entire ship up to the portal."

"Can we jump overboard?" Ulaume demanded, and his voice now sounded thin and distant. Space had become distorted.

"Into that?" Flick said, indicating the turbulent waters. "There is a vortex around us. How can we escape that?"

"We must do something!" Mima snapped. "We can't just stand here and wait for them to take us."

"This is your brother's doing," Tel-an-Kaa said to her coldly. "You might as well prepare yourself for a reunion, though I doubt it will be happy."

Lileem was having trouble with thinking clearly. Her mind felt muzzy, as congested as the clouds had been. Her fingers curled around the carving in her pocket. It was still cold. Maybe the Tigron had sent hara out in pursuit of them again, and was sitting at home on his throne in Immanion, fully aware of what was happening. But maybe he wasn't responsible at all. If he'd wanted to capture them, he could have done so at Atagatisel. Hadn't the Zigane mentioned at the time that she'd detected *two* groups of Gelaming near them? The thought occurred to Lileem then that Pellaz might have been trying to help them escape. Was this just wishful thinking? If it was, then it would be a big mistake to try and use the little carving to contact him. It would be very stupid to consider that; because a portal to Immanion was open, it might be possible to send out a strong message and ask for his help again.

Don't do it, she told herself. But already, she had closed her eyes. Her fingers gripped the carving firmly. Even in the midst of this chaos, she found it was possible to focus her thoughts. She imagined them as a pure beam of light shooting up through the center of the vortex, going beyond space and time, and somehow finding its way to Immanion. She imagined Pellaz sitting upon a great throne in a huge empty chamber. He was like a statue.

"Pellaz, hear me," she cried in her mind. "I call to you, Tigron, you who are lord of all Wraeththu. Hear me and come to my aid. We are your children and we in danger. Extend your powerful arm and smite our enemies."

She realized she was addressing him as if he was a dehar, but if the stories were true, and he was a har who'd risen from the dead, perhaps this was entirely appropriate.

The maddened waters were rising, and the entire world was held in the grip of chaotic elements. All around Lileem, hara were being thrown around the ship. She could hear their cries, distantly. Some crouched low, clinging on to whatever could keep them steady. Others had gone below deck. The shamans were screaming in rage and helplessness.

"Pellaz!" Lileem cried aloud. "Hear me and approach! I command you!"

She knew the others couldn't hear her. She had stepped out of time into a different place, an otherworld realm. She was in a building that looked like a temple, standing before a throne. In it, sat the Tigron and he *was* a statue, made of golden stone. He was hundreds of feet high and Lileem was so small, like an ant, before him. "Help us, Pellaz," she said. "Help us."

There was a sounding like mountains grinding together and the mighty statue raised one hand. Lileem heard his voice, inside her head. "Bring forth darkness to combat the endless light. Call upon the force that is strong in your heart and mind. I see this thing. You have wrenched it from the cauldron of creation."

Lileem heard an almighty thud, then another. The ground in this strange unearthly temple was shaking. Bits of stone fell down from the ceiling, which was invisible high above. Lileem turned. Something approached. Something huge. She glanced at the statue of the Tigron, but it was motionless. She heard a loud hiss and turned again at once.

A monstrous image of Aruhani filled a high doorway behind her. The dehar radiated dark power. He was the most beautiful and terrible thing she had ever imagined. He stamped a foot and the ground shook. He lunged forward and hissed again, and a great red tongue lashed out.

"Aruhani," Lileem said and her voice sounded tiny, like the whirr of an insect's wing. "Help us . . ."

The dehar paused. When he breathed, plumes of smoke poured from his nostrils. His eyes burned and his braids writhed like Colurastes hair. The sound of his breathing was like the rumbling of a volcano.

"Please . . ." Lileem said inadequately.

Aruhani stamped again and roared. Lileem had to cover her head because chunks of stone rained down from above. She cried out in terror and was thrown back into her own reality.

For some moments, she was confused. The rain of stone had become a rain of icy seawater, equally as bruising. In the brief time she'd been absent in her mind, the situation had worsened. She knew Flick and the others were standing by her, but could not see them. She closed her eyes and let her instincts guide her. Blindly, she groped for Flick's hand, drawn by the essence of his spirit. Her fingers curled around his and she spoke to him in mind touch. "Call upon Aruhani, Flick."

She heard his shocked response. "No!"

"Yes! Bring Mima and Ulaume to us. We must do it together. I know this. Don't question. Just do it. Trust me!"

The moment the four of them joined hands Lileem could see them again. Everything else around them was a frenzied mass of moving light. "Call Aruhani," she said in mind touch. "All of us. Now!"

Their combined effort was enough to conjure up the energy of the dehar. He was their focused intention, their desires, their need. He came as a giant, striding through the whirlpool. With one black talon, he tore a rent in the spiraling power, a fissure through which the ship fell with a cascade of water. It was like riding a tidal wave.

Lileem would afterward remember hardly anything of those moments. There were brief flickering images. Thrown into the water, her head colliding with something sharp. Limbs floundering around her. Cries. Screams. The sound of breaking timber. Down, down into the boiling black depths.

CHAPTER TWENTY-EIGHT

>-|-•>-•Θ•-<•-|-<

There are tales in the north of those who come out from the sea. Some say that survivors of shipwrecks are not really hara at all, but sea creatures clothed in borrowed flesh. It is said that these creatures walk the shore at night, singing in wailing voices to call forth their brothers from the depths. They are never happy on land.

Living in close proximity to the ocean, and attuned to its moods, the hara of the tribe of Freyhella have a host of superstitions associated with what they see as the most powerful element on earth. On that strange day, when the winds died, and the sky turned into a boiling soup of cloud, they took their fishing boats to dock. They stood upon the harbor of their town and watched fearfully all that occurred. They saw what at first they took to be a waterspout on the horizon, but the most sensitive among them spoke of winged creatures in the whirling phenomenon. They spoke of voices crying out in fear, the inner voices that only the inner ear can perceive. They spoke of magic bled of power, words that had lost all meaning.

When sky and sea appeared simultaneously to burst into one chaotic element and rush toward the land as a devouring tidal wave, the Freyhellans fled to the hills behind the town. The great wave broke upon the fierce black rocks around the shore and flung itself over the dwellings, shops, and workshops of the town, but nothing was destroyed. The Freyhellans descended the hills, and they found a strange sight. Fishes flopped in silvery heaps upon the eaves of the houses and seaweed draped the doors and windows. The main road was paved with shells and sand and the splintered spars of a dead ship. And on the roof of the Great Hall an octopus lay splayed out like a star.

The Freyhellans went down to the shore, knowing that they would find the dead in that place. Their shamans shook their staffs, which were hung with tassels of horsehair and dried weed and carved with powerful runes, to ward off any malevolent spirits. Rangy dogs with long tails ran among the wreckage, sniffing for survivors. As hara turned over the hanks of weed and sodden planks, they found many limp bodies. But the strangest thing of all, given the ferocity of what had happened, was that none of them were dead.

Lileem came to her senses in a small, dark room that smelled of tar. She was lying in a bed beneath a thick quilt and was wearing some kind of long shirt. For a moment she couldn't remember a single thing, like who she was and what her life had been. The light in the room was brownish, and she saw a porcelain bowl standing on a table, the only bright thing to be seen. A cloth hung over the edge of the bowl, and a slim figure emerged from the gloom and picked it up. As this individual approached her, Lileem recognized him as har. His hair was almost white, and hung over his chest in two thick braids, but his skin was dark.

"Lie still," he said in a strongly accented voice. Lileem could tell her language was not his native tongue. He placed the cloth over her forehead. It was damp and warm and smelled of lavender.

"My friends!" Lileem said. Her mouth and throat were dry and sore, and filled with the taste of salt.

"All of you survived," said the har, "which is a miracle. Be at rest. You will see them soon."

Lileem remembered then: the awful power of the elements, and she like a scrap of cloth hurled around in them. She should be dead. She knew she should be dead. "Tell me where I am," she said.

"This is Freygard, domain of the tribe of Freyhella," said the har. "And I am Galdra, chesnari of our leader, Tyr."

Lileem closed her eyes because her head was aching. Would they be safe here? Would the Gelaming assume they'd all been killed? She remembered calling upon Pellaz and how he had inspired her to summon Aruhani. Pellaz must know she was alive. But perhaps all that she had done was use her own energy to help them escape. The Tigron she had met might only have been a dehar, another Pellaz, created solely in her own mind.

Galdra wiped her face gently with the scented cloth and then offered her water to drink. Lileem told him her name. He clearly did not realize she was anything other than har.

The Freyhella are by nature superstitious, and therefore their leader, Tyr, interviewed the bewildered crew and passengers of *Night's Arrow* as soon as they were able to rise from their beds. He was anxious to know exactly what his hara had witnessed on the day the winds had died and whether there would be any repercussions for his tribe, practically or magically.

The day following Lileem's awakening, Galdra took her to a council chamber in the Great Hall, in the center of the town. Its ceiling was supported by vast wooden columns, covered in carvings. Tyr sat upon a throne of carved wood, on a raised dais, with a company of warriors arranged to either side of him. He was a tall har with frightening pale blue eyes. His hair was like unraveled silk, which had somehow got into a tangle. It fell over his breast, where an armory of metal amulets clanked on chains. Around his shoulders was a cloak of wolfskin.

Before the dais, stood Flick, Ulaume and Mima. Tyr was not paying any attention to them: he conferred with his hara. Lileem's companions appeared well, if exhausted. They were dressed, as she was, in Freyhellan garb of tunic and trousers, decorated with embroidered designs of sea creatures. Lileem went to them and embraced each in turn. The same words were on all their lips: "We should be dead," Lileem said nothing to this. She needed to speak to Flick in private about it first.

When Tel-an-Kaa strode into the chamber, only minutes after Lileem's arrival, Lileem did not recognize her. For a few moments, she thought this was a high-ranking har she had never met before, but then realized it was actually the Zigane, shorn of all her glamours and disguises. Tel-an-Kaa would speak for them, for she radiated authority.

Flick said to Lileem, in an undertone, "We have died after all. We are in Valhalla among the Norse gods." He had told her about the Norse legends long ago, in the lost days of curiosity and play at the white house.

Lileem smiled. "Then Tel-an-Kaa is the trickster Loki come to fox them."

"Let's see," said Flick.

Surprisingly, Tel-an-Kaa mostly told the truth. She said—perhaps guessing the independent Freyhella would not hold a high opinion of the Gelaming—

that she and her companions had been pursued by Gelaming, who wished to take them to Immanion. She said that some of them were former friends of the Tigron, and held sensitive information about his past. For this reason, the Gelaming were keen to capture them. She spoke of the efforts of the Roselane shamans to combat the magical attack, and how they had managed at the last moment to create a fissure in the vortex, thus enabling an escape. It was Roselane magic that had protected them during their tumultuous journey toward the land. Such was the power of the shamans.

Tyr seemed to accept this explanation, although he was clearly not happy about fugitives from the Gelaming being in his domain. "You will travel to Roselane now?" he asked.

"As soon as we are able," Tel-an-Kaa said. "Any help you could give us regarding transport would be much appreciated. I don't know what remains of our possessions, but we did begin our journey with a substantial amount of Parsic currency. You are welcome to that if you find it."

"Any ship that founders upon our shores is our property," said Tyr. "Therefore, your currency is ours anyway."

"Then I hope that in the spirit of kinship, and a mutual respect for freedom, you will lend us your aid regardless," said Tel-an-Kaa.

Lileem was greatly impressed by her courage.

Tyr appeared slightly stunned by the Zigane's forthright approach and perhaps found himself agreeing to help without realizing it. "We can provide a boat to take you upriver," he said. "Will that suffice?"

"We would also appreciate supplies," said Tel-an-Kaa.

Tyr nodded. "Galdra will see to it." He stood up. "You may leave."

Once outside the council chamber, Lileem and her companions praised Tel-an-Kaa for her handling of the situation.

"We need to be straightforward now," she said. "We cannot waste time. The Gelaming could reappear at any moment. I trust you are all ready to resume our journey?"

Lileem was disappointed they must move on so quickly, because she'd have liked to explore Freygard and learn about the Freyhella, but she could see the sense in Tel-an-Kaa's words.

Galdra, as Tyr's chesnari, was second in command of the Freyhella. He was as interested in their temporary guests as they were in his tribe, as he was second generation har, and liked to hear about harish life in other countries. He knew the language well because many hara had joined the Freyhellans fleeing from Varrs, Uigenna, or Gelaming. While some of his hara prepared a boat for the travelers, Galdra took them all to a feasting chamber in the Great

Hall. Here, he offered them a meal and for a few short hours they could enjoy good company in comfortable surroundings.

Tel-an-Kaa monopolized Galdra, which gave Lileem the opportunity to speak to Flick away from the Zigane's ears. She beckoned to Flick and led him to the hearth, which was some distance away from the table where all the others were sitting. "There's something I have to tell you," she said, "but I don't want Mima to hear it."

Flick glanced to where Mima sat talking with Ulaume. "That means Ulaume can't hear it either," he said. "He won't like that. He already thinks you confide in me too much. It's not really fair, Lee. He cares for you deeply."

"Oh, do shut up!" Lileem said. "This isn't about my relationship with Lormy. This is important. You can tell him everything later."

"Well, what is it?"

Lileem took a deep breath. She anticipated an unfavourable response. "I think Pell helped us escape the Gelaming."

Flick's eyes seemed to glaze over with a film of ice. "Now what makes you think that?"

"I called upon him. And he came. He told me we should invoke Aruhani."

Flick exhaled long and slow. "Lee, Pellaz knows nothing of the dehara, and knows nothing of you. This is not a time for games or fantasies."

"And I am no longer a child," Lileem said, "so don't speak to me as if I am. This isn't an idle fancy, Flick. I *feel* it."

"But why would Pellaz help us escape? It doesn't make sense. We've been led to believe he wants us—or at least me—in Immanion."

"We saw him at Atagatisel," Lileem said. "He let us go then. He helped us escape. I'm sure of it. And now he has done so again."

"We have no proof of that. It stretches belief, to say the least."

"We don't know everything," Lileem said, "and as Cobweb told Ulaume, we don't really know what's going on in Pell's head. Maybe he's more constrained as Tigron than he ever was as a normal har."

Flick cocked his head to one side and regarded Lileem through narrow eyes. "You know what?" he said. "You have a thing about the Cevarros. You have a secret liking for Terez and now you want to have a spiritual connection with Pellaz. You already have Mima as a roon friend: can't you be content with that or is it your aim to collect the entire family?"

Lileem could not repress her laughter. "Now that is an attractive thought! I'd not considered it, but perhaps you're right."

"Ah—so you do have a soft spot for Terez! I thought as much."

"I'm not sure it's that. He fascinates me. But anyway, it's irrelevant now, because we are so far away from him and I know now I can never . . ." She paused. "Stop sidetracking me. We were talking about Pellaz. You are prejudiced against him, and I understand your reasons, but can't you just have an open mind about this?"

"I find it hard to believe he'd know about Aruhani."

"Seeing as you've been trying so hard these past few years to uncreate the dehar you created?"

"What do you mean by that?"

"You know." Lileem knew this was not the time and place to introduce such a sensitive topic, but couldn't help herself. "Ever since the Uigenna took you, you've turned your back on all your work. Something happened, didn't it? Something you didn't like. I felt you call upon Aruhani, when I was crouched in the cellar of the white house with Mima. He came, didn't he?"

"Maybe I was playing with fire," Flick said in a fierce low voice. "I am not like Orien, or even Ulaume. I thought I was something, then I found out I wasn't. I'm not a great magus, Lee. I called up a demon and learned how dangerous that can be. That's all I'll say."

"You're wrong," Lileem said. "Whatever happened, you shouldn't turn away from the dehara. Aruhani helped us escape the Gelaming. He is not a demon."

"I created him from the darkest corners of myself," Flick said. "Perhaps he can be something else for you, but for me he will always be the amoral force that made me . . ." He shook his head. "You don't understand. I was like them, Lee. It was pelki, and I wanted it. Enjoyed it. I never want to feel like that again."

Lileem stared at him for some moments. She wasn't absolutely sure what he was trying to tell her, but it was nothing like she'd imagined. She'd believed Aruhani had made him violent, made him kill. He hadn't spoken of this before, she was sure. He hadn't even told Ulaume. "He is the dehar of life and death," she said, "as well as aruna, in all its aspects. Maybe you didn't know him then as well as you thought you did, and maybe you called upon the wrong aspect, or weren't specific enough, but you can't blame him for what happened."

"I don't. I blame myself. Aruhani came from me." Flick rubbed his face with his hands and pushed back his hair. For a few moments, he stared up at the smoke blackened beams of the ceiling, his fingers pressed against his scalp. "Strange I should speak of this now. I never thought I would."

Lileem embraced him and he laid his head on her shoulder. "It's gone," she said. "You let it out like Ulaume let out the screaming ghosts from Pell's old home."

Flick squeezed her briefly. "I wonder," he said.

A fog descended from the mountains and poured over the river. The Freyhellan long boat moored at the river docks looked ghostly in its misty shroud. Galdra accompanied the travelers to the boat to see them off, as did many other Freyhellans. Lileem felt as if they were leaving old friends; the visit here had been too brief. But perhaps a day would come when she could return. The Roselane hara began to embark while Lileem and her companions bid farewell to Galdra. A few Freyhellans would travel with them, and once the river was no longer negotiable, the passengers would leave the boat, which would then return to Freygard. Galdra had given them currency and generous supplies.

Just before Lileem and her party were about to board the boat, a har on horseback came up to Galdra and pulled his mount to a halt. "Tiahaar, I have a message."

Galdra paused in the act of embracing Ulaume in farewell, but didn't let him go. "What is it?"

"There is a har in the high meadows who summons the Megalithicans. He has horses and says that they must not ride the river. They must go with him."

Galdra released Ulaume. "Who is this har?"

"I know not. He would not give a name. He said the har Lileem would know to follow him."

Lileem glanced at Flick. Could it be Pell? "I'll go and see," she said. "I'll go at once."

"Wait!" Tel-an-Kaa snapped. "You can't be serious, Lee. It could be Gelaming."

"It isn't," Lileem said. "He knows my name."

"That is no basis for—"

"I'm going," Lileem said.

"I'll come with you," Mima said.

"No!" Without asking for permission, Lileem jumped up onto the back of a horse tethered nearby and called to the messenger. "Take me to him."

"Lileem!" Tel-an-Kaa cried and tried to grab hold of the horse's reins to prevent her leaving, but Lileem was too quick for her. She did not look back, but she heard Flick say, "Let him go. He knows what he's doing."

And Mima's voice: "I wish I did! We must follow them."

But whatever Flick said to that, Lileem did not hear.

The Freyhellan led the way out of town up into the forested hills behind it. Lileem could hear the muffled tocking of bells worn by sheep or cattle. Her guide led her to a sheer sloping meadow. Tall pines around it were mere black shadows in the fog.

"He is here somewhere," said the Freyhellan.

Lileem called, "Hello! It is I, Lileem!"

After a few moments, a figure emerged from the fog. He did not move, but the mist around him simply drew apart like a veil. Behind him were a number of spectral white horses. They stood with lowered heads, as if asleep.

"Wait here!" Lileem said to her guide, and leapt down from her horse. It was as if she stepped into a different world. The har before her was swathed in a cloak of shimmering gray fabric. The heavy hood was trimmed with wolf fur, which obscured most of the har's face, but for the mouth and chin.

Lileem went up to him. "I am Lileem. Who are you?"

The har stood motionless, unnaturally so. "I have brought you transport of a more suitable nature," he said, in a low, musical voice. "Whatever your destination, you may reach it quickly through this means."

"Are you Gelaming?"

"Yes, but no enemy of yours. The Tigron has sent me."

"He heard me," Lileem said softly, still amazed in spite of her conviction.

"There is little he does not hear," said the Gelaming. "Bring your companions to this place, and make haste. Bring only those closest to you. The others can travel by more conventional means."

"This could be a trap."

"Except that it's not and you know it." The har lifted long pale hands and threw back the hood of his cloak. Dark red hair fell forward over his shoulders. His face was elfin, the eyes large and dark. "I am Vaysh, the Tigron's aide. Only he and I know of this visit." The Tigron's aide could have stepped from an ancient myth: he seemed barely har, more unearthly than that, but perhaps all Gelaming appeared that way. They could cloak themselves with glamours as Tel-an-Kaa could.

"Why is Pellaz helping me?" Lileem asked. "How does he know of me? Does he know of the dehara? Does he know about Terez and—"

"Quiet!" said Vaysh. "I am not here to answer your questions, merely to facilitate your journey. You would be wise to fetch your companions at once, because there are others sniffing around this part of the world whose sole aim is to take you to Immanion."

"Why?"

"There are not many things the Tigron does not know," said Vaysh, "but Lord Thiede has his private agendas upon certain issues. He fears most what he cannot kill."

Lileem had no idea what the Gelaming was talking about. "Did Terez reach Immanion?" she asked. "You must tell me that at least."

"I have no knowledge of such a har," said Vaysh. "You called to Pellaz and he heard you. That is all I know."

"I'll bring my friends at once," Lileem said. "Don't go away."

Vaysh said nothing. He was as much like a statue as her vision of Pellaz had been.

Lileem's companions waited fearfully for her return. Flick wondered whether in fact she would and sensed the Zigane had the same concern. "Silly little fool!" Tel-an-Kaa muttered, more than once.

But very shortly after her departure, Lileem's horse came hurtling back. From the expression on her face, Flick could tell something amazing had occurred. She told them exactly what in excited, garbled words.

"Travel with the Gelaming?" Tel-an-Kaa asked scornfully. "I hardly think that is a wise idea."

"It isn't a trap," Lileem said earnestly. She turned to her companions. "Isn't this what we've all wanted, the Tigron's help? Didn't you all complain that Pellaz had forgotten you and turned his back on the past? Well, he hasn't, so stop being so stupid and come with me, will you? Vaysh might get impatient and leave. Hurry up!"

"I don't know," Tel-an-Kaa began, but fortunately Mima took control.

"Let's go," she said. "Let's not look these gift horses in the mouth. Are we going to be flying up into the sky? I, for one, don't want to miss that!"

"Me neither," Ulaume said. "Flick?"

Flick shrugged. "I'll go with the majority." He saw Lileem's furious expression. "Okay, okay, let's do it."

The Zigane was outnumbered.

Flick felt very uncomfortable with the whole idea, but if the offer was genuine, it would save them a lot of time, and as Mima had pointed out, this was hardly an experience they could refuse. They rode Freyhellan horses to the mountain meadow, and there Vaysh was still waiting for them. Lileem said it looked as if he hadn't moved a muscle since she'd left him. The horses behind him were magnificent and immense, even more so than the Varrish animals, which had been the largest Flick had ever seen. He sensed that the Zigane would take over the whole proceedings and speak to Vaysh, so before she could do this, Flick pushed his way to the front of the group. "I have two questions to ask you," he said, to the stern and haughty har before him, "and we will not go with you until you answer them."

Vaysh regarded him stonily. "I am not here to answer questions. I am here to help you on your journey."

"Is it true?" Flick asked. "I must know. Did Pell really die?" Despite what Seel had told him, part of him still believed that Thiede had spun some grand illusion.

"Yes," Vaysh replied.

"Was he made this Tigron thing against his will?"

"No. Are you ready? We should depart at once."

Two questions were not enough but the answers Flick had received effectively silenced him. In the world he inhabited, hara did not come back from the dead, or if they did, they were like Orien, mere shadows.

"You expect us to ride these Gelaming monstrosities?" Tel-an-Kaa inquired icily.

"Yes," Vaysh said. "Do not fear. I am quite capable of guiding you all."

"Then you will know of our destination, where we are."

"We will know of that, in any case."

Now it was Mima's turn to push to the front. "How much do you know?" she snapped. "Are you aware, for instance, who I am?"

Vaysh fixed her with a stare. "No. It is of little consequence to me who any of you are. Please, mount the horses. My time is precious."

"But—" Mima began.

Tel-an-Kaa reached out to touch her shoulder. "Hush," she said gently. "Say no more."

The Tigron may know many things, Flick thought, *but he does not know about the Kamagrian. Perhaps he cannot see them, as he sees the rest of us. He must be like a ghost, a powerful spirit, but he has limitations. The Pell I knew is dead. I must remember that.*

"Where do you wish to go?" Vaysh asked Tel-an-Kaa.

"Roselane in Jaddayoth," she replied, with clear reluctance. "Do you know of it?"

"I know little of Jaddayoth, you must send me enough information to find it."

Flick could tell the Zigane was far from happy about that. Perhaps she feared what Vaysh might pick up if she communicated with him by mind-touch, but she had no other choice. They were being given a free ride, and the journey otherwise could take months.

After the reality-splitting experience of otherlane travel, the one thing Flick was sure of was that he wanted to keep his horse. Unlike Seel had in the past, he didn't find the journey unsettling at all. In the space between the worlds, he felt utterly free, at one with the entity that bore him. Every care of his life fled away from him like a shrieking spirit. He laughed aloud and the sound left his essence in sparkling bubbles, leaving a trail behind him. This, he considered, was pure joy, pure being. It was like going through a spiritual cleansing.

When the horse leapt out into familiar reality once more, Flick was still laughing. His companions' mounts all slid to a halt, but he kept on riding, galloping ahead. He still felt as if he were flying. He was high above the ground because the horse was so big. They had emerged into the mountainous landscape of Roselane, where spires of stone reared toward a cloudy sky. Eagles soared high above and the land seemed to go on forever, unspoilt and seething with power. Flick heard voices calling him back, but he didn't care. He could very easily ride off into obscurity now. He had a magical Gelaming horse. He could go anywhere, except that he didn't know how to pass into the otherlanes. Vaysh had controlled the animals on their journey, perhaps to avoid giving Gelaming power away to lesser hara.

Eventually Flick brought the horse to a stamping halt in a high mountain meadow, a valley between immense cliffs. If this was Roselane, he knew he was going to enjoy staying there for a time. It was like being in the landscape of a visualization, such as those he'd once visited with Itzama, so much bigger than reality should be. If he went into one of the caves on the rock faces, perhaps he would meet the shaman again.

Flick dismounted and led the horse up the valley. It nudged his back with its nose, snorting. Occasionally, it strained away from his grip to graze upon the lush mountain grass, like any normal beast. Although it was huge, and very powerful, it appeared to have a sweet nature. Around them, the trees were bare, and already snow coated the high peaks, but Flick guessed this would be paradise in summertime.

His reverie was cut short by the arrival of Vaysh, who didn't look angry or impatient. His expression was impassive. He rode alongside Flick for a while and neither of them spoke. Then, Vaysh said, "Your friends are upset. You should return to them."

"I'm enjoying the solitude," Flick said. "I haven't been alone for a long time."

"I cannot stay. I must return the horses to Immanion."

Flick stopped walking and stroked his horse's neck. "Can't I keep him?"

Vaysh regarded him thoughtfully. "That is impossible."

"Pell's brother stole my horse," Flick said. It was a small lie, but perhaps worth it. "I think that deserves compensation, and the Tigron can surely afford it."

"Pell's brother . . ."

"Yes, the Tigron might be interested to know about him, but then doesn't he know everything already?"

Vaysh said nothing, but his expression was eloquent.

"You can tell him Terez is har, as is Dorado, who I have not met. The last time I saw Terez he vowed to find Immanion. Do I take it that quest has not been successful?"

"It occurred to me that the dark-skinned har in your company was once related to Pellaz," said Vaysh.

"An easy mistake to make," Flick said. If he was to take advantage of Kamagrian hospitality, he felt obliged to keep their secrets.

"He seemed to think I should know him."

"He is of high rank among his own tribe, that is all. Is the Tigron planning to meet us face-to-face at any point?"

"I have no idea," Vaysh said. "He is very busy."

"I heard he has a consort now."

"Yes. Caeru is Tigrina."

"And what of Cal? I presume you know of him."

"That is not my concern."

"You are a mine of information, aren't you?"

"I cannot discuss with you the matters pressing upon your mind. If you are so curious about them, perhaps you should have let those who pursued you take you to Immanion. Then, you would have had all your questions answered." Vaysh's scorn was withering.

Flick wished the har would just leave. "I want to keep the horse," he said. "I won't pry into your secrets. I don't know how to make him fly. I just want him."

Vaysh sighed through his nose and for some moments stared at the high peaks. Then, he came to a conclusion. "Keep him for now, but I might have to return and take him from you. His name is Astral. He is a *sedu,* which looks to you like a horse. The *sedim* are more than that, as you have discovered. If you attempt otherlane travel with Astral, it will fail. I will instruct him not to allow it."

"Do what you like. It seems to me he can be a worldly creature too. That is all I want."

Vaysh nodded curtly. "I will tell Pellaz of your request. I expect he will grant it." He turned his mount around and galloped it back down the valley.

For a few minutes, Flick remained where he was, soaking up the raw essence of the landscape, experiencing the pure dazed feeling that gripped his being. It didn't feel too bad, that was the thing. His heart felt lighter than it had for years.

CHAPTER TWENTY-NINE

Shilalama, effectively the capital of Roselane, had existed for centuries before Opalexian found her way to it and made it her headquarters. A long time ago, human ascetics had formed a community there, entranced by the wind-sculpted rock formations that had created a natural city in the high mountains. An air of spirituality and sanctity permeated the very stones of the city, and it was daily cleansed by pure fresh winds. In this place, Opalexian had sought to create her ideal community, as had many harish leaders. Hers differed in that she foresaw humans, hara, and parazha living together, their lives devoted to meditation and self-evolution.

Wishing to remain invisible to the harish population in neighboring territory, she had employed hara to speak on behalf of her people when the leaders of surrounding tribes had suggested a coalition, which had given birth to Jaddayoth, a union of twelve countries. Many of its hara were refugees from Megalithica, escaping Gelaming control. In the days when Flick and Ulaume first went to Roselane, the coalition of tribes was very new and still shaky. Some leaders within it were keen to establish strong links with Immanion, while others, still smarting from Gelaming interference in their affairs in Megalithica, were radically opposed to the idea. Indigenous hara, spawned from an ancient strand of humanity, were often resentful of newcomers, and many union meetings regularly collapsed into battles as competing leaders fought for dominance. Opalexian's hand, albeit an invisible one, did much to steer these nascent tribes toward some kind of harmony. The main problem was that each tribe developed swiftly very clear and well-defined religious and political beliefs, most of which were incompatible with one another. Ancient customs still prevailed in many areas, because the now ousted human population had adhered to shamanistic roots more than most. Empires had risen and fallen over the centuries, but the spirit of the land was very strong in that place, and had shrugged off human depredation. With the advent of Wraeththu, it had come into its own.

Spring came softly over the mountains, stealing up the slopes where a galaxy of white flower stars appeared overnight. When the sun shone in the afternoon, it conjured drowsy insects from their sleep. The air became dreamy, as the season flowed toward the intoxication of summer.

Flick rode Astral slowly on his patrols, shunning the company of others. He had the life he'd always craved: a normal, safe life. After they'd arrived in the city, Tel-an-Kaa had taken them to an unoccupied house and told them it was theirs. It was a two-story dwelling with sprawling low-ceilinged rooms and a good-sized yard at the back, planted with mature trees and plants. The Zigane had found jobs for them and had helped them settle in. Ulaume, being good with his hands, now worked at the Shilalama pottery. Their home was full of utensils they'd never need. Even though the Roselane were a peaceful tribe, they were not foolish, and understood the importance of guarding their territory from hostile intruders. Flick was now such a guard. He had the best horse in Shilalama, which could climb with the nimbleness of a mountain goat.

Despite the Zigane's earlier words to Lileem and Mima about how Opalexian might want to talk to them, no summons came from her palace, Kalalim. The newcomers quickly found out that Opalexian was rarely seen by any of her citizens. She obviously was not intrigued enough about the Tigron to question those who had met him. Or perhaps there was nothing they could tell her that she didn't already know.

Flick and his friends were absorbed into Roselane society, seamlessly and without effort. They were not regarded as more special than any other inhabitant, and this suited them completely. In Shilalama, Flick was just another har, and was expected to work for the community. He could enjoy simple pleasures and did not have to hide behind a disguise of dirt and rough clothes. There was nohar in Shilalama who would try to control or own him. In this land, he could walk once more the path to the dehara's altars. He had made peace with Aruhani. The Roselane were very interested in all he had to say about the gods. During the first winter Flick and the others spent in Roselane, a rather gaunt har named Exalan had come several nights a week to their home and wrote down every story that Flick could think of, Lileem adding her own details as they talked. The Roselane were keen to keep a record of every tribe's belief system, and Exalan worked for Opalexian, and therefore the high temple of the city. Ulaume had to tell Exalan all about Hubisag, but Flick knew there were a lot of less savory details left out of the account.

One night, lying in Flick's arms, Ulaume said, "Isn't it strange, how far we've come." And he meant in all senses.

"Do you ever think of Lianvis?" Flick asked.

"Not for a long time. Do you ever think of Seel?"

"Hardly," Flick replied. "It all seems so remote now."

There was a silence, then Ulaume said, "What about Pell?"

"I like to think he respects our decision. He's left us alone."

"I didn't make a decision," Ulaume said and there was bitterness in his voice. "I wonder whether Cobweb has told him about me."

Flick didn't want to talk about such things. The moment Astral had jumped out of nonreality into Roselane was the moment when Flick's life had changed for the better. The otherlanes had purified him. He did not want to shut out the past entirely, but neither did he want to dwell upon it. Lying there, he realized he felt so much more serene and complete than Ulaume did. It made him feel sad and protective.

"Are we chesnari, Flick?" Ulaume asked, a wistful voice in the darkness. "Is that what we are now?" There was a kind of finality to the question.

"You are my life partner, and I can't imagine life without you, so if that's chesnari, then yes. I suppose so."

"Good," Ulaume said. "At least that means I did *something* right."

"Lor, you did many things right. Don't be sad. There won't be many hara on this planet who didn't do things in the early days they'd rather they hadn't."

"I don't regret any of what I did," Ulaume said. "I haven't become a pious Roselane ascetic, Flick. I wouldn't be who I am without my history."

That made Flick think of Cal, a thought he attempted to banish at once.

"No doubt it's the same for him," Ulaume said, and Flick realized his thought, though swiftly quashed, must have been very loud indeed. After some moments, Ulaume said, "I just wish I hadn't been so stupid with Pell. I really do. Now, he'll never know who I'm capable of being."

That sounded like regret to Flick.

Sometimes, Flick wondered whether Astral missed the otherlanes and creatures of his own kind. He knew now that Astral was not a horse, but something that looked like a horse. He told everyone else that Vaysh had taken out of the beast all the things that made him different, but that wasn't true. Vaysh had indeed limited the extent of communication Flick could have with the creature, but Flick was still sure that when he thought in pictures, Astral understood some of what he was saying.

One morning, they went for a bareback gallop in one of the high meadows. Flick let Astral have his head, and he was clearly in the mood for spring, because he kicked up his heels a few times and nearly bucked off his rider. "Hey," Flick said, jerking the reins to remind Astral he had a passenger. "Don't be mean."

Astral skidded to a halt and then turned his head to regard Flick with a dark intelligent eye, a lock of his pure white mane hanging over it. If anything, he was the harish equivalent of horse, because surely no normal animal could affect such a seductive expression. Flick sighed and jumped to the ground. He unbuckled Astral's bridle and smacked him on the rump. "Go run, then. Have fun. Find yourself a mare."

Astral walked around in a circle for a while, sniffing the ground, then with head and tail high, charged off up the valley. Flick knew he'd return in a few hours.

Lileem had packed Flick a generous lunch, a task she had begun to undertake on a daily basis for the whole household recently, as she had become experimental with sandwiches. Now, Flick carried his satchel up the side of the valley, to a rocky platform. Here, he would lie down and stare at the sky for a while. When he was hungry, he would eat. Could life get any better?

Flick stretched out his body on the warm rock, his face wreathed in a contented smile. He listened to the breeze that blew over the higher crags, to the cry of birds. There was nothing else to hear. He was asleep when the shadow fell over him.

"Flick . . ."

He awoke at once. Mima had come to him. Something was wrong. He jumped up and turned quickly, facing a figure that was limned against the sun. Not Mima.

"Terez . . . ?" He couldn't have found them there, surely?

"No, Flick . . . it's me."

Clouds were moving to conceal the sun. The weather could change so quickly. *"Pellaz?"*

"Yes."

Flick walked warily around the ledge until the sun was behind him. Perhaps he was still asleep and a stray dream from the past had come to haunt him. But maybe Pellaz really was there, a radiant creature beyond all imagining, a divine version of his former self. His skin was golden brown, his hair a glossy black mane to his waist. His face and body were so perfect, Flick thought they could have been grown in a vat. Perhaps good living could do that to a har. Flick found himself laughing: the idea was too ridiculous. "It can't be you," he said.

"Why not? Because I haven't come to you before?"

"I didn't expect you to. Our lives diverged dramatically. You didn't have to come." He hesitated. "*Why* have you?"

Pellaz folded his arms. "I remember you so well, that innocent little thing at Saltrock. Not that I wasn't an innocent little thing either. If either of us had known . . ." He shook his head. "Somehow, I thought you'd be the same, which is stupid, considering how much I've changed."

"Time doesn't stand still," Flick said. He felt light-headed. This conversation was unreal. "The Gelaming have made a magnificent har of you, Pell. But then, that is what the rumors have told us."

Pellaz grimaced, as if made uncomfortable by the compliment, although Flick suspected he was merely being modest. "I've thought about finding you for a long time, Flick. But in some ways, it didn't seem right. All that I had, and was, had gone. I realized you might not want to be found. Seel told me you left Saltrock, after—"

"Don't," Flick said. Should he talk to the Tigron like that? It seemed the world was breaking apart like smoke before a rank wind.

"I know," Pellaz said. "I'm not here to rake over old coals. I'm here because . . ." He sighed. "I'm not a very good liar, even now."

"I heard you'd become quite good at it."

Pellaz shrugged. "Occasionally." He pulled a comical face. "Don't look at me that way. I'm still me inside, despite everything. Remember the good times, Flick. Those were fine days."

Flick sat down with his back against the cliff. His legs felt unsteady. "I have fond memories too. If we have to dwell on anything, let's concentrate on them. Are you here incognito, having escaped your viziers and generals for a while?"

Pellaz sat down beside him. "Something like that."

"What's it like being Tigron?" He clasped his hands around his knees and hoped Pell didn't notice how much he was shaking.

"Hectic most of the time. It's like a dream."

"Were you really dead?"

"Apparently. I can't remember. I just woke up one day and my whole life had changed."

"I spoke to you in a dream once. You said you wouldn't remember it."

Pellaz laughed.

"How did he do it?" Flick asked. "Everyhar says Thiede brought you back from the dead. We heard your head was blown off. Your body was burned. That was just a story, right? What really happened?"

Pellaz regarded him carefully. "I'm not sure. I *was* dead for a time, only it's hard to believe. I can't remember it. Thiede is very powerful. He called me back and created a body for me."

"No har can do that."

Pellaz shrugged. "Well, here I am, so I guess they can."

Flick reached for his satchel. He felt so disorientated; he needed something earthy and real to steady himself. "Are you hungry? I have lunch."

"Good."

Flick began to unwrap Lileem's package. "How did you get here? I mean, where's your horse?"

"I let him go to find Astral. That was how we found you, by the way. Peridot homed in on Astral. There were good friends. Now, he has no friends but you."

"I'm sorry about that," Flick said. "I wanted to keep him. Did Vaysh tell you your brother Terez stole my other horse?"

"Yes."

"Have you met Terez yet?"

Pellaz appeared distinctly uncomfortable now. "No. Thiede thinks it would be awkward. Terez does not fit into the picture very well. You know what it's like, Flick. We have to cast off our human lives. Terez is part of that, and much as I'm curious to see what kind of har he is, we've heard bad reports. That's sad."

"You wanted me to find your family," Flick said. "I did. I upheld my promise."

"I realize that," Pell said. "I shouldn't have asked you to do so, but I was young, newly incepted, and the past wasn't that far away then. I appreciate your loyalty though."

"Terez was a mess when I found him," Flick said. "He'd been partially incepted. Ulaume and I managed to complete the process, but it wasn't exactly a roaring success, hence the reports you've received, I expect. You do know about Ulaume, I take it?"

Pellaz smiled. "Yes. You and he are the last two hara I would ever have expected to end up together."

"We met at your old home," Flick said. "I was trying to fulfill my promise to you, and Ulaume had just been drawn there, following your spirit, or a vision of your spirit. He felt the exact moment when you died, you know. He lived it with you."

Pellaz raised his brows in surprise. "Are you sure?"

"As sure as I can be. Anyway, the cable farm was just ruins. Everyone was dead." This wasn't the whole truth, of course, but Flick had decided to be economical with facts for the time being. He wasn't sure how much Pell knew.

Pellaz nodded. "The old world has gone. We have to expect and accept that. I, more than any har, can't go back."

"Ulaume would like to see you," Flick said. "Whatever happened between you in the past, it affected him greatly. I think it changed him. For the better. Don't judge him on past experience."

"I don't," Pell said. "Once I did, and if I'd run across him, I'd probably have thrown him into a pit and never let him out, but I know better now. Ulaume was as much a product of his inception, and his tribe, as . . . well, *that* affects everyhar. Also, I know that you wouldn't be with him if he was as soulless as I once thought."

"We lived at the Richards house for a time, then the Uigenna chased us out."

"I should have sent help, but I didn't know about your situation then, Flick. My reinvented life was all so new. I hope you understand."

"Why should you have cared? You had become Tigron and your world was suddenly a lot bigger than it ever was before. Ulaume and I were just a small part of your past. Don't feel guilty about it."

"But Terez . . . Perhaps we—that is, the Gelaming—could have helped him more, changed the outcome. I haven't cast him off as much as I like to think, obviously."

He doesn't know about Mima, Flick thought. He would have to be careful. He mustn't let that slip out. "Don't you mind being pushed around by Thiede?"

Pellaz picked up a sandwich from where Flick had laid them out on greaseproof paper. "I let you keep the *sedu,* the horse, because I knew I could always use him to find you, when I wanted to."

"I should have realized that. Stupid of me." Flick hesitated. "You're not going to answer my last question, are you?"

Pellaz bit into the sandwich, chewed thoughtfully. "No. I'm surrounded by hara who fawn all over me, but I always knew that some from my past would resent what I'd become. Some from my present do too, come to think of it."

"Don't misinterpret my words," Flick said. "I'm not envious of you. Given the choice, I'd rather have my life than yours."

Pellaz smiled. "Well, one of the reasons I'm Tigron is because I think it's worth the price. I'm not bewailing my lot, Flick. I'm privileged and I enjoy it. Most of the time."

"Just the few awkward glitches from the past, eh?" Flick bit hungrily into his sandwich.

"Seel misses you," Pellaz said.

Flick nearly choked, but managed to swallow before spraying the Tigron with food. His laughter was genuine. "Is that what he says?"

"He thinks you were . . . *influenced* to leave Saltrock."

"I was. I heard a few home truths, that's all. It was the best thing." He wondered how long the conversation would go on before one of them said Cal's name.

"You know how it seems to me?" Flick said. "Some hara in the world seek power, others don't. You and Seel fall into the former category, Cal and I the latter." There, it was said. "It was perhaps the biggest thing we had in common for a while."

"Cal and you?" Pellaz said.

"Yes. We had a . . . thing for a while in Saltrock. Didn't Seel tell you about us?"

Pellaz shook his head.

It would have been so easy to descend into Ulaume mode and turn the knife. The idea held great appeal, but Flick could see the har he had once known looking out of that beautiful face beside him, and just couldn't bring himself to do it. "He loves you so much," he said softly. "I have never seen anyhar so much in love."

Pellaz turned away. "Some call it obsession."

"They can call it what they like, but I believe it's something that transcends death and distance. It's not over, Pell. It never will be."

Pellaz nodded, and Flick saw his throat convulse. He imagined the Tigron had swallowed tears so many times he could do it without thinking now.

"Thanks," Pellaz said in a husky voice. He stared at Flick unflinchingly. "Did he really do it, Flick? Seel said you were there . . ."

"Yes, he did it," Flick replied. "None of us can wipe that fact out, I'm afraid. I saw Cal come out of the Nayati. I never told Seel, but I knew Orien was dead long before anyhar else. I just couldn't bring myself to speak of it. I felt soiled, responsible . . ." He sighed. "It doesn't matter now."

"Seel always suspected that, you know."

"I thought he did. We weren't close enough to discuss it, Pell. I was just Seel's convenient servant."

"It's sad you think that way."

"He virtually kidnapped me in Galhea."

"He did that for me. He knows it was . . . unwise."

"And now he has a new family. As do you, I've heard."

Pell pulled a sour face. "Now that's another story, believe me. Thiede tricked me into it, although . . . It's a *long* story."

"Tell me, I'm interested."

Pell didn't speak for a few moments. Then he said, "I could *show* you."

"I'm not coming to Immanion. Please don't make an issue of it."

Pell laughed. "No, I didn't mean that. I can see you fit comfortably into this landscape. I meant this." He put down his sandwich and reached to take Flick's face in his hands.

Flick tried to pull away. "No."

"Don't be ridiculous," Pellaz said. "I won't pry. I just want to show you what happened."

To Pellaz, the sharing of breath was an efficient method of transferring information. Perhaps he was aware of what his living physical self could do to a har, and perhaps he took satisfaction in that, but while Flick wilted in drifts of perfumed essence, he merely told a story. He showed Flick a summer night in a town called Ferelithia, and a brief encounter with a har named Rue. This was before Pellaz had ever seen Immanion. That night was magical, a turning point: it was the night Pell and Rue conceived a pearl. And Pellaz just walked away from it into his big new life. Turned his back. When Rue turned up in Immanion, some time later, Thiede had declared Pellaz should take him as a consort and proclaim their son his heir. Simple. Only Pellaz was too tangled up inside about Cal, dying for love in a slow painful way, and in Rue he saw only a whipping post, because every time he saw Rue's face, he remembered the one he had loved and lost.

If Pellaz had wanted to dredge Flick's mind for facts in return, he could easily have done so, but he didn't. When he drew away, Flick fell backward and hit his head sharply on the rock behind him. He felt nauseous from more than the just the impact.

Pellaz touched the back of Flick's head and a blast of heat surged into

Flick's skull. Then it didn't hurt anymore. "Sorry," Pellaz said. "I should have warned you."

"That's some story," Flick said inadequately.

"That's part of why I don't judge Ulaume now," Pellaz said. "We all have our dark sides."

"A consort you despise and a broken heart. And you tell me it's worth being Tigron?" His lips were still numb.

"Yes, it's still worth it. I will achieve great things. I won't waste what's been given to me."

"The sacrificial king for all hara on earth."

"If you like. I used to be like you, but I'm not anymore. I can't be."

Flick wasn't quite sure what he meant by that. "And you're here just for the sake of old acquaintance?"

Pellaz raised his knees and rested his cheek upon them, gazing at Flick steadily. "I'm here because I wanted to talk to you, to somehar who isn't part of what I am now. I'm here because of who and what you are, Flick. I know, in you, I'll find refreshing honesty, something simple and straight forward, something clean."

"Is that a compliment?"

"I don't know. Is it?"

"You are very powerful and you can have what you want," Flick said. "Maybe you're looking for a confessional priest."

Pellaz laughed. "There's an idea! I'm enjoying this. I knew I would."

"This is bizarre. I feel we should know one another, and my memory tells me we do, but we don't at all."

"I know. But we can remedy that."

"Will you see Ulaume?"

Pellaz considered. "I don't think so. I sense neediness in him. He wants something from me. You don't."

"That puts me in a position."

"That's a pity."

Flick was already wondering whether he'd be able to tell Ulaume about this, and then, of course, there was Mima. Part of him wanted to tell Pellaz about Mima, because he knew how close they'd once been. Would he feel the same way about her as he did about Terez, if he knew she'd undergone a kind of inception? If Pellaz were anyhar but the Tigron, perhaps it would be safe to tell, but Flick knew the repercussions could be dreadful. They could ruin his life in Roselane.

"Can we do this sometimes?" Pellaz asked. "Just talk?"

"Do I have a choice?" Flick snapped, hearing Ulaume in his voice.

Pellaz was silent for a while. "I'd prefer to talk with you only if you wanted it."

"I don't know. There's Lor to consider. If I keep our meeting secrets, he'd sense I was hiding something, and I don't want to threaten our relationship. If I told him, he'd want to meet you too."

"But what do you want?"

Flick considered, and it didn't take very long. He knew what he wanted, but managed to stop himself saying it. "It'd be difficult, Pell. Of course I want to meet with the Tigron of Immanion in private. What har wouldn't? And of course I want to talk to an old friend. But . . ." He realized, ultimately, that it was Mima and Lileem, and knowledge of the Kamagrian, which stood between them, not Ulaume. If he continued to see Pellaz, whether secretly or not, he'd end up knowing about the Roselane.

"You have secrets, I know," Pellaz said. "See how good a friend I was, not looking at them? Are they that bad, Flick?"

"No," Flick answered. "One day . . . I'm sure that one day . . ." He couldn't think what to say. There might never be a time when Wraeththu could know about the Kamagrian.

"If you don't want to talk about what happened with you and Cal, you don't have to."

"I don't think it would do you any good."

"Now you sound like Thiede," Pellaz said. He stood up. "I will find you sometimes. We'll make no arrangements. And if you need me . . ."

"How?" Flick asked.

"I would be breaking every code of Gelaming law if I told you," he said, "because some of our technology, if you can call it that, is not for the every-har. That is all I'll say."

He went to the lip of the rock ledge and uttered a piercing whistle. The horses were not that far away. Perhaps they'd been eavesdropping. It dawned on Flick what Pellaz had meant: Astral. He was a means to contact Immanion any time, if Flick could only work out how. Vaysh had put restraints on the beast. Would Pellaz now remove them? He dared not ask, sensing his question would not be answered. It was up to him to work it out, if he ever had need to.

Then, there was another possibility.

Flick stood up and joined Pellaz at the edge of the rock. They watched the horses come toward them. "Did you help us on the ocean when the Gelaming came for us?" Flick asked. "Did you hear a call?"

Pellaz nodded. "A har in your company called upon me, but I had established a link with you, in any case. I was keeping an eye on things after what happened in Galhea. I sent out a troupe of hara to escort you to your destination, but the Roselane hid you from them. A pity. That would have avoided the unpleasant experience at sea."

Flick laughed. "I never realized! We ran from the wrong hara."

"Well, you had no way of knowing, so I can hardly blame you. Thiede sent hara out to look for you because he sensed a secret. Seel's and my fault, probably. Still, it was best you avoided capture. No doubt if you hadn't, you'd be set up as somehar's consort somewhere now, doing Thiede's work."

"Like Seel?"

Pellaz gave Flick a considered glance, but did not respond to the remark. "You have some powerful friends. You don't really need my help, certainly not now. Jaddayoth is spawning some interesting hara, as you are spawning interesting ideas about gods. We must talk of this sometime."

"Yes," Flick said. "I'm not sure I like the idea of being watched."

"It's a Gelaming habit I've picked up."

"A pity you couldn't have helped when I ran into Seel, then."

Pellaz laughed. "Oh Flick, don't you get it? I was at that party in Galhea. Nohar knew it, but I saw what happened. I had already vowed to find you one day, and then, there you were."

"Do you do that often?" Flick asked. "Spy on your friends? Did Cobweb and Seel know you were there?"

"No. I was there because I sensed I would learn something important, and I did." He kissed Flick briefly on the cheek. "There are no surprises, my friend."

After Pellaz had gone, Flick sat and stared at the sky for over an hour, but not in quite the same contented mood he'd enjoyed before. No surprises. Pellaz was wrong. There was a lot he didn't know.

There are so many things I should have asked him, Flick thought. *Next time . . .*

Flick lingered in the mountain meadows until long after sundown. He was sure that the moment he set foot in the house, his companions would sense at once that something enormous had happened. He dreaded looking into Ulaume's eyes. Like Cal had in the past, it seemed Pellaz had already made a liar of him. Pellaz and Cal were two halves of the same being. Did the Tigron know where Cal was now?

However, coincidence, the most potent of cosmic forces, was working in Flick's favor. When he finally mustered the courage to return home, he walked in on another enormous happening. The whole household had been thrown into a flustered panic, because a har had turned up for dinner. A har, who was now sitting at the kitchen table, filling the room with his dark, smoldering presence: Terez Cevarro.

CHAPTER THIRTY

Lileem had quickly discovered her vocation lay in caring for animals. Tel-an-Kaa had found a good job for her in Opalexian's personal stable, and now she cared for some of the finest horses in the land. Not as fine as Astral, of course, but still beautiful specimens.

For some weeks after their arrival in Shilalama, Lileem had meditated before her statue of the Tigron every night, but whatever brief contact she felt she'd had with him seemed to have vanished. He had helped them, but why had it ended there? He knew where they were. Gradually, her interest in him faded, because he seemed to have no relevance in Roselane and real life considerations took over.

Lileem had quickly made many friends among the Roselane, as had Mima, who with her prior experience in farming had secured a good position as a farm overseer on the outskirts of Shilalama. Again, Tel-an-Kaa had had a hand in making sure Mima had landed a decent job. Although it was her life's work to scour the world for straying Kamagrian and bring them to the fold of Roselane, the Zigane clearly had special feelings for Lileem and Mima. Whenever she was in the city, she would come for dinner, or invite them to her home. This friendship gave Lileem and Mima high status among the Kamagrian. Both of them, however, secretly felt they were closer to the hara they knew than to the parazha who were so eager to embrace them into their sisterhood. There was something about Kamagrian with which neither Lileem nor Mima felt entirely comfortable. Mima especially was contemptuous of the emphasis on the female side of their being. It was a subject that obsessed her and she'd come to the conclusion that all hara and parazha simply continued to identify with the gender they'd once been and that was the main difference between them. When Mima learned that some Kamagrian, who considered themselves among the most spiritual of their kind, had actually had their ouana-lim surgically removed, she was incensed. "That is not the message Opalexian should be giving parazha," she said. "It's irresponsible and sick."

Lileem just thought it was stupid and that the parazha concerned had problems that weren't really being dealt with. Meditation and prayer were all very well, but the physical body was important too. This, she decided, was what she and Mima liked most about Wraeththu. Aruna between Kamagrian was not as commonplace as it was among hara, where it was as much a part of social etiquette as sharing a drink or a meal. Many Kamagrian felt uncomfortable with their male aspects and sought to subsume them. She supposed that Wraeththu did the same with their female sides, although not so much in a sexual sense. What a tragic mess.

Tel-an-Kaa, for all her rhetoric and often bombastic nature, was more balanced than any other parage Lileem had met. She had seen the Zigane's real self, and it was not that much different from Ulaume or Flick. But Tel-an-Kaa would not hear a word against other parazha or their—to Lileem—misguided ways. She just said that all parazha should accept how their sisters wanted to live.

"They are just too *nice*," Mima once said scathingly of their new friends. "By Aru, I almost crave seeing Terez again, just to experience a bit of healthy dark!"

Her words, it transpired, were prophetic.

Lileem was alone in the house when a knock came at the front door. All their friends always came to the back door, which was never shut in warm weather, so Lileem knew it had to be a stranger who'd come calling. She'd just begun to prepare the evening meal, and went to answer the knock with a knife in one hand. She opened it and a black shadow fell over her.

"Hello Lee," said Terez, smiling. "Put down the knife. I hope there's no need for it."

"Terez!" Lileem exclaimed, in a voice she was sure sounded like a strangled squeak. "You're here! You found us!"

"Were you hiding from me?"

She stood aside to let him into the house. "We had to leave Megalithica so
quickly, we had no chance to tell you. I always wondered whether we'd see
you again."

"Well, you are."

She led him into the kitchen. "So much has changed."

"Yes," he said. He sat down at the table and rummaged in the leather
satchel he carried. "I hope you don't mind me turning up like this."

"Mind?" He'd never cared about that before. Lileem laughed nervously. "I
kind of missed you."

Terez pulled a smoking pipe out of the satchel. "When you were a harling,
you always used to watch me. I know you never liked what you saw. But, when
we used to meet on the river, it was you who was most welcoming. I noticed
that. Share a smoke?"

Lileem had been thrown into confusion by these disclosures. "Better not. I
have to get dinner ready." Strange how she could sound so calm, when in-
wardly war had just broken out. "There's wine in the larder. Do you want
some with that?"

"Okay."

She dried her hands on a towel. "Won't be a moment."

Terez lit his pipe. "Lileem the harling has gone for good. You're quite the
grown up har now, aren't you?"

"It happens. Time does that to a har, you know."

"Sorry, I keep remembering that grubby-faced imp back home and the
awkward coltish creature on the *Esmeraldarine*. Now, here you are, in full
flower."

Lileem knew her face was bright red and could do nothing to change it.
"You're not exactly the suppurating husk you once were, either," she said, and
fled the room.

She went into the larder to compose herself, convinced her heart would
burst from her chest at any moment. He was so much more handsome than
she remembered, if that was possible. Images of Terez prior to his re-
inception no longer seemed real. "Remember Chelone," she told herself.
"Don't be an idiot." She must never betray to him that she'd fantasized about
seeing him again a thousand times.

She brought out the flagon, crafted by Ulaume's own hand and decorated with pictures of inebriated hara, and poured him a gobletful with a steady hand. "Did you get to meet Pellaz?"

Terez pulled a sour face. "No. I did get to Immanion, but my dear brother is such an exalted har now, I couldn't get near him. I was heavily dissuaded, in fact, and old family ties have no importance now."

"We thought that might be the case." She sat down at the table with him, basking in the luxury of these moments alone with him.

Terez lit his pipe and took a long draw. "So, what exactly are you now, Lee? Have you found out? What about Mima?"

He had never spoken to her like this before. He had barely acknowledged her existence. Perhaps his travels had mellowed him. "Oh, we're fine," she said. "Same old freaks. Mima had a fling with a har in Galhea." She shrugged. "So . . ."

"I know you went to Galhea. I went looking for you and it became quite a quest to track you all down. My information as to your whereabouts came from Galhea. Took some time."

"Nohar knew where we were heading, other than to the eastern continent."

"It was difficult, but not impossible. I eventually managed to meet with two hara who'd escorted you to the coast."

"Leef and Chelone."

"That's right. I told them I was Mima's brother, and we look enough alike for that to sway them, so they told me you were heading for the northeast coast. I continued to ask around, and used the services of scryers, until I eventually found my way to Freyhella. They told me you were bound for Roselane in Jaddayoth, and that some Gelaming har had helped you on your journey. Is that right? Who was it?"

"Not Pell," Lileem said. "You are quite a sleuth, Terez. I wouldn't want to be an enemy of yours. There would be nowhere to hide."

Terez laughed and drank some of the wine. He shuddered.

"I know," Lileem said in sympathy. "It's my first batch, but it tastes okay after a few glasses."

"Hara round here are too open," Terez said. "It only took a few minutes to find out where you lived. Good job I'm not an enemy, isn't it?"

"There are no locked doors in Shilalama," Lileem said. "That's why we like it here."

"There seem to be a lot of humans here though. I saw several on my way here."

"There aren't that many," Lileem said. "Just a few refugees. They keep to themselves mostly and have dwellings in the hills beyond the city. They come to Shilalama for supplies and trade, but after a while, you don't even notice them. They're just neighbors." She hesitated. "Why have you looked for us, Terez?"

"You're my family, aren't you?"

"That never meant anything to you before."

He shrugged. "I found Immanion and it was the end of the path. A dead end. What next? Uigenna. No thanks. Other tribes? Too much effort. All I could think of was you four, and the pleasant evenings on the *Esmeraldarine*. We didn't get off to the best of starts, but I think we were friends in the end. I want to make the peace with Mima. Human family ties are supposed to mean nothing now, but I like to buck against tradition, even Wraeththu tradition. Pellaz has no interest in us, Dorado has vanished into haradom, so there is only Mima. And she *is* har, or thereabouts."

"She will be astonished to learn of your feelings!" Lileem said.

"No more astonished than I was when I realized they were there."

As Lileem continued to prepare the meal, now adding extra meat and vegetables to accommodate their surprise guest, she wondered whether, despite Roselane openness, she and her family should allow strangers to the tribe into their homes. In her experience, none came to Shilalama uninvited, or at least they were vetted by Opalexian's staff before being granted access. "Did anyhar try to stop you finding us here?" she asked.

"Not really. I said I was expected. Kept the family ties secret, of course, but . . . Where *are* the others?"

"Out working," Lileem said, then told him the details. He didn't seem that interested, which was a trait of the old familiar Terez.

Ulaume arrived home first and appeared quite pleased to see Terez, but you could never really tell with Ulaume. Claws might be extended later.

"Good to see your hair grew back," Terez said to him, which Lileem considered to be rather an insensitive remark. "The talk is that Wraxilan is dead now, so unfortunately I'll never get to punish him for you."

"That's a shame," Ulaume said. "It would have been nice if you'd brought me his head as a present."

Terez laughed. He appeared so at ease, and that was something entirely new for him. "If I'd had more time, I could have brought you a few Uigenna skins instead."

"Mmm, that would have been good. I need a new coat."

Mima, however, effectively squashed this playful reunion. When she walked in through the back door, her reaction to finding Terez in her kitchen was a cold "What are you doing here?"

"Seeking my sister," he answered smoothly.

She took off her coat and made a great fuss of putting her lunch satchel away. "I remember we once agreed we were no longer brother and sister."

"That was wrong. We are. We can't ignore it."

Ulaume excused himself from the room, and Lileem wished she could do the same, but unfortunately the bubbling pans needed supervising.

"Did you find our other brothers?" Mima asked. She got herself a goblet and poured a drink of Lileem's toxic wine.

"No. It's just you and me."

Mima regarded him thoughtfully, tapping the cup against her lips. "What do you want?"

"Peace," he said. "On your terms. I've missed you all."

Mima, surely, had to be as shocked by this admission as Lileem had been. It was in Mima's nature to be difficult and to draw this situation out for as long as possible, and Lileem hoped she wouldn't. She wanted them all to sit down to dinner with Terez and have a good evening. She wanted them all to be friends. She also knew she'd better not open her mouth, because if she did Mima would jump on her like a furious cat.

"I'm sorry," Terez said. "Will that do? What else can I say?"

Mima took a drink, hardened enough to its unique bouquet not to wince. "Okay," she said softly, in a measured tone, "but if this is to work, there's something you should know."

Don't, Lileem thought. *Please don't, Mima.* She had stared at the steaming pans for so long, her eyes were watering.

"Sure," Terez said cautiously.

"It was me who took you from the Uigenna," Mima said, then drained her cup noisily. Lileem glanced around quickly and saw tears in Mima's eyes, but Lileem could tell they were only an effect of the tart wine.

Terez just stared at his sister.

"Did you hear me?" Mima said, refilling her goblet. "I aborted your inception. It was me. I thought I was doing the right thing."

Terez looked away from her and stared down at the table. Silence was absolute, but for the inappropriately cheerful bubble of the pans. For long seconds, no one moved or spoke. Then Lileem saw that Terez was shaking. She glanced at Mima, who caught her eye. Mima's expression was cold, somehow accusatory, but also slightly puzzled. The sound Terez made was a dreadful thing, like the whines and howls when he'd been ill. It was low at first, a hideous continuous moan.

Lileem dropped whatever she was holding, and she would never remember what that was, and began to move across the kitchen toward Terez.

But Mima said, "No! Get out of here." She went to her brother and wrapped her arms around him.

Lileem left the room without looking back, heart pounding. She stood outside the door in the main hallway of the house and saw Ulaume sitting on the stairs. Together they listened to Terez sob in a choked strangled way for about fifteen minutes, and by then, the vegetables had begun to burn.

Mima opened the kitchen door and surprised Lileem and Ulaume who virtually had their ears pressed against it. "You'd better come in and salvage what you can," she said.

When Flick eventually came home, Ulaume and Lileem were engaged in cooking with rather more industry than it required and Terez was sitting stunned at the table, with Mima holding one of his hands. How this evening would progress, Lileem could not foresee.

She and Ulaume set the table and dished up the food, which was partly peppered with charred fragments. A paralyzing atmosphere gripped the room. Flick looked mortified, and none of them had yet told him exactly what had happened. He was sensitive and must have guessed for himself.

Terez roused himself to eat. He behaved like a polite child, which Lileem found really confusing. She wished he'd get back to normal. She wished Mima had kept her mouth shut. What was the point of telling him that? To absolve her own guilt: that was the point, she decided. But maybe Mima was right, and the only way she and Terez could ever be friends was if he knew the truth. That lie gnawed away at the foundations of their relationship and only by gouging it out could the situation between them improve.

Lileem conspired with Ulaume in an attempt to bring some kind of normalcy to the occasion. They tried to crack jokes and conduct their usual banter, but it was difficult. Lileem wondered what was wrong with Flick. Was he worried that if Terez became more of a regular fixture in their lives, he'd rekindle his relationship with Ulaume? It had seemed so intense between them after Terez's recovery. Now, perhaps remembering that time also, Flick was somber and appeared to be only half in the room with them.

Before the meal was finished, Terez pushed his plate away from him. "Mima, can we talk?" he asked.

"Yes," she answered.

He stood up and she led him into the yard at the back of the house.

"She *told* him," Lileem hissed at Flick, the moment the door was closed. "He knows what she did."

"Oh," Flick said. "That's . . . bad."

"It's not going to change anything," Ulaume said.

Flick smiled weakly. He took one of Ulaume's hands in his own and kissed it. "You know I love you, don't you?"

Ulaume laughed. "What? Has everyhar gone mad tonight?"

Flick said nothing.

"I know," Ulaume said. "Relax. I love you too."

The evening was cold now and the stars looked hard and sharp in the clear sky. Terez stared up at them and Mima stood behind him, hugging herself. She wished she'd put her coat on.

"You should have told me before," he said.

"I didn't know that," she said. "I really didn't know what to do for the best. You were so angry and you were . . . you were not the kind of har to trust. You were nothing like the annoying but cute little brother I'd once known."

Terez smiled mordantly at that. "I'm not going to ask why you did it. I know why. You were human and you didn't understand. You wanted to keep a living relative."

"That's it. Exactly."

"But you should have told me. Another thing you don't understand is what a relief it is to know the truth. I thought the Uigenna just abandoned me. You let me think that."

"Terez, I can't apologize for that, because I did not act in malice. The Uigenna are bad news, but I didn't really know that until after Flick and Ulaume came and told me what they knew. What I did to you was a tragic mistake, a desperate act. That's all there is to it. Believe me, I tortured myself about it for years, but ultimately I know there is no point to that. And if the two of us have any future, it has to be in truth. It's always lain between us, this dark secret and now it's out."

Terez sighed deeply. "I know. The strange thing is, it's irrelevant now, but it was a shock. I didn't expect to hear that."

"Are you angry?"

"I don't know. I was just back there for a while, that's all." He turned to her fully. "I haven't had a normal life, Mima. I'm an outsider, as you are, for different reasons. But I *am* har, through and through, and the fact that the feeling could spill from me in that way tonight only proves to me I'm right." He paused. "We both suffered. We were both in darkness for a long time. But if none of it had happened, you might be dead and I might be with the Uigenna, which I now realize would not have been the best path."

"With the benefit of hindsight, we could say that."

He put his head to one side and closed one eye, a gesture reminiscent of the boy he'd once been. "How are you?"

"Fine," she said. "It's good here. Bit tame, maybe, but safe."

He nodded. "Lileem told me you took aruna with a har. Is that right?"

"Yes. But . . . it's complicated. I take aruna with Lileem now, nohar else."

"Oh." He seemed surprised. "You are har, though, you and she?"

Mima smiled at him. "Yes, in our own way. We're not chesna, Terez. We're really close and I love her, but it's not . . . We're just finding a way. Comfort."

He smiled back and for long moments, they held each other's gaze. Then, he said, "Thanks, Mima."

She inclined her head. "Sorry I ruined your life."

They both laughed, hesitantly, then fell silent. "Come here," Terez said, and held out his arms.

Mima pressed herself against him, held him tight. "Don't ever believe them," she murmured, kissing his hair. "Family *does* matter. Ours does."

First thing the following morning, Mima did not go to work, but instead took Terez to Exalan in the government offices at Kalalim, to make sure it was acceptable for her brother to become part of their household. After speaking with Terez briefly, Exalan interviewed Mima in private. She told him that Terez knew nothing of the Kamagrian and believed herself and Lileem to be a strange kind of har.

"For the time being, let him think that," Exalan advised.

"But if he lives here, he's bound to notice differences in the parazha and hara around him. I'm not sure how to deal with that. What is the official line?"

Exalan smiled. "This is a rare circumstance—relatives from the past turning up—so there are no protocols for dealing with it. I will speak to Opalexian about it. But for now, if you are happy to be responsible for your brother, I can see no reason why he should not become part of your household. We are not Gelaming, Mima. We don't want to make harsh rules. The happiness of our citizens is of prime importance. I trust you will act wisely, should any difficult situations arise, and I am here to advise you, should you need me."

"Thanks."

"Take Terez to work with you. I'm sure you can find something to occupy his time."

"I will."

Mima was unsure how Terez would feel about this, as he'd been a loner for so long. Would he be prepared to fit into the community and work for it? Now that she'd truly found him again, she was anxious about losing him. But he seemed to accept the idea without reserve and said, "It'll be like old times, working the land."

"One thing you might notice," Mima was driven to say. "Shilalama is a sanctuary. Many of the hara here have had difficulties: strange inceptions, with unusual results. Many are similar to Lileem and me. It's polite not to ask questions or pry. Will you remember that?"

"I will be the spirit of discretion."

"As I said last night, this place can feel tame sometimes, but the hara here are a good tribe. There's nohar at the top wielding a big sword, and no pompous autocrats throwing their weight around. Therefore, cooperation and harmony are very important. We value these things. Even if the sweetness gets up your nose sometimes, just take a deep breath and smile back sweetly. Got that?"

Terez laughed. "Absolutely. I can't wait."

Lileem was concerned about Flick. He did not go out on patrol that day and after Ulaume had gone to work, went back to bed. Lileem went up to see him and he complained of feeling unwell. Hara were rarely sick. "What's wrong?" Lileem said. "You were fine before coming home last night. It's Terez, isn't it?"

"Partly," Flick mumbled.

"Don't worry," Lileem said, stroking his shoulder. "He's not going to take Ulaume off you."

Flick laughed in a strange, cruel kind of way. "No."

"You should go out again today. It's a bit overcast, but I'm sure it'll brighten up later. The mountain air will do you good. Take Astral for a wild gallop. Don't lie here moping."

"I want to lie down in a small confined space," Flick said. "Leave it at that, will you, Lee? Hadn't you better be going? You'll be late for work."

Lileem stood up with a sigh. "Okay, but I expect you to make us a superb feast for tonight."

Flick merely grunted and turned on his side. "We should be careful of the Cevarros," he said.

"What?"

"You heard." He pulled the quilt over his head.

Every day at work, Lileem waited impatiently for the moment when she could run back home. All she could think about was seeing Terez, thoughts which she kept to herself. Terez appeared to have adapted well to his new life, and although he had a tendency to say the wrong thing at the wrong time, which conjured the most intense silences known to the world, he was far from being the damaged har they had known in Megalithica. He flirted with Lileem, and maybe it was just joky affectionate play, but sometimes, when Lileem looked at him, the expression in his eyes stilled the breath in her throat.

Lileem believed that Mima would be the difficult one over Terez, but it seemed that Flick had assumed the role, and that was—well—it was inconvenient. Flick seemed to be changing, becoming introverted and secretive. One night, Lileem even overheard him having a heated argument with Ulaume, which was so unusual it was shocking. Ulaume wanted to know was what was wrong with his chesnari, but when he tried to talk about it, Flick simply lost his temper. This was not the Flick they all knew and loved, and even Ulaume was becoming strained and tense.

As the season flowered into summer and the mountains began to sing an exultant song of abundance and lushness, Flick sometimes stayed out all night. Ulaume didn't argue with him anymore, and this seemed to ease the situation at home, but Lileem could tell that Ulaume was bleeding inside about it. He would never be alone with Terez, clearly convinced this was the root of the problem. But Flick often wasn't there to notice this show of loyalty.

"It makes no sense to me," Ulaume once confided to Lileem, when the two of them sat up drinking one weekend night. Their yard was a riot of perfumed flowers and the warm night air was full of their scent. "Chesna is not about being possessive or frightened or threatened. It's a state of being. Hara take aruna with others all the time, whether in a chesna partnership or not. I *know* Flick. We all do. It's not like him to be this way."

No, it wasn't. And even though Lileem had consumed one and a half bottles of her own wine, it occurred to her then that perhaps Terez was not the reason for Flick's behavior.

"Maybe we're not chesna at all," Ulaume said gloomily. "Maybe we're kidding ourselves we are, because we've been thrown together."

"Don't say that," Lileem snapped. "I think maybe it has something to do with what happened with the Uigenna. Flick's got time to think now. He's punishing himself for that."

"He seemed fine when we first got here. More than fine. He'd put all that to rest."

That was true, and Lileem didn't really believe her own words either. It was a puzzle. "Perhaps you should . . ." She paused.

"What?"

"Well, when I was little, you found out about my friendship with Mima because . . . because you spied on me."

Ulaume stared at her with wide eyes. "Are you suggesting Flick is meeting somehar in secret?"

"No! I don't know what I'm suggesting, but aren't you curious to see what he gets up to on his own out there? Maybe the mountains are getting to him in a weird kind of way. I don't know. I just think there's more to all this than we imagine."

Ulaume sighed, and took a long drink. "You're not wrong there! I'll think about it."

"Perhaps," Lileem said, inspired by alcohol, "perhaps Astral can still take him into the otherlanes. Maybe that's what he's been doing, and he's become sort of addicted to it."

"I'd not thought of that."

"Well, it's worth investigating."

For a couple more weeks, nothing else was mentioned. Days flowed into balmy days and Lileem was sure the perfume of the mountain flowers had got into her blood. She felt drunk all the time, intoxicated and heady. Something momentous was approaching, and it was a marvelous feeling. In her heart, Lileem suspected what that might be. She was thinking of Terez, and that there always had to be a solution to everything, and that she would find the one she was looking for.

One night in bed, she asked Mima again about what had happened with Chelone. Mima now found this story extremely funny and she could tell it very well. She was often asked to recount it at friends' houses, because some Kamagrian had had similar experiences and liked to discuss them. When it was Mima's turn to talk, she'd have a roomful of parazha choking with laughter, which was often a welcome counterpoint to the stories of sadness and grief.

Now, Lileem laughed, as she always did, but her heart was racing. She had to wait for her moment, an appropriate pause in the story, but eventually, it came and she asked, "Would you do it again?"

Mima regarded her quizzically. "Hmm. Would I? Kaa tells us it's dangerous, life threatening."

"But is it?"

"Why?"

"I just wonder about things, that's all. So many parazha have been drawn to hara, and it's always ended up badly, but . . . I just wonder."

"Some of us would have to be brave enough to experiment and—who knows?—lives might well be lost in the process."

"You didn't die."

"I was lucky. Or so I've been told."

There was a silence.

"Be careful, Lee," Mima said softly, taking a lock of Lileem's hair in her hand. "I don't want to lose you."

It was difficult to keep things from Mima.

"The Roselane have few rules," Mima continued, "but we both know that is one of them. You'd be hard pressed to find a har round here who'd break it."

"I know," Lileem said. "It's just talk." She paused. "Will we live here forever until we die?"

Mima lay on her back, her arms behind her head. "I don't know," she said. "I really don't."

CHAPTER THIRTY-ONE

Midsummer, and its attendant festival, came and went, and now Shilalama prepared itself for the great Festival of the Mountain Walker, which lay between the summer solstice and the autumn equinox. This was the time when a strange atmosphere pervaded the land, the heat shimmered above the lichened rocks, and weird beings crawled forth from the cracks and hollows to haunt the high meadows at midday. The Mountain Walker was a noon ghost, the spirit of the land. In his presence, anything became possible. He was the heat of summer, the fire of the spirit and the Roselane lord of aruna. On his festival night, parazha cast off their restraints and abandoned themselves to pleasures of the flesh.

"Who knows," Mima commented, "we might get to see a side of our pious sisters we actually like!"

Lileem knew Mima didn't really mean this, as they now had good friends among the Roselane, hara and parazha alike, but it might be interesting to discover what the Kamagrian were like when they let down their hair. At the very least, it was curious that the entity they revered at this time was regarded primarily as masculine.

Tel-an-Kaa was home for the festival, which she claimed she never missed and, when she came around one evening, she tried to answer some of

Lileem's queries about it. They were sitting out in the yard, with a group of friends, including Terez and Ulaume. Flick, as usual, was absent.

"The Mountain Walker is our male aspect," Tel-an-Kaa said, "and we only let him out fully at certain times. He is the scent of growing things, the scent of the earth. He is the creatures that live upon it. He is the creative principle, the seed sower. He is ouana." She grinned. "I must stop talking about this. I have a strong urge to carry you off to bed now."

"Well, we could do that," Lileem said coquettishly, wholly aware of Terez sitting somewhere nearby, although she would not look at him.

"Unfortunately," Tel-an-Kaa said, "kind though the offer is, I have work to do tonight and must go to Kalalim shortly. But"—she winked at Lileem—"on the festival night, I intend to be off duty completely."

Everyone laughed then, and Mima said, "Okay, can I make a date with someone now please? Otherwise, it seems I'm going to be moping round alone that night!"

"No chance of that!" a parage said, conjuring more laughter.

They had all spoken quite frankly in front of Terez, who might now be wondering why the Roselane only let their male sides out at certain times of year. There was an excited expectant atmosphere in the yard, and Lileem wished the parazha could be like this more often. Perhaps an enterprising parage could begin to make changes in Shilalama.

Most of their guests stayed late, and dawn was approaching as Mima and Lileem said good-bye to the last of them and began carrying empty cups and bottles into the house. Lileem went back outside to fetch more and saw that Terez was sitting very close to Ulaume, his hand on Ulaume's shoulder. Ulaume was hunched up, his head hanging low. Terez whispered something in Ulaume's ear and Ulaume jumped to his feet, crying, "No!" He virtually knocked Lileem over as he pushed past her into the house.

Lileem went to gather up the cups around Terez's feet. "Whatever you just suggested was a bad idea," she said.

Terez shrugged. "It's ludicrous that he's here, all miserable, while Flick is out doing whatever he pleases. He should loosen up a bit. Give Flick something to be jealous for."

"He's not jealous of you."

"That's not what I've heard."

"Then don't make it any worse." She dared to look Terez in the eye then and saw at once he was very drunk. "Go to bed."

He stood up, unsteadily. "Is that an order, tiahaar?"

"Yes. Go on. Don't cause any more trouble."

Terez laughed and grabbed hold of her. "What? Like this?"

She held his gaze. "No, I don't call this trouble."

She couldn't help herself. She just put down the cup she was holding and embraced him in return. Sharing breath with him was like inhaling the scent of burning black flowers. She wanted to suck the breath from his lungs. She wanted to suck out his life.

He broke away from her lips and inhaled deeply. "Now I'm seeing stars," he said. "You're hungry."

"So are you. You're not getting much, are you?"

Terez laughed, still holding her tight. "The Roselane are not exactly to my taste, but . . . well, there's been the occasional fumble. What's your excuse?"

Lileem kissed his cheek. "Can you feel it? We both want to be ouana. Now how about that? How do you sort that out?"

"Lee, you are shocking," he said. "Mima would kill me."

"Only if you killed me," Lileem said. Reluctantly, she let him go. "Never mind that. Just go to bed and tomorrow this will seem like a dream."

He pulled her hair playfully. "One I've had before."

After he'd gone into the house, Lileem danced on the spot for over a minute.

Lileem knew that on the festival night, whatever plans others might have for her, she was going to take aruna with Terez. Like Mima had been in the past, she was driven and certain. She did not fear death, because she felt more than capable of dealing with any consequences. Lileem was far more experienced than Mima had been when she'd taken aruna with Chelone. If things got out of hand, Lileem was sure she could deal with it. What she couldn't deal with was the unbearable longing to be close to Terez. If she didn't do something about it, she'd go mad.

For the next few days, she paid him scant attention, all the while conscious of his puzzlement and confusion. She could feel him begging her to look at him, so they could exchange a glance. He needed to see something looking out of her, but she wouldn't give in. It was a powerful feeling.

Flick, not really to anyone's surprise, did not show any great enthusiasm for the festival, although he did agree to accompany Ulaume to the party being held in the grounds of Kalalim. Lileem was headachy with anticipation for the evening ahead, but she still had a moment of sadness when she thought about how Ulaume and Flick had somehow fallen apart. Since Terez had arrived, she'd been so wrapped up in her fantasies and dreams, she hadn't noticed that she'd lost a close friend. She couldn't remember the last time she and Flick had had a conversation. Soon, she must do something about it. They couldn't just let Flick slip away from them like this. It was obvious that he was deeply troubled, because as well as his long absences from the house, when he was present his mind seemed to be elsewhere. Flick had become sullen and short-tempered, traits he'd never had before.

The celebratory mood in the city that night was infectious, however, and even Flick seemed more like his old self as the five of them walked to Kalalim. Lileem hadn't yet had a drink, but felt intoxicated nevertheless and drew Flick away from the group. Mima was leading them all in a rowdy song and none of them paid any attention to Lileem and Flick hanging back from them a little.

Lileem took Flick's arm and murmured to him, "Are you in love with somehar else?"

He gave her a strange guarded look. "Is that what you think?"

"I'm looking for answers, however wild. I want my friend back, the one I used to talk with, the one who helped me through all kinds of problems. I love him very much, you see."

Flick took a deep breath. For a while, he did not speak, and Lileem let him have the silence. Then he said, "We'll talk. Tomorrow." He pulled on her arm to make her stop walking. "Lee, if I speak to you, you must vow on everything you hold sacred not to repeat it. Will you do that?"

She nodded. "Of course. You've kept my secrets often enough."

"It's big," he said.

She squeezed his arm. "I can tell."

"I've thought about confiding in you for weeks, but I don't want to compromise your position. The thing is, I'll lose my mind if I keep this to myself for much longer."

Lileem studied him for a moment. Was this about another har or the other-lanes? What else could it be? Had he simply lost interest in Ulaume? Lileem could not read Flick's thoughts. She could not even pick up the faintest glimmer. "Look, try to enjoy yourself tonight. Give that to Lormy at least. Don't hurt him anymore."

Flick grimaced. "That is uppermost in my mind, whatever any of you think."

The palace of Kalalim is an organic structure that appears to grow from the earth itself. Its spires are like twisted pinnacles of raw rock and are strung with many flags. On festival nights, when Opalexian opens her home to all in the city, visitors pass through a gatehouse into a square courtyard, and from there through a wide covered passage into the tiered gardens beyond. Kalalim houses the governmental offices of Roselane and because Opalexian is high priestess of their religion, the main temple is also part of the complex.

On the fated night of the Festival of the Mountain Walker, Kalalim was decorated with carnival extravagance. Even before Lileem and her companions arrived, the sparkling flowers of firecrackers filled the sky and musicians were playing loudly. A huge crowd had gathered in the sprawling gardens, perhaps the entire population of Shilalama. Hara, parazha, and humans alike were all dressed in festival costumes and many were masked, perhaps to hide their identities in an attempt to rid themselves of inhibition. The scent of roasting lamb mingled with the sugary aroma of frying sweet cakes. Opalexian, although absent from the celebrations herself, had donated vast quantities of wine and ale from her personal cellar. The Roselane might often be ascetic, but this didn't always extend to their diet. Improved Wraeththu and Kamagrian physiology meant that fewer foodstuffs were toxic to the body, and it would be a dour creature indeed who did not take advantage of that, at least at festival times.

Lileem and her companions found themselves a table near the main lake below the palace. Lanterns cast a pale yellow glow over the water, and the huge orange and black carp that lived within it clustered near the banks hoping for crumbs. In the places where stone steps descended into the lake, the surface was a seethe of slithery fins and scales.

Ulaume suggested some of them go to find drinks, and somehow, without too much obvious effort on Lileem's part, it ended up that she and Terez were left alone for a while, sitting on opposite sides of the table. When their hands rested on the wood, they were almost touching.

"This is better," Terez said. "Hara around here should do this more often."

Lileem could sense he felt awkward with her, perhaps not sure himself what he was feeling or why. "Are you glad you came here, or do you secretly crave your old life of the mysterious, romantic loner?" she asked.

He studied her for a moment, perhaps wondering whether she was mocking him. "It's not too bad. I can't think of anything better to do, and to be honest it's sometimes a relief to have a bed to fall into at the end of the day and know there'll be good food on the table."

Lileem wondered how he could say that without remembering his human family, who'd been slaughtered, but she didn't want to open up a line of conversation in that direction, so did not comment. "I'm glad you came," she said.

"I know," he said, "and *that* disturbs me." He glanced behind him, as if to check the others were not returning, then leaned closer toward her and spoke in a low voice. "What is this, Lee? I think of you all the time, and I gather I'm not supposed to."

She laughed. "We are not as dissimilar as you think."

"I don't think anything, because I have no idea what you are. You call yourself 'she,' but you look like a har to me. You taste like one. And every time you walk past me, and I catch a whiff of your scent, my body goes into shutdown. We shared breath, and under normal circumstances, that's just the beginning, but I don't know what to think about you."

"It's complicated," she said, "but we like each other, don't we? We can follow our instincts."

"Can we? I want to think so, but something bothers me. I don't know what it is. I get the impression that if anything happened between us, it'd have to be secret and that's not right."

"It'd have to be secret because there are . . ." She sighed. "Oh, Terez, I'm not sure what I can tell you. We can take aruna together, but there might be unexpected consequences."

"Meaning?"

"I'm a special kind of har, that's all. Arunic energy can manifest some strange things."

"Does this happen with Mima?"

"No, because she's the same as me. She had a peculiar experience in Galhea and since we came here, we've discovered it's happened before. We are safe with each other, but we've been told there are dangers in being close to normal hara."

"What kind of dangers?"

"Reality can go a bit squishy. Apparently."

He blinked. "What?"

"It's nothing I can't deal with, believe me. If I thought otherwise, I'd never have shared breath with you."

"Is this why you call yourself 'she'? Because you are apart from normal hara?"

"Oh, shut up," Lileem said, grinning. "I've simply got used to it. It doesn't mean anything. It just took a while for me to develop ouana characteristics, that's all. Everything's fine now."

Terez didn't appear to be convinced. "I think there's more," he said.

Lileem took his hands in hers and at once a tingling started up in her palms. They were both shooting off energy like the fireworks in the sky. "Trust me," she said.

He stared at her gravely, raised her hands to his nose, closed his eyes, and inhaled deeply, then said, "We'll see."

The others returned, bearing several large flagons of wine, and the five of them applied themselves to the task of getting drunk. Dancing had started in the courtyard of the palace, but after a few hours, this spilled out into the gardens, until the lake was surrounded by cavorting bodies. Musicians ran among them, playing fiddles, banging drums and tambourines or blowing pipes. The infectious riotous mood was impossible to resist and so it was that Lileem found herself dancing with Terez and they were spiraling away from the lake, toward the shadows of tall trees, where the grass underfoot was wet with dew and smelled like the elixir of life. The moment the darkness beyond the lantern light enfolded them, it seemed the sounds of the festival faded away. The song of the wind, high in the trees, was very loud. Terez and Lileem shared breath, still dancing, until they both came to a standstill and drew away from one another. Lileem could barely make out his features in the dim light. He took her hand and they walked in silence, deeper into the trees, where the gardens of Kalalim melded into the wild landscape beyond. They found a hollow, surrounded by gnarled ancient evergreen shrubs: a spidery nest of crackling old leaves.

Lileem was so intoxicated, by both the wine she'd consumed and the mind-altering effect of prolonged breath-sharing, she already felt as if reality was falling apart. The only thing that existed in the world was the combined essence of herself and this har. She had never felt like this with Mima. He put his hand beneath her shirt and she was sure her skin would be scorched. Flakes of it would turn black and float away, up into the night sky, to mingle with the cinders of the fires burning in the palace gardens.

She pulled away from his mouth, gulping for breath, feeling the night air sear her lungs. She could barely see: boiling specks of light occluded her vision. With great effort, she ordered her thoughts: *Remember what Mima said. Remember it!* Her head was aching so much she thought it might explode, while her body ached in a different way that was not pain. She pushed Terez onto his back, lunged to nip his throat, ripped open his shirt. In the dim light, his skin seemed to glow. He was perfect. He seemed to be half conscious and barely moved as she scrabbled to remove his clothing. For a moment she knelt over him, debating for the final time whether she could or should do this. Ultimately, reason had no say in the matter. She opened her trousers and pushed them down.

He made a strange sound as she entered him and his body shuddered beneath her. Lileem could not concentrate on observing effects. Neither could she be like Mima had been and bring this to conclusion swiftly. It was too sweet.

Dear, beautiful Aru, she thought, *god of all gods.*

Around her, the air was cracking open. She smelled an alien wind. So be it. Let it happen. She raised her head and her hair whipped around her face, tangled by cosmic breezes. There was a place. It was dark, so dark, and the sand there was scoured by an incessant storm. Booming sounds, like gargantuan machinery. An opening in the ground. Steps. Covered in sand. And the smell: like nothing. There is no smell like that. She felt she was climbing a ladder. A ladder of five rungs and when she reached the final rung, something would burst open, and there'd be another space beyond, and the rungs would be invisible in white light. It was the cauldron of creation and it would take them to this other place, the place of sand. In this place, all questions were answered.

At that moment, the tongue of her ouana-lim shot forth like the tongue of a snake and made contact with the fifth energy center within Terez's body. There was nothing she could do to prevent this. They both reached a climax and the otherworld shut down, like a series of great doors slamming, one by one.

Lileem poised shuddering, her upper body reared above Terez. She saw a shower of spectral light flecks falling down like snow. When they touched the ground, they disappeared.

Terez uttered a long, sighing groan. Lileem pulled away from him and lay by his side, cradling his head. His forehead and hair were damp. He was shaking and she thought it was from pain. She'd torn him, hurt him. "Terez," she murmured. "Say something. Speak to me."

For a moment, he was silent, then he said, "Did you see that place?"

"Yes."

"Where is it?"

"I don't know."

"It was so real. And we were there. Nearly. Not a good place."

"It was just different."

"No. Bad. I *know* it."

He went limp against her and she held him tight. The dark place. He'd been there before. She thought it was the place where he'd been trapped after Mima had snatched him from the Uigenna.

For an hour, Terez slept, his head on Lileem's chest. She lay on her back, staring up at the treetops and the stars beyond them. For a few short moments, she had been among the stars. She had not been in this world. Was this terrifying?

No. It was wondrous. It was perhaps the reason for her existence. She had a power, and only with hara could she access it. There were rumors that parazha had somehow disappeared completely, but that was because they were ignorant and afraid. Lileem did not feel that way. If she could get Terez and herself there, she could also bring them back. What was that place? She was convinced it was of great importance. It was the secret landscape that became accessible only if conditions were right. It might exist, right here and now, all around her, but invisible to her mundane perceptions. It was not like the otherlanes, not a rushing void, but a different world. She wanted to walk upon it. She wanted to descend the steps she had seen and find out what lay at the bottom.

Eventually, Terez stirred. He sat up and rubbed his face for several minutes, pressing his fingers deep into his eye sockets. Lileem was afraid he'd gouge out his own eyes. Then he shook his head wildly and stretched. "That, I presume," he said, "was what you meant about squishy reality."

"Yes. Wasn't it amazing?"

Terez made a noncommital sound. "I wish we'd brought something to drink with us. I feel like I could drain the lake."

"It's really important," Lileem said. "It's something we need to know. All of us."

"Mmm," Terez murmured, in a way that signified "absolutely not."

"Tell me you're not interested. Go on—be like all the little hara who just do what they're told and believe what they're told. Tell me this isn't yours for the taking."

She could feel his attention riveted upon her.

"What exactly did you see, Terez?"

"It felt, for a while, like I was back in that hideous no place," Terez said, "but now, I don't know. There's something underground."

"I know. We have to find it."

She could barely see him, but she could tell he was still staring at her. She could feel the stream of his thoughts. Whatever he might say, Terez wasn't afraid. He didn't fear anything. He was the only one. "I couldn't stop myself," she said, "but we finished it too quickly. Somehow, we have to go beyond that, and not lose control."

"And if we get there? What then?"

"We take a look around and come back."

"How, exactly?"

"The same way we got there."

He was silent.

"Terez," Lileem said, "we can live in Roselane, safe little lives, and then die. Or we can take a risk and do this, and perhaps find out something important. Don't you think this was meant to happen? You and me drawn to one another, the only two hara in the world who aren't stupid and scared, and are willing to take a chance?"

"You flatter me," he said dryly. "I'm scared shitless."

"But that doesn't mean you won't do it."

"No, it doesn't mean that." He groaned. "We can't do this tonight. I'm sore and possibly bleeding."

"I'm not," Lileem said. "Mima said it was more powerful when she was soume. That's what we have to do. You're more experienced than I am. I'm sure there are more than five centers in the soume-lam. You could hold the moment and go beyond the fifth center."

He laughed. "Not sure many hara are *that* experienced, Lee. What you're talking about—it sounds like conception. I've heard that there are two more energy centers, but they are only accessible during the intense aruna involved in creating harlings. Beyond the fifth center, we are no longer just in our own bodies. It is communion with the source of all things, inside us and outside us too. We could give birth to rather more than another world here."

"I don't care. In some ways, that would be a bonus, and a right smack in the eye to Tel-an-Kaa and her righteous kind, who say hara and parazha can't come together."

"What are you talking about?"

"Never mind. I'll explain another time. Are you brave enough, Terez? Are you as brave as I am?"

"Your strategy is transparent," he said, "and if I do this, it's not because I'm trying to prove anything."

"I know. It's because you want the knowledge, as I do. You were given a glimpse of something once, and you've never understood it. This is a way to find the answers."

Ulaume was not really surprised when he realized Flick was no longer around. He looked up at the mountains and there was a white specter gallop- ing up one of the hillsides. Even from this distance, Ulaume could tell it was Astral. The horse moved like no other: a sigh of vapor over the land.

Sighing, Ulaume went back to their original table, but all his friends had gone. Time to think. He had tried hard over the last few weeks to reach Flick, to claw out the root of the problem. Even Ulaume didn't really believe it was anything to do with Terez. But Flick was unreachable. He was distracted all the time, eaten up by something of which he could not speak. It had got to the point where there was no contact between them, and Ulaume lay awake many nights, with what seemed like yards of cold bed between him and Flick, knowing Flick was also awake, a thousand troubling thoughts cascading through his mind. Did he now have to accept that his chesna bond with Flick was over? Should he move out of the house? Should he find somehar with whom to spend the night? He rested his forehead against the table and groaned. It seemed an age ago when he and Flick had talked about being chesna. Simply by voicing it, Ulaume was sure he'd somehow killed it stone dead. And perhaps the first signal of the real trouble: the night when Terez had arrived and Flick had told Ulaume he loved him.

"Go home," Ulaume told himself aloud. *Think of the sand, of the silence, of Lianvis. Go back to him with a thousand new experiences to tell over a crackling camp fire.*

But he knew he could never be happy among the Kakkahaar again. Lianvis probably wouldn't even recognize him and no doubt had installed another har in Ulaume's place years ago.

A hand on his shoulder prompted him to raise his head. Not for one moment did he think it would be Flick, but he was sure it would be Lileem. Instead, he saw Tel-an-Kaa towering over him. She was clearly surprised to see him upset. "Are you all right?"

"No," he said. "If you're looking for Lee, I've no idea where she is."

Tel-an-Kaa sat down. "I can find her later. Don't worry. What's wrong?"

Ulaume knew he was about to open his heart to the Zigane, and once this was done, he'd have to make plans for the future. He took a deep breath and opened his mouth, but before the first words came out, Mima threw herself down beside him. "Lor, I need to talk," she said.

"Don't we all," he muttered.

"What's wrong with *you*?" Tel-an-Kaa asked Mima.

"Nothing," she said. "Family stuff." She paused meaningfully.

Tel-an-Kaa got to her feet and raised her hands. "Got the message. I'll go and look for Lileem."

"Do," said Mima and her voice was cold.

Ulaume waited until the Zigane was out of earshot, then said, "What's the matter?"

Mima scraped a hand through her hair, which was matted and wild from her frenzied dancing. Her breath smelled of wine. "Not sure," she said, "maybe nothing. Lor, Lee's missing and so's Terez."

"So? They might have gone home. You know what Lee's like. She sometimes can't hold her drink. Also, this is a massive crowd. You might simply have missed her. Nothing bad can happen to her here, Mima. Don't worry."

"She's not here, Lor, I know it."

Ulaume shrugged. He really didn't care. His whole life was lying in shattered little bits around his feet. "What do you want *me* to do about it?"

"I think . . . I think she and Terez have gone off together. I think she's going to do something stupid."

"Don't be daft."

"I'm not. You must have noticed the way they are with each other."

"It's just play. Terez knows Lileem is different. He wouldn't desire her, Mima. Nohar would."

"What the hell is wrong with you?" Mima snapped. "How can you be so . . . so . . . blind, prejudiced, and pompous! Not all hara think we're disgusting freaks!"

"Hey, I never said that!"

"Didn't you? How dare you! How fucking dare you!"

"Mima—" Ulaume began, but then she smacked him in the face. Instinctively, he smacked her back, on his feet in an instant. He could feel his hair stir around his shoulders and he could smell burning. "You'll never be har," he said. "You'll never have what you want. Look on me and weep, sister!"

Mima stared up at him, her eyes wide. He could see lamplight reflected in them. They were bright with tears. She blinked. "The woods are burning." Her voice was a ragged croak.

Ulaume had no idea what she meant by that. He uttered a sound of contempt and began to walk away, but Mima grabbed hold of his shirt. "The woods are burning!"

He turned to look out over the lake and beyond it, he saw a strange purple-red glow among the trees, like an autumn sunset. Other festivalgoers were beginning to notice it too. They moved toward the lake, talking excitedly and pointing, perhaps thinking the light heralded the beginning of another firework spectacle. It was an aurora, hanging amid and over the tall trees: a dancing curtain of light. If you looked at it with half closed eyes, it seemed as if the very air was cracking and the radiance was pouring through from another world.

Mima jumped to her feet. "By Aru!" she cried.

"What?"

She began to run toward the trees, dragging Ulaume with her. He didn't even attempt to ask where they were going or why. Mima's fear streamed off her in hot waves.

Many other hara and parazha had been drawn to investigate the source of the light, but Mima and Ulaume reached it first. In the trees, beyond the lake and far from the party, they found a nest of radiance, emanating from within a thicket of ancient bushes. Mima let go of Ulaume and threw herself in among the tangled branches, tearing them apart fiercely. Ulaume pushed his way in behind her. He had a glimpse, just a brief, blinding glimpse of two creatures of light, which became one creature of light. Then the whole night exploded with a tearing crash and the light shot outward. Ulaume and Mima were blown backward into the bodies of those who had followed them. For a moment, Ulaume thought the world had ended, but then there was only blackness, intense blackness, and a terrible silence.

He was lying on the ground, on his back. His spine hurt and he felt movement beneath it, realized he was lying on Mima's legs. She crawled out slowly from beneath him, staggered to her feet and went to investigate the thicket. Others were doing likewise, their voices low and frightened. A parage came forward with a lantern she must have taken from the side of the lake. This she gave to Mima, who disappeared among the branches. Ulaume could hear rustling, as if she was pawing through dry leaves.

After a few moments, she reemerged. "Nothing," she said.

"What was it?" the lantern parage demanded.

"I don't know," Mima replied, "there's nothing left to tell us."

Ulaume knew at once she was lying. Whatever differences he and Mima might have recently had, he knew they had to close ranks now. Mima didn't hand the lantern back to the parage who'd given it to her, even though she held out her hand to take it. It was clear Mima didn't want anyone else investigating the bushes. "It must just have been a phenomenon conjured by the celebration," Mima said, "an earth light, an expression of the festival."

In the lamplight, Ulaume could see that few were convinced by this. Some spoke of going to find Opalexian, even though she hadn't been spotted all evening. "Yes, do that," Mima said.

The onlookers began to wander back to the party and Mima drew Ulaume away from them. "Where's Flick?" she asked.

"Off riding in the night," Ulaume said. "What happened there, Mima?"

"We have to find him," she said. "At once. Terez and Lee have gone."

"What?"

Mima glanced at the last few stragglers, who glanced back at them. "Not here," she said. "Do you know where Flick is?"

"I saw Astral on one of the hills earlier. I think I know what direction he headed in, but—"

"Then we have to commandeer a couple of Kalalim horses for the rest of the evening."

"Mima—"

"They've gone, Lor, don't you get it? She took aruna with him. The worst has happened."

"Where are they? Where have they gone?"

"Aru, I don't know!" Mima snapped. "Somewhere else. Out of this world. Just gone."

"You don't know that for sure. I saw something, but I wasn't sure what it was."

Mima sighed heavily. "Lor, I just hid their clothes, as best I could. It was them."

"Can we bring them back?"

"I don't know! I need Flick. Why am I so stupid? I should have known this would happen."

If it was true, Mima seemed relatively calm, but Ulaume was aware of the fire in her eyes. She appeared calm because she was actually hysterical inside. He couldn't take it in. He couldn't believe it. But he knew that when any of them felt frightened, unsure, or confused, they turned to Flick for sense and clarity. "We'll find Flick. You're right. He'll know what to do. Come on. Some horse rustling is in order."

CHAPTER THIRTY-TWO

Flick's only intention that night was to put a stop to the madness, to try and put right all that had gone wrong in his life. He hadn't learned from his own mistakes and now was the time to change that.

He had seen Pellaz maybe half a dozen times since the first meeting, but what sent him out into the mountains, day after day, wasn't prearranged engagements, but only the hope of finding Pellaz in the place where they'd meet. It was like an addiction, destructive and selfish, and recently Flick had had the sense to admit to himself it was similar to how he'd felt about Cal. Pellaz wasn't damaged by the secret liaisons: Flick was. Their friendship wasn't about love, as Lileem had suspected, or even aruna. It was as if a mighty fiery angel had descended from the center of the universe to talk with Flick alone, and he craved it. His senses wanted to feast themselves upon the Tigron, not Pellaz Cevarro. Because even sitting near Pellaz, Flick was filled up with his power, his light, his energy. The sad thing was, he couldn't enjoy the fruits of this proximity, because it had to remain secret, when all he wanted to do was climb on to the roof of the house and shout it out to the whole of Shilalama. If he spoke at all, he would betray himself. So, it was better to be uncommunicative and moody, to hide behind that disguise. Keeping this from Ulaume was the hardest thing of all. But Pellaz was determined on that point. And, oh, how he needed to talk.

The Tigron had some firm friends in Immanion—Vaysh and a har named Ashmael—whom he trusted implicitly. He had loyal friends in the House of Parasiel too and was especially close to Seel and Cobweb. But all of them were intimately connected with the schemes and affiliations of the court of the Hegemony. All of them had their own views on the Tigron's affairs, and were not totally impartial. Flick was free of all this. He could bring a new eye to Pell's dilemmas, and because it was Flick's nature to help and seek solutions, Pellaz came to him more often than he'd originally intended.

So, now Flick knew all the intimate and miserable details of the Tigron's relationship with the Tigrina, Caeru, if such a hostile situation could ever be given that name. He knew that Pellaz feared that his own son, Abrimel, despised him, despite the fact Pellaz had done all he could to prove to the har that his feelings for Rue were separate and complicated, and soaked in bitter memories. Abrimel, apparently, wouldn't accept that. He and Rue were very close. Pellaz confessed he'd tried to build something with Rue, but it was impossible. For all his good intentions, he'd lose the desire for harmony the moment Rue did something to annoy him, which was fairly consistently.

After a couple of years playing the grieving victim at court, Rue had since begun to build his own connections and gather allies. He gave more public appearances than Pellaz did, and courted the devotion of the common hara. Most infuriating to Pell of all was the fact that Rue sucked up to Thiede and that Thiede, apparently, indulged him. Rue now owned a lot of land in Almagabra, as well as choice areas of Immanion itself. He was a har of substance and independence. He did his job well, and never spoke ill of the Tigron, all of which showed Pellaz in a bad light. When they appeared in public together, Rue's smile appeared genuine and he would make a display of small but affectionate gestures toward his consort. Hara noticed that Pell's was the sour face, the stiff posture. Hara in the street knew the rumors, and none of them could understand why their Tigron was so cold to the Tigrina. Any one of them would give an eye to have Rue at their side and in their bed.

What had begun as a personal issue—an issue of bruised hearts, sleepless nights, and the smell of lost years on the evening air—had turned into a political one. A few members of the Hegemony had opposed Thiede's plan for a Tigron, thinking more along the lines of a republic. Most had since come around, because they were sensible enough to realize Pellaz intended to do the best job he could. But now that he'd revealed his faults, Pell's enemies leapt upon them. A couple of underground journals in Immanion, which were sympathetic to his enemies, printed snide, if superficially careful, articles about him. They pointed out that he was young, untried, and nohar really knew his history. Despite Thiede's insistence to the contrary, Pellaz clearly did not take his position seriously and merely wanted to posture around the city, playing king. It was still up for debate as to whether Thiede had brought him back from the dead. The most vicious detractors thought he was a son of Thiede's, born to a har who'd probably suffered a worse fate than Caeru. And in the meantime, Rue drifted serenely through city life, always deferential, always listening, always ready with a smile.

Flick could not really blame the Tigrina for any of what Pellaz told him. What other options were left open to him? Fundamentally, Pellaz hated Rue because he wasn't Cal. There was a dark, infected sore spot at the heart of his life, and he couldn't speak openly of it to any of his friends, because they thought he was wrong. It wasn't that they liked Rue particularly—Cobweb was an expert at lampooning the Tigrina—but they couldn't understand why Pellaz just didn't play the game. It was as much a duty of his position as any other irksome task of state and he could not afford to betray failings. He should just get on with what he had to do, cut off his history with Cal as if it was an extra, useless, and necrotic limb. And besides, Rue was beautiful and good natured. He'd like nothing more than to heal the rift with his consort, so why make life more difficult than it could be? Thiede would never allow Cal back into Pell's life, so he might as well make the best of what he had. But how could Pellaz do that when he'd heard the rumors that Thiede held Cal in captivity? Thiede wouldn't talk to him about it, and that was the worst thing. Pellaz had listened to his friends. He'd tried to close down his heart, to let go of the past, but it kept rising up to haunt him. What were Thiede's plans for Cal? Was he trying to rehabilitate him? Was there a chance that, one day, he'd allow Pellaz and Cal to meet? There was so much unfinished business. Pellaz couldn't get on with his life properly until it was brought to a conclusion.

After the last occasion on which they'd met, Flick went away feeling dizzy with Pell's pain. He couldn't offer advice, because everything he wanted to say had been said before, by hara who were more aware than he was of the complexities of the situation. This didn't seem to matter to Pellaz. He just wanted to purge himself. There was never any danger of him finding out about the Kamagrian, because he wasn't interested in Flick's life. His time with his old friend was limited. Every second counted, and in those seconds, Pellaz needed to expel the floods of confusion and hurt he had to hide at home. Flick hadn't even been able to tell him that Terez was in Shilalama. He thought Pellaz wouldn't want to know. Neither did the Tigron want physical closeness. He could have any har he wanted, and for that reason perhaps, a friendship devoid of aruna was somehow more meaningful.

Flick had wanted to talk to Lileem about the situation, because she was the least emotionally involved in it. He'd begun to resent that he'd allowed Pellaz to take over his life and he was angry with himself that he'd let his dearest relationship, his chesna bond with Ulaume, fall into ruin. (It was frightening how quickly and easily that could happen.) And yet, when he argued with himself about it, and asked the question *Who would you rather never see again?* he could not bear the thought of losing Pellaz. If he told himself, *Well, in that case, go to Immanion. Give up your life in Roselane,* he didn't want to do that either. Now he knew that the term "being torn" really felt as if your body was being pulled apart by immense and implacable forces.

Still, he'd realized at the Festival of the Mountain Walker that he was on the brink of really losing everything. He'd let it go on for so long there was a chance that, should he reveal the truth, he'd lose Ulaume anyway. As to how Mima and Terez would react, he dared not conjecture. But it had to be done. As soon as he could, he would speak to Pellaz one last time, perhaps attempt to contact him through Astral, and tell the Tigron his decision. But, as Flick had learned was generally the case, circumstances conspired to change his plans.

Pellaz had never actually called to Flick. He hadn't needed to, because Flick was always in their meeting place at the times when Pellaz was most likely to be able to get away. But on the Festival night, Flick heard a call. It was insistent, desperate and commanding. "Come at once!" Flick's first impulse was to resist it, but perhaps because he'd made the decision to end—or at least change the circumstances of—his meetings with Pellaz, he decided he must respond to it.

It was easy to slip away from the crowd and run through the empty streets back home. He rode Astral bareback out of the city and up into the mountain meadows, where the spirit of the Mountain Walker felt very close indeed. Flick no longer even used a bridle on the *sedu,* as he'd learned to direct Astral through intention alone. Surely, the ability to jump from this reality was now very close. Astral galloped smoothly, his hooves barely touching the ground. The air was vibrating with power and dark shapes writhed at the corners of Flick's vision. Pell's call came louder, a deafening clamor in Flick's inner ear. Something had happened.

Pellaz was standing on the rock ledge where he and Flick had first met. A glowing nimbus surrounded his body; radiance so strong that Flick could see it with his physical eyes rather than just sense it. The Tigron's *sedu*, Peridot, was cropping the sweet grass below the ledge, and once Flick jumped down from Astral's back, the two creatures nuzzled each other and ambled off up the valley.

Pellaz stared down at Flick and did not speak until Flick had climbed up the rocks to join him. The Tigron's body was stiff, his eyes wide and wild.

"What's happened?" Flick asked.

"Hold me," Pellaz said. "Now."

Flick put his arms around him, and was aware at once of the sizzling energy coursing through the Tigron's body. He wasn't trembling on the surface, but inside he was shaking like a leaf. After a few moments, he pulled away from Flick's embrace and began to pace. "Cal is in Immanion," he said.

"You've seen him?"

"Yes. If you can call it that."

"Sit down, Pell. Explain." Flick sat against the rock face, but Pellaz wouldn't stop pacing.

"I knew Thiede had Cal. Everyhar knows it. He's being punished for what he did to Orien. I thought . . ." He shook his head. "It doesn't matter what I thought because it's just a fantasy. I believed Thiede was holding Cal in his ice palace—the place where he brought me back. It's a long way away in the north, and securely guarded. But Rue . . ." He grimaced. "This is the worst thing: Thiede told Rue he had confined Cal in a tower in the hills outside Immanion. I know that place. I've ridden past it a hundred times. It has no door. It's just empty, a skeleton, a prison. Thiede told Rue. Can you believe that? And Rue has used this information like a knife. I've been stabbed so many times, I'm dead. Again."

"Thiede must want you to know," Flick said carefully. "That's why he told Rue."

Pellaz didn't appear to hear these words. "I had to see for myself. You do understand that, don't you?"

Flick nodded. There was no need to say anything.

"I am Tigron. I go where I please. There must be a door. It's hidden, that's all. I can find it. I can open it through my will." He plunged his hands into his hair, pulled at it fiercely. "Of course I can. It's all just an illusion. And there it is, locked of course, but I hold that in contempt. So easy. I should smite Rue with that force, see him bubble and burn. I could do it."

He put his hands over his mouth, pacing, pacing.

"Pell," Flick began, but Pellaz was already speaking again.

"He was . . . top room. Not tied up or anything. His eyes . . . He wasn't there. It was just a body. Like I'd been, maybe, when I came back to this world. Thiede had done something to him." He stopped pacing.

Flick stood up. "What did you do?"

Pellaz uttered a caw of choked laughter. "What did I do?"

"Yes."

"Tried to bring him back. I shouldn't have."

"No! You didn't . . ."

Pellaz wheeled around to face Flick. "What would you have done? He is *me*. But I hate myself, apparently. What's left of him doesn't want me, Flick. It's over. I betrayed him."

"No," Flick said again, in a more assertive tone. "You didn't. Did he even recognize you?"

"He said I was dead. He knows that's not true, but he said it all the same."

"If Thiede had drugged him, he probably wasn't in his right mind. The last time I saw him he was consumed by his memories of you. He probably didn't dare believe you could be real."

"He knew," Pellaz said flatly. "He knows about Rue."

"Oh. Didn't you explain?"

"I tried, but he wasn't listening. I just wanted to hold him, to bring him back, for us to remember . . ." He pressed the heels of his hands against his eyes.

There was a silence, then Flick said, "Pell, did you . . . did you take aruna with him?"

"It wasn't that," Pellaz said sharply. "I can't call it that. What I did was violation and, yes, it brought him back a little. For all the good it did. He was insane, furious. I could have been the next Orien."

"Oh sweet Aru . . ." Flick breathed. He wanted to take Pellaz in his arms again, but that moment was past.

Pellaz stood with his back to Flick; his shoulders slumped. When he spoke, he sounded like the young har Flick had known in Saltrock. "How do I be good, Flick? How do I put this behind me and be the Tigron everyhar wants me to be? When will his ghost stop tormenting and torturing me? How could Thiede let me find that place and enter it? He knew what would happen."

"It's Thiede you should be mad at, not yourself," Flick said. "Pell, it's wrong. Thiede is playing with you all. What's his motive?"

Pellaz shook his head and said nothing. His hair hid his face.

"What interest did he have in me?"

Pellaz raised his head. "You?"

"When he sent Gelaming after us in Megalithica. What was the real reason for that?"

"Who cares?" Pellaz said coldly. "You're here. You're free. I could almost hate you for it."

"You're in danger of becoming as insane as Cal is," Flick said. "Give in to it, Pell. Become your pain. Be like him. End up in a gutter and Rue can dance on your bones. It'd be easy. Trust me."

Pellaz stared at him for long seconds. "Make it go away," he said at last.

"Only you can do that," Flick said. "Pell, things have got to change. Everything is stale and stagnant and—well, just bad. Cal is very sick. I think he always has been. I was wrong to say what I did to you when we first met up again. He *is* obsessed with you, and it's obvious he can never be part of your life again. You *must* let it go. It's for the best that Thiede has him locked up. You did need to see him for yourself. Much as I hate to say it, Thiede did the right thing in engineering that. Now, you have seen, and you must put it behind you."

"He is my life."

"He's an insane murderer!" Flick said, more harshly than he intended. "I'm sorry. That's not exactly how I feel about it. I can't hate Cal, because he's so ill, but neither can I forget the day that Orien died. I can still smell the blood, Pell, if I think hard enough about it."

"You don't know him like I do," Pellaz said, clearly avoiding further disclosures about that incident. "He can be healed. I know it. Part of the reason he's so sick is because of what happened to me. How can I blame him for hating me? He went mad for nothing."

Flick paused a moment. "I know," he said. "Don't think I haven't considered that myself. Of course, you also have to wonder whether he's always been that way. His life with you was just a respite. There's no point dwelling on it. Now is the time for change." He took a deep breath. "I'm sorry, Pell, but there's something I want to say. I'm sorry I have to say it now, but perhaps that's part of what needs to be."

"What?"

"I can't keep seeing you like this. If you want my friendship, it has to be honest and in the open."

"So you're abandoning me too?"

"No. Listen to me. Your brother is in Shilalama. He lives with us. I can't go on with this deceit. There's too much of it."

Pellaz uttered a cold laugh of disbelief. "You're saying this to me now? You think I care about these things after what I've just been through?"

"No, of course you don't care, but you should start to. If you want to start putting things right in your life, begin here. It'd be a small start perhaps, but a meaningful one."

Pellaz shook his head vigorously. "I can't," he said. "I can't be bothered with all the emotional fallout, the explanations, apologies, justifications . . . I'm too tired and beaten to deal with it."

"Then let me fix it so you don't have to," Flick said quickly, sensing a hint of capitulation on Pell's part. "Let me speak to Terez, and to Ulaume." He hesitated. "I may have to speak to some high-ranking hara in Shilalama too. I want to be honest, Pell. Cal made a liar of me once. I won't let it happen again. There are some important things you should know about this place, things that maybe Thiede already knows about and doesn't want you to be aware of, or maybe things that even Thiede doesn't know. It has nothing to do with Cal, or intrigues, or court scandals, or petty rivalries, but a lot to do with being a responsible ruler of Wraeththu. Do you hear me? Do you hear what I'm saying?"

"I showed you my true self," Pellaz said. "I showed you the dark, the rotten, the human bits that still lurk inside. Don't think I'm like this at home, Flick. I trusted you. Don't throw it back in my face."

"I'm not. A good Tigron would be a good listener. Have you gone deaf?" Flick thought that maybe he had gone too far with that.

Pellaz regarded him with narrowed eyes. "I need allies," he said. "Will I find that in my brother, in Ulaume? Will I find that in Shilalama?"

"By Aru, yes!" Flick said, not sure himself if that was the truth. "At least, meet your brother. If Thiede has decided Terez has no place in your life, perhaps it's time you made your own decision about it."

After a pause, Pellaz said, "Very well. Now tell me what it is I need to know about Shilalama." He had managed to pull himself together and draw the mask of Tigron over his face. He no longer appeared confused or upset. He was a har used to having his questions answered.

"I need to speak to certain individuals first," Flick said. "You'll have to trust me on that."

"There is nothing Thiede doesn't know."

"Maybe there isn't. But there are certainly things of which you are unaware."

Pellaz sighed deeply and nodded. "I will accept what you say and I will meet them. That is all. I can make no other promises. Remember that Ulaume has a bad reputation, and Terez, apparently, has earned one. I'm not sure it would be in my best interest to present them as friends, let alone relatives, in Terez's case."

"You slept with him every night of your life until you left home," Flick said softly. "Why do we have to abandon those whom we loved as humans, especially if they are har too? If you cannot forget Cal, how can you forget Terez . . . or Mima for that matter?"

"What has Mima to do with this?" Pellaz said. "Is she . . . is she still alive?"

Flick stared at him for some moments. He shouldn't tell, he knew he shouldn't. He was risking everything. "Yes," he said at last.

"You found her," Pellaz murmured, "when you went back to my home. You found her, didn't you?" His voice rose, and he grabbed hold of Flick's shoulders, his fingers digging painfully into the flesh. "Who else? Who else, Flick?"

"Let me go!" Flick said. "No one else. The others were dead, apart from Dorado, who was taken by the Uigenna."

Pellaz released him. "Why haven't you told me this before?"

Flick rubbed his bruised flesh. "You didn't give me space! You just dismissed that little task you made me swear to carry out. Remember? You've known that Terez is har for months, but you've never asked me about him. You didn't care."

"Did my brothers save Mima from the Uigenna?"

"No. She saved herself." He hesitated. "Pell, you should hear it from her, not me. It's an . . . extraordinary story."

"What do you mean? How can I?"

"She lives with us too."

Pellaz uttered a wordless sound and turned his back on Flick. It seemed as if he couldn't believe what he'd heard.

"Come back home with me," Flick said. "Now."

Pellaz did not turn to face him again for some moments. When he did, the mask was in place. "Yes, I will, although I cannot stay long."

Flick could barely trust that Pellaz had decided to cooperate. He whistled for Astral at once, and the horse came running with Peridot at his side. Before they mounted up, Flick said, "You might have to keep this meeting secret. You don't know how much I'm risking."

Pellaz laughed coldly. "You should know I'm good at keeping secrets," he said.

As they rode back down the moonlit valleys, Flick was thinking about whether he'd have to return to the festival and find his friends, or whether they'd already have gone home. He wondered how he should handle the situation. If he just sprang Pellaz on them without warning, no doubt a messy, emotional scene would ensue: the last thing Pellaz wanted. It might drive him away again immediately.

But, as usual, Flick found he could not make plans, because even before they reached Shilalama, two horses came galloping madly toward them, bearing Ulaume and Mima in a distraught state.

Flick uttered a low curse and directed a request at Astral to halt. He dismounted, sensing trouble, and not just the obvious.

"Flick!" Mima cried, throwing herself from her horse. Her attention was fixed directly on Flick. She didn't notice anything else.

"What is it?" he asked.

"Something terrible!" Mima exclaimed. "Where were you? Why did you leave? Lileem . . . Oh Aru, the worst has happened!"

"Hush!" Flick said. He took hold of her shoulders and glanced beyond her to Ulaume who was still seated on his horse. Ulaume was staring at Pellaz, and his expression was unreadable.

"Flick, what can we do?" Mima said, her face pressed against his shoulder.

"Tell me," he said. "What has Lileem done?"

Mima raised her head. At the same moment, Pellaz jumped down from Peridot and said, "Terez?"

Mima stiffened in Flick's hold. She gazed into his eyes as if afraid to look away.

"Yes," Flick murmured. "I was bringing Pell to you."

"How?" she asked. "How?"

Flick turned to Pellaz. "This is not Terez, this is Mima."

Pellaz stared at her, as he might stare at a wonder of the world. "Mima?" he said.

She stepped away from Flick and returned Pell's stare. She looked dazed. "Are you real? Has Lileem sent you?"

He frowned. "Who? No. Mima, I can't believe this. You look . . ." He shook his head.

"I am har," she said. "That is how I look."

"That's impossible."

"No, it's not. I'm your sister and you rose from the dead. The Cevarros are capable of anything." She laughed uncertainly. "How are we supposed to do this? This is a big reunion. There should be trumpets or something."

"Did Terez do this to you?"

"No," Mima said. She turned to Flick. "I can't deal with this now. You don't know what's happened."

"Then tell me," Flick said.

"Lileem and Terez—I think they took aruna together. They disappeared. I think it's like the otherlanes. I'm not sure. They've just gone. We need to get them back." She looked at her brother. "Is this why you're here? Can you help us?"

"I'm sorry," Pellaz said, "I have no idea what you're talking about. Mima, you look marvelous."

"Thanks, so do you." She appealed to Flick. "What do we do? Should we tell Kaa? I just don't know."

"Is this what you were trying to tell me?" Pellaz said to Flick. "About Mima, a woman becoming har?"

"Flick, what are we going to do?" Mima said.

"Be quiet, both of you," Flick said. "One thing at a time." He looked up for Ulaume, seeking support, but Ulaume had gone. There was no time to think about that. "We can't do anything about Lileem and Terez immediately. We don't know what's happened. You might be worrying over nothing."

"I found their clothes," Mima said. "There was a big light, and we saw them, just for a second, then they just weren't there. Where are they?"

"I don't know," Flick said. He felt as if he was about to disappear from reality himself and wondered how the universe expected him to deal with two such momentous situations at once. "We need to talk. Mima, Pell wanted to meet you and Terez. He needs to know the truth."

"Where do we begin?" Mima said. "I feel like I'm going to wake up from this crazy dream any moment."

"We all feel like that," Flick said. "And I hope Pell can help us. But first he needs to know what's going on."

"Can we tell the Tigron?" Mima asked, as if Pellaz wasn't standing there listening to them.

"Probably not," Flick said. "At least Kaa and her kind wouldn't want us too. But he's family, Mima. Haven't you always said that's important?"

She nodded and addressed Pellaz, who'd had the grace to remain quiet since Flick had asked him to. "I'm having difficulty accepting this is really you, but then after what I've seen tonight anything is possible."

"I have never dared think about you," Pellaz said. "This is as disorientating to me as it is to you. I'm glad to see you, Mima. This is a gift I'd never have expected."

She grinned, rather crookedly. "My brothers are adept at disappearing and reappearing in unbelievable circumstances. I only hope Terez keeps up the tradition."

Ulaume realized he had to accept that whatever hideous situation you can think of, fate will always devise something worse. It was clear to him now that Flick had been seeing Pellaz-har-Aralis, Tigron of Immanion, in secret and that this was why he'd lost interest in their chesna-bond. Who could blame him? Pellaz: beautiful, alive, and as distant as a star. He'd been a friend of Flick's once, and obviously still was: perhaps more than a friend. The Tigron's only memories of Ulaume, however, would be of a Kakkahaar whore who had once tried to strangle him with his hair. But how could Flick do this? How had he kept it so quiet?

It's bizarre, Ulaume thought, as he went to consume two bottles of Lileem's wine in the yard at home, *you think you know a har, but you really don't at all. How can the nicest har in the world turn out to be more deceitful, cunning, and sly than the most irredeemable of Kakkahaar?*

Now that he thought he'd lost Flick for definite, he realized how deep his feelings ran. He'd thought Flick had felt the same. Ulaume was convinced the otherlanes had somehow affected Flick. That damned spooky horse must have carried him off to Immanion the first chance it got.

I should find myself a suicidal Kamagrian, Ulaume thought, *and together we could pop out of existence. Perhaps there is another world. Perhaps Terez and Lileem are there now.*

He drank himself into deeper gloom, stretched out on a hard wooden bench. The dawn had begun, stealing over the land in an annoyingly serene and beautiful way. Ulaume only wanted to shoot the birds that sang rapturously in the oaks that lined the street beyond the yard. He really couldn't think what would happen to him next. Oblivion seemed the only option.

The sound of voices and doors opening and closing in the house advised Ulaume that Flick and Mima had come home. He wondered whether they had the illustrious Tigron with them. It seemed unlikely such a prestigious har would set foot in a humble dwelling like theirs, even though Pellaz derived from humble beginnings himself. Ulaume felt numb, incapable of rationalizing anything. The murmur of voices lulled him to sleep and as he drifted off, he imagined they talked about him, listing his faults. He imagined Pellaz told the others some of the terrible things Ulaume had done with Lianvis and that he should be thrown into a pit full of scorpions. Ulaume could hear them all laughing.

The laughter faded away and Ulaume was back in time. He dreamed of a powerful ritual, of Lianvis taking the life of a human child to curry favor with Hubisag. But when the moment came for the child to die, Ulaume did not help Lianvis kill. Instead, he called upon the dehar Aruhani, who manifested as a har with the lower body of a great serpent. The dehar spat poisonous fire that momentarily blinded Lianvis and his shamans. He carried Ulaume and the child up into the air in a black cloud that hid them from the world. In this cloud, Aruhani said, "It is your task to care for the little one now. Go into the wilderness, hide him from danger, and you will be absolved."

Ulaume woke with a start. His body was drenched with sweat because he was lying in the sun. His head ached in several different places, which made him smile sadly, because that was the sort of headache Lileem always had. He *had* cared for her. She was the child in the wilderness. And now, she had gone. Everything had gone.

"Ulaume?"

He opened his eyes and a black shadow stood over him. "Terez . . . ?"

"No." The figure hunkered down and Ulaume saw that it was Pellaz. "It seems that my siblings and I are always confused with one another." He looked so different and yet so similar to how Ulaume remembered. Ulaume couldn't think of anything to say.

"I'm sorry I've caused a problem," Pellaz said. "I have been meeting Flick for some time, and asked him not to tell you. I shouldn't have. It's not his fault."

Ulaume still could not speak, which he knew was most unlike him.

"I have heard so many strange and wonderful things. If my story is incredible, yours and Flick's is no less so. You left your tribe for the sake of a harling that wasn't even yours. That took guts."

"Don't patronize me," Ulaume said, finding his voice. "You've destroyed my life. Stupid of me to think I could have one." He tried to sit up and groaned. The effect of the alcohol would take a couple of hours to wear off, despite harish ability to shrug off the consequences of overindulgence. He decided to remain lying down, even if it did put him in a position of disadvantage.

"I have no idea what to say to you," Pellaz said. "I don't know you. The har that's been described to me by those who love you is not the one I met."

"We've all changed," Ulaume said.

"I haven't destroyed your life," Pellaz said. "I've only been talking to Flick, nothing more. I'm not trying to lure him to Immanion, if that's what you think. I just needed a friend."

Ulaume realized, even through the fog in his brain, that Pellaz was offering a lot. He was Tigron. He didn't have to explain himself. Flick must have asked him to. It was still too incredible to look upon him. The night of Hubisag's festival came back to Ulaume. He could remember the smell of the fire. He could remember his frustrated desire. But what made his heart hurt now was the thought of Flick inside the house.

Pellaz sat down on the ground beside Ulaume's bench. "I want to help with finding Terez and Lileem. I was thinking maybe Peridot, my *sedu,* could try to find them. Mima thinks that aruna between hara and parazha opens a portal to another realm. It's amazing . . ." He shook his head. "I feel like I've been fast asleep and have just woken up to find the entire world has changed."

"It has."

"Thank you for what you did for Mima. Without you, she would be dead."

"That was hardly her sentiment at the time. Anyway, Lileem did it, not me."

"You know what you did," Pellaz said. He drew in his breath. "There were differences between us once. I judged you."

"Don't," Ulaume said, "this is too embarrassing."

Pellaz reached out and took a lock of Ulaume's hair in his hand. "I heard what happened with the Uigenna. It must have been—"

"It was." Ulaume couldn't resist flexing that hair a little. It curled around Pell's wrist like a tiny snake.

Pellaz just watched it. He didn't move. "Come inside," he said.

"No," Ulaume said. "I appreciate you coming out here, but I don't need to hear it from you."

"Don't you?"

"No," Ulaume said. "I really don't."

Pellaz stood up and Ulaume's hair dropped from his wrist. "I'll tell him," he said.

"No. Say nothing."

Pellaz smiled. "I understand."

Ulaume thought about what he'd do if Flick didn't come out to find him. How long should he wait? He needed to use the bathroom, but didn't want to go slinking into the house. He didn't want to walk past them all.

The back door opened, and Ulaume was convinced it would be Mima, coming out to tell him to stop being stupid. But then Flick was there, looking down at him with uncertainty and concern. "Lor, do you want something to eat?"

Ulaume sat up. "That'd be good."

Flick hesitated.

"You're hovering," Ulaume said. "It's all right. I'm fine."

"Are *we*?" Flick pulled a sour face, and then growled. "Shit, that was a stupid thing to say. Of course we're not."

Ulaume pulled Flick down onto the bench beside him. "Do you want us to be fine?"

"Do you?"

"Mmm, I might go all human on you and demand some kind of commitment."

"I've been bad. I'm sorry. It's been a strange time."

"Kiss and make up?"

Flick smiled. "Okay."

Mima came out into the yard some minutes later. "I hate to break up this fond reconciliation," she said, "but Opalexian has got wind of Pell being here. We've been summoned to Kalalim."

Opalexian was the most reclusive of Kamagrian. Few hara or parazha ever saw her. It was said that she spent her time in meditation, trying to fathom out what Kamagrian and Wraeththu were, how they had come to be and where they were heading. She was reputed to be so powerful a psychic, it was no surprise her sensitive inner eyes and ears had known that Pellaz had come to her city. His charisma disturbed the ethers. He was too big a presence not to affect the very air in Opalexian's private chambers.

Hara and parazha drifting home from the festival in the early morning had witnessed Mima and Flick taking a magnificent and clearly powerful har into their home. Comments were made about how *that* particular household seemed to bring strangers home fairly regularly. Word reached Kalalim swiftly and by this time, Opalexian had been shocked out of her predawn devotions by an intrusion of forceful energy. It felt, to her, like an invasion of her city.

Neither Flick nor any of his companions had met Opalexian before. When they'd first arrived in Shilalama, they'd expected to be interviewed by her, not realizing how reclusive she actually was. They soon discovered that Exalan was her eyes and ears in the city, her right-hand har. When he spoke, it was with Opalexian's authority. However, that day, when Flick and Mima were taken into Exalan's private office, he was not alone.

A tall parage with long dark red hair, dressed in a simple black robe, stood before the window, while Exalan was seated behind his desk. The parage had bare feet and her clasped hands were concealed in the voluminous sleeves of her robe. Like Tel-an-Kaa in her true state, she was as androgynous as a har, but with a certain ambience that suggested she was Kamagrian rather than Wraeththu. Her face was beautifully sculpted, with wide almond-shaped eyes and high brows. She did not look very happy. Flick guessed at once who she was.

Exalan did not stand up as Flick and Mima entered the room, which normally he would have done, being a har of precise manners. Flick knew at once they were in deep trouble, and that a side of the Roselane they had not witnessed before might very well be about to manifest. Pellaz had been asked to wait outside, and even though Ulaume had offered to stay with him, Flick wasn't absolutely sure the Tigron would comply with that for long. No har or parage, however high-ranking they considered themselves to be, should ask the Tigron of Immanion to sit in a waiting room.

"You have a new outside visitor to your home," Exalan said to Mima. "May we ask if this is yet another member of your ever-expanding family?"

"It is my brother," Mima said.

"You seem to have an inexhaustible supply."

Flick had never heard Exalan be sarcastic before, nor use such a cold tone. His usual guise was of benign and humble servant of the city.

"It is my brother, Pellaz," Mima said, with some defiance.

The tall parage stepped forward. "We are aware of his identity," she said.

Exalan made a respectful gesture. "May I present Opalexian to you, High Priestess and First Parage of this city."

Mima ducked her head a little, but it appeared awkward and grudging. She was ready for a fight. Flick realized how immense a force the Cevarros could be if they closed ranks. Because Pellaz wanted strong hara around him, he would really benefit from having Mima back in his life. He needed Terez and Dorado too, probably. Flick wondered if the Tigron had realized this for himself yet.

"Facts," said Opalexian in a smooth, reasonable voice. Her tone was low, seductive. She reminded Flick very strongly of someone, but he couldn't think who. "Last night, there was a severe etheric disturbance in my garden. You investigated the phenomenon, were virtually first on the scene. You reported nothing. In the light of day, my staff searched the area and uncovered an amount of clothing and some very strange trace residue of a paranormal event."

She paused, but Mima offered nothing, her face set into an inscrutable expression.

"Almost simultaneously with this discovery, I become aware of a very powerful harish force in this city. Its signature is unique. It is the Tigron of Immanion."

Again a pause, and again Mima's silence.

Opalexian sighed through her nose. "I see. I ask myself if these two events are connected. Where are the other members of your household?"

"We were not told we all had to come," Flick said.

"Where are they?" Opalexian asked.

"We don't know," Flick said.

Opalexian stared at him, and he was sure she could see right into his mind, even though he wasn't aware of mind-touch. "I can only take a dim view of the Tigron being invited to my city. You are all aware that it is the wish of the Roselane for the Gelaming, if not Wraeththu as a whole, to remain ignorant of their existence. The Tigron's presence here puts every citizen in jeopardy. You were given sanctuary here, a home and a life. Is this how you repay us? I am waiting for your explanation, if indeed there is one, beyond the fact that Mima Cevarro cannot surrender her old human ties."

"No, I cannot!" Mima said, and Flick put a hand on her arm to restrain her.

"We can explain," Flick said. "This is not how it seems. As you know, Pellaz consented to come here. He is sitting outside this room like a common har. I hope you understand the message in that. It is not his intention to cause you trouble. He is here because of me, and because of his family."

"Tel-an-Kaa has informed me of the circumstances surrounding your journey to Shilalama. I am aware of Mima's and Terez's connection with the Tigron, and of yours. But in this city, all hara, parazha and humans are equal. Such weighty connections have no bearing here, and I had hoped you all felt the same. You accepted our way of life and have benefited from it. Where is Terez and the parage, Lileem?"

"I think you know," Mima said.

"I would like to hear it from you."

"We believe they took aruna together," Flick said, "with the inevitable consequences."

"And you summoned the Tigron here to ask for his aid?" Opalexian enquired.

"No," Flick said. "That was coincidence. I have been meeting him in the mountains for some time. I told him nothing about the Kamagrian, not until last night."

Opalexian took a deep breath, clearly having difficulty controlling herself. Flick sensed she'd like to bawl them out, but couldn't quite bring herself to do it and destroy the illusion of the character she had built. "It is forbidden for hara and parazha to become intimate," she said. "You all know this."

"Sometimes, feelings get in the way of common sense," Flick said. "That is the only explanation I can give."

"Your friends are lost to you now." Opalexian fixed Mima with a cold gaze. "I hope you realize you cannot risk doing something similar in an attempt to find them. If you do, you will all die."

"They are not dead," Mima said.

"Effectively, they are," Opalexian said. "The matter is closed, and you will deal with your grief as you see fit. Now, as to the other question—"

"Pellaz is not your enemy," Flick butted in. "He will speak for himself, of course, but in my opinion, it would be in your best interests to befriend him now. He will not betray you if you offer him loyalty."

Opalexian hissed and seemed to grow taller, her hair lifting from her head like a cat's fur. Flick realized who she reminded him of now: Thiede.

"I do not need some little har telling me how to conduct my affairs," she said. "I offer loyalty to none but my own tribe. The Gelaming are warmongers and tyrants. Their worldview has no empathy with mine."

"Pellaz is an individual," Flick said. "He is not the whole tribe of Gelaming. He has been placed into a role by Thiede. He is not entirely happy with it. He needs allies."

Opalexian raised an eyebrow, and Flick realized that with those last three words he had somehow captured her attention, and perhaps her cooperation. It came to him as a blinding revelation: Thiede and Opalexian were known to one another, and they were not in accord.

"I will speak to him," she said, "but first, I want the entire story from you two, with no details omitted—and, trust me, if you lie or prevaricate, I will know. We have methods of extracting information from the mind, so I suggest you cooperate willingly. It will save time, trouble, and possible hurt in the future."

"Your parazha have no idea what you're really like, do they!" Mima said. "Humble priestess, my ass!"

Opalexian smiled at this. "You are correct," she said. "Become accustomed to it."

CHAPTER THIRTY-THREE

Lileem came to her senses, buried naked in sand. She was lying on her back and only her face wasn't covered in the scouring, shifting granules. She opened her eyes to a sky blistered with huge stars, with the ammonite whorls of spinning galaxies, with great nebulas of purple and blue gases. Comets scrawled across the night, in a thousand different trails of light. The firmament was alive above her.

Before attempting to get up, she flexed each limb and mentally scanned her body for injury, but found none. If anything, she felt more alert and vital than she had for years. "I am alive," she thought, "and I am in another realm."

The landscape was immense, huge cliffs and pinnacles of obsidian rock rising all around her. They were so much younger than the mountains of her home plane, roughly sculpted, their sides raw and sharp. The sand beneath her feet was silver gray in the light of the stars, and it glittered with mica. There was no moon, but even so the light was brilliant. The air smelled of the same strange scent she'd experienced during aruna with Terez: there was no way to describe it, other than mustily sweet, but not unpleasant. At least she could breathe it. She hadn't considered that important fact when she'd planned to come here: the air might have been toxic. Was this not another sign that she was meant to come?

She must look for Terez. Not for one moment did she think he was hurt or dead. She was in a deep valley that looked as if it had been gouged from the rock by a gargantuan machine or perhaps a glacier. The sides of the cliffs were scored with horizontal crevices. There was no sign of life, either of plant or animal. Lileem began to walk around, carefully scanning the ground. She wondered how, if the air was breathable, there was no life. It didn't make sense.

She found Terez in a hole near to where she'd woken up. He was conscious and unhurt, but very disorientated. Lileem offered him an arm and he managed to haul himself out. For some minutes, he had to sit on the ground, breathing deeply. Lileem put her hands on his shoulders and blasted him with healing energy. Eventually, he reached up to touch one of her hands and said, "I'm okay."

Lileem stood up. "We did it," she said.

Terez looked around himself. "Anyone else here?"

"Doesn't seem so. We have to find the opening in the ground we saw. It must be around here somewhere."

Terez stood up beside her, caught hold of her shoulder to steady himself. "What is this place?"

"I think it's another realm of existence, another dimension," she said. "Look at the sky."

Together, they gazed at the stars. "It is beautiful," Terez said. "Amazing."

They walked up the valley for hours and then the sun came up. That, in itself, was magnificent. The sun was an incandescent inferno, so much bigger than the sun they knew. It rose above the horizon like a god. They could hear it: the sound of a thousand furnaces igniting at once. Before it rose fully, they could see white flames shooting from its surface, but once it had risen above the mountains its light was blinding. The black cliffs lost their color. It was like being in a void of white light. Terez and Lileem held onto each other's hands, because they could hardly see each other. They had become like cloudy ghosts.

"We should be burned," Terez said. "We should be blind."

"But we're not," Lileem said.

It was difficult to keep traveling, because they could barely see anything. Strange how in this place, it was easy to see at night, but the opposite during the day. Lileem could feel the heat on her skin, as she could smell the air, but it was not uncomfortable. She wondered whether the journey had changed them somehow, made them able to withstand the unfamiliar elements.

At midday, it became impossible to keep moving. They kept bumping into rocks. Terez noticed a faint shadow to their right and when they went to it, they found a narrow cave entrance. Once inside, they could see each other again. They groped their way deep into the rock and then sat down on the sandy floor. It should have been as black as pitch in there, but it wasn't. They could see each other quite easily.

"I'm not hungry or thirsty," Terez said. "Are you?"

Lileem thought about it. "No. We should be. Neither have I needed to take a pee or anything."

"Nor me. I don't feel hot or cold either. Something has happened to us."

"We'll just have to hope it's reversible."

"Of course we might be technically dead," Terez said. "We might be spirits now."

"That's a possibility," Lileem conceded. "Strange. I'm not that bothered."

"I wonder what Mima and the others are thinking," Terez said. "Will they have guessed what happened?"

"I think so," Lileem replied. "Mima will guess. I said a few things to her recently."

Terez wrinkled up his nose: an unrestrained childish expression. "You know, I've never felt this good in my skin before. Nothing is uncomfortable and my mind is just—hell, how do I describe it?—just peaceful."

"Perhaps we are dead, then."

Terez nodded. "Yeah." He smiled. "What a way to go!"

They did not feel a change of temperature on their skins, but they knew that night was falling, because the light faded in the cavern. Terez led the way back outside and as before the brilliant sky enacted its otherworld carnival overhead. Most important, they could now see they had wandered into an area where, even if creatures no longer inhabited it, at one time they had created buildings. An enormous structure of obsidian rose from the sand at the end of the valley. It was roughly pyramidal in shape, and many turrets, towers, and open-air walkways clustered all over it. The structure was not just an edifice; it was a mountain, carved from the glassy black rock. Beyond it, lay the ocean, a vast expanse of metallic water that shimmered with the reflections of stars.

The gates to the building, or perhaps city, were dwarfed by the size of the structure above them, but when Lileem and Terez reached them, they found the entrance was at least fifty feet high. Doors of obsidian stood open and sand had blown onto the floor beyond.

Inside was a vast chamber, with many dark entrances leading off it. It was empty but for a seated black statue, so huge it was impossible to see its face from below. Each of its feet was the size of a modest nayati. Was this a king or a god? It reminded Lileem of her vision of the Tigron. To walk around it would take a long time. Lileem touched the stone of the dais: it towered a good ten feet above her head. "This is not what we're looking for," she said. "We need to find the entrance to the underground place."

"Maybe it's beneath here," Terez said. "We should look."

"It'll take us a hundred years to explore all those passages," Lileem said.

"The way I feel, that won't be a problem."

"Time might not exist here, not in the same way we know it."

"Exactly."

It felt strange not to eat and drink, because those little rituals provided much of what anchored you to reality, to mundane life, to progression of the hours. Neither did Lileem or Terez feel the need to sleep. They explored the building for what seemed like days, and the sun did not rise again. There was no furniture, no other decoration or carvings, no indication of who had built the place or why: just endless chambers and corridors that would sometimes lead them out onto a balcony that overlooked the endless ocean. There were lots of stairways leading up, but none leading down. If there was a nether-world to this strange building, it was difficult to find.

Eventually, they found their way back to the main chamber and went out-side. A strange purple hue was cast over the land, and the stars were dimmer, which perhaps indicated the sun was about to rise again.

"How long have we been here?" Lileem wondered aloud. "Weeks, months?"

These were questions that did not require an answer. In their own realm, more time might have passed, or none at all. "We should investigate around the edge of the building," Terez said.

Not once had either of them suggested to the other that they should try to return to their own reality. They were consumed by the desire to find what they'd come to find. Beneath the ground lay a secret that was waiting for them to discover it. Sometimes they could hear it whispering to them in wordless songs.

The sun, when it rose, was not the same one they'd seen before. It was far dimmer: a violet globe surrounded by a crimson nimbus. It dyed the sky a magnificent imperial color and at the edge of its influence, the jewels of the heavens still shone. It was this sun that revealed the entrance to the hidden place that Terez and Lileem were seeking.

In the light of this new sun, the world appeared different. Lileem could discern details on the outside of the building she had not seen before: carvings of what looked like an ancient forgotten alphabet. The purple shadows across the gargantuan walls picked out faint outlines of what might have been depictions of creatures, but the light concealed as much as it revealed, for it had a shifting elusive quality.

While she was examining the walls, Terez scouted around at ground level. It was he who uncovered the dark shaft leading downward, its entrance partially covered by fallen boulders and moving shadows. The entrance led into a down-sloping passageway, which was triangular in shape. "This is what we came for," Lileem said and took the first steps into the darkness.

Beyond the meager light from outside, the walls exuded a faint radiance, so it was possible to see a few feet in all directions. Lileem's heart had increased in pace, and she realized it was the first time she'd been aware of her body's physical functions since she'd arrived in this strange realm.

The passage led deep below the ground, and as they progressed Lileem felt as if her head was under pressure. It was not a headache exactly, but more a feeling of uncertainty and anxiety. She mentioned it to Terez who said he felt nauseous.

"It's almost as if something's trying to make us turn back," he said.

"Do we carry on?" Lileem asked him. "It might be dangerous."

"Of course we carry on. If we're dead, we can't die twice."

They joked about being dead, but Lileem didn't really believe they were. Surely, if that were true, they wouldn't care about anything from their previous lives. They'd just drift off to become part of the cosmos itself, or else be in some kind of afterlife with other spirits. Perhaps it was time she worked out her idea of what the afterlife might be. She was sure it wasn't this.

It was impossible for them to determine how long they walked along the sloping passageway, but eventually they came to a circular chamber, around ten feet wide, and with a low ceiling. The walls of this chamber were carved with various lines and circles, which again suggested a language of some kind. Lileem walked around the chamber, one hand against the smooth walls. The place was built of a greenish soapy stone, with veins of darkness running through it. "Where is the light coming from?" she said. "It must be from the stone itself, but it doesn't seem that way. It just *is*."

"What was that?" Terez snapped.

"What was what?"

"A sound . . ."

They both stood still, ears straining. Then Lileem heard it: a distant thump from far below their feet. Simultaneously, the floor moved. At first Lileem thought it was some kind of earth tremor, but then she realized the floor had begun to drop. The chamber was a moving platform, and now they were going down.

Lileem put her arms around Terez. "This is it," she said. "For good or bad, we're going to find out . . ."

"What we're here for," he finished. They held each other tightly.

The platform moved down at a slow, regular rate, with a faint scraping sound. Below them, they could still hear the rhythmic thumping, which perhaps derived from the mechanisms that operated the platform. "Someone or something must be working this thing," Terez said.

"I don't think so," Lileem said. "I think it's automatic. It just started up because we stepped onto it."

"Let's hope it works the same way in reverse."

But maybe, Lileem thought, *we won't want or need to go back.* There might be another secret to uncover beyond and another and another. More realms to explore. It could be endless. Lileem pressed her forehead against Terez's shoulder. *Why don't I care? Why aren't I frightened to be so far away from my own world, and those I love? Why don't I worry about getting back? Do I have to make a decision about that?*

Entrances in the walls of the shaft reared into view, and the platform came to a halt. They were in another circular chamber: the end of the ride. The air smelled faintly metallic. Lileem chose a passageway at random and pulled Terez into it. She half expected the platform to rise again and leave them stranded, but it remained where it was. The walls in the passageway were veined with light. When Lileem touched them, she found they were warm.

Other passageways led off from the one they were following, and when they ventured into one of them, what they found beyond the threshold stopped them in their tracks. Was this a chamber or another corridor? It was difficult to tell. The space was high and narrow and appeared to be constructed of long vertical bricks in rows. On each brick was a symbol of light. The corridor, if such it was, stretched into the distance for as far as they could see.

Lileem was drawn to one wall and let her hands hover over the stones. She closed her eyes, and moved her fingers from left to right. She could feel differences in the air, as if energy vibrated more strongly in certain areas. Opening her eyes, she placed the first finger of one hand against a glowing symbol. At once, a hissing sound emitted from the wall and a slab of stone slid out, almost knocking her backward.

"Lee!" Terez cried, taking hold of her.

"I'm all right," she said. "Look . . ."

The stone that now poked out into the corridor and almost blocked their way was covered in marks, convoluted symbols of spirals and lines. Lileem touched them, and as she did so, a series of images flashed through her mind, a jumble of squiggles and dots. "These aren't bricks," she said to Terez. She touched the glowing symbol again and the stone retreated into the wall. Quickly, she touched another one and another stone slid out. It was different, of a pinkish color, and the symbols upon it were more angular and spare. Lileem sent it back into the wall, touched another one.

"What are you doing?" Terez said. He appeared reluctant to touch the stones himself. "What does this mean?"

Lileem did not answer for some moments, too intent on sliding different slabs in and out of the wall. Although their spines were of the same greenish stone, their inner sides were of many different kinds of stone, and the markings upon them also differed. Some were pictograms, like hieroglyphs, while others were nothing more than ranked series of dots. "I know what this place is," she said. "It's a library."

"We can't read what's here."

"Not yet, but we have all the time in the world."

"Wait," Terez said. He pulled Lileem away from the wall, his hands on her shoulders. "Lee, we must think about this. How long have we been here? Come on, we can't just lose ourselves in this dream. We should try to get home. We wanted to see if we could get here, and now we know we can, but we should also think about returning to the real world. We should think about it now."

"How can we?" Lileem snapped, pulling away from him. "Can't you see how important this is?" She gestured dramatically with her arms. "This place is a storehouse of knowledge, perhaps *the* storehouse, where the history of the universe is hidden. How can you even think about leaving here?"

"Because if we came here once, we can come again. We should try to get back, tell other hara about this."

"We might not be able to come back."

"Lee! Listen to yourself. Remember our world. Remember those we left behind. Remember your life."

"It's not important," Lileem said angrily.

"You don't mean that. Not really. Anyway, think about the responsibilities you have. Other hara and parazha might have ended up here. We need to get back to tell the world what really happens when we come together."

"There isn't anyone else around. We haven't seen a living soul. No har or parage has come here before."

"Then what happened to them? Think, Lee. Don't be selfish."

Lileem put her hands against the walls. She was hungry for knowledge. She was sure that if she looked at enough of the stone books, she'd find some in a language she knew. Time meant nothing here. She was free of the restrictions of the flesh. She could devote herself to study. *Why am I so obsessed?* she wondered. *What is it that calls to me here?*

"We should go now," Terez said. "Perhaps before it's too late."

Lileem stared at him for some moments. "We must come back."

"We will. But for now I want to feel alive again. I want to eat and sleep and *be*. This is not life. We must take aruna together again."

"If we can. I haven't felt the faintest tremor of desire since we came here."

"Which is not normal. Remember how we felt, how much we wanted each other. What has happened to that? Don't you want it back?"

Lileem smiled bitterly. "We have no idea whether aruna will even take us back home or somewhere else."

"No, but we have to try." He held out his hand. "Lee?"

She sighed through her nose and took his fingers in hers. "I know you're right, but . . . this place, it's reached right into me. Part of me belongs here."

"You made a promise to me that you could bring us home, remember?" Terez said. "Don't break it."

"So, what do we do? Try it here?"

"I think we should return to the place where we arrived in this realm. That would be the safest bet. Otherwise we might reappear in our world in the middle of a wall or something. At the very least, we'll find out whether the stone elevator works both ways."

When they retraced their steps to the circular chamber and it began to rise beneath them, Lileem could feel Terez's spirits soar. He was desperate to get home and had perhaps always felt that way. They had found the entrance to the underground world and that was what they had come for. Terez had had enough. He wasn't drawn to this realm like Lileem was.

As they began the long journey back along the deep valley, Lileem was already thinking in terms of how she might return here alone. It wasn't fair to drag somehar with her who didn't share her interest, or who was not prepared to surrender their mundane life to the search for knowledge. Lileem was now convinced her overwhelming desire for Terez had simply been an instinctive device to get her here. In the stone library resided the secrets of who and what she was. The genesis of Wraeththu and Kamagrian were hidden there, she was sure. It was the library at the end of the universe, the legendary Hall of Records that held the secrets of creations written by gods. No har, no parage, no human was ever meant to find it, because knowledge of this kind was not for mortal creatures. But beyond humanity, and its self-destruction, lay the accident of Wraeththu and Kamagrian, and the shared ability, bigger than the sum of its parts, which meant that together hara and parazha could plunder this secret realm. Did high-ranking hara and parazha already know this? Lileem would not be surprised to discover this was so. Perhaps they already came here and sought to keep it secret from those of lower caste. Humans had been confined in their flesh, denied access to worlds beyond their perception. Most had not even believed such realms existed.

This is how we are more developed than them, Lileem thought. *This must be our purpose, our meaning.*

But what use was this knowledge? Lileem and Terez found the place where they had been born into this world. They shared breath and touched one another, seeking the feeling that had drawn them together. But it was something they had left behind them. No spark of desire could be kindled here, no intimate sharing of body and mind. They were as empty as the bleak landscape around them. There would be no journey home.

CHAPTER THIRTY-FOUR

Flick knew he would never discover the whole truth about what the Tigron and Opalexian said to one another at their first meeting. He and Mima were sent from the room, as was Exalan, and Flick could tell Opalexian's aide was far from pleased about that. In the room where Ulaume was waiting for them, Exalan told them to return home, which they did.

The house seemed cold and desolate, empty as it was of Lileem and Terez's presence. Now, once the enormity of recent events began to settle in their minds, a sense of grief and loss crept into the dark rooms, made everything look cluttered and comfortless. Mima began to tidy up, perhaps seeking to bring back the spirit of place that seemed to have flown out of the windows.

Ulaume and Flick went to bed, exhausted and drained. Flick lay in Ulaume's arms and drifted into a troubled sleep, racked by fragments of disturbing dreams. Their whole life had shattered. He and Ulaume were together again, in mind and body, but things would never be the same. Opalexian was angry with them all, and it might be they'd have to leave Shilalama. Lileem and Terez were gone and they had no idea how to find them. The Gelaming horses might provide a means to travel in other worlds, but there were infinite other worlds, many of them perhaps bigger than the one they knew. Lileem and Terez could be anywhere. They could indeed be dead.

That evening, a messenger from Kalalim delivered another summons to the palace. Flick was sure they would now be asked to leave the city. Pellaz had not returned to them and because he had taken Peridot with him to Kalalim earlier, he might already have gone back to Immanion. The interview with Opalexian could have proceeded very badly. Flick was now regretting opening his mouth to Pellaz. He had been stupid. He should have just ended the meetings and put it all behind him. Instead, he had torn up the very fabric of their security. The Kamagrian would have been furious enough about Terez and Lileem. Why make matters worse by bringing the Tigron of Immanion into their city?

Opalexian received them in her private salon and her initial mien of relaxed sociability was intimidating, if not disorientating. Perhaps the meeting with the Tigron had not gone as badly as Flick had feared.

"Pellaz has returned to Immanion," she said to them, "but asked me to convey his apologies. He will contact you again presently."

"What of Lileem and Terez?" Mima asked. "Will you help Pellaz find them for us?"

Opalexian paused. "The Tigron has intimated he will undertake a search. However, I hold out little hope for his success."

It occurred to Flick then that Opalexian might not want Lileem and Terez to be found. They had transgressed one of the Kamagrian's laws, and it might not portray a desirable message to the populace if they returned safe and sound.

"What of us?" Flick asked. "Where do we stand?"

Opalexian made a languid gesture. "You are citizens of Shilalama. It is not our way to dole out punishments. In the event, your unwise and headstrong actions have yielded some interesting, and beneficial, results."

"Does that mean we can continue living here?" Ulaume asked.

"Yes, although if any of you attempt a similar experiment to that of your unfortunate friends, whichever one of you remains will be expelled. Is that not reasonable?"

"You're happy with the Tigron knowing about Kamagrian?" Flick asked carefully.

"We have come to an arrangement," Opalexian said. "That is all you need to know. I am assured of his silence, as he is assured of my . . . cooperation. The reason I have summoned you here tonight is to impress upon you that you must mention to no other citizen that Pellaz has been here. If anyhar or parage asks, you were merely visited by a high-caste friend from another Jaddayoth tribe. Invent your own story. But it had better be convincing, because I will be displeased should this information come out. That, incidentally, is the only other circumstance under which you will be removed from our community—far removed, I might add."

"Did you threaten Pellaz in a similar way?" Mima asked coldly.

Opalexian smiled. "I'm sorry this sounds like threats. Please put yourself in my position. My whole purpose is to safeguard the well-being of my tribe and strange though it may sound to you, I look upon you three as fondly as anyone else in this city. You are like naughty children, and you need to know the rules, but I trust you understand that now."

"You said Pell would contact us again," Mima said. "Does that mean he will return to Shilalama."

"He will not be seen in the streets," Opalexian said. "You will meet him here at Kalalim in future. Only Exalan and ourselves will know of these meetings. I have granted the Tigron access to you, Mima, because of your relationship. These things are not supposed to be of importance to hara and parazha, but because of Pellaz's unique position, this has to occasion an exception."

"So, we will be supervised."

"Not exactly. You will be given time alone together, if that is what you should wish."

But close enough for you to listen in, Flick thought.

Opalexian cast him a piercing glance and smiled.

Pellaz did not contact Flick, or any of the others, for over a month. Long though they talked into the night on a regular basis, trying to think of ways to find their lost friends, no ideas sprang to mind. They could not risk trying to duplicate the event, because they had no certainty they'd end up in the same place. And if Lileem and Terez *had* been torn apart or vaporized by what they'd done, it would be insane to follow their path.

The house felt different, as if the bricks themselves were grieving. Every day, Flick returned from his patrols and was still surprised not to see Lileem in the kitchen, laying out food and utensils for him to use. She'd always prepare the vegetables before he got home, and then act as his assistant throughout the cooking process, as if that was the greatest honor in the world. Flick hated cooking alone now, and if Mima or Ulaume offered to help, they only got on his nerves, because they didn't work with him in the same smooth way that Lileem had always done. During the day, Flick would have ideas and think, "I must tell Lee this," only to realize with a cold shudder that he could no longer do that.

Mima blamed herself, as was her nature. She should have paid more heed when Lileem had dropped hints she was interested in taking aruna with a har. She should have retold the story of her time with Chelone as the frightening thing it was, not just as a party joke. As for Terez, she had healed her rift with him only to lose him again. How could he be so stupid and rash? What had possessed him? And where was Pellaz now that she needed him? They'd had no time to re-forge their relationship or explore its new boundaries. How could she possibly care about her work on the farm when everything had turned out so terrible?

Ulaume was the least affected, and this was because he was convinced Lileem wasn't dead. Flick remembered his chesnari's certainty that Pellaz still lived, and how right that had turned out to be, so this gave him hope, which he tried to pass on to Mima.

Their friends in Shilalama guessed what had happened to Lileem and Terez, and it seemed this outrageous fact somehow contaminated the rest of the household. Visitors were few, and even Tel-an-Kaa kept her distance. Flick suspected Opalexian might have something to do with that. She wouldn't want to risk one of them letting the information about the Tigron slip out. Be-cause Flick habitually spent so much time alone during the day, the social snubbing affected him the least, but he knew that Mima suffered for it. She might have scorned the Kamagrian, but once their friendship froze away, she missed it. Flick was sure it would all blow over eventually, and he made the decision that at the next festival, he would do all that he could to win back their friends. If they were to continue living in Shilalama, this had to happen. Mima wouldn't hear of going anywhere else, because she wanted to be there, in case Lileem and Terez ever found their way home.

One night, sitting out in the yard as they did every evening, Ulaume pointed at the sky and said, "They are out there. Somewhere. I know it. Some-where in this universe or another, they are alive."

Flick poured out the last of Lileem's wine—they had drunk a lot these past few weeks. "We need Pell," he said. "Where is he?"

Flick rode out to his old meeting place with Pellaz every day, but the Tigron did not return. He even spent hours trying to communicate with Astral, begging the creature to summon Pellaz, pleading with him to find Lileem and Terez. But all Astral could offer in return was a kind of confused sympathy. Flick lacked the ability to truly commune with the *sedu,* and his desperate thoughts were merely a wordless scream in Astral's mind.

Then, just as Flick had given up hope of Pellaz ever contacting him again, a summons came from Kalalim. Exalan came to the house himself to deliver it. The Tigron had returned.

The meeting was ostensibly in private, but Flick was not deceived. In Opalex-ian's place, he too would make sure he heard every word of the conversation.

Pellaz embraced Mima warmly. His presence filled the room with power and light. He had brought them gifts from Immanion: beautiful clothes, perfume, exotic spices for the kitchen, a Gelaming ceremonial bridle for Astral, wrought with filigree silver and tiny diamonds.

"I would have come sooner," he said, "but I've been busy at home. Also, I don't want Vaysh suspecting anything. Nohar must know I come here. I'd been disappearing too regularly before, and it had to stop."

"What was the deal you made with Opalexian?" Ulaume asked.

Flick knew he wouldn't get an honest answer.

"The time is not yet right for Wraeththu to become aware of the Kamagrian's existence," Pellaz said. "There are too many other issues to be resolved first, too many different Wraeththu strands that need to find harmony and accord. Some hara would react very badly to this information. There could be hysterical purges of Kamagrian harlings, or any number of other fearful consequences. Wraeththu are still too new. The knowledge of Kamagrian could make them afraid that hara were reverting to a human state, that we cannot breed true. Fear makes hara do terrible things. I understand this very well. It may be years before the truth can come out, perhaps even centuries."

Flick couldn't imagine how so big a secret could be kept for such a long time.

"So, what do you get for your silence?" Ulaume insisted.

Pellaz stared at Ulaume for some moments, and Flick noticed a flicker of impatience in his gaze. "I am Tigron. I do not necessarily require something in return. I do what is best for harakind. My love for my race is unconditional, as is Opalexian's for hers. I am grateful to work in harmony with her."

"Work?"

"There is much we can teach one another," Pellaz replied.

"Such as how to control aruna between hara and parazha?" Mima asked hopefully.

Pellaz smiled sadly. "Not that, I'm afraid. None of us are yet advanced enough to understand it."

"Not even Thiede?" Flick asked.

"You know very well I can't confide in Thiede over this."

"But he knows everything, doesn't he?" Flick said. "He must know you've been here. He must know about the Kamagrian."

"No," Pellaz said. "He does not, and that's how it's going to stay for now. I'm not completely helpless. I have learned enough to protect my privacy."

"Will you help us find Lileem and Terez?" Mima said. "Please, Pell. We can't just forget about them. Ulaume knows they're alive, as he knew you were alive. He's never wrong." She turned to Ulaume. "Are you, Lor?"

Ulaume shrugged. "I don't believe so, not in matters of this kind."

Pellaz took a deep sighing breath. "I have tried to find them," he said. "Peridot knows what signature to look for in the otherlanes—one very similar to mine. He has found nothing. The otherlanes and the realms they connect are infinite. The task is virtually impossible. And, unlike Ulaume, I'm not convinced Terez is still alive. I'm sorry, Mima, I think we have to resign ourselves to his loss, and to Lileem's too. I know you were close to her and I appreciate how difficult this must be, but I've carried the burden of loss and grief for a long time, and I know you can live with it eventually. It becomes manageable and then it goes away. Life goes on. We have to move with it."

In a month, it appeared Pellaz had got over his consuming passion for Cal. This did not convince Flick one bit. He knew Pellaz wasn't telling the truth.

"You can't give up looking," Mima said.

"I have to," Pellaz said. "For one thing, I don't have the time. I could devote my life to this task and still not find them."

"Teach Flick how to ride Astral properly, then," Mima said. "You could do that. Then Flick could continue the search. Bring us all one of your weird horses. We could all try."

"I can't," Pellaz said. "The *sedim* are not horses exactly, Mima, and every one is accounted for. It was difficult enough to 'lose' Astral in the first place. Vaysh and I had to concoct a wild story about how he got swept off into the void by an energy storm. We impressed upon the other *sedim* not to reveal the truth, but who can say how they think and feel? We can't fathom their being, not really. I'm not sure to this day whether Thiede believes the story. There's no way I could risk bringing you more *sedim*. And if I removed the restraints on Astral, he'd 'show up' to other creatures of his kind while he was traveling. It's just impossible."

Flick had not realized before how difficult it must have been for Pellaz to arrange for him to keep Astral. He wished he'd known that, months ago. It would have meant a lot.

"There is one thing Opalexian has agreed to do for me," Pellaz said. "I have a human friend in Immanion, called Kate. In time, Opalexian will allow her to come to Shilalama and be made parage. It's the least I could do for her."

"And you trust this woman?" Mima said.

Pellaz smiled. "If somehar had made you the offer, and asked you to swear eternal silence, what would have been your decision? Particularly if you lived with hara. Imagine having to look at yourself every day in the mirror, watch yourself growing old, while your friends stayed the same. Imagine never being able to take aruna. I haven't told Kate about this yet, but I'm fairly confident what her response will be. When the time comes, I'd like you to care for her, Mima. Would you do that? Kate and I have had our ups and downs, not least because she is a close friend of Rue's but I care for her deeply. I would be grateful beyond words if your blood could incept her. It's the closest she could get to me. She is not like the pious Roselane, but a fun-loving and irreverent creature. You'd like her."

Mima's expression was stony. "Are you lining up a replacement for Lileem? If so, forget it."

"I wouldn't be so insensitive. I'm asking you, as a favor."

"All right," Mima said grudgingly, "if Opalexian knows how it should be done properly, I can shed a few drops of blood. I can't promise anything beyond that, however. I might not fancy her."

Pellaz laughed. "You don't know how much it cheers me to hear you talk like this." He took her in his arms again. "Kamagrian is a wondrous gift, Mima. It has given back to me the women I love."

Later, they joined Opalexian for a meal, and spent a pleasant evening in her company. Opalexian was conviviality itself. She drank a lot of wine and appeared to be genuinely tipsy, which indicated a level of trust. Flick knew that Pellaz and the Kamagrian priestess believed they'd sorted everything out, calmed ruffled tempers and dashed all hopes of Lileem and Terez being found. Gifts were offered to keep things sweet. Opalexian asked Mima if she would care to become overseer of the gardens of Kalalim. This would involve a big rise in status. A large house came with the job, and staff to look after it. Mima, Flick, and Ulaume could move into it within a week. Ulaume was good with his hands. It would please Opalexian if he would become her personal sculptor. She would like to commission statues of the dehara, which were, of course, so fascinating. Flick might like to open a temple to them in the city, in fact, to teach hara and parazha all about them. He could appoint a priesthood and devise rituals and ceremonies in the dehara's honor.

These were weighty gifts indeed. Flick was cynical about it. Was there any point in being angry? Probably not. Pellaz's arguments had been sound. There did seem to be little he could do about Lileem and Terez. Opalexian seemed to be taking Mima's relationship to the Tigron seriously. Her offers were genuine enough. *We might as well give in and enjoy it,* Flick thought. *To do otherwise would be stupid.*

So life caught them up in a hectic spin, when there was little time to brood about the past or what had been lost. The new house was beautiful, and attached to the palace complex. It had its own walled garden, with a terrace, and a series of waterfalls that brought back memories of Casa Ricardo. One of the many downstairs rooms was converted into a studio for Ulaume, where he had a sweeping view of the mountains. A staff of parazha came with the house, and Flick knew that the cook, a fearsome parage of short temper called Marmorea, would not look too happily upon him using her kitchen. The food she prepared was excellent, however. She often cooked with hot spices and peppers to remind Mima of home.

At the bottom of the long spacious garden was a small dark wood, and this afforded Pellaz the privacy he needed to visit their home. He would walk up the garden in the evenings, maybe once a month, leaving Peridot in the cover of the trees. The staff in the house believed him to be a high-ranking har from Garridan, and his visits always occasioned a flurry of excitement in the house, because the Garridan were mostly poisoners, and had a reputation for being dangerously romantic creatures. Pellaz would dress in black for these occasions, and his name to the staff was Artemisian.

Flick and the others found that their disapproving friends came flocking back after Opalexian waved her bounteous magical hand over their lives. On many occasions, hara and parazha dropped the hint that they would like to meet the dashing stranger who visited the house. They'd heard the rumors. Who was he? Mima, Flick and Ulaume ignored these less than subtle pleas. Artemisian was a har who guarded his privacy. He did not want to meet new faces.

Flick realized he had much to be thankful for in his life. Most hara would envy all that he had. High-ranking friends, an exclusive relationship with the most important har in Wraeththudom, a beautiful house, meaningful work, and a har he loved at his side. But still, he found himself thinking of Lileem and was plagued by the nagging doubt he hadn't done enough to try and help her. One night, in bed, he confided this thought to Ulaume, and Ulaume took Flick's face in his hands. "I haven't given up hope," he said. "I know that one day Lileem will return to us. I feel it in my heart."

His courage and conviction washed over Flick like the waves of a warm ocean.

"Trust me," Ulaume said.

"With my life," Flick murmured.

It was a special moment. Nothing was said, but Flick lay back and offered himself. There was a sweetness to this surrender he could not describe. His whole body ached. When he felt Ulaume inside him, he thought he might die from the feeling of completeness and love that swelled through his heart. Aruna had never been like this: so gentle, yet so intense.

There came a moment when Ulaume stopped moving and whispered, "We don't have to go on."

Flick stared into his eyes. "This is how much I trust you," he said. And he felt a part of him open up. It hurt a little, but soon the pain was forgotten in the overwhelming and blissful sensation that came afterward.

In this way, Flick and Ulaume conceived their first child.

The seasons stole over the land in their gowns of white, green, and russet. Clouds moved across the sky, from day to night, and the years passed. When Flick's son was born, he and Ulaume named him Aleeme, partly in honor of lost Lileem.

After a couple of years, the Tigron's friend Kate came to Shilalama, and as Pellaz had predicted she got on very well with Mima. The inception went through as planned, and not really to anyone's surprise, Mima consummated it with aruna. From thereafter, when Pellaz came to the house, he usually brought Kate with him. She was Katarin now.

It had become common knowledge in Immanion that Pellaz visited Jaddayoth on a regular basis, and he let it be known he stayed with Ulaume and Flick, although as far as everyhar else was concerned, they lived in Garridan rather than Roselane. Flick sometimes wondered how Seel felt about that, because he presumed Seel must know. The Tigron often yearned for times of peace and contemplation, and holidays with old friends in the beautiful mountainous country were just what he needed. He liked to take his human friend with him, even though it was rather frowned upon that he allowed her to ride the otherlanes. He had mentioned to friends that harish adepts in Garridan had taught Kate many meditational techniques to ensure longevity in humans, and this was why she did not appear to age as other humans did. No hara in Immanion questioned this, because to them it was unthinkable that Kate could have become in any way har.

Pellaz said he had learned that Thiede had released Cal from the tower, because Cal had renounced all ties to the Tigron. He was mostly rehabilitated and would now forge a new life somewhere else. Pellaz appeared to have accepted this.

Flick was sometimes dizzy with it all. Life was neat. No loose ends.

CHAPTER THIRTY-FIVE

The Festival of the Mountain Walker was only a few days away, and Flick was out in the orchard spraying the trees with an herbal insect repellent, Aleeme playing in the flower strewn grass at his feet. The sun was hot on Flick's head as its beams came down through the gently moving leaves. The drone of bees filled the air, because Ulaume had started an apiary at the end of the orchard. This might be the last year that Aleeme enjoyed this festival as a harling, because he was nearly seven years old, and the time for innocent play would soon be at an end. Flick looked down on his son affectionately. He looked more like his father than his hostling, but his hair, like Flick's was very dark. Flick supposed all harlings appeared enchanting, wondrous and special to those who had given them birth, but Aleeme's bright spirit was like a healing medicine. It was impossible to dwell on past darkness in his presence. Flick wished the harling could remain a child forever. He didn't want bad things to happen to his son. Who, for example, would they choose for his feybraiha? The only har Flick would really want for the job was Pellaz and he wondered whether that was a possibility. It seemed merely thinking his name conjured him up.

Flick felt the strange fracture in the air that signaled a portal to the other-lanes had opened, although Pellaz was adept at keeping his arrivals discreet. Peridot could jump through a crack, so he said.

Flick shaded his eyes and saw Pellaz, radiant as ever, strolling up through the trees. Aleeme spotted him and leapt to his feet with a cry of greeting. He ran toward the Tigron, and Pellaz swept him up in his arms and swung him round. Aleeme was all over him, chattering nonsensically, but as Pellaz released the harling he looked over and caught Flick's eye. His expression was grave.

"Hi," Flick said.

Pellaz came to him and kissed him on the lips. "You look wonderful," he said. "A dehar of the earth."

"Go inside, Lee," Flick said. "Tell Marmorea we have a guest for dinner."

Aleeme sped off, leaping into the air and making joyous whooping sounds.

"He's growing so fast," Pellaz said.

Flick nodded and folded his arms. "What is it?"

"A visit, what else?"

"Pell, I know you. You had 'something important' written all over your face just then."

Pellaz paused. "All right. I did want to wait until I had you, Lor, and Mima together, but I might as well tell you now."

"This sounds ominous . . ."

Pellaz smiled rather sternly. "It might be. Are you ready for Operation Rescue Senseless Relatives?"

Flick stared at him in disbelief. "What are you saying?"

"You heard. Of course, if we're successful, they can't stay here. I'll have to take them to Immanion. Opalexian believes I've dropped the matter."

"You never did," Flick said in wonder. He uttered a short laugh that threatened to turn to tears. "You never gave up."

"And you never trusted me," Pellaz said. "Of course I didn't give up, but Opalexian couldn't know that. I didn't tell you, either, because I didn't want to keep any of your hopes up, just in case I failed. It's taken me a long time, because I had to snatch moments when I could to continue the search. But I think I've found something at last."

Flick embraced him fiercely. "Pell, I can't believe this. Can you really bring them back after all this time?"

Pellaz held him at arm's length. "I don't know for sure. But I have a plan."

The rest of the day felt endless. Aleeme didn't want to go to bed because Artemisian was there: a har on whom he clearly had a big crush. Both Mima and Ulaume sensed a tension in Pellaz, and it was mentioned quite regularly throughout dinner. He managed to hold them off until Flick ordered Aleeme to go upstairs.

"So, what *is* on your mind?" Mima said. "Are you going to tell us now or what? Why haven't you brought Kate with you?"

"Don't overreact to what I'm about to say," Pellaz said.

"What *are* you going to say?" Mima said, eyes narrow.

"You and I, Mima, if you want to . . . tonight we could try to snatch Lileem and Terez back into our world."

Mima stared at him, her eyes glittering with the tears that welled almost instantly. Flick realized then: she had never forgotten. Like Pellaz, she'd learned to put bandages over the heart, but beneath them, wounds still festered. "You mean it?" she said in a husky croak.

He nodded. "Yes. I can't guarantee success, but we have a chance."

"But it's been so long. How are they? Are they the same? Where are they?"

"Hush," Pellaz said. "I can't answer your questions. Peridot and I have merely found Terez's signature in the otherlanes, that's all. You must realize that we will be attempting something no other har has done before: exit the otherlanes into an unknown world. The only reason I'm prepared to do it is because if Terez is alive, it must mean the realm he's in is not that hostile an environment. We have no way of knowing otherwise, which is why Wraeththu have not yet become great otherlanes explorers!"

"This is astounding," Flick said. "But surely dangerous."

Pellaz cast him a quick glance. "It is. If I'm wrong and we have to get out damn fast, I only hope we're not dead before we know it. But I don't think I'm wrong."

Ulaume had been silent so far, his eyes wide and dark. Flick reached for his hands beneath the table, and when he found them, clasped tightly in Ulaume's lap, the fingers were icy. Now Ulaume said, "Pell, the Hegemony would never allow you to do this. Risking your life in this way. It's unthinkable."

"I know," Pellaz said. "But they *don't* know. I feel confident about it. Believe me, I wouldn't be considering this if I had any doubts." He leaned forward, hands clasped on the table. "We don't know where Thiede got the *sedim* from, or how he made them, if that's the right word. But I've worked with Peridot for many years and I trust him. He is not a mindless animal. I've communicated my wishes to him and his response has been positive. He would not risk his own being for the sake of a stupid har, however grand and important that har might believe himself to be. If Terez is alive, Peridot will find him, and therefore—hopefully—Lileem as well. I've thought about all the possibilities. Terez could be a prisoner of another race, for example. The rescue might not be straightforward. But Peridot can jump in and out of the otherlanes in the blink of an eye. He can squeeze himself between the tiniest spaces." Pellaz reached out and took one of Mima's hands in his own. "I believe we can do this, but I need a companion. If we find the others, we'll need two *sedim* to bring them back."

Mima swallowed, her face wrinkling up as if she tasted something bitter. "Must I . . . must we take aruna together?"

Pellaz shook his head. "No, that's not necessary. But I do need your Kamagrian life force, which is why I've asked you rather than Flick or Ulaume. The combination of Kamagrian and Wraeththu energy is extremely potent, a vast resource we have not yet begun to tap. We know so little about it, and it's clearly fraught with dangers, but I do know that our conjoined force will be the focus to get us to the place where Lileem and Terez are. We can achieve this effect through means other than aruna. In this way, the outcome will be more controlled."

Mima nodded, her lips a thin compressed line. "Yes. Yes. I'll do whatever it takes." And if that had meant aruna with her brother, she'd have done that too.

"Flick," Pellaz said, "we'll need Astral for this. Mima must ride him."

"You'll remove the constraints?" Flick said.

"Yes. No other way, I'm afraid."

"But won't—"

"Don't mention it," Pellaz said. "We'll take a risk. I suggest we go to the place where we used to meet, Flick. It's far enough from Shilalama to guarantee privacy. I'd like you and Ulaume to accompany us, then return to this house and wait."

"That will be . . . hard," Flick said. "What if you don't return immediately? How do we explain Mima's absence? It could take years."

"I will do everything in my power to make this mission as swift as possible," Pellaz said, "as will Peridot. Astral is not as experienced, but Peridot will guide him. If you have to, say that Mima has come with me to Garridan to deal with a family emergency or something. Use your wits."

The sun had just set and the night air was still warm. The journey to Pell and Flick's old meeting place was around an hour and a half way from Shilalama, at a fast pace. Pellaz told Mima to ride Astral on the way there to familiarize herself with him. She'd ridden a *sedu* before, of course, on the way to Shilalama from Freyhella, but her memory of that journey was hazy. It had been so bizarre and so swift, her mind had blanked out most of the details.

Mima could not believe this was really happening, that in a few short hours she would literally be out of this world, her feet on the soil of an otherworld realm. It was incredible. If it happened, would she remain sane thereafter? So many times she'd prayed to the dehara, Aruhani in particular, and begged them to show her a way to bring Lileem back. Ulaume had never given up hope, but Mima's hope had vacillated. Sometimes, especially more recently, she'd been hit by a black depression, convinced that she'd never see Lileem or Terez again. Years had passed, but in private moments, when she dared to dwell upon it, it felt to Mima as if Lileem and Terez had disappeared only last week. Never, in all her wild imaginings, had she ever considered she would be doing this; voluntarily traveling to the no place where aruna, and its unpredictable dehar, had taken her lost friend and brother.

At the appointed spot, Pellaz asked his companions to sit in a circle and join hands. They sat beneath the rock on the sweet summer grass that was damp with evening dew. A great ghostly owl flew over their heads: surely an omen. Peridot and Astral stood motionless outside the circle, and for once their masks of being ordinary beasts of earth seemed to have slipped. They did not bow their heads to munch the grass, nor switch their tails, or toss their manes. They watched, with full and focused intention.

Mima took her brother's hand on the one side, and Ulaume's on the other. The moment she did so, she closed her eyes and it was like sharing breath. She was back at the white house with Lileem: it was a flickering grainy image, like the old movies she had seen what seemed like centuries ago. Her entire time with her adopted family flashed past her perception in seconds, then she was going further back, into a sunset and the smell of ripe cable fruit. She was brushing Pell's hair before a mirror by lamplight, and she was thinking: *He is so lovely, he should have been born a girl.* The moment Cal had set foot in their settlement, with all his languorous beauty, Mima had known that Pell would be lost. And that was before she even realized Cal was Wraeththu.

Pellaz squeezed her fingers and she sensed he must be picking up on her thoughts. His own were shrouded, but perhaps not. Perhaps the images in her mind came directly from him.

The Tigron drew in a slow deep breath through his nose. He called upon the power of the Aghama, the life force of creation. He called it down upon them. Mima could see it as a radiant beam that came from the center of the universe and held them in its light. They would travel this beam to other realms, to unimagined landscapes. Where her hand joined with Pell's, she felt as if the flesh was melting, as if she had begun to meld with him completely. Their bones would interlace like the twigs of trees growing close to one another in a deep dark forest.

"Think of Lileem," Pellaz said to her by mind-touch, "and do not let her go. Keep the image pure and strong and true. It is your lantern in the darkness."

He leaned toward her and put his mouth near her own. They did not touch but the streams of their breath mingled, causing myriad microscopic explosions in the air between them. The reaction kindled a new form of energy and where it existed, so the boundaries between the worlds became thin and unstable.

"Rise," Pellaz said aloud. "Mount Astral, Mima. Flick, Ulaume, stand back."

In a daze, Mima jumped up onto the *sedu*. The landscape around her had changed. It was as if she could perceive the essence of everything. The animal beneath her was so strange, she had to concentrate on the image of horse to stop herself leaping from its back with a scream of dread. She could hear the air fracturing, reality shattering, like guns firing in the distance or glass breaking underfoot. Astral connected with her as if his mind was a snake. A whip of intention lashed out and hooked into her consciousness. She could hear him speak. *We will open the way on the steam of your breath. Hold true, little one. Hold the lantern high.*

With a final ear-splitting crash, reality broke apart, Astral lunged forward, and Mima was hurled into the space between the worlds.

Rushing, vortex, waves of energy that she could smell and taste. A soaring ghost beside her that she could not see, but could only feel. The thing she rode: it had wings that were like oars that were like blades rotating. She wasn't riding it. She was *in* it. And this time, her awareness was fully awake and alert. She would not forget this journey. She was not a passenger, but a pilot and her navigator was the otherworldly being that enfolded her essence.

Few experience this, Astral told her. *Hara ride their dreams of flying horses and galloping limbs. Few perceive the truth of it.*

Pellaz called to her, *Keep the image strong. Hold it steady. It is Astral's guidance instrument.*

It was difficult to do that. Mima was having enough trouble trying to keep hold of her identity, so that she did not disintegrate into a billion motes of consciousness and scatter. Think, she told herself. Remember Lileem the harling. Remember her laughter. She couldn't keep one image in her head, but she relived many moments. In some ways, it was easier to offer Astral the feeling of her love for Lileem and into this, she poured her entire intention. This was the true beacon. In the midst of its pearly cloud, she thought, we have never been chesna, and we never will be, but we are sisters in skin and we share a history. I am coming for you, Lee. I will bring you back.

Then she saw it: a beautiful azure blue light in the maddening chaos of the otherlanes. It hung up ahead like a star. It was the light of Lileem's spirit. It was a lantern in a window in a tall dark tower. It was the great gout of radiance over a stormy sea that guided ships to dock. It was the candle of hope lit every evening high in a fortress, to show a rescuer where the princess was imprisoned. And Astral flew toward it.

Ever since she and Terez had tried, and failed, to get back home, Lileem had devoted herself to studying in the underground library. She had no means of writing anything down, so she had to memorize the symbols she saw. Terez spent his time exploring the great building above, seeking evidence of who might have built it and why. Occasionally, he went off into the landscape, searching for other buildings. He discovered that the purple sun revealed things in the chambers of the great pyramid. He'd occasionally seen what might have been furniture—strange objects. It was difficult to tell. Once, he'd found a room with painted walls. Images of birds surrounded him. When he and Lileem met up, usually by accident if she'd decided to come up from below for a while, he'd tell her what he'd discovered. But they met infrequently. Sometimes, Lileem didn't see him for what felt like years. They no longer existed in time, and when Lileem looked down at herself, she thought she might be becoming insubstantial, like a ghost. She and Terez had died, and this world they were in, it might be hell, because it was so lonely and so desolate, but Lileem could not see hell in a place where there was so much knowledge. She knew that Terez was unhappy, and maybe she could be too, if she thought about it, but mostly she was driven purpose. Everything that had gone before, her old life, no longer mattered.

She could only examine the stone books on the lower shelves of the library, because she could find no means to access the upper shelves, which towered at least a hundred feet over her head. But even so, she had enough to occupy her for an eternity. When she finally came across a book that she could read, she felt she had been rewarded for her industry and application. It slid out from the stack and she experienced a chill—the first physical sensation for an aeon. She saw the name of Aruhani, carved in stone.

Lileem pressed a hand against the word. The sight of it kindled memories of her old life. The book was covered in words, symbols, and pictures. The name might be coincidence, because in this place she would come across anything that had ever been thought of eventually, but below the word she saw an image of the dehar, almost exactly how Flick had described him. There was a symbol too and she realized it was a summoning glyph.

The words and markings were so tiny, and so many were crammed onto the stone, it was difficult to interpret them. First, she looked for other familiar words and was not surprised to find Miyacala and Lunil, but was pleased to discover Agave, who she'd invented as a child, and in adult life had considered not to be a bona fide dehar. But there were so many others, thousands. Mima felt excitement. She thought of Flick. She wanted him to know about this.

But he never will, she thought. *That is why this is hell. I am given proof or evidence, then condemned never to be able to share it.*

Lileem leaned her forehead against the stone for a few moments. She felt the ghost of a headache, far behind her eyes. The books were not heavy, despite appearances. She found she was hauling this one right out of the stack. She was going to take it to the upper place. She was going to make Terez look at it.

If there is a way to get home, she thought, *it lies somewhere within this library. I just have to keep looking for it.*

Aruhani had come to her. He had prodded her and made her remember the life she had left behind. She could not ignore this message.

Outside, no suns were in the sky and the stars wheeled overhead. Lileem found Terez beside the ocean, staring up. Her footsteps crunched upon the gravelly shore, but Terez did not look around. In the strange light, his naked skin looked like marble. *Once, I believed I loved him,* she thought. *This place has stolen that from me.*

"Terez," she said. "Look."

He did not respond immediately, but then turned slowly toward her. She held out the stone, which was almost half her height.

"You shouldn't bring those out here," Terez said. "It's forbidden."

"Who's here to forbid?" she asked. "Just look at it, will you."

She hunkered down and laid the stone out on the ground. Terez squatted beside her. "What am I looking for?"

Lileem pointed out the words. "Dehara," she said. "See? We didn't make it up."

"Maybe you did," Terez said, annoyingly unimpressed. "Whatever any creature thinks is recorded here. This is just your book, or Flick's book."

"No," Lileem said. "I know it's not."

Terez sighed. "What does it matter?" He stood up again and stared at the sky. "Somewhere, out there, perhaps in another layer of reality, lies home . . ."

Lileem was silent for a moment, then said, "I want to go back too, Terez. And I'm going to find a way how, I promise you. The information we seek lies in the library."

He glanced at her. "Maybe wanting to is the beginning," he said. "Maybe it's been you all along who has kept us here, because of that damned library. You haven't wanted to leave badly enough."

Lileem considered his words. He might well be correct. "Well, I do now," she said. If only they could find desire in this arid place, but she knew that route was closed to them. "I'll find a way. Come with me. Don't stay out here. It'd be quicker if we looked together."

They walked back along the shore with the cyclopean edifice looming over them, casting its gaunt shadow on the sea. It was necessary to climb long sloping dunes of silver-gray sand to reach the entrance to the library. Lileem and Terez waded up the dunes, their progress hampered by the shifting granules. The book felt heavy in Lileem's arms now.

Just as they reached the top, there was a great flash in the sky. Lileem almost dropped the stone. "What was that?"

It looked as if a star had exploded for much of the sky ahead of them was filled with pulsing, sparkling clouds. The ground was shaking, and there was a sound like thunder.

"A portal!" Terez cried, trying to scramble faster up the dune.

Lileem stumbled after him. "Another har and parage, do you think?"

"I don't know. Maybe Gelaming. They can go anywhere in creation, I'm sure. We must make them see us."

"Terez," Lileem said, "it might not be—"

Whatever words she was about to speak were swept away from her. An immense radiance burst out of the boiling sky with the sound of an entire city crumbling to destruction at once. Both Lileem and Terez ducked down, and a hot wind seared over them, blowing back their hair. Sand scoured their naked bodies. *Does this library have an owner?* Lileem thought. *And they have they just come back to it?*

She was afraid.

Terez dragged her to her feet and together they reached the top of the dunes. A short distance away, they could see two bizarre creatures, crouched on the ground outside the pyramid. Were they creatures? They could equally have been machines. In some ways, they were like giant insects, because they had wings and their segmented bodies appeared to be made of some metallic substance that shifted with many colors like oil. The wings were similar to insect wings in that they moved so fast they were simply a blur, but Lileem could see that they were rotating rather than flapping. There was also something about the creatures that reminded her of sea animals. Their legs were like a crab's or spider's legs, with their bodies hanging between them. Their heads were long and triangular like a sea horse's. They had three enormous faceted eyes. It was only when she heard her name called aloud that Lileem realised the strange creatures had passengers or riders.

"Lileem!"

She knew that voice, even after so long. "Terez," she cried. "It's Mima!"

"I know," he said and there was fear in his voice, as if he thought this was a terrible, cruel illusion.

"Come on!" Lileem began to run toward the creatures.

The creatures appeared to be surrounded by a shimmering bubble of sparkling air. Lileem careered into it and then found she was lying on her back on the ground, the stone book on top of her. Something had repelled her with immense force.

She stood up quickly, and put out a hand toward the light. Something pressed against her hand. She couldn't push through it.

"Lileem," Mima called. "Come to me. Come now. There isn't much time."

"I can't!" Lileem wailed.

"Try!"

Terez was at her side now and together they pushed against the resistant air. They could make no impression on it. "This isn't real," Terez was saying, over and over, but he kept trying to break through the barrier.

"Terez!"

Everything was happening so swiftly, Lileem hadn't inspected who rode the other creature. Her whole being was intent on reaching Mima, on going home and there was no time for thought or consideration. But now, she turned her attention to Mima's companion. She knew him at once, not just because he looked so like her visions of him, but because he was surrounded by golden light, by power.

"It's your brother," Lileem said. "Terez, it's Pellaz. He's come for us."

Pellaz leapt down from his peculiar mount and came to the side of the bubble. He looked like a dehar and perhaps he was. "Concentrate," he said. "This world is responsive only to one-way portals. There is no way back. Peridot and Astral are holding open the portal they made, but they are weakening. You have to break through this barrier. You must believe you can."

Terez took Lileem's hand in his own. "I believe it!" he said fiercely.

Pellaz closed his eyes briefly, then extended one shining hand toward them. It came through the barrier as if through water and it dripped with opal fire. Terez grabbed hold of it. Pellaz would pull them through, together. "Now!" Terez yelled to Lileem.

She hesitated, then let go of Terez's hand and ran back the short way to where the stone book lay in the sand. She heard them all calling to her, urgently, angrily, but she couldn't help herself. She couldn't leave this place with nothing. They'd suffered too much. The book felt so heavy now. She could barely pick it up, but if there was one last thing she could do in her life, it must be this. She staggered back to Terez, whose expression was demented.

"Lee! Drop that thing. Hurry. What the fuck are you doing?"

"Drop it!" Pellaz shouted at her. "You can't bring it with you."

Lileem ignored him. She held it close against her body with one arm, feeling the muscles rip beneath its weight. Its surface felt rough now and it ground against her naked skin. She must ignore the weight. She must believe she could do this. With her free hand, she grabbed hold of Terez's fingers and she saw that her own were bleeding.

Pellaz uttered a fearsome cry and hauled them through the barrier. Lileem felt her skin tear. It hurt so much. But then they were through. She gripped the stone book with both arms. Her legs were buckling beneath her. Terez and Pellaz carried her between them to Mima's mount. Mima was looking down, in terror, her hair swirling round her head as if she were underwater.

"Lileem, drop the stone!" she cried. "They can't lift you. Lee, do what I say!"

"No," Lileem said. "I can't leave it behind. Please."

Both Terez and Pellaz were trying to wrench her arms apart, but it was as if her limbs had turned to stone. Nohar could move her. One of them slapped her face, but she didn't let go.

"This is insane!" Terez cried. "For fuck's sake, Lee. We have to go. We need to go."

Lileem uttered an anguished wail. Terez and Pellaz were trying to lift her up to Mima, but she was too heavy.

"If you don't let it go, we'll have to leave you here," Pellaz said harshly. "Is that what you want?"

"Wait!" Mima cried. She leaned down. "Pass it to me, Lee."

"No!" Pellaz said. "We can't risk taking anything back."

Lileem saw Mima's face above her and it shone as her brother's face did. She was as powerful and beautiful as Pellaz, as strong as a dehar. Lileem collapsed to her knees and with all her strength held up the stone to Mima. "Please. It's about the dehara. Please."

Mima leaned down and, as if the stone weighed nothing at all, took it from Lileem and put it before her. The creature she rode uttered a high pitched cry and its rotating wings rose higher.

"Quickly!" Pellaz said. "The portal is fragmenting." He and Terez managed to lift Lileem up behind Mima. She took hold of Mima's waist, clasped her numb arms around her.

Beside them, Terez and Pellaz mounted the other creature. Jagged stripes of red light fractured the protective bubble around them. Lileem felt a strong sucking wind that sought to bind them to this world. Her vision was blurred, but she was sure that millions of small scuttling creatures were pouring out of the pyramid, coming to claim and devour them. She heard Mima cry, "Astral, we are ready!" The creature's wings were turning frantically now. Hazily, Lileem could see an otherlanes portal opening before them, but it was weak, and kept partially closing again.

"Aru," Lileem prayed. "You tore the skin of the vortex that would have taken us at sea. Do this again now. Hold wide the gates. Be with us."

Whether the dehar heard and obeyed her command in this alien place, she did not know. She did not see his image or feel his presence, but suddenly the creature she rode shot up vertically into the air and, with a mighty crack, reality splintered. The portal opened wide like a yawning mouth and they plunged through it.

CHAPTER THIRTY-SIX

$\succ\!\!\cdot\!\!\leftrightarrow\!\!\cdot\!\!\ominus\!\!\cdot\!\!\langle\!\leftrightarrow\!\!\cdot\!\!\prec$

Flick sat beside Lileem's bed, gazing upon her. He and Ulaume had finished bathing her body carefully and now she lay naked on top of the quilt. They didn't want to put covers over her, because her skin was covered in scratches and grazes, some of them quite deep. She looked emaciated, and this was hardly surprising. Terez, who'd fared better than Lileem, had already told everyone how he and Lileem hadn't eaten or slept for years. It was a miracle they had survived in that alien place.

Pellaz said that he'd considered taking all four of them back to Immanion immediately, rather than stopping off in Shilalama first, but Astral and Peridot had been weakened by their experience, and it was easier for them to follow the trail they'd recently made. They had intimated to Pellaz that they could not have remained in the otherworld realm for more than a few minutes, because the place worked its own peculiar hold on any creature that found its way there. If you didn't leave at once, you might never leave at all. Pellaz said that on the way back, he had felt Peridot's fear and the fact that such a creature, revealed in the other realm for perhaps what it truly was, could be so terrified was the most unsettling thing of all.

Lileem sighed and shuddered in her sleep. The skin on her face was raw and her arms and hands were badly cut. Mima had told Flick about Lileem's obsession with bringing a heavy stone slab back with her. "The strangest thing was," Mima said, "when we broke through from the otherlanes into this world, I wasn't holding a slab at all. It had turned into an old, cracked stone bowl. Inside, it's covered in strange markings."

"It must have been the journey," Flick said. "The stone changed in the same way the *sedim* changed. Maybe."

As for how the *sedim* had appeared in that realm, Pellaz was unsure if that was their true form or not. It might be that in different worlds, they took different forms. The moment they'd leapt out of the otherlanes, they'd transformed back into white horses. In any event, the journey had exhausted the creatures. They needed to rest before attempting another otherlane jump.

Flick left Lileem to sleep and went downstairs. The house was quiet, but soon Aleeme and the staff would be rising from their beds. Lileem and Terez could be kept secret for only a short time, and the *sedim* would not be ready to leave before the household was awake. Lileem was also patently in no condition to travel.

Mima and Pellaz had taken Terez to Mima's room and were no doubt still deep in conversation with him. Ulaume was making an early breakfast. His cooking left a lot to be desired, but Flick was so tired he didn't complain. The stone bowl Lileem had brought back with her stood on the kitchen table. It was a small, unremarkable looking thing, like an ancient artifact dug up from the site of a vanished city. Flick picked it up and examined it. The markings inside it were unfamiliar. He sensed no peculiar emanations. It was dead stone.

Ulaume placed a plate of burned toast in front of Flick. "Carbon's good for you," he said lightly. "Keeps you regular."

"Thanks." Flick munched the toast with effort, but gratefully drank the coffee Ulaume placed beside his plate. "What's going to happen?" Flick said. "Will Opalexian be angry?"

"Who knows?" Ulaume replied. "She and Pell are fairly close now. She might have mellowed." He glanced at the clock on the wall. "Mima and Pellaz have done something nohar has ever done before. Opalexian will know about it, I'm sure. She'll have *felt* it. Shall we place bets on when we'll be summoned to Kalalim?"

"Any time now," Flick said. "I'm already bracing myself for it."

In fact, Opalexian made no move until midmorning. By that time, Flick had instructed their housekeeper, Silorne, to keep away from the rooms where Terez and Lileem were sleeping. He explained they'd received unexpected guests in the night, who had undertaken an arduous journey and needed peace and quiet. This appeared to satisfy the housekeeper for now. Pellaz and Mima did not sleep, and neither did Ulaume or Flick. They were all waiting for the storm to break.

Before noon, a covered carriage drew up in the driveway outside the main entrance to the house. From this, stepped a parage who was concealed by a heavy hooded cloak. Silorne answered the door and conducted the visitor into the living room, where Flick and the others were gathered, drinking coffee and discussing what had happened. The parage paused at the threshold and waited for the housekeeper to depart. Then she threw back the hood of her cloak. It was Opalexian herself. She uttered no greeting, but said directly to Pellaz, "I know why you did it. I just wish you hadn't." It was not an opening thrust to which it was easy to respond.

Pellaz regarded her thoughtfully, then spoke in a measured tone. "I intend to take Lileem and Terez to Almagabra. I can protect them. I have an estate outside the city where they can stay. No har or parage need ever know what has happened."

"That is out of the question," said Opalexian, coming into the room. She did not sit down. "I wish you had informed me of your wild plan. Of course, you must tell me the details later. But for now we must make arrangements for our willful charges. I have taken my time in coming here, because I wanted to consider the matter. It is my decision that Lileem must remain here in Shilalama. Your brother is your responsibility, but he cannot stay here. They must be separated. Our task is to ensure they never discuss this matter with anyone, har or parage."

"Perhaps we should ask them what they would like to do," Pellaz said.

"Don't be absurd." Opalexian sniffed imperiously. "What condition are they in?"

"Terez is fine," Pellaz said, "but Lileem sustained minor injuries. They are both exhausted. You cannot speak to them yet."

Opalexian nodded thoughtfully. "Can you keep Terez from Thiede in Almagabra?"

"No, but I can do my best to keep my brother's experiences private. It is known that he lives with Flick and Ulaume. He understands he must tell nohar about Shilalama or the Kamagrian. I have told nohar in Immanion anything about Terez's disappearance. I will say it is my choice to have him with me in the city."

"Once Thiede realizes Terez is not a scavenging Uigenna wretch, he will want to use him, Pellaz."

"Possibly. I will do all that I can to protect him."

"Make sure you do. Thiede must not know what has occurred. If he discovers the truth, whether it's your fault or not, our agreement comes to an end."

Pellaz stared at her coldly. "You can be sure I want to avoid that."

Flick could tell that both Mima and Ulaume were as curious as he was about what that agreement entailed, but none of them felt brave enough to ask.

"I'm glad we have an understanding," Opalexian said. "The time for initial preparation draws near." She glanced at Mima. "Your brother and I have much to discuss. Can you provide us with a private room?"

"Of course," Mima said. There was an icy edge to her voice.

"Also, the moment that Lileem is fit to talk, send me word. She must speak to no one, including yourselves, until she has spoken to me. Is that clear?"

Mima inclined her head. "As cut glass."

"Good. Now, if you would be so kind, conduct Pellaz and I to the private room." Opalexian took in all the occupants of the room with one sweeping, chilling glance. "This household is nothing but trouble. I expect it is the influence of Cevarro blood. Now Thiede can have two of them on his hands. I almost pity him." She smiled at Pellaz. "But, of course, the best is yet in store for him. Are you ready, tiahaar?"

Pellaz stood up. "More than so."

Lileem was quite ill for some weeks after her return. Every day, she'd sit out in the garden, in a chair beneath the apple trees, her hands lying loosely in her lap. She didn't talk much and she didn't read. She was consumed by grief.

In the otherworld, her feelings for Terez had been frozen, but once she'd regained consciousness, in her new bed in the new house, they came crashing back. She felt exactly how she'd felt on the night of the festival, when she and Terez had taken aruna together. Her first thoughts were of him, and the first thing she said to Ulaume, who happened to be in the room when she awoke was, "Where's Terez?"

From the look on Ulaume's face, she feared that Terez had died. But then Ulaume told her the truth. She would never see Terez again. As if losing him wasn't bad enough, she also had to contend with another, perhaps deeper, sense of bereavement. Although in many respects she was glad to be home, she found she missed the otherworld. At night, when she looked at the sky, she yearned for the majestic splendor of the wheeling alien stars. When the sun rose, she thought of the incredible sunrises she had seen. She wanted to see them again. But it was not just for the magnificent landscape that she grieved. She was sure that some unbelievable truth about Wraeththu and Kamagrian lay hidden in the library. Her stone book had not survived the journey to this world, and that was sad, because she'd wanted so much to share it with Flick.

Part of me stayed behind, she thought. *I am still there, wandering through the corridors, seeking, seeking.*

The only thing that might have made the loss of the otherworld bearable was being able to be with Terez and that was not possible.

So much had happened to her friends in her absence: the new house, new jobs, a harling for Flick and Ulaume, and most important of all, Pellaz. She'd missed all that, and it hurt. Mima cared for her still, but now she had a roon friend in Almagabra too. Things were not the same.

Perhaps to cheer Lileem up and to bring her back into their family, Flick and Ulaume decided to undertake a blood-bond ceremony. It would be like a festival. It would be a happy day. Lileem tried to be interested, but she felt so tired all the time. Every morning, she woke up thinking she had something important to do. Then she'd remember where and who she was, and that the important thing had gone.

Opalexian came to the house and questioned her in a grueling manner and Lileem was too weak not to tell the truth.

"You must never do this again," Opalexian said. "You do understand that, don't you? Pellaz and Mima risked their lives for you, as did the *sedim*. You cannot be so selfish as to put those who care for you in such a position again."

"But the library," Lileem said. "It's important."

"You saw what you wanted to see," Opalexian said. "The dehara exist because you and Flick dreamed them into being, fueled them with your thoughts. That is how all gods are created. You take the formless stuff of creation and shape it with your mind, as you shape statues of clay with your hands. It's my belief you were in a realm of pure thought. You and Terez created a world around you, because your senses needed it. You might have gone insane, otherwise. Perhaps there was no world, no landscape, but only a formless vortex of power." Nevertheless, she took Lileem's bowl with her to Kalalim, and didn't give it back.

When Lileem watched Aleeme at play, it made her weep. She remembered being a harling herself and how the world had been full of wonder then. Aleeme would run up to her and throw flowers into her lap. "Don't cry," he'd say. So she'd cry some more.

Opalexian was concerned about Lileem's depression and sent her personal healers to help. This did some good and after a few months, Lileem was able to function again. Her body recovered, even if her heart still felt as heavy as the stone she'd tried to bring back to this world with her.

Flick and Ulaume arranged to perform their blood-bond in the spring.

Lileem asked, tentatively, if Terez would come. The answer was no. Opalexian had forbidden Terez to return to Shilalama, under any circumstances. Once, Mima went to visit Terez at Pell's estate in Almagabra. Pellaz came to fetch her. Lileem could tell Mima felt guilty because Lileem couldn't go. "Just give him my love," Lileem said.

When she returned, Mima took care not to enthuse too much about her visit. She spoke a lot about Pell's wonderful country estate, but very little about Terez himself. Lileem asked about him, and Mima said, "He's well, Lee. Pell takes care of him."

"Does he miss me?"

"Of course."

Lileem could tell this was not the truth. Terez was her Chelone: the har who'd desired her, but whose desire could not withstand the terrible reality of their intimacy. He believed she'd kept him from home for years, and perhaps she had. He'd left Shilalama without saying good-bye to her, angry because she'd nearly ruined their chance to get home when it came. She dreamed of him nearly every night. She dreamed of them together, taking aruna like normal hara. It was too painful. Eventually, she asked Opalexian's healers for medicine to stop her dreaming.

Old friends came to visit Lileem and sometimes, late at night, when much wine had been consumed, some were brave enough to ask questions about what had happened with Terez. Lileem kept the promise of silence that she'd sworn to Opalexian, but not because she wanted to please the Kamagrian leader. She knew that Opalexian was right: no other parage should attempt what Lileem had done. Although Lileem believed it was the most important thing that had ever happened to her, she didn't think any parage of her acquaintance was fit to follow in her footsteps. Such knowledge did not concern them. They lived the safe life that Opalexian had designed for them. When asked, she would say, "It was the worst thing I ever did. I'm lucky to be alive. It's damaged me forever."

Her friends could look at her haunted eyes and know this was the truth. Eventually, the questions stopped. Lileem had become useful to Opalexian: she was a living example of what could happen if a parage was stupid enough to take aruna with a har.

Mima, Flick, and Ulaume all tried to encourage Lileem to talk, to share her feelings, but it was difficult. She felt there was no point to it. They could not help her and the things that made her sad would never change.

The blood-bond ceremony ended up as a huge party, with every high-ranking Roselane invited as guests. Flick and Ulaume spoke vows to one another that they'd taken months to craft perfectly, and Opalexian herself offici-ated. In the orchard of their home, with all the trees in full blossom, she cut their arms lightly and bound them together. She spoke the words of a beauti-ful ritual, conjuring tears in the eyes of all who listened.

Lileem stood beneath the trees, with white petals falling down upon her. She thought how lovely Ulaume and Flick looked, and how close they were. At one time, they'd virtually hated one another, and bizarrely enough, it had been Terez who'd brought them together. Aleeme stood gravely at Opalexian's side, hand-ing her ritual items when she needed them. Lileem could tell it would not be long before he was adult. Mima stood at the front of the crowd with Pellaz and Kate, tears of joy running down her face. Pellaz had his arm around his sister. They were like twins.

Lileem watched them all, and it was as if she was a ghost who had come back to the living to observe their happiness on this special day. *I will not be here for long,* she thought. But where she would go, she had no idea.

That night, she lay awake with her bedroom window open, her arms behind her head. She could hear Ulaume and Flick taking aruna together in the room next door, but the sounds of it didn't conjure similar responses in her own body as they'd always used to do. Flick and Ulaume were in such raptures, she was almost tempted to bang on the wall to get them to shut up. *Is this how my life's going to be?* she thought. *Will I never feel that special way again?*

The following morning at breakfast, Flick and Ulaume were all over each other and seemed drunk. Their constant mutual pawing got on Lileem's nerves. When Ulaume got up to leave the table, Flick grabbed hold of him and started kissing his stomach, over and over.

Mima, sitting between Pellaz and Kate, who'd stayed the night, let out a whoop of delight. "You've made another pearl, haven't you?" she cried.

Aleeme yelled, "Yay, a brother!"

Flick and Ulaume started laughing. Then Mima was out of her seat, hug-ging them both. Lileem felt sick. She went outside.

Pellaz followed her out. It was strange how quickly she'd become used to his presence, he who had once seemed like a god to her. They'd talked about the connection she'd felt with him. He'd been amused to hear her story of him as a gigantic statue. The reality to him was far more commonplace.

He'd heard her call and had perceived her personal power, in the form of the dehara. He'd simply pointed out the obvious, he thought: use what you al-ready have.

Lileem sat down on an ornamental wall and he sat beside her. He didn't say anything for a while, and she was grateful. Her nose was running. She wiped it with her hands.

"It's hard for me, seeing things like that," Pellaz said, referring to Flick and Ulaume. "It makes me think about my own blood-bond, and how Rue and I will never have what Flick and Ulaume have. Making harlings isn't as easy as they make it seem, you know. It shows how deep their love runs. Their relationship is perfect. To be frank, it turns my stomach to witness it."

Lileem thought he didn't really mean that. He was trying to make her feel better, because he sensed she couldn't join in with the household happiness and that she felt bad about that. "Pell, can you take me away?"

He sighed. "No. You know that I can't."

"Why?"

"Opalexian would not want me to."

"You are Tigron. How can her feelings matter that much? You could take me anywhere. You must know other hara somewhere I could live with. Somewhere far far away."

"I can't upset her," Pellaz said. "She has me in a fierce hold."

"How?" Lileem turned her head to look at him. "You made a deal with her, I know. What was it? You can tell me. I won't breathe a word, I promise. I'm just a ghost."

"Opalexian believes she can exorcise ghosts," Pellaz said. He picked up a stone from the gravel path and threw it onto the lawn. "She will do something for me that Thiede will not."

"What?"

Pellaz lowered his eyes, stared at the ground. "She will heal Cal."

"I thought he was healed," Lileem said. "Flick told me the whole story, and that Thiede had let him go. Flick said it was all over."

Pellaz glanced at her. "He has been released, but he is still very sick."

"How do you know?"

"I asked Opalexian to find out, when I first met her. He still suffers, as Thiede wants him to. He needs to be healed of all that's been done to him, by Thiede and even by those who came before. By the Uigenna, by human parents, everyone."

"So you can be together again?"

"I don't know," Pellaz said. "Opalexian says she will try. I don't know her plans exactly. All I know is that I have to keep silent and hope and dream. I have to trust that, one day, Cal and I will both know the truth about one another, because there are so many lies, so many barriers. I have to hope we can meet in a place out of time and remember all that we were. I will never forget him, and I know he'll not forget me either. If anyone can draw the poison, I believe Opalexian can. I have to trust her. I have to give her what she wants, because this is the only thing that matters to me."

"I hope it works," Lileem said. "I really do."

Pellaz smiled tightly. "We'll see. You're just as much of a worry. You're so unhappy. I wish I could take you away, give you a new life, but . . ."

"I know. I have to be punished for being bad. I'm stuck here in this great big prison."

"Perhaps you should speak to Opalexian, tell her how miserable you are. She isn't the evil witch queen she makes herself out to be, you know."

"I'll try. I wonder if she'd let me be like Tel-an-Kaa and roam the world looking for parazha. But then, I suppose I'm not to be trusted."

Pellaz squeezed her leg. "Then show Opalexian that you are. She can't keep you confined here forever. If you think I can help in any way, just ask."

"Well, you could speak to her first . . ."

"All right. I will. When we next meet."

"Thanks, Pell." She leaned over kissed his cheek. Beautiful Pellaz. Kind Tigron. How tragic he should be so sad inside.

A few weeks after Flick and Ulaume's blood-bonding, Aleeme began to display signs of approaching feybraiha. Flick told Ulaume of his desire to ask Pellaz to be their son's first aruna partner, and Ulaume agreed this might be a good idea. They said nothing to Aleeme, because they sensed he would be delighted with their choice and would be extremely disappointed if Pellaz refused.

Gelaming engineers had perfected a piece of technology that aided the amplification of mind-touch messages, so that mind "mail" could be sent easily over greater distance. Pellaz had brought one of these units to Shilalama and Flick's household was the first in Roselane to own such a device. Very shortly afterward, Opalexian received a similar gift from the Tigron. Now, Flick could contact Pellaz whenever he needed to, and after his discussion with Ulaume about Aleeme, he sent a message to Immanion, asking Pellaz if he could spare them an hour or so very soon.

Pellaz arrived at their home the following day. He said he'd been to visit Opalexian first, and wanted to speak to Lileem about something he'd discussed with the Kamagrian leader, but first he sat down with Flick and Ulaume at the bottom of the garden to hear what they had to say. Flick voiced their request carefully. Now that he had to speak to Pellaz personally, he realized he was asking quite a lot. It was a privilege indeed for anyhar to have the Tigron as their first aruna partner, and if Pellaz indulged all of his friends in this manner, he'd spend a lot of time that he could ill afford, educating young harlings in arunic skills. Pellaz paused before answering, and when he did, it was to decline, but not because of the reasons Flick had anticipated.

"This is a great honor you're offering," Pellaz said, "but I can't help you. Thiede has changed me, Flick. If I took aruna with such an inexperienced har as Aleeme, it could damage him severely. I'm more like Thiede now and my essence is strong. I'm sorry."

Flick was not particularly surprised. "We're stuck," he said. "We know no hara here we consider worthy of the task. Most of our close friends in Shilalama are Kamagrian."

"What you need," Pellaz said, "is another harish family with second-generation sons."

"This might sound incredible, but we're the only hara in this city who've had sons," Ulaume said. "Remember, this is the territory of pious Roselane. The hara who end up here are mostly like monks."

Pellaz laughed. "That has not escaped me!" He cupped his chin with one hand, pondered for a few moments. "Let me think."

"Are there any families of your acquaintance who might help?" Ulaume asked.

Pellaz drew in his breath slowly. "Yes," he said at last.

Flick could tell the family Pellaz had in mind was controversial. He knew before the Tigron spoke what he would say.

"I could speak to Seel and Swift in Galhea," Pellaz said. "Or, more importantly, I could speak to Azriel. He's not a child any longer, of course, but he is second generation. He's Swift's son, and a fine har. He will be experienced now, and he is pure-born. He would be my recommendation."

"They'd never allow it," Ulaume said.

Flick said nothing. He wondered how Pellaz could be so insensitive.

"Things are different now," Pellaz said. "Seel does not harbor the same feelings for you as he used to do, Lor. I—and Cobweb too—have made sure of that."

"And we should care?" Flick said coldly. "There's no way I'll allow a son of mine to go anywhere near a har of Seel Griselming's blood."

"Flick, that is irrational," Pellaz said patiently. "What do you think, Lor?"

Ulaume glanced at Flick. "I don't know," he said uncertainly. "If Flick feels strongly about this, I have to support him."

"Never mind Flick's feelings," Pellaz said. "What are yours?"

"What?" Flick cried. 'Pell, what's the matter with you?'

"Hush," Pellaz said. "Hear me out. Well, Lor? You know that the House of Parasiel is very prominent. It would be good for Aleeme to undergo feybraiha there. It would be good for the rest of your family too."

Ulaume was virtually squirming in his seat. "Well, I have no objections personally . . ."

"Thanks," Flick said. "How short is your memory? Remember how Seel behaved with you."

"I also remember how Cobweb and Swift behaved," Ulaume said, carefully. "It would be a great honor for Aleeme, Flick. You know that."

"Seel would never comply," Flick said. "I don't care how old Azriel is now. Seel is his hostling and no doubt still rules him with an iron fist."

"That's not true," Pellaz said. "I've told you a hundred times he wants only to make peace with you. He knows I see you all the time, as you know I see him. This is ridiculous. How long ago was it that you left him?"

"I thought we were supposed to be hiding here in secret," Flick said. "Parading into Galhea with you is hardly a surreptitious act."

Pellaz laughed. "You don't have to hide anymore, Flick. You are under Opalexian's protection. I don't know how much Thiede knows about her, but he's aware that the Roselane tribe has a very strong leader. He wouldn't risk upsetting her, I'm sure. You are quite safe now. Hara in Immanion know you don't live in Garridan. I've been building roads for you. I want to see a day when you and Ulaume can visit me in Immanion openly."

"These are all interesting ideas," Flick said, "and it's even more interesting that you haven't mentioned them to us before. But can we get back to the main subject? Aleeme's feybraiha."

"Flick, think about it," Pellaz said. "I know what you wanted: a safe, unadventurous life, and in many ways you have it. But Fate has conspired to make you a har of status, not just in my eyes, but in Opalexian's too. Your name is known in Immanion. And that brings me to another matter you should consider. You and Ulaume should think about taking a second name."

"Why?" Flick said. "We don't need one."

"You have started a family," Pellaz said, "and your sons will go on to have sons. You should have a family name. I believe it is important."

"You're right," Ulaume said. "I hadn't considered that."

"Your sons can't remain here in Shilalama all the time," Pellaz said. "As you've already found out, it presents difficulties. You and Ulaume have each other, Flick, but think about Aleeme's future, and that of your unborn son.

Would it be fair to deny them a full life? At the very least, you should allow them to be educated somewhere in Almagabra."

Flick was angry at everything the Tigron had said, because he knew Pellaz was right. It would benefit Aleeme to get to know other hara abroad, especially ones like the Parsics. He was almost an adult, and what did Shilalama really offer a full-blooded young har? Aleeme was not a greatly spiritual har. He would want more from life than meditation in the mountains and he had no companions his own age here. Their friendship with the Tigron would afford Aleeme advantages of which most hara could only dream. It would be selfish to deny him these privileges. "I'll have to think about this," Flick said. "You've given us a lot to consider."

"Don't think too long," Pellaz said. "Remember that Aleeme should spend some time with the one who is chosen for him before the feybraiha takes place." He paused. "Will you give me permission to speak to Seel and Swift? The rift between you and Seel should be healed. It is pointless. If you want an apology, I'm sure Seel will be prepared to give it."

That means that Pellaz will command him to apologize, Flick thought. He looked at Ulaume. "What do you think, Lor? You're more impartial than I am."

"I think it's . . ." Ulaume shrugged. "I think it would be good for Aleeme."

Flick sighed. "All right, then. But I don't want apologies or scenes. I don't want to be close to Seel again, nor to discuss the past in any way, but I can be cordial, if that's what it takes."

"I'm delighted to hear it," Pellaz said. He braced his hands on his knees. "Now, I'd like to speak to Lileem. I have good news for her."

"What's that?" Flick asked. "What did you discuss with Opalexian? Will she allow Terez back here?"

"No," Pellaz said, "but she has agreed to allow Lileem to work overseas with Tel-an-Kaa, as a kind of apprentice. She's confident Kaa can keep an eye on Lee. Lileem asked me to help her in this matter, and I have. After her experiences in the otherworld, she needs to travel, to spread her wings."

Flick had no idea Lileem felt that way. She clearly talked more with Pellaz than she did with her own family. That hurt. "So, it seems you're arranging for most of our household to flee the nest," he said, sharply.

"Oh, come on," Pellaz said. "It's obvious you and Lor will eventually have this big old house overrun with harlings! You won't lose anyhar, Flick. The world is a different place now. It's easy to keep in touch."

Flick harbored a faint hope that Seel would object to Azriel taking part in Aleeme's feybraiha. This was not just because of the aversion he still had to Seel, but also because once events were set in motion, it would be the beginning of Aleeme leaving home. It would be a great wrench for Flick to lose his firstborn son, not to be able to see him every day, even if Aleeme did deserve everything that Pellaz could give him.

Once Flick had given his consent, Pellaz wasted no time, perhaps concerned that Flick would change his mind. He returned to Shilalama only two days later to say that the House of Parasiel would be honored to help with Aleeme's feybraiha. The Tigron came with a written invitation from Cobweb in his hand. Flick, Ulaume, and Aleeme would be welcome in Galhea as soon as was convenient. Azriel was pleased he had been chosen, and Cobweb wanted to supervise contact between his highharling and Aleeme for two weeks before the feybraiha ceremony took place.

After the invitation had arrived, Flick then hoped that Opalexian would intervene, because she disapproved of her citizens interacting with the world of Wraeththu. Annoyingly, she gave her blessing. She trusted Flick and Ulaume, and she trusted the Tigron. This alliance might help Kamagrian's position when the time came for them to reveal themselves to the world. The only stipulation she made was that Mima should not go to Galhea, not just because she was Kamagrian, but because it was obvious she was related to the Tigron. For the time being, it was preferable for Mima to keep a low profile. This disappointed Mima, not least because she was very fond of Aleeme and wished to part of his coming of age rite, but she accepted Opalexian's decision. She already knew that she was lucky Opalexian allowed her to visit Pellaz occasionally. Lileem, however, would be permitted to attend the feast day of the rite. Tel-an-Kaa, as a good friend of the Parsic family, would be invited, and Lileem could be present as the Zigane's new assistant. Tel-an-Kaa would teach her how to disguise herself, because she'd need this skill in order to carry out Kamagrian work in Megalithica. A gathering at Galhea, among friends, would be a good opportunity for her to practice appearing like a human female.

Finally, Flick turned to his son, harboring the faintest hope of all that Aleeme would be upset or frightened and would refuse to go to Galhea. No such luck. Aleeme was nervous about aruna with a stranger, but excited about the prospect of going abroad, of traveling the otherlanes with Pellaz.

It's going to happen, Flick thought glumly. *I should know by now that life never stays the same.*

While Flick was brooding over his forthcoming meeting with Seel, Ulaume invented a second name for their family: Sarestes, taken from the names of both Saltrock and Colurastes. He didn't think Kakkahaar should be included.

The date was named, the arrangements finalized. The Sarestes family would travel with Pellaz to Megalithica as soon as Ulaume's harling was born and had hatched from its pearl. The household staff would look after the harling while its parents were away. Flick hoped he had not invoked dark gods in trying to prevent the visit to Galhea. What if the universe intervened by harming Ulaume or the harling, so that they couldn't go anywhere? While Ulaume groaned in pearlbirth, Flick paced around praying to all the dehara. "I want to go," he said to them. "I really want to go."

The pearl was delivered without hitch and a short time later, the pearl hatched. A new Sarestes was born. They named him Orien.

A couple of days before the journey to Galhea, Pellaz arrived at the Sarestes house with a companion—Cobweb Parasiel. Cobweb, aware of the past friction between Flick and Seel, felt it would be a good idea for Flick to meet somehar from Galhea prior to arriving there. Flick appreciated this gesture. Cobweb made a great fuss of the new harling and treated Aleeme like an adult. In a very short time, the household took him to its heart.

Lileem, as usual, felt uncomfortable around the cozy domestic scenes and asked Pellaz if they might speak in private. An idea had been brewing in her head for some days. She'd debated whether to act on it or not, but now, on impulse, she decided she had to. She took Pellaz out into the garden, into the last of the evening.

"I haven't thanked you properly for what you did," she said.

"That's okay," Pellaz said. "Everyhar's been preoccupied with other things. I don't need thanks. Glad to help."

"There's one more thing I want to ask you," Lileem said.

"Ask."

"When we go to Galhea, it's not Shilalama, is it?"

"Well no, of course not."

"So you wouldn't really be breaking any promises to Opalexian if you took your brother there."

"Lee—"

"No, don't just refuse. I want to talk to him, Pell. It's unfinished business. I don't intend to do anything stupid." She didn't know what she intended. She dared not think.

Pellaz stared at her, but she could not meet his eyes. "Are you sure about this?" he asked. "You don't look it."

"I'm sure. Please ask him."

Pellaz rubbed his face. "I don't know. I'll have to think about it. I can't make a decision now."

"It's important to me. Very important."

"Very well. I'll think about it. You should know that, despite everything, and the way Terez seemed when he left here, he would like to speak to you too."

"Has he asked you something similar?"

Pellaz didn't reply. "Don't get your hopes up. You'll have to wait and see."

The next morning, Lileem went early to Exalan's office and requested an audience with Opalexian. The Kamagrian leader consented to this, perhaps imagining Lileem wished to discuss her forthcoming new role. Few hara or parazha could simply walk into Opalexian's quarters and ask to see her, but the Sarestes were exceptions. Lileem reflected that Opalexian had become a lot more accessible in general since they'd first moved to Shilalama. That could only be a good thing.

Opalexian received Lileem in her morning room and there Lileem made her request. She asked for the bowl she had brought back with her from the otherworld.

"Why do you want it?" Opalexian asked.

"Because I'm leaving Shilalama soon, and I want to take it with me," Lileem said. "I know it's an important artifact, simply because of where it came from, but I need it to remind me of things, that's all." She risked a smile. "If ever I'm tempted to be bad, I can look at that cracked old thing and count my blessings. It has sentimental value."

Opalexian regarded her keenly. "Are you happy now, Lileem?"

"Yes. I'm grateful for everything you've given me. I want to work for Kamagrian to the best of my abilities. I won't disappoint you."

Opalexian continued to stare at Lileem for several long, excruciating moments. Then she went to a cupboard in the room, took a key from the pocket of her robe, and unlocked the cupboard door. She took the cracked stone bowl from within.

Lileem swallowed with difficulty. The sight of the artefact made her head spin. She could remember everything so well.

"I know you are bright," Opalexian said, holding up the bowl before her and turning it in her hands. "I wish more parazha were like you, Lileem. Many are troubled and damaged and afraid. You are something else, and I think it's because the good hara who brought you up gave you such love and care. Many of your sisters do not enjoy such fortune. You are what they all should be, I think."

"I know I'm lucky," Lileem said. She licked her lips. They felt as dry as shed snakeskin.

Opalexian turned to her and held out the bowl. "Take it," she said. "Tel-an-Kaa speaks well of you too, you know. You could be one of our brightest stars, Lileem. Don't forget that."

"I won't." Lileem took the bowl. It was icy cold in her hands and surprisingly heavy.

Opalexian nodded thoughtfully. "Good. Kamagrian need parazha like you."

Don't do this to me, Lileem thought and knew then that even without mind-touch, she and the Kamagrian leader were having a secret conversation.

Opalexian took Lileem's face in her hands and kissed her brow. "Go with my heart," she said. "Go, my pioneering daughter. Have faith. Be strong. I am often not a good mother, but I know when it is time for chicks to flee to the nest, to follow their own path."

Lileem felt tears gather in her eyes. *I don't want to have to do this,* she thought, *and yet I do.* "Good-bye," she said.

"May the dehara go with you," Opalexian said.

CHAPTER THIRTY-SEVEN

Seel realized he was extremely nervous of seeing Flick again. He knew of Flick's continued antipathy toward him and had been aghast when Pellaz had voiced the request concerning Aleeme's feybraiha. That was the Tigron's work, Seel was sure. Pellaz didn't like loose ends and when he had the opportunity to interfere in a matter and put it right, he generally took it. He was like a more benign version of Thiede.

The party from Shilalama arrived midmorning, and Cobweb was with them. Seel was sitting in a sun-soaked sitting room in Forever, on the edge of his seat, fraught with nerves. When the portal opened and the *sedim* poured through into the garden from the otherlanes, Seel did not move. He heard Swift's office door open and close. He heard his chesnari's footsteps across the great hall of the house and the front doors creak wide. He heard voices. Greetings. *Go out there,* he told himself. *It'll be more difficult later if you don't.*

Without further thought, he rose to his feet and left the room. Swift had already conducted their guests into the hall. When Swift saw Seel, he came to his side and put an arm around him. All Seel could see was Flick. Everyhar else was a blur.

You don't have to worry, Seel thought, *the har standing there, just feet away from you, is somehar completely different to the Flick you knew. He is not the one who wept in a lake of blood in your kitchen. He is not the one whose eyes were always dark and wounded. He is not even the scruffy waif you locked away in a room upstairs. He is himself, not your guilt.*

Seel stepped forward, taking Swift with him. "Welcome," he said. "Welcome to our home."

Flick inclined his head a little and introduced his son. Aleeme did not look much like Flick had in his youth, although he had similar dark hair. Second-generation hara were very different to their parents. They were never weighed down with the baggage of past history. They stood taller.

"Azriel is out at the moment," Seel said. "We thought you should all settle in before you meet him."

"I'll show you your rooms," Cobweb said. "They overlook the lake." He began to lead the Sarestes toward the stairs.

Ulaume paused by Seel before following the others. "Thank you for this," he said.

Seel shook one of his hands briefly. "We are happy to be involved."

And it was over, that first difficult meeting. Swift took Seel back into the sitting room and held him close.

"There should be one other here," Swift said softly.

Seel tightened his arms. "I know." He could not speak Cal's name.

Lileem did not like having to pretend to be female, but Tel-an-Kaa insisted. "Why can't I just be har?" Lileem complained, indicating with disgust the long gypsy skirts Tel-an-Kaa had dressed her in. Lileem preferred trousers.

"We have our job to do," Tel-an-Kaa said. "You know why we affect the appearance of being human. Stop being difficult."

They were staying in an inn in Galhea and later that day would go to Forever for Aleeme's feybraiha feast. Lileem had slipped the little otherworld bowl into the pocket of her skirt, and now kept touching it. The future was a boiling mass of uncertainty. Her mind was a blank. She felt driven, but refused to think about it. Far easier to worry about the way she was dressed and the way her loose hair got tangled up in everything. Walk past a door and it caught on the frame. Trees would grab her and priceless ornaments would be swept crashing to the floor. Lileem usually wore her hair in braids, but the Zigane said a loose glossy cloud looked more feminine. When she sat down, she sat on the hair and it hurt. She kept forgetting to brush it to the side. *I have Kakkahaar hair, that's the trouble,* Lileem thought. *Too damn long.*

She had trained with the Zigane for some months now and had learned how to pick up traces of lost Kamagrian in the ethers and to put out a call to them, a beacon to draw them to safety. There was some satisfaction in this work, because already she had located two wandering souls, who had been confused and terrified, and who had looked upon her as a powerful angel of salvation. Tel-an-Kaa praised her efforts all the time. It sounded contrived to Lileem. She sensed what lay beneath it. The Zigane feared Lileem would one day just slip away. Her fears were justified.

Perhaps in another attempt to keep Lileem from straying, Tel-an-Kaa had initiated a physical relationship between them, and in those moments of intimacy complied with Lileem's desire for them both to be like hara, to call each other that. Perhaps she looked upon it as an erotic fantasy Lileem had, but to Lileem it was simply the way she was meant to be. She knew she was testing the Zigane, seeing how far Tel-an-Kaa would go to keep her happy. Aruna with the Zigane was like eating dried prunes after having once feasted on ripe plums. It could never be like it had been with Terez, but so what? When plums were out of season, prunes were better than nothing. This metaphor made Lileem laugh whenever she thought of it, which was sometimes at inappropriate moments. She never told Tel-an-Kaa why she was laughing.

At midday, they hired a carriage to take them to Forever. The event would begin with lunch in the gardens, next to the lake. Cobweb had invited everyhar who was anyhar in Galhea, because he thought Flick and Ulaume should meet them. The gardens were heaving with guests, who were all desperate to get a glimpse of, if not a few words with, the Tigron of Immanion. The Sarestes were treated like celebrities because they were friends of Pellaz. Lileem spotted Flick, surrounded by a group of hara, and grinned. He looked distinctly uncomfortable. Poor Flick. He must be hating this. Ulaume was nearby, regaling a troupe of admirers with some anecdote or another. He appeared to be in his element. And there was Aleeme, all grown up and beautiful, casting shy glances at the handsome young har who would later teach him the amazing skills of Wraeththu's most delicious pastime. Lileem sighed. She should have had a proper feybraiha too. At least she'd had Mima, who was perhaps one of the closest parazha to har. Lileem wished other Kamagrian could be more like her.

Lileem wandered around the garden, unable to shed Tel-an-Kaa, who stuck to her side like glue. She was looking for Terez, but it appeared that Pellaz hadn't brought him after all. If that was the case, Lileem wanted to leave. She couldn't join in with the party spirit, because the event only reminded her of everything she could never have. It would be rude to leave, though. She was here for Aleeme and must remember that, even if Aleeme was too busy to speak to her.

Midafternoon, Pellaz himself conducted a ritual in the grounds of the house to initiate Aleeme into the first level of the Wraeththu caste system, Ara. Not that Ulaume and Flick ever thought about such things. It was probably meaningless, really. How many hara concentrated on learning the magical path, in order to achieve higher levels? Not a lot, in Lileem's opinion. It was just a pretty ceremony, a preamble to the arunic feast that awaited Aleeme later on. Foreplay.

Lileem drank apple wine and amused herself by being short with Tel-an-Kaa. The Zigane appeared to appreciate Lileem was troubled, and didn't take offense, which was hardly the reaction that Lileem had been hoping for. A good row might make her feel better.

More food and drink was brought out. Lileem stood by the tables and consumed vast amounts of wine. Tel-an-Kaa conversed with hara nearby, but kept casting covert glances back at Lileem as if to make sure she was still there. *I'm not going anywhere,* Lileem thought.

That evening, there would be a party with music and dancing. Beforehand, Aleeme went into the house to change his clothes and no doubt receive final instructions from his parents concerning the activities of the later part of the evening, when he would have to return to his bedroom and wait alone for Azriel to come to him. Lileem realized she was so consumed with envy about this that she was literally seeing red. Everything had a ruddy tinge to it, which was not just an effect of the splendid sunset.

Lanterns were lit in the trees and the great window doors to Forever's function room were thrown wide to the night. Inside, the house was lit by candles and boughs of evergreen had been fixed to the walls. Displays of white flowers and dark green leaves covered every surface that wasn't covered in food and drink. The Parsics had spared no expense for their guests. This would be an occasion to remember.

Lileem stood against a wall, still drinking wine. At last she'd managed to freeze the Zigane off. Tel-an-Kaa had given up on her, and Lileem didn't blame her. Hara had begun to dance to the reel of pipes and drums. Flick must have been drinking too, because he was smiling now.

Again I am ghost at the threshold, Lileem thought. *I am standing at the edge of the light, looking in.*

She saw Swift bow to Ulaume and lead him onto the dance floor. She saw Aleeme so radiant he looked like a star. Every happy face was like a grinning demon to her. She needed to get away. Empty glass too. Better refill it. She was just about to move away, when her skin prickled unaccountably. She glanced quickly at the doors to the terrace. A tall dark har stood there, gazing around himself. Lileem nearly vomited with shock. It was Terez. He had arrived late. Perhaps Pellaz had instructed him to. He was dressed in Gelaming attire, his black hair shining over his shoulders and breast. To somehar half blind, it would be obvious he was closely related to the Tigron. Pellaz walked across the room to his brother and took him by the arm. He led him back to the high table, where the families of Aleeme and Azriel were sitting. Most of them, anyway. As if this thought was an invocation, Lileem felt a presence sidle up beside her and jumped a little. She turned and saw a fair-haired, bony-faced young har had come to stand next to her.

"You're having fun, aren't you," he said in a cold sarcastic tone. He was skinny, but somehow good enough to eat.

"Go away," Lileem said. "Do it now, because this is a party and I mustn't be impolite. If you stay, I shall be forced to swear at you."

"It's a shit party," said the har. "A shit party for sheep."

Lileem examined him for a moment. She was jolted by a sense of recognition for a har she had never met. "You must be Cal's son," she said. "Tyson. I've heard about you."

The har gave her a mordant glance. "You're a friend of that Flick's aren't you?"

"Yes."

Tyson grimaced. "And he's a big friend of Pellaz-tiahaar-wonderful. There are insanity warrants as well as death warrants, you know. One time, Aralis signed one for my hostling. Signed it in blood."

Lileem made a vague sound. This was not what she wanted. "Oh well, as we all know, first generation are all neurotic. Just thank everything that's sacred you don't have to be like them. Look, is there something more interesting we can do? I'm really bored and really drunk. I don't mean anything roony by that, by the way, in case you were wondering."

Tyson sniggered. "You're weird. That's why I came over. I can spot weird hara really easily, only you're not har. I asked Kaa about you. She said you're human. You don't seem like it. You do seem pissed off, however."

"Yeah, well," Lileem said. "What do you do for fun?"

"I've got some sheh, and some smoking weed. We could go outside and seek oblivion beneath the stars."

"Better than this oblivion," Lileem said. "Lead on."

She followed Tyson to the garden, stealing a glance at the high table as she did so. Terez was paying close attention to Pellaz, rather in the manner of a devoted hound sitting at the feet of its master, tail thumping against the floor. He must have felt Lileem's attention upon him, however, because for a moment, he turned his head to stare right at her. Lileem's body went hot, then cold. She held his dark gaze with her own for a moment, but then Terez's eyes appeared to become unfocused. He looked right through her, and turned back to his brother with a smile. There hadn't even been a ghost of the past in his eyes, and Lileem was sure he'd recognized her. She felt as if a giant fist had come hurtling across the room and had smacked her in the eyes. She was virtually seeing stars.

"You coming?" Tyson asked impatiently.

They went outside.

Tyson took her to a secluded spot near the ornamental lake. Few hara were outside as most of the guests were dancing in the house. Lileem sat down on the damp grass. She felt surprisingly numb. She didn't want to weep at all. Tyson sat beside her and began to pack a pipe with smoking mix. As he worked, Lileem admired his slim wrists and dextrous fingers. His pale hair fell heavily over his eyes, and he looked exactly how she'd imagined Cal would look. Her head was spinning a little. It would be a mistake to smoke anything. She'd had enough intoxicants already.

"Is there fresh water anywhere around here?" she asked.

"Sure," Tyson said. "There's a stream in the trees over there. Are you okay?"

"Need a drink," Lileem said. She scrambled to her feet, ripping her skirt as she did so and then stumbled off in the direction Tyson had indicated. She could hear the sound of running water.

Her skirt ripped even more as she fought through brambles to get to the water. She was half tempted to take it off completely. When she reached the stream, she collapsed onto its bank, and for some moments had to sit completely still so that her head would stop spinning. Her stomach roiled and then she was being sick into the tall grass. She heaved until she thought her stomach would bleed. *Stupid to have drunk so much, really stupid.*

Wiping her mouth, she took out the bowl from the pocket of her skirt. She realized she could see her surroundings quite well, because beams of strong moonlight shone down upon her. When she looked up, she could see an immense full moon through the branches of the trees. "Hi, Lunil," she said and blew a kiss toward the sky.

She leaned toward the stream and scooped up some of its bright glittering water with the bowl. The moonlight and the water made the symbols on the bowl's inner sides appear darker and more distinct. The language of gods, impenetrable and mysterious. Lileem threw back her head and drank. Water ran down her chin, onto her clothes. It ran over her fingers. And as she drank, she felt every symbol, every mark, flow into her. She drank of the gods, imbibed their being. When the bowl was drained, she looked into it. There were no marks on its sides. She uttered a long, ululating howl, like a wolf. Suddenly, life seemed fine again.

Lunil had flown out of the moon. He was a great shining figure in the sky, with stars in his hair. As she gazed upon him, so more spectral radiant figures gathered round him, flying from every corner of the universe to display themselves to her. There were thousands of them, mighty angels and dehara that filled the firmament. Each of them sang his own song to her, his own magic. Lileem felt a wrench within her and opened her mouth. She thought she was going to be sick again, but could not move. Her head was forced far back on her neck. The dehara sang and a stream of black motes spiraled out of Lileem's mouth and flew up into the sky. They changed into birds as they rose toward the moon. The symbols of the dehara had left her body, but she still knew them. They were with her always.

Above her, the sky shook with a sound like a thousand angel choirs crying out. The radiant figures exploded like immense fireworks. Sparks showered down. Then Lileem realized they really were fireworks. Aleeme had mounted the stairs that led to the bedroom. The Parsics had lit up the sky for him. Lileem could hear the cheers from the house.

Tyson must have wondered what had happened to her, if indeed he'd hung around waiting. Lileem scrambled to her feet. It was only then that she realized the little cracked bowl was no longer in her lap. Her ripped skirt was covered in a fine powder, like dust, like ash. She gathered some of it up in one hand, held it tight.

Lileem clawed her way back to the lake and found that Tyson was still sprawled there on his back, smoking his pipe. She didn't know how long she'd been away.

"What have you been doing?" Tyson asked her. "Weird sounds."

"I've been communing with gods," Lileem said.

Tyson sniggered. "Still want smoke?"

"No, I think you heard I've had more than enough tonight."

Tyson was silent for a moment, puffing on his pipe. Lileem heard its stem tap against his teeth. Then he said, "I don't have to be like him, do I?" It wasn't a question; it was a revelation.

"No," Lileem said. "You don't. I don't know your hostling, but I know Pell. He's okay, really. It wasn't his fault, what happened. They had their tragedy, and it was big. I can't see the sense of making it bigger."

Tyson laughed softly. "Yeah."

"You should talk to Pell. It might help you both."

Tyson sat up. "Cobweb has got this stuff that makes you feel better. If you had some of that you could drink some more. Want me to fetch some?"

Lileem hiccupped, and her throat burned. "That might be good."

"Okay, wait here." He stood up, hesitated. "What's the deal with you?"

"I'm not human," Lileem said.

"Thought so," Tyson said. "Won't be long."

Lileem sat and stared at the water that lapped at the banks. She could see the ghostly outlines of some kind of folly across the lake. This was a really good place. Her fist was still closed around a handful of dust. She imagined Terez coming to her, how she wouldn't hear him approach, but would know when he was there. She wouldn't turn to him or say anything. He would hunker down beside her and for some time they would be silent. She would be able to smell him. She remembered that scent so well. What would there be to say, really? The fact that he had come to her would be enough.

Lileem sighed deeply. Terez was a Gelaming noble now, groomed and elegant. He'd had other hara since her: she knew he didn't share her feelings, although she didn't blame him for it. She just couldn't have what she wanted in this world. But there was another life, another world. In that place, she would never experience love, but as she couldn't in her own reality either, that didn't really matter.

I can have knowledge there, she thought, *and the wheeling skies, and the suns, and the mighty waters. I want to explore it more fully, immerse myself in it without responsibility to any other. I want to let it change my being.*

There were no soft footsteps on the path behind her, no familiar scent. Instead, she heard Tyson returning to her, humming beneath his breath. He sat down beside her and threw a small glass bottle into her lap.

"Here, drink that."

"Open it for me," Lileem said. She still held tightly the dust in her hand.

Tyson picked it up, unscrewed the top, and held it to her lips. His skin, so close to her, smelled like burned spice. She drank the bitter fluid and even the burning trail it left in her throat made her feel slightly better.

"Cobweb is a powerful witch," Tyson said. "The things he brews up can kill or cure in seconds."

Lileem laughed, swallowed with difficulty.

"What are you, then?" Tyson asked her.

"Har," she said, "but also different. I look like this because I work with the Zigane. We search for human refugees."

"I know," Tyson said. "Why are you angry? Didn't you want your friend to be with Azriel?"

"No, it's not that," Lileem said. "Private stuff. Unfinished business. Rubbish, really."

Tyson took hold of her free hand and immediately it felt as if her flesh started to sizzle. She could pull away now, if she wanted to.

"Forget it," he said. "Why should Azriel and Aleeme have all the fun?"

He put a hand upon her face and drew her to him. This was so dangerous. She didn't want to harm him. But already, she could hear the faint murmur of a distant sea. The sparks of spiraling stars fizzed in her hair. She put her mouth against his. His lips were beautiful and his essence was the dark roar of stormy skies. Her being was so attuned to the otherworld, merely the sharing of breath was enough to take her there

She was out of her body looking down and saw them together in the clear moonlight. She saw them become enshrouded in a shifting pearly essence. A portal was opening around her, and she must be strong enough to step through it and cast Tyson from her. She couldn't risk taking him there. The moment was so close. Part of her was estranged from her flesh, waiting and calculating, while another swooned in the beauty of touching another har once more. If only she could have this. If only . . .

Now. She had to call to her body as if it was a reluctant younger sister. "Come! Leave this place!" The portal appeared like a flight of shining stairs, where angels would walk between the worlds. The dust in her hand was the link to it, the contact between her and Tyson the vehicle. Joy filled her being. There was no better way to leave this world for the last time.

Then she saw him, strolling down the path to the lake. His face was troubled, but because of her heightened sense of awareness, she could perceive the flame inside him, the flame that had never flickered or faltered: the flame that burned for her alone. Terez. She cried out, and her body pulled away from Tyson. Terez had come to her. The radiance around her became brighter and brighter and there was a sound like the limbs of trees breaking off and falling to the forest floor.

A mighty flash of light erupted as the portal opened wide. Lileem was drawn to it, as a spirit is drawn to death. Now, she was fighting it, howling like a maddened ghost. The pull was too strong. She opened her closed fist and the remains of the bowl spun about her, like stinging shards of diamond.

Terez and Tyson would be blinded by the light, but only for a moment. When their vision cleared, Terez would see only Tyson by the lake and drifting over him would be a strange dust, the ancient sand of a far and unimagined world.

EPILOGUE

There was once a festival night that surpassed all others. It was the night when the world of Wraeththu changed, when hara, consciously or not, turned purposefully to approach their potential. Because of that night, Ulaume and Flick came together. Because of that night, Lileem had a childhood and youth spent with hara. It changed her, and made her the parage who could step out of reality to search for truth.

Looking back over the years, Flick often thought about how so many events had been initiated by the night when Pellaz had left his first physical body: lives had been touched and turned, dehara had come down from the heavens. A harling had been born, a very special one. Flick could not mourn for Lileem again, because Opalexian had told him Lileem had made the choice to go back to the otherworld. Her own special festival night had changed her in such a way that she could no longer live happily in this reality. Flick did not want her to be unhappy.

"I let her go," Opalexian said, "because she understands now. If she ever returns, it will be in a time when the world needs what she has learned for it."

"Our purpose, all along," Flick said, "was to care for her."

"Not just that," Opalexian told him. "Your search for knowledge too, was of great importance."

Flick had tried hard to live a small life, but couldn't really have it. Fate had given him certain things to keep him sweet, but it had tasks for him too. Pellaz had slowly, but firmly, guided him into the world of Wraeththu. Although Flick and Ulaume still lived in Shilalama, and the Kamagrian were still perhaps the world's greatest secret, there were now temples to the dehara in the city of Immanion. Pressure for Flick to write down all that he had learned was overwhelming, but eventually he asked Exalan to do it. "Don't give them a holy book," he said, "give them the encouragement to dream for themselves."

It amused Flick to think that his name and his work were taught to harlings in schools. No doubt they believe him to be some profound, sagacious individual, but he knew that essentially he hadn't changed at all. Exalan, as his scribe and assistant, enjoyed the status more.

Some years after Lileem's second disappearance, it became common knowledge that Thiede was Wraeththu's progenitor. Whether Thiede allowed this information to leak out himself or some other enterprising har put all the facts together and came up with the right conclusion, not even Pellaz ever discovered. Thiede remained inscrutable on the matter, although he did not appear to be that distressed the truth was out.

Wraeththu was surging toward a dazzling future, changes occurring all the time. The western countries were mostly free of belligerent tribes and in other lands, new harish nations were forming all the time. Most remaining humans lived in autonomous reserves, while others were content to live with hara who were disposed to permit it. Those who still dwelled beyond Wraeththu influence were of no threat.

Pellaz and the Hegemony governed all cooperative tribes from Immanion, but nohar was under any illusion that they had supreme control. Thiede held the reins, as he always had. If, sometimes, decisions were made that were not wholly acceptable, most hara were content with the way things were. It appeared to the majority of hara that everything had slipped comfortably into place. They were free and they could explore their being without fear.

One day, Opalexian summoned Flick to Kalalim alone. It was a glorious afternoon and the city dozed peacefully in the sunlight. Opalexian sat in her office, and the windows were closed, despite the heat. The atmosphere was somewhat stifling. Flick realised at once she had something important to say to him, and his first thought was of Lileem. He had never given up hope that she would return home again.

He sat down before Opalexian's desk, waiting to hear.

"Flick, I have a proposition for you," she said.

"Tell me."

She rose from her seat and padded, bare foot, around the desk to stand beside him. "You might remember that Pellaz and I once had an agreement."

"Yes. He never told me what it was."

"He asked me to heal Cal."

"Cal." Even now, the name made Flick go cold. "Did you?"

"If Cal and Pellaz were ever to come together, it would change everything."

"Which is why Thiede has never allowed it," Flick said. "But I'm curious: why and how could it change things? At the end of the day, they were just two hara in love."

"Their union would make what Lileem and Terez did look like nothing," Opalexian said. "It would initiate many things, not least a change for Kamagrian."

"Do you want that?"

Opalexian sighed deeply. "Thiede would not want it."

"Does he know about you?"

"Flick, I am his sister."

This did not come as a shock to Flick. If anything, the information put matters perfectly into perspective.

"Not in the normal way," she added hastily. "We were created by similar means, and neither of us really know what that was. We do know that someone, or something, created us for a purpose, and like Thiede did with his Tigron, it took a few attempts to get it right. I was an earlier attempt. If any others survived, it is not known to us. They certainly didn't have the effect on the world that Thiede and I did. Thiede does not believe that Kamagrian should be encouraged or enlarged. He thinks it is a mistake and is happy for me to gather parazha here in Shilalama, to keep them out of the way. I do not think that parazha born to hara are freaks or throwbacks. That is a point that Thiede and I have never agreed on."

"Do you have a lot of contact with him?" Flick asked.

"Not now. We did not discover one another until long after Thiede had established the first Wraeththu tribes. We met, fought, met again, and have maintained an uneasy alliance ever since. It is a long story, and one day I will tell it to you. All I want you to know for now is that it is my wish for Cal to become Tigron."

"What?" Flick said. "You can't mean that."

"He and Pellaz should be one. Tigron is not one individual, but two. Thiede will never allow this, because he would be disempowered. His war with Cal has been long and bloody. It is a private war and an abomination. Terrible things have been done to Cal."

"He probably deserved most of them. I know him. I know what he's capable of and also what he isn't. He is the most selfish har on earth, populating a universe of one. It would be insane to give him power. I shudder to think what he'd do. Most likely, he'd destroy the world and laugh as it burned."

"And while hara think of him that way, it will never happen," Opalexian said. "Think about it."

"I don't want to!" Flick shook his head in disbelief. "This can't be so."

"It is my belief that Thiede influenced Cal in such a way that he would do atrocious things. I'm surprised he didn't have Cal killed at the same time as Pellaz, but maybe that is because he couldn't. Perhaps Cal has higher powers protecting him in some way. Whatever the reason, it interfered with Thiede's plan. He certainly didn't intend to lose Orien. It must tear at his heart to this day that he was so immersed in recreating Pellaz, he was unable to save his dearest friend. He was, at that time, physically incapable of action. Still, his disability in that respect worked in my favor. I have been working some time toward a certain conclusion, even before Pellaz came to me and made his innocent request. For years before that, I had sought, painstakingly, to undo what Thiede had done to Cal."

"You have known of him all along?"

Opalexian nodded. "When Thiede made his Tigron, an operation I observed from afar with the greatest fascination, I saw what he let slip through his fingers. I saw Cal. Unfortunately, part of the redemption process has required Cal to descend deeper into madness and despair."

"You mean you've tortured him as much as Thiede has?"

"Yes. There is no other way. You don't understand these things, Flick. It is very complex. Because of the magnitude of what must happen, and its subtle effects, I couldn't simply bring Cal here and heal him. He had to heal himself, and that was hard, because he lacked the will to do so. It has taken me many years to guide him along a better, stronger path. I have been groping in the dark, and sometimes the things I have laid my hands upon in that darkness were not what I desired."

"What has this to do with me?"

"The final stage is in preparation. Cal will be brought to Shilalama. I will tell him all that he needs to know and the last healing will take place. Then he will be sent to Immanion. At that point all hara and parazha had better flee to their storm cellars, because the hurricane will be devastating. Its mighty winds will fly to every corner of the earth."

Flick felt numb. He couldn't take in what he'd heard. It couldn't be true.

"Will you help me?" Opalexian said softly.

Flick stared at her for some moments. "What are you asking me to do?"

"Take him to the dehara in trance. Give him knowledge of them and their strength. Tel-an-Kaa can work with you on this, because she will be responsible for the final phase of Cal's healing. She has been involved for some time in this process."

"You want me to see Cal? Here?"

"Yes. I know how you must feel about this, but I hope you appreciate I wouldn't ask you if it wasn't important to me."

"I can't," Flick said. "I've done many things because others have wanted me to, but I can't do this."

"Will you not at least think about it?"

"About what? Destroying Thiede? That's what this is really about, isn't it?"

Opalexian went back to her seat. "Cal knows you. He will trust you. It will help him become all he should be if you could be with him now."

"No," Flick said. "The answer is no and it always will be. I've played my part in various political games, and it will never happen again."

"I know what you're thinking," Opalexian said. "You're thinking about going home and sending a message to Pellaz to warn him. Remember that Pell wanted this. He asked me to help him."

"He didn't ask for this," Flick said. "What you're offering him is a choice between Thiede and Cal, only he doesn't know he has to make it. At the very least, he should be made aware of the consequences."

"He doesn't have a choice," Opalexian said. "I can be just as ruthless as Thiede has ever been. For this reason, as a precaution, I have had your communication equipment, and your *sedu* temporarily impounded. They will be returned to you in due course."

Flick stood up. "I suppose I should be angry, but I can't be bothered. You think you know everything, but I guarantee there will be unexpected results from this. If Cal is involved, I doubt the outcome will be wholly to your liking."

"It *will* happen," Opalexian said. "I'm saddened you won't be part of it, but I won't stoop to forcing you. I hope you realize that Thiede wanted to keep you from me. He understands your significance, which is why he attempted to intercept your journey here."

"I won't be part of your schemes—yours or Thiede's."

"Very soon, Flick, you're going to have to accept Cal and let go of the past."

"He's no innocent," Flick said. "He has been abused and manipulated, but part of him has never been touched. In my opinion, the worst part. In some ways, I want him to enjoy power, because then you're really going to have trouble on your hands, but in others way I hope he doesn't, because of what it could mean for hara and parazha everywhere."

"It means he will be your Tigron," Opalexian said. "Go home and get used to the idea. I don't want us to fight, Flick. You have done many good things, and I respect you greatly. Once this is over, I will send word. I will tell you the outcome myself."

"You and Thiede are so alike. It's obvious why you could never be friends. The world isn't big enough for both of you, is it?"

Opalexian laughed. "In some ways, you are right, but I won't be like him. I won't be holding the strings of power and tweaking them on a whim. If I wanted that, Thiede would have been dead years ago."

"Will he die now?"

"Go home, Flick. You have made your feelings clear and I have nothing else to say to you."

Flick left Kalalim in a daze. He wanted to speak to Seel about this. He *should* speak to Seel, but Opalexian had made sure that was impossible. None of them had the power to make a difference. It was already done. "Aru help you, Pellaz," Flick murmured aloud. "Aru help us all."

When he reached the market quarter, he almost didn't notice the two hara talking to a Roselane har at one of the stalls. But their unusual attire and the fact that they were obviously outsiders commanded his attention. He noticed first the bright gold hair and came to a standstill.

Cal was already here.

Flick felt faint and had to reach out for support to the wall beside him. There could be no mistake. He knew that face, that hair, that *being*. Flick ran into a side street. If he ran fast enough, he might escape the present and leap into the past, the day before yesterday, some time last year. Any time but this. *No more,* he prayed to whichever dehar might be listening, *I beg you. No more.*

He kept on running all the way home.